READER'S DIGEST

CONDENSED BOOKS

FIRST EDITION

Published by
THE READER'S DIGEST ASSOCIATION LIMITED
25 Berkeley Square, London W1X 6AB.

THE READER'S DIGEST ASSOCIATION SOUTH AFRICA (PTY) LTD.
Nedbank Centre, Strand Street, Cape Town

Printed in Great Britain by Petty & Sons Ltd., Leeds

Original cover design by Jeffery Matthews A.R.C.A.

ISBN 0 340 20319 6

READER'S DIGEST CONDENSED BOOKS

THE GREAT TRAIN ROBBERY
Michael Crichton

BLIND LOVE
Patrick Cauvin

BROWN ON RESOLUTION
C. S. Forester

WHERE ARE THE CHILDREN?
Mary Higgins Clark

AMONG THE ELEPHANTS
Iain and Oria Douglas-Hamilton

COLLECTOR'S LIBRARY
EDITION

In this volume

THE GREAT TRAIN ROBBERY
by Michael Crichton (p.9)

For most people, "The Great Train Robbery" is the brutal crime perpetrated by Ronald Biggs and associates in 1963. In fact, this book tells of the original "Great Train Robbery", a far more fascinating operation. It took place over a hundred years earlier when its ingenuity and brazen impertinence won it the title of "The Crime of the Century"

In presenting his thrilling version of how this coup was planned and executed, best-selling novelist Michael Crichton not only brings the arch-criminals vividly to life, but also recreates all the glamour and squalor of the Victorian Underworld.

BLIND LOVE
by Patrick Cauvin (p.151)

This international best-seller is, quite simply, a love story—but a love story with a difference. It tells of a middle-aged schoolmaster who lives an uneventful and unassuming life, until he meets a young woman who is rich, beautiful—and blind.

Patrick Cauvin writes of these two strangely starred lovers with a profound understanding of human nature and of the problems of blindness and loneliness. He describes their uncertainty, awkwardness and happiness with extraordinary delicacy and skill.

It is a novel that goes straight to the heart.

BROWN ON RESOLUTION
by C.S. Forester (p.243)

This famous novel about the lone Leading Seaman, who challenged the whole might of a hostile German cruiser with no more than a rifle, is one of the great classics that established Forester as England's finest naval writer. His deep understanding of ships and sailors, his brilliant ability to create suspense and to describe what it is really like to be in action make this a book that can be read with pleasure, again and again.

WHERE ARE THE CHILDREN?
by Mary Higgins Clark (p.327)

Nancy Eldredge has a home, a husband and two beautiful children. Her haunted past from seven years ago seems safely buried, until suddenly the most dreaded nightmare strikes: the children disappear. Suspected by the police, doubted even by her husband, Nancy cannot say where they have gone.

AMONG THE ELEPHANTS
by Iain and Oria Douglas-Hamilton (p.411)

This is the story of a young man who was so fascinated by elephants that he went to live among them. During the five years he spent observing the massive herds in Tanzania's famous Lake Manyara National Park, he came to love not only the exotic world of Africa but also a beautiful girl called Oria. She was to become his wife, mother of his children and co-author of this unforgettable book.

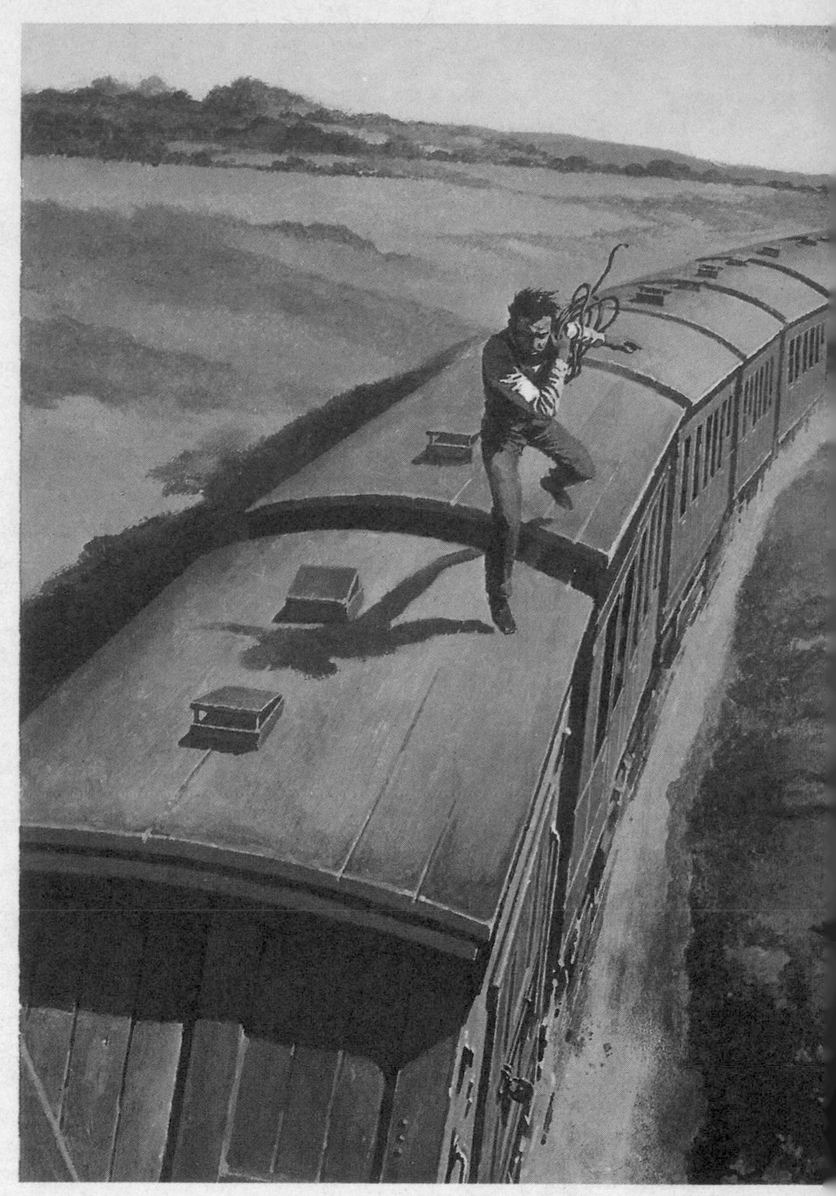

Illustrated by Gino D'Achille

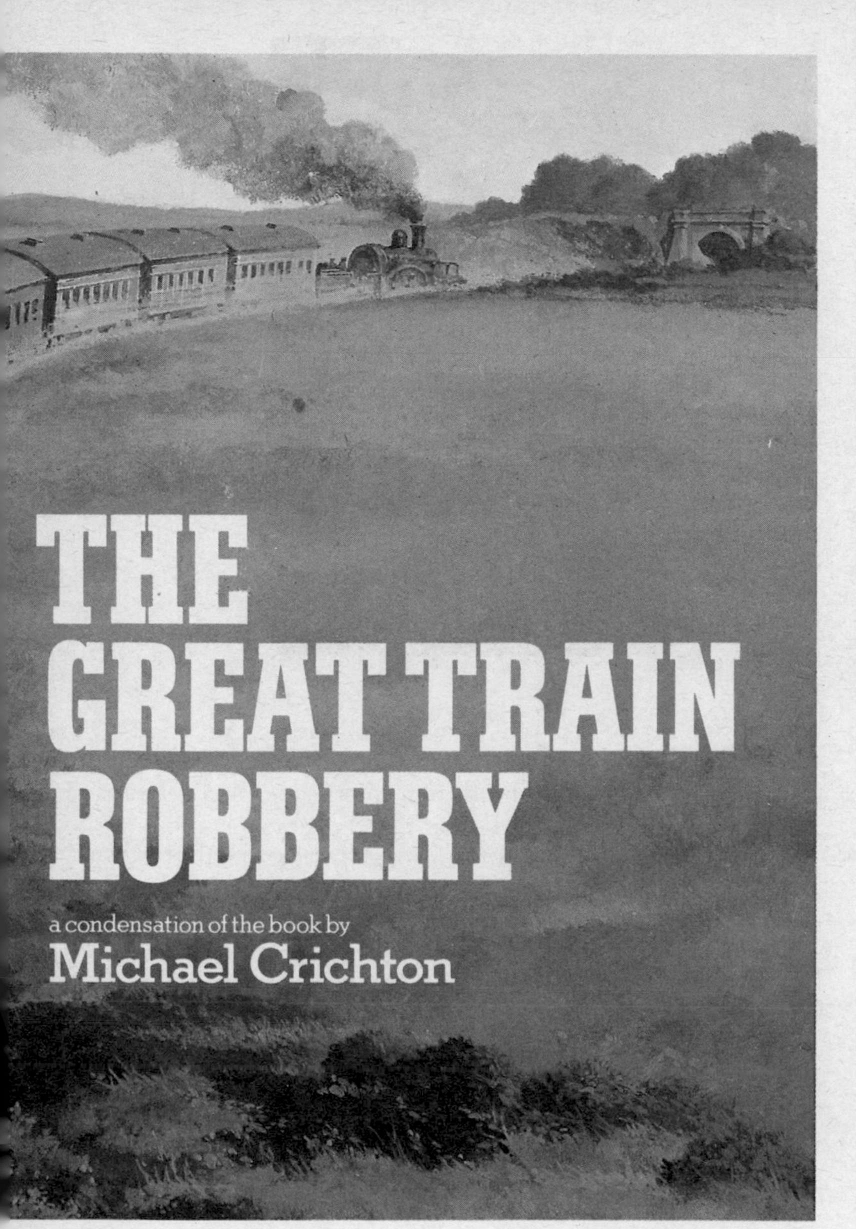

THE GREAT TRAIN ROBBERY

a condensation of the book by

Michael Crichton

Published by Jonathan Cape, London

Edward Pierce

In 1855 three men, named Pierce, Agar and Burgess—each from a very different social class—combined their talents and their opportunities to commit the cleverest crime of the Victorian Age—the first, and still the most sensational, Great Train Robbery.

So much is history. What are not known now are the details of this strange trio's lives and of how they planned the crime. Yet in this fascinating novel, part-thriller, part-documentary, Crichton has brought their story vividly to life, as he follows the conspirators and the men they duped from Mayfair to the slums of Seven Dials, and down the Folkestone line from London Bridge. . . .

Robert Agar

Richard Burgess

It is difficult, after the passage of more than a century, to understand the extent to which the train robbery of 1855 shocked the sensibilities of Victorian England. The sum of money stolen—£12,000 in gold bullion—was large, but not unprecedented, and the meticulous organization of the crime was similarly not unusual. Yet the Victorians always referred to this robbery in capital letters, as The Crime of the Century.

To understand why they were so shocked, one must understand something about the meaning of the railways. Victorian England was the first industrialized society on earth, and it evolved with stunning rapidity. At the time of Waterloo, England was a predominantly rural nation of thirteen million people. By the middle of the nineteenth century, the population had nearly doubled, and half the people lived in urban centres.

These new Victorian cities glittered with more wealth than any society had ever known—and they stank of poverty as abject as any society had ever suffered. Yet there was also widespread public complacency, for the fundamental assumption of Victorians was that progress, material as well as moral, was inevitable. We may find that complacency laughable today, but in the 1850s it was a reasonable attitude to adopt.

During the first half of the nineteenth century, the price of bread, meat, coffee, and tea had fallen; the price of coal was almost halved; the cost of cloth was reduced 80 per cent. Factory working hours had been reduced from seventy-four to sixty a week for adults, and from seventy-two to forty for children. Gaslights glowed throughout the cities; steamships made the crossing to America in ten days instead of eight weeks; the new telegraph service provided astonishing speed in communications.

But of all the proofs of progress, the most striking were the railways. In less than a quarter of a century, they had altered every aspect of English life. In September 1830, the Liverpool & Manchester Railway opened and, in its first year of operation, the number of railway passengers carried between these two cities was twice the number that had travelled the previous year by coach. The social impact was extraordinary. By 1850, five thousand miles of track criss-crossed the nation, providing cheap and increasingly swift transportation for every citizen, and the railways had come to symbolize the material progress which would lead inevitably to the eradication of social evils. So what was really so shocking about The Great Train Robbery was that it suggested that the elimination of crime might not be an inevitable consequence of such progress. Crime could no longer be likened to the plague, which had disappeared with changing social conditions. A few daring commentators even had the temerity to suggest that crime was not linked to social conditions at all. Such opinions were, to say the least, highly distasteful.

They remain distasteful to the present day, little more than a decade after another spectacular English train robbery. Indeed, our moral attitudes towards crime account for a peculiar ambivalence towards criminal behaviour itself. It is feared, despised, and vociferously condemned. Yet it is also secretly admired. This attitude was clearly prevalent in 1855, for The Great Train Robbery was not only shocking and appalling. It was also "daring", "audacious" and "masterful".

We share with the Victorians another attitude—a belief in a "criminal class", by which we mean a subculture of professional criminals who make their living by breaking society's laws. Without question, such a subculture existed in mid-Victorian England. Many of its features were brought to light in the trial of the chief participants in The Great Train Robbery.

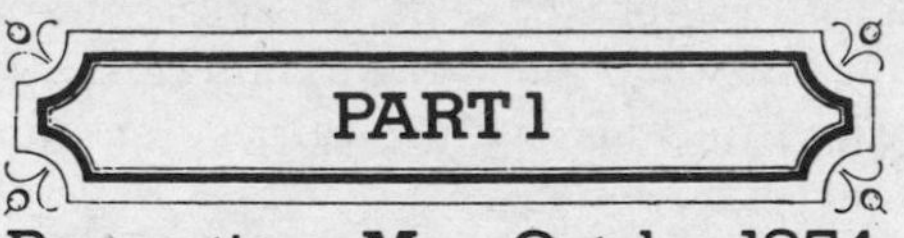

PART 1

Preparations: May–October 1854

CHAPTER ONE

Forty minutes out of London, passing through the rolling green fields and cherry orchards of Kent, the morning train of the South Eastern Railway attained its maximum speed of fifty-four miles an hour. Riding the bright blue-painted engine, the driver in his red uniform could be seen standing upright in the open air, while at his feet the engineer crouched, shovelling coal into the furnaces. Behind the engine and tender were three yellow first-class coaches, followed by six green second-class carriages; and at the very end, a grey, windowless luggage van.

As the train clattered down the track on its way to the coast, the sliding door of the luggage van opened, revealing a desperate struggle inside: a slender youth in tattered clothing was striking out against a burly, blue-uniformed railway guard. Although weaker, the youth made a good showing, landing one or two telling blows. Indeed, it was only by accident that the guard, having been knocked to his knees, should spring forward in such a way that the youth was caught unprepared and flung clear of the train through the open door, so that he landed tumbling and bouncing like a rag doll upon the ground. The guard, gasping for breath, looked back at the fast-receding figure of the fallen youth.

After a minute or two, the youth stirred. In great pain, he raised himself up on one elbow, but he instantly collapsed back to the ground, gave a final convulsive shudder, and lay wholly still.

Half an hour later, an elegant black brougham carriage with rich crimson wheels came down a dirt road parallel to the railway tracks. The driver drew up his horse, and a most singular gentleman emerged, fashionably dressed in a dark green velvet frock coat and high beaver hat. The gentleman climbed a hill, pressed binoculars to his eyes, and swept the length of the tracks. Immediately he fixed on the body of the prostrate youth, but he made no attempt to approach him. On the contrary, he remained standing on the hill until he was certain the lad was dead. Only then did he climb into his waiting carriage and drive northward towards London.

THIS SINGULAR GENTLEMAN was Edward Pierce, and for a man destined to become so notorious that Queen Victoria herself expressed a desire to meet him—or, barring that, to attend his hanging—he remains an oddly mysterious figure. In appearance, Pierce was a handsome, red-bearded man in his early thirties. In his speech, manner and dress he seemed to be a gentleman, and well-to-do; he was apparently very charming. He claimed to be an orphan of Midlands gentry, to have attended Winchester and then Cambridge, and was a familiar figure in many London social circles. A bachelor, he maintained a London house in fashionable Mayfair. But he spent much of the year travelling, and was said to have visited not only the Continent but New York as well.

Contemporary observers clearly believed his aristocratic origins; the very idea of a highborn gentleman adopting a life of crime was so titillating that nobody really wanted to disprove it. Yet there is no evidence that Pierce came from the upper classes; indeed, almost nothing of his background prior to 1850 is known. Even his name is doubtful: various trial witnesses claimed to have known him as John Simms, or Andrew Miller, or Robert Jeffers.

The source of his obviously ample income was equally disputed. Some said he was a silent partner in a highly successful firm that manufactured sports equipment. Others said that he owned several public houses, and a smallish fleet of cabs, headed by a sinister cabby, named Barlow, with a white scar across his forehead. This was more likely true, for the ownership of pubs and cabs was an occupation where underworld connections were useful.

It is not impossible that Pierce was a well-born, educated man; the Victorian underworld supported many such figures down on their luck. But, in general, these educated men were petty criminals of a pathetic sort. Edward Pierce, on the other hand, was a master cracksman, who over the years had accumulated sufficient capital to finance large-scale criminal operations, thus becoming what was called "a putter-up". And towards the middle of 1854 he was already well into an elaborate plan to pull the greatest theft of his career, The Great Train Robbery.

ROBERT AGAR—a known screwsman, or specialist in keys and safe-breaking—testified in court that when he met Edward Pierce in late May, 1854, he had not seen him for two years.

Agar, at the time of the meeting, was twenty-six years old, and in fair health except for a bad cough, the legacy of his years as a child working as a matchstick dipper in Bethnal Green. The premises of the match manufacturer's firm had been poorly ventilated, and the air was filled with that poisonous white vapour of phosphorus that might cause a person's lungs to decay, or his jaw to rot off. Agar, however, had nimble fingers, and when he took up the trade of screwsman, he was immediately successful. For six years he was never apprehended.

Agar testified that the meeting with Pierce occurred at the Bull and Bear public house. Located at the periphery of the notorious criminal slum of Seven Dials, this well-known flash house was, in the words of one observer, "a gathering place for all manner of females dressed to represent ladies, as well as members of the criminal class, who could be seen at every turning." It was also frequented by gentlemen of quality with a taste for low life, and the conversation of two fashionably dressed young bloods lounging at the bar while they surveyed the women in the room would have attracted no particular attention.

Agar recalled that the conversation began without greetings or preliminaries.

Agar said, "I heard that Spring Heel Jack's left Westminster."

"I heard that," Pierce agreed, rapping with his silver-headed cane to draw the attention of the barman. Pierce ordered two glasses of the best whisky, which Agar took as proof that this was to be a business discussion.

"I heard," Agar said, "that Jack was going on a south swing to dip the holiday crowd." In those days, London pickpockets left in late spring, travelling north or south to other cities. A pickpocket's stock in trade was anonymity, and one could not dip a particular locale for long without being spotted by the crusher on the beat.

"I also heard," Agar continued, his eyes on Pierce's face, "that Jack took the train, and was doing some crow's peeping for a particular gent who is putting up."

"He might have done," Pierce said.

"I also heard," Agar said with a sudden grin, "that you are putting up."

"I may," Pierce said. He sipped his whisky, and stared at the glass. "What have you heard I am putting up for?"

"A robbery," Agar said. "For a ream flash pull."

Pierce turned away from the bar and looked at the women in the room. Several returned his glances warmly. There was a brief silence. "How's the touch?" he asked finally.

"Ever so nice," Agar said. To demonstrate, he held out his hands, palms flat, fingers wide: there was no tremor.

"I may have one or two little things," Pierce said.

"Spring Heel Jack held his cards close," Agar said. "He was all swelled mighty and important, but he kept it to his chest."

"Jack's put in lavender," Pierce said curtly.

This was, as Agar later explained it, an ambiguous phrase. It might mean that Spring Heel Jack had gone into hiding or that he was dead. Agar didn't inquire further. "These one or two little things, could they be tricky?"

"Very tricky," Pierce said.

"Inside or outside?"

"I don't know. You'll want a tight lip. If the first lay goes right enough, there will be more."

Agar downed his whisky, and waited. Pierce ordered him another. "Is it keys, then?" Agar asked.

"It is."

"Wax, or straightway haul?"

"Wax."

"On the fly, or is there time?"

"On the fly."

"Right, then," Agar said. "I'm your man. I can do a wax on the fly faster than you can light your cigar."

"I know that," Pierce said, striking a match on the counter top and holding it to the tip of his cigar. Agar gave a slight shudder; he did not himself smoke and every time he smelled the phosphorus and sulphur of a match, it gave him a twinge, from his days in the match factory.

He watched Pierce puff on the cigar until it caught. "What's the lay to be, then?"

Pierce looked at him coldly. "You'll know when the time comes."

"You're a tight one."

"That," Pierce said, "is why I have never been in." Later, other witnesses disputed this claim, saying that Pierce had served three years in a Manchester prison.

At the trial, Agar said that Pierce gave him a final word of caution about keeping silent, and then moved away from the bar, crossing the smoky, noisy Bull and Bear to bend briefly and whisper into a pretty woman's ear.

CHAPTER TWO

Mr. Henry Fowler, forty-seven, knew Edward Pierce in rather different circumstances. Fowler admitted that he had little knowledge of Pierce's background: the man was clearly well-heeled and amusing for an occasional dinner. He recalled an episode at Pierce's home in late May, 1854. It had been a dinner of eight gentlemen; the conversation chiefly concerned a new proposal for an underground railway within London itself. Fowler found the idea tedious, and he was disappointed when it was still discussed over brandy in the smoking room. He drank his brandy with a growing sense of fatigue. Indeed, he was thinking of taking his leave when Mr. Pierce asked him about a recent attempt to rob a gold shipment from a train.

It was only natural that Pierce should ask Fowler, for he was the brother-in-law of Sir Edgar Huddleston, of the banking firm of Huddleston & Bradford, Westminster. Mr. Fowler was the general manager of that prosperous enterprise, which specialized in dealings in foreign currency. When England and France had declared war on Russia two months previously, in March, 1854, the firm of Huddleston & Bradford was designated to arrange for the payment of British troops fighting the Crimean campaign. It was precisely such a consignment of gold that had been the object of a recent attempted theft.

"A trivial endeavour," Fowler declared, conscious that he was speaking on behalf of the bank. The other men in the room were substantial gentlemen who knew other substantial gentlemen. Mr. Fowler felt obliged to put down any suspicion of the bank's inadequacy in the strongest possible terms. "Yes, indeed," he said. "Trivial and amateurish."

"The villain expired?" asked Mr. Pierce, puffing his cigar.

"Quite," Mr. Fowler said. "The guard threw him from the train at a goodly speed. The shock must have killed him instantly."

"Has he been identified?"

"Oh, I shouldn't think so," Fowler said. "The manner of his departure was such that his features were considerably—ah, disarrayed. At one time it was said he was named Jack Perkins, but the police have taken no great interest in the matter. The whole manner of the robbery speaks of the rankest amateurism."

"I suppose," Pierce said, "that the bank must take considerable precautions."

"My dear fellow," Fowler said, "considerable precautions indeed! I assure you, one doesn't transport twelve thousand pounds in bullion to France each month without the most extensive safeguards."

"We should all be most curious to know the nature of your precautions," Pierce said. "Or is that a secret of the firm?"

"No secret at all," Fowler said, taking the opportunity to withdraw his gold watch from the pocket of his waistcoat, flick open the cover, and glance at the dial. It was past eleven; he should retire; only the necessity to uphold the bank's reputation kept him there. "In point of fact, the precautions are of my own devising. And if I may say so, I invite you to point out any weakness in them." He glanced from one face to the next.

"Each gold bullion shipment is loaded within the confines of the bank itself, which I hardly need mention is wholly impregnable. The bullion is placed in a number of ironbound strongboxes, which are then sealed. A sensible man might regard this as protection enough, but of course we go much further." He paused to sip his brandy.

"The sealed strongboxes are taken by armed guard to the railway station. The convoy follows no established route, nor timetable; it keeps to populous thoroughfares, and thus there is no chance that it may be waylaid on the road to the station. Never do we employ fewer than ten guards, all trusted and long-standing servants of the firm, and all heavily armed. At the station, the strongboxes are loaded into the luggage van of the Folkestone train, where we place them in two of the latest Chubb safes."

"Indeed?" Pierce said, raising an eyebrow. Chubb safes were universally recognized as the finest in the world.

"Nor are these the ordinary line of Chubb safes," Fowler continued, "for they have been specially built to the bank's specifications. Gentlemen, they are on all sides constructed of one-quarter-inch tempered steel, and the doors are hung with interior hinges which offer no external purchase for tampering. Why, the very weight of these safes is an impediment to theft, for they each weigh in excess of two hundred and fifty pounds and are bolted to the floor of the luggage van."

"Most impressive," Pierce said.

"So much so," Fowler said, "that one might in good conscience consider this to be adequate safeguard for the bullion shipment. And yet we have added still further refinements. Each safe is fitted with two locks, each requiring two keys."

"Two keys? How ingenious."

"Not only that," Fowler said, "but each of the four keys—two to each safe—is individually protected between shipments. Two are stored in the railway office itself. A third is in the custody of one of the bank's senior partners, Mr. Trent, a most reliable gentleman, as some of you may know. I myself am entrusted with the fourth key."

"A considerable responsibility, I should think," Pierce said.

"I must admit I felt a certain need for invention in the matter," Fowler admitted, and then lapsed into a dramatic pause.

It was a Mr. Wyndham, who was a bit stiff with drink, who

finally spoke up. "Well, damn it all, Henry, will you tell us where you have hidden your bloody key?"

Mr. Fowler took no offence, but smiled benignly. "I keep it," he said, "about my neck." And he patted his starched shirt front. "I wear it at all times, even while bathing—indeed, even in my sleep." He smiled broadly. "So, gentlemen, you see that the crude attempt of a mere child from the dangerous classes can hardly be of concern to Huddleston & Bradford, for the little ruffian had no more chance of stealing that bullion than I have of—well, of flying to the moon." Here Mr. Fowler allowed himself a chuckle at the absurdity of it all. "Now, then," he said, "can you discern any flaw in our arrangements?"

"None whatsoever," said a Mr. Bendix, and Mr. Pierce added, "I must congratulate you, Henry. It is the most ingenious strategy."

"I rather think so myself," Mr. Fowler said.

Soon thereafter, Mr. Fowler took his leave, arising with the comment that if he were not soon home to his wife, she should think him dallying with a judy—"and I should hate to suffer the pains of chastisement without the antecedent reward." His comment drew laughter from the assembled gentlemen; it was, he thought, just the right note on which to depart, although there was more truth to the statement than he would care to admit.

"I shall see you out," Pierce said, also rising.

CHAPTER THREE

England's railways grew at such a phenomenal rate that the city of London was overwhelmed, and never managed to build a central station. Instead, each of the lines, privately built, ran their tracks as far into London as they could and then erected a terminus. But in the mid century this pattern was coming under attack. The dislocation of poor people, whose dwellings were demolished to make way for the incoming lines, was one argument; another focused on the inconvenience to travellers forced to cross London by coach to make connections from one station to another.

After the construction of Victoria Station and King's Cross in

1851, there was a moratorium on further construction. This left several of the new lines at a disadvantage, and one of these was the South Eastern Railway, which ran from London to the coastal town of Folkestone, some eighty miles away. The South Eastern had to lease space at London Bridge Station from the London & Greenwich Railway.

Located on the south shore of the Thames near its namesake, London Bridge was the oldest railway station in London. It was originally constructed in 1836. Never popular, the station was attacked as "inferior in design and conception" to such later stations as Paddington and King's Cross. Yet when the station was rebuilt in 1851, the *Illustrated London News* recalled that the old station had been "remarkable for the neatness, artistic character, and reality of its *façade*" and regretted that it had disappeared, "to make room, apparently, for one of less merit."

One must admit that the new terminus was most unsatisfactory. Victorians regarded the train stations as the "cathedrals of the age"; they expected them to blend the highest principles of aesthetics and technological achievement, and many stations fulfilled that expectation with their high, arching, elegant glass vaults. But the new London Bridge Station was depressing in every way. An L-shaped two-storey structure, it had a flat, utilitarian appearance, with a row of dreary shops under an arcade to the left, and the main station straight ahead, unadorned except for a clock mounted on the roof. Most serious, its interior floor plan—the focus of most earlier criticism—remained wholly unaltered.

The traffic supervisor's offices consisted of three rooms in a remote section of the terminus—two rooms for clerks, and a larger office for the supervisor himself, with a storage area for valuable checked items. All the rooms had glass frontings. The whole suite was located on the first floor of the terminus and accessible only by an ironwork staircase leading up from the station platform. Anyone climbing or descending the stairs would be in plain view of all the passengers, porters, and guards on the platforms below.

The traffic supervisor was named McPherson. He was an elderly Scotsman who kept a close eye on his clerks, seeing to it that they did no daydreaming out of the window. Thus no one in the office noticed when, in early July, 1854, two travellers took up a position on a bench on the platform, and remained there the entire day. Nor did anyone notice when the same two gentlemen returned the following week, and again spent a day on the same bench, watching the activity in the station and frequently checking their pocketwatches while they apparently awaited their train.

In fact, Pierce and Agar were not employing pocketwatches but rather stopwatches. After the second day of watching the routine of the clerks, the changes of the guards and the arrival and departure of visitors to the office, Agar finally looked up the iron staircase to the office and announced, "It's bloody murder. She's too wide open. What's up there, anyway?"

"Two keys I happen to want," Pierce said.

Agar squinted up at the offices. If he was disappointed in Pierce's answer he gave no indication. "Well," he said, in a professional tone, "if it's two bettys you want, I reckon they are in that storage area"—he nodded, not daring to point a finger—"you see the cupboard?"

Pierce nodded. In the storage area was a shallow, wall-mounted lime green cupboard. It looked like the sort of place keys might be stored. "I see it."

"There's my money, on that cupboard. Now you'll cool she has a lock on her, but that will give us no great trouble. Cheap lock."

"What about the front door?" Pierce said, shifting his gaze. Not only was the cupboard locked, but the frosted door, with SER stencilled on it, had a large brass lock above the knob.

"Appearances," Agar snorted. "I could open her with a ragged fingernail. The problem is the crowds."

Pierce nodded, but said nothing. This was essentially Agar's operation, and he would have to figure it out. "Two keys is four waxes. Four waxes is nigh on a minute, to do it proper. But that doesn't count cracking the outside, or the inside cabinet." Agar looked around at the crowded platform, and the clerks in the office. "Bloody flummut to try and crack her by day," he said. "Too many people about."

"Night?"

"Aye, at night, when she's empty."

"At night, the crushers make rounds," Pierce reminded him. They had already learned that during the evening, when the station was deserted, the policemen patrolled it at four-or-five-minute intervals. "Will you have time?"

Agar squinted up at the offices. "Not unless they were already open. Then I can make my entrance neat as you please, and I do the waxes quick-like, and I'm gone in less than two minutes flat."

"But the offices will be locked," Pierce said.

"I'm thinking of a snakesman," Agar said.

Pierce looked up. The supervisor's office had a broad glass window; through it, he could see Mr. McPherson, in his shirtsleeves, with white hair and a green shade over his forehead. And behind McPherson was a window for ventilation, a window no more than a foot square.

"A proper snakesman can make it through," Agar said. A snakesman was a child adept at wriggling through small spaces. Usually he was a former chimney sweep's apprentice. "And once he's in the office, he unlocks the cupboard, and he unlocks the door from the inside, and he sets it all up proper for me. That will make this job a bone lay, and no mistake," he said, nodding in satisfaction.

"If there's a snakesman."

"Aye."

"And he must be the devil's own," Pierce said, looking again at the window, "if we are to break that drum. Who's the best?"

"The best?" Agar said, looking surprised. "The best is Clean Willy, but he's in Newgate Prison, and there's no escaping that."

"Perhaps Clean Willy can find a way out."

"Nobody can find a way," said Agar. "It's been tried before."

"I'll get a word to Willy," Pierce said, "and we shall see."

Agar nodded. "I'll hope," he said, "but not too excessive."

The two men resumed watching the offices. "Here comes the esclop," Agar said, meaning a policeman.

Pierce saw the police constable, and flicked his stopwatch: seven minutes forty-seven seconds since the last circuit.

"You see a lurk?" Pierce said.

Agar nodded to a baggage stand in a corner, not more than a dozen paces from the staircase. "There'd do."

The two men remained seated. At seven o'clock, the clerks left the office to return home. At seven twenty, the supervisor departed, locking the door after him. The two men remained another hour, until the last train had departed, and they were too conspicuous. They remained just long enough to clock the constable on night duty as he made his rounds of the station.

Pierce glanced at the second hand on his stopwatch. "Five minutes, three seconds," he said. "Can you do it?"

"Of course I can do it," Agar said. "If I have a snakesman like Clean Willy."

The two men left the railway station. As they stepped into the fading twilight, Pierce signalled his cab. The cabby with a scar across his forehead whipped up his horse and clattered towards the station entrance.

"When do we knock it over?" Agar said.

Pierce gave him a gold guinea. "When I inform you," he said. And then he got into the waiting cab and rode off into the deepening night darkness.

BY THE MIDDLE OF July, 1854, Pierce knew the location of three of the four keys he needed to rob the safes. Two keys were in the traffic supervisor's office. A third hung around the neck of Henry Fowler. To Pierce, these three keys presented no major problem. The real difficulty centred around the fourth key. Pierce knew it was in the possession of Mr. Trent, but he did not know *where*—and this lack of knowledge represented a formidable challenge indeed, and one that occupied his attention for the next four months.

A few words of explanation may be useful here. In 1854, Alfred Nobel was just beginning his career and would not discover dynamite for another decade. Combination locks had not yet been invented, and safe manufacturers were careful to employ the heaviest construction materials available to discourage thieves from stealing the whole safe outright. As the master safe-cracker, Neddy Sykes, said at his trial in 1848: "The key is everything in a lay, the problem and the solution."

A key, if one stops to think about it, is really rather small. It can be concealed almost anywhere on a person's body, or in a room—particularly in a cluttered Victorian room, where even so ordinary an item of furniture as a waste-paper basket was likely to be covered in cloth, layers of fringes, and decorative rings of tassels. Furthermore, the Victorians themselves adored secret compartments and concealed spaces; a mid-century writing desk was advertised as "containing 110 compartments, including many most artfully concealed from detection".

The first question was whether Mr. Trent kept his key in the bank. Junior clerks of Huddleston & Bradford took their dinner at one o'clock at a pub called the Horse and Rider, across the street from the firm. Here Pierce struck up an acquaintance with a young clerk named Rivers.

Normally, the servants and junior clerks of the bank were wary of casual acquaintances, for one never knew when one was talking to a criminal out of twig; but Rivers was relaxed, in the knowledge that the bank was impregnable to burglary—and perhaps because he had a deal of resentment towards the source of his employment.

In this regard, one may profitably record the "Rules for Office Staff" posted by Mr. Trent. These were as follows:

1. Godliness, cleanliness and punctuality are the necessities of a good business.
2. The firm has reduced the working day to the hours from 8:30 a.m. to 7:00 p.m.
3. Prayers will be held each morning in the main office.
4. Clothing will be of a sober nature. The clerical staff will not disport themselves in raiment of bright colour.
5. A stove is provided for the benefit of the clerical staff. It is recommended that each member of the clerical staff bring 4 lb. of coal each day during cold weather.
6. No member of the clerical staff may leave the room without permission. For calls of nature clerical staff may use the garden beyond the second gate.
7. No talking is allowed during business hours.
8. The craving of tobacco, wines or spirits is a human weakness, and as such is forbidden to the clerical staff.

9. Members of the clerical staff will provide their own pens.
10. The managers expect a great rise in the output of work to compensate for these near Utopian conditions.

However Utopian, the working conditions of Huddleston & Bradford led Rivers to speak freely about Mr. Trent. "Bit of a stiff, he is," Rivers said. "Snapping his watch at eight thirty sharp, and God help the man whose omnibus is late."

"Demands his routine, does he?"

"With a vengeance. He's vain, too: grew whiskers longer than yours, he did, on account of the fact he's losing the hair up top." During this period, whiskers on gentlemen was a new fashion, and opinion was divided on its benefits.

"He has this brush I hear," Rivers went on. "Dr. Scott's electric hairbrush, comes from Paris."

"What's it do?" Pierce inquired.

"Cures headaches, dandruff, and baldness, too," Rivers said, "or so it's claimed. Mr. Trent locks himself into his office and brushes once an hour, punctual." Here Rivers laughed at the foibles of his employer.

"He must have a large office."

"Aye, large and comfortable. He's an important man, Mr. Trent."

"Keeps it tidy?"

"Aye, the sweeper's in every night."

Pierce did not recall the rest of the conversation for he now knew what he wanted—that Trent did not keep the key in his office. If he did, he would never leave the place to be cleaned in his absence, for sweepers were notoriously easy to bribe.

But even if the key was not in the office, it might still be kept in the bank. To determine if this was so, Pierce could strike up a conversation with a different clerk, but he was anxious to avoid this. Instead, he chose another method.

TEDDY BURKE, twenty-four, was working the Strand at two in the afternoon, the most fashionable hour. Like the other gentlemen, he was decked out, wearing a high hat, frock coat, narrow trousers, and a dark silk choker. This outfit had cost him a pretty, but it was essential to his business, for Teddy Burke was one of the swell mobsmen.

In the throng of gentlemen and ladies who browsed among the elegant shops no one would notice that Teddy Burke was not alone. In fact, he was working his usual operation, with himself as dipper, a stickman at his side, and two stalls front and back, four men, each as well dressed as the next.

On this fine early summer day, the air was warm and redolent of horse dung, despite the busy working of a dozen street-urchin sweepers. There was heavy traffic of carts, brightly lettered omnibuses, four-wheel and hansom cabs, and from time to time an elegant chariot drove past, with a uniformed coachman in front and liveried servants standing behind. Ragged children darted among the traffic and turned cartwheels under the horses' hoofs for the amusement of the crowd, some of whom threw them a few coppers.

Teddy Burke was oblivious of the excitement, and of the rich array of goods in the shopwindows. His attention was wholly fixed upon the quarry, a fine lady wearing a heavy flounced crinoline skirt. His gang was in formation. One stall had taken up a position three paces ahead; another was five paces back. The stalls would create confusion should anything go wrong. Teddy Burke planned to work the quarry on the fly, the most difficult kind of dip, as she moved from one shop to the next.

"Right, here we go," he said, and the stickman moved alongside him. It was the stickman's job to take the pogue once Teddy had snaffled it, thus leaving Teddy clean, should there be any hue and cry and a constable to stop him.

Together with the stickman, he moved so close to the woman that he could smell her perfume. He could see her handbag on her right arm.

Teddy carried an overcoat draped across his left arm. A sensible person might have asked why a gentleman would carry an overcoat on such a warm day; but the coat looked new, and he could have conceivably just picked it up from one of the nearby shops. In any case, the overcoat concealed the movement of his right arm across his body to the woman's handbag. His fingers prised it open, searched deftly for the purse, and touched it; he took a deep breath, praying that the coins would not clink, and lifted it out.

Immediately he eased away from the woman, shifted his overcoat to his other arm, and in the course of that movement passed the purse to the stickman. The stickman drifted off. Ahead and behind, the stalls moved out in different directions. Only Teddy Burke, now clean, continued to walk along the Strand, pausing before a shop that displayed crystal decanters imported from France.

A tall gent with a red beard was admiring the wares in the window. He did not look at Teddy Burke. "Nice pull," he said.

Teddy Burke blinked.

The speaker was too well-dressed to be a plainclothes crusher, and he certainly wasn't a nose, or informer. Teddy Burke said carefully, "Are you addressing me, sir?"

"Yes," the man said. "Shall we walk awhile?"

Teddy Burke shrugged and fell into step alongside the stranger. They walked for some minutes in silence. "Do you think you can be less effective?" the man asked after a time.

"How do you mean, sir?"

"I mean," the man said, "can you buzz a customer and come out dry?"

"On purpose?" Teddy Burke laughed. "It happens often enough without trying, I can tell you that."

"There's five quid for you, if you can prove yourself a prize bungler."

Teddy Burke's eyes narrowed. There were plenty of magsmen about, who often employed an unwitting accomplice to take a fall in some elaborate scheme. Teddy Burke was nobody's fool. "Five quid's no great matter."

"Ten," the man said, in a weary voice.

"What's the lay, then?" Teddy Burke said.

"Lots of bustle, just enough to set the quarry to worry, make him pat his pockets."

"Who's the quarry, then?" Teddy Burke said.

"A gent named Trent. He's about sixty, has a grey beard, long sidewhiskers and a considerable paunch. He arrives at his office, just before eight thirty. The Huddleston & Bradford Bank."

REGENT
CIRCUS

Teddy Burke whistled. "Westminster. Sticky, that is. There's enough crushers about to make an army."

"But you'll be dry. All you've to do is worry him."

Teddy Burke walked a few minutes, thinking things over. "When will it be, then?"

"Tomorrow morning."

"All right."

The red-bearded gentleman gave him a five-pound note and informed him he would get the rest when the job was done.

"What's it all about, then?" Teddy Burke asked.

"Personal matter," the man replied, and slipped quickly away into the crowd.

AS DAWN CAME, the silence of respectable central London was broken by the crowing of cocks and the mooing of cows, sounds incongruous in an urban setting. But in those days animal husbandry was still a major London industry and during the day a major source of traffic congestion. It was not uncommon for a fine gentleman to be delayed in his coach by a shepherd with his flock. By modern standards the division between city and country life was blurred.

When the Horse Guards clock chimed seven o'clock, the first of that urban phenomenon—commuters—appeared on their way to work, conveyed by "the Marrowbone stage", that is, on foot. These were the armies of women and girls employed as seamstresses in the sweatshops of West End dress factories, where they worked twelve hours a day for a few shillings a week. At eight o'clock, the shops along the great thoroughfares took down their shutters; apprentices and assistants dressed the windows in preparation for the day's commerce. Between eight and nine o'clock was rush hour, and the streets became crowded with men. Everyone from government clerks to bank cashiers, from stockbrokers to soap-boilers, made their way to work on foot, in omnibuses, tandems, dogcarts—altogether a rattling, noisy traffic jam. In the midst of this, the street sweepers began their day's labours, collecting the first droppings of horse dung. And they were busy: an ordinary London horse deposited six tons of dung on the streets each year, and there were at least a million horses in the city.

Pierce and Agar, crouched on a rooftop overlooking the imposing façade of the Huddleston & Bradford Bank across the way, watched an elegant brougham, delicately sprung, with gleaming dark polished wood carriage and lacy-spoked wheels come down the street towards them.

"There he is now," Agar said.

Pierce checked his watch. "Eight twenty-nine. Punctual, as usual."

The brougham pulled up to the door of the bank, and the driver jumped down to open the door. Mr. Edgar Trent stepped down to the pavement.

"Watch, now," Pierce said.

At the very moment that Mr. Trent stepped to the ground, a well-dressed young man jostled him roughly, muttered a brief apology over his shoulder, and moved on in the rush-hour crowd. Mr. Trent walked the few steps forward to the impressive oak doors of the bank, then stopped, in mid stride.

"He's realized," Pierce said.

On the street below, Trent looked after the well-dressed young man, and immediately patted his side coat pocket, feeling for some article. Apparently, what he sought was still in its place, his shoulders dropped in relief, and he continued on into the bank.

Pierce grinned and turned to Agar. "Well," he said, "that's what we need to know."

"What's that, then?" Agar said.

"We need to know," Pierce said slowly, "that Mr. Trent brought his key with him today, for this is the day of—" He broke off abruptly. He had not yet informed Agar of the plan, and he saw no reason to do so until the last minute. A man with a tendency to be a soak, like Agar, could loosen his tongue at an unlikely time.

"The day of what?" Agar persisted.

"The day of reckoning," Pierce said.

"You're a tight one," Agar said. And then he added, "Wasn't that Teddy Burke, trying a pull?"

"Who's Teddy Burke," Pierce said.

"A swell, works the Strand."

"I wouldn't know," Pierce said, and the two men left.

"Cor, you're a tight one," Agar said again. "That *was* Teddy Burke."

Pierce just smiled.

IN THE COMING DAYS, Pierce learned a great deal about Mr. Edgar Trent's daily routine. Mr. Trent was a rather severe gentleman; he rarely drank, never smoked or played at cards. He was the father of five children ranging in age from a four-year-old son to a twenty-nine-year-old daughter; his first wife had died in childbirth some years before and his second wife, Emily, was thirty years his junior and an acknowledged beauty.

The Trent family resided at No. 17 Highwater Street, Mayfair, in a large Georgian mansion. Altogether, twelve servants were employed: a coachman, two liverymen, a gardener, a footman, a butler, a cook and two kitchen assistants, and three maids. There was also a governess for the three youngest children.

Mr. Trent kept two bulldogs, which were walked twice a day, at seven in the morning and at eight-fifteen at night, by the cook's assistants. The dogs were penned in a run at the back of the house.

Mr. Trent himself followed a rigid routine. Each day, he arose at 7:00 a.m., breakfasted at 7:30, and departed for work at 8:10. He invariably lunched at Simpson's at one o'clock, for one hour. He left the bank promptly at 7:00 p.m., returning home no later than 7:20. Mr. Trent and his wife went out of an evening twice in the course of a week; they generally gave a dinner once a week and occasionally a large party. On such evenings, an extra maid and manservant would be laid on, but these people were obtained from adjacent households; they were very reliable and could not be bribed.

The servants were content. They were all well-treated and loyal to the household, particularly to Mrs. Trent. When the Trents were away most of the servants remained in the mansion. At no time, it seemed, were there fewer than eight people residing in the house.

The tradesmen who came each day to the side entrance of the house worked the entire street, and they were a close-mouthed lot, careful never to associate with a potential thief.

All this information Pierce accumulated slowly and carefully, with some help from Agar. He adopted various disguises when he talked with servants in pubs and on the street; he also loitered in the neighbourhood, observing the patterns of the house, but this was a dangerous practice.

According to his own testimony, by the end of July, Pierce had made no progress. "The man afforded no purchase," Pierce said, speaking of Trent. "No vices, no weaknesses, no eccentricities."

Clearly, there was no point in breaking into a twenty-three-room mansion on the off chance of coming upon the hidden key. Pierce had to have more information.

He had failed in every attempt to strike up a personal acquaintance with Mr. Trent. Henry Fowler, who shared with Pierce an occasional gentleman's evening on the town, had been approached on the subject of Trent, but Fowler had said the man was religious, proper, and rather a bore in conversation; and he added that his wife, though pretty, was equally tedious. (These comments, when brought forward in trial testimony, caused Mr. Fowler considerable embarrassment, but then Mr. Fowler was confronted with much greater embarrassments later).

Pierce could hardly press for an introduction to such an unappetizing couple. Nor could he approach Trent directly, pretending business with the bank; Henry Fowler would rightly expect that Pierce would bring any business to him. Nor did Pierce know anyone except Fowler who was acquainted with Trent.

By the beginning of August Pierce was considering several desperate ploys—such as staging an accident in which he would be run down by a cab in front of the Trent house, or a similar episode in front of the bank. But these tricks would require some degree of genuine injury to Pierce, and understandably he kept postponing the matter.

Then, on the evening of August 3rd, Mr. Trent suddenly changed his established routine. He returned home at his usual time, 7:20, but he did not go indoors. Instead, he went directly to the dog run at the back of the house and put one of his bulldogs on a leash. Petting the animal elaborately, he climbed back into his waiting carriage and drove off.

When Pierce saw that, he knew he had his man.

CHAPTER FOUR

Not far from Southwark Mint was the livery stable of Jeremy Johnson & Son. It was a smallish establishment, quartering perhaps two dozen horses in three wooden barns. A casual visitor to this stable might be surprised to hear, instead of the whinny of horses, the predominant sound of barking, growling, snarling dogs. But the meaning of those sounds was clear enough to frequenters of the place. Throughout London, there were many reputable establishments that operated a side business of training fighting dogs.

Mr. Jeremy Johnson led his red-bearded customer back through the stables. He was a jovial old man with most of his teeth missing. "What is it you'll be wanting?" he asked.

"Your best," Pierce said. "I am very particular."

"Oh, I can see that," Johnson said. "You're seeking a learner, so as to polish him yourself?"

"No," Pierce said, "I want a fully made dog."

"That's dear, you know, very dear." Johnson mumbled. He pushed open a creaking door, to a small courtyard at the rear. Here were caged dogs on all sides. The dogs yelped and barked as they saw the men.

"Very dear, a made dog," Johnson said. "Takes a proper long training. First we gives the dog to a coster, and he jogs the dog day and day again—to toughen him, you know."

"I understand," Pierce said impatiently, "but I—"

"Then," Johnson continued, "then we puts the learner in with an old gummer—or a young gummer, as the case is now. Lost our gummer a fortnight past, so we took this one"—he pointed to a caged dog—"and yanked all the teeth, so he's the gummer now. Very good he is, too. Knows how to worry a learner."

Pierce looked at the gummer. It was a young dog, barking vigorously. All its teeth were gone, yet it continued to snarl and pull back its lips menacingly. The sight made Pierce laugh.

"Yes, yes, 'tis a bit of a joke," Johnson said, moving around the enclosure, "but not when you get to this one here. Now here, there's no joking. Here's the finest taste dog in all of London, I warrant."

This was a mongrel, larger than a bulldog, and parts of its body had been shaved. Pierce knew the routine: after the sparring bouts with a gummer, a young dog was put into the pit with a taste dog, to acquire the final skills for the kill. The usual practice was to shave the vulnerable parts of the taste dog, encouraging the learner to attack those areas.

"This taster," Johnson said, "has put the touches on more champions than you can name. You know Mr. Benderby's dog, the one that bested the Manchester killer last month? Well, this taster here trained Mr. Benderby's dog." Johnson squinted at Pierce. "You want your dog for ratting? We have special trained ratters," Mr. Johnson said. "A touch less dear, is why I mention it."

"I want your very best made dog."

"And you shall have it, I warrant. Here is the devil's own, right here." Johnson paused before a caged bulldog that weighed about forty pounds. The dog growled but did not move. "See that? He's a confident one. He's had a good mouthful or two, and he's as vicious as ever I saw."

"How much?" Pierce said.

"Twenty quid."

After a lengthy silence, Pierce said, "I want your *best* dog." He pointed to the cage. "This dog has never fought. He has no scars, I want a trained veteran."

"Well, then," Johnson said, looking away as if embarrassed, "there *is* one more animal, but he's very special. This way."

He led Pierce out of the enclosed courtyard to another area where there were three dogs in somewhat larger pens. They were all heavier than the others; Pierce guessed they must weigh fifty pounds, perhaps more. Johnson tapped the middle cage.

"This'un," he said. "This'un turned felon on me," Johnson rolled up his sleeve to reveal a set of jagged white scars. "Thought I'd have to top him off, but I brought him back, nursed him, and trained him special, because he has the spirit, see, and the spirit's everything."

"How much?" Pierce said.

Johnson glanced at the scars on his arm. "This'un I was saving—"

"How much?"

"Couldn't let him go for less'n fifty quid, beg pardon."

"I will give you forty."

"Sold," Johnson said quickly. "You'll take 'im now?"

"No," Pierce said. "I'll call for him soon."

"Then you'll be putting a little something down?"

"I will," Pierce said, and gave the man ten pounds.

"Damn me," Johnson said after he had gone. "Man buys a made dog, then leaves him. What're we up to today?"

CAPTAIN JIMMY SHAW, a retired pugilist, ran the most famous of the sporting pubs, the Queen's Head, off Windmill Street. A visitor on the evening of August 10th, 1854, would be greeted by a most peculiar spectacle, for although the pub was notably dingy and cheap, it was filled with all manner of well-dressed gentlemen who rubbed shoulders with hawkers, costers, navvies, and others of the lowest social station. Yet nobody seemed to mind, for everyone shared a state of excited, noisy anticipation. Furthermore, nearly everyone had brought a dog. There were all sorts: bulldogs, terriers, various mongrels. Some nestled in the arms of their owners; others were tied to the legs of tables. All were the subject of intense discussion and scrutiny.

The few decorative features of the Queen's Head reflected this same interest in dogs. There were stuffed dogs in dirty glass boxes mounted over the bar and prints of dogs by the hearth.

Captain Jimmy moved about the room calling, "Give your orders, gentlemen." Then, at nine o'clock, he gave the order to "light up the pit" and the entire assembled company began to file towards the upstairs room, each man carrying his dog, and each man dropping a shilling into the hand of a waiting assistant.

The first floor of the Queen's Head was a large room, as low-ceilinged as the ground floor. This room was devoid of furnishings, and dominated by the pit—a circular arena six feet in diameter, enclosed by slat boards four feet high. The floor of the pit was whitewashed, freshly applied each evening.

As the spectators arrived, their dogs immediately came alive, jumping in their owners' arms, barking vigorously, and straining on the leashes. Captain Jimmy said sternly, "Now you gentlemen that have fancies—shut 'em up," and there was some attempt to do this, but it was hardly successful, especially when the first cage of rats was brought forth.

Captain Jimmy held the rusty wire cage over his head, waving it in the air; it contained perhaps fifty scampering rats. "Nothing but the finest, gentlemen," he announced. "Every one country born. Who wants to try a rat?"

By now, fifty or sixty people had crammed into the narrow room. There was money in every hand, and lively bargaining. Over the general din, a voice from the back spoke up. "I'll have a try at twenty. Twenty of your best for my fancy."

"Weigh the fancy of Mr. T.," Captain Jimmy said, for he knew the speaker. The assistants rushed up and took the bulldog from the arms of a grey-bearded, balding gentleman. The dog was weighed.

"Twenty-seven pounds!" came the cry, and the dog was returned to its owner.

"That's it, then, gents," Captain Jimmy said. "Twenty-seven pounds is Mr. T.'s fancy dog, and he has called for a try at twenty rats. Shall it be four minutes?"

Mr. T. nodded in agreement.

"Four minutes it is, gentlemen, and you may wager as you see fit. Make room for Mr. T."

The grey-bearded gentleman moved up to the edge of the pit, still cradling his dog in his arms. The animal was spotted black and it snarled at the rats. Mr. T. urged his dog on by making snarling and growling noises himself. "Let's see them," Mr. T. said.

The assistant opened the cage and reached in to grab the rats with his bare hand. This was important, for it proved that the rats were indeed country animals, and not diseased. The assistant picked out "twenty of the finest" and tossed them down into the pit. The animals scampered around the perimeter, then finally huddled together in one corner, in a furry mass.

"Are we ready?" called Captain Jimmy, brandishing a stop-watch in his hand.

"Ready," said Mr. T., growling to his dog.

"Blow on 'em! Blow on 'em!" came the cry from the spectators, and various dignified gentlemen puffed and blew towards the rats, raising their fur and sending them into a frenzy.

"Aaannnddd . . . *go*!" shouted Captain Jimmy, and Mr. T. flung his dog into the pit. Immediately Mr. T. crouched down until his head was just above the wooden rim, and from this position he urged his dog on with instructions and growls.

The dog leapt forward into the mass of rats, striking out at them, snapping at the necks like the true and well-blooded sport that he was. In an instant he had killed three or four.

The betting spectators screamed and yelled no less than the owner, who never took his eyes from the combat. "That's it!" shouted Mr. T. "That's a dead one, drop 'im, now *go!* Grrrrrr! Good, that's another, drop 'im. *Go!* Grrr-rugh!"

The dog moved quickly from one furry body to the next. Then one rat caught hold of his nose and clung tightly; the dog writhed, got free, and raced after the others. Now there were six rats killed.

"Two minutes past," called Captain Jimmy.

"Hi, Lover, good Lover," screamed Mr. T. "Go, boy, go!"

The dog raced around the arena, pursuing its quarry; the crowd screamed and pounded the wooden slats to keep the animals in a frenzy. At one point Lover had four rats clinging to his face and body, and still he kept going, crunching a fifth in his strong jaws. In the midst of all this furious excitement, no one noticed a red-bearded gentleman of dignified bearing who pushed his way through the crowd until he was standing alongside Mr. T.

"Three minutes," Captain Jimmy called. There was a groan from several in the crowd. Three minutes gone and only twelve rats dead; those who had bet on Mr. T.'s fancy were going to lose.

Mr. T. himself did not seem to hear the time. His eyes never left the dog; he barked and yelped; he writhed with his dog; he snapped his jaws and screamed orders until he was hoarse.

"Time!" shouted Captain Jimmy. The crowd sighed and relaxed. Lover was pulled from the arena; the three remaining rats were deftly scooped up by the assistants.

The ratting match was over; Mr. T. had lost.

"Bloody good try," said the red-bearded man, in consolation.

THE PARADOXES inherent in Mr. Edgar Trent's behaviour at the Queen's Head pub require some explanation.

In the first place, a banker, a devout Christian, and a pillar of the respectable community would normally never think to associate himself with members of the lower orders. Yet there were a few places in Victorian society where members of all classes mingled freely, and chief among these were sporting events—the prize ring, the turf, and, of course, the baiting sports.

Animal baiting had been a cherished form of amusement throughout Western Europe since medieval times. But in Victorian England animal sports were dying out rapidly. The baiting of bulls or bears, common at the turn of the century, was now quite rare; cockfighting was found only in rural centres. In London in 1854, only three animal sports remained popular, and all concerned dogs.

Nearly every foreign observer since Elizabethan times has commented on the affection Englishmen lavish upon their dogs, and it is odd that the very creature most dear to English hearts should be the focus of these sadistic "sporting events".

Of the three dog sports, dogs set against other dogs was considered the highest "art". But dogfights were relatively uncommon, since they were ordinarily battles to the death, and a good fighting dog was an expensive article.

Even less common was badger-baiting. Here a badger would be chained in an arena, and a dog or two set loose to worry the animal. The badger's tough hide and sharp bite made the spectacle particularly tense and highly popular, but a scarcity of badgers limited the sport.

Ratting was the most common dog sport. Although technically illegal, it was conducted for decades with flagrant disregard for the law. Throughout London there were signs reading, "Rats Wanted" and "Rats Bought and Sold"; there was, in fact, a minor industry in ratcatching since a sporting pub with a well-attended rat pit might buy two thousand rats a week—and a good country rat could fetch as much as a shilling. At the same time, reputable gentlemen felt no unease at participating in ratting sports; they considered themselves "staunch supporters of the destruction of vermin", and nothing more.

ONE SUCH STAUNCH SUPPORTER, Mr. T., retired to the downstairs rooms of the Queen's Head pub, which was now virtually deserted. Signalling the solitary barman, he called for a glass of gin for himself and some peppermint for his fancy. He was in the process of washing his dog's mouth out with the peppermint—to prevent canker—when the red-bearded gentleman came down the stairs and said, "May I join you for a glass?"

"By all means," Mr. T. said, continuing to minister to his dog.

Upstairs, the sound of stamping feet and shouting indicated the beginning of another episode of the destruction of vermin. The red-bearded stranger had to shout over the din. "I perceive you are a gentleman of sporting instinct," he said.

"And unlucky," Mr. T. said, equally loudly. He stroked his dog. "Lover was not at his best this evening." He ran his hands over the dog's body, probing for deep bites, and wiped the blood of several cuts from his fingers with his handkerchief. "But he came off well enough, and will fight again."

"Indeed," the red-bearded man said, "and I shall wager upon him again when he does."

Mr. T. showed a trace of concern. "Did you lose?"

"A trifle. Ten guineas, it was nothing."

Mr. T. was well enough off, but not disposed to think of ten guineas as "a trifle". He looked again at his drinking companion, noticing the fine cut of his coat.

"I am pleased you take it so lightly," he said. "Permit me to buy you a glass, as a token of your ill fortune."

"I count it no ill fortune at all," returned the red-bearded man. "Indeed, I admire a man who may keep a fancy and sport him. I should do so myself, were I not so often abroad on business."

"Oh, yes?" said Mr. T., signalling to the barman.

"Why, only the other day, I was offered a most excellently made dog," said the stranger. "I could not make the purchase, for I have no time myself to look after the animal."

"Most unfortunate," said Mr. T. "What was the price asked?"

"Fifty guineas."

The waiter brought the drinks. "I am myself in search of a made dog," Mr. T. said.

"Indeed?"

"I should like a third to complement my stable, with Lover and Shantung. But I don't suppose. . . ."

The red-bearded gentleman paused discreetly before answering. The training, buying, and selling of fighting dogs was, after all, illegal. "If you wish," Pierce said at last, "I could inquire whether the animal is still available."

"Oh, yes? That would be very good of you." Mr. T. had a sudden thought. "But were I you, I should buy it myself. After all, your wife could instruct the servants in the care of the beast."

"I fear," replied the red-bearded man, "that I have devoted too much of my energies these past years to the pursuit of business concerns. I have never married." And then he added, "But of course, I should like to."

"Of course," Mr. T. said, with a most peculiar look coming over his face.

CHAPTER FIVE

Victorian England was the first society to constantly gather statistics on itself, and generally these figures were a source of unabashed pride. Beginning in 1840, however, one trend was worrying: there were increasingly more single women than men.

Here was a problem of considerable gravity. Women of lower stations in life could take jobs as seamstresses, flower girls, or any of a dozen lowly occupations. These women were of no pressing concern. But the problem presented by the daughters of the middle- and upper-class households was different. These young ladies possessed education and a taste for genteel living. And they had been raised from birth for no other purpose than to be "perfect wives". It was terribly important that such women should marry, or they became pitiful social misfits.

In practice, an unmarried daughter of a professional man could use the one unique attribute of her position, education, and become a governess. But by 1851, twenty-five thousand women were already employed as governesses and there was, to say the least, no need for more. Her other choices were much less appealing: she might perhaps be a shop assistant, a clerk, a telegraphist, or a nurse, but all these occupations were more suitable for an ambitious lower-class woman than a gentlewoman of quality. If a young woman refused such demeaning work, her spinsterhood imposed a considerable financial burden upon the household.

In short, there was intense pressure for marriage—any sort of decent marriage—felt by fathers and daughters alike. The Victorians tended to marry relatively late, but Mr. Edgar Trent had a daughter Elizabeth, now twenty-nine and of "wholly marriageable condition"—meaning somewhat past her prime. It could not have escaped Mr. Trent's attention that the red-bearded gentleman might be in need of a wife. The gentleman himself expressed no reluctance to marry, thus there was no reason to believe that he might not be drawn to Elizabeth. With this in mind, Mr. Trent contrived to invite Mr. Pierce to his house in Highwater Street for Sunday tea, on the pretext of discussing the purchase of a fighting dog from Mr. Pierce. Mr. Pierce accepted the invitation.

Elizabeth Trent was not called as a witness at the trial of Pierce, out of deference to her finer sensibilities. But accounts of the time give us a picture of her. She was of medium height, rather darker in complexion than was the fashion, and her features were, in the words of one observer, "regular enough without being what one might call pretty." Then, as now, journalists were inclined to exaggerate the beauty of any woman involved in a scandal, so that the absence of compliments about Miss Trent's appearance probably implies "an unfortunate aspect". She apparently had few suitors, and must surely have been impressed with Pierce, that "dashing, intrepid, fine figure of a man with charm to burn".

By all accounts, Pierce was equally impressed by the young lady. A servant's testimony records their initial meeting.

Mr. Pierce was taking tea on the back lawn with Mr. Trent and Mrs. Trent. They watched as bricklayers patiently erected a ruined building, while nearby a gardener planted picturesque weeds. This was the last gasp of a nearly one-hundred-year English fascination with ruins; they were still so fashionable that everyone who could afford a decent ruin installed one in his grounds.

Pierce watched the workmen for a while. "What is it to be?" he inquired.

"We thought a water mill," Mrs. Trent said. "It will be so delightful, especially if there is the rusted curve of the waterwheel itself. Don't you think so?"

At that moment Elizabeth arrived, wearing a white crinoline. "Ah, my darling daughter," Mr. Trent said, rising, and Mr. Pierce rose with him. "May I present Mr. Edward Pierce, my daughter Elizabeth."

"I confess I did not know you had a daughter," Pierce said. He bowed deeply at the waist, took her hand, and seemed about to kiss it but hesitated. He appeared greatly flustered by the young woman's arrival on the scene.

"Miss Trent," he said, releasing her hand awkwardly. "You take me quite by surprise."

"I cannot tell if that is to my advantage or no," Elizabeth Trent replied, quickly taking a seat at the tea table and holding out her hand until a filled cup was put in it.

"I assure you, it is wholly to your advantage," Mr. Pierce replied. And he was reported to have coloured deeply at this remark.

Miss Trent fanned herself; Mr. Trent cleared his throat; Mrs. Trent picked up a tray of biscuits and said, "Will you try one of these, Mr. Pierce?"

"With gratitude, madam," Mr. Pierce replied.

"We are just discussing the ruins," Mr. Trent said, in a somewhat overloud voice. "But prior to that Mr. Pierce was telling us of his travels abroad. He has recently returned from New York."

It was a cue; his daughter picked it up neatly. "Really?" she said, fanning herself briskly. "How utterly fascinating."

"I fear it is more so in the prospect than the telling," Mr. Pierce replied, avoiding the glance of the young woman to such a degree that all observed his abashed reticence. He was clearly taken with her; and the final proof was that he addressed his remarks to Mrs. Trent. "It is a city like any other in the world, if truth be told, and chiefly distinguished by the lack of niceties which we residents of London take for granted."

"What business took you to New York?" Mr. Trent asked.

"If I may be so bold," Mr. Pierce continued, ignoring the question, "and if the delicate ears of the ladies present shall not be offended, I shall give an example of the savagery which persists in the American lands, and the rude way of life which many persons there think nothing remarkable. Do you know of buffaloes?"

"I have read of them," said Mrs. Trent, her eyes flashing. "The buffaloes are large beasts, like wild cows, and shaggy."

"Precisely so," Mr. Pierce said. "The western portion of the American country is widely populated with these buffalo creatures, and many persons make their livelihood in hunting them. Some seek the flesh of the animals, which is reckoned like venison, and some the hide, which also has value."

"They lack tusks," Mr. Trent said. Mr. Trent had lately financed an elephant-killing expedition on behalf of the bank, and at this very moment an enormous warehouse at the dock was filled with five thousand ivory tusks.

"No, they have no tusks, although the male of the species possesses horns."

"Please go on," Mrs. Trent said, her eyes still flashing.

"Well," Pierce said, "on occasion, the men who hunt these buffaloes drive the beasts over some cliff in a mass. But that is not common. Most frequently, the beast is dispatched singly. In any event—and here I must beg excuses for the crudity of what I must report—once the beast has terminated existence, its innards are removed."

"Very sensible," Mr. Trent said.

"To be sure," Pierce said, "but here is the peculiar part. These buffalo hunters prize as the greatest of delicacies the small intestines of the beast."

"How are they prepared?" Miss Trent asked. "By roasting over a fire, I expect."

"No, madam," Pierce said, "for I am telling you a tale of abject savagery. These intestines are consumed upon the spot, in a state wholly uncooked."

"Dear God," said Mrs. Trent.

"Now, then," Pierce continued, "it happens upon occasion that two men may have joined in the killing, and immediately afterwards each falls upon one end of the prized intestines, trying to gobble up this delicacy faster than his opponent."

"Gracious," Miss Trent said, fanning herself more briskly.

"Not only that," Pierce said, "but in their greedy haste, the buffalo hunter often swallows the portions whole. This is a known trick. But his opponent, recognizing the trick, may in the course of eating pull from the other the undigested portion from his mouth. And thus one man may gobble up what another has earlier eaten, in a manner of speaking."

"Oh, dear," said Mrs. Trent, turning quite pale.

"How quaint," said Miss Trent bravely, with a shivering voice.

"You really must excuse me," said Mrs. Trent, rising.

"My dear," Mr. Trent said.

"Madam, I hope I have not distressed you," said Mr. Pierce, also rising.

"Your tales are quite remarkable," Mrs. Trent said, turning to leave. Mr. Trent hastened after her.

Thus Mr. Edward Pierce and Miss Elizabeth Trent were briefly alone on the back lawn of the mansion, and they were seen to exchange a few words. Miss Trent later admitted to a servant that she found Mr. Pierce "quite fascinating in a rough-and-ready way," and it was generally agreed in the Trent household that young Elizabeth was now in possession of that most valuable of all acquisitions, a "prospect".

CHAPTER SIX

Between 1801 and 1851, London tripled in size. With a population of two and half million, it was by far the largest city in the world, and yet it continued to grow. Already, the now familiar pattern of expansion was termed "the flight to the suburbs". Outlying areas that at the turn of the century had been villages and hamlets—Marylebone, Islington, St. John's Wood, and Bethnal Green—were thoroughly built up, and the newly affluent middle classes were deserting the central city for these areas where the air was better, the noise less bothersome, and the atmosphere in general more pleasant and "countrified".

Of course, some older sections of London retained a character of great elegance and wealth, but these were often cheek by jowl with the most shocking slums. The genesis of these was poorly understood at the time, but the now familiar pattern was recognizable: a region of the city would be cut off from circulation by newly constructed thoroughfares; businesses would depart; disagreeable industries would move in, creating noise and air pollution; ultimately, the region would become decrepit and populated only by the lowest classes.

These slums were profitable for landlords. A lodging house, or nethersken, of eight rooms might take on a hundred boarders, each paying a shilling or two a week to live in hugger-mugger promiscuity, sleeping with as many as twenty members of the same or opposite sex in the same room. While some proprietors of lodging houses lived in the area—and often accepted stolen goods in lieu of rent—many owners were substantial citizens, landlords *in absentia* who employed a tough deputy to collect the rents.

During this period there were several notorious rookeries, but none was more famous than the six acres in central London that comprised the rookery of St. Giles, called "the Holy Land". Located not far from the theatre district of Leicester Square, the prostitute centre of the Haymarket, and the fashionable shops of Regent Street, the St. Giles rookery was strategically located for any criminal who wanted to "go to ground".

Contemporary accounts describe the Holy Land as "a dense mass of houses, through which narrow and tortuous lanes curve and wind. There is no privacy here, the streets are thronged with loiterers, and the rooms crowded to suffocation". There are references to "the stagnant gutters . . . the filth choking up dark passages . . . and children swarming everywhere, relieving themselves as they please".

Such a squalid, malodorous and dangerous tenement was no place for a gentleman, particularly after nightfall. Yet in late August, 1854, a red-bearded man in fashionable attire walked fearlessly through the narrow lanes. The vagrants watching him no doubt observed that his silver-headed cane looked ominously heavy, and might conceal a blade. There was also a bulge about the trousers which implied that he was armed. And the very boldness of such a foolhardy incursion probably intimidated many of those who might be tempted to waylay him.

Pierce himself later said, "It is the demeanour which is respected among these people. They know the look of fear, and likewise its absence, and any man who is not afraid makes them afraid in turn."

Pierce went from street to stinking street, inquiring after a certain woman. Finally he found a lounger who knew her.

"It's Maggie you want? Little Maggie?" the man asked, leaning against a yellow gas lamp-post.

"She's a judy, Clean Willy's doll."

"I know of her. Pinches laundry, doesn't she? Aye, she does a bit of snow, I'm sure of it." Here the man paused significantly.

Pierce gave him a coin. "Where shall I find her?"

"First passing up, first door to yer right," the man said.

Pierce continued on. He walked down the street, past vague shadows, and here and there a woman whose clothing glowed in the night—matchstick dippers with patches of phosphorus on their garments. Dogs barked; children cried; whispers and groans and laughter were conveyed to him through the dark. Finally he arrived at the nethersken, with its bright rectangle of yellow light at the entrance shining on a crudely hand-painted sign which read: LOGINS FOR THRAVELERS.

Pierce entered the building, pushing his way past the throng of dirty, ragged children clustered about the stairs; he cuffed one briskly, to show them there was to be no plucking at his pockets. He asked after the woman named Maggie, and was told she was in the kitchen.

The kitchen was the centre of every lodging house, and at this hour it was a warm and friendly place, a focus of heat and rich smells. A half-dozen men stood by the fire, talking and drinking; at a side table, several men and women played cards while others sipped bowls of steaming soup; tucked away in the corners were musical instruments, beggars' crutches, hawkers' baskets, and pedlars' boxes. He found Maggie, and drew her to one side. He gave her a gold guinea, which she bit. One couldn't be too careful with gold guineas, but this one was genuine, and she flashed a half-smile.

"What is it, then, guv?" She looked calculatingly at his fine clothes. "A bit of a tickle for you?"

Pierce ignored the suggestion. "You dab it up with Clean Willy?"

She shrugged. "I did. Willy's in Newgate."

"You see him?"

"I do, once and again. I goes as his sister, see."

Pierce pointed to the coin she clutched in her hand. "There's another one of those if you tell Willy he should break at the next topping. It's to be Emma Barnes, the murderess. They'll hang her in public for sure. Tell him: break at the topping."

She laughed. "There's no breaks from Newgate—topping or no."

"Tell him *he* can, or he's not Clean Willy," Pierce said. "Tell him to go to the house where he first met John Simms, and all will be well."

She shook her head. "How can he break from Newgate?"

"Just tell him," Pierce said, and turned to leave.

"I'll tell," she said, and slipped the gold coin into her shoe. Pierce turned away from her and retraced his steps, leaving the Holy Land.

CHAPTER SEVEN

The execution of the notorious axe murderess Emma Barnes on August 28th, 1854, was a well-publicized affair. On the evening prior to the execution, the first of the crowds began to gather outside the high granite walls of Newgate Prison, where they would spend the night in order to be assured of a good view of the spectacle the following morning. That same evening, the gallows was brought out and assembled by the executioner's assistants.

The owners of nearby rooming houses that overlooked Newgate Square were pleased to rent their rooms for the evening to the better class of ladies and gents eager to get a room with a good view over the site. Mrs. Edna Molloy, a virtuous widow, knew perfectly well the value of her rooms, and when the well-spoken gentleman named Simms asked to hire the best of them for the night, she struck a hard bargain: twenty-five guineas.

Mr. Simms paid her on the spot, thus she paid little attention when, later in the day, he and his party filed upstairs to the hired room. The party consisted of two other men and two women, all smartly turned out in good clothes.

When the party entered the room, Simms—or Pierce, as he was better known to the others—stepped to the window and looked down at the gathering crowd. The square was dark, lit only by the glare of torches around the scaffold where the crossbar and trap were taking shape.

"Never make it," Agar said behind him.

Pierce turned. "He has to make it, laddie."

"He's the best snakesman in the business, but he can't get out of there," Agar said, jerking his thumb towards Newgate Prison.

The second man now spoke. "If it can be done, Clean Willy can do it." He spoke slowly, and gave the impression of a man who formed his thoughts with slowness. Pierce knew he could be quick in action, however, for this was Barlow, the reformed buzzer turned rampsman—a pickpocket who had degenerated to plain mugging—whom he had hired five years ago as his private cabby. Stocky, rugged Barlow, with the white knife scar across his forehead, was precisely what he wanted for a buck cabby, a man holding the reins to the cab, ready to make the getaway—or ready for a bit of a shindy if it came to that. And Barlow was loyal.

Pierce looked at the women. They were the mistresses of Agar and Barlow, which meant they were also their accomplices. He did not know their names and he did not want to. He regretted the very idea that they must be present on this occasion—in five years, he had never seen Barlow's woman—but there was no way to avoid it.

"Did you bring the trimmings?" Pierce asked.

Agar's woman opened a picnic basket. In it, he saw a sponge, medicinal powders, and bandages. There was also a carefully folded dress. "All I was told, sir."

"The dress is small?"

"Aye, sir. Barely more'n a child's frock, sir."

"Well enough," Pierce said, and turned back to look at the square once more. He stared at the granite walls of Newgate Prison.

"Here's the supper, sir," said Barlow's woman. She was an obvious soak. You could smell the gin breath across the room. Pierce looked back at the supplies of cold fowl, jars of pickled onion, lobster claws, and a packet of dark cigars.

"Very good, very good," he said, as he sat down at the table. "I'll have a leg of that chicken, and we shall disport ourselves as best we can while we wait."

PIERCE SLEPT part of the night; he was awakened at daybreak by the noise of the crowd which had now swollen to more than fifteen thousand. Pierce knew that the streets would be filled with ten or fifteen thousand more, making their way to see the hanging on their route to work. Employers hardly bothered to keep up a pretence of strictness on any morning when there was a hanging; it was an accepted fact that everybody would be late.

The gallows itself was now finished; the rope dangled in the air above the trap. Pierce glanced at his pocketwatch. It was 7:45 a.m., just a short time before the execution itself.

In the square below, the crowd began to chant: "Oh, my, think I'm going to die!" There was a good deal of laughter and stamping of feet.

They all went to the window to watch.

Agar said, "When do you think he'll make his move?"

Pierce said, "Whenever he thinks best."

The minutes passed slowly. No one in the room spoke. Finally, Barlow said, "I knew Emma Barnes—never thought she'd come to this."

Pierce said nothing.

At eight o'clock, the chimes of St. Sepulchre signalled the hour, and the crowd roared in anticipation. There was the soft jingle of a prison bell, and then a door in Newgate opened and the prisoner was led out, her wrists strapped behind her. In front was a chaplain, reciting from the Bible. Behind was the city executioner, dressed in black.

The crowd saw the prisoner and shouted "Hats off!" Every man's hat was removed as the prisoner slowly stepped up the scaffold. Then there were cries of "Down in front! Down in front!" They were, for the most part, unheeded.

Pierce kept his gaze on the condemned woman. Emma Barnes was in her thirties, and looked vigorous enough. But her eyes were distant and glazed; she did not seem to see anything. She took up her position and the city executioner fitted the rope to a chain around her neck.

The clergyman read loudly, keeping his eyes fixed on the Bible. The city executioner strapped the woman's legs together with a leather strap; then slipped a black hood over her head. At a signal, the trap opened with a wooden *crack!* that Pierce heard with startling distinctness; and the body fell, and caught, and hung instantly motionless.

There was a moment of utter silence, and then the excited roar of discussion. Pierce knew that most of the crowd would remain in the square, watching for the next hour, until the dead woman was cut down and placed in a coffin.

"Will you take some punch?" asked Agar's canary.

"No," Pierce said. And then he said, "Where is Willy?"

CLEAN WILLY WILLIAMS, the most famous snakesman of the century was inside Newgate Prison beginning his escape. He was a tiny man, and he had been famous in his youth for his agility as a chimney sweep's apprentice; in later years he had been employed by the most eminent cracksmen, and his feats were now legendary. It was said that Clean Willy could climb a surface of glass.

Certainly the guards of Newgate, knowing the celebrity of their prisoner, had kept a close watch on him these many months, just in case. Yet they also knew that in the more than seventy years since the building was finished, no convict had ever escaped from Newgate. Designed by George Dance, "one of the most meticulous intellects of the Age of Taste", every detail of the building had been set forth to emphasize the harsh facts of confinement. Thus the proportions of the window arches had been "subtly thickened in order to intensify the painful narrowness of the openings". The stones of the fifty-foot-high walls were so finely cut that they were said to be impossible to scale. Yet even if one could manage the impossible, it was to no avail, for encircling the top of the walls was an iron bar, fitted with revolving, razor-sharp spiked drums. And the bar was also fitted with spikes. No man could get past that obstacle.

With the passing months, as the guards grew familiar with the presence of little Willy, they ceased to watch him closely. He was not a difficult prisoner. He never broke the rule of silence, never spoke to a fellow inmate; he suffered the "cockchafer"—or treadmill—for the prescribed fifteen-minute intervals without complaint or incident; he worked at oakum-picking with no surcease. Indeed, there was some grudging respect for the cheerful way the little man went about the routine. He was a likely candidate for a foreshortened sentence in a year or so.

Yet at eight in the morning on August 28th, 1854, Clean Willy had slipped to a corner of the prison where two walls met, and with his back to the angle he was shinning straight up the sheer rock surface, bracing with his hands and feet. He dimly heard the chanting of the crowd: "Oh, my, think I'm going to die!" as he reached the top of the wall and without hesitation grabbed the bar with its iron spikes. His hands were immediately lacerated.

From childhood, Clean Willy had had no sensation in his palms, which were thickly covered with scar tissue. It was the custom of homeowners of the period to keep a hearth burning right to the moment when the chimney sweep and his child assistant arrived, and if the child scorched his hands in hastening up the still-hot chimney, that was not any great concern. So Clean Willy's hands had been burned again and again, and he felt nothing now as the blood trickled down from his slashed palms, ran in rivulets along his forearms, and dripped and spattered on his face.

He moved slowly along the revolving spiked wheels, down the full length of one wall, then to the second wall, and then to the third. It was exhausting work. He lost all sense of time, and never heard the noise of the crowd that followed the execution. He continued to make his way around the perimeter of the prison yard until he reached the south wall. There he paused and waited while a patrolling guard passed beneath him. The guard never looked up, although Willy later remembered that drops of blood landed on the man's cap.

When the guard was gone, Willy clambered over the spikes—cutting his chest, his knees, and his legs, so that the blood now ran very freely—and jumped fifteen feet down to the roof of the nearest building outside the prison. No one heard the sound of his landing, for everybody was attending the execution.

From that roof he jumped to another, and then another, leaping six- and eight-foot gaps without hesitation. Once or twice, he lost his grip on the shingles and slates of the roofs, but he always recovered. He had, after all, spent much of his life on rooftops.

Finally, less than half an hour from the time he began to inch his way up the prison wall, he slipped through a window at the back of Mrs. Molloy's lodging house, padded down the hall, and entered the room rented by Mr. Simms and his party.

Agar recalled that Willy presented "a ghastly aspect, most fearsome. He was barely conscious and bleeding like a stuck saint." He was revived with the vapours of ammonium chloride from a cut-glass inhaler. His clothes were stripped off by the women who pretended no modesty but worked quickly; his many wounds were staunched with styptic powder and sticking plaster, then bound with surgical bandages. Agar gave him a sip of coca wine for energy, and beef-and-iron wine for sustenance. He was forced to down some tincture of opium for his pain. This combined treatment brought the man to his senses, and enabled the women to clean his face, douse his body with rose water, and bundle him into the waiting dress. A bonnet was placed over his head, and boots laced on his feet; his bloody prison garb was stuffed in the picnic basket.

No one among the crowd of more than twenty thousand paid the slightest attention when the well-dressed party departed from Mrs. Molloy's boarding house—with one woman so faint that she had to be carried by the men into the waiting cab—and rattled off into the morning light. A faint woman was a common enough sight and, in any case, nothing to compare to a woman turning slowly at the end of the rope, back and forth, back and forth.

CLEAN WILLY was taken to Pierce's house in Mayfair, where he spent several weeks in seclusion while his wounds healed. It is from his later testimony to police that we first learn of the mysterious woman who was Pierce's mistress, and known to Willy as "Miss Miriam".

Willy was placed in an upstairs room, and the servants were told that he was a relative of Miss Miriam's who had been run down by a cab in New Bond Street. From time to time, Willy was tended by Miss Miriam. He said of her that she was "well-carried, a good figure, and well-spoke, and she walked here and there slow, never hurrying." This last sentiment was echoed by all the witnesses, who were impressed by the grace of the young woman; her eyes were said to be especially captivating.

Willy recalled only one conversation with her. He asked, "Are you his canary, then?" Meaning was she Pierce's accomplice in burglary.

"Oh no," she said smiling. "I have no ear for music."

From this he assumed she was not involved in Pierce's plans, although this was wrong. She was probably the first of the thieves to know Pierce's intentions,

At the trial, there was considerable speculation about Miss Miriam and her origins. A good deal of evidence points to the conclusion that she was an actress. This would explain her ability to mimic various accents and manners of different social classes; her tendency to wear make-up in a day when no respectable woman would let cosmetics touch her flesh; and her open presence as Pierce's mistress. In those days, the dividing line between an actress and a prostitute was exceedingly fine.

Pierce himself was rarely in the house, and on occasion he was gone overnight. Clean Willy recalled seeing him once or twice in the late afternoon, wearing riding clothes and smelling of horses.

"I didn't know you were a horse fancier," Willy once said.

"I'm not," Pierce replied shortly. "Hate the bloody beasts."

Pierce kept Willy indoors after his wounds were healed, waiting for his "terrier crop" to grow out. In those days, the surest way to identify an escaped convict was by his short haircut. By late September, his hair was longer, but still Pierce did not allow him to leave. When Willy asked why, Pierce said, "I am waiting for you to be recaptured, or found dead."

This statement puzzled Willy, but he did as he was told. A few days later, Pierce came in with a newspaper under his arm and told him he could leave. The body of a young man had been found floating in the Thames, and police authorities had identified him as the escaped convict from Newgate.

The same evening Willy went to the Holy Land where he found Maggie. Willy lived off her earnings as a laundry stealer, never venturing outside the sanctuary of the rookery. He had been warned by Pierce to keep his mouth shut, and he never mentioned that he had had help in his break from Newgate. Maggie reported of this period, "He took his ease, and spent his time cheerful, and waited for the cracksman to give his call."

CHAPTER EIGHT

Of all the fashionable sections of London, none compared to the spongy, muddy pathway in Hyde Park called the Ladies' Mile, or Rotten Row. Here, weather permitting, were literally hundreds of men and women on horseback, all dressed in the greatest splendour, radiant in the golden sunshine at four in the afternoon.

It was a scene of bustling activity; the horsemen and horsewomen packed tightly together; the women with little uniformed foot pages trotting along behind their mistresses, or sometimes accompanied by stern, mounted duennas, or sometimes escorted by their beaus. And if the spectacle of Rotten Row was splendid and fashionable, it was not entirely respectable, for many of the women were of dubious character. These were members of the highest class of prostitute and, like it or not, respectable ladies often found themselves competing with these smartly turned-out demimondaines for masculine attention.

Beginning in late September, 1854, Edward Pierce began to meet Miss Elizabeth Trent on riding excursions in the Row. The first encounter was apparently accidental, but later, by a sort of unstated agreement, they occurred with regularity. The unattractive young

woman apparently never thought it strange that Mr. Pierce should single her out from among the throng of stunning beauties in Rotten Row. Her life began to form itself around these afternoon meetings; she spent all morning preparing for them, and all evening discussing them.

At the trial, Pierce summarized their conversations as "light and trivial", and recounted only one in detail. This occurred some time in the month of October, 1854. It was a time of political upheaval and military scandal; the nation had suffered a severe blow to its self-esteem. The Crimean War was turning into a disaster. The British troops were badly trained, badly supplied, and ineptly led. Lord Raglan, the military commander, was sixty-five and "old for his age". Raglan often seemed to think he was still fighting Waterloo, and referred to the enemy as "the French", although the French were now his allies. By October, this ineptitude culminated in Lord Cardigan's charge of the Light Brigade, a spectacular feat of heroism which destroyed three-quarters of his forces in a successful effort to capture the wrong battery of enemy guns.

Nearly all upper-class Englishmen were profoundly concerned. But on that warm October afternoon in Hyde Park, Mr. Pierce gently guided Elizabeth Trent into a conversation about her father.

"He was most fearfully nervous this morning," she said.

"Indeed?" Pierce said, trotting alongside her.

"He is nervous every morning when he must send the gold shipments to the Crimea. He is a different man from the very moment he arises."

"I am certain he bears a heavy responsibility," Pierce said.

"So heavy, I fear he may take to excessive drink," Elizabeth said, and laughed a little.

"I pray you exaggerate, Miss Elizabeth."

"Well, he acts strangely. You know he is entirely opposed to the consumption of any alcohol before nightfall."

"I do, and most sensible, too."

"Well," Elizabeth Trent continued, "I suspect him of breaking his own regulation, for each morning of the shipments he goes alone to the wine cellar, with no servants to accompany him. He is insistent upon going alone. Many times my stepmother has chided him that he may stumble on the steps to the basement. But he will have none of her entreaties. He spends some time in the cellar, then emerges and makes his journey to the bank."

"I think," Pierce said, "that he merely checks the cellar for some ordinary purpose. Is that not logical?"

"No, indeed," Elizabeth said, "for at all times he relies upon my stepmother to deal in the stocking and care of the cellar, and the decanting of wines before dinners."

"Then his manner is most peculiar. I trust," Pierce said gravely, "that his responsibilities are not placing an overgreat burden upon his nervous system."

"I trust," the daughter answered, with a sigh. "Is it not a lovely day?"

"Lovely," Pierce agreed. "Unspeakably lovely, but no more lovely than you."

Elizabeth Trent tittered. "I am so happy," she said.

"And I am happy with you," Pierce said, and this was true, for now he knew the location of all four keys.

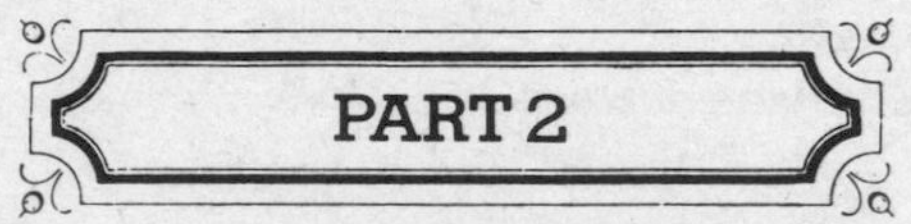

PART 2

The Keys: November 1854-February 1855

CHAPTER NINE

Mr. Henry Fowler, seated in a dark recess of the taproom at the lunch hour, showed some agitation. He twisted his glass in his hands, and he could hardly bring himself to look into the eyes of his friend Edward Pierce. "I do not know how to begin," he said. "The matter is a trifle indelicate."

"Speak forthrightly," Pierce advised, "as one man to another."

Fowler gulped his drink and set the glass back on the table with a sharp clink. "Very well. The fact is that I have a strong craving for a young virgin."

"How may I help?" Pierce asked, already knowing the answer.

"Some days ago, you did happen to mention that, as a bachelor, you might have knowledge—ah, that you might make an introduction on my behalf to a fresh country girl."

Pierce frowned. "It is no longer so easy as it once was. But there is a woman I know who often has a fresh or two. I can make discreet enquiries."

"Oh, thank you, thank you," Fowler said, and called for another drink.

"You may expect a communication from me in a day or so, but I warn you that a true fresh may be expensive. They are much in demand, you know."

Two days later, Mr. Fowler received by penny post a letter addressed to him by Pierce. In it he was told to present himself in four days' time, at eight o'clock, at a house in Lichfield Street near St. Martin's Lane. Mr. Fowler sent off a quick note of thanks to his friend Pierce for his assistance.

When Henry Fowler found himself at the address given to him, he eyed the establishment with some trepidation, for the exterior was not particularly prepossessing. Thus it was a pleasant surprise when a knock at the door received an answer from an exceedingly beautiful woman, who asked him to address her as "Miss Miriam".

Standing in the hall, Fowler saw that this house was not one of those crude establishments where beds were obtainable for five shillings an hour; on the contrary, here the furnishings were plush velvet, with rich drapings and fine Persian carpets. Miss Miriam comported herself with extraordinary dignity as she requested a large sum; her manner was so well-born that Fowler paid without a quibble before being directed to an upstairs room.

Once in the room, Henry Fowler could scarcely believe his eyes. Here was a delicate creature, rosy-cheeked and wonderfully young. Her very bearing bespoke her uninitiated state. Her name was Sarah, and she explained that she had lately come from Derbyshire, that her parents were dead, and that she had an older brother off in the Crimea. She talked of these events almost gaily, though she seemed to be nervous.

The room was superbly furnished; it was red and elegant, and the air was softly perfumed with the scent of jasmine. Fowler looked about briefly, for a man could never be too careful. Then he bolted the door and turned to face the girl.

"Well, now," he said. "Shall we . . . ah . . ."

"Oh, yes, of course, sir," she said, and began to undress him. He submitted passively, and soon was naked.

She touched the key which hung round his neck on a silver chain. "What is this?" she asked.

"Just a—ah—key," he replied.

"You'd best take it off," she said, "it may harm me."

He took it off. She dimmed the gaslights, and then disrobed. The next hour or two was so magical to Henry Fowler that he did not notice that a stealthy hand slipped around one of the heavy red velvet curtains and plucked away the key from atop his clothing; nor did he notice when, a short time later, the key was returned.

THE DAY AFTER Mr. Fowler had his assignation, Mr. Pierce prepared to crack the mansion of Mr. Trent. Involved in this plan were five people: Pierce, who had some inside knowledge of the layout of the house; Agar, who would make the wax impression of the key; Agar's woman, who would act as "crow", or lookout; and Barlow, who would be a "stall", providing diversion. There was also the mysterious Miss Miriam. She was essential to the planned housebreak, for she would carry out what was called "the carriage fakement". This was one of the most effective methods of breaking into a house, and relied upon a solid social custom of the day—the tipping of servants.

In Victorian England, roughly ten per cent of the entire population was "in service", and nearly all were poorly paid. The poorest paid were those whose tasks brought them in contact with visitors: the butler and the footman relied on tips for most of their annual income. Thus the notorious disdain of the footman for insubstantial callers—and thus, too, the "carriage fakement".

By nine o'clock on the evening of November 12th, 1854, Pierce had his confederates in their places. Agar's woman lounged across the street from the Trent mansion. Barlow had slipped down the alley towards the tradesman's entrance and the dog pens at the back of the house. Pierce and Agar were concealed in the shrubbery next to the front door. When all was in readiness, an elegant carriage drew up to the kerb in front of the house, and the bell was rung.

The Trent household's footman heard the ring, and opened the door. He saw the carriage drawn up at the kerb. Dignified and conscious of tips, the footman was certainly not going to stand in the doorway and shout into the night to inquire what was wanted. He went down the steps to the kerb to see if he could be of service. Inside the carriage he saw a handsome, refined woman who asked if this was the residence of Mr. Robert Jenkins. The footman said it was not, but Mr. Jenkins' house was around the corner, and he gave directions.

While this was happening, Pierce and Agar slipped into the house through the open front door. They proceeded directly to the cellar door. It was locked, but Agar employed a picklock, and had it open in a moment. The two men were inside the cellar, with the door closed behind them by the time the footman received his shilling from the lady in the carriage.

In the light of a narrow-beam lantern, Pierce checked his watch. It was 9:04. That gave them an hour to find the key before Barlow provided his diversion to cover their escape.

Pierce and Agar moved stealthily down the creaking stairs into the depths of the cellar. They saw the wine racks, locked behind iron gratings. These locks yielded easily to Agar's attentions, and at 9:11 they entered the wine cellar proper.

Pierce could make only one assumption about the hiding place of the key: since Mrs. Trent was the person who usually went into the cellar, and since Mr. Trent did not want her coming across the key by accident, the banker probably hid his key high up. They first searched the tops of the racks with their fingers. There was soon a good deal of dust in the air, and Agar, with his bad lungs, had difficulty suppressing his cough. Several times his stifled grunts were sufficiently loud to alarm Pierce, but the Trent household never heard them.

Soon it was 9:30. Now time was beginning to work against them. Pierce searched more frantically and became impatient, hissing his complaints to Agar.

Fifteen more minutes passed, and Pierce began to sweat. And then, with startling suddenness, his fingers felt something cold on the top of the wine-rack crossbars. The object fell to the ground with a metallic clink. A few moments of scrambling around on the earthen floor of the cellar, and they had the key.

"That's for a safe all right," said Agar.

"Right," Pierce said, sighing. He took the lantern and held it for Agar. Agar fished two wax blanks from his pockets. He held them in his hands to warm them a moment, and then he pressed the key into them, first one side, then the other.

"Time?" he whispered.

"Nine fifty-one," Pierce said.

"I'll do another," Agar said, and repeated the process with a second set of blanks. This was common practice among the most adept screwsmen, for one never knew when a blank might be later injured. When he had two sets, Pierce returned the key to its hiding place.

"Nine fifty-seven."

"Crikey, it's close."

They left the wine cellar, locking the grating behind them, and slipped up the stairs to the main cellar door. Then they waited.

Barlow, lurking in the shadows near the servants' quarters, checked his own pocketwatch and saw it was ten o'clock. Carrying a bag, he moved to the dog kennels. Three dogs were there, including the new gift of a made dog from Mr. Picrcc. Barlow bent over the run and pushed four squeaking rats out of the bag and into the enclosure. Immediately, the dogs began to raise a terrible din.

Barlow slipped off into the shadows as he saw the lights come on in one window after another in the servants' quarters.

Pierce and Agar, hearing the commotion, opened the cellar door and moved into the hall, locking the door behind them. There was the sound of running footsteps at the back of the house. They unfastened the locks and bolts of the front door, let themselves out, and disappeared into the night.

They left behind them only one sign of their visit: the unlocked front door. They knew that in the morning the footman, being first to arise, would come upon the front door and find it unlocked. But he would remember the incident of the carriage the night before, and would assume that he had forgotten to lock up afterwards.

CHAPTER TEN

The ease with which Pierce and his fellow conspirators obtained the first two keys gave them a sense of confidence that was soon to prove false. Almost immediately after obtaining Trent's key, they ran into difficulties from an unexpected quarter; the South Eastern Railway changed its routine.

The gang employed Miss Miriam to watch the routine of the London Bridge offices, and in late December, 1854, she returned with bad news. The railway company had hired a jack who now guarded the premises at night. Since they had been planning to break in at night, this was sour news indeed.

"Why?" Pierce asked. "In God's name, *why*?"

In later courtroom testimony, it emerged that the South Eastern Railway management changed hands in the autumn of 1854. Its new owner, Mr. Willard Perkins, was a gentleman whose concern for the lower classes was such that he introduced a policy of employing more people "in order to provide honest work for those who might otherwise be tempted into lawlessness." The extra jack was hired for this reason alone.

According to Agar, Pierce covered his disappointment quickly. "What's his rig?" he asked.

"He comes on duty at lock-up each night, at seven sharp," Miss Miriam said.

"And what manner of fellow is he?"

"He's a ream esclop," she replied, meaning a real policeman. "He's forty or so. But I'll wager he doesn't sleep on the job, and he's no lushington."

"Is he armed?"

"He is," she said, nodding. "And he sits up at the top of the steps by the door, and does not move at all. He has a small paper bag at his side, which I think is his supper." Miss Miriam could not be sure of that, because she dared not remain watching too late in the day for fear of arousing suspicion.

"Crikey," Agar said in disgust. "Sits right by the door? He's coopered that ken for sure."

"Not coopered," Pierce said, "just a little more difficult. We don't know the full night routine. We never had an all-night watch." At night the station was deserted, and loiterers and tramps were briskly ordered off by the policemen making their rounds. "A concealed man could remain all night in the station. Do you happen to know of a skipper?"

"A skipper?" Agar said, in surprise. "I can find one. But what's the lurk, then?"

"We'll pack him in a crate," Pierce said.

The term "skipper" did not imply an occupation, but rather a way of life, and more specifically a way of spending the night. During the mid century, a sizeable fraction of London's growing population lacked both shelter and the means to pay for it. Such people spent their nights outdoors. Their favourite places were the so-called "Dry-Arch Hotels", meaning the arches of railway bridges, but there were other haunts. Skippers were people who routinely sought barns and outhouses. At this time even rather elegant households frequently lacked indoor plumbing; the outhouse was a fixture among all classes, and it was increasingly found in public places as well. The skipper would wedge himself in and sleep away the night.

The reason Pierce wanted a skipper, of course, was to obtain someone who could tolerate cramped quarters for many hours. He first arranged for a packing crate to be built and delivered to his residence. Agar then obtained, by his own accounting, "a very reliable skipper named Henson", who was later reported to have found his shipping crate "ever so wide" as he was nailed inside it.

The crate was placed strategically within London Bridge Station. Through the slats, Henson was able to watch the behaviour of the night guard. After the first night, the crate was hauled away, painted another colour, and returned to the station again. This routine was followed three nights in succession. Then Henson reported his findings. None of the thieves was at all encouraged.

"The jack's solid," he told Pierce. "Regular as this very clock." He held up the stopwatch Pierce had given him to time the activities. "Comes on at seven prompt, with his little paper bag of supper. Sits on the steps, always alert, never a snooze, greeting the crusher on his rounds."

"What are the rounds?"

"First crusher works to midnight, goes every eleven minutes round the station. Sometimes he goes twelve, and once or twice thirteen minutes, but regular it's eleven for him. Second crusher works midnight to the dawn. He keeps to no beat but goes this way and that, popping up here and there with a wary eye in all directions. And he's got himself two barkers at his belt," he explained, meaning that the man was armed with two pistols.

"What about the jack who sits by the office door?" Pierce said. "Does he ever leave his place?"

"No," the skipper said. "He sits right there, and he hears the church bells ringing the hour. Now, at eleven o'clock, he opens his bag, and eats his tightener, always at the ringing of the clock. Now he eats for maybe ten, fifteen minutes, and he has a bottle of beer and then the crusher comes around again. Now the jack sits back, taking his ease, and he waits until the crusher comes once more. Now it's half-past eleven or thereabouts. And then the crusher passes him by, and the jack goes to the W.C."

"Then he *does* leave his place," Pierce said. "How long is he gone?"

"I was thinking you might want to know," Henson said. "He's gone sixty-four seconds one night, and sixty-eight the next night, and sixty-four the third night. Always near about eleven thirty. And he's back to his post when the first crusher makes the last round, quarter to midnight."

"He did this every night?"

"Every night."

"Yes," Pierce said, "beer does have that effect. Now does he leave his post at any other time?"

"Not to my eye."

"And you never slept?"

"What? When I'm sleeping here all the day through on your nice bed, here in your lodgings, and you ask if I kip the night away?"

Pierce thanked the skipper, paid him a half-crown for his troubles, allowed himself to be whined and cajoled into paying an additional half-crown, and sent the man on his way. As the door closed on the skipper, Agar shook his head, "Sixty-four seconds. That's not your kinchin lay"—not exactly robbing children.

"I never said it was," Pierce said. "But you keep telling me you're the best screwsman in the country, and here's a fitting challenge for your talents: is it a coopered ken?"

"Maybe," Agar said. "I got to practise the lay. And I need to cool it close up. Can we pay a visit?"

"Certainly," Pierce said.

CHAPTER ELEVEN

The twentieth-century urban dweller's attitude of fear or indifference to a crime in progress would have astounded the Victorians. In those days, any person being robbed or mugged immediately raised a hue and cry, and the victim got an immediate response from law-abiding citizens around him. There were several reasons for the willingness of the populace to get involved in a crime. In the first place, London's Metropolitan Police, though the best in England, was only twenty-five years old, and people did not yet believe that crime was "something for the police to take care of". Second, firearms were rare, and finally, the majority of criminals were children, often extremely young, and adults were not hesitant to go after them.

In any case, an adept thief took great care to conduct his business undetected, for if any alarm were raised, the chances were that he would be caught. For this very reason thieves often worked in gangs, with several members acting as stalls to create confusion. Such gangs sometimes staged a fracas to cover illegal activities, and this manoeuvre was known as a "jolly gaff". A good "jolly gaff" required careful planning and timing.

On the morning of January 9th, 1855, Pierce looked around the cavernous, echoing interior of London Bridge Station and saw that all his players for his "jolly gaff" were in position. Pierce himself would perform the most crucial role, that of the "beefer". He was dressed as a traveller, as was Miss Miriam. She would be the "plant". A few yards distant was the "culprit", a child, nine years old, scruffy and noticeably out of place among the crowd of first-class passengers. Pierce had himself selected the boy from among a dozen children in the Holy Land; the criterion was speed. Farther away still was the "crusher", Barlow, wearing a constable's uniform with the hat pulled down to conceal the white scar across his forehead. Finally, not far from the steps of the traffic supervisor's office was the whole point of the ploy: Agar, disguised in his finest gentleman's clothing.

As it came time for the London & Greenwich eleven-o'clock train to depart, Pierce scratched his neck with his left hand. Immediately, the child came up and brushed rather abruptly against Miss Miriam's right side, rustling her purple velvet dress. Miss Miriam cried, "I've been robbed, John!"

Pierce raised his beef: "Stop, thief!" he shouted, and raced after the bolting child. "Stop, thief!"

Startled bystanders immediately grabbed at the youngster, but he was quick and slippery, and soon tore free of the crowd and ran towards the back of the station. There Barlow in his policeman's uniform came forward menacingly. Agar, as a civic-spirited gentleman, also joined in the pursuit. The child was trapped; his only escape lay in a desperate scramble up the stairs leading to the railway office.

The little boy's instructions had been explicit: he was to get up the stairs, into the office, past the desks of the clerks, and back to a high rear window opening out onto the roof of the station. He was to break this window in an apparent attempt to escape. Then Barlow would apprehend him.

The child burst into the South Eastern Railway office, followed by Pierce. "Stop him, he's a thief!" Pierce shouted and, in his own pursuit, knocked over one of the clerks. The child was scrambling for the window. Then Barlow, the constable, came in.

"I'll handle this," Barlow said, in an authoritative voice, but he clumsily knocked one of the desks over.

"Catch him! Catch him!" Agar called, entering the offices.

By now the child was scrambling up onto the traffic supervisor's desk, going towards the window; he broke the glass with his small fist, cutting himself. McPherson, the supervisor, kept saying "Oh, dear, oh, dear," over and over.

"I am an officer of the law, make way!" Barlow shouted.

"Stop him!" Pierce screamed, allowing himself to become quite hysterical. "Stop him, he's getting away!"

Glass fragments from the window fell on the floor, and Barlow and the child rolled on the ground in a struggle that took rather longer to resolve itself than one might expect. The clerks watched in confusion. No one noticed that Agar had turned his back on the commotion and was trying several of his jangling ring of bettys in the lock on the door to the office, until he found one that worked. Nor did anyone notice when Agar then moved to the side wall cabinet, trying the lock with one key after another until he found one to open it.

Three or four minutes passed before the young ruffian—who kept slipping from the hands of the red-faced constable—was finally caught by Pierce. The constable gave the little villain a good boxing on the ears, and the lad handed up the purse he had stolen. He was carted away by the constable. Pierce dusted himself off, looked around the wreckage of the office, and apologized to the clerks and the supervisor.

Then the other gentleman who had joined in the pursuit said, "I fear, sir, that you have missed your train."

"By God, I have," Pierce said. "Damn the little rascal."

And the two gentlemen departed—the one thanking the other for helping corner the thief, and the other saying it was nothing—leaving the clerks to clean up the mess.

It was, Pierce reflected, a nearly perfect jolly gaff.

LATER THAT SAME DAY, in the afternoon, Clean Willy arrived at Pierce's house to be given the lay.

"It'll be tonight," Pierce told him. "Once it's dark, you'll go up to London Bridge, and get onto the station roof. Cross to the broken window. It's in the supervisor's office. Little window, barely a foot square."

"What then?"

"Get through it into the office. There you will see a green cabinet mounted on the wall." Pierce looked at the little snakesman. "You'll have to stand on a chair to reach it. Be very quiet; there's a jack posted outside the office, on the steps."

Clean Willy frowned.

"Unlock the cabinet," Pierce said, "with this key." He nodded to Agar, who gave Willy the first of the picklocks. "Unlock and open the cabinet and wait. Around ten thirty, there'll be a bit of a shindy. A soak will be coming into the station to chat up the jack. Then you unlock the main door to the office, using this key here" —Agar gave him the second key—"and then you wait."

"What for?"

"For eleven thirty, or thereabouts, when the jack goes to the W.C. Then Agar comes through the door you've unlocked, and he makes his waxes of the keys that we hope are inside the cabinet. Then he leaves, and you lock the door right away. By now, the jack is back. You lock the cabinet, put the chair back, and go out the window, quiet-like."

"You popped me out of Newgate for this?" Clean Willy said. "This is no shakes, to knock over a deadlurk," meaning an empty building.

"It's a deadlurk with a jack posted at the door, and you'll have to be quiet-like, all the time."

Clean Willy grinned. "Those keys mean a sharp vamp."

"Just do the lay," Pierce said, "and quiet."

THAT EVENING a characteristic London pea-soup fog, heavily mixed with soot, blanketed the city. Clean Willy, easing down Tooley Street, one eye to the façade of London Bridge Station, was not sure he liked the fog. It was so dense that he could not see the first storey of the terminus.

But Clean Willy knew a lot about the way buildings were constructed, and by eight o'clock he was on the terminus roof.

The main portion was roofed in slate; over the tracks the roofing was glass, and he avoided that. Moving cautiously through the fog, he edged round the building until he found the broken window in the supervisor's office. He noticed the office was in some disarray, as if there had been a struggle there during the day. He reached through the jagged hole in the glass, turned the lock, and raised the window, perhaps nine by sixteen inches. He wriggled through it easily, stepped down onto a desk top, and paused.

He had not been told the walls of the office were glass. Through the glass, he could see down to the deserted tracks and platforms of the station below. He could also see the jack on the stairs, a paper bag at his side.

Carefully, Clean Willy climbed down off the desk. His foot crunched on a shard of broken glass; he froze. But if the guard outside heard it, he gave no sign. After a moment, Willy crossed the office, set a chair next to the high cabinet, and stepped onto it. He plucked the twirl Agar had given him from his pocket, and picked the lock. Then he sat down to wait, hearing distant church bells toll the hour of nine o'clock.

Agar, lurking in the deep shadows of the station, also heard the church bells toll for nine o'clock. Another two and a half hours, and he had been wedged behind this baggage stand for two hours already. He sighed and wondered, for the thousandth time, what Pierce intended to do with these keys which he had spent eight months getting. All he knew was that it must be a devilish flash pull. But what *was* it? The question preoccupied him more than the mechanics of timing a sixty-four-second smash and grab. He was a professional; he had prepared well and was confident. His heart beat evenly as he stared across the station at the jack on the stairs, as the crusher made his rounds.

THE DRUNKEN IRISHMAN with the red beard and slouch hat stumbled through the deserted station singing "Molly Malone". As he shuffled along, it appeared he was so lost in his song that he might not notice the guard on the stairs.

But he did, and he eyed the guard's paper bag suspiciously before making an elaborate and wobbly bow.

"And a good evenin' to you, sir," the drunk said.

"Evening," the guard said.

"And what, may I inquire," said the drunk, standing stiffer, "is your business up there, eh? Up to no good, are you?"

"I'm guarding these premises here," the guard said.

The drunk hiccupped. "So you say, my good fellow, but many a rascal has said as much. I think, sir, we shall have the police to look you over."

"Now, look here," the guard said.

"You look here, and lively, too," the drunk said, and abruptly began to shout, "Police! *Po-lice!*"

"Here, now," the guard said, coming down the stairs. "Get a grip on yourself, you scurvy soak."

At that moment, the constable came running around the corner, drawn by the shouts of the drunk.

"Ah, a criminal, officer," said the drunk. "Arrest that scoundrel," he said, pointing to the guard, who had now moved to the bottom of the stairs. "He is up to no good."

The constable and the guard exchanged open smiles.

"You find this a laughing matter, sir?" said the drunk, turning to the copper. "This man is plainly up to no good."

"Come along, now," the constable said, "or I'll have you in lumber for creatin' a nuisance."

"A nuisance?" the drunk said, twisting free of the constable's arm. "I think you and this blackguard are in cahoots, sir."

"That's enough," the constable said. "Come along smartly."

The drunk allowed himself to be led away by the copper, and the guard sighed and climbed back up the stairs to eat his dinner. The distant chimes rang eleven o'clock.

For Pierce, the most delicate part of his performance was the conclusion, when he was led by the constable out into Tooley Street. Pierce did not want to disrupt the policeman's regular rhythm on the beat, so he had to disengage himself rather rapidly.

As they came into the foggy night air, he breathed deeply, and made a show of straightening up, as if the night air had sobered him. "Well, my dear fellow, I am most grateful for your ministrations and I can assure you that I can carry on well from here."

"You're not going to be creating another nuisance?"

"My dear sir," Pierce said, standing still straighter, "what do you take me for?" He bowed to the crusher and wandered into the fog, singing "Molly Malone".

Pierce went no farther than the end of Tooley Street. There, hidden in the fog, was a cab.

"How'd it carry off?" Barlow asked.

"Smart and tidy," Pierce said. "I gave Willy two or three minutes to unlock the door; it should have been enough."

And he slipped back towards the station.

BY ELEVEN THIRTY, Pierce had taken up a position where he could see the traffic office stairs and the guard. The copper made his round; he waved to the jack, who waved back. The copper went on; the jack yawned, stood, and stretched.

Pierce took a breath and poised his finger on the stopwatch button. They would have only sixty-four seconds.

The guard came down the stairs, and moved off towards the W.C.

Pierce hit the button, and counted softly, "One . . . two . . . three . . ."

Agar was already running hard, barefooted to make no sound. He dashed up the stairs.

"Four . . . five . . . six . . ."

Agar reached the door; it opened and Agar was inside. The door closed.

"Seven . . . eight . . . nine . . ."

"Ten," Agar said, panting, looking around the office. Clean Willy, grinning, took up the count.

"Eleven . . . twelve . . . thirteen . . ."

Agar crossed to the already opened cabinet. He removed the first of the wax blanks from his pocket, and then looked at the keys in the cabinet.

"Crikey!" he whispered. Dozens of keys hung in the cabinet, large and small, labelled and unlabelled, all hanging on hooks. He broke into a sweat in an instant.

"Seventeen . . . eighteen . . . nineteen . . ."

Agar was going to fall behind on the count. He knew it with

SER

sickening suddenness. He stared helplessly at the keys. He could not wax them all; which were the ones to do?

"Twenty . . . twenty-one . . . twenty-two . . ."

Clean Willy's droning voice infuriated Agar. He stared at the cabinet in a rising panic. He remembered what the other two keys looked like; perhaps these two keys were similar. He peered close at the cabinet; the light in the office was bad.

"Twenty-three . . . twenty-four . . . twenty-five . . ."

"It's no bloody use," he whispered to himself. And then he realized something odd: only one hook had two keys on it. He quickly lifted them off. They looked like the others he had done.

"Twenty-six . . . twenty-seven . . . twenty-eight . . ."

He set out the first blank, and pressed one side of the first key into the blank, holding it neatly, plucking it out with his fingernail; the nail on the little finger was long, one of the hallmarks of a screwsman.

He took the second blank, flipped the key over, and pressed it into the wax to get the other side. He held it firmly, then scooped it out.

"Thirty-two . . . thirty-three . . . thirty-four . . ."

Now Agar's professionalism came into play. He was falling behind—at least five seconds off his count now—but he knew that at all costs he must avoid confusing the two keys. It was common enough for a screwsman under pressure to make two impressions of the same side of a single key; with two keys, the chance of confusion was doubled. Quickly but carefully, he hung up the finished key.

"Thirty-five . . . thirty-six . . . thirty-seven . . . Lordy," Clean Willy said. He was looking out of the glass windows, to where the guard would be returning in less than thirty seconds.

Swiftly, Agar pressed the second key into his third blank. He held it there just an instant, then lifted it out. He pocketed the blank, and plucked up his fourth wax plate. He pressed the other side of the key into it.

"Forty-four . . . forty-five . . . forty-six . . . forty-seven . . ."

Abruptly, while Agar was peeling the key free of the wax, the blank cracked in two.

"Damn!"

He fished in his pocket for another blank. His fingers were steady, but there was sweat dripping from his forehead.

"Fifty-one . . . fifty-two . . . fifty-three . . ."

He drew out a fresh blank and did the second side again, plucked the key out, hung it up, and dashed for the door, still holding the final blank in his fingers. He left the office without another look at Willy.

"Fifty-six," Willy said, immediately moving to the door to lock it up.

Pierce saw Agar exit, behind schedule by five full seconds, his face was flushed with exertion.

"Fifty-seven . . . fifty-eight . . ."

Agar sprinted down the stairs, three at a time, and across the station to his hiding place.

"Sixty-two . . . sixty-three . . ."

Agar was hidden.

The guard, yawning, came around the corner, still buttoning up his trousers. He walked towards the steps.

"Sixty-four," Pierce said, and flicked his watch.

The guard took up his post at the stairs. After a moment, he began humming to himself, very softly, and it was a while until Pierce realized it was "Molly Malone".

CHAPTER TWELVE

"The distinction between base avarice and honest ambition may be exceeding fine," warned the Reverend Noel Blackwell in his 1853 treatise, *On the Moral Improvement of the Human Race*. No one knew the truth of his words better than Pierce, who arranged his next meeting at the Casino de Venise, in Windmill Street. This was a large and lively dance hall, brightly lit by myriad gas lamps. Young men spun and wheeled colourfully dressed girls. The total impression was one of fashionable splendour, which belied a reputation as a notorious place of assignation for whores and their clientele.

Pierce went directly to the bar, where a burly man in a blue uniform with silver lapel markings sat hunched over a drink. He appeared distinctly uncomfortable in the casino. "Have you been here before?" Pierce asked.

The man turned. "You Mr. Simms?"

"That's right."

The burly man looked around at the women, the finery, the bright lights. "No," he said, "never been before. Bit above me."

"Let me buy you another drink," Pierce said, raising a grey-gloved hand. "Where do you live, Mr. Burgess?"

"I got a room on Moresby Road," the burly man said.

"I hear the air is bad there. You married?"

"Aye." Burgess showed a flash of impatience. "What's this all about, then?"

"Just a little conversation," Pierce said, "to see if you want to make more money."

"Only a fool doesn't," Burgess said shortly.

"You work the Mary Blaine," Pierce said.

Burgess nodded and flicked the silver SER letters on his collar: the insignia of the South Eastern Railway.

Pierce already knew a good deal about Richard Burgess, a Mary Blaine scrob, or guard on the railway. He knew where Burgess and his wife lived; he knew that they had two children, aged two and four, and he knew that the four-year-old was sickly and needed the frequent attentions of a doctor, which Burgess and his wife could not afford.

He knew that Burgess fell into the lowest-paid category of railway employee, and was paid but fifteen shillings a week. His wife made ten shillings a week sewing, which meant that the family lived on a total of about sixty-five pounds a year. It was little wonder that Burgess felt uncomfortable in a place that charged two shillings a drink.

"What's it to be?" Burgess said, not looking at Pierce.

"I was wondering about your eyesight."

"My eyes are good enough."

"I wonder," Pierce said, "what it would take for them to go bad."

Burgess sighed, and did not speak for a moment. Finally he said in a weary voice, "I done a stretch in Newgate a few years back. I'm not wanting to see the cockchafer again."

"Perfectly sensible," Pierce said. "And I don't want anybody to blow my lay. We both have our fears."

Burgess gulped his drink. "What's the sweetener?"

"Two hundred quid."

Burgess coughed, and pounded his chest with a thick fist. "Two hundred quid," he repeated.

"That's right," Pierce said. "Here's ten now, on faith." He set the money on the bar top.

"A pretty sight," Burgess said. "What's the lay?"

"All you need to do is worry over your eyesight."

"What is it I'm not to see, then?"

"Nothing that will get you into trouble."

Burgess turned stubborn. "Speak plain," he said.

Pierce sighed. He reached for the money. "I'm sorry," he said. "I fear I must take my business elsewhere."

There was a moment of silence. Finally, Burgess reached over with his other hand and plucked away the two five-pound notes. "Tell me what I do," he said.

"It's very simple," Pierce said. "Soon you will be approached by a man who will ask you whether your wife sews your uniforms. When you meet that man, you simply . . . look away."

"That's all? For two hundred quid?"

"That's all."

Burgess frowned for a moment, and then began to laugh. "You'll never pull it," Burgess said. "There's no cracking those safes, wherever I look. Few months past, there's a kid, works into the baggage car, wants to do those safes. Have a go, I says to him, and he has a go for half an hour, and he gets no further than the tip of my nose. Then I threw him off smartly."

"I know that," Pierce said. "I was watching."

Burgess stopped laughing.

Pierce withdrew two gold guineas from his pocket and dropped them on the counter. "There's a dollymop in the corner—pretty thing, wearing pink. I believe she's waiting for you," Pierce said, and then he got up and walked off.

THE DEMAND for all kinds of consumer goods in Victorian England was insatiable, and the response was specialization. It is in the mid-eighteenth century that one first hears of cabinet makers who made only the joints of cabinets, and of shops that sold only certain kinds of cabinets. The increasing specialization was apparent in the underworld as well, and nowhere more peculiar than in the figure of the "eel-skinner". His principal business was making eel-skins, or coshes. The earliest eel-skins were sausage-like canvas bags filled with sand, which muggers and thieves could carry up their sleeves until the time came to wield them on their victims. Later, eel-skins were filled with lead shot.

As firearms became more common, eel-skinners turned to making bullets, and in early January, 1855, a Manchester eel-skinner named Harkins was visited by a gentleman with a red beard who said he wanted to purchase a quantity of LC shot.

"Easy enough done," the skinner said. "I make all manner of shot, and I can make LC right enough. How much will you have?"

"Five thousand," the gentleman said.

The eel-skinner blinked. "Five thousand—that's a quantity." He stared up at the ceiling and plucked at his lower lip. "Bless me, that's more'n fifty pounds of shot all in. Fifty pounds of lead, and the casting—that'll take some time."

"I need it in a month," the gentleman said.

"A month. . . . Let's see, now . . . casting at a hundred a mould . . . yes, well. . . ." The eel-skinner nodded. "Right enough, you shall have five thousand within a month. You'll be collecting it?"

"I will," the gentleman said, and then he leaned closer, in a conspiratorial fashion. "It's for Scotland, you know."

"Oh, well, yes, I see that plain enough," the eel-skinner said, though the reverse was clearly true. The red-bearded man put down a deposit and departed, leaving the eel-skinner in a state of marked perplexity. He would have been even more perplexed to know that this gentleman had visited skinners in Newcastle-upon-Tyne, Birmingham, Liverpool, and London, and placed identical orders with each of them, so that he was ordering a total of two hundred and fifty pounds of lead shot. What use could anyone have for that?

FOR MANY MONTHS now, the first war correspondent in history, William Howard Russell, had been in Russia with the Crimean troops, and his despatches to *The Times* about the bungling of the war had aroused furious indignation at home.

Despite such provocative news, however, the despatches which most intrigued Londoners in January concerned a man-eating leopard that menaced Naini Tal in northern India. The "Panar man-eater" was said to have killed more than four hundred natives, and accounts were remarkable for their lurid detail. Stories of the leopard became the delicious talk of dining rooms among company given to raciness; women coloured and tittered while men—especially men who had spent time in India—spoke knowledgeably about the habits of such a beast, and its nature.

When, therefore, on February 17th, 1855, a caged, fully grown leopard arrived at London Bridge Terminus, it created a considerable stir—much more than the arrival, a short time previously, of armed guards carrying strongboxes of gold, which were loaded into the SER luggage van and placed in two Chubb safes.

Here was a full-sized, snarling beast, which roared and charged the bars of its cage as it was loaded onto the same luggage van of the London-Folkestone train. The animal's keeper accompanied the beast and before the train departed explained to the crowd of curious onlookers that the beast ate raw meat, that it was a female four years old, and that it was destined for the Continent, where it would be a present to a well-born lady.

The train pulled out of the station shortly after eight o'clock, and the guard on the luggage van closed the sliding side door. There was a short silence while the leopard stalked its cage and growled intermittently; finally the railway guard said, "What do you feed her?"

The animal's attendant turned to the guard. "Does your wife sew your uniforms?" he asked.

Burgess laughed. "You mean it's to be you?"

The attendant did not answer, but opened a small leather satchel and removed a jar of grease, several keys, and a collection of files. He went immediately to the two Chubb safes, coated the four locks with grease, and began fitting his keys. Burgess watched the process: he knew that rough-copied keys would not work on a finely made safe without polishing and refining.

"Where'd you make the impressions?" he said.

"Here and there," Agar replied, fitting and filing.

"Are you taking the gold today, then?" Burgess asked as Agar managed to get one of the safe doors open. Agar did not answer; he stared transfixed for a moment at the strong-boxes inside. "I say, are you taking the gold today?"

Agar shut the door. "No," he said. "Now stop your voker."

Burgess fell silent.

For the next hour Agar worked on his keys. Ultimately, he had opened and closed both safes. When he was finished, he wiped the grease from the locks. Then he cleaned the locks with alcohol and dried them with a cloth. Finally he placed his four keys carefully in his pocket, and sat down to await the arrival of the train at Folkestone station.

Pierce met him at the station and helped to unload the leopard. "How was it?" he asked.

"The finishing touches are done," Agar said, and then he grinned. "It's the Crimean gold, isn't it? That's the flash pull."

"Yes," Pierce said.

"When?"

"Next month," Pierce said.

The leopard snarled.

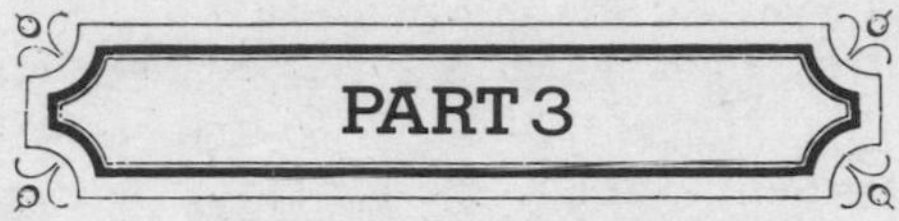

PART 3

Delays and Difficulties: March–May 1855

CHAPTER THIRTEEN

The plan was extremely simple. Pierce and Agar were to board the train in London, each checking several satchels filled with lead shot onto the baggage van. Agar would again ride in the van, and while Burgess looked away Agar would open the safes, remove the gold, and replace it with lead shot. The satchels with the gold would be thrown from the train at a predetermined point, and collected by Barlow. Barlow would then drive on to Folkestone, where he would meet Pierce and Agar.

Meanwhile, the gold strongboxes—still convincingly heavy—would be transferred to the steamer going to Ostend, where the theft would be discovered by the French authorities hours later. By then, enough people would have been involved in the transportation process so that there would be no particular reason to suspect Burgess. In any case, British-French relations were at a low level because of the Crimean War, and it would be natural that the French would assume the English had carried out the theft, and vice versa.

The plan seemed utterly foolproof, and the robbers prepared to carry it out on the next gold shipment, scheduled for March 14th, 1855. But on March 2nd Czar Nicholas I of Russia died suddenly. News of his death caused considerable confusion in business circles. For several days the reports were doubted, and as a result of the general uncertainty the gold shipment was delayed until March 27th. By then, Agar was desperately ill with an exacerbation of his chest condition, and so the opportunity was missed. Pierce and his fellow conspirators were obliged to wait until April.

The next shipment was set for April 19th. The robbers were getting their information on shipment schedules from a girl named Susan Lang, a favourite of Henry Fowler's. Susan somehow got her facts wrong: the gold went out on April 18th, and when Pierce and Agar arrived at London Bridge Station in time to board the April 19th train, Burgess informed them of their error. To maintain appearances, Pierce and Agar made the trip anyway, but Agar testified in court that Pierce was in "a very ugly humour indeed" during the journey.

The next shipment was scheduled for May 22nd. To prevent any further snags, Pierce took the rather risky step of opening a line of communication between Agar and Burgess. Burgess could reach Agar at any time through an intermediary, a betting-shop proprietor called Smashing Billy Banks.

On May 10th, Agar came to Pierce with a piece of ghastly news—the two safes had been removed from the South Eastern Railway's luggage van and returned to the manufacturer, Chubb, for "overhaul".

"Overhaul?" Pierce said. "What do you mean? Those are the finest safes in the world." He frowned. "What's wrong with them?"

Agar shrugged.

"You bastard," Pierce said, "did you scratch the locks when you put on your finishing touches?"

"I greased her lovely," Agar said. "I know they look as a routine for scratches. I tell you, she had nary a tickle on her."

Agar's calm demeanour convinced Pierce that the screwsman was telling the truth. Pierce sighed. "Then *why*?"

"You know a man who will blow on the doings at Chubb?" Agar asked.

"No," Pierce said. "And I wouldn't want to try a cross at Chubb's." The safemaker's firm was unusually careful about its employees. He stared into the distance thoughtfully.

"What is it?" Agar asked.

"I was thinking," Pierce said, "that they would never suspect a lady."

WHAT ROLLS-ROYCE would become to automobiles, Chubb had long since been to safes. The head of that venerable firm, Mr. Laurence Chubb, did not later remember—or pretended not to remember—a visit by a handsome young woman in May, 1855. But an employee of the company was sufficiently impressed by the lady's beauty to recall her in detail.

She arrived in a handsome coach, with liveried footmen, and swept imperiously into the firm. She was extremely well dressed and spoke with a commanding manner; she demanded to see Mr. Chubb himself.

When Mr. Chubb appeared a few moments later, the woman announced that she was Lady Charlotte Simms; that she and her invalid husband maintained a country estate in the Midlands and that recent incidents of thievery in the neighbourhood had convinced her that she and her husband needed a safe.

"Then you have come to the best shop in Christendom," said Mr. Chubb.

"So I have been previously informed," Lady Charlotte said, as if not at all convinced.

"What is it, specifically, that your ladyship requires?"

Here Lady Charlotte, for all her imperiousness, seemed to falter. She gestured with her hands. "Why, just some manner of, ah, large safe, you know."

"My lady," said Mr. Chubb, "we manufacture steel safes and iron safes; portable safes and fixed safes; safes with a capacity of six cubic inches and safes with a capacity of twelve cubic yards; safes mounted with single locks and double locks."

This recitation seemed to put Lady Charlotte even further off her form. "Well," she said, "I, ah, I don't know . . ."

"Perhaps if your ladyship looks through our catalogue?"

"Yes, excellent."

"This way, please." Mr. Chubb led her into his office and seated her by his desk. He drew out the catalogue and opened it to the first page. The woman hardly looked at it.

"Mr. Chubb," she said, in an earnest tone, "I must beg your assistance. I am quite at a loss and I can tell nothing from pictures. Can you perhaps show me some of your safes?"

"My lady, forgive me," Mr. Chubb said, rushing round the desk to help her to her feet. "Of course. If you will follow me into the workrooms I can show you the various safes we make."

He led Lady Charlotte back into the long workroom behind the offices. Here a dozen men were busy hammering and welding. The noise was so loud that Mr. Chubb had to shout for Lady Charlotte to hear, and the good woman herself fairly winced from the din.

"Now, this version here," he said, "has a one-cubic-foot capacity, and is double-layered, sixteenth-inch tempered steel, with an insulating layer of dried brick dust of Cornish origin."

"It is too small."

"Very good, my lady, too small. Now, this one here"—he moved down the line—"has a capacity of two and a half cubic feet."

"Still too small."

Mr. Chubb led her deeper into the workroom. Lady Charlotte coughed delicately in a cloud of brick dust.

"Now, this model here—" Mr. Chubb began.

"There!" said Lady Charlotte, pointing across the room at two safes. "That's the size I want."

They crossed the room. "These safes," said Mr. Chubb, "represent the finest examples of our workmanship. They are owned by the Huddleston & Bradford Bank, and are employed in the Crimean gold shipments, where naturally security is of the utmost. However, these are generally sold to institutions, and not to private individuals. I naturally thought—"

"This is the safe I want," she said, and then looked at them suspiciously. "They don't appear very new."

"Oh, no, they are nearly two years old now."

This seemed to alarm Lady Charlotte. "Two years old? Why are they back? Have they some defect?"

"No, indeed. A Chubb safe has no defects. They have merely been returned for replacement of the undercarriage mounting pins. You see, they travel on the railway, and the vibration works on the bolts which anchor the safes to the luggage-van floor."

"These locks are burglarproof?" Lady Charlotte asked.

"Oh, absolutely. So much so that in two years no villain has ever even attempted to break them."

Lady Charlotte nodded thoughtfully. "Very well," she said. "Please load one of these safes into my carriage."

"My lady," Mr. Chubb said patiently, "we must construct the safe to your order."

Lady Charlotte appeared quite irritated. "Well, can I have one tomorrow morning?"

Mr. Chubb gulped. "Tomorrow morning—um, well, as a rule we require six weeks to construct a safe. On occasion we can manufacture one as quickly as four weeks, but—"

"Four weeks? That is a *month*. I wish to purchase a safe *today*."

"Yes, my lady, quite. But as I have attempted to explain, each safe must be built, and the shortest time—"

"Mr. Chubb, you must think me an utter fool. I have come here for the purpose of buying a safe, and now I discover you have none to sell but on the contrary will only construct one for me in a month's time. Within a month the brigands of the neighbourhood will very probably have come and gone, and your safe will not in the least interest me, or my husband. I shall take my business elsewhere. Good day to you, sir."

With that Lady Charlotte swept out, and Mr. Laurence Chubb was heard to mutter in a low voice, "Women."

CHAPTER FOURTEEN

Although they now knew that the overhaul did not include changing the locks on the safes, one week later the thieves' plans were thrown into still further disarray when a letter was delivered to Pierce. Written in a graceful hand, it read:

> My dear Sir:
> I should be most greatly obliged if you could contrive to meet with me at the Palace, Sydenham, this afternoon at four o'clock for the purpose of discussing some matters of mutual interest.
> Most respectfully, I am,
> William Williams, Esq.

Pierce looked at the letter in consternation and read it aloud to Agar.

"Clean Willy's got himself a screever for this one," Agar said, staring at the penmanship.

"Obviously," Pierce said. "But why?"

"You going to meet him?"

"Absolutely."

THE CRYSTAL PALACE, an enormous three-storey glass building covering nineteen acres, had been erected in 1851 in Hyde Park, to house the Great Exhibition of that year, and it impressed every visitor who saw it. Indeed, even in drawings the Crystal Palace is stunning to the modern eye, and to see more than a million square feet of glass shimmering in the afternoon light must have been a remarkable sight.

After the exhibition, the Great Hall was taken down and moved to Sydenham, in South-East London. Here, shortly before four o'clock, a brass band concert was in progress when Edward Pierce entered the vast structure to meet Clean Willy. Pierce saw Clean Willy sitting in one of the rows to the left. He also saw Agar, disguised as a retired army officer, apparently snoozing in another corner. The band played loudly. Pierce slipped into the seat alongside Willy.

"What is it?" Pierce said, in a low voice.

"I'm needing a turn," Willy said.

"You've been paid."

"I'm needing more," Willy said.

Pierce shot him a glance. Willy was sweating, and he was edgy. "Willy," Pierce said, "if you've turned nose on me, I'll put you in lavender."

"I swear it's no flam," Willy said. "Money is what I need and that's the end of it."

Pierce withdrew two five-pound notes from his wallet. "Don't blow on me," Pierce said, "or I'll do what must be done."

"Thank you, sir, thank you," Willy said, and quickly pocketed the money.

Pierce left him and came out of the Palace into the park. He walked quickly to Harleigh Road, where he paused to adjust his top hat. The gesture was seen by Barlow, whose cab was drawn up at the end of the street.

Then Pierce walked slowly down Harleigh Road, moving with all the appearance of a relaxed gentleman taking the air. At the end of Harleigh Road, he hailed a cab and rode it into town to Regent Street, where he got out. He walked along Regent Street casually, never once glancing over his shoulder, but pausing frequently to look in shop windows and to watch the reflections in the glass. He did not like what he saw, but he was wholly unprepared for what he next heard, as a familiar voice cried out, "Edward, dear Edward!"

Groaning inwardly, Pierce turned to see Elizabeth Trent. She was shopping, accompanied by a livery boy who carried brightly wrapped packages. "I—why, I must say, this is an extraordinary surprise," Pierce said, bowing and kissing her hand.

She snatched her hand away. "Edward," she said, taking a deep breath. "I did not know what had become of you."

"I must apologize," Pierce said smoothly. "I was very suddenly called abroad on business, and am sure my letter from Paris was inadequate to your injured sensibilities."

"Paris?" she said, frowning.

"Yes. Did you not receive my letter?"

"Why, no."

"Damn!" Pierce said, and then immediately apologized for his strong language. "It is the French," he said, "they are so ghastly inefficient. If only I had known. When you did not reply to me in Paris, I assumed that you were angry. . . ."

"I? Angry? Edward, I assure you," she began, and broke off. "But when did you return?"

"Just three days past," Pierce said.

"But now that you are returned to England," Elizabeth Trent said, "I trust we shall be seeing you at the house once more."

Here it was Pierce's turn to be greatly discomfited. "My dear Elizabeth," he said, stammering. "I do not know how to say this," and he broke off. "When I did not hear from you in Paris, I naturally assumed that you were displeased with me, and . . . well as time passed. . . ." Pierce suddenly straightened. "I regret to inform you that I am betrothed."

Elizabeth Trent stared. Her mouth fell open.

"Yes," Pierce said, "I have given my word to a French lady."

"A *French* lady?"

"Yes. I was most desperately unhappy, you see."

"I do see, sir," she snapped, turned abruptly and walked away. Pierce remained standing on the pavement trying to appear as abject as possible, until she had driven off in her carriage. Then he continued down Regent Street, and anyone who observed him might have noticed that now there was nothing about him that indicated the least remorse.

At Windmill Street he entered an accommodation house that was a known dollymop's bunk, but one of the better class.

In the plush velvet hallway, Miss Miriam said, "He's upstairs. Third door on the right."

Pierce went upstairs and entered a room to find Agar seated, chewing a mint. "Bit late," Agar said. "Trouble?"

"I ran into an old acquaintance," Pierce said. "What did you see?"

"I cooled two," Agar said. "Both riding your tail nice-like. One's a crusher in disguise; the other's dressed as a square-rigged sport. Followed you all the way down Harleigh Road, and took a cab when you climbed aboard."

Pierce nodded. "I saw the same two in Regent Street."

"Probably lurking outside now," Agar said. "How's Willy?"

"Willy looks to be turning nose," Pierce said. "What's to be done with him?"

"I'd bump him," Agar said.

"I don't know about bumping," Pierce said, "but he won't have another chance to blow on us."

"What'll you do with the officers?"

"Nothing for the moment," Pierce said. "I've got to think a bit." And he sat back, lit a cigar, and puffed in silence.

The planned robbery was only five days away, and the police were on to him. If Willy had sung, and loudly, then the police would know that Pierce's gang had broken into the London Bridge Station offices.

"I need a new lay," he said, and stared at the ceiling. "A proper flash lay for the coppers to discover."

CHAPTER FIFTEEN

The institutions of any society are interrelated, even those which appear to have completely opposite goals. Almost immediately the organized police force was formed, Victorians witnessed the new force making relationships with its avowed enemy, the criminal class. These relationships were much debated in the nineteenth century, and they continue to be debated to the present day.

In 1855, the principal figure in the Yard was Richard Mayne, "a sensible lawyer", who had done much to improve the public's attitude towards the Metropolitan Police. Directly under him was

Mr. Edward Harranby, and it was Harranby who oversaw the ticklish business of working with informers.

In the late afternoon of May 17th, Harranby had a conversation with his assistant, Mr. Jonathan Sharp.

Sharp said to him, "The snakesman blew, and we have had a look at our man."

"What sort is he?" Harranby said.

"He appears a gentleman. Probably a cracksman or a swell mobsman. The snakesman says he's from Manchester, but he lives in a fine house in Mayfair. He doesn't know the exact location."

"Can we assist his powers of memory?"

Sharp sighed. "Possibly."

"Bring him in. I'll have a talk with him. Do we know the intended crime?"

Sharp shook his head. "The snakesman says he doesn't know, except this fellow's planning a flash pull."

Harranby turned irritable. "That is of remarkably little value to me," he said. "Who is on this gentleman now?"

"Cramer and Benton, sir."

"They're good men. Keep them on his trail, and let's have the nose in my office, and quickly."

"I'll see to it myself, sir," the assistant said.

CLEAN WILLY, very nervous, was drinking at the Hound's Tooth pub. He left there about six and headed straight for the Holy Land. He moved swiftly through the evening crowds, then ducked into an alley; he jumped a fence, slipped into a basement, crawled through a passage into an adjoining building, climbed up the stairs, and came out onto a narrow street.

At the end of the street he turned into the entrance of a lodging house. Immediately he knew that something was wrong; normally there were children yelling and scrambling all over the stairs, but now they were deserted. He paused, and was just about to turn and flee when a rope snaked out and twisted around his neck, yanking him into a dark corner.

Clean Willy had a look at Barlow, with the white scar across his forehead, as Barlow strained on the garrotting rope. Willy coughed, and struggled, but Barlow's strength was such that the little snakesman was literally lifted off the floor, his feet kicking in the air. This struggle continued for the better part of a minute, and then Clean Willy's body sagged.

Barlow let him drop to the floor. He unwound the rope, removed the two five-pound notes from the snakesman's pocket, and slipped away. Many minutes passed before the children re-emerged and approached the corpse cautiously. Then they stole the snakesman's shoes, and all his clothing, and scampered away.

SITTING IN THE third-floor room of the accommodation house with Agar, Pierce finished his cigar and sat up in his chair.

"We are very lucky," he said finally. "If Willy blew, he'd tell them we knocked over the London Bridge Station."

"I doubt he'd blow so much, right off. He'd likely tickle them for a bigger push." An informant let out information bit by bit, with a bribe from the police at each step. "Anyway, where's the luck, then?" Agar said.

"In the fact that London Bridge is the only station in the city with more than one line operating from it."

"Aye, that's so," Agar said, with a puzzled look.

"I was thinking of the London & Greenwich line," Pierce said. "It would be pleasant if the crushers were in Greenwich."

"So you're needing a bone nose to pass them the slang? In that case Chokee Bill will do you proper."

"Chokee Bill? That old mick?"

"Aye, he did a stretch in Newgate. But not for long."

"Oh, yes?" Pierce was suddenly interested. A shortened prison sentence often implied that the man had made a deal to become an informer. "Got his ticket-of-leave early, did he?"

"Uncommonly early," Agar said. "And the crushers gave him his pawnbroker's licence quick-like, too."

"So he's in the uncle trade now?" Pierce said.

"Aye," Agar said. "But they say he deals barkers now and again."

Pierce considered this at length, and finally nodded. "Where's Bill now?"

"His uncling shop is in Battersea, on Ridgeby Way."

"I'll see him now," Pierce said, getting to his feet.

"Don't make it too easy," Agar warned.

Pierce smiled. "It will take all their best efforts." He went to the door.

"Here, now," Agar called to him, with a sudden thought. "It just came to me mind: what's there for a flash pull in Greenwich of all places?"

"That," Pierce said, "is the very question the crushers will be asking themselves." He grinned at Agar's perplexed look and left the room.

When Pierce came out of the accommodation house, it was twilight. He immediately saw the two crushers lurking at opposite corners of the street. He made a show of looking nervously about, then walked to the end of the block, where he hailed a cab.

He rode the cab several blocks, then jumped out quickly at a busy part of Regent Street, crossed the thoroughfare, and took a hansom going in the opposite direction. To all appearances, he was operating with the utmost cunning.

In fact, Pierce would never bother with the crossover fakement to dodge a tail; it rarely worked, and when he glanced out of the small back window of the hansom cab, he saw that he had not thrown off his pursuers. He proceeded directly across the Thames to Battersea, to see Chokee Bill.

THE IMAGE OF A respectable and well-dressed gentleman entering the dingy premises of a Battersea pawnbroker may seem incongruous from a modern perspective. But Victorian middle-class people were drawn to the broker more for the anonymity of the loan than the cheapness of it. This was, after all, an era when many people equated economic prosperity and good fiscal management with moral behaviour; to be in need of a loan implied some kind of misdeed.

Pierce found Chokee Bill, a red-faced Irishman, sitting in a back corner. Chokee Bill jumped to his feet quickly, recognizing the dress and manner of a gentleman.

"Evening, sir," Bill said. "How may I be serving you?"

Pierce looked around the shop. "Are we alone?"

"We are, sir, as my name is Bill, sir." But Chokee Bill got a guarded look in his eyes.

"I am looking to make a certain purchase," Pierce said. As he spoke, he adopted a broad Liverpool dockyard accent, though ordinarily he had no trace of it. "I need certain rare items."

"Rare items," Chokee Bill repeated. "What manner of rare items, sir?"

"Objects of metal," Pierce said, looking directly at the pawnbroker. He found all this circumspection tedious, but it was necessary to convince Bill.

"Metal you say?"

Pierce made a deprecating gesture with his hands. "It is a question of defence, you see. I have valuables, property, articles of worth. . . . Do you take my meaning?"

"I take your meaning," Bill said. "And I may have such a thing as you require."

"Actually," Pierce said, looking around the shop again, "actually I need five."

"*Five barkers?*" Chokee Bill's eyes widened in astonishment. "That's a goodly number."

Pierce immediately edged nervously towards the door. "Well, if you can't snaffle them—"

"Wait now," Bill said, "I'm not saying can't. All's I said is five is a goodly number."

"I was told you had them at hand," Pierce said.

Chokee sighed. "They're not here, sir. A man doesn't keep barkers about in an uncle shop."

"How quickly can you get them?"

As Pierce became more agitated, Chokee Bill became more appraising. Pierce could almost see his mind think over the meaning of a request for five pistols. It implied a major crime, and no mistake. As a blower, he might make a penny or two if he knew the details.

"It would be some time, sir," Bill said.

"How much time?"

There followed a long silence. "A fortnight would be safe."

"A fortnight!"

"Eight days then."

"Impossible," Pierce said, talking aloud to himself. "In eight days, I must be in Greenw—" He broke off. "No," he said "Eight days is too long."

"Seven?" Bill asked. "Thursday next?"

"At what hour?"

"A question of timing, is it?" Bill asked, with a casualness that was wholly unconvincing.

Pierce just stared at him.

"I don't mean to pry, sir," Bill said quickly.

"Then see you do not. What hour on Thursday?"

"Noon."

Pierce shook his head. "We will never come to terms. It is impossible and I—"

"Here, now. What hour Thursday must it be?"

"No later than ten o'clock in the morning."

Chokee Bill reflected. "Will you be coming yourself to collect them?"

Once again, Pierce stared at him. "That hardly need concern you. Can you supply the pieces or not?"

"I can," Bill said. "But there's an added expense for the quick service."

"That will not matter," Pierce said, and gave him ten gold guineas. "You may have this on account."

Chokee Bill looked at the coins, turned them over in his palm. "I reckon this is the half of it."

"So be it."

Bill nodded. "Will you be needing shot as well?"

"What pieces are they?"

"Webley 48-bore, rim-fire, holster models."

"Then I will need shot."

"Another three guineas for shot," Chokee Bill said blandly.

"Done," Pierce said. He went to the door, and paused. "A final consideration," he said. "If, when I arrive Thursday next, the pieces are not waiting, it shall go hard with you. Think on it." And he left.

IT WAS NOT QUITE dark; the street was dimly lit by gas lamps. He did not see the lurking crushers but knew they were there somewhere. He took a cab and drove to Leicester Square, where the crowds were gathering for the evening's theatrical productions. He entered one throng, bought a ticket for *She Stoops to Conquer*, and then lost himself in the lobby. He was home an hour later, after three cab changes and four duckings in and out of pubs. He was quite certain he had not been followed.

CHAPTER SIXTEEN

The morning of May 18th was uncommonly warm and sunny, but Mr. Harranby took no pleasure in the weather. Things were going very badly and he had treated Mr. Sharp with notable ill temper when he was informed of the death of Clean Willy. When he was later informed that his tails had lost the gentleman in the theatre crowd—a man they knew only as Mr. Simms, with a house in Mayfair—Mr. Harranby had flown into a rage.

But Mr. Harranby's rage was now controlled, for the Yard's only remaining clue was sitting before him, looking very red-faced. Harranby frowned at Chokee Bill.

"Now, Bill," Harranby said, "This is a most serious matter. Five barkers tells me there is something afoot, and I mean to know the truth behind it."

"He was tight with his words, he was."

"I've no doubt," Harranby said heavily. He fished a gold guinea out of his pocket and dropped it on his desk before him. "Try to recall," he said.

"It was late in the day, sir, and I was not at my best," Bill said, staring pointedly at the gold piece.

Harranby would be damned if he'd give the fellow another. "Many a memory improves on the cockchafer, in my experience," he said.

"I've done no wrong," Bill protested. "I'm honest as the day is long, sir. There's no call to put me in the stir."

"Then try to remember," Harranby said.

Bill twisted his hands in his lap. "He comes into the shop near six, he does. Dressed proper, with good manner, but he speaks a wave lag from Liverpool, and can voker romeny."

Harranby glanced at Sharp, in the corner. From time to time even Harranby needed some help in translation.

"He had a Liverpool sailor's accent and he spoke criminal jargon," Sharp said.

"Aye, sir, that's so," Bill said, nodding. "Wants me to snaffle five barkers, and I say five's a goodly number, and he says he wants them quick-like, and he's nervous, and he's showing plenty of ream thickers to pay up on the spot."

"What did you tell him?" Harranby said, keeping his eyes fixed on Bill. A skilled informant like Chokee Bill was not above playing each side against the other.

"I says to him, five's a goodly number but I can do it in time. And he says how much time, and I says a fortnight. This makes him cool the cockum for a bit, and then he says he needs it quicker than a fortnight. He starts to say he's off to Greenwich in eight days, but then he catches himself, like."

"Greenwich," Harranby said, frowning.

"Aye, sir, Greenwich was on the tip of his tongue. So I says how long? And he says seven days, and no later than ten o'clock."

"Seven days," Harranby said, "meaning Thursday next. Go on."

"So I says I can do it. And he gives me ten gold pushes, and he takes his leave and says he'll be back Thursday."

"What else?" Harranby said.

"That's the lot," Bill said.

There was a long silence. Finally Harranby said, "What do you make of this, Bill?"

"It's a flash pull and no mistake."

Harranby tugged at an earlobe, a nervous habit. "What in Greenwich has the makings of a proper flash pull?"

"Damn me if I know," Chokee Bill said.

Harranby paused. "There's another guinea in it for you if you can say."

A fleeting look of agony passed across Chokee Bill's face. "I wish I could be helping you sir, but I heard nothing."

Harranby waited a while longer, and finally dismissed the pawnbroker, who snatched up the guinea and departed.

When Harranby was alone with Sharp, he said again, "What's in Greenwich?"

"Damn me if I know," Sharp said.

"You want a gold guinea, too?"

Sharp said nothing. He was accustomed to Harranby's sour moods. He sat in the corner and watched his superior light a cigarette and puff it reflectively. Sharp regarded cigarettes as silly, insubstantial little things. They had been introduced the year before by a London shopkeeper, and were mostly favoured by troops returning from the Crimea.

"Now, then," Harranby said. "Let us begin from the beginning. We know this fellow Simms has been working for months on something, and we can assume he's clever."

Sharp nodded.

"The snakesman was killed yesterday. Does that mean they know we're on the stalk?"

"Perhaps."

"Perhaps, perhaps," Harranby said irritably. "We must *decide*, according to principles of deductive logic. Let us stick to the facts of the matter. Now, then, what else do we know?"

The question was rhetorical, and Sharp said nothing.

"We know," Harranby said, "that this fellow Simms, after months of preparation, suddenly finds himself in desperate need of five barkers. He has had months to obtain them quietly, one at a time, creating no stir. But he postpones it to the last minute. Why?"

"You think he's playing us for a pigeon?"

"We must entertain the thought, however distasteful," Harranby said. "Is it well known that Bill's a nose?"

"Surely there are suspicions about."

"Indeed," Harranby said. "And yet our clever Mr. Simms chooses this very person to arrange for his five barkers. I say it smells of a fakement." He stared moodily at the tip of his cigarette. "I don't like it, but we may be giving this Simms fellow too much credit. We must assume he is really planning on Greenwich. But what is there in Greenwich to steal?"

Sharp shook his head. Greenwich was a small seaport town, chiefly known for its naval observatory, which maintained the standard of time—Greenwich Mean Time—for the nautical world.

Harranby began opening drawers in his desk, rummaging. "Where is the damned schedule?" Harranby said. "Ah, here it is." He brought out a small printed folder. "London & Greenwich Railway . . . Thursday . . . Ah. Thursdays there is a train leaving London Bridge for Greenwich at eleven fifteen in the morning. Now, what does that suggest?"

Sharp looked suddenly bright-eyed. "Our man wants his guns by ten, so that he will have time to get to the station and make the train."

"Precisely," Harranby said. "All logic points to the fact that he is, indeed, going to Greenwich on Thursday. And we also know he cannot go later than Thursday."

Sharp said, "What about buying the five guns at once?"

"Well, now," Harranby said, warming to his subject, "you see, by a process of deduction we can conclude that his need for the guns is genuine, and his postponing the purchase to the last minute—on the surface, a most suspicious business—springs from some logical situation. The exact reason does not matter. What matters is that he needs those guns for some crime in Greenwich."

"Bravo," Sharp said, with a show of enthusiasm.

Harranby shot him a nasty look. "Don't be a fool," he said, "The principal question still stands before us. *What is there to steal in Greenwich?*"

Sharp said nothing. He stared at his feet. He heard the scratch of a match as Harranby lit another cigarette.

"We may deduce that this lengthy planning is directed towards a major crime with high stakes," Harranby said. "In addition, we know our man is a seafaring person, so we may suspect his crime has something to do with dockyard activities in some way. Thus we may limit our inquiry to whatever exists in the town of Greenwich that fits our—"

Sharp coughed. "I was only thinking sir, that if it is Greenwich, it's out of our jurisdiction. Perhaps we ought to cable the local police and warn them."

"Perhaps, perhaps. If wc were to cable Greenwich, what would we tell them? Eh?"

"I was only thinking—"

"Good God," Harranby said, standing up behind his desk. "Of course! The cable! The cable is in Greenwich."

"Do you mean the Atlantic cable?" Sharp asked.

"Certainly," Harranby said, rubbing his hands together. "Oh, it fits perfectly. Perfectly!"

Sharp remained puzzled. He knew, of course, that the proposed transatlantic cable was being manufactured in Greenwich; the project had been under way for more than a year and represented one of the most considerable technological efforts of the time. There were already undersea cables in the Channel, linking England to the Continent. But these were nothing compared to the twenty-five hundred miles of transatlantic cable.

"But surely," Sharp said, "there is no purpose in stealing a cable?"

"Not the *cable*," Harranby said. "The *payroll* for the firm. An enormous project, and the payroll must be equal to the undertaking. That's our man's objective. And if he is in a hurry to leave on Thursday, he wishes to be there on Friday—"

"*Payday!*" Sharp cried.

"Exactly," Harranby said. "You see the process of deduction carried to its logical conclusion."

"Congratulations." Sharp said cautiously.

"A trifle," Harranby said. He was still vcry exciled, and clapped his hands together. "Oh, he is a bold one, our friend Simms. To steal the cable payroll—what an audacious crime! Come along, Mr. Sharp. We must journey to Greenwich, and apprise ourselves of the situation at first hand."

CHAPTER SEVENTEEN

Mid-century Victorians of all classes accepted a kind of ruthlessness in their dealings with one another that seems outrageous today. A case in point is Sir John Alderston and his crate of wine.

Captain John Alderston was knighted after Waterloo, in 1815, and in subsequent years he became one of the prosperous owners of the South Eastern Railway. Alderston's single vice was a passion for card games, and his outstanding eccentricity was that he preferred to wager personal belongings instead of hard cash. Apparently this was his way of viewing card-playing as a gentlemanly pastime, and not a vice. The story of his crate of wine, which had its origins just a week before The Great Train Robbery, never came to light until 1914, some forty years after Alderston's death, when his family commissioned a biography by an author named William Shawn. The relevant passage reads:

> A family member recalls that Sir John returned home one evening in a mood of great distress after an outing for card-playing with several associates who also owned a share of the railway. In his play, Sir John had lost a case of Madeira, twelve years old, and he was exceedingly reluctant to part with it. Yet he promised to put it aboard the Folkestone train, for delivery to the winner, who resided at that coastal town.
>
> Sir John fretted and fussed, condemning the gentleman who had won, and suspecting aloud that the man had cheated in clandestine fashion. With each passing day, he became more convinced of the man's trickery. Finally he instructed his manservant to load the wine on the train, placing it in the luggage van with a deal of ceremony and filling-in of forms. When the train arrived in Folkestone, the crate was discovered to be empty, and a robbery of the precious wine was presumed. The guard in the van was dismissed and Sir John paid his wager with the funds from the insurance.
>
> Many years later, he admitted to his family that he had loaded an empty crate onto the train. He was overcome with guilt, especially for the discharged railway employee, to whom he contrived to pay an anonymous annual stipend over a period of many years, such that the sum paid was vastly in excess of the value of his wine. Yet to the last, he felt no remorse for the creditor, one John Banks. On the contrary, during the last days of his mortal existence, when he lay in his bed delirious with fevers, he was often heard to say, "That blasted Banks is no gentleman, and I'll be damned if he'll get my Madeira, do you hear?"

Back in 1855, the mysterious disappearance of this same wine was to figure prominently in the plans of Edward Pierce for, partly at the behest of the insuring agency, it caused certain immediate changes to be made in the railway security procedures.

ON THE EVENING of May 21st, just a few hours before the robbery, Pierce was dining with Miriam, in his house in Mayfair. Shortly before nine thirty, Agar came storming into the dining room, making no apologies for his abrupt entrance.

"Burgess," he said, in a breathless voice. "He's downstairs."

Pierce frowned. "You brought him *here*?"

"I had to," Agar said. "Wait till you hear."

Pierce left the table and went downstairs to the smoking room where Burgess was standing, twitching his blue guard's cap in his hands.

"What's the trouble?" Pierce said.

"It's the line." Burgess said. "They've changed everything."

"What have they changed?" Pierce said.

Burgess spoke in a headlong torrent: "I first came to know this morning, you see, I come to work proper at seven sharp, and there's a cooper working on me van, hammering and pounding. And there's a smith as well, and some gentlemen standing about to watch the work. And that's how I find they've changed all manner of things, I mean the running of the car the way that we do, all changed, and I didn't know—"

Pierce frowned impatiently. "Tell me what is changed," he said.

Burgess squeezed his hat until his knuckles were pale. "For one, they have a new jack the line's put on, started today—a young one."

"He rides with you in the baggage van?"

"No, sir," Burgess said. "He only works the platform."

Pierce shot a glance at Agar. It didn't matter if there were more guards at the platform. "What of it?" he said.

"Well, it's the new rule, you see. Nobody rides in the baggage car, save me as guard." Burgess said. "That's the new rule, and there's this new jack to keep it proper."

"I see," Pierce said. That was indeed a change.

"There's more," Agar said gloomily.

Burgess nodded. "They've gone and fitted outside locks to the luggage-van doors. Now they lock up in London Bridge, and unlock in Folkestone."

"*Damn*," Pierce said. He began to pace back and forth in the room. "Why have they changed the routine?"

"It's on account of the afternoon fast train," Burgess explained. "Seems it was robbed last week. Gentleman lost a valuable parcel somehow—collection of rare wine, I hear it to be. Anyhow, he puts a claim to the line or some such. The other guard's been dismissed, and there's all bloody hell to pay. Supervisor his very self called me in this morning and dressed me down proper. And the new jack at the platform's the station supervisor's nephew. He's the one locks up, just before the train pulls out."

"Rare wines," Pierce said. "God in heaven, *rare wines!* Can we get Agar aboard in a trunk?"

Burgess shook his head. "Not if they do like today. Today, this nephew, McPherson, makes the passengers open every trunk large enough to hold a man. Caused a considerable fray."

"Can we distract him and slip Agar in while he's not looking?"

"Never's he not looking. He looks like a starved rat after a flake of cheese."

Pierce plucked his pocketwatch from his waistcoat. It was now ten o'clock at night. They had ten hours before the Folkestone train left the next morning. Pierce could think of a dozen clever ways to get Agar past a watchful Scotsman, but nothing that could be quickly arranged.

Agar's face was the very picture of gloom. "Shall we put off until next month, then?"

"No," Pierce said. He immediately shifted to his next problem. "Now, this lock they've installed on the luggage-van door. Can it be worked from inside?"

Burgess shook his head. "It's a padlock—hooks through a bolt and iron latch, outside."

"Could it be unlocked during one of the stops—say, Redhill—and then locked again at Tonbridge, farther down the line?"

"Be a risk," Burgess said. "She's a fat lock, big as your fist, and it might be noticed."

Pierce continued to pace. Agar and Burgess watched him. Finally Pierce said, "If the van door is locked, how do you get ventilation?"

Burgess said, "Oh, there's air enough. That van's shoddy made, and when the train gets to speed, the breeze whistles through the cracks, and through the slappers in the roof."

"What're they?" Pierce said.

"Slappers? A slapper's what your railway folks call a manner of trap. She's a hinged door up in the roof, and inside you've a rod to open or shut it. They fit two slappers to a coach, facing opposite ways. That's so's one is always away from the wind."

"And you have two of these slappers in the luggage van?"

"Aye, that's true," Burgess said, "but they're not proper, because they're fixed open, you see, no hinging, and so when it rains there I be, soaked through—"

"The slappers give access to the interior of the luggage van?"

"They do." Burgess paused. "But if you're thinking of slipping a bloke through, it can't be done. They're no more than a hand's breadth square, and—"

"I'm not," Pierce said. "Now, you say you have two slappers? Where are they located?"

"On the centre of the roof," Burgess said. "No more than three paces separate."

"All right," Pierce said. "You've told me what I need to know." He turned to Agar. "This padlock on the outside. Is it hard to pick?"

"I don't know it," Agar said, "but a padlock's no trick. They're made strong, but they have fat tumblers, on account of their size. Some a man can use his little finger for the betty, and tickle her broke open in a flash."

"Could I?" Pierce said.

Agar stared at him. "Easy enough, but you might take a minute or two."

Pierce turned back to Burgess. "How many second-class coaches are there on the morning train?"

"Six, as often as not, seven near the weekend. Sometimes, midweek, they run five."

Pierce looked at Agar: Agar had figured it out. The screwsman shook his head. "Mother of God," Agar said, "you've lost your mind, sure as I stand here. What do you think, you're a mountaineer? You're Mr. Coolidge himself?" Mountaineering was a new sport, only three or four years old, and the most notable of the English practitioners, such as A. E. Coolidge, had become famous.

Pierce said, "I know Mr. Coolidge. I met him on the Continent last year. I climbed with him in Switzerland and I learned what he knows."

Agar was speechless. He stared at Pierce for any sign of deception, but Pierce had turned back to Burgess. "I want you to go home now, and sleep, and get up tomorrow and go to work as usual. Just do your regular day of work, and don't worry about anything."

Burgess glanced at Agar, then back to Pierce. "Will you pull tomorrow, then?"

"Yes," Pierce said. "Now go home and sleep."

When the two men were alone, Agar exploded in anxious fury. "This is no simple kinchin lay tomorrow." He threw up his hands. "Make an end to it, I say. Next month, I say."

Pierce calmly went to a sideboard and poured two glasses of brandy.

"I've waited a year for this," he said finally, "and it will be done tomorrow."

"Done?" Agar exploded again. "Done *how*?"

"There is a bone lay," Pierce said, "but there are things for you to do. Go to your lodgings, and come back with your finest clothes, and quickly."

When Agar departed speechless, Pierce sent for Barlow.

"Do we have any rope?" Pierce said.

"No, sir. Could you make do with bridle leather?"

"No," Pierce said. He considered a moment. "Hitch up the horse to the flat carriage and get ready for a night's work. We have a few items to obtain."

CHAPTER EIGHTEEN

On the morning of May 22nd, when the guard McPherson arrived at London Bridge Station to begin the day's work, he was greeted by a most unexpected sight. There, alongside the luggage van of the Folkestone train, stood a woman in black—a servant, by the look of her, but handsome enough, and sobbing most piteously. The object of her grief was not hard to discover, for near the poor girl, set onto a flat baggage cart, was a plain wooden coffin. Although cheap and unadorned, the coffin had several ventholes drilled in the sides. And mounted on the lid was a kind of miniature belfry, containing a small bell, with a cord running from the clapper down through a hole into the coffin.

Although the sight was unexpected, it was not in the least mysterious to McPherson—or, indeed, to any Victorian of the day. Nor was he surprised to detect the reeking odour of advanced corporeal decay emanating from the ventholes.

During the nineteenth century, both in England and in the United States, there arose a peculiar preoccupation with the idea of premature burial. To modern thinking, it is all exaggerated and fanciful; it is difficult now to recognize that for the Victorians, premature burial was a genuine fear shared by nearly all members of society. Nor was this widespread fear simply a neurotic obsession. There was plenty of evidence to lead a sensible man to believe that premature burials did occur, and that such ghastly happenings were only prevented by some fortuitous event. Most cases involved victims ostensibly drowned, or electrocuted, but there were other instances where a person might lapse into a state of apparent death.

In fact, the whole question of when a person was dead was very much in doubt—as it would be again, a century later, when doctors struggled with the ethics of organ transplantation. But it is worth remembering that physicians did not understand that cardiac arrest was wholly reversible until 1950; and in 1850 there was plenty of reason to be sceptical about the reliability of any indicator of death.

Victorians dealt with their uncertainty in two ways. The first was to delay interment for several days and await the unmistakable olfactory evidence of the beloved one's departure from this world. The second method was technological; the Victorians contrived an elaborate series of signalling devices to enable a dead person to make known his resuscitation. A wealthy individual might be buried with a length of iron pipe connecting his coffin to the ground above, and a trusted family servant would be required to remain at the cemetery, day and night, for a month or more, on the chance that the deceased might suddenly awake and begin to call for help. Persons buried in family vaults were often placed in spring-loaded coffins with a complex maze of wires attached to arms and legs, so that the slightest movement of the body would throw open the coffin lid. Many considered this method preferable to any other, for it was believed that individuals often returned from a state of suspended animation in a mute or partially paralysed condition.

The fact that these spring-loaded coffins popped open months or even years later (probably the result of some deterioration in the spring mechanism) only heightened the widespread uncertainty about how long a person might lie dead before coming back to life, even for a moment.

Most signalling devices were costly, and available only to the wealthy classes. Poor people adopted the simpler tactic of burying relatives with some implement—a crowbar or a shovel—on the vague assumption that if they revived, they could dig themselves out of their predicament.

There was clearly a market for an inexpensive alarm system, and in 1852 George Bateson received a patent for the Bateson Life Revival Device, described as "a most economical, ingenious and trustworthy mechanism, promoting peace of mind amongst the bereaved at all stations of life".

"Bateson's belfry", as it was known, was a plain iron bell mounted on the lid of the coffin, over the deceased's head, and connected by a cord or wire through the coffin to the dead person's hand, "such that the least tremor shall directly sound the alarum". Bateson's belfries attained instant popularity, and within a few years a substantial proportion of coffins were fitted with these bells.

That morning, McPherson had more important things to worry about than the weeping servant girl and the coffin, for he knew that the gold shipment from Huddleston & Bradford would be loaded upon the railway van at any moment.

Through the open door of the van, he saw Burgess. McPherson waved, and Burgess responded with a nervous greeting. McPherson knew that his uncle, the supervisor, had yesterday given Burgess a good deal of sharp talk; Burgess was no doubt worried to keep his job, especially as the other guard had been dismissed. McPherson assumed that this accounted for Burgess's tension. Or perhaps it was the sobbing woman. It would not be the first time a stout man had been put off his mark by a female's piteous cries. McPherson turned to the young girl and proffered his handkerchief.

"There now, Missy," he said. "There, now . . ." He sniffed the air. Standing close to the coffin, he noticed that the odour seeping out of the ventholes was certainly rank. But he was not so overcome by the smell that he failed to observe the girl was attractive, even in her grief.

"Oh, please, sir," the girl cried, taking his handkerchief. "Oh, please, can you help me? The man is a heartless beast, he is."

"What man is that?" McPherson demanded.

"Oh, please sir, that guard upon the line. He will not let me set my dear brother here upon the train, for he says I must await the other guard. Oh, I am most wretched," she finished, and dissolved into tears once more.

"He would not let your brother be put aboard?"

Through sobs and sniffles, the girl said something about rules.

"Rules?" he said. "A pox on rules, I say." He noticed her heaving bosom, and her pretty narrow waist.

"Please, sir, he is most firm about the other guard—"

"Missy," he said, "I am the other guard, and I'll see your dear brother on the train with no delay."

"Oh, sir, I am in your debt," she said, managing a smile through her tears.

McPherson was overwhelmed. "Just you wait," he promised.

He turned to chastise Burgess for his overzealous adherence to the rules, but at that moment he saw the first of the grey-uniformed, armed guards of Huddleston & Bradford, bringing their bullion consignment down the platform.

The loading was carried out with sharp precision. First, two guards entered the van, and made a quick search of the interior. Then eight more guards arrived, in neat formation around two flatcarts, each pushed by a gang of sweating porters—and each piled with rectangular, sealed strongboxes. At the van, a ramp was swung down, and the porters pushed first one, and then the other, of the laden flatcarts up into the van, to the waiting safes.

Next an official of the bank, a well-rigged gent with an air of authority, appeared with two keys in his hand. Soon after, the supervisor arrived with a second pair of keys. They inserted their keys in the safes and opened them. The bullion strongboxes were loaded into the safes, and the doors were shut with a massive metal clang. The keys were twisted in the locks; the safes were secured.

The man from the bank took his keys and departed.

"Mind your work this morning," the supervisor said to his nephew. "Open every parcel large enough to hold a knave, and no exception." He sniffed the air. "What's that ungodly stink?"

McPherson nodded over his shoulder to the girl and the coffin a short distance away. It was a pitiful sight but his uncle frowned. "Scheduled for the morning train, is it?"

"Yes, Uncle."

"See that you open it," the supervisor said, and turned away.

"But Uncle—" McPherson began, thinking he would lose his newly gained favour with the girl by insisting on such a thing.

The supervisor stopped. "No stomach for it? Dear God. You're a delicate one." He scanned the youth's agonized face. "All right then, I'll see to it myself," and he strode off towards the weeping girl. It was at that moment that they heard an electrifying, ghastly sound: the ringing of Mr. Bateson's patented bell.

In later courtroom testimony, Pierce explained the psychology behind the plan. "Any guard watches for certain happenings. I knew the railway guard suspected some fakement to smuggle a

living body onto the van. Now, a vigilant guard will know a coffin can easily hold a body; he will suspect it less, because it seems too obvious.

"Yet, he will likely wonder if the body is truly dead, and if he is vigilant he will call to have the box opened, and spend some moments making a thorough examination of the body to insure that it is dead. He may feel the pulse, or he may stick a pin here or there. Now, no living soul can pass such an examination without detection.

"But how different it is if all believe that the body is not dead, but wrongly incarcerated. Now all emotions are reversed: instead of suspicion, there is hope. Instead of a respectful opening of the casket there is a frantic rush to break it free, and in this the relatives join willingly.

"And then, when the lid is raised and the decomposed remains come to light, how different is the response of the spectators. Their desperate hopes are dashed in an instant; the ghastly truth is immediately apparent at a moment's glance. The relatives are wildly distraught. The lid is quickly closed—and all because of reversed expectations."

At the sound of the bell, which rang only once, the sobbing girl let out a shriek. The supervisor and his nephew broke into a run, quickly covering the short distance to the coffin.

By then the girl was in a state of profound hysteria, clawing at the coffin lid with her fingers. "Oh, my dear brother—oh, Richard, dear Richard—oh, God he lives. . . ." Her fingers scrabbled at the wooden surface, and her tugging rocked the coffin so that the bell rang continuously.

The supervisor and his nephew instantly caught the girl's frantic anxiety, but they were able to proceed with more sense. The lid was closed with a series of metal latches, and they began to open them.

In a few moments, the men were at a fever pitch of intensity. And all the while, the girl cried, "Oh, Richard—dear God, make haste, he's alive!" and all the while, the bell rang from the rocking coffin.

The commotion drew a crowd of some size, which stood a few paces back on the platform, taking in the bizarre spectacle.

"Oh hurry, hurry, lest we are too late," the girl cried, and the men worked frantically. Indeed, only when they were at the final two latches did the supervisor hear the girl cry, "Oh, I knew it was not cholera, he was a quack to say it."

The supervisor froze, his hand on the latch. "Cholera?" he said.

"Oh hurry, hurry," the girl cried. "It is five days now I have waited to hear the bell. . . ."

"You say cholera?" the supervisor repeated. "Five days?"

But the nephew, who had not stopped throwing off the latches, now flung the coffin lid wide.

"Thank God!" cried the girl, and threw herself down upon the body inside, as if to hug her brother. But she halted in mid-gesture, which was perfectly understandable. With the raising of the lid, a foul stench rolled forth in a near palpable wave, and its source was not hard to determine; the body lying within, dressed in his best Sunday clothes, hands folded across the chest, was already in a state of obvious decomposition. The exposed flesh at the face and hands was bloated and puffed, a repellent grey-green colour. The lips were black, and so was the partially protruding tongue.

The supervisor and his nephew hardly saw more of that horrific spectacle before the feverish girl swooned on the spot. The nephew instantly leapt to attend her, and the supervisor, with no less alacrity, closed the lid and began shutting the latches.

The watching crowd, when it heard that the man had died of cholera, dissipated with the same swiftness. In a moment, the station platform was nearly deserted.

Soon the girl recovered from her swoon, but she remained in a state of profound distress. She kept asking softly "How can it be? I heard the bell. I heard it plain, did you not?"

McPherson did his best to comfort her, saying that it must have been some sudden gust of wind that had caused the bell to ring.

The supervisor, seeing that his nephew was occupied with the poor child, took it upon himself to oversee the loading of luggage into the van of the Folkestone train. When at last the malodorous coffin was loaded into the van, he took a certain delight in warning Burgess to look after his health, since his fellow passenger had fallen victim to King Cholera. Then he barked a final order to his nephew to get on with the job and lock up the van, and returned to his office.

All this time, Pierce had been on the platform. He had been among the crowd that witnessed the episode of the opened coffin. It had proceeded precisely as he had intended, and Agar, in his hideous make-up, had escaped detection.

When the crowd dissipated, Pierce had moved forward to the van, a porter at his side. The porter had been carrying some rather odd luggage on his trolley, and Pierce had had a moment of disquiet when he saw the supervisor himself take up the job of overseeing the loading of the van.

A thoughtful man might wonder why a gentleman of quality travelled with such small and extremely ugly satchels. Their leather was coarse and the stitching at the seams was crude and obvious. Furthermore, although the gentleman's porter was a burly character, he was clearly straining under the weight of each small satchel.

Pierce had watched the supervisor's face while the five bags had been loaded, one after another, but the supervisor, somewhat pale, had not noticed them at all.

Pierce drifted away, but did not board the train. Instead, he remained near that end of the platform, apparently curious about the recovery of the woman who had fainted. In fact, he was lingering in the hope of seeing the padlock that he would soon be attempting to pick.

At last, when the supervisor went back to his office and the young woman made her way towards the coaches, Pierce fell into step beside her.

"Are you fully recovered, miss?" he asked.

"I trust so," she said.

They merged with the boarding crowd at the coaches. Pierce said, "Perhaps you will join me in my compartment for the duration of the journey?"

"You are kind," the girl said, with a slight nod.

"*Get rid of him.*" Pierce whispered to her. "I don't care how, just do it."

Miriam had a puzzled look for only a moment, and then a hearty voice boomed out, "Edward! Edward, my dear fellow!" A man was pushing towards them through the crowd.

Pierce waved a delighted greeting. "Henry," he called. "Henry Fowler, what an extraordinary surprise."

Fowler came over and shook Pierce's hand. "Fancy meeting you here," he said. "Are you on this train? Yes? Why so am I, the fact of the matter—ah. . . ." His voice trailed off as he noticed the girl at Pierce's side. He displayed some discomfiture, for in terms of Henry Fowler's social world all the signals were mixed. Here was Pierce, dressed handsomely and showing his usual polish, standing with a girl who was pretty enough, but by her dress and manner a very common sort. Then, too, the girl had been weeping; it was all most perplexing and unusual, and—

Pierce put Fowler out of his misery. "Forgive me," he said, turning to the girl. "I should introduce you, but I do not know your name. This is Mr. Henry Fowler."

The girl, giving him a demure smile, said, "I am Brigid Lawson. How'd you do, sir."

Fowler nodded a vaguely polite greeting, struggling to assume the correct stance towards an obvious servant girl (and therefore not an equal) and a female in distress (and therefore deserving of gentlemanly conduct). Pierce made the situation clearer. "Miss, ah, Lawson, has just had a most trying encounter," Pierce said. "She is travelling to accompany her deceased brother, who is now situated in the van. But a few moments past, the bell rang, and there was hope of revival and the casket was opened—"

"I see, I see," Fowler said.

"—but it was a false alarm," Pierce said.

"And thus doubly painful, I am certain," Fowler said.

"I offered to accompany her on the journey," Pierce said.

"And indeed I should do the same," Fowler said, "were I in your place. In fact . . ." He hesitated. "Would it seem an imposition if I joined you both?"

Pierce did not hesitate. "By all means," he said cheerfully. "That is unless Miss Lawson. . . ."

"You are ever so kind, you two are," the girl said, with a brave but grateful smile.

"Well, it's settled, then," Fowler said, also smiling. Pierce saw that he was looking at the girl with interest. "But would you like to come with me? My compartment is at the front." He pointed up the line of first-class coaches.

Pierce had intended to sit in the last compartment of the third first-class coach. From there, he would have the shortest distance to travel, when the time came, to reach the luggage van at the rear.

"Actually," Pierce said, "I've my own compartment, down there." He pointed towards the final first-class carriage. "My bags are already there, and I've paid the porter, and so on."

"My dear Edward," Fowler said, "How did you get yourself back there? The choice compartments are all towards the front. Come along. I assure you, you'll find a forward compartment more to your liking, and particularly if Miss Lawson feels poorly. . . ."

"Nothing would delight me more," Pierce said, "but in truth I have selected my compartment on the advice of my physician, after experiencing certain distress on railway journeys. This he attributed to the effect of vibrations originating in the engine, and therefore he's warned me to sit as far back from the source as possible." Pierce gave a short laugh. "He said in fact that I should sit second-class, but I cannot bring myself to it."

"And little wonder," Fowler said. "There is a limit to healthy living, though you cannot expect a physician to know it. Very well then, we shall all ride in your compartment."

Pierce said, "Perhaps Miss Lawson feels, as you do, that a forward carriage would be preferable."

Before the girl could speak, Fowler said, "What? And steal her away from you, leaving you solitary upon the journey? I would not think of it. Come, come, the train will soon leave. Where is your compartment?"

They walked along the train to Pierce's compartment. Fowler was in unshakable good spirits, and chattered at length about physicians and their foibles. They stepped into Pierce's compartment and closed the door. Pierce glanced at his watch: it was six minutes to eight. Time was short to get rid of Fowler, particularly as it had to be done in such a way that no suspicion would be aroused.

Mr. Fowler was still talking, but his focus was directed towards the girl, who gave every appearance of rapt attention. "It's the most extraordinary luck, running across Edward today. Do you travel this route often, Edward? I myself do it no more than once a month. And you, Miss Lawson?"

"I been on a train before," the girl said, "but I never gone first-class; only my mistress, this time she buys me a first ticket, seeing as how, you know. . . ."

"Oh, quite, quite," Fowler said, in a hearty, chin-up manner. "One must do all one can for one in times of stress. I must confess, I am under no little stress myself this morning. Now, Edward here, he may have guessed the reason for my travel, and therefore my stress. Eh, Edward?"

Pierce had not been listening. He was staring out of the window, considering how to get rid of Fowler in the remaining few minutes. "Do you think your bags are safe?" he said.

"My bags? Bags? What—Oh, in my compartment? I have no bags, Edward. I carry not so much as a case of briefs, for once in Folkestone, I shall remain there just two hours, hardly a space of time to take a meal, or smoke a cigar, before I am back on the train, homeward bound."

Smoke a cigar, Pierce thought. Of course. He reached into his coat pocket, and withdrew a long cigar, which he lit.

"Now then, dear girl," Fowler said, "our friend Edward here shall surely have surmised the purpose of my journey, but I fancy you are still in the dark."

The girl was, in fact, staring at Mr. Fowler with her mouth slightly open.

"The truth is that this is no ordinary train, and I am no ordinary passenger. On the contrary, I am the general manager of the banking firm of Huddleston & Bradford, and today, aboard this very train—not two hundred paces from us as we sit here—my firm has stored a quantity of gold bullion for shipment overseas to our brave troops. Can you imagine how much? No? Well, then—it is a quantity in excess of twelve thousand pounds, my dear child."

"Cor!" the girl exclaimed. "And you're in charge of all that?"

"I am indeed." Henry Fowler was looking plainly self-satisfied, and with reason. He had obviously overwhelmed the simple girl with his words, and she appeared to have entirely forgotten Pierce.

That is, until Pierce's cigar smoke billowed in grey clouds within the compartment. Now the girl coughed in a delicate suggestive fashion, as she had no doubt observed her mistress to do. Pierce, staring out of the window, did not seem to notice.

The girl coughed again, more insistently. When Pierce still made no response, Fowler took it upon himself to speak. "Edward," he said. "I believe your tobacco causes Miss Lawson some distress."

Pierce looked at him and said, "What?"

"I say, would you mind—" Fowler began.

The girl bent forward and said, "I feel quite faint, I fear, please," and she extended a hand towards the door, as if to open it.

"Just look, now," Fowler said to Pierce. Fowler opened the door and helped the girl—who leaned rather heavily upon his arm—into the fresh air.

"I had no idea," Pierce protested. "Believe me, had I but known—"

"You might have inquired before lighting your diabolical contraption," Fowler said, with the girl leaning against him, so that much of her bosom pressed against his chest.

"I'm most dreadfully sorry," Pierce said. He started to get out himself to lend assistance.

The last thing Fowler wanted was assistance. "You shouldn't smoke anyway, if your doctor has warned you that trains are hazardous to your health," he snapped. "Come, my dear," he said to the girl, "my compartment is just this way, and we can continue our conversation with no danger of noxious fumes."

"Dreadfully sorry," Pierce said again, but neither of them looked back.

A moment later, the whistle blew and the engine began to chug. Pierce stepped back into his compartment, shut the door, and watched London Bridge Station slide away past his window as the morning train to Folkestone began to gather speed.

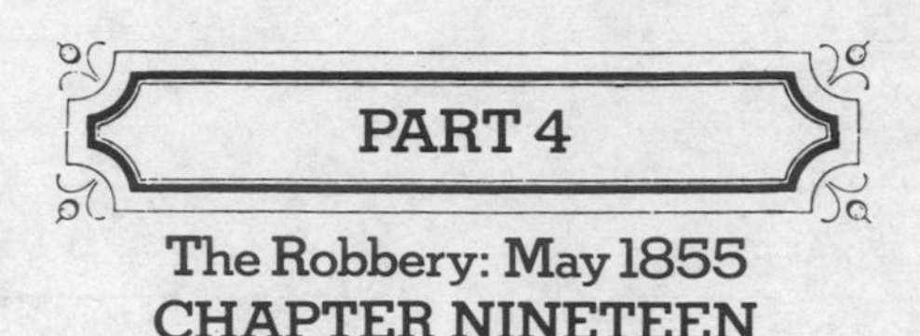

PART 4

The Robbery: May 1855

CHAPTER NINETEEN

Burgess, locked in the windowless luggage van, knew by now the location of the train at any moment by the sound of the track. He heard first the smooth clacking of the wheels on the well-laid rails of the yard. Then, later, the hollow, more resonant tones as the train crossed Bermondsey on the elevated overpass for several miles, and, still later, a transition to a deader sound and a rougher ride, signalling the beginning of the southward run outside London.

Burgess had no inkling of Pierce's plan, and he was astonished when the coffin bell began to ring. He attributed it to the sway of the train, but a few moments later there was a pounding, and then a muffled voice. Unable to make out the words, he approached the coffin.

"Open up, damn you," the voice said.

"Are you alive?" Burgess asked, in tones of wonderment.

"It's Agar, you damnable flat," came the answer.

Burgess hastily began to throw the catches on the coffin lid. Soon after, Agar—covered in a dreadful green paste, smelling horribly, but acting in normal enough fashion—got out of the coffin and said, "I must be quick. Get me those satchels there."

Burgess hurried to do so. "But the van is locked," he said. "How will it be opened?"

"Our friend," Agar said, "is a mountaineer."

Agar opened the safes and removed the first of the strongboxes, breaking the seal and taking out the dull gold bars of bullion—

each stamped with a royal crown and the initials "H & B". He replaced them with small bags of shot, which he took from the satchels.

Burgess watched in silence. "A mountaineer?" he said finally.

"Yes," Agar said. "He's coming over the tops of the train to unlock us."

"When?" Burgess said frowning.

"After Redhill, returning to his coach before Ashford. It's all open country there. Almost no chance of being seen." Agar did not glance up from his work.

"Redhill to Ashford? But that's the fastest part of the run."

"Aye, I suppose," Agar said.

"Well, then," Burgess said, "your friend is mad."

AT ONE POINT in the trial of Pierce, the prosecutor lapsed into a moment of frank admiration. "Then it is not true," said the prosecutor, "that you had any experience of the recreation of mountaineering?"

"None," Pierce said. "I merely said that to reassure Agar."

"Had you, perhaps, some past experiences of athletic or physical endeavour which persuaded you of your ability to carry out your intended plan?"

"None," Pierce said.

"Well, then," said the prosecutor, "I must inquire, if only for reasons of human curiosity, what on earth, sir, led you to believe you might succeed in such a palpably dangerous undertaking as clambering about on a swift-moving railway train?"

Journalistic accounts mention that at this point the witness smiled. "I knew it would be no difficulty," he said, "despite the appearance of danger, for I had on several occasions read in the press of those incidents which are called railway sway, and I had similarly read of the explanation, offered by engineers, that the forces are caused by the nature of swiftly moving air. Thus I was assured that these forces would operate to hold my person to the surface of the coach."

At this point, the prosecutor asked for further elucidation, which Pierce gave in garbled form. The truth was that he undertook his climb over the carriages with a sense of confidence that was completely unfounded. Briefly, the situation was that, around 1848, when railway trains began to attain speeds of fifty or even seventy miles an hour, a bizarre new phenomenon was noted. Whenever a fast-moving train passed a train standing at a station, the carriages of both trains had a tendency to be drawn together in what was called "railway sway". In some cases the carriages heeled over in such a pronounced fashion that passengers were alarmed, and indeed there was sometimes minor damage to coaches.

Railway engineers, finally admitted their perplexity outright. No one had the slightest idea why "railway sway" occurred, or what to do to correct it. Trains were then the fastest-moving objects in human history, and the behaviour of such swift vehicles was suspected to be governed by some set of physical laws as yet undiscovered. The confusion was precisely that of aircraft engineers a century later, when the "buffeting" phenomenon of an aircraft approaching the speed of sound was similarly inexplicable.

However, by 1851 most engineers had decided correctly that railway sway was an example of Bernoulli's law, a formulation of a Swiss mathematician, which stated, in effect, that the pressure within a moving stream of air is less than the pressure of the air surrounding it. This meant that two moving trains, if they were close enough would be sucked together by the partial vacuum of air between them. A solution to the problem was soon adopted: the parallel tracks were set farther apart, and railway sway disappeared.

One can readily understand the erroneous conclusions Pierce drew. Apparently he believed that the airstream around the moving carriage would act to suck him down to the carriage roof, and thus help him to maintain his footing as he moved from car to car. The truth is that Bernoulli's law would not operate in any way on his body. He would simply be a man exposed to a fifty-mile-an-hour blast of rushing air, which could blow him off the train at any moment.

Nor was this the extent of his misinformation. The very fact that high-speed travel was so new left Pierce, along with his contemporaries, with very little sense of the consequences of being thrown from a fast moving vehicle. Pierce had seen Spring Heel Jack dead after being thrown from the train. But he had regarded this with no sense of inevitability. At this time, the hazard of falling from a speeding train was thought to lie in the precise manner of the fall: a lucky man could pick himself up with a few scrapes, while an unlucky man would break his neck on impact.

The prosecutor asked, "Did you take any manner of precaution against the danger of a fall?"

"I did," Pierce said, "and they caused me no little discomfort. Beneath my ordinary external garb, I wore two pairs of heavy cotton undergarments, which had the effect of making me unpleasantly heated, yet I felt these protective measures necessary."

Thus, wholly unprepared, Edward Pierce slung a coil of rope over his shoulder, opened the compartment door, and clambered up onto the roof of the moving carriage. His only true protection lay in his complete misunderstanding of the danger he faced.

THE WIND STRUCK HIM like an enormous fist, screaming about his ears, stinging his eyes, tugging at his cheeks and burning his skin. He had not removed his long frock coat, and the garment now flapped about him.

For a few moments he was totally disorientated by the unexpected fury of the shrieking air that passed him; he crouched, clutching the wooden surface of the coach, and paused to get his bearings. He found he could hardly look forward at all because of the particles of soot blown back from the engine. Indeed, he was rapidly covered with a fine black film. Beneath him, the coach rocked in an alarming fashion.

He nearly abandoned his intent in those first moments, but after the initial shock had passed he determined to go forward with his plan. Crawling on his hands and knees, he moved backwards to the end of the coach, and paused at the space over the coupling that separated his carriage from the next. This was a gap of some five feet. Moments passed before he gathered the nerve to jump to the next car, but he did so successfully.

From there he crawled painfully down the length of the car. His frock coat was blown forward, covering his face and flapping around his eyes. After some moments of struggle he shook it off and saw it sail away, twisting in the air. The whirling coat looked enough like a human form to give him pause; it seemed a kind of warning of the fate that awaited him if he made the slightest error.

Freed of the coat, he was able to make more rapid progress; he jumped from one coach to the next with increasing assurance, and eventually reached the luggage van. Atop the van, he gripped an open slapper, and uncoiled his length of hemp. One end was dropped down the slapper, and after a moment he felt a tug as Agar, inside the van, picked it up.

Pierce moved to the second slapper. He waited there, his body curled tight against the constant, unyielding blast of the wind, and then Agar's ghastly green hand reached out, holding the end of the rope. Pierce took it; Agar's hand disappeared from view. Pierce now had his rope slung from one slapper to the next. He tied the loose ends about his belt, and then, hanging on the ropes eased himself over the side of the van until he was level with the padlock.

In that manner he hung suspended while he twirled the padlock with a ring of keys, trying one after another and operating, as he later testified, "With that degree of delicacy which circumstances permitted." Altogether, he tried more than a dozen keys, and he was beginning to despair when he heard the scream of the whistle.

Looking forward, he saw a tunnel, and an instant later he was plunged into blackness and churning sound. The tunnel was half a mile long; there was nothing to do but wait. When the train burst into sunlight again, he continued working with the keys, and was gratified when almost immediately one of the picks clicked smoothly in the mechanism. The padlock snapped open.

Now it was a simple matter to remove the lock, swing the crossbar free, and kick the door with his feet until Burgess slid it open. The morning train passed the sleepy town of Godstone, but no one noticed the man dangling on the rope, who now eased down into the interior of the luggage van and collapsed on the floor in absolute exhaustion.

AGAR TESTIFIED that in the first moment that Pierce landed inside the luggage van, neither he nor Burgess recognized him: "I cool him first, and I swear he's some muck Indian, so black he is and his dunnage torn all about, and I says, the cracksman's hired a new bloke to do the lay. And then I see it's him himself, right enough."

Surely the three men must have presented a bizarre picture: Burgess, neat and tidy in his blue railway uniform; Agar, dressed splendidly in a formal suit, his face and hands a cadaverous bloated green; and Pierce, his clothing shredded and sooty black from head to foot.

But they all recovered quickly, and worked with swift efficiency. Agar had completed the switch; the strongboxes, with their new treasure of lead shot, were re-sealed, the safes were locked up again; the five leather satchels stood by the van door in a neat row, each laden with gold bullion.

Pierce got to his feet and took his watch from his waistcoat, an incongruously clean object. He snapped it open: it was 8.37.

"Five minutes," he said.

Agar nodded. In five minutes, they would pass the most deserted stretch of track, where Pierce had arranged for Barlow to wait and pick up the flung satchels. Pierce sat down and stared through the open door at the countryside rushing past.

"Are you well, then?" Agar asked.

"Well enough," Pierce said. "But I don't cherish going back."

"Aye, it's frazzled you proper," Agar said. "You're a sight and no mistake. Will you change when you're snug in the compartment again?"

Pierce, breathing heavily, was slow to comprehend. "Change?"

"Aye, your dunnage." Agar grinned. "You step off the train at Folkestone as you stand now and you'll cause no end of stir."

Pierce watched the green, rolling hills flash past the open door. Here was a problem he had never considered. But Agar was right:

he couldn't step out at Folkestone looking like a ragged chimney sweep, especially as Fowler was almost certain to seek him out to say goodbye. "I have no change," he said.

Agar laughed heartily. "Then you'll play the proper ragamuffin, as you've made me play the stiff."

"It's nothing funny," Pierce snapped. "I have acquaintances on the train who will surely see me and mark the change."

Agar's merriment was quashed instantly. He scratched his head with a green hand. "And these same of your acquaintances, they'll miss you if you're not there at the station?"

Pierce nodded.

"It's the devil's own trap, then," Agar said. He looked around the van, at the various trunks and pieces of luggage.

"Give me your ring of tickles, and I'll break a pit or two, and we'll find some square-rigged duns to fit you."

He held out his hand to Pierce but Pierce was looking at his watch. It was now two minutes to the drop-off point. Thirteen minutes after that, the train would stop in Ashford, and by then Pierce had to be out of the luggage van and back in his own compartment. "There's no time," he said.

"It's the only chance—" Agar began, but broke off. Pierce was looking him up and down in a thoughtful way. "No," Agar said. "Damn you, no!"

"We're about the same size," Pierce said. "Now be quick."

He turned away and the screwsman undressed, muttering oaths. Pierce watched the countryside. They were close now: he bent to position the satchels at the lip of the open door.

Now he saw a tree by the roadside, one of the landmarks he'd long since set for himself. Soon there would be the fence . . . There it was . . . and then the old abandoned cart. A moment later, he saw the crest of a hill and Barlow beside the coach.

"Now," he said and, with a grunt, flung one satchel after another out of the moving train. He watched them bounce on the ground one by one. He saw Barlow hastening down the hill towards them. Then the train went around a curve.

He looked back at Agar who had stripped and held his fine duds out for Pierce. "Here you are, and damn your eyes."

Pierce took the clothes, rolled them into as tight a ball as he could manage, wrapped the parcel with Agar's belt, and, without another word, swung open the door and jumped into the wind. Burgess closed the van door, and a few moments later the guard and Agar heard a clink as the bolt was thrown, and another clink as the padlock was locked once more. They heard the scratching of Pierce's feet as he scrambled up to the roof; and then they saw the rope, which had been taut across the roof from slapper to slapper, suddenly go slack. The rope was pulled out. They heard Pierce's footsteps on the roof a moment longer and then nothing.

"Damn me, I'm cold," Agar said. "You'd best lock me back up," and he crawled into his coffin.

Pierce had not progressed far on his return journey before he realized he had made still another error in his planning: he had assumed it would take the same amount of time to go from the van to his compartment as it took to go from his compartment to the van. But the return trip, against the blast of the wind, was much slower. He was further burdened by the parcel of Agar's clothing, which he clutched to his chest, leaving only one hand free to grip the roofing. Within minutes he realized that he would still be crawling along the rooftops when the train reached Ashford Station; and then he would be spotted, and the jig would be up.

Pierce had a moment of profound rage that this final step in the plan should be the only thing to go irretrievably wrong. The fact that the error was entirely his own doing merely increased his fury.

Squinting ahead, he saw Ashford Station, a tiny red rectangle with a grey roof in the far distance. In less than a minute the train would be near enough so that passengers on the platform could see him. He knew, of course, what he must do, but he did not think about it. He got up and ran, sprinting forward, leaping from one car to the next without hesitation, half blinded by smoke.

Somehow he made it safely to the first-class coach, swung down, opened the door, dropped into his compartment, and immediately pulled the blinds. The train was now chugging very slowly and as Pierce collapsed into his seat he heard the hiss of the brakes and the porter's cry: "Ashford Station . . . Ashford . . . Ashford . . ."

Pierce sighed. They had done it.

CHAPTER TWENTY

Twenty-seven minutes later, the train arrived at Folkestone, and all the passengers disembarked. Pierce emerged from his compartment, appearing, he said, "far better than I deserved, but far from sartorial correctness, to put it lightly."

Although he had hastily employed handkerchief and spittle to clean his face and hands, he had discovered the soot on his flesh to be most recalcitrant. As he had no mirror he could only guess at the condition of his face, but his hands were no cleaner than pale grey.

Except for the top hat, all his clothing fitted poorly. The trousers were almost two inches short of an acceptable length, and the cut of the coat, although elegant enough, was of the extreme and showy fashion that true gentlemen of breeding avoided. And, of course, he reeked of dead cat.

Thus Pierce stepped out onto the crowded Folkestone platform with an inner dread. He knew that most observers would put down his appearance as a sham: it was common enough for men who aspired to be gentlemen to obtain secondhand goods, which they wore proudly, oblivious to the ill fit of the garments. But Pierce was all too aware that Henry Fowler would spot the peculiarity of Pierce's appearance in an instant, and would wonder what was amiss. He would almost certainly realize that Pierce had changed clothing for some reason during the ride, and he would wonder about that as well.

Pierce's only hope lay in keeping his distance from Fowler. He planned, if he could, to make off with a distant wave of goodbye and an air of pressing business. Fowler would certainly understand a man who looked after business first. And from a distance, with the intervening throng of people, Pierce's bizarre dress might possibly escape his eye.

As it happened, Fowler came charging through the crowd before Pierce could spot him. Fowler had the woman beside him and he did not look happy.

"Now, Edward," Fowler began crisply, "I should be forever in your debt if—" He broke off, and his mouth fell open.

Dear God, Pierce thought, it's finished.

"*Edward*," Fowler said, staring in astonishment.

Pierce's mind was working fast, trying to anticipate questions, trying to come up with answers; he felt himself break into a sweat.

"Edward, my dear fellow, you look *terrible*. When you told me you suffered from trains, I hardly imagined. . . . Are you all right?"

"I believe so," Pierce said, with a heartfelt sigh. "I expect I shall be much improved after I dine."

"Dine? Yes, of course, you must dine at once, and take a draught of brandy, too. Your circulation is sluggish, from the look of you. I should join you myself, but—ah, I see they are now unloading the gold which is my deep responsibility. Edward, can you excuse me? Are you truly well?"

"I appreciate your concern," Pierce began, "and—"

"Perhaps I can help him," the girl said.

"Oh, capital idea," Fowler said. "Most splendid. Splendid. She's such a charmer, Edward, and I leave you with her." Fowler hurried off down the platform towards the luggage van, turning back once to call, "Remember, a good strong draught of brandy's the thing." And then he was gone.

Pierce gave an enormous sigh, and turned to the girl. "How could he miss my clothes?"

"You should see your countenance," she said. "You look horrible." She glanced at his clothes. "And I see you've a dead man's dunnage."

"Mine were torn by the wind."

"Then you've done the pull?"

Pierce only grinned.

PIERCE LEFT the station shortly before noon. The girl remained behind to supervise the loading of her brother's coffin onto a cab. Much to the irritation of the porters, she turned down several waiting cabs claiming she had made arrangements in advance for a particular one.

This cab did not arrive until after one o'clock. The driver, an ugly brute with a scar across his forehead, helped with the loading, then whipped up the horses and galloped away. No one noticed when, at the end of the street, the cab halted to pick up another passenger, an ashen-coloured gentleman in ill-fitting clothes. Then the cab rattled off, and disappeared from sight.

BY NOON, the strongboxes of the Huddleston & Bradford Bank had been transferred, under armed guard, from the Folkestone railway station to the Channel steamer, which made the crossing to Ostend. They were then transported, under armed guard, to the Ostend railway terminus for shipment to Paris by train the following morning.

On the morning of May 23rd, French representatives of the bank of Louis Bonnard et Fils arrived at Ostend to open the strongboxes and verify their contents, prior to placing them aboard the nine o'clock train to Paris.

Thus, at about 8.15 a.m. on May 23rd, it was discovered that the strongboxes contained a large quantity of lead shot sewn into individual cloth packets, and no gold at all. This astounding development was immediately reported to London by telegraph, and the message reached Huddleston & Bradford's offices shortly after 10:00 a.m. Immediately it provoked the most profound consternation in that firm's brief but respectable history, and the furor did not abate for months to come.

PREDICTABLY, the initial reaction of Huddleston & Bradford was sheer disbelief that anything was amiss. The French cable had been composed in English and read: GOLD MISSED NOW WHERE IS, and was signed VERNIER, OSTEND.

Confronted by this ambiguous message, Sir Edgar Huddleston announced that there had been, no doubt, some silly delay with the French customs authorities and he predicted the whole business would be unravelled before teatime. Mr. Bradford, who had never made the slightest attempt to conceal his intense and lifelong loathing for all things French, assumed that the filthy Frogs had misplaced the bullion, and were now trying to fix the blame on the English. Mr. Henry Fowler, who had seen the gold shipment safely onto the Channel steamer, observed that the signature "Vernier" was an unfamiliar name, and speculated that the cable might be some sort of practical joke. This was, after all, a time of increasingly strained relations between the English and their French allies.

Cables requesting—and later demanding—clarification flashed back and forth across the Channel. By noon, it appeared that the steamship crossing from Folkestone to Ostend had been sunk and the bullion lost in the mishap. However, by early afternoon it was clear the steamer had had an uneventful passage, but almost everything else was vastly more confused.

Cables were now being fired off to all conceivable parties by the Paris bank, the French railway, the English steamship line, the British railway, and the British bank, in dizzying profusion. As the day wore on, the tone of the messages became more acrimonious and their content more ludicrous. The whole thing reached a sort of pinnacle when the manager of the South Eastern Railway in Folkestone telegraphed the manager of the Britannic Steam Packet Company, also in Folkestone: QUI EST M. VERNIER. To this, the steamship manager shot back YOUR SCURRILOUS ALLEGATIONS SHALL NOT GO UNCHALLENGED.

By teatime in London, the desks of the chief officers of Huddleston & Bradford were heaped with cables, and office boys were despatched to gentlemen's homes to inform their wives that their husbands would not be home for dinner. The earlier atmosphere of unruffled calm and disdain for French inefficiency was now fading, replaced by a growing suspicion that something might actually have happened to the gold. And it was increasingly clear that the French were as worried as the English—M. Bonnard himself had taken the afternoon train to Ostend. He was a notorious recluse, and his decision to travel was viewed as a most significant event.

By seven o'clock in London, when most of the bank's clerks went home for the day, the mood of the officers was openly pessimistic. Sir Edgar was snappish; Mr. Bradford had the smell of gin on his breath; Mr. Fowler was pale as a ghost; and Mr. Trent's hands trembled. There was a brief moment of elation around 7.30 p.m. when the customs papers from Ostend, signed by the French the previous day, arrived at the bank. They indicated that at 5.00 p.m. on May 22nd the designated representative of Bonnard et Fils, one Raymond Vernier, had signed for nineteen sealed strongboxes from Huddleston & Bradford containing, according to the declaration, twelve thousand pounds sterling in bullion.

"Here is their bloody death warrant," Sir Edgar said, waving the paper in the air, "and if there's been any irregularity, it is wholly upon French heads." But this was an exaggeration of the legal situation, and he knew it. Soon after, Sir Edgar received a long cable from Ostend:

> YOUR CONSIGNMENT NINETEEN (19) STRONGBOXES ARRIVED OSTEND YESTERDAY 22 MAY AT 1700 HOURS ABOARD SHIP "ARLINGTON" SAID CONSIGNMENT ACCEPTED BY OUR REPRESENTATIVE WITHOUT BREAKING SEALS WHICH APPEARED INTACT CONSIGNMENT PLACED IN OSTEND STRONG SAFE WITH GUARD NIGHT 22 MAY FOLLOWING OUR CUSTOM NO EVIDENCE TAMPERING SAFE GUARD CHARACTER RELIABLE MORNING 23 MAY OUR REPRESENTATIVE BROKE SEALS YOUR CONSIGNMENT FOUND CONSISTING QUANTITY LEAD PELLETS FOR GUN BUT NO GOLD PRELIMINARY INQUIRY REGARDING ORIGIN PELLETS SUGGESTS ENGLISH MANUFACTURE REVIEW OF BROKEN SEALS SUGGESTS PREVIOUS BREAK AND SECONDARY SEALING SKILFUL NATURE NOT AROUSING SUSPICION AT ORDINARY INSPECTION IMMEDIATELY NOTIFYING POLICE OFFICIALS ALSO GOVERNMENT IN PARIS REMINDING ALL OF BRITISH ORIGIN BRITISH RAILWAY BRITISH STEAMSHIP BRITISH SUBJECTS GUARDING THROUGHOUT REQUEST YOU INFORM BRITISH AUTHORITIES I AWAIT YOUR SOLUTION TO THIS TRUE PUZZLE.
>
> LOUIS BONNARD, PRESIDENT
> BONNARD ET FILS.

Sir Edgar's reaction to the cable was reported to be "A heated and forceful expletive, provoked by the stresses of the moment and the lateness of the hour". It was nearly ten o'clock at night before he was finally calm enough to say to Mr. Bradford, "I shall notify the Minister. You notify Scotland Yard."

EVENTS OF SUBSEQUENT days followed a certain predictable pattern. The English suspected the French; the French suspected the English; everyone suspected the English railway officials who in turn suspected the English steamship officials, who in turn suspected the French customs officials. British police officers in France, and French police officers in England, rubbed shoulders with private detectives hired by the banks, the railway, and the shipping line. Everyone offered some sort of reward for information leading to the arrest of the villains, and informants on both sides of the Channel quickly responded with a dazzling profusion of tips and rumours.

The most widespread belief, on both sides of the Channel, was that the robbery was some kind of inside job. The complexity and neatness of the theft surely pointed to inside co-operation. Thus every individual who had the slightest relationship to the Crimean gold shipment came under scrutiny, and was interrogated by the authorities. The zeal of the police to gather information led to some unlikely circumstances: the ten-year-old grandson of the Folkestone harbourmaster was tailed by a plainclothesman for several days. Such incidents only increased the general confusion.

No significant progress was made until June 17th, nearly a month after the robbery. Then, at the insistence of the French authorities, the safes in Ostend, aboard the English steamship and on the South Eastern Railway were all returned to their respective manufacturers in Paris, Hamburg, and London for dismantling and examination of the lock mechanisms. The Chubb safes were discovered to contain telltale scratches inside the locks, as well as traces of metal filings. The other safes showed no signs of tampering.

This discovery focused new attention on the luggage-van guard Burgess, who had been previously questioned and released. On June 19th, Scotland Yard announced a warrant for his arrest, but the same day the man, his wife and his two children vanished without a trace, and were not found subsequently.

It was then recalled that the South Eastern Railway had suffered another robbery from its luggage van, only a week prior to the bullion theft. The clear implication of lax management by railway authorities fed the growing public suspicion that the robbery must have occurred on the London-Folkestone train, and the press began to refer to The Great Train Robbery.

All during July and August, 1855, The Great Train Robbery remained a sensational topic in print and conversation. Although no one could figure out quite how it had been done, its evident complexity and audacity soon led to the unquestioned belief that it must have been carried out by Englishmen. The previously suspect French were now deemed too limited and timid even to conceive such a dashing endeavour.

The English newspapers printed every shred of rumour, hearsay and speculation about the robbery; but the plain fact was that throughout the summer months no single new development occurred, and inevitably interest began to wane. Having wallowed in a delightful orgy of anti-French sentiment, having deplored and applauded the villains themselves, having relished the foibles of bankers, railwaymen, diplomats, and police, the public was now ready to see its faith restored in the basic soundness of banks, railways, government, and police. In short, they wanted the culprits caught, and quickly.

But the culprits were not caught. Officials mentioned "possible new late developments in the case" with ever less conviction. Newspapers featuring stories of the robbery sold fewer copies.

By October, The Great Train Robbery was no longer of interest to anyone in England.

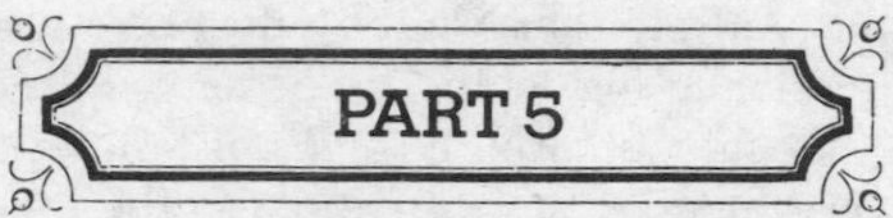

PART 5

Arrest and Trial: November 1856–August 1857

CHAPTER TWENTY-ONE

November 5th, Guy Fawkes Day, had been celebrated in England since 1605. But the celebration, observed the *Illustrated London News* in 1856, "has of late years been made subservient to the cause of charity as well as mere amusement. On Wednesday evening a grand display of fireworks took place on the grounds of the Merchant

Seamen's Orphan Asylum, Bow Road, in aid of the institution. The grounds were illuminated and a band of musicians was engaged. In the rear of the premises was a gibbet, from which was suspended an effigy of the Pope; and around it were several barrels of tar, which at the proper time were consumed in a most formidable blaze. The exhibition was attended by a large concourse of people, and the result promised to be of considerable benefit to the funds of the charity."

Any combination of large crowds and distracting spectacles was, of course, also of considerable benefit to pickpockets and cut-purses, and the police that night were very busy indeed. In the course of the evening, no fewer than thirteen "vagrants, vagabonds and petty villains" were apprehended by officers of the Metropolitan Force, including a female who was accused of robbing an intoxicated gentleman.

This arrest was made by one Constable Johnson, a man of twenty-three, who was walking the asylum grounds when, by the flaring light of the fireworks exploding overhead, he observed a female crouched over the prostrate form of a man. Fearing the gentleman might be ill, Constable Johnson went to offer help, but at his approach the girl took to her heels. Constable Johnson gave chase, apprehending the female a short distance away when she tripped on her skirts and tumbled to the ground. Observing her at close hand to be "a female of lewd aspect" he at once surmised that she was robbing the gentleman, in his intoxicated stupor, and that she was the lowest form of criminal, a "bug-hunter". Constable Johnson promptly arrested her.

The saucy minx put her hands on her hips and glared at him in open defiance. "There's not a pogue upon me," she declared, which words must surely have given Constable Johnson pause. He faced a serious dilemma.

In the Victorian view, proper male conduct demanded that even women of the lowest sort be treated with caution and consideration for the delicacy of their feminine nature. The woman claimed to have no stolen goods on her person; and if this was true, she would never be convicted. He could not search her: the very idea that he might touch the woman's body was unthinkable. His only recourse was to escort her to the station, where a matron would be called to perform the search. But the hour was late; the matron would have to be roused from her bed, and the station was some way distant. In the course of being escorted through dark streets, the woman would undoubtedly have many opportunities to rid herself of incriminating evidence.

Furthermore, if Constable Johnson brought her in, called for the matron, raised all manner of fuss and stir, and it was then discovered the girl was clean, he would look a proper fool. He knew this; and so did the girl.

Altogether it was a situation not worth the risk or the bother, and Constable Johnson would have liked to send her off with a scolding. But Johnson had recently been advised by his superiors that his arrest record left something to be desired; he had been told to be more vigilant, and there was the strong implication that his job hung in the balance.

So Constable Johnson decided to take the bug-hunter in for a search—to the girl's open astonishment, and despite his own rather considerable reluctance.

DALBY, THE STATION SERGEANT, was in a foul humour, for he was called upon to work on Guy Fawkes night and he resented missing the festivities.

He glared at Johnson and the woman at his side. The woman gave her name as Alice Nelson, and stated her age was "eighteen or thereabouts". Dalby sighed and rubbed his face sleepily as he filled in the forms. He sent Johnson off to collect the matron. He ordered the girl to sit in a corner. The station was deserted, and silent except for the distant pop and whistle of fireworks.

After a space of time, the judy spoke up. "If you granny I've a pink or two beneath me duds, see for yourself." Her tone was lascivious; the invitation was unmistakable, and she began to scratch her limbs through the skirt in languorous fashion.

"You'll be finding what you want, I reckon," she added.

Dalby sighed.

The girl continued to scratch. "I know to please you," she said, "and you may count on it, as God's me witness."

"And earn the pox for my troubles," Dalby said. "I know your sort."

The girl lapsed into silence. She ceased scratching herself, and soon enough sat up straight in her chair.

"Let's strike a bargain," she said, "and I warrant it'll be one to your liking."

"There's no bargain to be made," Dalby said, hardly paying attention. He knew this tedious routine, for he saw it played out, again and again, every night he worked at the station.

"Set me to go," the girl said, "and you'll have a gold guinea."

Dalby sighed, and shook his head. If this creature had a gold guinea on her, it was sure proof she'd been bug-hunting.

"Well, then," the girl said, "you shall have ten." Her voice now had a frightened edge.

"Ten guineas?" Dalby asked. That at least was something new; he'd never been offered ten guineas before. He hesitated. In his own eyes he was a man of principle, but his weekly wage was fifteen shillings, and sometimes it came none too promptly. Ten guineas was a substantial item and no mistake. He let his mind wander over the idea.

"Well then," the girl said, taking his hesitation for something else, "it shall be a hundred! A hundred gold guineas!"

Dalby laughed. His mood was broken, and his daydreams abruptly ended. In her anxiety the girl was obviously weaving an ever wilder story. A hundred guineas! Absurd.

"You don't believe me?"

"Be still," he said.

There was a short silence while the girl chewed her lip and frowned. Finally she said, "I know a thing or two."

Dalby stared at the ceiling. It was all so predictable. After the bribe had failed, there came the offer of information. The progression was always the same. Out of boredom, as much as anything else, he said, "And what is this thing or two?"

"I know who did the train robbery lay."

"Mother of God," Dalby said. "but you're a clever judy. Why do you know that's the very thing we're all wanting to hear—and hear it we have, from every blasted muck-snipe, smatter-hauler and bug-picker who comes our way. Every blasted one knows the tale to tell." He gave her a wan smile.

In fact, Dalby was feeling something like pity for the girl. She was such a down-and-out, hardly able to formulate a reasonable bribe. In truth, Dalby seldom was offered information about the train robbery any more. That was old news, and nobody cared.

"I know the screwsman did the pull," the girl said. "I can put you to him swift enough."

"Aye, aye, aye," Dalby said.

"I swear," the girl protested, looking ever more desperate.

"Aye, but I suppose," Dalby said, "that you'll find this gent for us if only we set you free for a bit of hunting him down, isn't that right?" Dalby looked at the girl to see her expression of astonishment. These types are always astonished to hear a crusher fill in the details of their tale.

But it was Dalby who was surprised, for the girl very calmly said, "No. I know exact where he's to be found."

"But you must lead us to him?" Dalby said.

"No," the girl said. "He's in Newgate Prison."

Several moments passed before Dalby fully appreciated her words. "Newgate Prison?" he said. "What's his name then?"

The girl grinned.

Soon after, Dalby called for a runner to go to the Yard and notify Mr. Harranby's office directly, for here was a story so strange it very likely had some truth in it.

BY DAWN, the basic situation was clear to the authorities. The woman, Alice Nelson, was the mistress of one Robert Agar, recently arrested on a charge of forging five-pound notes. Agar had protested his innocence; he was now in Newgate Prison awaiting trial.

The woman, deprived of Agar's income, had turned to various crimes to support herself. According to a later official report she showed "a most overpowering apprehension of confinement". In any case, she turned nose on her lover, and told all that she knew, which was little enough—but enough for Mr. Harranby to send for Agar.

CHAPTER TWENTY-TWO

"A thorough comprehension of the devious criminal mind," wrote Edward Harranby in his memoirs, "is vital to police interrogation." Harranby certainly had that comprehension, but he had to admit that the man seated before him, coughing, presented a particularly difficult case. He and Sharp were in their second hour of questioning, but Robert Agar stuck to his story.

In interrogations, Harranby favoured the introduction of abrupt new lines of inquiry to keep the villains off balance. But Agar seemed to handle the technique easily.

"Mr. Agar," Harranby said. "Who is John Simms?"

"Never heard of 'im."

"Who is Edward Pierce?"

"Never heard of 'im. I told you that."

"Isn't this man Pierce a famous cracksman?"

"I wouldn't know."

Harranby sighed. He was certain Agar was lying. "Well now, Mr. Agar. How long have you been forging?"

"I didn't do no soft," Agar said. "I swear it wasn't me. I was in the pub downstairs, having a daffy or two is all."

"You are innocent?"

"Aye, I am."

Harranby paused. "You're lying," he said. "We'll see you in the stir for many years."

"There's no blame upon me," Agar said, getting excited.

"Lies, all lies. You're a counterfeiter, pure and simple."

"I swear," Agar said. "I'd not do any soft. There no sense to it—" Abruptly, he broke off.

There was a brief silence in the room, punctuated only by the ticking of a clock on the wall. Harranby had purchased the clock especially for its tick, which was steady, loud, and irritating to prisoners.

"Why is there no sense to it?" he asked softly.

"I'm honest is why," Agar said, staring at the floor.

"What honest work do you do?"

"Local work. Here and there."

That was possible enough. In London at that time there were nearly half a million unskilled labourers who worked at various odd jobs.

"Where have you worked?"

"Well, let's see, now," Agar said, squinting. "I did a day for the gasworks at Millbank, loading. I did two days at Chenworth hauling bricks. A week past I did some hours for Mr. Barnham, cleaning his cellar."

"These employers would remember you?"

Agar smiled. "Maybe."

Here was another dead end for Harranby. Employers of casual labour often did not recall their workers.

Harranby found himself staring at the man's hands. Then he noticed that the little fingernail on one of Agar's hands was long. A long fingernail might mean all sorts of things. Some sailors wore a nail long for luck; clerks who used seals kept a nail long to pluck the seal from the hot wax. But for Agar. . . .

"How long have you been a screwsman?" Harranby said.

"Eh?" Agar replied with an expression of elaborate innocence. "Screwsman?"

"Did you make the keys for the safes?"

"Keys? What keys?"

Harranby sighed. "You've no future as an actor, Agar."

"I don't take your meaning, sir," Agar said. "What keys are you talking of?"

"The keys for the train robbery."

Here Agar laughed. "Cor," he said. "You think if I was in on that flash pull I'd be doing a bit of soft now?"

Harranby's face was expressionless, but he knew that Agar was right. It made no sense for a man who had participated in a twelve-thousand-pound theft to be stamping out five-pound notes a year later.

"There's no use pretending," Harranby said. "We know that Simms has abandoned you. Why are you protecting him?"

"Never heard of 'im," Agar said. "Can't you see that plain?"

Harranby paused and stared at Agar. It was time for a different approach. He picked up a piece of paper from his desk, and put on his spectacles. "Now, then, Mr. Agar," he said. "This is a report on your past record. It's none too good."

"Past record?" Now his puzzlement was genuine. "I've no past record."

"Indeed you do." Harranby said, running his finger along the print on the paper. "Robert Agar . . . Hmmm . . . twenty-six years old . . . hmm . . . born Bethnal Green . . . hmm . . .Yes, here we are. Bridewell Prison, six months, charge of vagrancy in 1849, and Coldbath, one year eight months, charge of—"

"Not true, I swear it, not true!"

Harranby glared at the prisoner over his glasses. "It's all here in the record, Mr. Agar. I think the judge will be interested to learn it. What do you suppose he will get, Mr. Sharp?"

"Fourteen years transportation, at least," Sharp said, in a thoughtful way.

"Australia," Agar said, in a hushed voice.

"Well, I should think," Harranby said calmly. "Boating's the thing in a case like this."

Agar was silent. Harranby knew that although "transportation" was popularly portrayed as a much-feared punishment, the criminals themselves viewed banishment to Australia with equanimity. Many villains suspected that Australia was agreeable, and to "do the kangaroo hunts" was unquestionably preferable to a long stretch in an English prison. Indeed, at this time Sydney, in New South Wales, was a thriving, handsome seaport of thirty thousand. In addition, it was a place where "personal history is at a discount, and good memories and inquisitive minds are particularly disliked. . . ." A man like Agar could view transportation as, at the very least, a mixed blessing.

But Agar was greatly agitated. Plainly, he did not want to leave England. Seeing this, Harranby was encouraged.

"That will be all for now," he said. "If in the next day or so you feel that you have something you wish to tell me, just inform the guards at Newgate."

Agar was ushered out of the room, and Sharp asked, "What were you reading?"

"A notification from the Buildings Committee," Harranby said, "to the effect that carriages are no longer to be parked in the courtyard."

AFTER THREE DAYS, Agar informed the Newgate guards that he would like another audience with Mr. Harranby. On November 13th, he told Harranby everything he knew about the robbery, in exchange for the promise of lenient treatment and the vague possibility that one of the institutions involved—the bank or the railway or even the government itself—might see fit to present him with a stipend from the still outstanding offers of reward for information.

Agar did not know where the money was kept. He said that Pierce had been paying him a monthly stipend in paper currency. The criminals had agreed that they would divide the profits two years after the crime, in May of the following year, 1857.

Agar did, however, know the location of Pierce's house. On the night of November 13th, the forces of the Yard surrounded the mansion of Edward Pierce, or John Simms, and entered it with barkers at the ready. But the owner was not at home; the frightened servants explained that he had left town to attend the P.R., or prize ring, spectacle the following day in Manchester.

TECHNICALLY, boxing matches in England were illegal, but they were held throughout the nineteenth century, and drew an enormous, loyal following. The necessity to elude authorities meant that a big match might be shifted from town to town at the last minute, with vast crowds of enthusiasts following all over the countryside.

The match on November 19th between Smashing Tim Revels, the fighting Quaker, and the challenger, Neddy Singleton, had been moved from Liverpool to a small town called Eagle Welles, and eventually to Warrington, outside Manchester. The fight was attended by more than twenty thousand supporters, who found the spectacle unsatisfactory.

In those days, the P.R. had rules that would make the event almost unrecognizable to modern eyes. Fighting was done bare-fisted, the combatants being careful to regulate their blows in order to avoid injury to their own hands and wrists; a man who broke his knuckles or wrists early in a contest was almost certain to lose. Rounds were of variable duration, and fights often went fifty or even eighty rounds. Knockouts were not sought. On the contrary, the proper fighter literally battered his opponent into submission.

Neddy Singleton, hopelessly outclassed by Smashing Tim from the start, adopted the ruse of dropping to one knee whenever he was struck, in order to halt the fight and allow him to catch his breath. The spectators hissed and booed this ungentlemanly trick, but nothing could be done to prevent it, especially as the referee —charged with giving the count of ten—called out the numbers with a slowness that demonstrated he'd been paid off smartly by Neddy's backers.

With thousands of spectators standing about, including every manner of ruffian, the men of the Yard were at some pains to operate unobtrusively. Agar, with a revolver at his spine, pointed out Pierce and the guard Burgess from a distance. The two men were then apprehended with a whispered suggestion that they come along quietly or take a bit of lead for their trouble.

Pierce greeted Agar amiably. "Turned nose, did you?" he asked with a smile.

Agar could not meet his eyes.

"Doesn't matter," Pierce said calmly. "I've thought of this as well. You'll lose your share, you know."

At the periphery of the crowd, Pierce was brought before Mr. Harranby.

"Are you Edward Pierce, also known as John Simms?"

"I am," the man replied.

"You are under arrest on a charge of robbery."

To this Pierce replied, "You'll never hold me."

By nightfall on November 19th, both Pierce and Burgess were, along with Agar, in Newgate Prison. Harranby quietly informed government officials of his success, but there was no announcement to the press, for Harranby wanted to apprehend the woman known as Miriam, and the cabby Barlow, both still at large. He also wanted to recover the money.

ON NOVEMBER 22ND, Mr. Harranby interrogated Pierce for the first time. The interview was remarkably brief. Pierce was ushered into the office and asked to sit in a chair, isolated in the middle of the room. Harranby, from behind his desk, directed his first question with customary abruptness.

"Do you know the man called Barlow?"

"Yes," Pierce said.

"Where is he now?"

"I don't know."

"Where is the woman called Miriam?"

"I don't know."

"Where," said Harranby, "is the money?"

"I don't know."

Harranby appraised him for a moment. There was a short silence. "Perhaps," Harranby said, "a time in 'the Steel' will strengthen your powers of memory."

"I doubt it," Pierce said, with no sign of anxiety.

When he had been taken from the room Harranby said to Sharp, "I shall break him, you may be sure of that." The same day, Harranby arranged for Pierce to be transferred from Newgate Prison to the House of Correction at Coldbath Fields, also called the Bastille. "The Steel" was not ordinarily a holding place for accused criminals awaiting trial. But it was a frequent ruse for police to send a man there if some information had to be "winkled out" of him before the trial.

"The Steel" was the most dreaded of all English prisons. Chief among its features were the "cockchafers", narrow boxes in a row where prisoners remained for fifteen-minute intervals, treading down a wheel of twenty-four steps. The daily regimen of the prison was so debilitating that even after a short sentence of six months, many a man emerged "with the steel gone out of him" —his body damaged, nerves shot, and resolution so enfeebled that his ability to commit further crimes was severely impaired.

As a prisoner awaiting trial, Pierce could not be made to undergo the harsh routine for the convicted inmates, but he was obliged to follow the rules of prison conduct, and if he broke the rule of silence, for example, he might be punished by a time at the cockchafer. Thus one may presume that the guards frequently accused him of speaking, and he was "softened up".

On December 19th, after four weeks in "the Steel", Pierce was again brought to Harranby's office. Harranby had told Sharp that "now we shall see a thing or two," but the second interrogation turned out to be as brief as the first.

"Where is the man Barlow?"

"I don't know."

"Where is the woman Miriam?"

"I don't know."

"Where is the money?"

"I don't know."

Mr. Harranby, the veins standing out on his forehead, dismissed Pierce with a voice filled with rage. As Pierce was taken away, he calmly wished Mr. Harranby a pleasant Christmas.

"The cheek of the man," Harranby later recorded, "was beyond all imagining."

MR. HARRANBY was under considerable pressure from several fronts. The bank of Huddleston & Bradford wanted its money back, and made its feelings known to Harranby through the offices of none other than the Prime Minister, Lord Palmerston himself. The inquiry from "Old Pam" was in itself embarrassing, for Harranby had to admit that he had put Pierce in Coldbath Fields, and the implications of that were none too gentlemanly. But Pierce remained in Coldbath until February 6th, when he was again brought before Harranby.

"Where is the money?"

"In a crypt, in St. John's Wood," Pierce said.

Harranby sat forward. "What was that?"

"It is stored," Pierce said blandly, "in a crypt in the name of John Simms, in the cemetery of Martin Lane, St. John's Wood."

Harranby drummed his fingers on the desk. "Why have you not come forth with this information earlier?"

"I did not want to," Pierce said.

Harranby ordered Pierce taken to Coldbath Fields once more.

On February 7th, the crypt was located, and the appropriate

dispensations obtained to open it. Mr. Harranby, accompanied by Mr. Henry Fowler, opened the vault at noon that day. There was no coffin in the crypt—and neither was there any gold. Upon re-examination of the crypt door, it appeared that the lock had been recently forced.

Mr. Fowler was extremely angry at the discovery, and Mr. Harranby was extremely embarrassed. The following day, Pierce was returned to Harranby's office and told the news.

"Why," Pierce said, "the villains must have robbed me. I always knew Barlow was not to be trusted."

"So you believe it was Barlow who took the money?"

"Who else could it be?"

There was a short silence. "Do you not care," Harranby said, "that your confederates have turned on you in this fashion?"

"It's just my ill luck," Pierce said calmly. "And yours," he added, with a slight smile.

"BY HIS POLISHED DEMEANOUR," Harranby wrote, "I presumed that he had fabricated still another tale to put us off the mark. But in further attempts to learn the truth I was frustrated, for on the first of March, 1857, a *Times* reporter learned of Pierce's capture and he could no longer conveniently be held in custody."

Harranby demanded to know how the reporter had been put on to the story, but *The Times* refused to divulge its source. A guard at Coldbath who was thought to have given out the information was discharged, but nobody was ever certain one way or the other.

In any case, the trial of Burgess, Agar, and Pierce was set to begin on July 12th, 1857.

CHAPTER TWENTY-THREE

The trial of the three train robbers was greeted by the public with the same sensational interest it had earlier shown in the crime itself. Burgess, the most minor of the players, was brought to the dock of the Old Bailey first. The fact that this man knew only parts of the whole story only whetted the public appetite for further details. Agar was interrogated next, but like Burgess was a distinctly limited man, and his testimony served only to focus attention on the personality of Pierce himself, whom the press referred to as "the master criminal".

Pierce was still incarcerated in Coldbath Fields, and as neither the public nor the press had seen him, there was plenty of freedom for eager reporters to conjure up wild and fanciful accounts of the man's appearance, manner, and style of living. It was said that he lived with three mistresses in the same house; that he was the illegitimate son of Napoleon; that he took cocaine and laudanum; that he had previously been married to a German countess and had murdered her in Hamburg. There is not the least evidence that any of these stories is correct, but it is certainly true that the press whipped up public interest to the point of frenzy, and Pierce's house in Mayfair was broken into on three occasions by avid souvenir hunters. *The Times* complained that this fascination with a criminal was "unseemly, even decadent", and went so far as to suggest that the behaviour of the public reflected "some fatal flaw in the character of the English mind".

Thus, it is one of the odd coincidences of history that by the time Pierce began his testimony, at the end of July, the public and the press had turned their attention elsewhere. For, quite unexpectedly, England was facing a new trial of national proportions: a shocking and bloody uprising in India.

Indeed, reports of the dreadful aftermath to the siege of Cawnpore had only just reached England. A thousand British citizens, including over three hundred women and children, had been under fire for twenty-one days. Then, on June 25th the rebel sepoys had offered the survivors safe passage by ship to Allahabad. The evacuation had begun at dawn on June 27th by means of forty riverboats. As soon as the last Englishman had climbed aboard, the sepoys had opened fire. Nearly every man had been killed. The surviving women and children had been taken to a house and held there in suffocating heat until, on July 15th, several men entered the house with sabres and knives and slaughtered everyone present. The dismembered bodies had been dumped into a nearby well, and were said to have filled it.

The English at home, on hearing this news, screamed for bloody revenge. At such a moment, the appearance of a criminal in the dock of the Old Bailey, for a crime committed two years past, was of very minor interest. But there were some reports on the inside pages of the dailies, and they are fascinating for what they reveal about Edward Pierce.

He was brought before the bar for the first time on July 29th: "handsome, charming, composed, elegant and roguish". He gave his testimony in an even, utterly calm tone of voice, but his statements were inflammatory enough. He referred to Mr. Fowler as "a fool" and Mr. Trent as "a nincompoop". These comments led the prosecutor to inquire of Pierce's views of Mr. Harranby, the man who had apprehended him. "A puffed-up dandy with the brains of a schoolboy," Pierce announced, drawing a gasp from the court, for Mr. Harranby was in the gallery as an observer. Mr. Harranby was seen to colour deeply.

Even more astounding than Mr. Pierce's words was his general demeanour, for he carried himself extremely well, and proudly, apparently giving no hint of moral remorse for his black deeds. Quite the opposite, he seemed to demonstrate an enthusiasm for his own cleverness. "He appears," noted the *Evening Standard*, "to take a degree of delight in his actions which is wholly inexplicable."

This delight extended to a detailed accounting of the foibles of other witnesses, who were themselves most reluctant to testify. Mr. Trent was fumbling and nervous, and greatly embarrassed, while Mr. Fowler recounted his own experiences in a voice so low that the prosecutor was continually obliged to ask him to speak up.

There were a few shocks in Pierce's testimony. One occurred on the third day of his appearance in court.

"Mr. Pierce, are you acquainted with the cabby known as Barlow?"

"I am."

"Can you tell us his whereabouts?"

"I cannot."

"Can you tell us when you last saw him?"

"Yes. I saw him last six days ago, when he visited me at Coldbath Fields."

(Here there was a buzzing of voices within the court, and the judge rapped for order.)

"Mr. Pierce, why have you not brought forth this information earlier?"

"I was not asked."

"What was the substance of your conversation with Barlow?"

"We discussed my escape."

"Then I take it, you intend with the aid of this man to make your escape?"

"I should prefer that it be a surprise." Pierce said calmly.

The consternation of the court was great, and the newspapers were outraged: "A graceless, unscrupulous, hideous fiend of a villain," said the *Evening Standard.* There were demands that he receive the most severe possible sentence.

But Pierce's calm manner never changed. He continued to be casually outrageous.

PIERCE CONCLUDED his testimony on August 2nd. At that time, the prosecutor, aware that the public was perplexed by the master criminal's cool demeanour, turned to a final line of inquiry.

"Mr. Pierce," said the prosecutor, rising to his full height, "I put it to you directly: did you never feel, at any time, some comprehension of unlawful behavings, some moral misgivings, in the performance of these various criminal acts?"

"I do not comprehend the question," Pierce said.

The prosecutor was reported to have laughed softly, "Yes, I suspect you do not; it is written all over you."

At this point, His Lordship cleared his throat and delivered the following speech from the bench: "Sir, it is recognized truth of jurisprudence that laws are created by men, and that civilized men agree to abide by these laws for the common good of society. For it is only by the rule of law that any civilization holds itself above the squalor of barbarism. This we know from all the history of the human race, and this we pass on in our educational processes to all our citizens.

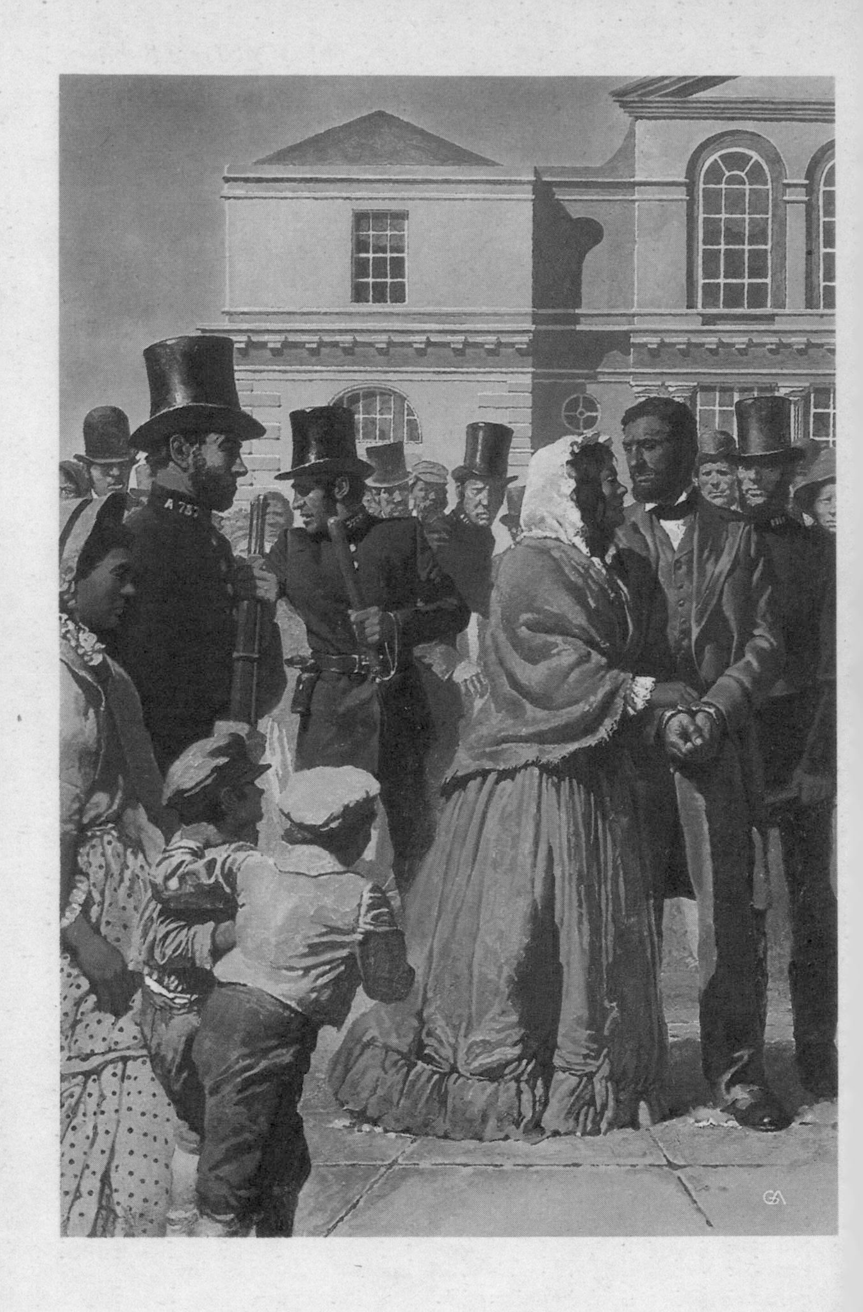

"Now, on the matter of motivation, sir, I ask you: why did you conceive the plan, and execute this dastardly and shocking crime?"

Pierce shrugged. "I wanted the money," he said.

FOLLOWING PIERCE'S testimony, he was handcuffed and escorted from the courtroom by two stout guards, both armed. As Pierce left the court, he passed Mr. Harranby.

"Good day, Mr. Pierce," Mr. Harranby said.

"Goodbye," Pierce replied.

Pierce was taken out of the back of the Old Bailey to the waiting police van, which would drive him to Coldbath Fields. A sizeable crowd had gathered on the steps of the court. The guards pushed away the crowd, which shouted greetings and expressions of luck to Pierce. One scabrous whore, slipping forward, managed to kiss the culprit full on the mouth, before the police pushed her aside.

It is presumed that this whore was actually the actress Miss Miriam, and that in kissing Pierce she passed him the key to the handcuffs, but that is not known for certain. What is known is that when the two van guards, coshed into insensibility, were later discovered in a gutter near Bow Street, they could not reconstruct the precise details of Pierce's escape. The only thing they agreed upon was the appearance of the driver—a tough brute of a man, they said, with an ugly white scar across his forehead.

The police van was later recovered in a field in Hampstead. Neither Pierce nor the driver was ever apprehended. Journalistic accounts of the escape are vague, and all mention that the authorities showed reluctance to discuss it at length.

IN AUGUST, 1857, Burgess, the railway guard, pleaded the stresses of his son's illness, claiming that it had so warped his moral inclinations that he fell in with criminals. He was sentenced to only two years in Marshalsea Prison, where he died of cholera.

The screwsman Robert Agar was sentenced to transportation to Australia for his part in The Great Train Robbery. Agar died a wealthy man in Sydney, New South Wales, in 1902.

Mr. Harranby died in 1879 while flogging a horse, which kicked him in the skull.

Mr. Trent died of a chest ailment in 1857; his daughter Elizabeth married Sir Percival Harlow and had four children by him.

Henry Fowler died in 1858.

Pierce, Barlow, and the mysterious Miss Miriam were never heard from again. In 1862, it was reported that they were living in Paris. In 1868, they were said to be residing in "splendid circumstances" in New York. Neither report has ever been confirmed.

The money from The Great Train Robbery was never recovered.

Michael Crichton

A Conversation with Josh Greenfeld

When Michael Crichton graduated from Harvard Medical School in 1969, he had a choice: either he could practise medicine or become a full-time writer. (He had already published five thrillers under *noms-de-plume.*) Crichton, fortunately, opted for books, and both *The Andromeda Strain* and *The Terminal Man* became films as well. Crichton himself has since directed two films, both based on stories he has written.

Standing six feet nine inches tall, Crichton is now an easily recognizable figure in Hollywood, and his home serves as a repository for a modern art collection including works by Oldenburg, Warhol and Lichtenstein.

When I met him recently I asked him how *The Great Train Robbery* came about.

MC: I was in a period when all I knew was that I didn't want to do any more science fiction for a while. One day I came across a reference to a train robbery, just a couple of hundred words, and I thought: "Isn't that interesting?"
JG: It was an actual case?
MC: Oh yes. The broad outlines are all true.
JG: What exactly attracted you to the idea?
MC: I think it was the avoidance of cliché. I was very taken by the idea that the safe itself could be the real roadblock. You know, so many books and movies these days presume you just blow up the safe. In the 1850s you had to go through all that trouble to get the keys.
JG: In the real case was it a Crimean military payroll?
MC: Yes.
JG: And did a bank manager have one of the sets of keys?
MC: There it gets fictional. In the actual case there were three guys who stole the keys, rode in the train, polished the keys, waited until the next shipment, stole the money and finally got turned in by a girl. That's all I know.
JG: You've been to London?
MC: Oh yes. When I was at Cambridge in 1964.
JG: And you returned to London for research?
MC: No. I felt it would be cheating, and I was also sort of interested in keeping gaps in the book. I didn't want the usual omniscient narrator, but instead that "I'll-tell-you-everything-I-was-able-to-find-out" quality.
JG: The novel certainly gives out a lot of information that seems "real".
MC: Most of it is authentic. I went to the Los Angeles library and picked up books on Victorian cities, underworld language and all that. But sometimes I'd make things up.
JG: Much of the language is arcane. Did you consider having a glossary?
MC: Originally I was going to. But the publishers said people will find it very irritating unless you explain as you go along.
JG: *The Great Train Robbery* will surely become a film. Do you want to direct it?
MC: Oh yes. There are so many things you think of while you're writing—such as how the people are walking, the manner in which the conversation is building—that you just can't translate to anybody else. And after writing, directing is fun. There's nothing like writing to make you want to get back of the camera again.

J.G.

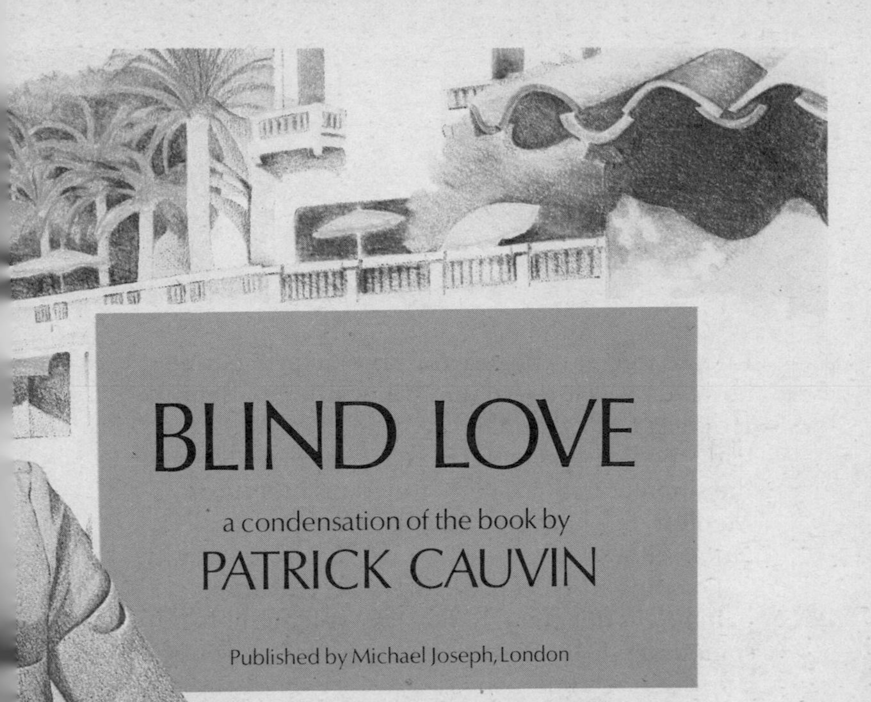

BLIND LOVE

a condensation of the book by

PATRICK CAUVIN

Published by Michael Joseph, London

Title page illustration by Clare Davis.

Life, so they say, begins at forty. Jacques Bernier, however, was forty-six and still waiting patiently. He wasn't exactly unhappy: at least schoolmasters had long holidays and this year he was off to spend the summer with his grown-up daughter near Menton. But he wasn't exactly what you'd call *happy* either. . . .

Possibly, when you are forty-six, waiting patiently is not enough. Possibly you ought to *do* something. Like give up smoking. Or buy yourself a new suit. Or fall in love.

That is fine, but what happens when you fall in love with a girl who cannot see? Can you both be happy? Can the sighted ever really understand the blind?

Patrick Cauvin has told this story with freshness, innocence and truth. It is tender. It is often hilariously funny. It is also a revelation of what it means to be blind and to be very much in love.

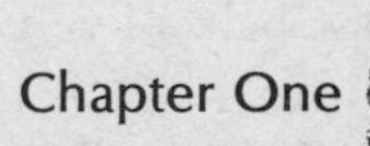

Chapter One

"Bernier!"

I turned round. "What's up?"

It was Briette—the students called her Bri-Bri—running towards me in the sunlight. The reflections of the sun in the school windows were so brilliant I couldn't see her properly. I stopped in the middle of the playground, surrounded by boys and girls and sunshine.

She was the athletic type, sprinting like a Girl Guide, elbows close in to her sides. As one of my colleagues, from the department of natural sciences, I'd known her for fourteen years—at weekends she looked after gangs of adolescents, dragging them off to the forests that surround Paris. Her wholesome good spirits terrified me.

Also she was involved passionately—if I may put it that way—in sex education. Her locker was crammed with gigantic coloured charts depicting men and women with transparent bellies and bemused expressions, set about with informative arrows and complicated scientific terminology.

She was partial to shock tactics. There was an occasion last year when, as the two of us were standing on the staircase surrounded by students, she unrolled a really breathtaking poster and brandished it like a revolutionary standard.

"What do you think of it?" she cried. "Speaking as a schoolmaster, of course."

My forehead covered with sweat, I fled before the sound of her voice could die away in the ancient corridors, thoroughly ashamed to possess all that complicated plumbing, those glands, that immodest tangle of veins. I'm sure the fifth-formers looked at me disapprovingly. I'm sure they did.

Anyway, today was June 28, the last day of the school year, prize-giving day, the day for speeches and the inevitable school play. Jacqueline Briette ground to a halt in front of me. With her round spectacles like headlights and her large square teeth, she reminded me of the front of a fifties Cadillac.

She tossed me her news like a fast ball. "I've got my transfer, Bernier! For next term!"

Her transfer. She'd been dreaming of it for years. She was a native of the Haute-Garonne, and she'd been trying to get back there ever since the end of the war. But there'd always been some teacher with more diplomas who got the job.

It was a funny thing, but I didn't like the idea of her leaving. I didn't like change. I suppose I was just an old stick-in-the-mud. I returned to my office year after year, and if they painted the walls or changed the desks even, it made me unhappy.

Not that I'd ever been a close friend of Briette's: her jolly hockey-sticks personality got me down. All the same, she'd been around for so long that without her something would be missing.

"I'm glad for your sake," I murmured.

Together we went into the school hall. At once I began to feel terribly hot. I really ought to have got myself a lightweight suit—perhaps even a linen suit like the one Versin, one of the sixth-formers, was wearing. Except that he was only eighteen, and had the build of a cowboy. It wasn't as if I had any wish to look young.

Although the curtains had been drawn over the bay windows of the hall, the place was stifling. Some of our colleagues were already installed on the stage. It was going to be rough—more than two hours of listening to the headmaster repeat last year's speech, which was the same as the year before's. Still, I ought to be well used to it by now.

"Good morning, Monsieur Bernier." That was old mother Rebolot, who taught chemistry. She was wearing a floral print, with a butterfly over her left breast, wild roses over her right, lavender heather here and there . . . the whole of it encasing thirteen stone. Close to retirement, soon she too would be gone.

I sat down beside Briette, next to one of the potted palms. It was an odd thing about those plants—they only appeared on speech days, never at any other time.

"Well, well, my dear Bernier, and are you looking forward to your holiday?" That was Meunier, history and geography, quite a personality, the life and soul of any party. For years he'd been hiding my napkin ring on average twice a week. We're all jokers in the teaching profession.

The children filed in. The sound of voices rose. Two hundred people sat in front of us—dear Lord, how hot it was! Thank heaven the very next day I'd be in . . . it was hard to say exactly where, what with the holiday rush and the chance of my wretched car battery letting me down. Perhaps I shouldn't have accepted Anne's invitation, but we saw so little of each other these days, my daughter and I.

"Ladies and gentlemen, quiet, if you please. . . ."

Carnot was shouting himself hoarse. It wasn't much fun being assistant head, not when your passion was trout fishing. Every time I was invited to his house I went through the ritual of admiring his rods, reels, spoons and artificial flies. Needless to say, I knew nothing whatever about fishing. But I was fond of Carnot.

Briette leaned towards me. "Where are you going this summer?"

My shirt came unstuck when I moved. "To the Midi, above Menton."

"To visit friends?"

"That's right." I'd never mentioned Anne. The school board knew about my marriage, no one else. I'd had to write it in on the forms. Family status: divorced, one child.

"A little silence, if you don't mind. . . ." Duverrier, the headmaster, climbed onto the stage, raised his arms. "If you don't mind." Slowly the noise subsided, a sea receding with the tide. Duverrier smiled, enjoying his power to calm the restless ocean. Once a year Duverrier played Neptune.

Total silence. Then, suddenly, something behind me exploded. I jumped as if catapulted from my chair. The Marseillaise! It happened every year but somehow I always forgot. The blare of the loudspeaker hidden behind the palms a few feet away almost broke my left eardrum. Squeezed against patriotic Briette, who was beating time with her flat heels, I could only endure stoically.

At last we resumed our seats, the final crash of the cymbals still buzzing in my head. Next year I'd make very sure that I found out where they'd put the loudspeaker and give it a wide berth.

In front of us the ocean had subsided again. Neptune had the floor. "It makes me very happy, once again to see us all gathered together in this hall—parents, children, teachers—for this little ceremony that not one of us feels is antiquated, but which for me is . . ."

Never before had I noticed the vast amount of hair growing out of the bursar's ears, like seaweed. How could any sound penetrate that thicket? Luckily I had no scissors with me—the temptation would have been hard to resist.

". . . And to whom do we owe such results? To you, the parents, who have helped us, whose support and constant vigilance have . . ."

My hands were damp. Twenty-seven minutes. Neptune was breaking his own record—he always said the same thing, but each year it took him longer. Anyway, this time tomorrow, if all went well, I'd be in Lyon.

At the loud storm of applause I jumped, and frantically clapped my clammy palms. I suddenly realized how thirsty I was.

"Have you time for a drink?" Briette whispered. She was offering me one for the road at Marcel's, the café on the corner. I'd order a Ricard with lots of water, a whole jugful. I could see it, smell it.

The prizegiving began. Neptune shook hands with each winner. It was the form master who actually presented the books.

"*Chapoteau, Viviane.*" I glimpsed the top of Viviane Chapoteau as she dithered in front of Duverrier, paused in front of her teacher, then vanished.

"*Évrard, Philippe.*" He was very tall, I could see him above the others. It was always the same, they began with the ten-year-olds. My students would be last. Patience!

"*Devinard, Nathalie.*" I wondered how things would be at Anne's. She hadn't said anything about the house in her letter, just that she and Frédéric were expecting me.

"*Villeneuve, Françoise.*" I didn't know much about Frédéric: I'd only met him two or three times. But I'd got the impression that he thought of me as a harmless old codger—which wasn't too bad. It's no use expecting too much, these days.

"*Frémier, Jacques.*" Perhaps they were right not to get married. At any rate, it didn't worry me that Anne was living with him. Maybe I wasn't really such a fuddy-duddy. Besides, fifty years ago Frédéric would have been considered a good match—after all, it was he who had bought that house in the village, or rather his parents who had paid for it. Nowadays he was just another young fellow in jeans who was taking forever to get his degree, and meanwhile tanned himself in the Alpes-Maritimes and slept with my daughter.

At last it was my turn to hand out prizes. "Excuse me, excuse me. . . ." I edged down the row, crushing as few feet as possible and clearing my throat in order to make myself heard above the growing uproar.

"*Trinardier, Albert.*" He'd done a paper on Hemingway. He was a good lad. He stood in front of me and we shook hands. How stupid it was—we'd been together for a whole year and now, just when we were parting, we shook hands for the first time. I handed him his book.

"Goodbye, sir."

I was unexpectedly moved. I wanted to call him by his first name, just once. "Goodbye, Trinardier, Albert."

People laughed, a little embarrassed. It was just like me, to funk it, to crack a little joke and leave it at that. I just had to hope he understood.

"*Caranel, Emilie.*" They called her Caramel of course—she was a pert little thing, with reddish hair, and she'd won second prize. She was mad about Baudelaire. "Goodbye, Caramel."

"Goodbye, Monsieur Bernier." Her eyes glistened. I'd never realized she had such long lashes.

Three more came to get their books. Then I returned to my seat, mission accomplished.

The chairs, table and plants were removed, and the play began. Four scenes from *Andromaque*, the children draped in sheets, Pyrrhus in a toga that didn't quite hide his gym shoes. It was a great success. There were lots of fans in the audience.

Everything was wound up very quickly. I drank my two Ricards with Briette on the café terrace. I shook a hundred hands. "Have a nice holiday." "Have a good time." "See you in September. . . ." I went out onto the boulevard, a bit fuddled by the drinks, feeling a little sad but also gay. I had two months ahead of me, as empty as blank pages. It was up to me to fill them.

I HAD MEANT to take a cold shower, but at the first drop I turned on the hot. I have a sensitive skin, you see.

My last clean towel. Well, it was time for the year to be over—I'd do the washing in October.

There I stood, naked, in front of the bathroom mirror. Hmm . . . five foot eight, eleven stone, a little heavy but nothing to worry about. Legs good: no sign of varicose veins. Chest good also, though I hated to see the hair on it turning grey. Still, I was twenty twenty-five years ago, so it wasn't surprising.

Stomach tucked in, biceps flexed: the result wasn't too bad, taking all in all. It was silly, really, the way I couldn't ever stand in front of a mirror without acting the fool. Would I ever be too old to play Tarzan in the bathroom?

Orange briefs. There I'd clearly been influenced by the ads. I'd waited so often on the métro in front of a huge poster showing three tanned, husky young men in coloured briefs drinking whisky on a yacht that I'd finally bought a pair. Anyway, it was the holidays, a good time to try something new. The yacht could come later.

It was one o'clock, and I still had plenty to do: ask the concierge to forward my mail, pay my rent, pack my suitcase. And check the blasted car battery.

First of all, the suitcase. I always found it depressing to open my wardrobe. All my suits were grey, my shirts white, my sweaters sober, my shoes black. Actually, the one bright thing I owned was that pair of briefs. I'd arrive on the Riviera looking like an undertaker's assistant.

Occasionally I had been tempted to buy myself something really trendy, but such things were usually sold in select boutiques no bigger than a postcard, full of Swedish salesgirls, so somehow I'd never quite got round to it.

The bell rang. It was Madame Morfoine, the concierge. "The post, Monsieur Bernier." Evidently she wanted to chat. Usually she never came upstairs. "Well, Monsieur Bernier, so you're leaving tomorrow?"

"Yes indeed, Madame Morfoine. Tomorrow morning."

She eyed my open suitcase. "You teachers are lucky. Two and a half months' holiday!"

"Yes indeed, madame. The profession has its good sides. . . ."

"And where are you going—if I'm not being too curious?" She always said that. She was quite capable of asking, "And how many women are there in your life—if I'm not being too curious?"

"To a little village in the Midi. . . . Oh, and by the way, would you mind forwarding my mail?"

Finally she went away, with Anne's address and a ten-franc note clenched in her fist. It made me happy, the thought of seeing Anne again. It had always been so hard, when she was little, to take her back on Sunday evenings to her mother. I used to take her to the Walt Disneys—for three years, until she was ten, she never missed a single Disney film. Often I sat through them twice. Once we saw *Peter Pan* three times in a row, eating liquorice all the time. I was sick that night. She was fine.

When she was ten she began wanting to see love stories: whenever *Gone With The Wind* was being shown she'd brandish the entertainment section of the paper under my nose and off we'd rush to the métro. I must have seen that film in every single Paris district. I knew it by heart.

I'd bring her back at eight thirty. "Good night, Anne. See you next week."

"See you Sunday, Papa."

In the summer I'd take her to the zoo. The time we spent standing in front of those bears!

For my birthday she'd do me a drawing, and I still had all eleven of them. The first was of a house with a green sun and a curious object with skinny legs that she claimed was a lamb. The last was a charcoal drawing of a dancer, carefully shaded. It was clever: she'd been sixteen at the time.

Then one day my ex-wife, Catherine, announced that she was going to Canada, "to start a new life", as she put it. I had shared her life for eighteen months, a short enough period but one that had seemed endless to both of us. She hesitated to take Anne with her, to a new country, a new language, and she wondered if I would. . . .

In short, Anne came to live with me. We repainted my rooms, she stuck pictures all over the walls, the years passed. Anne the schoolgirl, Anne the college student, Anne in love, Anne gone.

A postcard during the holidays, from time to time a phone call, an Algerian restaurant where I would treat her, whenever she was free, to a *couscous*. She'd done very well. I watched for the credit titles on TV and saw her name quite often: designer, Anne Bernier. It pleased me. But she lived at a pace that took my breath away. I couldn't possibly keep up.

And then, three weeks ago, as we ate our steaming *couscous*, she leaned her elbows on the checked tablecloth. "How would you like to spend your holidays with me?"

"If you promise you won't take me to *Gone With The Wind*."

She laughed then. She was beautiful when she laughed, far more beautiful than her mother. And she knew how to dress, unlike me. She told me about the house, in the hills just outside Sainte-Agnès, with a marvellous view and no sound except the crickets. I could rest there, read, work if I wanted to. Of course, Frédéric would be there too, but. . . .

"You do like Frédéric, Papa?"

"Of course I do." I had nothing against Frédéric—except that he was sleeping with my daughter. And that was just me being stuffy.

"So that's fixed? You will come?"

I raised my glass. "To our holiday together."

We parted in a gay mood, delighted with each other.

Good Lord! It was almost four and I hadn't finished packing. And what about the car? That rotten battery worried me sick. And with 87,000 kilometres on the clock I always had the feeling that when I reached the top of the next hill my old Citroën would drop dead from sheer exhaustion.

To be honest, that car terrified me. I could easily have taken a train, bought a sleeper. Then I'd have arrived on the Riviera fresh and rosy-cheeked among the palm trees. Instead, I'd be stuck to my seat, dripping with sweat, risking death every second . . . and it wasn't even a question of money. I could quite well have afforded to travel by train—except that I'd completely forgotten to book a seat. And anyway Carnot had assured me it was ridiculous to go by train if you owned a car. For a while, therefore, I'd convinced myself that driving was fun: the sense of freedom it gave you, the feeling that you could stop any time you wanted.

But now that it was almost time to go, my palms were sweating at the thought of having to drive over a thousand kilometres in a junk heap with burned-out cylinders. I'd never make it. If I got as far as Fontainebleau it'd be a miracle.

I cooked myself some spaghetti. Put myself in an Italian mood. After all, Sainte-Agnès was only a few miles from the frontier.

I lit a cigarette and saw that I had only a few left. What if I tried to stop smoking over the holidays? I'd be out in the open air. I should take the opportunity to clean out my lungs. Anne was always telling me how bad smoking was for me. She used terrible words like heart attack, cancer, emphysema. I really ought to try. I'd buy just one more packet for the road, but as soon as I got there I'd stop.

I'd take some exercise too. I'd been planning that for the last ten years. I could see myself trotting through the thyme and the rosemary in the soft morning air. I would come back tanned, muscular, my lungs clean. I could just hear fat old Rebolot on my return. "My dear Bernier—you look twenty years younger!"

The water for the spaghetti was boiling. I dropped in the long sticks, grated the cheese. I would go to bed early, and set the alarm for four thirty. A quick shave, the suitcase shoved in the boot, and I'd be off. The motorway would take me all the way to Avignon. Nothing could be easier. Then across Provence to Anne's place. She'd be waiting at the door just like in a Walt Disney film.

Plate, fork, knife, and I was ready to eat. It was only five o'clock, but I could eat at any time I pleased, now I wasn't tied to the school canteen. Besides, I hadn't eaten since noon.

Outside, the white sun beat against my window. The Parisians were going to fry this summer; the city would be like an oven. The thought made me laugh—perhaps I had a mean streak. Tomorrow, at this time, I would be far, far away.

"*FOOL! ROAD-HOG! CRETIN!*"

People in big Peugeot 404s were all the same. Bastards. And they all weighed at least fifteen stone.

All that fuss, just because I'd overtaken a gigantic articulated lorry that was crawling along at fifteen k.p.h. There was nothing else on the road I was up to passing, and I certainly wasn't going to miss the golden opportunity. So I'd signalled, and pulled out. And then that moron had appeared on the horizon, blasting his horn, flashing his lights. Evidently his dearest wish had been to drive me off the road altogether. I lurched a bit, and by the time I was back in the right lane he was probably in Marseille.

I'd managed to get past Fontainebleau after all. Just one thing was bothering me—my old heap was running magnificently. No creaks, no groans, no smell of burning. It was too good to be true. When disaster struck it would be a real corker.

Lyon, 380 km. It was going to be hot. Already I could feel the sun through the windscreen, through my nylon shirt. And it was only just past eight. Time for a Gauloise? Just one, to celebrate the start of my holiday?

Ecstasy. The grey-blue smoke drifted langorously in the yellow sunlight. The road was straight, I had two fingers on the wheel, a cigarette between my lips, an eye on the rearview mirror. I was on top of the world. . . . And how about a little music? The radio sounded like an asthmatic with a cold, but sometimes a tune came wheezing through.

> *Aime-moi, aime-moi*
> *Quand je suis dans tes bras*
> *Je dis: Oh! la la la la la la!*
> *Aime-moi, aime-moi. . . .*

Terrible. I'd seen the singer on TV. Some of the children had stuck her picture in their notebooks. Seeing it had brought the generation gap home to me.

". . . *three kilometres of blocked traffic at Nogent-le-Rotrou, better take the Émeraude route. Drive carefully, holidaymakers. In ten minutes we'll have another report. You're listening to Johnny. . . .*"

So much for the radio. There were caravans ahead, three in a row. I was about to pass. A quick look in the mirror—not a Peugeot 404 in sight. I pulled out, hurtled by, all three of them, like a champion.

My old jalopy was going like the wind, eating up the road, not a sign of trouble.

At the next garage I stopped to fill up. There was no need to queue, not at the pump for Regular. I took the opportunity to get out and stretch my legs. Then I parted with thirty francs—petrol was getting more expensive every day—and parked my racer outside a shop. These motorways were astonishing—their service stations were getting to look like shopping centres.

I got out, stared into the shop window. And then I saw *it*. I'd thought I was too old for love at first sight. But there it was, exactly what I needed. A simple, two-button suit, blue denim, stitched pockets, flared trousers. My dream.

The mean side of me made me glance at the price tag—only 150 francs! So I could afford it too. I could hardly breathe. Usually it took me at least three weeks to make up my mind. To buy something straight off, on impulse, that was real adventure.

I looked in the shop. There was only one saleswoman, and thank heaven she didn't look like an emancipated Swede. I made up my mind. How wonderful it would be to arrive wearing something new. Anne would be delighted. Frédéric quite speechless. And anyway, it was holiday time.

I went in. She approached me, not at all forbidding. And I could count on the fingers of one hand the salesgirls who didn't frighten me. "I'd like to see the suit in the window, please. The blue one."

"Certainly, monsieur." She thought it quite natural that I wanted it. "It's very light and comfortable. There's a hot summer ahead and you've picked a very popular style. Would you like to try it on?"

She produced a tape measure and measured my waist. I retired to the changing room bearing the object of my desire. Dressing rooms worried me—the curtains had a way of sliding along the rod, leaving sizeable gaps. I always felt that dozens of old ladies were peering in, nudging each other at my crumpled socks, sniggering at my shirt-tail flapping over my backside.

Methodically I removed my shoes, then my trousers, and pulled on the new pair, all fresh and airy. I zipped up the fly, examined myself. Perfect. Now the jacket. Impeccable. Was it really me? I felt buoyant, elegant, nonchalant. The suit was a delightful combination of the ambassador and the cowboy. I went out.

"It fits you perfectly. It doesn't need the slightest alteration."

"I admit I'm tempted. But don't you think it's a little too . . . too youthful?"

Her eyes widened in astonishment. "Not at all. You're just the type to wear it. Only yesterday a man bought one just the same, and he was at least sixty. I wouldn't hesitate, if I were you."

Sixty! That decided me. "I'll take it."

"You'll keep it on?"

The woman was full of good ideas. I went back into the dressing room, gathered up my old outfit and handed it to her, transferred my keys, wallet, pen, and wrote a cheque. She made up the parcel and I walked out into the sun. It was definitely a gala day. I had just bought a fantastic ensemble, the weather was marvellous, I was going to see Anne, I was twenty years younger.

I drove off. At the first whirr of the starter my car had leapt forward like a thoroughbred. The traffic was heavy in Vienne; at Lyon too there was a jam. Then the road cleared.

Valence, 85 km. It was nearly two o'clock. For the first time in years I felt really hungry. Usually I ate without much interest. Now, suddenly, I craved something delicious—perhaps a green salad with tomatoes, a bottle of dry rosé, a grilled steak. Not for me a sandwich bought at the service station. Today was a gala day.

I drove for another thirty kilometres until I saw a blue road sign showing a plate with knife and fork crossed. Just looking at it made me even hungrier. So there I was, facing the window, resplendent in my new suit. The sun flooded the room, making the glass tables sparkle. The decanter of rosé shone, my plate was heaped with salad, rice, olives, hard-boiled eggs, and little cubes of something I didn't recognize. I felt like a king.

A fat, anxious-looking man approached my table. "May I sit here?"

"Help yourself."

In a furious voice he ordered sausage and sauerkraut. "Are you having trouble with your radiator?" he asked me.

Frankly, I didn't even know if my car had a radiator. I seldom dared look under the bonnet. "No, everything seems all right," I told him casually.

He looked disappointed, and started on his sausage so disconsolately that I felt guilty. "But I *am* having trouble with my battery," I said.

He stopped eating, his fork in mid-air. "How old is it?"

"About five years."

He snorted. "Then it's had it. I buy one every three years."

That was a blow. Fortunately my steak arrived just then and cheered me up.

Trying to sound as if I knew something about cars, I said, "I think it's still pretty good. One of these days I'll have to replace the points, though."

I'd heard Carnot say this often enough, and I thought it sounded impressive. But my companion just grunted, and returned to his sausages, so I quickly finished eating, paid my bill, and left. Some people were only happy when they'd got you worried.

The car started like a dream. So much for my battery being

done for! I turned on the radio: it was a pop group, but I left the wretched thing on. When you wore clothes like mine you had to live up to them. I started to whistle. Everything was fine.

Chapter Two

I arrived under a golden setting sun that lit only the humpy-tiled roofs, the church tower, the surrounding hills. I'd had to ask the way three times. At the last stop a little old man with a basket had leaned in, filling the car with a scent of figs.

"When you leave the village you must turn left just before the wash-house. Keep going a short way and you'll see the house. Take care—the goats are brought in at just about this time and they're not very bright."

I thanked him and drove off. After twelve hours at the wheel I was exhausted. The road the old man had indicated was a narrow, stony affair. I was worried for my poor thin tyres, so when the farmhouse came in sight I pulled over and walked the rest of the way. I felt a twinge of disappointment: Anne wasn't waiting for me at the door.

Instead, a young man sat on the steps. Stripped to the waist and barefoot, he was fiddling with a piece of wire. For a moment I thought I'd come to the wrong place. "Does Anne Bernier live here?" I asked him.

He took his time, went on twisting the wire. "Yes."

I couldn't stand people like that. People who finished what they were doing before they condescended to answer. "I'm her father."

The lout didn't appear impressed. But he did move his long legs to let me pass, and shook my hand. "Greetings. I'm Max."

I managed a smile. Then Anne appeared, radiant, wearing a loose T-shirt and a khaki skirt. She kissed me on both cheeks and hurried me inside. "Oh, I'm so pleased to see you. Come on in—you must be worn out."

It was so dark I could only just make out a few benches, some pots of paint, and various young people lying on mats on the floor. There seemed to be at least a hundred.

"Sit down. I'll make you some coffee. We've some friends staying."

A few arms waved limply from the mats—a gesture of welcome, I supposed. I waved back, and sank down on a bench. Seemingly I was to spend my holiday living in some sort of commune.

As I drank my coffee and answered Anne's questions, I looked them over. A girl in a long skirt was lying on her stomach, trying to read in the last of the daylight, a boy's frizzy head resting on her backside.

"Any trouble with the car?"

"No. Everything went beautifully."

Anne put her head on one side, as if to examine a picture. "You've bought a new suit."

I choked into my coffee. "Yes. Well, it was so hot . . ."

"You look great." She hugged me. Then she turned away. "Kim—will it be ready soon?"

Kim stuck her head in through the hatch, brandished a wooden spoon. She was tiny, with curly red hair. "We eat in five minutes."

"Come and meet my father. Papa—this is Kim Spander. You must have seen her on television."

I shook hands with Kim, who still clutched her spoon. At that moment Frédéric came in, sporting an Indian shirt. Max followed him, still busy with his bits of wire. "Welcome, Monsieur Bernier. I hope you had a good trip?"

I had no time to answer. Anne grabbed me and whisked me off upstairs. "You must come and see your room."

It was tiny, but quite magnificent: red-tiled floor, whitewashed walls, an old brass bedstead, a table in front of the window. She looked at me. "What d'you think?"

"It's perfect."

She laughed. "Have you brought any papers to correct?"

I laughed too. "Not one. I don't have a thing to do. Are there any books around?"

"The room next door is full of them. You can't get any in the village, but Menton is only twenty-five kilometres away. You'll find everything you want there. Now I'll show you the bathroom."

"Wait a minute—I left my bag in the boot. I'll go and get it."

She crossed the room and leaned out of the window. "Frédéric, will you bring up Papa's suitcase?"

"I can get it," I protested. "I'm not seventy yet."

She became all motherly. "You're tired—why not take a bath? Kim's making *boeuf en daube*. I told her you liked it. If you need anything, just shout."

She was already at the door when I got up my courage to remark, "There seems to be an awful lot of you!"

"Ten, with you." Not quite a hundred, then. "See you."

I went through to the bathroom and closed the door. Through the walls a vague commotion could still be heard, clattering plates, laughter. And I a man who detested gangs of people, who was thoroughly unsociable. I'd been tricked, ambushed! Well, we'd just have to see how it went, but if it hadn't been for Anne I'd already have been far away. I might have known that she wouldn't be able to live without crowds of people.

The shower did me good. Then I stretched out in the bath. It felt so good I began to drop off. Sleep came gently, the coloured bath tiles gradually blurring, the light fading. . . .

Aime-moi, aime-moi
Quand je suis dans tes bras
Je dis: Oh! la la la la la la!
Aime-moi, aime-moi. . . .

I nearly split my head open on the soap dish. Without doubt, that was the loudest record player I'd ever heard. There were shouts of protest and the volume was lowered a little. I soaped myself, trying to keep my mind blank.

Tap-tap-tap on the door. I leapt up, hit my head again, wrapped a flowered towel round my waist, opened the door.

It was the girl in the long skirt, with my suitcase. "I've brought you your bag."

"Ah! Er . . . yes, well . . . thank you very much." I clutched at my towel.

"My name is Françoise." It was a good thing she didn't hold out her hand. I'd have looked pretty silly then.

"Er . . . that's nice. And I'm Jacques Bernier."

She gave me a sort of military salute. I nearly imitated her, then remembered my towel and sat down instead, quite exhausted, on the bathroom stool. She went away. Thank God. An unmarried man like me could only take just so much excitement. I returned to my room, put on my shirt and trousers. Finally, throwing caution to the wind, I went down to dinner without my socks.

I descended the stone staircase, my heart in my mouth. And no wonder. I'd fallen among hippies.

THE INTRODUCTIONS took place while the *boeuf en daube* was being served, to the sound of scraping benches. I already knew Max—it was explained that the wire things he made were models for abstract sculptures that sold very well in America. This staggered me. I'd never have thought of earning my living twisting wire round bits of wood.

Every now and then Kim, the dancer, would leap in the air, kicking her legs. Françoise, in the long skirt, worked in a shop. There were two bearded gurus—Antoine and Virgil. One of them had a girl, a Bohemian creature enveloped in a black shawl who kept staring at me as if she expected me to disintegrate from old age at any moment.

From the other end of the table, Anne called to me, "How do you like the set-up here?"

I tried to think of an original answer. It would have been nice to impress the young people. "It's excellent. From now on I'll never live in any other way."

One of the gurus sniggered. "Me too. I'm going to stay here at least until December."

Laughter. Everyone talked at once. "Put on a record," Frédéric suggested.

Françoise swayed off to one end of the room. Kim shouted something I couldn't make out. Behind me, an orchestra blared. The Bohemian's voice rose above the hubbub. "So you're a teacher, are you?"

At once I was wary. "Yes . . . ?"

"How can anyone be a teacher, these days?"

"I agree it's difficult. But somehow I manage to survive each year until the end of June."

Max's head bobbed up. "I thought the kids shot at you as you entered the classroom."

"It hasn't happened yet. Next year perhaps it will."

Frédéric picked at his teeth with his fingernail. "Don't your students read Mao? He says that if a teacher is boring they have every right to fall asleep in his class."

Françoise protested. "It's not a question of right—it's a necessity. I often slept in class at the university."

They were launched then—and in the racket I was quite forgotten. I wouldn't last three days in such an atmosphere.

The Bohemian downed her wine in a single gulp. "You're not saying a word, Franz."

I had quite forgotten him. He was an Austrian and a strict vegetarian. For the last half-hour he'd been munching celery, watching us all with infinite sorrow.

Frédéric leaned back, put his feet on the table. "It's your turn to do the washing-up, Antoine."

Antoine protested, so I offered my services. I wanted to demonstrate my good will towards the community.

Everybody demurred. Françoise left the bench and curled up in an armchair near the fireplace. The others sprawled about on the floor and argued wearily. Frédéric had installed Anne on his knee. The other guru, eyes closed, took up a yoga position. Kim cleared the table, still doing little leaps and *entrechats*. As she passed Franz he stroked her legs with innocent grace, but she paid no attention.

I was bored. I was also anxious in case one of them became aggressive and started bombarding me with questions. I didn't have their quick wit, I didn't quite understand their language, their jokes. Possibly they were nice enough people. So why the hell didn't they show it? I glanced at my new slacks. For a few hours they'd given me the illusion of youth. But now, tonight, I felt old.

I got up. "Excuse me. I'm worn out. I think I'll go to bed."

Anne followed me out, hugged me, a hint of anxiety lurking in her eyes. "What do you think of them?"

I made an effort. "A nice crowd. Likeable."

She went back to them, reassured.

And there I was, alone in my room. I wondered what they were saying about me. "He's not bad, your father." "Not much to say for himself." "He looks a bit bewildered." Or else—and this would be worse—they wouldn't even mention me, as if I hadn't existed. I could hear them laughing. They seemed to be having a better time since I'd left. Next day I discovered they'd got to bed around four. Apparently it had been "a really weird evening".

WHAT I DREADED most were mealtimes, when we were all together. The rest of the time I could manage. I would go for strolls in the hills, taking a whodunnit with me, and install myself under a tree. After four pages I'd doze off. While I slept the sun would move round. I acquired a fine tan. Kim congratulated me. "When you arrived you were the colour of the evening paper."

I spent part of one afternoon with the Bohemian who came out to join me, still wrapped in her shawl, even though it was eighty in the shade. She was far from stupid. She'd read a lot, worked in various shops, sold advertising space. I felt that if I'd asked her to go to bed with me she'd have consented with disarming naturalness—a favour one did for members of one's own crowd. Not that I'd have dreamt of making such a suggestion—I was far too full of hang-ups.

The evenings were interminable. Guru Virgil made everyone laugh a lot, but I never found him in the least funny. I smiled until my muscles ached. And I went to bed early.

Then, one night, just as I was about to drop off, I had an idea. In the morning I'd go into Menton. I needed to be alone. The thought cheered me up enormously.

I OPENED the shutters on a steel-grey sky, clouded, leaden. The ivy on the wall rustled softly, as if waiting for the strong winds that usually accompany sudden summer storms. The weather suited my plans, gave me an excuse to go off and buy some new books. What was there to do in such weather except read?

I went downstairs. Anne appeared soon after, yawning, and turned on the radio. I buttered my roll and told her I was going to Menton. I was afraid that one of the crowd would want to come along but there were no candidates.

I drove off, rain spattering the windscreen, laying the dust. I heard a rumble of thunder; the rain stopped. I opened the window, letting in the damp air. It smelt of solitude. It was an eternity since I had last been alone.

When I was a child I'd often come to Menton. I remembered a square near the Casino. I'd played in the sand while my mother sat on a bench, knitting. All around were towered palaces, giant colonnades. High above my head, cupolas, domes . . . it was Baghdad, Alexandria, Moscow, all rolled into one.

At a turn in the road the coastline appeared and my memories shattered. Tower blocks concealed the beach. *Sun Marina, Riviera Beach.* Glass and plastic cafés, snack bars, car parks. What had become of the square of long ago?

I parked the car, and walked towards the old town. That particular area didn't seem to have changed very much. Everything was a little smaller, though. Unless it was I who had grown. I lit a Gauloise, felt better. I'd climb the steps of the jetty and walk out to the sea wall.

I reached the lighthouse. The sea looked sickly, made of *papier mâché*. Not a single ship in sight, only one of those pedal boats, the couple in it drifting dismally. On the rocks beyond the jetty a few fishermen eyed their lines. I liked to watch people fish—not exactly a lively spectator sport, but it always fascinated me.

The clouds over Italy were breaking up and timid patches of blue were appearing. I felt fine, Anne's little band of savages completely forgotten. But I had to think about buying some books. It was getting on for noon and the shops would be closing.

There were people about as I returned along the jetty: children chasing each other, young couples strolling, laughing, exchanging quick little kisses. They had probably only met a few days ago, and already they were kissing. How quickly things happened nowadays! And how slow had been the holiday loves of my youth, so complicated, so full of pretences. At seventeen I'd played at being a man of the world—at forty-five I still wasn't one. These boys seemed so mature, so at ease with themselves and with their girls.

Perhaps it was because they were better-looking than I'd ever been—taller, slimmer, gayer. Perhaps it was the food they ate, or the sun lotions they used. Either way, at the sight of them, I became an envious old man. Suddenly a thousand years old.

At the bookshop, I thought of other things. There I was in my element. Bookshops all had the same smell—sometimes I wondered if my love of literature didn't begin with its smell. Certainly I tended to sniff each book before I read it.

The best-sellers were by the cash register. I glanced at them, then headed for the paperbacks. In the end I chose eight: two Balzacs, one Gide, one Cocteau to improve my mind, and four whodunnits. The cashier put them all in a large carrier bag. I'd bought enough to last me a week. Then I'd come back for more.

A bistro near the old town was still not too crowded, so I decided to treat myself to a restaurant lunch. I settled myself at a tiny table between a Dutch family and some Spanish house-painters and ordered *spaghetti bolognese:* sixteen francs with a carafe of rosé and coffee. Afterwards I wandered out into the street, carrying my large bag. With the entire afternoon to kill I was assailed by a familiar anxiety: what on earth could I do?

I walked to the Casino, and there I had an inspiration. Outside it an extraordinary poster showed a green-eyed monstrosity, its enormous teeth stained with blood, its huge claws crushing a dozen buildings. It was also hugging a pleasant-looking young lady who didn't seem very happy. I sympathized with her. At one side was a notice: *Two o'clock performance.*

Not a moment to lose! I rushed to the ticket window and marched in as if I were leading a regiment to battle.

It is within these ancient cellars that the finishing touches are given to cheeses that tomorrow will be shipped all around the world. . . .

With the cinema in darkness and the usherette shining her torch in my eyes like a fascist interrogator, I could see very little. There seemed to be hardly anyone there—a few lovers in the back rows, some pensioners, and myself. The film progressed with agonizing slowness. A dozen or so chaps in hospital gowns were loading cheeses onto trucks. I sighed, and sank back into my seat.

. . . *And thus, day after day, deep within the barren soil, the wondrous adventure of soft cheeses brings forth. . . .*

"Oh, do get on with it!"

I sat up. Who'd said that? Then I spotted her, slouching in the row in front of me, three seats to my left, her knees up, the tight denim of her jeans visible in the shifting light from the screen. At that moment I only knew three things about her: she was bored with cheese, she was blonde, and at the cinema she liked to make herself really comfortable.

. . . *In these cold-storage warehouses they will remain until they are shipped to your local supermarket. Their unique aroma. . . .*

At last, for the final scene, triumphant music burst forth. A flaming sun set behind the Auvergne mountains. It was too much for me—I applauded frantically. For someone as shy as myself it was ridiculous, but I just couldn't help it.

The girl in front of me laughed, and when the lights came on she turned round. I saw her face for the first time. She wasn't a young girl but a woman of about thirty-five. She had soft lips, and a curl on the side of her cheek, just like a comma. She was very pretty. "You must be very keen on cheese," she said.

"But of course. I always carry a variety of brands, a different one in each pocket."

She laughed again, then turned back to face the screen so that all I could see was the top of her head. She wasn't looking for a pick-up—I was sure of that. She wasn't the type. She wore a blue shirt with patch pockets, hardly the uniform of a tart. Besides, already she seemed completely to have forgotten me.

The usherette came down the aisle with her choc-ices. She paused, gazed wearily round at the tiny audience, then went back up again. There was complete silence, as if we were all dead. The lights dimmed. Soft music.

A commercial: *The records you are listening to can be bought at the Discodisc Shop, 36, Avenue Gambetta.*

I could still hear my neighbour's laugh. It hadn't been in the least embarrassed; just easy and spontaneous. Clearly she was a very poised, self-assured person. After all, she hadn't hesitated to speak to me first—a thing I'd never have dared. Now, when I leaned sideways, I caught her yawning widely enough to break her jaw.

I sat back. I didn't want her to catch me staring. It wasn't any good my dreaming. She was still young, beautiful. She could have any man she wanted. And it certainly wouldn't be a stuffy old schoolmaster.

The lights were extinguished. A clash of cymbals and there, on the wide screen, in scarlet letters: THE MONSTER OUT OF THE BEYOND. The show had begun.

WEARING A FLIMSY nightgown, Teresa was about to slip between raspberry-striped turquoise sheets when the telephone rang.

"Is that you, darling?"

"Yes. I'll be late home. I'm needed here at the laboratory."

"Don't worry, darling. Everything is fine. I'm not in the least anxious."

Actually, you could see her hands shaking. In an earlier scene she'd dropped a pile of plates. It was subtle, this film.

"Go straight to bed, honey. Tordo has escaped into the desert. You can sleep in peace."

Tordo was the name of the monster.

Teresa replaced the receiver, sighed and went to bed.

Teresa was the wife of a scientist who was trying to perfect a weapon that would annihilate Tordo. The monster itself had no particular characteristics, apart from an unattractive countenance and an ability to pulverize the Empire State Building.

Teresa had closed her eyes. Something was about to happen. An immense shadow filled the screen. Through the window you could see a gigantic eye pressed against the pane. The music throbbed. Suddenly Tordo went into action, smashing the window and seizing the girl between his thumb and forefinger. Teresa screamed.

My neighbour sat up very straight and in spite of the racket I heard her gasp. As Tordo strode away over blocks of houses I leaned forward. "Have no fear. I am here," I said, dramatically.

She turned towards me, her face blotched with purple from the screen. "Do you think he's going to kill her?"

"I doubt it. The film's not yet half over."

Scene followed scene, but we were no longer watching. All I wanted was to talk to her, to be with her somewhere else, to quit this idiotic film that no longer interested either of us. But to suggest such a thing needed more nerve than I possessed. My heart was pounding: in the past I'd missed so many opportunities, this time I was determined not to fail. If it had been Frédéric or Max in my place, they'd have changed seats, taken her in their arms. . . .

I leaned further forward. "Forgive me, but I think this film is boring you as much as it is me. Why don't we go? I could buy you a drink. I swear I'm not just trying to pick you up."

Never in my life had I been so proud of myself. I could hardly believe it was I who had spoken. For a moment she said nothing. Then she stood up. "All right."

In the darkness she stumbled on the stairs. I took her arm and we went out together.

The sun was shining. Summer was at its height. She leaned against the wall and stood, her face upturned. "What time is it?"

"It's four thirty."

"I must be back here by five," she said. "My sister will be waiting to take me home." She smiled. "I'm blind, you see."

"TWO BEERS, PLEASE."

Her eyes were bright, reflecting the sea and also the corner of a parasol. But they could see neither. I felt amazingly calm. It was strange to be able to watch someone without being afraid they'd think you were staring. I could examine her at my leisure, her mouth, her forehead. When she drank her beer a little foam gathered in the corner of her lips. She put the glass down, using her little finger as a guide, touching the surface without groping.

"Who are you?" she asked.

"Well, I . . . well, it's very simple. I teach literature in a school and just now I'm on holiday." I felt that she was still waiting. Or perhaps one always felt the need to say more to blind people, to compensate a little for their handicap. "I live in Paris. I'm divorced, and—"

She stopped me. She had delicate fingers, no rings, only a small gold chain on her wrist. "It's more fun to guess. You're about thirty."

"No. I'm forty-two."

What a petty liar I was! Either I should have told the truth or taken off a good fifteen years. Instead, I'd deducted a paltry three.

"I'd never have thought it. You have a young voice."

That put new heart into me. She took out a packet of Gitanes and some matches. Instinctively my hand went to the lighter in my pocket, but I stopped in time. She lit her cigarette, inhaled deeply, then leaned back in her chair.

"Do you have a moustache?"

"Do I sound like a man with a moustache?"

"I'm not sure. Perhaps."

I took out a Gauloise. "All right, yes, I do have a moustache. I'm tall, tanned, my ears stick out, I played in *Gone With The Wind*, and my first name is Clark. Who am I?"

Suddenly she pointed her cigarette at me. "You're smoking. Yet when I took out my cigarette you didn't offer me a light. Why?"

Right from the beginning I'd felt I would say the right things, tell her what she wanted to hear. "I prefer to light my own cigarettes and I thought you might too. Besides, you manage very well without any help."

She tapped the end of her cigarette with her thumbnail and the ash landed neatly in the ashtray. She must have located it earlier and remembered exactly where it was. "My name is Laura Bérien. I live in Paris, I'm thirty-four, and I get gentlemen in cinemas to offer me glasses of beer."

She had a very fine profile. There was something about the line of her neck that made me want to throw her over my saddle and gallop away to the ranch of our dreams where we'd live to the end of our days amid kisses and twittering birds and tame

Indians. I'd have to be careful. The days of adolescent love were long past.

She stubbed out her cigarette. "I wonder what happened to poor Tordo. I hope they didn't kill him."

"Of course not. Teresa fell in love with him. So they got married and had lots of little monsters."

Momentarily she was thoughtful. "What did Teresa look like?"

"A girl, two eyes, a nose, a mouth—there must be millions like her."

She touched her own cheeks with the tips of her fingers. "At first I was afraid I wouldn't remember what I looked like."

I gazed at her. She grew more beautiful with every minute. There was a short silence. "How did it happen?" I said.

She shrugged. "Medical terms are so complicated. Apparently it was a rare eye disease. A gradual weakening of the optic nerve. For a few months the light grew dimmer, then suddenly it went out."

"Did it happen a long time ago?"

"Four years." She sat up straight and put her hands on her knees. All at once she smiled again. "And I still don't know if you have a moustache."

"No, I don't have a moustache. But I have green eyes and a hairy snout. My name is Tordo."

She laughed then, her eyes focused on me so that for an instant I was sure she could see me. The whole thing was a hoax.

"Would you please tell me the time, Tordo?"

Good Lord—I'd quite forgotten. It was five to five. I slipped a ten-franc note under the beer mat. For me the holidays would finish early that year. They'd have been short, but I'd never forget them.

I wanted to say her name. "It's nearly five, Laura. I'll take you back. Will you hold my arm, or would you rather . . . ?"

She stood up. "We'll walk arm-in-arm. Even people who aren't blind walk that way."

We strolled down the boulevard. "My sister will be waiting in front of the Casino. She has a dark blue Citroën, with a dent in the nearside front mudguard."

"Will it worry you if she sees me with you? I can leave you at the corner if you'd prefer it."

The curl shifted against her cheek as she shook her head. "No, it doesn't matter. But you're a very sensitive monster."

We were there. Her hair smelled of lemons. I wanted to remember that scent exactly. . . . When I released her my hand retained the feel of her softly rounded arm. With a boyish gesture she put her hands in her pockets. Just then I saw the car. I had twenty seconds left.

"Laura . . . Laura, could I see you again?"

See you. Clumsy words, words that for her had no meaning. She lowered her head. I couldn't see her face. Behind us I heard the car door open. She'd be taken away. I was too late.

Then, as simply as if she were asking me to pass the salt, she said, "Come by any afternoon. Villa Caprizzi, on the Gorbio road."

Her sister came up and hugged her. But her eyes were on me all the time. They weren't at all alike. Her chin was weak and there were unfriendly lines round her mouth. If Laura asked her what I looked like she wouldn't paint a flattering picture.

Laura introduced us. "Edith—this is Tordo, the monster out of the beyond."

Edith was taken aback. "Delighted to meet you," she murmured.

But her heart wasn't in it. I watched the car disappear round the corner, convinced that I would stay there, glued to the spot, until the end of time—or certainly until the beginning of the new school year.

Back at the farmhouse, singing boisterously, I set the table for dinner. It was only then that I realized I had left my bag of books in the cinema. And I didn't care. Nothing could have bothered me less.

I COULDN'T SLEEP. It was difficult to believe what had happened to me—after twenty long years of emotional calm I had fallen madly in love! Laura. . . . I'd go to see her the very next day. If I'd been only eighteen perhaps I'd have pretended I was busy, pretended I had a very full social life, but not now. Knowing she was expecting me, I couldn't have borne to spend a single day away from her.

But was she really expecting me? Perhaps it was she who had the full social life. I might arrive and find her place packed with people, smart people, interesting people, and Laura in the middle of them all, greeting me with, "Come in and meet my friends. Folks, this is Jacques Bernier, professional seducer. He tried to proposition me in the cinema."

They surrounded me, leering at me. Suddenly it seemed that they all resembled Tordo. I yelled aloud and clutched at my pillow. The nightmare passed. Laura . . . I wished I understood what it was to be blind. What do you see when you don't see anything? Then, slowly it dawned on me that I who had always hated to be stared at, I'd found the perfect answer: I'd fallen in love with a woman who couldn't see me.

Chapter Three

"What on earth was the matter with you last night? You screamed as if your throat was being cut." Anne was arranging flowers, sucking her finger where the thorn of a rose had pricked it.

"I had a nightmare," I said.

She eyed me. "You look very spruce, all shaved and shiny. Are you going out again?"

"Certainly I am. And if you're planning to hire a detective to follow me, I warn you he'd better have his wits about him."

Françoise was wearing a bikini—its two pieces would have fitted into the palm of my hand. She was outside on the terrace, covered with a yellowish cream that smelt of antiseptic. "I bet your father's driving the girls crazy down in Menton."

Frédéric looked up from his paper. "What's she like?" he asked.

What really annoyed me was that they didn't believe a word of it. They were being kind, teasing me, assuming that an old dodderer like me had finished with women long ago. Still, for the sake of peace I played along. "She's eight, she has long pigtails, and she gives me all her sweeties."

As I was leaving Anne called after me, "Don't get yourself hijacked. We'll expect you back for dinner."

I waved, and got into the car. An address was buzzing in my head: *Villa Caprizzi, on the Gorbio Road.*

"TWO BEERS, PLEASE."

Laura smiled as the waiter walked away. "Well? What did you tell them?"

"I told them I had a date with an eight-year-old girl with pigtails."

Part of her was in the shade. She moved slightly till she was all in the sun. "How old is your daughter?"

"Anne was twenty-four last October."

Laura was wearing a plum-coloured sweater, and yesterday's jeans. Going to see her had been childishly simple. I'd rung at her gate and she'd run down the steps like a ballet dancer. "I've come to treat you to another glass of beer," I said.

"No, today it's my turn." She called back into the house, "Edith, I'm going out."

Without waiting for an answer she'd come through the gate. Once in the car she touched the windscreen, the steering wheel. "I like these little Citroëns," she said.

I whistled in admiration, we laughed, and now we were on the terrace of the Continental. All around us people were eating huge multi-coloured ice-creams. My hands were trembling, and I didn't seem to be able to control them.

She was toying with her glass. "You know, a funny thing happened to me last year in this café. Edith was at the hairdresser and I was waiting for her here. Suddenly someone sat down at my table and a voice asked, 'How about us two taking a ride?' I was flabbergasted. I asked the man what right he had to think I would go anywhere at all with him. He said, 'Because you've been staring at me for the last ten minutes.'" She laughed. "Ever since then, whenever I'm out I shift my head from time to time, just to be safe."

There was a pause. Very quietly, I moved my chair a few inches round the table: her eyes followed me. "That's very good," I said.

"You know, yesterday, when you said you were blind I thought you were pulling my leg."

"Really? I'm so glad to hear it. I've learned to tell a lot, just by sound. I'm like a one-woman radar station."

I took a long gulp of beer. "I have a confession to make. I slept very badly last night, and when I woke up I was remembering all those stupid films where you see a woman in hospital, her head all swathed in bandages. Then a sexy surgeon arrives, unwraps the bandages, you get a close-up of him looking anxious. Gradually her eyes focus. Finally she cries out, 'I can see! I can see!'"

She seemed to look away. Not that for her it made the slightest difference. "It's nice of you to imagine such things. I'm sorry to have to disappoint you, but for me the film doesn't end that way. No miracle operation is possible. Does that upset you?"

"On the contrary, it suits me very well. There's a Chaplin film in which the blind woman gets back her sight and finds him so ugly she doesn't even recognize him. I'd hate that to happen to me."

"You underestimate yourself," she said quietly. "Edith has given me quite an attractive picture of you."

I was astonished. "You'll have to excuse me for a few minutes. I must send Edith a shopful of red roses."

She laughed, pushed back her chair. I noticed yet again the enchanting curl on the side of her cheek. For a time we were silent, happy just to be together.

Then, suddenly, I saw Anne and Françoise down on the pavement, just a few feet away, licking ice-cream cones. I leaned across to Laura. "We've got company," I murmured.

Laura waited, said nothing. Anne was the first to see us. She seemed visibly impressed, as if she thought her father had done rather well for himself. She stopped in her tracks. "Should I keep on walking as if I hadn't seen you? Or may I come up and say hello?"

I felt proud of her—she always knew just what to do in complicated situations. "Laura—I'd like you to meet my daughter. And this is her friend Françoise."

Laura was the first to hold out her hand. The gesture was so natural that neither girl noticed. "I'm so glad to meet you. As you can see, I've grown quite a bit since yesterday."

Anne took refuge in her ice-cream. "That's just like him. Telling us he had a date with an eight-year-old."

Laura waved vaguely. "Sit down and join us."

Anne and Françoise exchanged glances. "No," Anne said, "we'd like to but we've got shopping to do. We're having a party tomorrow night and. . . ." She paused. "I tell you what—why don't you come? It won't be much, just a sort of get-together. We'll eat outside, have a bonfire, sing some songs. But we'd be awfully pleased if you. . . ." I knew she wouldn't stop until Laura had agreed to go. "You see, the fact is my poor father is bored stiff with the whole lot of us. I'm so glad he's got to know you."

Before I could protest Laura had raised her hand for a turn to speak, as if in school. "Of course, I'd be delighted to accept. It's really very nice of you to ask me. But—just in case you haven't yet noticed—I really ought to warn you about something. I'm blind."

Anne stopped licking her cone. Françoise gaped. "Well, no," Anne said. "I hadn't noticed."

Laura's laugh was as relaxed as always. "Then I was right to mention it."

For a moment Anne was at a loss. "But I don't see . . . I mean, what difference does it make . . . ? I mean—Oh hell, I don't know *what* I mean!"

I went to her rescue. "It doesn't matter. Laura's already said she'll come. Now run off and do your shopping."

Laura held out her hand and Anne shook it gratefully. "See you tomorrow night," she said.

They went, leaving the two of us alone again. When Laura spoke there was a hint of anxiety in her voice. "Does it worry you that your daughter should know you're trying to seduce a blind woman?"

"I'm not trying to seduce you."

She gave a little laugh. "You never stop trying."

"Me? Good Lord—all I did yesterday was offer you a glass of

beer, and I came to fetch you today hoping you'd do the same for me. Nothing more and nothing less."

"All right, all right—we'll say no more about it. Anyway I should have asked you how you felt about tomorrow night. Will it bother you if I come?"

Her hand lay on the table and I took it in mine. She left it there and neither of us moved for a long time.

THE PLACE they'd chosen for their campsite was a good way up the mountain, and we'd walked there in single file along a goat track, Françoise in the lead, a bottle of vodka in each hand. Max stumbled behind: he was carrying a huge haversack of food, and besides, he'd already been at the *vin rosé*. Laura chatted as we climbed, the wind wrapping her long skirt around my legs as I guided her. She was in excellent form and had made quite an impression on Virgil, talking to him knowledgeably about twelve-tone music. When we came upon the lighted bonfire, she took a deep breath. "Roast lamb. It smells good."

We were all very gay. I had appropriated a bottle of wine for the two of us, but it wasn't enough. As always, Anne urged me to do my recitation from *Le Cid*, taking all the parts myself. I put up a battle—until, that is, Laura joined in against me. Perhaps it was the wine I had drunk, but I thought I detected a note of tenderness in her voice. So I gave in.

It was a great success, and Laura applauded like mad. I felt a bit embarrassed, took a sentimental drink from her glass. I looked into her eyes and saw the stars and the firelight reflected. Someone began to play a guitar, the notes falling like slow cascades of shimmering water. "Suddenly everything's so quiet," Laura murmured. "What are they all doing?"

It was the first time she had asked me such a question. It was sweet to me, but also painful. "The fire is dying, Max and Kim are dancing, Virgil is playing the guitar. I can't see the others. It's like one of those Mediterranean travel posters, with the stars unbelievably bright. Soon it'll be dawn."

She shivered briefly, and my hand touched her cheek as I draped my jacket over her shoulders. The party was over. The others would sleep on blankets and Virgil would go on playing his guitar. "Shall we go back now?" I whispered.

Her eyelashes cast long shadows on her cheeks. "If you like."

We stood up. Anne saw us and came over. "Are you off?"

Laura nodded. "I've had a marvellous time. I really mean it."

Anne beamed. "I'm so glad. You're sure you weren't bored?"

I felt Anne wasn't just being polite—she truly did want Laura to have had a good time.

Laura put her hands on Anne's shoulders. "I've laughed a lot, I've drunk a lot, and thanks to you I feel very, very happy. Please believe me."

We walked away down the path and I didn't turn round, even though I knew that Anne, like a little worried sentinel, was watching us, erect in the dawn light, while behind her the last wisps of smoke climbed in the still air and the ashes crumbled.

THE SOUND of the guitar had long since died away. Nearby, a tiny trickle of water ran over the stones of a mountain spring. I guided Laura's hand till the water slid between her fingers. She knelt and drank, her face among the moist wild grasses. In the faint morning light a drop glistened as it ran down her chin and neck.

I kissed her. I was no longer afraid. This was happening to me, Jacques Bernier. My jacket slid from her shoulders and I felt her arms around my neck.

Her hands moved to my face, seeking, touching. She'd know me now, my forehead, my nose, my mouth. Until she had finished I scarcely dared breathe.

"Well? Do I pass?"

"You'll do." She laughed gently and her fingers returned to my face, but this time with tenderness. I felt full of joy, gloriously alive.

"Laura—listen to me. I'll take you home. Pack your bag, I'll pack mine, and we'll be off."

Her forefinger traced the line of my lips. "I . . . I must—"

I kissed her again. I was quite reckless—after so many years of dull routine I wasn't going to let the chance of happiness escape me. "Say yes, Laura, or I'll throw you over the cliff."

"All right. We'll go. But what'll poor Edith say?"

"I don't give a damn. Anyway, what *will* she say?"

"I expect she'll understand. Not that it matters."

It was daylight by the time we reached her villa but the shutters were still closed. At the gate I took her in my arms and her lips tasted of the dawn and I thought we would go on kissing for ever.

She leaned back against the wall, breathless, her fingers gripping my arm. "I want to tell you something."

All at once she seemed so vulnerable. "What is it, my dear?"

"I'm afraid." She gestured almost despairingly and hugged me closely to her. Her whisper tickled my ear. "It's four years since I've made love."

"Are you afraid you've forgotten how?"

Her smile returned. I'd won. It was time, I told myself, to be entirely frank with her. "Laura—the other day I took a few years off my age. I'm nearly forty-six. And another thing—if either of us is terrified at this moment, it's me."

Her smile was there to stay. Satisfied, I left her, went back to the car, sat smoking for some minutes before I drove off. I wanted to think about things, savour to the full the happiness that had suddenly come to me. In a few hours we'd go away.

Together.

TOUCH AND SMELL were what were going to matter. I'd have to buy some super-sharp razor blades and I'd have to shave more carefully. Under my jaw there were places I usually missed. I'd also get myself some decent after-shave—the stuff I was using just then had been given me three years before by some of my less imaginative students, and it stank of aniseed. Even on the métro, at eight in the morning, it had won me some pretty dirty looks.

No, I'd treat myself to something more subtle, virile yet delicate. If such a thing existed.

As for the rest of me, well, a few toning-up exercises would probably take care of that slight thickening at my waist and thereabouts. I settled myself on the cold tiles of the bathroom floor and tried to remember the exercises my gym teacher used to put us through when I was at school. I reached forward, touched my toes, did my best to get my chin down onto my knees. The gap remained a good six inches.

Oh well. I took a deep breath and moved on to the next exercise. Leaning back, lifting first one leg and then the other. Perhaps a little song would help me bear the agony:

Aime-moi, aime-moi
Quand je suis dans tes bras
Je dis: Oh! la la la—

Somebody was pounding on the bathroom door. "Will you be done soon, or had I better come back this afternoon?"

I grabbed my dressing gown, tried to look dignified, opened the door. It was Max. "I've been waiting here a good twenty-five minutes."

I was genuinely surprised. "How quickly time passes!"

He smiled humourlessly and went past me into the bathroom. Before closing the door he called out, "Are you really leaving us?"

"Yes, I am. Almost at once."

"Then I'll say goodbye. And good luck."

He was a friendly chap. "Goodbye, Max. And when you next have an exhibition, don't forget to send me an invitation."

"That's a promise."

He closed the door. I returned to my room; I was sorry to be going. At first they'd all terrified me, but now . . . well, for all their extravagant talk and trendy behaviour they were really very simple people—probably a good deal more simple and genuine than I myself.

I closed my suitcase. Anne came quietly into the room and sat down on the bed. "You're going away with Laura?"

"Yes."

She smoothed the bedspread with her hand, and sighed.

"Is anything the matter?" I asked.

She smiled, a little uneasily. "I suppose not. After all, you're a grown man. . . . But have you thought how things will end?"

"Since they haven't even started yet I really can't say." She lowered her head, and went on stroking the bedspread. I sat down beside her. "Listen, Anne, it's all very simple. I'm leaving here to go off with a woman. Is that so terrible?"

"It could be."

"Why? Don't tell me you're jealous."

"It's not that. But there's something you seem to think so unimportant that I hardly like to mention it. Laura is blind."

I went to the window and leaned out. The crickets were making such a noise I was afraid she mightn't hear me. "I know Laura is blind. What difference does that make?"

She joined me at the window. "None at all. Forget what I said, it doesn't matter. Where are you both going?"

"I haven't the faintest idea. We're going—that's enough."

She stepped back a little, looked at me with a mixture of pride, tenderness and anxiety. "You know, beneath your venerable exterior you're really quite a lad."

It was time to leave. I kissed her and we went downstairs together, through the empty rooms.

"Say goodbye to them all for me."

"Of course I will."

Outside the sun was burning hot. I got into my car and Anne leaned in at the door. "You're not going to get married, are you?"

"I promise to do nothing without asking you first."

I started the engine. Above the various rattles, Anne shouted, "That's the first time I've seen you drive off without getting in a fret about your battery."

She was right. I hadn't given it a thought. "My dear girl, if I have any trouble with the battery I'll stop at a garage and buy a new one. I detest a man who goes on about his battery. If I met one I'd avoid him like the plague."

Anne stood back and waved. I put the car in first. "*Ciao.*"

"*Ciao. Bon voyage.*"

She dwindled in the mirror, then a curve in the road hid her from view. I'd done it. In fifteen minutes I'd be with Laura.

"WE'LL HAVE TWO tomato salads, please. Then—"

The corners of the patron's mouth turned down tragically. I thought he was going to announce the demise of his entire family.

"I haven't any more tomato salad."

Laura was toying with her fork. "That's all right. I'll have melon instead."

The man threatened to collapse. "I haven't any more melon."

I glanced at the menu. "That's a pity. Never mind—we'll have the eggs mimosa."

His despair was total. "I haven't any more eggs mimosa."

Laura began to laugh. The man raised his arms hopelessly. "What am I to do? It's after three o'clock. You came so late."

"All right then. What *do* you have?"

He was comforted. "We have sauerkraut. My wife is an Alsatian. Winter or summer, we have sauerkraut."

I squeezed Laura's arm. "Will sauerkraut do you?"

"It'll do me fine."

The sauerkraut wasn't bad: it had a special flavour that went well with the Ricards that we drank. Then we had cheese, and a *baba au rhum*.

Laura pushed back her plate. "I couldn't manage another mouthful. Would it be all right if I loosened my belt?"

"It's strictly forbidden really, but I'm broad-minded. Besides, I've already loosened mine."

She leaned towards me. "I think that's rotten. Taking advantage of my infirmity to make an exhibition of yourself."

She undid the belt of her jeans and as she stretched her legs under the table her knees touched mine. "This is a nice place," she said. "Where are we?"

"I don't really know. We must have driven about five hundred kilometres. Would you like to stop?"

"I think so."

I called to the patron. "Do you have a room for us?"

He nodded. "In the annexe—everything here is taken. It's not very grand, you understand, but at least it's clean. If you'd like to look at it—?"

"We'll take your word for it."

By now it was nearly five o'clock, and the restaurant was quite empty. I turned to Laura. "Tell me about your work. So far you haven't said a thing about it."

"I . . . well, I work for an organization which finds jobs for the handicapped. With the aid of a tape recorder and a special telephone I've managed to make myself completely indispensable. Besides, it seems that test questions put by blind people get much more truthful answers than ones put by ordinary social workers."

"You mean people don't lie to a blind person?"

"Let's say they lie less."

"What sort of questions do you ask?"

"All sorts. But I specialize in work-related interpersonal relations. That sounds impressive, doesn't it?" She buckled her belt and stood up. "Shall we go for a walk?"

The path down to the village was steep, and I held her very close, my arm round her shoulders. The village street was arcaded, cool and shadowy, with a smell of wet stones where the women had sprinkled water in front of their doors. We walked slowly. Broken staircases led to narrow passages overlooking the hills. A dog followed us, it's cold nose nuzzling Laura's hand.

In the square, in front of the Café des Sports, men were playing bowls, their voices strangely hollow, trapped under the heavy foliage of the trees.

"I'll buy you a drink at the café. It's just opposite."

The heat had abated. It was the hour when the colours of the countryside were most vivid: the sky above us was a deep blue and beyond the rooftops a mountain towered, motionless in the yellow splendour of the summer.

She couldn't see it. The green leaves against the sky were no longer a part of her world. But I didn't grieve, for I knew that, as I placed the ice-cold glass in her hand, the shadows were meaningless and happiness was within our grasp.

THE BEDROOM.

She finished smoking her Gauloise while I brought up the luggage. Certainly I was afraid, but I'd expected that and it didn't matter.

She'd found her way to the window. She breathed in the soft night air, then turned. "The room—what's it like?"

"It's small and neat and clean. It's like a hotel room."

I sat down on the bed. Dzzzzoiiinnng!

I was still vibrating like the clapper of a bell when Laura, alarmed, cried out, "What on earth have you broken?"

"I haven't broken anything. I merely sat down on the bed."

I lifted the mattress. There was no box spring, just some metal coils that were throbbing like a thousand harps.

Laura placed the palm of her hand in the middle of the bed and pressed lightly. Dzzzzoiiinnng!

When the noise had finally subsided, I said, "Let's sit down together."

Dzzzzzoiiiiinnnnng! I should have timed it. It must have been at least a minute and a half before silence returned. Laura began to giggle. "This," I said, "is the official nuptial chamber. When the villagers hear *dzoing* they hurry up here carrying torches and congratulate the happy couple."

I was about to slide the mattress onto the floor when I heard a key turn in a lock. The voices that followed sounded so close that I felt sure invisible people had entered our room.

First, a woman's voice: "For God's sake, Alexander, stop arguing and clean your teeth."

Alexander started to whistle a pop tune. A suitcase was opened, and tissue paper rustled.

A little girl's voice, presumably his sister: "Ma—where'd you put my dressing gown?"

Her father: "Where *have* you put my dressing gown—how many times do I have to tell you?"

Alexander: "Anyway, it's too hot for a dressing gown."

His mother: "Leave your sister alone. Just clean your teeth."

Laura whispered in my ear, "Are you sure they're not here in the room with us?"

I had an idea. "Just listen to this," I whispered back. Then I emitted a series of sepulchral coughs. At once, next door, all noise suddenly ceased.

Woman's voice, distinctly tinged with anxiety: "Is that you coughing, Alexander?"

Man's voice: "Why don't you leave him alone? It came from next door."

Laura stepped back and sat down on the bed, releasing the full orchestra of springs. There was a moan of fear, then the man's voice again: "There's nothing to be afraid of. It was only a bed squeaking."

Then, in a loud voice, Laura called out, "Have you cleaned your teeth yet, Alexander?"

Prepared for any emergency, I pulled two blankets off the bed, grabbed Laura's hand and dragged her out into the corridor. We just had time to hear Alexander reply "Yes, Ma," before we ran off down the stairs and into the night.

THERE WERE no stars, nothing but our bodies, close together between the blankets. I could scarcely see her. I kissed her cheeks, tasted salty tears upon them. "Laura—what's the matter?"

Her voice trembled. "I don't know. I just don't know."

I stretched out beside her and withdrew my hands from her breasts. "Don't you want me to?"

"Oh, yes. Terribly. I just don't know what's wrong with me."

I wrapped her tightly in the blanket and we sat up, quietly smoking our cigarettes, not moving or speaking for a long time. Then, slowly, she turned to me. I can still hear her voice, the voice of a woman who had triumphed over darkness, battled alone, and won.

"Jacques, it's going to be all right. I think it's going to be all right now."

Chapter Four

Charny, 3 km.

She gritted her teeth. The speedometer needle touched thirty-five, wavered, went up to forty. "I'm going to change into top."

She let in the clutch, changed gear, accelerated away, everything beautifully synchronized. The steering wheel remained rock steady. She must have been an excellent driver once.

"There's a turn coming up," I said. "Gradual, to the right."

She changed down, slowed to ten k.p.h. Sweat trickled between my shoulder blades. "It'll be easy enough. You'll feel the road's camber. Careful—here it is."

She braked and I saw her knuckles whiten as the car swerved a little—but she regained control just as I was about to grab the wheel. The road ahead was straight and clear.

"There—you've done it. You can go a little faster now. There's no need to look so worried."

"I keep seeing huge things about to smash into us."

"D'you want to stop?"

"At the next kilometre marker."

The country ahead was flat as far as the eye could see. We might have been in the Beauce; I was never quite sure where that particular region began or ended. In any case, we were on a vast level plain.

"All right, you can stop now. You've done your kilometre."

The stone was there, partly hidden by the tall summer grass. *Charny, 2 km.* She braked, shifted into neutral, and kissed me. Then we changed places.

"How did you like it?"

"It was fun. Do you know what worried me most?"

"The mud on the windscreen."

"Don't be silly. It was the thought that you might be helping me with your hand on the wheel without my knowing. But you saw how well I managed."

"Like an old hand."

She laughed happily. "How fast did we go?"

"Forty."

She whistled. I wanted to ask if she used to be a fast driver, but there was a tacit understanding between us that we didn't allude to the past, to the time when she could see.

I felt marvellous. It was four days now since we had left and everything had gone smoothly, without a single hitch. Life was all happiness and love. Two days ago she'd suddenly had this wonderful idea. The hotels were packed, and it had taken us ten tries to find a room even. The restaurant had been crowded with holidaymakers, all loudly exchanging recipes for shrimp sauce, for sunburn lotions, for ways to keep the children quiet. I'd been on the point of getting a terrible headache when Laura's hand had crept across the table, between the salt and the bottle of rosé, to rest on mine. She had the sensible look on her face that had by then become familiar to me.

"Listen," she said. "Everyone else is heading south. Why don't we go in the opposite direction?"

"What a brilliant idea. Tomorrow we'll drive up to Paris."

The very next day we'd begun the long drive back.

Now she yawned and stretched. "How far are we from Paris?"

"We'll be there in about two hours. Would you like to sleep a little? Or would you rather we sang something?"

"Let's sing."

We couldn't go far wrong: there was just the one duet we both knew, it was from *Carmen*.

She'd first sung it when she was thirteen, wearing a checked apron and a round white collar, at a party to celebrate the Mother Superior's birthday: it had been sandwiched between a nocturne by Fauré and tea in the garden with *petit fours*. For my part, I had once had a neighbour who was a retired infantry captain, mad on music but very deaf. Every day he'd played three records, always the same and always in the same order. The last was the duet from *Carmen*, and it had become engraved indelibly on my memory.

Laura's voice climbed. She wanted to run away with a matador, the trollop! I beat on the steering wheel in my agitation.

Carmen, il est temps encore . . .
Carmen, il est temps encore . . .

But she had no respect for her soldier lover, and defied me. Our voices blended, it was masterly.

Oh! ma Carmen, je t'aime encore,
Oh! ma Carmen, je t'a-do-ore.

Then she'd said goodbye to me and I was about to stab her. But first I had to pass a ten-ton lorry. That done, I ran my sword through her.

She expired, fell against the curtains. I broke down completely.

C'est moi qui l'ai tuée . . .
Ma Carmen, ma Carmen-en adorée . . .

"You shouldn't smoke so much," Laura told me. "Your voice cracked on the high notes."

She put her hand on my knee. In spite of the sound of the engine, after the racket we'd been making it seemed suddenly very quiet. "Being with you makes me very happy," she said.

I wasn't good at expressing my feelings. In fact, sometimes it was so hard to get the words out that I ended up saying nothing. They were like clothes, hanging in a cupboard: I wanted to get them out, air them, but I was afraid they'd been stuck there so long they'd smell of moth balls. . . . So I didn't tell her that I loved her.

Instead, "Since we get on so well together," I suggested, "why don't we stay together a bit longer?"

Her lips touched my ear. "Why not?"

Through the half-open window, a warm July breeze wafted in. The haze directly ahead meant we had almost reached Paris.

WHEN WE arrived at her flat I'd hardly had time to put down the suitcases before she was showing me her favourite game: she called it her "dice with death".

It worked like this. The four rooms of her flat had connecting doors. First she opened them all, then she returned to the entrance hall, then she began. She ran flat out through all the rooms, spun round in the last, and tore back to me, missing the door frames by no more than an inch. Finally she flung herself into my arms.

"What d'you think of that?"

I was cold with sweat. "What would happen if a draught blew one of the doors shut?"

"You guess."

"Splat?" I suggested.

"Right first time. But so far there's never been a draught."

"You've been very lucky."

Foolishly I'd thought that to live with a blind person you had to be something of a male nurse, keeping everything very calm, perhaps doing a little reading aloud to a background of soft music. Instead I was stuck with a maniac who specialized in indoor races, going to SF films and driving my motor car. Which all went to prove how dangerous it was to have preconceived ideas.

She took my hand and showed me round. The walls, the ceiling, even the floor, were painted white. Against it the few fine pieces of furniture, inherited from her family, looked quite lost.

"When I first went blind I had everything repainted," she said. "It seemed to me that if the inside of my home was dark, then it would be even darker in my mind. For a long time I used to go to sleep with the lights on."

Laura, alone in a twofold darkness, turning on the lights like a frightened child. There were times when I couldn't bear the thought. I lifted her in my arms.

"What shall we do now?"

"I'll give you one guess."

As her back touched the sheets, she whispered in my ear, "Well, you poor old man, how's your sex life now?"

"I can't complain. How about you then, Grandma?"

"IT'S NUMBER SEVENTEEN, the building just on the corner."

"Have you been here often?"

"Just a couple of times."

I found a parking space a little farther on. It was nine thirty and we were a little late for the party. The waiter had taken ages to bring me the bill. To the left, the dome of Les Invalides shone in the moonlight.

"Perhaps I ought to have brought a bottle of something."

She shook her head. "There's always something to drink. Besides, these people are my friends."

We went up in the lift to the fourth floor. Laura was looking her best. She was wearing a pleated white linen dress, her only jewellery a large silver ring. She had put on her make-up with extraordinary skill.

"Tell me, will they have the lights on up there?"

She laughed as the lift stopped and we got out. "Don't worry. They know you're coming. Are you nervous?"

"A little. Shall I ring?"

"Go ahead."

The door opened immediately, as if the man had been standing waiting on the other side. His eyes were shut, not like a sleep-walker's, but somehow permanently.

"Good evening, Simon," Laura said.

"Ah! It's you, Laura. We've been expecting you. And you've brought your friend. That's good."

I couldn't imagine how, but he knew I was there. I shook hands with him, then he put two fingers on my shoulder and guided me towards a group of people sitting in the middle of the room. A young woman gave me a drink. I noticed that they could all move around without the slightest difficulty, but not one of them, with the exception of Simon, crossed the room diagonally. Instead they stayed near the walls, where they could be sure of not bumping into things. That explained why the chairs were all in the centre of the room.

"Good evening, Laura. It's Maxime."

The man who addressed her was young and very handsome, one of the few men there who wore his hair long. He made a greater impression on me than the others. His pupils were white, the irises slightly veiled and almost colourless. His gestures were slow and graceful.

Laura chatted with him. They smiled at each other. He seemed to be staring at her with his dead man's eyes. He was different from the others, and he frightened me. But I left them together: I didn't want her to think I didn't trust her. And besides, I'd have her to myself again soon enough.

"Monsieur Bernier—we were wondering if we could ask you something. . . ." It was Simon, with the girl who had given me my drink.

"Of course. Ask away."

"It's a trap really," he said. "You see, we all read Braille here, but some of us are voracious readers and it's just not enough. So one purpose of these little meetings is to invite a sighted person and ask him to read to us. We record each reading and hope to build up a sort of audio-library. Would you be our reader tonight?"

"Of course. I'd be happy to. But I'm not a very good reader."

"I'm sure that's not true. May we begin quite soon?"

So Laura had ambushed me. But I'd get my revenge. I crossed to her, took her arm. "Laura—might I have a word with you?" I led her to the centre of the room. "Are you sure they're all blind?" I whispered.

"Of course I'm sure. Apart from you, we're all blind. What're you driving at?" There was a trace of anxiety in her voice.

"You'll soon see."

I took her glass, carefully placed it on the floor, then drew her close to me. With my right hand I pulled down the zipper of her dress and caressed her back. Then I kissed her fiercely.

She struggled, twisted her mouth away. "Have you gone mad?"

Without loosening my hold, I pushed her towards the wall. "Don't worry, they can't see us," I whispered.

"Oh!" Her exclamation was muffled. Then she, too, entered into the spirit of the thing, and kissed me back. A few inches from my right elbow a lively conversation about the stock market was in full swing. It seemed that even among the blind there were bloated capitalists.

"Stop it, darling, you're smothering me!"

When I zipped up her dress the man next to me gave a slight start. Simon called the party to order. It was high time.

"*THIS MORNING the world shines like a forgotten, unpicked fruit, like an orange in the dense foliage of an orange tree. . . .*"

It was odd that they should have chosen this piece—it was all about colour and light. They were listening, but their heads were turned away as if they weren't: it was hard to realize that people could pay attention properly when they weren't looking at you.

Laura's hand was toying with a fold in the curtain. Maxime stood near her, pale and handsome. He looked for all the world like Count Dracula, free during the hours of darkness from his crypt in the family mansion. The silence was broken only by my voice and by the faint rustle of the tape recorder.

Stealthily I turned to the last page and quickly glanced at it without interrupting the reading. One hundred and sixty-five pages, and I was only on the. forty-fifth. Would I ever make it to the end?

"*Good morning, beautiful wild rose, my companion in solitude, you have blossomed in front of my door during the night. . . .*"

No time to take a drink. I was chained to my book like a convict. What if I skipped a chapter or two? The sooner I finished, the sooner I'd be alone again with Laura.

I had just turned a page when I heard a click. It was the end of the tape. Simon got up with the sigh of a man emerging from a marvellous dream, and turned off the recorder.

"Thank you. You've been very kind. It's hard to explain how much the readings mean to us."

If shame could have killed, I'd have been a dead man. I'd been in a position to contribute something really important to their lives, and all I'd thought of was how I could skip a few pages.

"I know you must be tired," Simon went on, "so you'd better stop now. Someone else will finish the book for us."

Everyone started to leave. In the car Laura snuggled up to me with a sigh of contentment. "Home, James," she murmured.

We drove back in the warm hush of the night. Like other couples we had spent an evening with friends, and now we were going home.

A couple, just another ordinary couple.

"HEY, MEN. Cockroach is pinching all the nails!"

Cockroach dived between my knees. I grabbed at Laura, but she had already bumped against the fence and was covered with wet paint from shoulder to elbow.

"Damn! Be careful—you've got paint on your blouse."

Two loose planks twisted sideways and three grubby little children came through the gap. The tallest, a girl, had wrinkled socks and a freckled face. The boys with her were so dirty it was hard to tell where their skin ended and their T-shirts began.

"Seen a bloke runnin' away, 'ave you?"

"Yes, he ran into us. You can see what happened."

They stared at Laura's sleeve. "It was Cockroach what done it," said boy number one. "'E's been tryin' to 'ammer nails into us."

"That's right," said the girl. "He's round the twist."

"Hey, Pamela," said boy number two, "what the lady needs is turpentine, That'll fix it."

"Where'll I find a thing like that?" Laura asked.

"We've got lots," said boy number two, "else I wouldn't 've said."

As we squeezed through the fence after them I remembered reading something about the place in the papers. It was an adventure playground on a building site where all work had stopped on account of persistent strikes. We could hardly move without climbing over thick planks, stooping under beams, stepping over the children who were busy hammering nails, drilling holes, painting, shrieking at each other. Seemingly it was one of those sociological experiments that was working out very well. There, right in the middle of the city, the children were building shacks, putting up walls, having a marvellous holiday.

Two boys as thin as sticks were carrying a long wooden plank towards us. I pushed Laura back against a piece of rusty corrugated iron to let them get by. Pamela, the girl in the wrinkled socks, turned to her. Her chin was as pointed as the tip of a penknife. "Can't you see where you're going?"

"No," Laura said. "I'm blind."

"Gimme your hand, then. The gentleman can take yer other."

We walked a few steps. The two boys cleared a path for us as if they were motorcyclists in front of an official limousine. "Get out of the way. The lady's blind."

"Such is fame," Laura murmured.

Twenty-five or so of them surrounded us as we sat down on a pile of paving stones that looked like part of a demolished barricade. Pamela was offering us a tin of turpentine when a bearded man approached, shoving the crowd aside. "No adults allowed in here," he said.

I told him it was Pamela who'd suggested we come in.

"Well, if the kids invited you, that's different."

He walked off while I dabbed at the paint with my handkerchief soaked in turpentine.

It was strange to be in Paris in July, sitting on a pile of rubbish, surrounded by dozens of children. It was, of course, Laura who interested them. They muttered among themselves, then one of the boys came forward. His hair was plastered down with brilliantine, he had eyes the colour of prunes, and there were bandages on every single one of his fingers.

"Can't you really see nothing, lady?"

"Not a thing." She caught a drop of turpentine that was trickling down her arm.

A little girl in a flowered apron who was standing behind the others called out, "What about me? Can't you see me?"

I thought they were going to turn on her. A frizzy-haired child whom they called Mohammed, shouted back, "The lady said she can't see, stupid! If she can't see, then she can't see. Not even you."

I put the turpentine on one side and lit a cigarette. Mohammed watched my every move—I was sure he smoked like a chimney himself. I handed the cigarette to Laura. "Do you want to go?" I asked her.

"No—why? These stones are hard, but otherwise I'm fine."

The children laughed and I began to question them, to find out what they thought about things. "This place—is it fun here?"

"Not bad. It's not the seaside, mind."

"The seaside?" another put in. "Do me a favour. The seaside stinks worse nor this place, any day."

A little chap sitting on a plank leaned forward, almost losing his balance. "Garn. It don't never. And I bet you never been to the seaside neither."

"Fat lot you know about it."

"I do so. I been there, see?"

"So?"

"So nothing. So there ain't no stink."

Laura laughed. The children looked at her: blind, young, beautiful, and so happy. I put my hand on her shoulder. "You must admit this is all a bit different from the Riviera."

The little girl in the apron had come closer. Suddenly, in a strident voice, she demanded, "Is everything sort of black then, when you're blind?"

Everybody froze. It was a funny thing, the way children could so easily be embarrassed. They could have killed that little girl for saying such a thing, but it was too late now so they just stood there, feeling terribly uncomfortable.

"Not at all," Laura answered. "I don't see things all black. Black is a colour, and I can't see colours."

She spoke so naturally that everybody breathed again. Now it was Pamela's turn. "If things ain't black, then what *are* they?"

I saw how well Laura understood the children's curiosity. "It's hard to explain," she said. "I tell you what—Pamela, give me your hand."

The child offered her grubby little paw. The others watched in silence.

"Look at Pamela's hand," Laura began. "She can't see with her hand. Her hand will tell her all sorts of things about the world, but it can't see. Things aren't black, not to a hand. Well, when you're blind, that's what it's like. No colours, no black, no white."

A murmur of understanding went round the crowd.

Then, "Would you like to see our hut?" a girl asked us. She hadn't spoken before and the invitation, coming from her, was a sort of gift offering.

The hut was in one corner of the site, near a tree that was probably the last in the whole neighbourhood. Mohammed told us its trunk had been so caked with soot that they'd taken a ladder and washed it down. And why not—the Arc de Triomphe had been scrubbed, so why not their tree? They'd built the hut behind it and it wasn't yet finished: they were planning to put on a second storey, but they weren't quite sure how.

Laura strolled along surrounded by children, three of them clinging to each arm. And as for me, well, I ended up giving all my Gauloises to Mohammed and the bigger boys. I knew it was weak-minded of me, and bad for their lungs, but I defy anyone, faced with a gang of children spending their summer holidays in the foul air of Paris, to do otherwise.

As we were leaving, Laura hugged and kissed at least a dozen little girls who had followed us as far as the fence. Then she ducked through, I went after, and we found ourselves again on the cracked pavement outside. She seemed happy, yet at the same time a bit upset.

We walked arm-in-arm through what was left of Les Halles, narrow streets where you could still smell the aroma of ancient cheeses, finishing up in one of the last cafés still to serve coffee in glasses, sitting at a rickety table, eating chips out of a greasy paper bag. She was on top of the world: the children and all their questions had filled her with energy and enthusiasm.

"Where would you like to go now?"

"Take me to a restaurant, somewhere really grand."

"You'll have to get changed. In those jeans, with all that turpentine on your shirt, I doubt if they'd even let you in to do the washing-up."

"Then you must buy me a mink coat."

"Nobody wears mink coats in July."

"You're only saying that because you're an old miser."

I paid for our coffee. "I tell you what the newspapers'll say. 'Lecherous schoolmaster in his mid-forties, unable to satisfy the excessive demands of his blonde companion, crazed with sorrow, strangles her with her bra strap.'"

She giggled. "'Lecherous schoolmaster in his mid-forties. . . .' What'll those reporters think of next? Anyway, since your modest income won't allow you to keep me in the style to which I've been accustomed, you can be my guest instead."

We crossed the Seine as boats glided past below us. She liked the murmur of the water, and its evocative smell. In the square of Notre-Dame a guitar player was singing the blues. Laura leaned dreamily over the embankment, listening to him.

"Paris is a strange city," she said. "It's full of places where you wouldn't think you were in a city at all."

"That's its real charm."

I felt she was growing melancholy, partly on account of the guitar player and his slow, plaintive chords. I moved away from her as quietly as possible, and came up on her other side. Then I put on a falsetto voice and a phony accent. "Excuse me, ma'am, but which exactly is that church over there?"

"It's Notre-Dame," she answered.

"I thought Notre-Dame had two towers. That one has just the one. Why is that?"

For a moment she was disconcerted, then she came at me, laughing so much that she had hardly any strength left. All the same, she managed to land several painful blows to the body. It took us a while to recover. Her lips were close to mine as she whispered, "You're terrible. Your jokes are in the worst possible taste. Honestly, one day you'll open a manhole, then push me into it."

"I'm saving that up for the end of the week."

We walked along the quays towards the Odéon. Her hand was in mine. We had been together in Paris for eight whole days.

IT WAS JUST like the Hall of Mirrors at Versailles, but more sinister. We had scarcely taken three steps towards the damask-covered tables before the waiters fell upon us. One, an alarmingly moustachioed man in tails who looked as if he had been cast in bronze, drew back Laura's chair.

"We thought you were away on holiday, Mademoiselle Bérien."

Another handed me a menu covered in embossed leather. They knew she was blind and didn't offer her one.

"A cocktail to begin with?"

Laura was very much at her ease. "A Manhattan, not too strong."

"And for monsieur?"

I was trying to remember what they drank in whodunnits. Crooks tended to have cocktails on almost every page. Then I got it. "I'll have a Cuba libre."

Moustachio bowed deeply, then departed. I expressed my admiration at the chandeliers and the fake Gobelin tapestries. Laura was delighted. "It's not so bad, is it? I've been here a few times with Edith—she loves this sort of place."

"Me too. I've always had a weakness for museums. I just hope I won't use the wrong fork. Shall I read you the menu? If I start now I might just about finish before they close."

Moustachio returned, moving as if he were mounted on ball bearings. "Are mademoiselle and monsieur ready to order?"

"Perhaps you could give us a few suggestions."

We discussed the menu with some acrimony. I had intended to

order a magnificent steak with fried potatoes: instead I was forced to make do with a filet mignon, some fancy kind of mushroom, and potatoes *ducales*. Whatever they were.

My protests amused Laura enormously. "Be quiet now, or I'll order you some snails *á la Montpensier*. Edith had them once and she described how the waiter cooked them right here, before her very eyes, in a lot of little chafing dishes. All the other diners were absolutely fascinated."

At the next table, three Dutch women had just settled themselves. Together they must have weighed over a ton. Laura finished her Manhattan and leaned towards me. "I can hear new voices," she said. "It's terrible the way, what with my sad affliction and all, you can make eyes at strange women just as much as you like."

I choked over my glass. A waiter turned to glare at me like a reproving Medusa. Obviously this was no place for frivolity.

"What are you laughing at?"

I put my glass down. "I'll describe these newcomers to you. The best-looking one resembles a pressure cooker, her neighbour is as fat as a barrel, and as for the third—"

Her laughter stopped me, and her fingers stroked my arm. "Jacques, I want you to know that ever since I walked out on that film in Menton, I haven't stopped feeling happy for a single moment."

I caught my breath. What she had just said meant a lot to me. But I kept things light. It didn't do to show one's feelings. "That's because I'm a professional life-and-soul-of-the-party."

She tilted her head, the way a mother does when she knows her child is lying. "I'm sure you're not really like that."

Me? That dull old schoolmaster? "No, perhaps I'm not, I expect it's you who inspires me. No, I don't expect—I *know*."

My filet mignon had just arrived. Inadvertently I touched the plate—it was so hot it burned my fingers, raising a considerable blister. Only then did the waiter warn me. "I suggest that monsieur take care. The plates are hot."

Clearly he was out to get me.

Laura was munching her way enthusiastically through her exotic main course. I asked her if it was good.

"Taste it," she said, holding out her fork on which were impaled little rubbery cubes covered with a pinkish sauce. I chewed manfully, and swallowed. It tasted like a mixture of artichokes and chewing gum. I offered her a piece of my filet.

Laura rested her chin in her hands. "How's it going, my dear lecherous schoolmaster?"

"It's going very well. Except that this sort of place always makes me want to take off my shoes. How d'you explain that?"

She answered in her best sociologist's manner. "It's a characteristic manifestation of class-consciousness. You're a middle-class man who would like to register his disapproval of upper class ostentation by a grotesque action of great political significance."

"What about you? Don't you ever have such impulses?"

"Of course I do. Mine is to dance on the table."

"I'd like to see that. Why don't you give it a try?"

"First you must order me some dessert. I'll have the black-currant tart. For you I recommend the cherries in maraschino."

"If I asked for a plain yoghourt d'you think they'd send for the police?"

"That's a chance you'd have to take. Pour me some wine."

We were on our second bottle and her cheeks were very pink.

"Afterwards we'll have some champagne," she said.

"You're really celebrating tonight."

"Why not? It's my birthday."

Suddenly I felt dreadful. "Why didn't you tell me?"

"What would you have done about it?"

"At least I could have wished you a. . . ."

"Well, it's not too late for that."

The table was so wide I was afraid of upsetting something if I leaned across it. So I got up, went round it, took her face in my hands and kissed it. "Happy birthday, dear Laura."

"Darling—thank you."

The waiters must have been having fits. I returned carefully to my place. It was odd, the way wine could affect your legs.

"Waiter!"

Just before he arrived I was able to whisper to her, "It's a new one. The others must have been rushed off to hospital."

This one resembled a sort of vertical snake.

"Blackcurrant tart, please, some cherries in maraschino, and a bottle of champagne."

At that he bowed deeply, and respectfully hurried away.

"AND THREE makes five, plus five makes ten. Thank you, monsieur."

The sunlight on the glass of the door hurt my eyes. My eyelids burned and every time my feet hit the pavement a gong sounded in my head. Luckily I found a chemist that was open—during the summer holidays it was a rare phenomenon. I hoped the fizzy aspirin would do us both some good.

While I was putting her to bed she told me the story of her life, repeating herself over and over again. I don't think I slept much. Later that morning we spent some time sitting together on the edge of the bath. She couldn't stop moaning.

I held her in my arms. "Jacques, I'm so ashamed. I shouldn't have drunk so much. A blind person ought to know how to behave herself."

In the end I went and bought a bunch of carnations, two bottles of mineral water, a packet of noodles, six eggs in a plastic box and a tin of sardines. When she smelt the fragrance of the carnations she ran to kiss me, then stopped short, her face twisted with pain. She too had gongs in her head. We calmed them with a massive dose of aspirin.

It was perhaps our best, most tender morning. Since leaving Menton everything had been so hectic that both of us welcomed this quiet time together. I brewed tea with mint, cooked the noodles, felt I was showing a hidden talent for nursing.

For a while we hardly spoke. When she asked me for a cigarette I knew she was on the mend. As for me, I was still feeling decidedly liverish. Usually I was very careful with my diet, and sometimes even took a couple of pills before meals.

She stroked my cheeks. "Don't you feel well?"

"My liver's acting up a bit."

"Haven't you any medicine for it?"

"I'm afraid not. I left my pills in Menton."

"You never told me you had trouble with your digestion. Why?"

"I try not to think about it. Besides, I didn't want to spoil the picture."

For the very first time I saw her face shut itself off from me. "What on earth do you mean, 'spoil the picture'?"

I felt too seedy to want an argument. "It doesn't matter. Let's not talk about it. We're in no fit condition."

She jumped up, very much alive. Evidently she had recovered a lot quicker than I. "Well, I don't know about you, but I'm in excellent condition to discuss it. And I'll tell you what you're trying to do—you're like a child, making up a fairy story, ignoring anything in the real world that, as you put it, might spoil the picture. We're too old, Jacques, you and I, to be featured on the cover of *True-Love Romance.*"

I knew she was right, and that annoyed me. "That's nonsense! I've a perfect right to try to forget that I'm forty-five and you can't see. There's no need to make an issue out of it."

"But why do you *want* to forget? You're forty-five and I'm blind—but we manage very well, don't we?"

"I still prefer not to think about it," I mumbled.

She laughed bitterly. "Well, I don't. I'm what they call a handicapped person—it's no use pretending otherwise. And I don't see why you, if you've got these drops to take, shouldn't be able to—"

"They're not drops, they're pills."

"Then why don't you take your damn pills and be done with it? It's no use being afraid I'll notice you aren't eighteen any more—I already have. You're forty-five, and I love you. There now—you've made me say it. But you mustn't think that being in love has made either of us any younger. When we go to bed together I'm perfectly aware it isn't a young adolescent who's holding me in his arms."

I was taken back. "I didn't think we did too badly."

She laughed. "I never said we did. But it's no use thinking—"

I grabbed her wrists and we fell to the floor. She struggled, tried to pull my hair, but I had a firm grip on her and didn't intend to let go. She twisted about a bit more, then gave up.

"How's your liver now?" she panted.

"Forget my damn liver. Just repeat after me, 'Jacques darling, you're a perfect lover.'"

"Jacques darling—" She jabbed me in the ribs so hard that I was forced to let her go. Not to put too fine a point on it, I wasn't exactly in top condition. I called a truce.

In the late afternoon we went out and I bought myself some liver pills. Also some sticking plaster—she'd grazed her foot during our wrestling match. On account of us the chemists had had a good day. We returned home at peace with one another. I felt like a child who had been found out in a lie, and been forgiven. My conscience was clear. Tomorrow was another day.

I should have known better. All too often life was just like a bad Western: it was only when things were at their quietest that real danger came along.

On the landing, by the door to Laura's flat, a man was waiting. Maxime. I was afraid to let him come in.

THE WHISKY in his glass was dead level. The hand holding it was steady. I was glad that Laura couldn't see him: his features were classic, finely chiselled. But behind his apparent calm a fire smouldered.

Laura had been just finishing her rehabilitation course at the Institute for the Blind when Maxime first joined it. He'd already twice attempted suicide and had refused for a long time to learn Braille. In his home all music, even the radio, was forbidden. For over a year he hadn't uttered a word. Then a change came over him and he seemed to want to live again. I didn't know the reason, but I suspected that Laura was a good part of it.

"You're a schoolmaster, Monsieur Bernier?"

The words were innocent enough. But from his tone of voice I knew quite well what lay behind them: "What the hell are you doing here, Bernier, in the world of the blind?"

"Yes. I teach literature."

He smiled contemptuously. Either he was making no attempt to hide his feelings or his blindness prevented him from controlling his facial expressions.

"You must forgive me, Monsieur Bernier, but schoolmasters have always struck me as being singularly lacking in imagination. They enter the classroom at six and don't leave till they're sixty."

Laura stirred in her chair. She was clearly uneasy.

"It's true," I said, "we do lead routine lives. But I'll tell you a secret—adventure bores me."

He toyed with his glass and a shadow passed over his face. "You like to sound paradoxical, Monsieur Bernier. But I'd like to ask you just one question: would you consider living with a blind person an adventure?"

Laura was very pale. "Maxime, I don't think this sort of conversation is called for. I'd be grateful if you'd—"

He interrupted her. "Monsieur Bernier, you're going to discover one thing very quickly. In the country of the blind neither the one-eyed nor the sighted are kings."

He radiated an almost brutal power. My voice shook. "I don't think I understand you."

Laura tried again to intervene, but Maxime was launched, and nothing would stop him. "A blind person isn't simply someone who can't see. He's a person quite different from other people, with different ways of thinking, of feeling, of loving and hating. I can promise you one thing: he has nothing, absolutely nothing in common with the world of sighted people."

Laura listened to him in silence, her knuckles white on the arm of her chair. I stood up and lit a cigarette. "Obviously, when one part of the whole changes, then the whole changes also. Then what?"

"Then what? It's really quite simple. Blind people belong to a group apart—we can communicate only with each other. You know that, and so does Laura."

She shivered as he spoke her name. "We've talked about this so often, Maxime. You know how I feel. In you there's a need to break off all contact with the sighted world, to become part of a closed society. Whereas for me . . . for me there's just a world in which I'm blind and Jacques can see. That's all. And there's nothing anyone can do about it. So let's drop it, shall we?"

Slowly Maxime uncrossed his legs. His face was blank. He spoke calmly, without passion, each word razor sharp. "You're both victims of an illusion. You've fallen for all that idealistic stuff about mutual understanding; you believe in friendship between whites and blacks, between Jews and non-Jews, between Algerians and Frenchmen. Yet you know perfectly well that the truth is different, that every time two races meet the result isn't harmony, but slavery, the ghetto, bitter warfare. And if a fundamental barrier exists between black and white, it's nothing in comparison to the universe that separates the blind from the sighted."

Laura made a quick instinctive gesture, as if to ward off a ball flying at her. "I think we should end this conversation, Maxime."

He was jealous, of course. He wanted Laura and I had her. All the rest was talk. He was silent now and we finished our drinks without speaking.

Perhaps he was right, though. Even before he'd begun I'd felt an outsider, being the only one there who could see. In time, perhaps, I would come to believe that Laura was too different for me ever to understand her. Then, perhaps, I would realize that she belonged to Maxime, that his world and hers were the same. She already knew perfectly well that he was young and rich and handsome. Dear God, how could I compete, I who was middle-aged and poor and ordinary?

"Will you have supper with us?"

My tone wasn't very encouraging. Maxime stood up. "No, thank you. I'm expected elsewhere."

Walking ahead, Laura brushed lightly against him as she went to open the door. My heart was pounding: it was always when people were leaving that the really important things were said. He knew I'd be listening, but that wouldn't stop him.

"See you soon, Laura. You're on the wrong path, you know. This man is your last link with the sighted world. It's broken with you, but you haven't yet broken with it. When that happens you'll turn to me. And it'll happen sooner than you think."

The door slammed, Laura came back to me, her lips trembling. She leaned against me, her forehead against my chest. "He's mad. He's scared me since the very first time we met."

My voice was unsteady. "Don't worry, darling. Dracula has gone off now to suck the blood of some solitary passerby. Forget about him."

She nodded. I knew it wasn't easy to forget things to order. The words he had spoken lingered in the room, lay heavily between us. She sighed. "Sick. He's really sick. . . ."

The seed he had sown in her mind was evil. I seized her shoulders, determined to be stronger than he. "I, Jacques Bernier, by the grace of our Holy Father the Pope and in obedience to my sovereign, offer you, Lady Laura, aid and assistance. For you alone I promise to overcome the powerful and terrifying Prince of Darkness. I suggest that, you on your mare and me on my noble palfrey, we push off from here at the crack of dawn."

"Where d'you want to go?"

"I haven't the faintest idea."

She clapped her hands. "Belgium! I've always wanted to go to Belgium."

"Do they have beer?"

"Pale and strong."

"And mussels?"

"The best. With fried potatoes."

"Church bells?"

"Carillons of them."

"Then we'll go."

Chapter Five

"I swear it's as flat as the palm of my hand. There's nobody around. Just follow your nose."

We were on the beach at Ostend. She hopped from one foot to the other. "I know you'll beat me. I haven't raced in four years."

"I haven't raced in thirty, so neither of us is exactly in good training. Let's see who's first in the water. It's only about a hundred yards."

"Aren't there people swimming?"

"I told you, not a soul. They're all stuffing their faces with lunch. Come on now—one, two, three, *go!*"

The sand pushed up between my toes, my knees pumped up and down as I pounded off down the beach. Laura dashed ahead of me. She was veering to the left but it didn't matter: the beach was quite deserted. I was panting heavily, she was well in the lead, my feet were becoming clogged with sand . . . she was going to win. I spurted, gained a metre or so, wheezing like a grampus.

She heard me and groaned, then ran faster, as if her life depended on it. I didn't want to lose so I tackled her while she was in full flight and we collapsed together on the wet sand by the edge of the sea. "You swine—I was winning!"

We lay there, gasping for breath. After three tries I managed to say, "You know, that little black bikini really suits you."

"Shall we go in?"

"That's what we came for."

Laura was jumping up and down in the shallow water. "Gosh, it's cold."

"That's only because you're scared. I've already dived right in."

"I don't believe a word of it."

We had to walk a long way out before the water even came up to our waists; it seemed as if we'd have to go on walking for ever. For no apparent reason Laura suddenly started shadow-boxing, leaping about like a flying fish.

"Are you quite sure you're feeling all right?"

"Go to hell. I've had to be careful for far too long. Now, just for once, I don't have to be afraid of knocking over a tea-plate or poking out someone's eye. I'm going to make the most of it. If you don't like it, then watch out!"

She plunged in. With her hands cupped like a seashell she threw water at me, her aim amazingly accurate. It was hard to run in the water but she thrashed ahead, then dived in and swam off. I went in more carefully, did a sedate breast-stroke, keeping my head well above the water.

She reappeared on my left, doing the crawl like a champion. "Where are you?"

"Over here."

She clutched at me and I stood up. We still weren't out of our depth but by now the water reached halfway up our chests.

"Kiss me, my love."

Wet, salty lips—a sea-scented kiss, full of summer.

Off we went. At first I couldn't keep up with her, then she slowed down. After swimming quite a distance we lay on our backs, resting. Out of the corner of my eye I could see her, floating gently like a boat at anchor.

"I don't know where I am any more," she said. "I can't orientate myself at all. But it doesn't matter in the least. There's absolutely nothing to bump into. Only the sea can do that for you."

We turned round and began to go back, dawdling to prolong the pleasure. Once out of the water the sharp wind at once gave me goose pimples. I'd forgotten our towels so we lay down on the sand, our faces turned to the sun. I covered her with the hot dry sand and gradually she stopped shivering.

Her eyes were closed and her hand kept shaping and reshaping the same little pile of sand. Away to our left the first family had just arrived: umbrellas, folding chairs, shrimping nets. It was time to go.

Laura stood up. "Where are we going for lunch?"

"I've no idea. But I'll buy you the best mussels in the North Sea."

She hesitated for a moment, then turned purposefully away towards the sea. "Wait for me. I'm going back in once more."

Alone now, she walked away. Already the waves were breaking around her knees. A strange feeling came over me as I watched her: for the first time I was seeing her as a stranger might. Everything I knew of her disappeared—her smile, her past, her unique ways of smoking, drinking, loving. All that was left was the figure of a woman gradually merging with the sea. I felt this was what she really wanted, just to be a body moving in space, experiencing only this elemental pleasure.

I wanted to join her, but held myself back. The instinct that had prevented me from offering her my cigarette lighter at the café told me she wanted to be alone. I stood at the edge of the water, my toes curling in the wet sand.

When she returned, a haze of irridescent water glistened in her hair. Lowering her head, she shook it violently.

"Everything all right?"

At the sound of my voice she veered towards me, holding out her wet hands. "Fine."

The bathing hut smelled of wood and fresh paint. Sand was sticking to my back and in a bit of cracked mirror I saw I was badly sunburned. I'd have to tell her. Anyway, she'd find out soon enough, in a day or two, when my nose began to peel.

She was waiting for me outside, wearing a different skirt. Her head bent to one side, she was brushing the sand from her hair.

"I haven't seen that skirt before."

She twirled round like a mannequin. "You haven't seen anything yet. I've brought along a pair of flared Mexican slacks that'll cause a sensation."

We climbed the dunes and the steps up to the sea wall. We found an inn, built of weathered black bricks, and went in. It smelled of brine and some kind of disinfectant. A few minutes later we were stuffing ourselves with food. Once again I had forgotten to bring my pills.

LATER, we set off for Bruges.

"On my right a wooden windmill, in the Flemish style."

"Are the sails turning?"

"No."

Twenty seconds of silence.

"On my left, another windmill."

No answer. I let ten seconds pass. "Still another windmill, larger than the others."

"This must be real windmill country."

At the fifteenth windmill Laura gently put her hand on my knee. "Jacques, will you do me a favour?"

"Certainly, my love. Anything at all."

"Just tell me exactly how many windmills you've seen since we left Ostend?"

"None at all. Windmills belong in Holland."

She sank back. "You know what you can do, don't you?"

We came to the outskirts of the city. Suddenly I felt wretched. All that magnificence, the statues, the glint of the sun on the gilded columns and balconies, the reflections in the dark water of the canals . . . she'd never see any of it. And what words could I possibly find to do justice to this exquisite city, this spectacular *coup de théâtre*, this poem in stone?

We left the car just as the church bells began to sound a carillon. Pigeons fluttered above us and the heavy banners snapped in the wind. She tossed her head back, smiled. It was then that I knew there was nothing to fear. Bruges would live in her memory; it was already part of her.

THE HOURS passed swiftly, punctuated by the music of the bells. We'd been in Bruges three days, drinking beer on café terraces overlooking the grey canals, strolling along the cobbled streets, daydreaming in parks where little old ladies in cotton stockings and dark shawls hurried by, making for the cathedral at all hours of the day.

We dined regularly at an Italian restaurant. The first time we were there Laura knocked over the salt and the waitress realized at once that she was blind. Since then she'd been especially kind, and brought us extra-large helpings.

I finally wrote to Anne. It felt like a thousand years since I had left her—I'd almost forgotten what she looked like. I asked to be remembered to everyone, hoped they were having good weather. . . . I didn't know what else to say: I'd never been much good at putting happiness into words.

"Jacques?"

"Mmmm?"

She was dipping a piece of roll in her cup. It was ten o'clock and she hadn't finished breakfast. Life was like that.

"Would it bore you if we went shopping?"

"Of course not. Why?"

"I'd like to get Edith a present. It would be a way of saying I'm sorry for having left so abruptly."

"What would she like?"

"A ring, I think. She seldom wears them but she adores them."

We went out into the crowded streets. In crowds I'd got into the habit of holding Laura very close, my arm round her shoulder. We'd worked out other little tricks. For example, when we were going up or down a kerb I'd walk a little more slowly, my leg very close to hers so that she could feel exactly what I was doing. That way she hardly ever stumbled.

I spotted a smart boutique, featuring Indian scarves, Afghan coats, necklaces from Nepal—all probably manufactured somewhere just round the corner. I guided Laura to a counter where rings were heaped in a sort of large bowl. She dug around in them. "We'll have to go somewhere else. These are all junk."

We left. There were flower sellers under the arcades and on the corner, a big department store. Inside, it was so crowded that I drew back.

Laura squeezed my arm. "Don't be nervous. I'll look after you."

Together we found the escalator. "I'm going to buy you something, too," she said. "What would you like?"

"You should have warned me . . . I honestly can't think."

I steered her between the counters, towards the jewellery department. She was happy, and very excited.

"Can I help you, monsieur, madame?" The saleswoman had the air of a startled rabbit, accentuated by a slight moustache.

"I'm looking for a ring, something without a stone, a heavy sort of ring in stainless steel or some such. Please let me feel each one. I can't see."

The startled rabbit blushed, searched among the jewellery cases, anxious to please. I wondered why she should be so embarrassed that Laura had told her she was blind. Human nature was a mystery.

She watched as Laura fingered each ring. "That one might suit. What do you think, madame?"

It was a design of interlocking cubes, big enough to cover the entire knuckle. Laura put it on. "Does it shine?"

"No, madame. The finish is matt."

She sighed, stroked an affair of circles and ovals that seemed to attract her, then set it aside. "I'll take this one, please."

"Which one would you have chosen for yourself?" I said.

"The same one. I always buy Edith what I'd like for myself."

I turned to the startled rabbit, whose nose was still twitching. "We'll take two, if you have them."

Laura moved close to me. "I'm very touched. The other's for me?"

"Brilliant! Right first time. And your thigh against mine is most disconcerting."

The startled rabbit heard me and her nose twitched worse than ever. She hurried away to wrap up the two rings.

"I shouldn't let you do this," Laura told me. "With a gold-digger like me you soon won't have a penny left out of your schoolmaster's tiny pittance."

I pressed my finger against the tip of her nose. "Don't worry. I've managed to put quite a bit away under my mattress. I was planning to buy a little thatched cottage with it for my declining years, but it doesn't matter. I can always go to an old people's home."

The saleswoman returned with two parcels wrapped in green and gold marbled paper. When I'd paid, Laura firmly took my arm.

"Now it's my turn. Conduct me to the men's department."

Her tone was so commanding I had no alternative but to obey. Once there she began a rapid sort of finger ballet, touching the shirts, feeling the sweaters, whisking from counter to counter.

"What you need, Jacques, is a nice turtleneck sweater."

"But for heaven's sake, it's the middle of July!"

"And the evenings are chilly. As soon as there's the slightest breeze, your teeth begin to chatter. I notice these things."

"I don't deny it. But I've a perfectly good jacket."

"Precisely, I'm fed up with that jacket. With a sweater you'll look positively athletic."

"But I'm not the athletic type."

She wasn't listening: her fingers stroked a particular sweater, then held it up against my chest. "This ought to fit. But you'd better try it on."

Remembering the perils of changing rooms, I attempted a small subterfuge. "Not this one. It's quite hideous—all yellow and green and blue stripes. It's horrible."

Laura was about to give in when a saleswoman suddenly appeared. "Can I help you, madame?"

Laura smiled a slow, Machiavellian smile. "Would you tell me, please, the exact colour of the sweater I'm holding?"

The saleswoman didn't seem a bit surprised. She was evidently used to all sorts of silly questions. "It's written on the label, madame. The colour is grey."

There was a short silence. I coughed discreetly.

"Thank you so much," Laura purred. "And you're quite sure it doesn't have any yellow and green and blue stripes?"

"Quite sure, madame. It only comes in solid colours."

Laura turned to me. "You're so sharp, one day you'll cut yourself."

I dug into the pile and brought out a brown one. "This is brown. I prefer this colour."

And there I was, back in a changing room. The curtains wouldn't close, of course, but left the usual gap. I took off my shirt and tried on the sweater. It wasn't at all bad.

I returned to Laura, tucking in my stomach, thrusting out my chest, and she felt me, pulling solicitously at the neck.

"It's not tight under the arms, is it?"

"Not at all. It's perfect."

"We'll take it. And now we'll have a look at some shirts."

I protested. "But I've got plenty of shirts."

"White shirts. And I've had enough of them. I want to choose you something gayer. Take me to the shirt department."

Once there, I had to stick out my neck so that a third saleswoman, the sporty type this time, with damp hands, could measure it. She also checked my shoulders and the length of my arms. Belgians really took their work seriously.

She was particularly concerned with the length of my arms. She found them unusually long. That upset me. "Hadn't you noticed, mademoiselle," I snapped, "the way I'm forced to walk with my hands trailing on the ground?"

She tittered so loudly that a good thirty people turned to stare.

Laura chose three shirts: a maroon one (I'd held out for at least one dark colour) and two with bold stripes. I could just imagine myself turning up at school in them—the children would queue up to have a look.

As we were passing the T-shirt counter I said, "You know what I'd like best of all? A T-shirt with 'I love Mickey Mouse' written across the front."

She squeezed my hand. "Are we in the T-shirt section?"

I thought she was really going to buy me one. But the T-shirt she bought was for herself, and she kept it on: a black and green affair that fitted her like a glove and made her look heartbreakingly young. She smiled at me, and suddenly I felt as if we were meeting like two young lovers at the edge of a Flemish canal—one of those straight, silent canals that flowed between banks of thistles and sad-looking trees towards the sea. Perhaps it was her blindness that made this happen, the way she was able to isolate herself from the surrounding crowds. All I know is that the moment she smiled at me the busy department store disappeared and there she was, waiting for me near the canal, a flower in her hand.

She took my arm, brought me back to earth. "Come along," she said, "we haven't finished our shopping yet."

I thought we were going to buy up the entire shop—we rushed from department to department, spending money like water. Finally I called a halt. "That's enough, Laura. I need a drink. If I don't get one in the next three minutes I shall faint dead away."

We left, our arms loaded, and collapsed with all our purchases in an elegant café near the Flanders bridge. Through the stained-glass of the window I could see the rooftops of the mansions on the other side of the river. I drank my beer in a single gulp, then began to sort through our enormous pile of parcels. There were records, a china tobacco jar to take back to Simon in Paris, a large scarf for a friend of Laura's whom I didn't know, a suede jacket for Laura—apparently a great bargain—my turtleneck, my shirts, and socks—ten pairs.

When she'd ordered them from the saleswoman the enormity of the number had quite appalled me. "But why ten?" I'd demanded.

"Because it's far more sensible than washing your only pair every night in the hotel washbasin."

I tried to tell her I'd managed like that perfectly well for the last twenty years, but I might as well have saved my breath. I now had ten pairs of new socks. She was revolutionizing my entire life.

She was drinking; her eyes shone above the white foam of the beer and she wiped her lips with the back of her hand like a badly-brought up child. "Didn't we have fun?"

"Yes, Laura. Yes, we did."

We'd certainly had fun.

IT LOOKED as if the weather was going to turn nasty on us. Above the city, the evening sky was filled with heavy clouds. The streets were empty and the canal reflected only the darkening horizon. Even the café we were in was dismal.

Laura yawned and so did I. It was one of those moments that sometimes happen—life seemed to be pausing, resting before it went on again. We felt calm, and a little sad. Conversation died between us. All we could do was wait for life to start up again.

"How about going home?"

"If you like."

She too was making no particular effort, evidently feeling it would have been a waste of time. Then, in a small voice, she added, "This place seems spooky. I'm sure the cellar is full of dead bodies."

We left. Laura kept stroking my sweater. "You're really warm and snug, aren't you Jacques?"

She was quite right—I wore it all the time. The wind on the quays was as cold as November.

Laura shivered. "What a country! I should have put on my new jacket."

A cinema advertisement was tacked to the wall but the street lights were so dim that I let go of her hand for a second to get close enough to read it. She kept on walking.

The film was a thriller. Perhaps it'd be worth a try.

Then I heard a shout and turned round. There were three people under a street lamp, a man, Laura looking terrified, and a small boy lying on the ground. The man stooped over the boy, then looked up without finding out if the child had been hurt, and yelled, "Can't you look where you're going?"

As I hurried towards them Laura answered, "No, I'm afraid I can't."

I knew she wouldn't say she was blind, that was up to the man to work out for himself. He scooped the child up and set him on his feet. He was a coarse creature with a face as round as an Edam cheese. Not realizing we were together he winked at me, then turned to Laura. "I don't mind you looking for customers beside the canal, but next time watch out where you're going."

I suppose it was wrong of me, but before I'd had time to think I blurted out, "Can't you see she's blind, you dirty bastard?"

Either I had shouted too loudly, or he just didn't want to understand. He just fastened on the insult. "What was that you called me? I didn't quite catch it."

He leaned forward, a stupid, evil expression on his face, and cupped his hand behind his ear as if he were deaf. He had a good forty pounds advantage over me, and he knew it. "What did you call me? I'm not sure I got it."

I felt a powerful urge to take to my heels. Instead, I actually heard myself saying, "I called you a dirty bastard."

I saw the blow coming and took it on my shoulder. Laura flung herself against me but didn't block a beautiful opening for a jab at the man's face. I gave it everything I'd got, and felt I'd smashed every knuckle. He retreated, his nose bleeding.

"Get the police, Marcel. I'm bleeding."

Laura flailed one arm in the direction of his voicc, all the time clutching me so tightly that it hurt. I was trembling like a leaf. "You swine—I told you I was blind. *Blind!* Do you think I'd have knocked your child down on purpose?"

He was breathing heavily, his mind working so slowly you could almost see the ideas trundling round in his head. Finally he said, "I'm bleeding. He's going to pay for this."

He started towards me. It was now or never.

I stepped back, Laura still clinging to me, till the wall was at my back. I had forty years of compromise, of defeat behind me—now I'd had enough. And I couldn't bear the thought that Laura might guess how petrified I was. I'd have to stand up to this bull-headed lunatic.

I shook Laura off and met him head on. I must have landed another one because I heard him grunt. Then everything went black, the ground rushed up to meet me, and my face was in the dirt. I heard a great roaring sound. Then I came to, saw trouser legs, heard men talking excitedly in Flemish. I scrambled to my feet. Laura was explaining things to two men. I staggered towards her, bits of enamel grating between my teeth.

We left soon after. Another group had gathered across the street to watch. I was painfully aware of the way they all stared after us.

THE LIGHTS in our bedroom dazzled my eyes. I sat down, my legs like water, my hands still trembling a little. It was the left side of my jaw that hurt the most. Laura was bathing it with a wet cloth.

"What made you call him a dirty bastard?" she said gently.

"Because that's what he was."

She pulled back my lip and began testing my teeth. "Isn't that one a bit loose?"

She looked so worried it made me laugh. "I've lost a crown, but otherwise they're fine. You should have warned me that he had a sledgehammer up his sleeve."

"You've been very lucky. Lie down now, I'll make you a hot compress."

I stretched out on the bed while she went to the bathroom. I'd watched this scene in various films: the hero, a real tough guy, lying back, having the honourable wounds of battle ministered to by this sexy bird. Now, for once, it was I who was the hero.

The only trouble was that usually the hero had come out on top, whereas tonight. . . . But at least I had landed just one real haymaker. That was something to remember.

"Laura—you know, it's a pity you couldn't see what I did to him. I got one nasty one through to him, the sort of thing Carlos Monzon is always trying to do and doesn't always come up with."

"Who on earth is Carlos Monzon?"

"He's a boxer. A world champion."

She came back into the room with another hot cloth. Pressed

against my cheek, it seemed to draw off all the pain. It felt very pleasant.

"The man mountain came towards me . . . very scientifically, I watched for an opening. The moment he lowered his guard, wham! I let him have it."

She laughed. Though she was still slightly anxious, she was beginning to relax. "I thought you were the strictly non-violent type. What got into you?"

I snorted. "You must be joking. I'm a born fighter. It was a good thing he ran away, otherwise I'd have made mincemeat of him."

She tied the hot cloth under my chin with a towel, pulling the two ends tight and knotting them on top of my head. "There . . . I bet you look just like a beautiful Easter egg. You know, I'm afraid I really hurt that child. He must have been running when I crashed into him. In a way that man was right to make such a fuss. If you can't see you shouldn't be walking about alone."

"You weren't alone. I was close at hand. And anyway, you've a right to walk alone. It's not as if you were a public menace."

"But I am—and anyway I was frightened. Suddenly everything about me was dangerous. When I first became blind I often had nightmares about walking along a busy main road. I'd hear the screech of tyres, horns honking. That man's voice brought it all back to me."

She began to tremble, tried to hide it, pushed my hand away from her arm. "You can never depend on a blind person, Jacques. The slightest thing and she cracks up completely."

I didn't know what to say: for the first time I saw how vulnerable she was, how hemmed in with dangers. To Laura the edge of the pavement, a staircase, a passing cat, almost anything could prove fatal. My attention had been distracted from her for just a few seconds, she'd gone on alone, and. . . . "It was my fault. I shouldn't have let you go on without me."

Her reply was sharp. "We can't go around chained together."

I raised my voice. "I don't see why we should have a quarrel. We happened to run into a nutter who was spoiling for a fight. That kind of thing can happen to anyone."

She laughed, but her eyes were filled with tears and she began to sob pathetically. We held each other close for a long time, and then I went to fetch a cloth from the bathroom to wipe her face.

"Don't bother," she said. "We've used them all up on your jaw."

The crisis had passed, so I played the fool a bit, making boxing match noises: the shouts of the crowd, the gong, the advice of the trainer. Unsurprisingly, the guests next door began to bang on the wall; they weren't exactly overjoyed to be given a re-run of a boxing fight at after one in the morning.

Laura had cheered up now. "They're probably not sports fans," she whispered. "We'd better go to bed."

The incident was over. As we were getting into bed, she turned to me. "Tomorrow, what d'you say to moving on?"

"Good idea."

She hesitated. "Shall we go back to Paris?"

"Capital! We'll return to the capital."

She kissed me on the forehead.

"Good night, Laura."

"Good night, Carlos Monzon."

Chapter Six

The trumpets sounded, and the prince appeared. A few rapid strides and he had seized the jewelled hands of the queen. She drew herself up and her scarlet fingernails seemed to tear at the silk of her bodice. . . .

Laura sighed. "I'm bored."

"Would you like to leave?"

"*Shhhhh!*"

The fellow behind us looked most unfriendly. Obviously he didn't want to miss a word of the play—he'd probably bought season tickets. We shut up, paid attention to the argument on the stage. . . .

The curtain finally fell to a light spattering of applause. There can't have been more than fifteen of us in the whole theatre. And two acts still to come. I had a feeling we wouldn't stick it out to the end. As we made our melancholy way to the bar, the handful of spectators eyed each other suspiciously, as if wondering why any of them had come in the first place.

We crossed the foyer. In the bar a single customer was staring resignedly into his glass.

"Do we have to go back in?" Laura murmured.

"I'd just as soon not."

We left, through corridors reeking of expensive dust. It was marvellous to be outside, under the neon-lit leaves of the chestnut trees. We strolled away down the boulevard like a couple of lifelong Parisians. The flower stalls were still in business and at one, in the middle of all the roses and carnations, was a sign which announced: *Tomorrow, July 25—Saint Jacques's Day.*

My name day. But what really struck me was the fact that we had been together now for three whole weeks, Laura and I. It seemed incredible: I'd have sworn that we couldn't have been gone from Menton for more than a week.

"D'you know what day this is?"

"It's Friday the twenty-fourth."

Another surprise. Unlike me, she hadn't lost contact with reality, and I couldn't resist pointing it out. "I'd have expected your mad passion for me to make you lose count of the days."

She didn't answer at once. We continued on past several bright shop windows. Then, abruptly, she said, "I know it is the twenty-fourth, because on the thirty-first I have to be in New York."

I had often read in books that when someone received a shock, "everything began to spin", or even, "suddenly everything went black". But for me it wasn't at all like that. The statue in the Place de Clichy didn't budge an inch and the street lamps went on burning as brightly as ever. Everything remained exactly the same. Except for one thing: in seven days Laura would no longer be with me. Nothing had changed except the future.

She had her own life, of course, her friends, her work. She might be blind, but she was still young, pretty, intelligent, and there were millions of other men in the world. After all, what had really happened during those last three weeks? We'd had a good time; we'd helped each other to turn just another ordinary holiday into something special; nothing more and nothing less. Certainly life hadn't begun for her the day she met me in a Menton cinema.

"You haven't said anything. . . ."

She had told me once that it was difficult to lie to a blind person. Anyway, I had no wish to. "I was thinking about you going away. Why didn't you mention it before?"

"What was the point? Life isn't much fun when you're counting the days. I didn't want you waking up every morning, thinking only fourteen days . . . now only another week."

I cleared my throat. "How will you get to America?"

"I'm going with Edith. I've been asked to help run a psychiatric institute there."

"Will you . . . enjoy that?"

"I've no idea. I'm going there to find out for myself, and then decide. I don't have to accept."

"No. You don't have to accept."

She stopped abruptly and pointed straight ahead, towards the Place Blanche. "Listen. . . ."

The sounds were distant: klaxons, grinding noises, a mixture of shouting and distorted music. Then, closer, a recognizable song:

Aime-moi, aime-moi
Quand je suis dans tes bras
Je dis: Oh! la la la la la la. . . .

Laura smiled. But, perhaps for the first time since I had met her, it wasn't a real smile. "It's a fair of some sort," she said.

I too made an effort. "Shall we go? I've got some loose change in my pocket."

"Let's!"

We plunged into the crowd, the air reeking of waffles, nougat and caramel. People were milling around in front of the "Thousand and One Nights". Nearby was a wrestling booth. Laura made us stop and listen to the barker's patter.

Three men were on the platform: one, skinny and nervous, was jumping frantically around, shadow-boxing; the second, wearing a leopard skin, was named "The Strangler"; the third was a burly fellow in red tights and hood, with a black bat across his chest.

"And here, ladies and gentlemen, is a man whose face nobody can bear to look at, who has never been beaten in the two thousand matches he has fought . . . The Vampire of Düsseldorf. . . ."

Laura leaned towards me. "How about trying that deadly uppercut of yours? After all, now is your big. . . ."

I couldn't hear the rest of what she said because of all the shouting and the shrieks of the children as they rushed up and down the fake snow on the "Russian Mountains" next door.

"Would you like some peanuts?" I yelled.

The man had his stall between the "Ghost Train" and a fortune teller with all sorts of diplomas. I bought some peanuts for Laura and a licorice sweet for myself. In the centre of the sticky black spiral was a little pink sugar pearl. I chomped the whole thing up, every bit. As we came to Professor O'Brien's menagerie (lions from Africa, crocodiles from the Amazon, tigers from Bengal) I decided to take a chance.

"How would you feel about getting married?"

She fumbled in her bag, brought out a peanut, rolled it to and fro in her hand, then tossed it up and I caught it between my teeth. She leaned her head on my shoulder and we walked away, amid the crack of rifle shots, the blare of horns, the shouts, the singing, the laughter.

Only seven days were left.

THE DAYS PASSED so quickly. Neither of us mentioned the question of marriage again, and then, suddenly, in two days she would be gone, leaving by plane for Nice. I was to take her to the airport, Edith was to meet her at the other end, everything had been arranged. Neatly rounded, like a sad melody.

That evening we had a guest—Simon. I was delighted to have him: there was so much goodness and gentleness in Simon that I felt it was myself, not he that was the afflicted one. We talked a lot about literature—I was completely at home with him.

Once, when he and I were alone for a few minutes, he seemed to want to talk about Laura. I could see he took a friendly interest and was concerned about us as a couple. But then Laura came back into the room and, to my regret, we had to change the subject. If Laura and I did decide to get married, Simon was the person I'd go to for advice. He knew so much about the world of the blind that was unfamiliar to me—he might be able to tell me if we'd make a success of it. We'd managed to be happy for twenty-three days. Perhaps that was the most I should hope for.

"TURN ROUND and tell me how nice I look."

I swung round in my chair. She was standing in the middle of the living room, a white cane in her hand, wearing dark glasses. I'd never before seen her like that, and I didn't know what to say. Clearly, however, some reaction was expected.

"I didn't realize you had the full kit. . . ."

She laughed. "Edith thinks I should get a seeing-eye dog too, but I wouldn't know where to put it."

"You do use the cane, though?"

"Only when I go out alone, and that's not very often. I used it more in the beginning. Mini skirts were the rage then and once, when I went out in one, I heard a woman say, 'Blind people really ought to dress more decently'. Other people expect you to be earnest and a little sad, and if you're not, it shocks them. They think a blind woman who laughs must be a fake."

I wondered why she was displaying herself to me with all the outward trappings of her affliction. Perhaps she wanted to convince me that her blindness was more important than the fact that she was a woman.

She touched my arm and ran her fingers up to my cheek. "Ten o'clock in the morning and you're still unshaven and in your pyjamas. You're getting idle, Bernier. You're a hopeless case."

Her fingers moved to my forehead, my eyelids. Suddenly she broke down completely, sobs bursting from her as if a taut canvas had been ripped by a knife. She collapsed onto the floor, curled up in a tight ball, weeping pitifully as only a woman can. I didn't know what to say, how to comfort her. I knelt beside her.

"Hush . . . hush now. What's the matter, darling?"

Gradually she calmed down, her body still shaken from time to time by long shudders, like the last tremors of an earthquake. With her head in the crook of my arm, she whispered, "Pay no attention, Jacques. I do this now and then."

"What is it that makes you suddenly so unhappy?"

I knew by the tone of her voice that her answer was going to be important for both of us. "Up to now I've been gay, but I wouldn't want you to get the idea that it's easy or that I'm always so cheerful. I do my best to make you think my blindness isn't important to me, that it's something I can easily overcome. . . . Well, it's not, Jacques. There are some things you can never overcome—d'you hear me? *Never*!"

She shouted the last word. I stood up, shattered, my arms hanging uselessly at my sides.

Her voice broke. "I work a bit, I play around with you, I laugh, but there's one thing I never forget, not for a single second: once, four years ago, I still had my sight."

I saw myself in the mirror on the wall: my face was deathly pale. For an instant I wondered if everything had been a performance, right from the beginning. Had she only been pretending to laugh, pretending to love me, pretending to be happy?

"The other night you asked me to marry you," she went on. "The least I can do is to warn you that Laura isn't just a devil-may-care creature who doesn't give a damn about being blind. There's no such thing as a blind person who doesn't mind being blind."

"But Laura—"

"Let me finish. Laura is a girl who's eaten up with anger and misery. She may seem to be doing all right for most of the time, but. . . . I'll tell you a secret, Jacques. You remember the second time I went into the water at Ostend? The weather was beautiful, and I'd been so happy? Well, suddenly I was tempted to swim out to the open sea and just drown. Even though I love you. . . ."

She lowered her head, unable to put into words the terrible barrier that lay between her and the rest of the world.

". . . Maxime has thought about all this more than most of us, and he believes he's found the answer: he cuts himself off from everyone who can see, he behaves as if he belonged to a different species, he has nothing to do with them. Usually I find this attitude overdone, far too extreme. Only now and then do I wonder if perhaps he's right after all."

I reached for a cigarette. My fingers, yellow with nicotine, were trembling. I should really try to cut down.

She sat in silence for a while, her chin on her knees, her arms around her legs, her face still streaked with tears.

Finally, "Why don't you say something?"

"Because once you get started it's impossible to get a word in edgeways."

The beginning of a smile formed on her lips. It was a good sign. All the same, we'd always joked, made light of things. Now, suddenly, we must be serious with one another.

I found my voice. "Believe it or not, I've never doubted for a minute that being blind is no joke. We've spent almost a month together and I honestly believed we could go on. I suggested marriage only because perhaps I'm a bit old-fashioned. If you object, it really doesn't matter. After all, it'll save me having to buy a new suit, and send out invitations. . . . I just want to say this to you: I don't know if it's possible for a sighted person and a blind one to be lastingly happy together. All I do know is that Laura Bérien and Jacques Bernier can be."

She sighed. "You must feel you have a vocation for nursing."

I lost patience with her. "You've just been telling me what's going on in *your* head—don't start analysing what's in mine too!"

"Stop shouting at me. The woman downstairs will complain."

"This time, Laura, you won't stop me. I'm going to say what needs to be said." I knelt in front of her, took her head in my hands, and talked for a long time. I in my crumpled pyjamas, unshaven, and she in an old pair of slacks and her Shetland sweater, her face in a mess, her hair all anyhow.

". . . and besides, I'm getting old. I'm fed up with living alone, eating scrambled eggs and doing the washing-up once a week. I've asked you to marry me because it's you I want. It's as simple as that. I want to marry you. Don't look for fancy motives. If you say yes, I'll be very happy. If you say no . . . well, that's the way things are."

She laughed softly, tenderly. "You won't jump in the Seine?"

I raised my right hand. "I promise."

For a moment she went off into a dream. Then she put her hand on my arm. "There's so little time before I leave. . . ."

My watch said twelve thirty. Tomorrow at this time we'd be on our way to the airport. I kissed her.

"We've got twenty-four hours, Laura. An eternity."

THE MAN in the cap stood just in front of me, blocking the view, so that I didn't see them come round the turn.

"There they are!"

Just behind the hedge their caps flashed in the sun. Laura dug her fingers into my arm. The sound of pounding hooves grew nearer. Laura was jumping up and down.

"Can you see our horse?"

Just then I saw him, the jockey crouching, his backside higher than his head, thwacking with his whip.

"He's running third—he's catching up. Now he's about to pass. There he goes! He's way out in front."

Clumps of turf flew up and the ground trembled as they raced by.

"Will he win?" Laura yelled.

I leaned forward as far as I dared. "Yes, he's made it, he's made it—he's won!"

She was smiling like an angel as the rest of the horses thundered by. I grabbed her—we hadn't exactly netted a fortune, but all the same it was a marvellous feeling.

The man in the cap turned round to us. "Don't get so excited. There's still another lap to go."

A blow, certainly. Laura's face fell. "Do you think number six has a chance?"

The man looked at her, then at me, an expression of amused astonishment in his eyes. "Number six? He's king of the also-rans. What made you choose him?"

It wasn't much use trying to impress him—he looked as if he had been born in a paddock and would die queueing up at the tote. With all the respect that the amateur owes the professional, I confessed, "We've been backing number six in every race."

He shook his head in pity. "You come to the races often?"

"No," Laura admitted. "This is our first time."

I stood up on tiptoe. "Look out! Here they come!"

Without a word, the man in the cap handed me his binoculars.

"Well?" Laura asked. "What's our also-ran up to?"

Where was that blasted number six? I surveyed the field, couldn't see hair nor hide of him. Dear God, it just wasn't possible! Yes, there he was, right at the back, clearly in distress, his jockey egging him on as if he were on a sinking raft. I recognized his apple-green cap. It was him all right.

I handed back the binoculars. "He's at least half a lap behind," I told Laura. "He looks as if he's running backwards."

She tore up our tickets disconsolately. "He started off too fast. He should have kept something in reserve."

The expert chuckled. "Even if he'd started off at a slow trot, he'd still have been dead on arrival. It's not his fault, he has bad asthma. Any jockey will tell you that. When he wheezes at Auteuil you can hear him in Chantilly."

Laura laughed. "The one time we have a bet we choose a horse with asthma. You don't have a tip for the next race, do you?"

"You do as you please, of course," said the man. "But I reckon number seven is going to run away with it."

"Thank you so much," Laura said, then turned towards me pleadingly. "Just one last bet?"

I scolded her sternly. "I knew you'd drag me down to bankruptcy. You're a compulsive gambler and you won't stop till I'm reduced to thieving or murder to pay off your outrageous debts. How many men have committed suicide because you brought them to utter ruin?"

"Just one last fling on number seven. You heard what the man said."

"It's no use trying to get round me. But I'll buy you a beer instead."

Very few people were at the bar. I settled Laura in front of a glass of beer and went to place a bet on number seven in the fourth race, number eight in the fifth, number nine in the sixth—just to be safe.

The beer was foaming, and ice-cold. We made ourselves comfortable. The weather was beautiful, the air smelled of the countryside, and it wasn't yet four o'clock. But I shouldn't have been looking at my watch.

It was funny how we'd happened to come here. She'd felt like going out into the country, but it wasn't easy from Paris. I suggested the Bois de Vincennes, but when we found ourselves driving past the race course we decided to come in here instead.

The bell rang and the horses were at the post. I was all keyed up. We asked each other riddles, just to pass the time.

Then the loudspeaker announced that the winner was number twelve. Laura was very disappointed. "We'd better go. This isn't our lucky day."

That wouldn't do. I was forced to make a confession. "We'll have to hang on. I've bet on the next two also."

"You swine—and you accuse me of being the compulsive gambler! Which horses?"

"Belle Fontaine and Tanagra."

Her face lit up. "Well, that's different. One of them is bound to win. I feel it in my bones."

A SLOW foxtrot, the lights subdued, the piano relaxed and easy, the chap on the drums stroking them with soft metal brushes. We hadn't danced very much, only the slow ones—those were the only ones I knew. We were still a bit shaken up by the afternoon's final big thrill: Tanagra had won by a length.

We'd decided to get rid of all our winnings in the one evening, which explained the ritzy night club, the champagne and the foxtrots. We'd been treated to a strip tease, and also a singer with bad adenoids who gave a bad imitation of Frank Sinatra. Now our foxtrot was over, and I led Laura back to the table. I couldn't take my eyes off her—I wanted to remember her face for ever. The thought was constantly with me: after tomorrow I won't see her ever again.

"Champagne?"

"Please."

Silence settled over us. Already, it seemed, I must face the fact that part of her was no longer with me. The pianist was playing a solo, an American song that had been popular a few years before but now sounded somehow tired. Laura sat dreaming, her chin in her hand. She was very beautiful. I wouldn't even try to describe her . . . she was simply Laura. And she was leaving me.

Two guitars joined the piano. Not a slow foxtrot, but something I thought I could manage. "May I have this dance, dear lady?"

She smiled and stood up: we glided away across the floor, beneath a mirrored ball that scattered light like flecks of confetti.

"Dance closer to me," she whispered.

I knew I tended to hold my partner as if some imaginary barrier separated us. The old me, very old-fashioned and proper. I could feel the warmth of her, and smell her scent. It just wasn't possible that this was the end.

She raised her head as if she had guessed that I was about to speak. "I don't think I'll be staying in New York," she said.

The music changed to a waltz. Few people were dancing, there was plenty of space, so I followed the music. I, who had never learned to dance, I began to whirl her around and around. . . . We circled the floor at least fifteen times, Laura twirling, her head thrown back, laughing.

Finally we stopped, dizzy with tiredness and champagne. I sank into my chair, my heart ready to burst.

It had been our last day, and probably my luckiest. Tanagra had won and Laura would come back.

"*ALL PASSENGERS for . . . flight three-two-seven for Teheran . . . please go to gate number. . . .*"

The voice echoed between the walls of the concourse at Orly as if between steep mountains. I pulled Laura back out of the way of a luggage trolley.

"Wait for me here. I'll have your ticket checked."

Usually completely at a loss when it came to formalities, I found the right ticket office immediately. The booking clerk ran her finger down the list of passengers for Nice, tore off a coupon and handed me two cards, giving me instructions.

"Laura Bérien is blind," I said. "Would it be possible for. . . ."

Her expression didn't change. "Don't worry, she'll be looked after by the air hostess during the entire trip." She picked up a banana-shaped telephone. "Hello? A blind woman on flight two-fourteen. Laura Bérien. That's right, to Nice. Thank you."

Listening to her, I got the impression that Air-Inter ran a special service for blind people. I went back to Laura. She was wearing the ring I had given her, her fingers toying with the frames of her dark glasses. I didn't know what to say.

"Jacques—what'll you do for the rest of your holiday?"

That was something I hadn't cared to think about—another six interminable weeks. I couldn't go back to Menton, walk down its streets, stare at the closed shutters of the Villa Caprizzi, wander about on endless pilgrimages.

"I'm not sure . . . I expect I'll stay in Paris, go for long walks, visit some museums. And I'll go and see Simon."

She lowered her head. "I wish I wasn't going away."

"What about all those films where a girl just like you is on the point of boarding a plane? Her lover drags himself miserably back to his car. Then, suddenly, the girl turns, runs back, knocking over piles of luggage. She reaches his car just as he's about to drive off, tears open the door, and throws herself in. The last scene shows the car moving off. Her head's on his shoulder, tears of pure happiness running down her cheeks."

She laughed. "Was that the film where the girl who was blind in the beginning got her sight back at the end?"

"The very one."

Why hadn't I asked her to stay? It shouldn't have been difficult to tell her how tired I was of hearing about her ridiculous trip to New York. To tell her that I loved her and couldn't do without her. It was my need to appear broadminded, to understand that she had to go because of her work, because it was a chance of a lifetime, that had ended us up at Orly airport, not knowing what the hell to say to one another.

I swallowed. "You'll write to me?"

"Of course."

"And I'll reply. But there's . . . a certain difficulty. I expect you can guess what it is."

Her fingers reached out and touched my face. "I know Edith will have to read me your letters, but I've nothing to hide from her. Write to me as passionately as you like. She won't mind."

"I'll try. And I'll add a nice word to her at the end."

Twenty minutes more.

A Hindu family had taken the row of seats opposite us. One of the children was swinging his leg rhythmically back and forth, as if counting the seconds.

"If . . . if you do come back, when d'you think it'll be?"

"November, I think."

Late autumn was usually a beautiful time of the year in Paris. At the weekends I'd take her out to the forests, to inns with low oak beams. There were so many things we hadn't yet done.

The boy was annoying me, kicking at the seat like a human metronome. And we had so little time. . . .

Laura jumped up. "I haven't a single cigarette."

"Don't move. I'll go and get you some."

"No—let me come with you."

She really didn't want to leave—otherwise she wouldn't have insisted on coming with me. Then the bell announcing a departure sounded and my heart sank.

"Forty Gauloises, please."

I stuffed one of the packets into her jacket pocket. She opened it at once, tearing the paper the wrong way, which wasn't like her.

"All passengers on Air-Inter flight two-fourteen to Nice are requested to go to gate number seven."

So that was that. Everything was coming to an end. We went back into the waiting room. The child was still beating time with his foot. I picked up her travelling bag.

"There's no need to hurry," Laura said. "They always give you plenty of time."

I put my hand on her shoulder, my fingers tense. "The fact is, my dear . . . well, I'm sure I haven't told you often enough how much I love you. I . . . I'm going to be lost without you."

Abruptly, as if suddenly dazzled by a bright light, she put on her dark glasses. "I'm wondering if perhaps the girl in your film did the right thing."

"*All passengers for flight number two-fourteen. . . .*"

"Laura Bérien?"

It was the air hostess. She must have spotted the dark glasses.

"I'm Laura Bérien."

"I'm responsible for looking after you and seeing that you're comfortable. If you need anything at all, please don't hesitate to ask. I'll be close at hand all through the journey."

"Thank you."

The girl cast a rapid, inquisitive glance at me. "I'll come and get you in a few minutes. Please give me your ticket now."

We were alone again.

"Well, here we are!"

"Yes, here we are!"

We laughed together. I'd never noticed before how white her teeth were. And there were tiny wrinkles at the corners of her eyes.

"Are you going straight home?"

"No—first I'll make sure that you're safely on board. Then I'll wave my handkerchief till my arm drops off."

The hostess was coming back, all briskness and efficiency.

"Here comes your bodyguard."

"We might kiss," Laura said.

"That was my intention."

Her lips tasted fresh and sweet, like sugared raspberries. The hostess reached us, put her hand on the shoulder of Laura's sucde jacket. The other passengers were already piling into a small bus that waited below us on the tarmac.

"Goodbye, Laura."

She waved with her free hand as the hostess took her off. The girl was chatting, showering her with attention, but Laura didn't respond. Then they were gone.

There really wasn't much point in my staying. I had no idea which plane would be hers and I preferred to spare myself the idiocy of gluing my eyes to one particular flight while in fact she might be going away on quite another. The sky was wonderfully clear and blue, no sign of bad weather, nothing to fear at all really . . . apart from mechanical failure or a hijacking.

Forcing myself to turn away, I went back across the departure lounge. The child was still there, opposite where we'd been sitting, but now his leg was still, like the pendulum of a stopped clock.

I put my hand in my pocket, came across the envelope that had been there since that morning, forgotten. It was a letter from Anne. It was strange that it should have arrived just then, as if, with Laura gone, my past was asserting itself. I hadn't even read the letter. Perhaps I was an unnatural father, but I hadn't given Anne much thought during the past month. Now I had all the time in the world.

I sat down, opened the letter. It was, for Anne, a long letter. She was fine, had two TV shows lined up in the autumn, Frédéric was as nice as ever and they were still in love.

> Just now the two of us are alone here. Max was the last of the gang to leave. I think perhaps they all scared you when you first arrived. I wonder if you went off with Laura partly to escape from their rowdiness.

How silly she was. Nothing would have stopped me from going off with Laura—even if Anne had begged me to stay I'd have refused. Up to then there'd been so little of the romantic novel in my life, not even anything you'd call a full life really. . . .

> I'm perfectly aware that you're a grown man, and not without common sense, and you may think I'm just plain jealous. But this thing is so serious that right from the beginning I've hesitated to say a word. I've discussed it all with a friend who's a specialist in such matters, though, and he's confirmed just how difficult it is to live with a handicapped person. Even if things seem easy for you today, I can't believe they'll go on being so easy tomorrow.

Did she think I hadn't considered all that? And I'd come up with two answers—the first was enough really—I loved Laura. The second was more selfish—it was my last chance of love. I was getting older, there wouldn't be another. If Laura didn't come back to me, then there'd be nothing but exam papers, friends, a lonely retirement. I'd grow old alone, and I didn't want that.

> Frédéric keeps telling me it's none of my business, and of course he's right. But he's also wrong, because anything that happens to

you concerns me. I'd like you not to make a big mistake, to be happy. So all I can say is, be careful, Father. Look both ways before you cross the street. . . .

Like a slender diamond bird, a plane silently glided past the window. I'd answer Anne tonight, write her a good long letter.

I rose from my seat. By now Laura's plane must have left, and suddenly I was afraid that I wouldn't be able to remember her face. Like an idiot, I didn't have a single photograph of her. Perhaps it was just as well—photographs were the privilege of sighted people. It was the same for both of us now, we would see each other only with the eyes of memory until she returned.

Outside, the sun beat down mercilessly. The metal of the car was scorching. I opened the windows to let some air in. She would come back. She'd said she would and I must believe her.

But perhaps her life over there would make her forget: a few weeks in America and Jacques Bernier, an unimportant schoolmaster on his summer holiday, would gradually fade. Besides, she might find her new work fascinating. All sorts of things might delay her return, or even prevent it forever. . . .

As I started the car a large Peugeot 404 shot out in front of me, then braked. The driver gestured his apology and waved me on. It was a miracle, the first time a member of that killer breed had ever behaved like a human being. Soon after, I passed three heavy lorries, honking my horn gaily, and turned the radio on full blast. The road ahead was clear.

Perhaps it didn't mean a thing. But I was sure then that my love, my blind beloved, would come back to me.

Patrick Cauvin

Patrick Cauvin—real name Claude Klotz—was born in Marseille in 1932. He progressed (socially as well as geographically!) to Paris when his parents bought a house there in 1938, and it was in the capital that he went to school all through the war years. He was, so he says, most definitely not an enthusiastic student.

After university he was immediately called to the colours and sent to serve his country in Algeria. The army appealed to him even less than school had done, and he enlivened the boredom of service life by doing a bit of writing: popular song lyrics, short stories, children's books. He also tried his hand as a painter, but with little success.

All things come to an end, however, even National Service. Back in civvie street at last, he suddenly discovered where his real vocation lay and became (like his hero, Jacques Bernier) a teacher of literature in a secondary school. But he continued to write in his spare time, and published several crime novels. Then, at the beginning of 1974, he wrote *Blind Love*, achieving with it an immediate international success. The book has been translated into all the principal European languages and a film based on it is already in the making.

Married, with two children, Patrick Cauvin teaches in a school on the outskirts of Paris. He is fascinated by American films, by anything to do with the sea, and by football. Unlike many novelists, he doesn't find authorship at all a difficult or mystical process: he writes quickly, in longhand, and enjoys every moment of it. His next book—about the changing relationship between a father and his young son—will soon be on its way to eager publishers throughout the world.

A
CLASSIC
OF OUR
TIME

BROWN ON RESOLUTION

a condensation of the book by

C. S. Forester

Illustrated by Michael Turner and Betty Maxey

Published by Bodley Head, London

1893 A shy naval officer, travelling from Greenwich to London, blushes as a lady in his compartment smiles at him. . . .

1914 A brave young seaman lies dying among the desolate, burning rocks of a Pacific island. . . .

The strange destiny that linked these men—and so brought destruction on the German cruiser *Ziethen*—was founded in unconventional passion and crushed by an act of extraordinary, but unselfconscious, courage. Their story, as told by C.S. Forester in this absorbing and unusual early novel, with all the genius for creating character and action that he was to show later in his books on Hornblower, has deservedly become a classic of our time.

Chapter One

Leading Seaman Albert Brown lay dying on Resolution. He was huddled in a cleft in the grey-brown lava of which that desolate island is largely composed, on his back with his knees half drawn up in his fevered delirium. Sometimes he would mumble a few meaningless words and writhe feebly onto his side, only to fall back again a second later. He was dressed in what had once been a sailor's suit of tropical white, but now it was so stained and draggled, so torn and frayed, it was only a few thin, filthy rags feebly held together.

His face was swollen and distorted, as were his hands, being quite covered with hideous lumps as a result of the poisoned bites of a myriad of flies, a cloud of which hung murderously over him. His feet, too, although a few fragments of his shoes still clung to them, were horribly swollen and bruised and cut.

Yet Albert Brown was not dying because of the biting flies, or even because of the hideous condition of his feet. For the dingy rags on his right shoulder were stained a sinister brown, those at his back were similarly stained, and his right breast was covered with a black, oozing clot of blood from a bullet wound.

Brown lay at the edge of the central portion of the island. Up above him rose the bare lava of the highest point of Resolution, a distorted muddle of naked rock bearing a million razor edges—razor edges which explained the frightful condition of his feet. Just at Brown's level, stretching along at each side (for Resolution is a hog-backed island bent into a half-moon) began the cactus, ugly, nightmarish plants, clustering together thicker and thicker on the lower slopes, each bearing a formidable armament of spikes which explained the tattered condition of Brown's clothes.

Stretched out in the scanty shade cast by the cacti, there lay iguanas—mottled crested lizards—somnolently stupid. Overhead wheeled seabirds, and occasionally a friendly mockingbird would hop close round Brown's dying body and peer at him. Down at the water's edge, where the Pacific broke against the lava boulders, there massed a herd of marine iguanas, industriously gnawing the seaweed on which they lived, while round them strayed marvellous scarlet crabs and other representatives of the amphibious life of this almost unknown member of the Galapagos Islands.

The sky above was of a glaring, metallic blue, from which a burnished sun poured a torrent of heat upon the land beneath. No trace of human life could be seen around the whole wide horizon, save only for Leading Seaman Albert Brown, huddled in his cleft, and hunger and thirst and fever and loss of blood were soon to make an end even of him. Perhaps in years to come some exploring scientist would happen across his bleached bones and would ponder over that broken rib and that smashed shoulder-blade.

IT ALL BEGAN more than twenty years earlier, with Lieutenant-Commander R. E. S. Saville-Samarez, R.N., seated in the train which was carrying him from the Royal Naval College, Greenwich, and a not very arduous course of professional study therein, towards London and a not very closely planned week of relaxation therein. He sat in his first-class carriage and looked, now at his newspaper, now out of the window, now at the lady who was seated demurely in the opposite corner of the carriage.

The commander was not much given to prolonged reading, nor to prolonged following of any one train of thought. He thought, as was only natural, of the influence of first-class certificates upon promotion, and he wondered vaguely if he would ever attain the security and authority of captain's rank with its consequent inevitable climb to the awesome heights of an admiral's position. Admirals in one way were mere commonplaces to the commander, for he came of a long line of naval ancestors, and an uncle of his was an admiral at that moment, his grandfather had commanded a ship of the line during the Crimean War, and *his* grandfather had fought at the Nile and had been an admiral during the reign of George IV.

But he did not think long about admirals for he felt restless and fidgety, and he wished that the lady was not in his carriage so that he could put his feet up on the opposite seat and smoke. He glanced across at her, and found, to his surprise, that she was contemplating him in a manner difficult to describe—detached yet friendly; certainly not in the way a lady ought to look at a man with whom she was alone in a railway carriage in the Year of Our Lord 1893. The commander was quite startled; he looked away, but his eyes strayed back stealthily as soon as he was sure her gaze was averted. No, she was not at all *that* sort—no one could be with that placid, calm look. But she was a fine woman, with her stylish sailor hat and her smart costume with its leg-of-mutton sleeves. As he looked, she turned and met his gaze again, and he flushed with shy embarrassment down his sunburnt neck and hurriedly looked out of the window. But once again his eyes stole back, inevitably. And she was smiling at him.

Agatha Brown's father was a Nonconformist greengrocer; but, as his Nonconformist friends would hurriedly explain when speaking of him, a greengrocer in a very large line of business. His big shop at Lewisham employed a dozen assistants, and he had two other shops besides. Long ago he had climbed high enough to leave off living over his shop and to take instead a substantial house beside Greenwich Park. Here he lived with his three sons and his daughter (his eldest child) who managed the house in the efficient and gracious manner possible in that era. His wife was dead and much regretted, but, thanks to Agatha's domestic efficiency, not greatly missed in the economic sphere.

That morning Agatha had risen as usual at six-thirty, and had helped one maid with the breakfast while the other looked to the fires. She had poured out tea for Will and Harry and sat at table with them while they hurried through breakfast, and had closed her eyes and clasped her hands devoutly when Dad, having come back with George in the trap from market, read prayers, what time the other two stood impatiently waiting to get off to their business of managing the shops at Woolwich and Deptford. Then Dad, too, ate his breakfast, and read his newspaper, and of course being preoccupied with that could not attend properly to his table manners. He drank his tea, noisily, through his moustache, and although Agatha had listened to the performance daily for twenty-nine years somehow on that particular day she found it unusually distasteful. She told herself that it was time she had a change, and realized that although she was that very day going for five days' stay with a bosom friend at Ealing, that amount of change would not suffice her. Her first reaction was to promise herself a dose of senna that evening (senna was Agatha's prescription for all the ills flesh is heir to) and her second was to consider senna inadequate. Only slightly introspective though she was, Agatha found herself surprised at being in such an odd frame of mind.

Then when Dad had taken his departure Agatha had busied herself with the stupendous task of leaving everything in the house prepared for her five days' absence. When she left the house at four o'clock with her little suitcase, she felt lighthearted and carefree; the tingle of her clean starched underlinen was pleasant to her; she was free of the house and all its troubles for five whole days. But all the same she did not want to spend five days at the home of Adeline Burton at Ealing. The Burton household was very like the Brown household, when all was said and done. And then she found herself in the same carriage as Lieutenant-Commander R. E. S. Saville-Samarez.

She liked him at first sight, and at first sight she knew him for what he was, a naval officer of the best brand of British stupidity. She liked his good clothes and his smooth cheeks (Agatha, as she regarded these last, felt a revulsion of feeling against the fashionable hairiness of 1893). She knew he would speak to her soon, and she knew she would answer him.

Agatha's smile set the coping-stone on Samarez's unsettledness. His hands fluttered to his pockets.

"Mind if I smoke?" he asked hoarsely.

"Not at all," said Agatha. "I should like it."

That, of course, was at least four words more than any lady ought to have said. Samarez feverishly pulled out his silver cigarette case and matchbox, lit a cigarette and drew a deep lungful of smoke in an unthinking effort after self-control.

Agatha was still smiling at him, a placid, innocent smile. Samarez simply had to go on talking to her, and the Englishman's invariable opening topic came to his lips.

"Beastly weather," he said, with a nod through the carriage window, where February sunshine fought a losing battle against February gloom.

"I rather like it, somehow," said Agatha. "Of course, you find it very different from the tropics," she went on, to Samarez's amazement. How on earth could she tell he had been to the tropics?

"Er—yes," he said. "Beastly hot there, sometimes."

"China station?" she asked. Agatha's knowledge of the Navy was only what might be expected of a secluded young woman, but she had heard the blessed words "China station" somewhere and they drifted into her mind now and were seized upon gratefully.

"Yes," said Samarez, more amazed than ever, "that was my last commission."

The China station was a pleasant source of conversation. Thanks to the exaltation of her mood, Agatha was able to talk—or rather to induce Samarez to talk—without displaying any annoying ignorance, and by the blessing of Providence they chatted really amicably. Samarez's heart warmed to this charming woman, so refined, so friendly without being cheap, with such a musical contralto voice and such a ready laugh. When they reached London Bridge Samarez realized with a little chill of disappointment that in a few more minutes he would have to separate from this friend.

Friends at the moment were scarce. Samarez had a week's leave on his hands, and he was almost at a loss as to how to employ it. On the China station, stifling under the awnings, the most delectable spot on earth had appeared to be the dining-room of the Junior Army and Navy Club, but now it did not seem half so attractive. Above all, Agatha Brown was a woman. Samarez had at present nothing more in his mind but companionship. He wanted to talk to a woman, and so far women had not counted for much in Samarez's life.

They rattled through Waterloo Junction, and now were rumbling on to Charing Cross railway bridge. Through the window he could see the wide, grey river, and the lights of Charing Cross Station were close at hand. Agatha glanced up at her suitcase in the rack, in evident mental preparation for departure. Samarez stood up in the swaying carriage; his hands flapped with embarrassment.

"L-look here," he said, "we don't want to say goodbye yet. Let's—let's have dinner somewhere."

He stood holding to the luggage rack, appalled by the realization that he was guilty (if the lady chose to find him so) of an ungentlemanly action. His innocent eyes pleaded for him. And Agatha's eyes softened; for he was so like an artless little boy begging for more cake. She felt motherly and not a bit daring as she said yes.

Once out of the train Samarez, despite his elation, displayed all the orderly logic of the disciplined man of action. Agatha's suitcase and his own leather kit-bag were ticketed-in at the cloakroom, a cab was summoned, and with a flash of brilliance he recalled the name of the one restaurant which in those days was suitable for ladies and tolerant of morning dress. The cab-horse's hoofs clattered across the station courtyard and out into the Strand, and they sat side by side as the lamps went by.

Pleasant it was, and each was conscious of a comforting warmth from the other. Each felt supremely befriended and deliciously expectant—of what they could not say. The drive passed far too quickly; to Agatha it hardly seemed a moment before she found herself being helped from the cab by the restaurant porter.

From opposite sides of the table each regarded the other. It was too good to be true, for the one that he should be sitting with a woman of good sense and irreproachable morals (to a sailor such an encounter is all too rare an occurrence), and for the other that she should be in a restaurant at all (this was nearly Agatha's first experience of restaurants) let alone with a clean-bred, good-looking young man. Samarez ordered a good dinner and summoned the wine waiter. The very mention of the word "wine" caused Agatha to start a little, for the worthy Mr. Brown was a staunch, even violent abstainer. But here of course, amid the gilding and the gay people and the supple-backed waiters, it was all different.

Dinner passed by in a delicious dream. Agatha's acquaintance with food so far had been of the roast beef and apple tart order. When she consulted Mrs. Beeton, it had been for the purpose of designing substantial meals for the hearty Browns, and the refinements of foods had passed Agatha by, so that now each succeeding course came as a new and delicious revelation. Not even the necessity of tactfully observing which implements Samarez employed and imitating him could mar her enjoyment, and the wine, warming and heartening, was the finishing touch.

She leant forward towards Samarez and talked without a care, and he talked back with what seemed to him to be positively dazzling wit. Once or twice his head went back and he chuckled deep down in his chest with wrinkles round his eyes in a manner which brought a pain into Agatha's breast, and made her long to stretch out her barren arms and draw his rough head down to her bosom. She imagined herself rubbing her cheek against his short rebellious hair, and the mere thought turned her faint with a strangely maternal longing.

"Well, I'm blest," said the commander suddenly. "Do you know, I've been talking to you all this time and I don't even know your name."

"It's Agatha," said Agatha—that much of her name was tolerable to her, although the "Brown" always rankled—"and I don't know yours either."

Samarez hesitated for one regretted second; he was sure that it was unwise to tell one's name to a strange woman, but this woman was so different.

"It's a very long one," he said, "but it begins with Richard."

"I shall call you Dickie," said Agatha decidedly, and she finished her coffee as though to seal the bargain.

So dinner was finished, and they had no possible excuse for lingering. Yet both of them were most desperately unwilling to part. Their eyes met again and again across the table, and conversation died. Fate simply forced them, with sinking hearts, to rise from the table. Samarez waited for her in the foyer in a restless and unsettled state of mind.

And Agatha, adjusting her veil in the cloakroom, felt on the verge of tears. It was past seven o'clock and she really must reach Ealing and the Burtons' by nine at the latest; and most emphatically she did not want to leave Dickie. But she had not the faintest idea what she did want.

At the door circumstances forced them further towards separation.

"Cab, I suppose?" said Samarez huskily.

They climbed into a four-wheeler, and Samarez, still retaining a grain of sanity, directed the driver to Charing Cross Station. Agatha had clean forgotten the luggage left there. Restlessly Samarez took off his hat and wiped his forehead. A passing street lamp lit up his boyish face and his rumpled hair.

"Oh," said Agatha uncontrollably. One hand went to his shoulder, the other fumbled for his lean brown hand in the darkness. Samarez turned clumsily with his arms out to her, and all their unhappiness melted away under their wild kisses.

Chapter Two

It was the lights at the courtyard entrance of Charing Cross which brought them back momentarily to reality. Agatha's face was wet with tears, her hat hung by one hatpin, as their embrace came to an end. The cab halted outside the station and a porter tore open the door.

"I—I can't get out," stammered Agatha, shrinking away into a corner.

Samarez climbed out and shut the door.

"Wait!" he flung at the driver, and pelted into the station. It was only a matter of seconds before he came back, suitcase and kit-bag in hand. He opened the door of the cab, and Agatha came to life again out of her mazed dream.

"Where to, sir?" asked the cab driver.

"Where to?" echoed Samarez stupidly.

"I don't know—Ealing, I suppose," said a little voice from the depths of the cab.

"Ealing," said Samarez to the cab driver.

"Ealing, sir? Ealing Broadway, sir? Right, sir," said the cab driver, and the door slammed to, with Samarez and Agatha in blessed solitude once more.

Passion had them greatly in thrall. Agatha's hat came off and the tears flowed freely from her eyes as she pressed against Samarez with all the abandon her corseted waist permitted. Agatha had forgotten she was twenty-nine, of strict Wesleyan upbringing. Years of bottled-up emotion were tearing her to pieces. Somehow or other she found herself speaking, her hands on his breast and her face lifted to his.

"Of course, I've *got* to go to Ealing," she said. It was a statement made in the hope of contradiction.

"What are you going to do there?" asked Samarez.

"I'm going to stay with friends. They're expecting me."

The little voice whispering in the darkness added fresh fuel to the flames of Samarez's passion. Into the back of his mind leapt the sudden realization that in the cab lay her luggage and his, all their necessaries for days.

"Can't you put them off?" he asked, hardly realizing what he was saying. "Send them a wire. Don't go."

"Oh, my *dear*," came the answering whisper.

Samarez leaned out of the window and redirected the cabman.

When they arrived at the hotel the porter was discreet; the reception clerk was friendly; in fact, no one in the hotel thought twice about them, because Agatha looked the last person in the world to share a bedroom with a man who was not her husband, and her glove concealed the absence of a wedding ring. In the dignified seclusion of the hotel bedroom Samarez's enforced calm fell away. He opened his arms to her and she came gladly to them, giving herself with a delicious, cool relaxation. She felt fantastically motherly towards this tousle-headed boy even during his greediest caresses, and when he sighed out his content with his face upon her bosom she clasped him against it with the same gesture as she would have used to a child.

And the next day, and the day after, and the day after that this maternal attitude became more and more marked. No twinge of conscience came to ruffle the serenity of her soul; she was flooded with a sense of well-being that was not diminished by the necessity for writing to Adeline Burton a careful letter explaining that an unforeseen domestic crisis had compelled her reluctantly to postpone her visit at such brief notice. Agatha would come some other time, as soon as she could, if Adeline did not mind. The lies which Agatha wrote flowed so naturally from her pen that she did not give them a thought.

Samarez, on the other hand, was somewhat troubled of conscience on those occasions when it occurred to him what he was doing. Agatha had a blossoming innocence which she displayed at every moment. She clearly had not even toyed with the idea of dallying with men. Her underclothing proved that, if nothing else did. It was exquisitely neat, with a myriad tucks and gatherings, but it was not to be called frivolous. She was a respectable member of a respectable family, who had bestowed her virginity on him just as she might have given half a crown to a beggar. It made Samarez queerly uncomfortable. And yet, after three days' intimacy, she was far less attainable than ever before. Something was still out of reach, and he was piqued in consequence. He tried to buy presents for her, to lavish money on her for clothes and jewellery, but whenever he tried she put the suggestion aside with a smiling negative. Samarez was not to know that Agatha's main reason for refusal was the impossibility of subsequently explaining away these gifts to her family.

So it was with a queer mixture of pique and gentlemanly feeling that, after three days, Samarez proposed marriage to her. He did not want to; he held the strongest possible opinion regarding the unsuitability of marriage for naval officers, and he did not believe in marriage much, anyway. But he proposed, and as he did so he regarded her anxiously, at the same moment annoyed with himself for throwing away his future and comforted by the knowledge that he was doing the "right thing" And Agatha, her hands on his shoulders, looked deep into those anxious eyes before she slowly shook her head.

"No, Dickie," she said, "it would be better if we didn't. But it was awfully nice of you to ask me."

Although she was keenly alive to the extent of the sacrifice Samarez had proposed making, she saw the unwisdom of marrying a man whom one only loved as one might love a pet St. Bernard.

So that after five days the affair came to an end. Five days during which Agatha had had a glimpse of the sort of life led by women who are not greengrocers' daughters; of good food, of leisure, of ample spending. Truth to tell, the waste of money and time, by the end of the five days, had so worked upon Agatha's mind that she was quite glad of the prospect of returning home to economical housekeeping and domestic industry. And Samarez had begun to cease to interest her—he was not a tremendously interesting fellow, as a matter of fact.

Yet the parting was painful. Samarez clung to her as they kissed goodbye in the hotel bedroom, with his hand to her breast. Agatha's eyes were wet, although she realized she was doing the sensible thing, and it was very gently that she put his hands aside. He held her hand in the cab as they drove to Charing Cross, and he even tried to make one last appeal after she had boarded the train for Greenwich. She only shook her head and smiled, however, and two minutes later Samarez was alone on the platform, watching the train round the bend in the distance, trying obstinately not to feel relieved.

Chapter Three

Agatha arrived home to find everything quite normal. No hint had reached the Browns that she had not been staying with the Burtons, and she told one or two placid lies which gave a little local colour to the idea that she had been there. Her exalted mood died away.

Within a week it seemed incredible to her that she could have been guilty of such terrible conduct; she had forgotten the state of mind which had led her into it; she felt and hoped that it had only been a very vivid and shocking dream. She ceased in consequence to carry the ring Samarez had bought her on the ribbon round her neck.

Yet very soon she became actively aware that it could not have been a dream. For a time she thrust her fears behind her and went on grimly with her household affairs, but they continually recurred to her. She was worried about them, and uncertain of what she ought to do. She knew Samarez's name and ship (of course she would!) and for a moment thought of writing to him, but she put the idea aside as unworthy. But as the symptoms became unmistakable and she began to fear discovery she grew more worried, and it was a positive relief when the storm broke. Mr. Brown came home one day at five—rather earlier than his usual time.

"I want to talk to you," he said.

"Well?" said Agatha, quite calm now that the crisis had come.

"I met Burton this afternoon, quite by accident. And he said what a pity it was you weren't able to go over to Ealing and stay there the last time it was arranged."

Mr. Brown stared at his daughter from under his heavy eyebrows. The thing was incredible to him—and yet—and yet. . . . His doubts led him to work himself up into a rage.

"Didn't you tell me last February you were going to stay there, and didn't you come back and say you had?" he blared.

"Yes," said Agatha.

"Well, where did you get to? Where the *devil* did you get to?"

Agatha made no reply.

"You made me look such a bleedin' fool when Burton said that to me," raved Mr. Brown—the adjective showed he was nearly beside himself. "Where the devil did you get to? Was—was it a *man*?" he demanded. "Tell me this minute, girl."

Agatha knew it was no use telling Mr. Brown about Samarez. He wouldn't understand. She didn't understand herself.

"My God, it was!" said Mr. Brown. "Who was it? Tell me, or I'll—"

"It wasn't anybody you know, Dad," said Agatha.

"Damned if I care. Tell me his name and I'll find him. I'll teach him."

"No you won't, Dad. I won't tell you."

"You won't? We'll see, my girl."

"Yes, we'll see," said Agatha. Her old exalted mood was coming over her again, leaving her outwardly calm but inwardly rejoicing. Mr. Brown stared at her serene face, and his rage simmered down into incredulous astonishment.

"But he didn't do you any *harm*, Aggie, old girl, did he?" wheedled Mr. Brown.

Agatha met his eyes, and nodded with certitude.

"You would say he did, Dad," said Agatha.

The flush of Mr. Brown's anger gave way to a yellow pallor. His very bulk as he sat in his chair seemed to diminish.

"What am I to do?" he pleaded. "Whatever will the Chapel say?" Upon Mr. Brown dawned the awful realization that despite his three shops and his fine house, the Chapel would find huge stores of food for gossip in this catastrophe. The finger of scorn would be pointed at him; nevermore would the proud privilege be his of passing round the plate at morning service.

The arrival of his two eldest sons prolonged the discussion. Will and Harry were brimful of the ferocious energy which had carried their father to such heights in the world of greengrocery, and, unlike him, they were still young and able to reach instant, Napoleonic decisions.

"People mustn't know about it," said Will positively, "that's certain. Agatha will have to go away for the—as soon as it's necessary. We'll have to say she's gone to stay with friends."

"That's it," chimed in Harry, "and the . . . the child will have to be boarded out when she comes back."

The three of them looked to Agatha for agreement, and found none. Her face was as though cut in stone.

"No," she said, "I won't have him boarded out. I'm going to be with him, always."

The pronoun she used displayed her silly, baseless hope that her child would be a son, but it passed unnoticed.

"Don't be silly," said Harry, with immense scorn.

"You'll have to do what you're told," sneered Will. "Beggars can't be—"

Will's speech broke off short as he caught sight of a flash of triumph in Agatha's face, and was reminded by it of a forgotten factor. He met the eyes of his father and his brother with some uneasiness.

For fifteen years ago, when Mr. Brown had just begun to be successful in business, he had followed the prudent example of thousands of others by investing his savings in house property and deeding it over to his wife. It was a wise precaution, ensuring the possession of capital and the necessaries of life even if bankruptcy were to strip Mr. Brown nominally of all he possessed. Mr. Brown had seen to it that his wife made a will in his favour, and had thought no more about it. But on his wife's death a wretched pettifogging lawyer from the purlieus of Deptford had produced a will of more recent date (made, in fact, as soon as Mrs. Brown was aware of the cancer which would cause her death) by which all her property was left to her daughter Agatha. It had been Mrs. Brown's one exceptional action in life and had been undoubtedly inspired by the desire to render Agatha free of that dependence upon mankind which even Victorian ladies found so exasperating on occasion.

Dad and the boys, as soon as they had recovered from their astonishment, had tried to laugh the matter off. Dad had gone on collecting the weekly rents of the six houses in Beaconsfield Terrace as usual, and as usual had devoted them to his own purposes without rendering account. But those houses were Agatha's all the same, as was the hundred pounds a year clear which they brought in. Will and Harry and Mr. Brown looked at each other with an uneasy suspicion of defeat.

"I'm not a beggar," said Agatha, "so I *can* be a chooser if I like. I'm going to live with my boy wherever I like."

Will boiled over with rage at being thus contemptuously treated by a mere woman—and especially at the thought of all that goodly money being taken out of the family. For a second or two brother and sister stood and glared at each other. But Agatha rallied all her waning moral strength, turned away and walked slowly from the room.

Upstairs in her bedroom she packed with calm, unthinking deliberation the suitcase which had accompanied her on that wonderful trip to London nearly three months before. She included her jewel case with her few petty pieces of jewellery; then, struck by a sudden thought, she opened it again, took out the wedding ring Samarez had bought her, and slipped it onto the third finger of her left hand. Then, suitcase in hand, she descended the stairs and walked slowly to the front door. She opened the door and went out down the pretentious, tiny carriage drive and turned left towards the station. When she reached the station and found there was no up train for half an hour she could not bring herself to wait; instead she boarded the down train and travelled on it for a couple of stations, and then changed trains and returned back through Greenwich. And so Will and Harry, sent out to make peace at any price by a despairing Dad ten minutes after she had left the house, quite missed her.

Chapter Four

So it was that at midsummer, 1893, a pleasant-faced widow, Mrs. Agatha Brown, came to live in lodgings at Peckham. Her sympathetic landlady soon knew all about her—about the husband, rather a bad lot, seemingly, who had been in the greengrocery trade and had died suddenly of some rather vague disease, but leaving his widow well provided for by the standards of that place and time; about the happy event which was to be expected shortly; about her general friendlessness and the dislike with which her late husband's family regarded her for intercepting the legacies they had come to look upon as their due. Mrs. Rodgers became a great admirer of Mrs. Brown. Mrs. Brown had round her that tremendous aura of "independent means" which implies so much to a working-class dependent for its daily bread upon the whim of an employer. Mrs. Brown paid splendidly regular money for her furnished rooms, but she paid only a tiny amount more than the lowest market value, so that contempt could not creep in to adulterate Mrs. Rodgers's admiration. Mrs. Brown always knew how much of her butter and tea and other supplies she had left, so that Mrs. Rodgers's first tentative stealings were calmly checked. Mrs.

Rodgers bore no ill will—quite the contrary. She was soon a very subservient ally.

Mr. Deane, too, who had drawn up the astonishing will, was very helpful and kind. He shook his head sympathetically when Agatha told him about family trouble which had led her to leave home, and he readily consented to take upon himself the management of Agatha's six houses in Beaconsfield Terrace. He looked up sharply when Agatha explained that at her new address she was known as Mrs. Brown, and when he noticed the expression on her face he pulled his white whiskers and looked down at his notes again in embarrassed fashion.

Agatha had drifted to 37 Colchester Street, Peckham, as a result of a brief examination of the small advertisements in the local paper; it was the first address she had called at, and she was satisfied. She also went to the local doctor for examination and decision on her condition. Doctor Walters's verdict was in agreement with her own. He, too, looked at her sharply, guessing shrewdly that there was more in her history than she was likely to tell him. But he did all his duty and more; he prescribed a regimen for her, gave her information on points of which she was quite ignorant, and finally obtained for her two or three books which more or less gave her guidance towards the approaching great event.

In the nineties expectant mothers were treated as invalids; the books took it for granted that Agatha would be really unwell, whereas she had never felt better in her life. But she took the written word for gospel, and therefore sat carefully by a closed window and watched the petty pageant of the streets while she stitched and stitched and dreamed in all the unreality of occupied idleness.

For, although the books assumed her to be an invalid, they offered some compensation at least in the array of garments they prescribed as necessary for the "little stranger". This "little stranger" had to have binders, matinée jackets, veils and shawls and a christening gown, socks and gloves, daygowns and night-gowns of flannel exquisitely embroidered in silk—and Agatha made every blessed thing herself, stitching away patiently by the window.

There was another matter in which she took an interest, though. One day while casually glancing through the newspaper a name caught her eye, and with a slight sense of shock she looked again. The name was that of Lieutenant-Commander R. E. S. Saville-Samarez, and it occurred halfway down a list headed "Naval Appointments". Agatha had not realized before that by the aid of this list she would be able to follow Samarez's professional career, and the discovery stimulated her attention. She found there was another column which sometimes appeared, headed "Movements of H.M. Ships", and thus she could trace Samarez wherever the Lords of Admiralty might send him.

Day passed after day, and week after week. It called for quite an effort to make herself realize that her time was at hand. But within the last few weeks a new portent had appeared in Salisbury Road, next to Colchester Road. A board had spread itself there, bearing the legend, "Nursing Home—Surgical, General, Maternity"

Agatha made her arrangements with Doctor Walters's full approval; for the doctor, with happy memories of hospital experience and trained assistance and proper appliances, was thoroughly dissatisfied with the makeshifts he usually had to employ in practice.

So it was with a strange excited feeling that one day Agatha walked round to the Salisbury Nursing Home with Mrs. Rodgers at her side, carrying the historic suitcase. Agatha liked it all: she liked the bare, clean rooms and the trim, efficient nurses and the cheerfully unsympathetic aspect of the place, for Agatha was mostly of a Spartan turn of mind.

The grit that had carried her father from errand-running to wholesaling took Agatha into maternity without a tremor or a regret. The slight pains came; Doctor Walters called, was unhesitatingly cheerful, and went away again. And then the real pains came, wave after wave of them, so that she found herself flung into a sea of pain of an intensity she had not believed possible.

Then it was all over and she was free to hold her child on her arm for a few wonderful minutes. It was a boy of course.

Chapter Five

She called him Albert; goodness knows why. She had hesitated over "George", but had put it aside in case she ever encountered her family again. George was her father's name, as well as her favourite brother's, and she would not have them think that the child was called after them. Albert was all her own; she knew personally no one of that name at all, and perhaps this satisfied her jealous desire for possession, while about the name there clung a flavour of association with the Royal Family which endeared it to her rather bourgeois little heart.

Agatha returned to 37 Colchester Road. It was comfortable and she did not want to seek out a new resting place. Moreover, she soon began to establish a business connection in the locality. Albert's marvellous garments were the admiration of all who saw them, and the tale of them was told round about. It was not long before Agatha received tentative inquiries as to whether she would mind making similar things for other Peckham babies. Agatha had found that even the labour of looking after the finest baby in England left her with much free time, and idleness was abhorrent to her. She accepted commissions eagerly, and it was not long before she found that she had little spare time left. There was not much profit to be made, but still there was a little, and Agatha, although she had found it easy enough to live on a hundred pounds a year, was eager to increase her income and accumulate savings. Mr. Deane, the solicitor, had looked at her incredulously when she had told him it was her intention to make Albert an officer in the Navy; he had declaimed in his soft-spoken way at the expense as a waste of money, but Agatha cherished the ambition none the less. She set her round chin firmer still and bent to her sewing with renewed forcefulness.

So Albert Brown grew up in a world of many sections. Upstairs there was his mother, who spoke to him softly and clearly, and whom he knew by experience it was best to obey promptly. On the other hand, he knew that if he could manage the perilous descent of the stairs there would be a warm welcome for him from Mrs.

Rodgers, who was always ready with a word, or a piece of bread and butter covered with brown sugar, or an unimaginative although ready part in whatever game he chose to devise. Yet Mrs. Rodgers, with all her endearments, did not bulk one half as large in Albert's affection as did his mother, who played games really well, and who read entrancing books to him, and whose voice, with its sweetness and purity of intonation, was worth a thousand times as much as Mrs. Rodgers's hoarse utterance. Outside the house there was the Street with its myriad attractions—the carts with their big horses, hides glistening and nosebags tossing; and errand boys and sweeps and road-mending gangs. Beyond the Street was the Park, where little boys could run madly up and down and hoot and scream and look at the boats on the pond and make friends with stray dogs and gallop back to where Mother was sitting. The Park and the Street and Upstairs and Downstairs were all exceedingly splendid places, and if the earthrending unhappiness of childhood ever got a grip on you then there was always Mother's sweet-scented breast on which to pour out your woes and Mother's soft arms to go round you. Soon the world had a fifth quarter, which was School, presided over by a deity called Miss Farrow, who on terrible occasions wielded the cane with dreadful results upon such small boys as dared to be naughty.

Watching the development of her child with all the terrible detachment of a mother born to be gushingly affectionate and restrained by a hot ambition, Agatha came early to the conclusion that her son was not of greatly above the average brains, and much more amenable to discipline than ever she could picture Nelson or Drake to be in their childhood. He was in fact orderly and law-abiding. She felt a little twinge of disappointment; surely a child so lawlessly conceived ought to be vastly different from the ordinary herd! But her plans, so often lovingly revised before Albert's arrival, were easily capable of covering even this state of affairs. The calm foresight of a woman with only herself and her child to consider began to plan a new system of training aimed at guiding young Albert's footsteps with security along the thorny road of Admiralty.

Perhaps if Albert's father had been a stockbroker Agatha's

thoughts would have been directed towards stocks and shares. As it was, the fact that he was an officer in the Royal Navy gave her the first necessary impetus towards adopting the Navy as her hobby. Chance had shown her how to study naval appointments and movements in newspapers; and from this it was but a step to those books of reference which described every fighting ship in the world, and in which she could study each successive ship to which Samarez was appointed. It was not long before Agatha had quite a knowledge of armaments and tonnages and displacements. The Library had all sorts of books to interest her; she read "Lives" of various admirals, and naval histories, and *Letters of Lord Nelson*. With pathetic cunning she began to lead young Albert's thoughts in the same direction. If Albert had no genius, then orderly training and astute education of taste might serve the same purpose.

Mr. Deane, the solicitor, could not understand Agatha's repeated demands that he should ascertain for her the conditions of entry on *Britannia*, and the costs of a naval education. He ventured to point out that if Agatha persisted in her decision to send young Albert to the Navy she could count him lost to her from the age of twelve. Agatha fully realized it already, and set her jaw as she told him so. Agatha believed that self-sacrifice was the primary duty of mankind; that man (and much more so woman) was born to sorrow; and that she should give up her child seemed to her right and proper, especially if the Navy benefited. The British Navy was to her the noblest creation in the world. Mr. Deane sighed impatiently; he had been brought up in a world where women never had any ideas of their own and never, never dreamed of acting contrary to masculine advice.

Perhaps it was this impatience of his which impelled him along the steep and slippery road on which his footsteps were even then straying. Perhaps he could not bear to see good money wasted on Albert Brown, and he embezzled it as the only method of prevention. Joking apart, Agatha's insistence must really be taken into account in estimating the circumstances of the misdeeds of that venerable old hypocrite.

Temptation certainly came his way. A whole series of road improvements and tramway extensions had led to the sale of a great deal of house property lately—Agatha's included. Mr. Deane found himself in charge temporarily of a large amount of his clients' capital. Mr. Deane—the awful truth appeared later—led two lives, one in the company of a damsel of a class which the newspapers sometimes designated as "fair Cyprians". Mr. Deane's expenses were naturally in excess of his income. Mr. Deane endeavoured to right such a state of affairs by tactful speculation, and selected the South African market as the field of his activities. Mr. Deane lost money, for South African securities slumped heavily before the threat of war. Mr. Deane shrank from the thought of suicide, or of prison and poverty, so he gathered together what remained of his clients' negotiable assets and departed for Callao, accompanied by the fair Cyprian. The Official Receiver found much work to do in clearing up the ruin left by Mr. Deane.

Agatha's money had nearly all vanished. The Official Receiver sorted out for her a tiny fraction of the original capital, but it was woefully small. Agatha set her lips and turned with energy into continuing her life's work, still without reference to her family. She would not go back to them, nor crave their help. She would not have them say, "I told you so". The fine sewing which she had done before to earn luxuries now was called upon to supply necessities. Lucky it was that she had built up a connection, and that not much further effort was needed to establish herself in the good graces of the local big drapers and gain herself a small but assured market. No *Britannia* for Albert now, alas.

So fine sewing continued to earn the daily bread of Agatha and Albert. One more set of plans had to be devised for Albert's future. If he was not to receive a commission in the usual way then he must gain one in the unusual way. Commissions sometimes were gained by the lower deck, so Albert must begin as a seaman and work his way upward. If he started with sound ideas on his profession, with enthusiasm and a good general education, it might well come about. Agatha kept money in the bank against that day, when he would need an outfit and some money to spend, and flung herself with ardour into the business of providing Albert with the grounding she thought necessary.

That was easy enough, for Albert was an amenable little boy. A board-school education was of course all his mother could afford for him, but a board-school education backed up by strong home influence will do as much for any boy up to eleven years of age as any other form of education. So that even while Agatha was entering upon the study of the higher aspects of Sea Power she was at the same time helping Albert with his sums and beginning his first tentative introduction to Drake and Nelson.

Tentative indeed, for Agatha found it impossible to bestow upon Albert the high dramatic insight which infused her dreams. Ships were just ships to ten-year-old Albert. He could not be impressed by the mighty pageant of England's naval history. The Nile and Trafalgar were to him mere affairs where Englishmen asserted their natural superiority over Frenchmen. He was a matter-of-fact young man, and Agatha duly realized the fact with vague disappointment. Even Agatha, with all her dreams and insight, could not foresee the sprouting of the grain she was sowing in such seemingly inhospitable soil.

Chapter Six

So years followed years and each succeeding year dragged more heavily and more painfully than did the one before. To Agatha it seemed as if retribution was being exacted from her for her sin. Fine sewing sank steadily in value; private customers fell away—a falling marriage rate and birth rate broke her on their wheel. The shops which had first bought her output had grown larger and had amalgamated, and gradually she was squeezed out from supplying them. Agatha's earnings grew smaller, and there were often weeks when she had to draw upon her hoarded capital to meet Mrs. Rodgers's weekly bill.

Nor was this all. Physical pain had come into her life. Sometimes it was slight, and Agatha could seemingly set it aside unnoticed. But at the other times it was sharper and more intense.

It had begun to come upon her when Albert was eleven, when he had grown into a thickset freckled boy with unruly hair just like his father's. He had done more than his masters had expected of him by winning a scholarship and proceeding from the Council School to a Secondary School. Agatha's careful supervision of his studies thus bore its first fruit. She was proud of his progress even while she had to reconcile herself to the fact that he was only an ordinary little boy—just as his father must have been.

When the pain came upon her, she tried to accept it in the philosophic spirit with which she had accepted all the other buffetings of Fate. Pain was natural to a woman at her time of life. She lost her smooth, placid good looks. Her cheeks fell inwards and her mouth compressed itself into a harder line. Wrinkles came between her eyebrows as a result of the continual distortion of her forehead during the agonizing bursts of pain.

Young Albert, full of the pressing and immediate interests of a new school, did not notice the gradual change which came over his mother. He did not even notice at first his mother's unaccountable fits of sudden abstraction and convulsive gripping of the arms of her chair.

But there came a time when even Agatha could no longer endure the torment, nor explain it to herself as natural in a woman of forty-three. For the second time in her life she yielded up her body to Doctor Walters's anxious examination and for the second time listened to his verdict. A different verdict this time, delivered sadly instead of jovially. Even as he spoke Agatha realized that what he was saying was not news to her—it only voiced a fact she had refused to admit to herself. Doctor Walters's heart was wrung with pity. He told her what he had found, told her of the operation which would be necessary—and strove to keep from his voice any hint of what he knew would be the end even after the operation. Agatha unflinchingly looked him in the face as he spoke; it was Doctor Walters who avoided a meeting of the eyes.

So Albert came home from school to a new world, a world where Mrs. Rodgers had to deputize for a mother who was in hospital. He went on at school, but now his Wednesday and Saturday afternoons were spent on journeys to the hospital and in a few fleeting, worried minutes in a chair beside his mother's bed.

She died hard, died game, as befitted the daughter of a self-made man. She rallied round despite the fearful things they did to her with knives. There was one afternoon when she stretched her arm out suddenly from the bedclothes (a frightening arm; suffering had stripped the smooth flesh from it and left it a skinny bundle of bones and tendons) and pointed at him.

"Albert," she said, "Albert, you know about the Navy? You know you're going to join the Navy?"

"Of course, Mother," said Albert.

"Promise me, then, boy," said Agatha.

"Of course I will, Mother. Of course."

Next time Albert came he found a feebler, stranger mother still. She did not know him. Opium had her. Each succeeding visit found her muttering and dreamy. Agatha's life went out of her while she floated above a vast grey sea sombrely tinted with opium, while around her loomed up the immense silhouettes of the battle squadrons, the grey, craggy citadels of England's glory and hope. Their funnel smoke swirled round her, veiling the worried freckled face of the child of her sin, and she smiled happily.

Chapter Seven

Albert, now aged fourteen and a half, could not join the Navy until he was fifteen and a quarter. He said goodbye to his school with hardly a twinge of regret; he had early been impregnated with Agatha's fatalistic tendencies and he could accept the inevitable without complaint. Totally without introspection and without much notice for the circumstances in which he found himself, he was never more than vaguely unhappy during the following nine months.

The school sympathetically found him an office boy's position with a City firm. The only part of his life that he really hated was the bowler hat which convention compelled him to wear, even at fourteen years old, and it was not until afterwards that he realized how much he detested everything connected with an office boy's life. He swept out the front office, he filled inkwells, he took messages, painfully learning his way about London in the process; he copied letters; he experienced the endless boredom and occasional fierce spasms of work which everyone in an office experiences. And since ordinary diligence and honesty were habitual to him and he had good average brains, he was looked upon with approving eyes, and after six months his wages were raised from five shillings a week to seven and sixpence. This official recognition gave him no thrill; office life was a mere marking of time before he took the tremendous stride towards the goal he not merely desired, but considered inevitable.

When Albert Brown was fifteen years and three months old all but one week he approached the chief clerk and gave him the week's notice which the law demanded. The chief clerk looked Albert up and down and whistled softly in surprise.

"What in hell do you want to leave for?" he demanded. "Or are you just playing up for another rise?"

"Don't want a rise," said Albert. "I only want to give notice."

"Well, you *are* a looney," decided the chief clerk. "You're getting on well. In another six months you'll be junior clerk here. Why do you want to leave?"

"I'm going to join the Navy," said Albert.

"Whe-e-e-ew," said the chief clerk; he was certain that Albert was crazy.

Authority at Whitehall, when Albert presented himself, received him with open arms. This was the kind of stuff they needed for the Navy—an orphan without a relation in the world, and a sturdy, well-set-up young man of undoubted physique. Educated too, with the very best of characters from his school and the City office. Albert's birth certificate (Agatha, fifteen years ago had rendered herself, unknowingly, liable to imprisonment on account of a false declaration to the registrar) was duly inspected and passed. He had no legal guardian and no next-of-kin. That was all quite uninteresting; the Navy of course did not know (neither did Albert) that Albert Brown was the only son of Captain Richard E. S. Saville-Samarez, C.B., M.V.O.

Yet, however it was, Albert was a man of mark after six months at Shotley Barracks. His was not an original mind, but a Secondary

School education which had gone as far as the beginnings of trigonometry and mechanics was not common at Shotley. Albert had the natural self-containedness of the only child; he was accustomed to independent action; even those hated months in the City office had served their turn in broadening his mind and accustoming him to keeping his head in encounters with strangers. His memory was good, and little of the hard-earned knowledge gained at school had faded during his City life. The very elementary mathematics taught at Shotley were child's play to him. The severely practical instruction in seamanship was a joy to his logical mind and his fingers were deft in their work and powerful when strength was demanded.

Albert's career moved logically onward through musketry and swimming and elementary gunnery and seamanship and drill, from second-class boyhood to first-class boyhood, from Shotley Barracks to H.M. Training Ship *Ganges*, until at last even first-class boyhood was left behind and he became a full-blown Ordinary Seaman in the newly commissioned third-class cruiser, *Charybdis*, which left Portsmouth late in 1912 to continue the old tradition (sadly weakened by new strategical arrangements) of showing the flag in Eastern waters and to maintain the very necessary policing of those rather disorderly shores.

Albert Brown was not romantic, and it is doubtful if any emotion came to him as England vanished from sight. But his love for his country, his delight and pride in her naval might were real enough, an essential part of him. Brown, however, had no use for words, and he turned solidly to his duty as the thrust of *Charybdis*'s screws bore him away from the land for which he was ready to give his life.

Chapter Eight

The beginning of the war found *Charybdis* at Singapore. There was a buzz of joy throughout the lower deck; opinion had grown stronger and stronger that Germany's huge naval effort could only end in war between England and Germany. In anticipation of a North Sea clash the English sailor had been steadily withdrawn from the Mediterranean and the Pacific, so that at the very time when England's Navy was stronger than ever it had been there was a smaller English force than ever before in Eastern waters. And that summer night when the First Fleet went speeding northward to its station at Scapa, the "preparative" flashed by wireless to the few scattered units which flew the White Ensign in the Pacific.

For there was cause for some anxiety there. Vice-Admiral Maximilian von Spee was lost in the vast expanse of the ocean; he had cannily cleared from Tsing-tao and no one knew where he might appear or where he might strike. His armoured cruisers, *Gneisenau* and *Scharnhorst*, held the big gun records of the German fleet, and there were light cruisers with him too. Also, Muller with *Emden* and von Lutz with *Ziethen* were free to attach themselves to him, so it was obvious that he had a fast-moving, hard-hitting squadron which any English fleet without battleships might be chary of encountering.

No one knew where he might appear, or at what he might strike; on the high seas there were fleets bearing Australian troops, New Zealand troops, Indian troops, English troops. If one such fleet were left unconvoyed he might deal it one of the most terrible blows given in war. At every point of danger there had to be stationed against him a squadron of strength superior to his own, and England was woefully short of cruisers. The naval might of England had definitely asserted its superiority, but here in the Pacific there was this one rebel, hopeless and desperate, who might yet strike a fierce blow or two before Fate overtook him.

That in the end Fate would overtake him there was no doubt whatever. When, very soon, the Japanese declared war and besieged Tsing-tao, he had no harbour left him. Coal could only be obtained with difficulty, the myriad spare parts he would need would be unobtainable, the myriad small defects which would develop would be irremediable. Sooner or later, whether or not he encountered an enemy, he would have to call the game lost and seek internment in some neutral port. But were he not hunted down and destroyed the material damage he might do would be enormous, and the damage to British prestige would be more serious still. So messages flew back and forth summoning all the scattered Pacific units of the British fleet into groups converging on the million square miles wherein he lay concealed.

The lower-deck ratings of *Charybdis* thought nothing of the task. They put a happy trust in their officers, who would bring a superior force against von Spee; and if they were not in superior force, then English grit and English gunnery would take no heed of odds. No man aboard *Charybdis* but would eagerly have accepted the chance to fight in that obsolescent cruiser against *Scharnhorst* or *Gneisenau* with their deadly 8-inch guns. And for the terrible superiority of their 5.9 guns over the almost obsolete Mark IV 4.7 which *Charybdis* carried they cared nothing.

Albert Brown, through what his mother had told him, had a more intimate knowledge of the facts and probabilities. He knew, as did the others, of the imminent hunt for von Spee, but he had a clearer appreciation of the difficulties. *Charybdis* could not hope to fight successfully any one of the majority of von Spee's squadron, and she had hardly speed sufficient to escape danger. *Scharnhorst* or *Gneisenau*, those big armoured cruisers, would blow her out of the water instantly. *Ziethen*, an earlier and smaller armoured cruiser, would have hardly more difficulty. But if death came to him—well, he died, and that was the end of speculation. If not—wartime and an expanding Navy meant promotion. He was Leading Seaman now, though still only twenty. The commission he hardly dared to think about seemed at last a faint possibility. Brown knew it was the first step in promotion which was the hardest to come by.

So *Charybdis* left Singapore hurriedly and drove eastward, obedient to the flickering wireless, into the deserts of the Pacific. This was the very beginning of the war, before Japan had turned against Germany and sent her army to Kiaochow and her navy in a wide sweep south-eastward after von Spee. *Charybdis* took her course across the China Sea; she nosed her way through the Carolines, exploring that straggling group of flat, miserable islands, and from there threaded her way on to the Marshalls. On the opposite side of the world an anxious Admiralty awaited her reports, for the Carolines and Marshalls were German possessions, and there, if anywhere, would von Spee be found. But a thousand miles of sea leaves much room in which a small squadron can be lost, and *Charybdis* missed contact with von Spee by the barest margin of twenty-four hours. *Charybdis*'s negative reports, relayed round the world, came in to puzzle the naval staff more than ever. They were at a loss to think where von Spee could have hidden himself. The Australian Navy was on its guard to the southward; the Japanese fleet was sweeping down from the north; a concentration was gradually taking shape at the Falklands. Contact with von Spee must be made. He might even pass the Panama Canal and appear in the West Indies, and break across the Atlantic in a desperate effort to reach home. The wireless orders summoned *Charybdis* farther yet across the Pacific, south again to a secret coaling station and onward towards Panama.

Von Spee, striking across the South American coast, had ordered *Ziethen* (Captain von Lutz) to steer for Australian waters. *Ziethen*, with her large displacement, her ten 6-inch guns and thick armour, would be a match for any of the British light cruisers, and being in no way homogeneous with von Spee's own squadron, could be well spared. And a thousand miles from land *Ziethen* encountered *Charybdis*.

Charybdis saw a smudge of smoke on the horizon. She steered towards it. Soon *Ziethen*'s three tall funnels could be descried through glasses. Captain Holt of *Charybdis* ran through his memory to pick out which remembered silhouette was hers.

"That's *Ziethen*," he said. "Now where are the others?"

For a few minutes both ships held on slightly divergent courses, each anxious to ascertain whether the other was in the company of others. But they were alone upon a waste of water.

"Fight or run?" said Captain Holt to himself, knowing the answer as he said it.

Run? He must not run. He could not fight *Ziethen*, but it was his duty to shadow her by virtue of his half-knot superiority in speed until someone came up who *could* fight her. But shadow a ship of superior force over two thousand miles of dangerous sea with only such a tiny additional speed? The odds would be a hundred to one that he would lose her—and his professional reputation. He must fight then—old 4.7s against new 5.9s, four thousand tons against eight thousand. Luck might aid him; a sea fight is always a chancy business. At the worst he might do *Ziethen* some serious damage before *Charybdis* sank, and *Ziethen* seriously damaged meant *Ziethen* rendered useless, for she had no place where she might effect repairs.

"Action stations" had gone long ago; steam was being raised in all boilers; the propellers were beating a faster rhythm as both ships worked up to full speed, swinging round each other before rushing in to grapple. Captain Holt put the glasses to his eyes again and spoke casually to the man at the wheel. Round it went, and *Charybdis* heeled as she swung sharply under maximum helm at high speed. The captain was making the most of his chances, closing the range as rapidly as possible to avoid as much as he could being hit without being able to hit back. Even as *Charybdis* came round the wireless signalman was sending out, over and over again, the message telling of the encounter, giving latitude and longitude, trying to inform the expectant British fleet where *Ziethen* was to be found. And while he did so *Ziethen*'s operator was "jamming" hard. No message could hope to get through that tangled confusion, especially over a distance of thousands of miles.

But *Ziethen* was ready for *Charybdis*'s manoeuvre. Well did Captain von Lutz appreciate the superiority of the 6-inch over the 4.7. He put his helm over too, and *Ziethen* came round until the courses of the two ships were almost parallel, and, as *Charybdis* turned further, he continued his own turn until it almost seemed as if he were running away. It was a pretty sight, those two great ships wheeling round each other on the blue, blue Pacific with a blue sky over them and peace all about them. Only the spread smudges from the heavily smoking funnels marred the picture.

"Out of range still, curse them!" groaned *Charybdis*'s gunnery lieutenant, hearkening to the monotonous chant of the range-taking petty officer.

A sudden little haze became apparent round *Ziethen*, and almost simultaneously tall pillars of water shot up from the surface of the sea two hundred yards from *Charybdis*'s bow. *Charybdis* heeled again under pressure of helm in her effort to close. The tall fountains of water shot up again, this time only a hundred yards from the quarter; some of the water splashed onto *Charybdis*'s deck.

"Bracketed, by God!" said the gunnery lieutenant, and then, in surprised admiration of a worthy opponent, "Good shooting! Damn good shooting!"

Charybdis turned sharply to disconcert the German range-takers, but the next salvo pitched close alongside, flooding the decks with water. Down below the level of the water, under the protective deck, the stokers were labouring to supply the steam which was being demanded so insistently; but *Ziethen*'s stokers were labouring too. Victory might well incline to the ship which first reached her maximum speed; speed would enable *Charybdis* to close, or enable *Ziethen* to keep away and continue to blast her enemy with salvoes to which no reply was possible. Once only did the gunnery lieutenant see his beloved guns in action. They fired at extreme range, on the upward roll, but it was a vain hope. The gunnery lieutenant groaned his bitter disappointment when he saw the tall columns of water leap half a mile on the hither side of the enemy. But the anguish of the gunnery lieutenant's soul ended with his groan, for *Ziethen*'s next salvo came crashing fair and deadly upon *Charybdis*'s deck; five 6-inch shells falling together. They blew the gunnery lieutenant into unrecognizable rags; they dashed to pieces the range-taking petty officer and his instrument; they wiped out the crew of No. 4 gun; they left the superstructure riddled and funnels tottering; they started fires here, there, and everywhere, so that the executive officer and his hose-party, choking in the smoke, could not cope with one half of the work.

Nor was that one salvo all. Salvo followed salvo, with barely half a minute between them. *Charybdis* reeled beneath the blows; smoke poured from her in increasing volume, but her vitals, her motive power, were down below her protective deck, and she could still grind through the water with undiminished speed. The captain was down and dying, torn open by a splinter, and it was the commander who gave the orders now; dead men lay round the guns, and the stewards were bearing many wounded down below to the surgeon; scratch crews manned the guns, which flamed and thundered at hopelessly long range. Yet fierce resolution, half a knot more speed and a slightly converging course all did their work. The high-tossed pillars of water crept nearer to *Ziethen*, and soon a shrill cheer from a gun-layer, cutting through the insane din, greeted *Charybdis*'s first hit. There were dead Germans now upon *Ziethen*'s deck.

But *Charybdis* was a dying ship, even though the thrust of her screws still drove her through the water. Her side was torn open; she would have been wrapped in flame were it not that the shells pitching close alongside sometimes threw tons of water on board and extinguished some of the fire. Her guns still spoke spasmodically through the smoke and the White Ensign still flew overhead. When the oldest navy met the newest, pride left no room for surrender; barbaric victory or barbaric death were the only chances open to the iron men in their iron ships. For every single shell which was flung at *Ziethen* a full salvo came winging back, five shells at a time, with the range known to a yard. Even as *Charybdis* made her last hit her death was in the air. It smote her hard upon her injured side; it detonated the starboard magazine so that a crashing explosion tore the ship across. The hungry sea boiled in; the stokers and the artificers and the engineers whom the explosion had not killed died as the water trapped them below decks. In thirty seconds *Charybdis* had passed from a fighting ship to a twisted tangle of iron falling through the sunlit upper waters of the Pacific down into the freezing darkness of the unfathomed bottom. Above her vast bubbles came boiling up to the surface; a smear of oil and coal dust marred the azure beauty of the Pacific, and at its centre floated a little gathering of wreckage, human and inhuman, living and dead—nearly all dead.

Chapter Nine

The record of Brown's doings while *Charybdis* fought *Ziethen* is not material to this history. He was only a part of a whole, and whatever he did the credit belongs not to him, but to the Navy, the tremendous institution which had trained him and disciplined him. If in the last few desperate moments he fought his gun without superior direction, that was because handling a 4.7 under all conditions had been grained into his nature. To Brown should go all the glory and honour for what he was to do on Resolution. For he acted on Resolution without orders, on his own initiative, under conditions where training could not help him.

That was all still in the future, however, and to the German boat's crew which picked him up as they pulled through the scattered wreckage he was merely a half-stunned, stoutly-built fellow of medium height, very freckled, with hard grey eyes and fair hair—one of only three survivors. He was very badly shaken, having been blown from the deck to the water when the magazine exploded and he was hardly conscious of holding on to a stray rolled hammock which came to the surface providentially near him when *Charybdis* sank. He lay limp in the bottom of the boat as it rowed back to *Ziethen*, and he had to be assisted to the ship's deck.

All Brown wanted at that time was to allow his weakness to overcome him, to fall to the deck and sleep heavily, but the exigencies of war would not allow him that luxury. He was the only one of the survivors of *Charybdis* who was even half conscious, and Captain von Lutz, bearing on his shoulders the responsibility for *Ziethen* and her crew, must know at once how *Charybdis* came to be where she was; whether she had consorts near who could have heard her wireless and whether the meeting was intentional or accidental.

They did not treat Brown unkindly; they dried him and gave him spirits and wrapped him in a comfortable woollen nightshirt and allowed him to sit in a chair in the dispensary beside the sick-bay while he was being questioned.

Brown rolled dazed eyes over his questioners as he sat huddled in his chair. The bearded officer with all the gold braid must be *Ziethen*'s captain; the young officer was a sub-lieutenant; the shirt-sleeved man was the surgeon, and the naval rating in the background was the sick-bay steward.

Fierce and keen were the captain's questions, uttered in guttural English. Brown made halting replies, his eyelids drooping with weariness. He told of *Charybdis*'s slow progress eastwards across the Pacific. No, he did not know of any other English ship near. At this point the captain called upon the sub-lieutenant to interpret, and the sub-lieutenant duly informed Brown in pure English that a

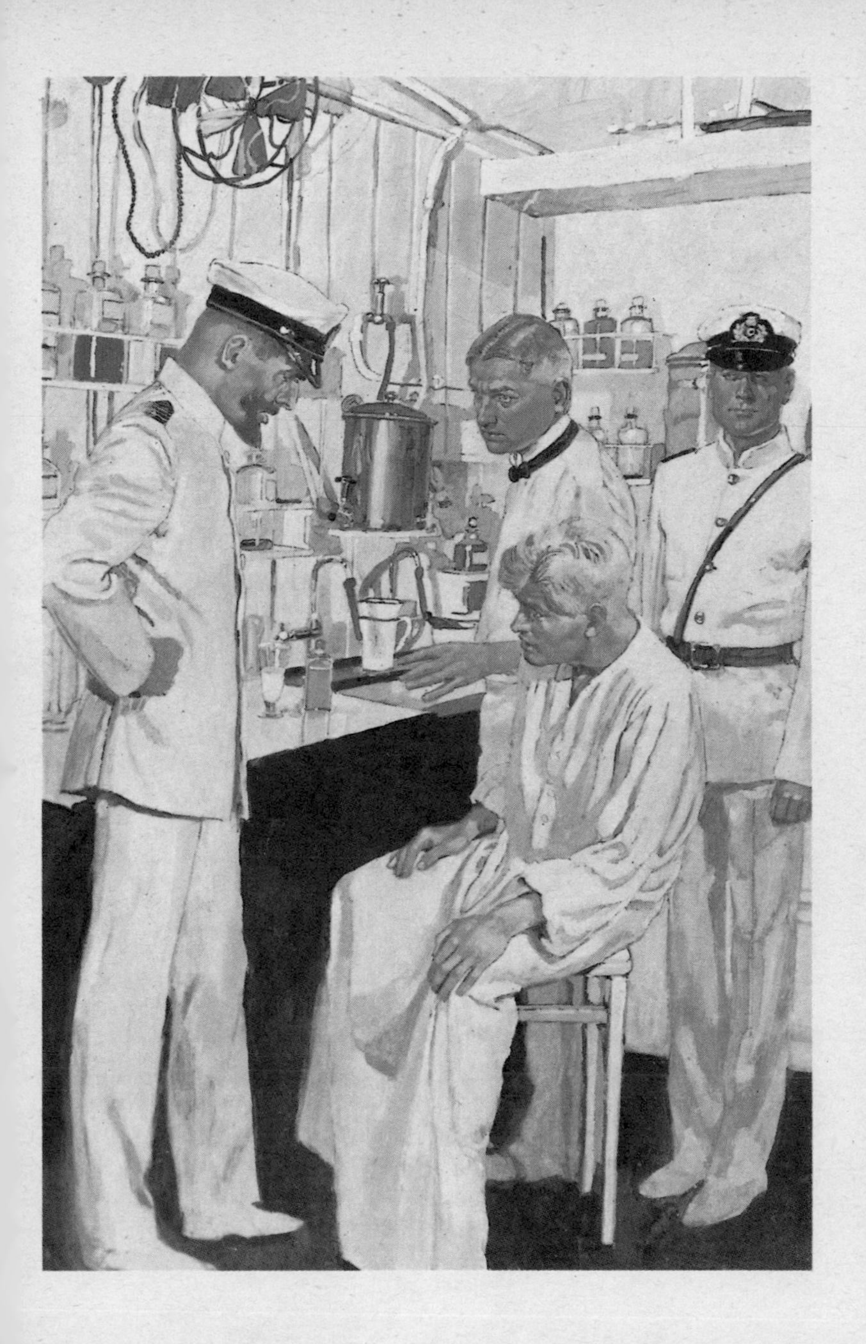

prisoner who made false statements was guilty of espionage, and as such was liable to be shot.

"Yes," said Brown.

"Was *Charybdis* expecting to encounter *Ziethen*?"

"I don't know," said Brown.

"What was her course and destination at the time of meeting?"

"I don't know," said Brown.

Now, did he want to be well treated while he was on board?

"Yes," said Brown.

Then let him answer their questions sensibly. Whither was *Charybdis* bound?

"I don't know," said Brown, and at this point the medical officer intervened, and Captain von Lutz left testily. Brown had been speaking the truth when he said he did not know; but he had a shrewd idea all the same, and had he told von Lutz of his suspicions he might have relieved that officer of a great burden of worry. But that was no way Brown's business. Captain von Lutz's ill-timed threat had reminded him of this fact at the very moment when, in his half-dazed condition, he was likely in reply to kindly questioning to have told all he thought.

The surgeon summoned the sick-bay steward and another colleague, and between them they tucked Brown into a cot, put a hot bottle at his feet (shock had left him cold and weak) and allowed him to sleep. And while Brown slept *Ziethen* came round on her heel and headed back eastward.

For *Charybdis* had not gone to the bottom quite without exacting some compensation. One of her 4.7-inch shells had struck *Ziethen* fair and true a foot above the waterline, and a yard forward of the limits of her armour belt. There the shell had smashed a great hole through which the sea raced in such a volume that the pumps were hard put to it to keep the water from gaining until, after the battle, a sweating work party had got a collision mat over the hole. Examination of the damage showed it to be extensive. Nowhere else on all the side of the ship could a shell of that calibre have been put to better use. The forward armour plate, starboard side, was buckled and loose on its rivets; there was a hole in the skin ten feet across, one-third of it below water, and, worst of all, the bulkhead and watertight door between the injured compartment and the boiler compartment were involved in the damage as well. The ship was actually in danger; in smooth water she had nothing to fear, but, given a Pacific gale two compartments might fill and *Ziethen* would go to join *Charybdis* on the bottom.

Clearly it meant the postponement of *Ziethen*'s projected raid on the Australian convoys. She must find a haven of some sort where she could rest while her shattered hull was patched. A neutral port would mean almost certain internment, or if she were not interned, her presence would be broadcast far and wide, and on her exit from neutral waters she would find awaiting her an overwhelming force of the enemy. She must therefore find somewhere a deserted piece of land from which news would not spread, where she would be able to find shelter while her artificers forged and fixed new plates, and where it was unlikely that enemy warships would find her. In the Pacific there was more than one such haven, but the nearest was far superior to all others: Resolution Island, that last, most northerly outlier of the Galapagos Archipelago. So *Ziethen* set her course for Resolution, a thousand miles away, while a relay of sweating artificers down in the Stygian depths of her toiled to keep her pumps at work.

BROWN SLEPT all the rest of the day and most of the night. In the morning he looked about him; he was alone. The interior of the cabin was a cool white, and a whirling electric fan helped out the portholes in their business of ventilation but the air which came in hardly seemed to cool the cabin. For *Ziethen* was almost on the Equator, and iron decks and iron bulkheads meant sweltering heat under a vertical sun. Brown was used to the heat; two years in the tropics had made such a state of affairs almost normal to him.

He had not much time to think before the sick-bay steward entered the cabin. His jolly German face creased into a smile as he saw Brown conscious again. He put a thermometer into Brown's mouth, and smiled again as he read it and noted the result on a chart. He spoke to him amicably, and grinned as he realized that Brown did not understand a word he said. He made Brown comfortable as dexterously as a nurse might, and waddled away with a friendly look over his shoulder. Ten minutes later he returned with the surgeon.

"Bedder, eh?" said that officer with a glance at the chart. He took Brown's wrist and produced his watch simultaneously, felt his pulse and nodded.

"Any bain any blace?" he asked.

"No, sir," said Brown.

"You can haf breagfast, den."

The surgeon spoke to the steward, who vanished and returned almost at once. He brought good grey bread and tinned butter, and coffee which was not as good as either; but Brown relished it all. The steward also brought him clothes—shirt and jumper and loose trousers, and socks and shoes; they were the white-duck uniform of a German sailor, and Brown put them on, a little troubled by the minor differences between it and the English naval uniform—the collar, for example, had to be buttoned awkwardly inside—but the general fit was not too bad.

Later he was led once more into the presence of the captain and searchingly questioned. Brown did his best not to give information; he fell back when hard-pressed upon a stolid stupidity. And since it was extremely probable that a mere leading seaman from an isolated cruiser should know nothing, the captain in the end dropped the inquisition. And, after all, it is doubtful if anything Brown could have told him would have added to Captain von Lutz's information. The captain was about to dismiss him when the sub-lieutenant interposed with a respectful question. The captain exchanged a few sentences with the sub-lieutenant, and uttered his verdict.

Brown heard of the decision on his return to the sick-bay.

"You are to helb here," said the surgeon to him.

Brown could only stare without understanding, and the surgeon explained in a fatherly manner.

"What are we to do wit you on board here?" he asked. "Pud you in prison? You gan ztay and helb nurse your vrients."

The plump steward led him into the adjoining ward of the sick-bay. There lay two men. One had his head half swathed in bandages, through which once more a red stain was beginning to show. Through a hole in the bandages over his mouth came a continued bubbling groan. Half a forehead and one eye remained uncovered to show Brown that beneath the bandages lay what had once been the homely, friendly features of Ginger Harris, a messmate of his and a bosom friend of two years' standing. There was no hint of recognition in that one eye of Ginger's when it opened; all Ginger's thoughts were at present concentrated upon himself. Later, when Brown saw what was beneath the bandages, he was not at all surprised.

The second cot was occupied by a leading signalman, whom Brown did not know at all well, and he hardly recognized him because he was so exceedingly pale—even his lips were white—that he was more like a soulless visitor from another world. Brown wondered what was the injury from which he was suffering. He looked inquiringly at the fat steward, who indicated a bulge beneath the bedclothes, whirled his arms round like a windmill, said "Sh-sh," and tapped his leg. Brown grasped his meaning; the leading signalman had come within reach of one of the *Charybdis*'s gigantic propellers as she sank and had lost his leg.

So he and these two wrecks were the sole survivors of the four hundred and odd men who had constituted the crew of *Charybdis*. It had been a vain, frantic sacrifice. Brown could picture back in England the arrival of the news of the loss of *Charybdis* with all hands. The tea parties would say, "Dear me, how sad!" and go on talking about cancer of the womb; and the business offices would say, "Mismanagement somewhere, of course," and revert to the Cesarewitch or the delinquencies of office boys. Brown knew how little the people for whom he was fighting appreciated his services and those of his fellows. But none of this affected his determination to do his duty; his duty to the Navy, to himself and (although he would not think of it in those words) to the memory of his mother.

Later he found himself jeering bitterly at himself for his highfalutin determinations. He was a prisoner in the hands of the enemy, and helpless. He could think of no means to hold back *Ziethen* from her mission of destruction. As soon as her side was repaired she would go off capturing and sinking British ships. And there was nothing he could do. He knew too much about the internal discipline of a ship to hope to disable the engines or bring off any other boy's-adventure-book coup. Helplessness and despair and loneliness combined to force him into the utter black misery of the twenty-year-old during the three days that *Ziethen* was ploughing her crippled way to Resolution.

Chapter Ten

The Galapagos Archipelago is a group of volcanic islands, bisected by the Equator, about six hundred miles from the South American coast. They support no inhabitants—mainly because they have little water—and they are sufficiently distant from the ordinary trade routes to remain comparatively unvisited. Their flora and fauna have followed their own lines of evolution without interference from the mainland, so that they boast their own special species. The monstrous Galapagos tortoises gave the Archipelago its collective name, but the individual islands were christened by the Englishmen who called there on sundry occasions. Albemarle, Indefatigable, Chatham, Barrington, Resolution and the rest are all reminiscent of ships or admirals or statesmen.

Resolution is the loneliest and least visited of all the islands. Once it was a volcanic crater, but it has been extinct for a thousand years or more, and the Pacific has broken in at one point so that in shape it is an incomplete ring of towering cliffs surrounding a central lagoon half a mile across. The entrance gives twenty fathoms of water; the centre of the lagoon is of unplumbed depth. The cliffs themselves (the ring is nowhere more than a quarter of a mile thick) are of lava in huge tumbled jagged blocks with edges like knives, the lower slopes covered thinly with spiky cactus, the upper slopes naked rock. The extreme highest ridge, however, where the wind has had full play, has been somewhat weathered down, so that the lava edges have been blunted, and are disguised by a layer of smaller pumice.

One glimpse of that central lagoon convinced Captain von Lutz that here indeed was the sheltered harbour he desired. Cautiously he made his entrance, with a picket boat ahead, taking soundings as he went. As *Ziethen* entered the lagoon, the stifling heat of the place closed in upon her with crushing force, for the cliffs cut off the wind and the sun beat down upon their sloping surfaces, pitilessly reflecting inward.

Very slowly *Ziethen* swung sideways. An anchor roared from her hawse-hole and took grip of the bottom away from the vast depths of the central throat of the old crater. Tide and propellers and rudder were balanced against each other while another anchor was got away from the stern, and soon *Ziethen* was riding safely in the heart of Resolution. It was a sound piece of seamanship which Brown thoroughly appreciated.

And as soon as mooring was completed, *Ziethen*'s crew sprang into furious action. Alone on a sea where every man's hand was against them, it was dangerous to linger within sight of land however deserted. Repairs must begin at once. The stokers were set to work clearing the starboard bunkers and transferring their contents to the port side. The gunnery lieutenant supervised a party which laboured to empty the starboard magazines and fill the port ones. Even the starboard battery twelve-pounders were unshipped with infinite labour, and taken across. To expose a foot of a ship's bottom necessitates the transference of hundreds of tons—and even that is a dangerous and chancy matter in a ship whose sides are plastered with armour plate.

That evening Brown was allowed on deck under the friendly chaperonage of the fat steward. He looked up at the towering cliffs, and felt the increasing heel of the deck, and it dawned upon him that if those cliffs were in the possession of an enemy with a gun—a six-inch—a twelve-pounder even!—*Ziethen*, heavily listed, would be helpless. Her decks could be swept, the repairing party overside could be wiped out, and the mending of the side could be postponed indefinitely, until either the ship was sunk or she remedied her list again and cleared off in disgust to some new refuge; and refuges as good as Resolution were necessarily few. He scanned the desolate cliffs again. They were barely more than a quarter of a mile away at any point, within easy rifle-shot, in fact. Rifle-shot! An idea sprang into Brown's brain, and the blood surged hot beneath his skin. He turned away from the fat steward lest he should betray his sudden agitation. But again and again he peered up at the cliffs, turning over in his mind the details of his plan, searching for flaws in it and debating consequences.

Back in the sick-bay, while listening for the feeble cry of the leading signalman, or the sound of Ginger Harris's agony, he plunged more seriously into his plans. If he could delay *Ziethen*'s repairs for a time, or if (as he hardly hoped) he could drive her away unrepaired, he would have achieved much. Somewhere, of course, British ships were seeking her out, and the longer she could be kept in one spot the more chance they would have of finding her. The news of the sinking of *Charybdis* must have brought many ships hot upon the trail. (Brown did not know that *Charybdis*'s wireless messages never got through and the loss of *Charybdis* was at long last ascribed to internal causes.) To hold *Ziethen* helpless for a few days might well settle the matter. It might cost him his life, but that was a price he expected to pay. Agatha Brown's influence was bearing its fruit, and perhaps his heritage on the male side from a long line of fighting naval ancestors had something to say in the matter too.

Brown's escape from *Ziethen* was absurdly simple. This of course was largely because he was not expected to want to escape—who on earth would desire to be marooned on a barren and waterless island? At the foot of the gangway outside the sick-bay stood an arms rack. In the rack stood twelve rifles, and above them hung twelve sets of equipment. For *Ziethen* was a raiding cruiser, and must be ready at a moment's notice to send away an armed boarding or landing party. The rifles and equipment stood ready for the use of one of the boats' crews. Brown had noted them casually more than once, but now he opened the door and stole out to examine them more closely. The rifles were heavily greased, as was necessary in the tropics. The equipments were ready for instant use. He felt the ammunition pouches; they were full—sixty rounds per set. Pouches at the back of each belt contained two days' emergency rations. The water-bottles were empty, however. Brown removed two, tiptoed back and filled them, and drove the corks well home. Inside the door he listened carefully, heard no one coming, and slipped out again. He replaced one water-bottle in its sling and buckled the other to the belt of the same set of equipment. He emptied the pouches of another set and filled his pockets with the ammunition. He put a third day's rations into the pouch of the set he proposed taking with him, and his preparations were complete.

But to be ready to depart was one thing; to transfer to the mainland of Resolution was quite another. Brown realized how easily his plan might fail at this point, and how discovery would mean the punishment cells and the end of all his hopes. He weighed the chances and decided he might perhaps succeed. All that was necessary, in fact, was a cool head and moderate good fortune.

Outside it was now tropically dark; the young moon had not quite cleared the highest ridge of Resolution to light the lagoon. Brown lifted the full set of equipment, put it over his shoulders, and buckled it about him. He took a rifle, slung it on one shoulder, and, unobserved by the watch, stole up the gangway. In five seconds he was crouched beneath the port-side boat, as it swung in its davits. With noiseless rapidity he set about his preparations for the next step.

With his knife he cut the lashings of the boat cover, reached inside and pulled out, after a small search, two of its lifebelts. One of them he bound about his rifle as tightly as he could; it would be a sorry fiasco if the weapon were to sink and he were to arrive on Resolution safe but unarmed. The other he bound about him. Then he fished out one of the boat's lines and dropped the end very, very quietly overside. Slinging his rifle again, he gripped the rope and lowered himself down. He was hampered by the bulkiness of the lifebelt and the mass of his equipment, but patience and brute strength saved him from swinging with a crash against the steel side of the ship; he went down foot by foot, cautiously.

At last he felt the sea at his ankles, and by the time he had reached the end of the rope it was at his waist. He let himself fall the rest of the way, sinking until the water closed over his head in his effort to avoid a splash before the lifebelt brought him to the surface again. The rest was easy. Lying as much on his back as the lifebelt would allow, and clinging like grim death to his rifle, he struck out gently with his feet along the ship's side; the water was as warm as milk. Heading steadily past *Ziethen*'s stern he moved away by almost imperceptible degrees. It was half an hour before his slow, powerful strokes bore him to the side of the lagoon, and he had to swim along the side for another ten minutes before he could discover a bit of beach which shelved sufficiently to allow him to clamber up. There he unfastened the lifebelts, dropped them in a cactus clump, and set his face in the darkness towards the steep, horribly tangled slope before him.

Brown knew nothing of the Galapagos Islands—truth to tell, he did not know that he was on one of them—and he was hardly expecting the appalling effort which the climb demanded. The island was a mass of lava blocks welded together, overgrown with cactus; to make a yard's progress involved hauling oneself up a six-foot block guarded with razor edges, tearing through spiky cactus at the same time. In a very short time his hands and feet were raw, his clothes were in rags, blood was running from his scratches, and he was streaming with sweat. After fifty yards of progress body and mind were numb with fatigue, but he still toiled on. One thought cheered him during that desperate struggle: if his progress was slow that of a landing party would be equally so, and with his rifle in a point of vantage he would be able to hold any number of men back. So, gasping with fatigue, finding handhold and foothold in the dark, heaving himself up with gigantic efforts, he forced his way to the top, and there, on a projecting knuckle of rock which would be an advantageous, strategic position, he lay down to wait until dawn, his rifle at his side. Instant sleep closed over him as he lay, face downward with his head on his arms.

Chapter Eleven

But while Brown was crawling up the steep side of Resolution, and while he was asleep on the projecting saddle of rock, many things had happened. Tremendous news had reached *Ziethen* from the wireless stations on the South American mainland; von Spee had struck his first blow upon the ring of enemies which had closed in upon him. Admiral Sir Christopher Cradock had encountered him, with two weak armoured cruisers against two powerful ones.

He could have refused battle; he could have fallen back on a slow battleship which was wallowing along two hundred miles away, but he had refused to lose touch with an enemy who had already proved so elusive. He had gone boldly into action, hoping to do von Spee enough damage to cripple him, but he had not been so fortunate as had been *Charybdis* in her battle with *Ziethen*. *Good Hope* and *Monmouth* had sunk with all hands under the guns of *Scharnhorst* and *Gneisenau*, and von Spee was now for a brief space master of all the Southern Pacific coast.

The nitrate ships, vital to the manufacture of British explosives, were cowering in Chilean ports while an exasperated Admiralty in London was hurriedly searching for the wherewithal to close the gap which von Spee had hewn in the ring they had flung round him. In the last desperate matter of national life or death von Spee's victory was unimportant—what were two obsolete armoured cruisers to a Navy which could put thirty Dreadnoughts into line? But to the life of a Cabinet it was supremely important. With von Spee triumphant in the Pacific, the Cabinet's prestige might well be so shaken as to ensure its fall; and the results of such an overturn were incalculable.

Well was it, indeed, that *Ziethen* in her damaged condition had not dared to let loose her wireless and announce the destruction of *Charybdis*. Once let her repair herself so that she could move about and evade pursuit, and she would be emboldened to proclaim her victory; the streets of London would be full of posters: "Another Naval Disaster in the Pacific", and the Cabinet might come crashing down. That is what Captain von Lutz realized as he read the stream of wireless messages, and, fired with impatience, he hastened below to inspect the achievements of the ship's smiths and artificers who were preparing the plates which were to close the yawning hole in *Ziethen*'s side. Not a moment was to be lost. Twelve hours from dawn would see *Ziethen* out once more in the Pacific, blazoning the destruction of *Charybdis* to all the world, and privately informing a German secret agent in Peru of her need for coal and of the rendezvous whither a collier should be sent.

Even the news that the captured English sailor had escaped and taken a rifle with him did not disturb Captain von Lutz's state of pleased anticipation; the escape of the sailor could do no harm—von Lutz wondered why the sailor had bothered to arm himself seeing that they would not trouble to pursue him—and the captain contented himself with putting into prison the kindly sick-bay steward and the marine sentry of the upper deck, for purely disciplinary reasons.

BROWN AWOKE when dawn was rushing into the sky. He was very sore and tired and thirsty; but he gratified his thirst only to the extent of two swallows from his water-bottle. He looked to his rifle. As he had hoped, the thick grease with which it had been smeared had kept the water from the metal, and no trace of rust appeared on it or in it. He opened the chamber of the butt, extracted oil-bottle and pull-through, and cleaned the barrel ready for action. He had never before handled a Mauser rifle, but the supreme simplicity of the mechanism held no secrets for him. He filled the magazine and lay ready for action.

Below him, a scant quarter of a mile away, the *Ziethen* lay immobile nearly at the centre of the lagoon. The water round her was smooth, glassy, save for the strong ripple which Brown's powerful eyesight could detect about her stern and her anchor chains as the rapid tide swirled round them. She lay like a ship of the dead; even from her funnels there came only a shimmering hint of internal activity.

Yet as the light improved Brown could see white-clad figures on her deck and upper works, and he fingered his rifle, sighting on them each in turn, while refraining from pulling the trigger. He wanted every cartridge for more important work than casual killings. Later the white flag with the black cross soared upward; the day was officially begun on board *Ziethen*. Immediately afterwards there was a stir of activity on the starboard side, and Brown could see that repair work had begun. Two bo'sun's chairs were lowered down the side, one to each extremity of the hole made by *Charybdis*'s shell, and white-clad figures scrambled down Jacob's ladders onto each of them. The damaged plates were to be unriveted and removed while new ones were preparing. Brown laid his rifle to his shoulder and his cheek to the butt.

Slowly the sights came into line. Through the U of the backsight could be seen a tiny triangle of white—the white of the jumper of the man on the bo'sun's chair. Up into the U crept the wedge of the foresight; it moved steadily upward until its tip was exactly in line with the top of the U. There it stayed for a tiny instant of time, while Brown, mindful of his musketry training at Harwich, steadied his breathing, took the first pull of the trigger, and slowly squeezed the trigger back farther through the final tenth of an inch. Then the rifle went off and the echo of its report ran menacingly round the circle of cliffs.

Maschinistmaat Zimmer had set cheerfully about his task of drilling out the rivets around the broken plate. He whistled to himself as he adjusted his tools, and he even cracked a joke or two with the other men swinging beside him in the bo'sun's chairs. Then something hit him hard on the left side close to his heart, and for an instant he knew pain, agonizing pain, before darkness shut in upon him. He was dead as his knees gave way under him and he fell back over the rail of the chair; his feet caught under the lower rail, and he hung head down, grotesquely inert.

Leading Seaman Brown snicked the bolt of the Mauser out and in, aimed again coolly and rapidly, and fired. The other man on Zimmer's bo'sun's chair fell dead even as he looked round to see what had happened to Zimmer; one man on the other chair died as he turned to see whence came the firing; the fourth man crumpled up as, panic-stricken, he sprang towards the Jacob's ladder.

Brown fired three more shots into the groups of men who swarmed to the side of the ship on the upper deck out of curiosity; they took effect, and in a few seconds the upper deck was deserted. At *Ziethen*'s side, absurdly small, the white corpse of Maschinistmaat Zimmer dangled, and above him lay two white splotches which were the bodies of his mates. The fourth man had fallen into the sea.

It was an apt picture of the simultaneous power and helplessness of modern machinery. On the one hand lay *Ziethen*, with her ten 6-inch guns and her hundreds of crew, and on the other a lad of five foot eight, aged twenty, dominating her in consequence of his rifle. Brown was not a marvellously good shot, but to hit four men with four shots at a quarter of a mile when they are entirely exposed and conspicuous in white against a dark background does not call for marvellous shooting. Brown had won the first trick, and he snuggled down into his niche on the saddle of rock to await the next development.

On board *Ziethen* there was fury at the death of four messmates and friends. Captain von Lutz, the angriest man on the ship, strode out upon the bridge; but a bullet smacked against a stanchion close at his ear and sang off into the distance. Even Captain von Lutz, one of the cleverest minds in the Imperial German Navy, did not realize the difficulty of the task before him. He gave abrupt orders to clear away the steam pinnace so that a landing party could arrest this fellow and bring him on board to be dealt with.

Brown lay patiently in his niche. Where he lay he could command the stern and the whole starboard side of the ship. His rifle was pushed forward between two blocks of lava which gave him almost perfect protection; the straggling cactus was an efficient screen, and the bulge of the saddle and the nick in its tip gave him command of most of the face of the cliffs even where he lay. He was perfectly satisfied with his position; he saw that his magazine was filled and submitted patiently to the scorching heat, which was beginning to roast him slowly.

Suddenly the next development made itself apparent. Round *Ziethen*'s stern, shooting swiftly for the shore, came her steam pinnace, with twenty men aboard. Brown's rifle cracked out again and again, taking swift toll before the men in her flung themselves down under shelter.

The helmsman dropped, shot through the breast, but the officer in command, the gold flashing on his white coat, grasped the tiller and held her to her course as Brown's next bullet tore the cap from his head. Next second the boat was out of sight under the steep drop of the bare rock at the water's edge. Brown recharged his magazine.

The lieutenant in command of the landing party realized, in the instant that he grasped the helm, that this was not going to be the simple arrest of a nearly helpless man. It dawned upon him that a man with a rifle a hundred yards away can take a severe toll of a mass of men rushing upon him. So he restrained the tendency of his men to bundle out of the pinnace and rush wildly up the slope. Under shelter of the steep bank he spread them out over the fifty yards of the bank's extent. He saw that they had their rifles loaded. He got them all into position, and then he gave the word for a simultaneous rush.

But here began the second lesson. No one who had not attempted it could realize that the word "rush" had no place in the vocabulary of Resolution. The dreadful razor-edged blocks of lava and the clustered cacti made anything like rapid progress impossible.

Brown, motionless in his cranny, saw appear below him a line of men's heads at the water's edge, and he promptly put a bullet through one of them. The other heads developed shoulders and bodies and legs and came towards him, falling out of sight behind lava blocks, rising into full view again as they struggled over them, creeping up towards him at a ridiculously slow pace. He fired deliberately, waiting for each shot until a man had heaved himself up into full view. A man's whole body at a hundred yards makes a superb target. Brown had fired six shots and hit six men before the "rush" died away. No man seeing his companions killed at each side of him could bring himself to heave himself up and expose himself to the next shot. The dozen survivors stayed behind the cover they chanced to have at hand, and lay without attempting to make further upward progress. They pushed their rifles forward and began to fire up at the hidden death above them.

Despite the numerical odds against him, all the advantages were still with Brown. No one yet in the attacking party had a clear knowledge of his hiding place; thanks to the two close blocks of lava and the cacti, he was thoroughly hidden. To an attacker all that might be in sight was a rifle muzzle and two or three square inches of face in deep shadow, and it would call for keener eyes, if unaided by chance, than the human race possessed to detect that much in the possible thousand square yards of rock and cactus where he might be hidden. Brown was not hampered to any such extent. He was higher up and could see farther over the edges of the lava blocks. He had more enemies to shoot at, and those enemies occupied positions taken up by chance in the heat of the moment. He was cool and unflurried by exertion.

Bullets began to shriek overhead in the heated air, to raise clouds of pumice-dust when they hit the rock, or to cut their way rustling through the fleshy cactus leaves. Not one came within ten yards of Brown. Coolly, he began to take toll of his attackers. Here there was a shoulder, there a leg, over there a head and shoulders completely exposed. He took deliberate aim and fired, shifted his aim, fired again, slewed round carefully to avoid any exposure of himself, and fired once more. Each shot echoed flatly round the cliff; the noise of the report was no guide whatever to the position of the marksman. Shot after shot went home. Wounded men lay groaning in hollows and crevices. Dead men lay with their faces on their rifles. Very soon the few survivors dared not fire back, but crouched down, afraid to move. The lieutenant, mad with rage, leaped to his feet to shout to his men, and received a bullet full in the face which flung him over backward. Silence descended again. Brown blew gently down the breech of his rifle barrel, peered through narrowed eyes for any sign of his enemies, and resumed his waiting, eyes and ears alert. For an hour nothing happened save for one attempt on the part of an unfortunate to stretch his cramped limbs, an attempt which secured him a bullet through the knee which drained the lifeblood out of him in half an hour.

So that a duel of patience ensued between the watcher on the cliff above and the dwindled half dozen down below. After the rude reports of the rifles the stillness of Resolution once more took possession. The sun climbed steadily upward, pouring down a stream of brassy heat, and in the centre of the lagoon *Ziethen* swayed idly at anchor. As the heat increased, the objects on the island took on an unreal appearance as the air above them shimmered hazily. Minutes dragged by like hours, but the sailors at the base of the cliff dared make no movement.

On *Ziethen* everyone was puzzled at what had happened. They had watched the landing; they had seen men fall; they had heard the firing abruptly increase and die away to nothing; but they could not explain the sequence of events. They could see the pinnace against the shore, and the boat guard sitting therein, but save for three or four dead bodies they could see nothing of the landing party, which was not surprising considering the tangle of rocks and cactus into which it had fallen. The opinion on board was that the attack must have moved up into some gully unnoticeable from the ship, driving its quarry before it. At that rate the danger to workers on the ship's damage must have vanished. Captain von Lutz, impatient to have his ship ready for action again, gave the order for a further party of artificers to recommence work.

Brown saw the white-clothed figures descend the Jacob's ladders. He gave them plenty of time; they sent up the bodies of their predecessors to the upper deck by a rope hoist, and then they began work. As they began he opened fire, and once again the echoes of his shots ran flatly round the island. The little white figures collapsed in the bo'sun's chairs. The sudden firing over their heads roused the men crouching down the cliff, and they, wearied with waiting and conscience-smitten about the non-fulfilment of their duty, took up their rifles once again. Someone down there had at last formed a shrewd guess as to where Brown was hidden, and as the rifles resumed their clatter bullet after bullet began to hit the rocks near him. One of them even drove dust into his eyes. Brown realized the danger. He paid no attention at present to the other riflemen firing at him, but, lying deadly still, peered this way and that through the slit between his two blocks of lava for his one keen-eyed or quick-witted enemy. He saw part of him at least—a bit of white jumper and dark collar, deep in the shadow of a rock, and beyond the rock another bit of white which was probably the end of a trouser leg. Their owner was still firing away enthusiastically, and at each shot a bullet came buzzing nearby. Brown took aim, sighting for the edge of the collar against the white jumper. At a hundred yards he could not miss; as he pressed the trigger he saw the jumper jerk and his target rolled struggling into view; some fair-haired boy, not so very unlike Brown himself, striving ridiculously to hold together his shattered right shoulder with his left hand. Brown turned his attention to the others, whose bullets were ploughing into the cliff face twenty yards on either side of him. One of them he killed and the fire of the others ceased abruptly again as they crouched down in their hollows. As they did so,

Brown observed the boat guard standing up trying to see what was going on. Him Brown killed too, without mercy as without rancour.

It was nearly noon by now. Brown had delayed the repairs of *Ziethen* for six hours already. That in itself was a vast achievement.

Chapter Twelve

The next incident in the battle of Resolution was a tribute to the power of the rifle which lay in Brown's hand. There was a flutter of white from *Ziethen*'s upper deck, a flutter of white long repeated. Then two figures climbed down the Jacob's ladders, and in one of them, even at that distance, Brown could recognize the rather portly form of the surgeon. Out of sheer rigidity of mental pose Brown found himself pointing the rifle at him before he remembered the white flag and desisted. The newcomers bent over the writhing, shrieking figures on the bo'sun's chairs, busied themselves with bandages and splints, and soon (but every minute meant delay to *Ziethen*) the wounded men were hoisted inboard and their attendants climbed up after them.

And as they went there was a sudden commotion at the foot of the cliff. Someone there could not bear the heat and strain any longer. Also he was the nearest to the water's edge. He flung himself suddenly, on all fours, down a little precipice, rolled down another, crashed through a cluster of cactus and tumbled over the last descent to the water. A bullet from Brown's rifle tore past his ear as he did so, but in his flustered panic he never noticed it.

His example was infectious. The other survivors of the landing party rose simultaneously and flung themselves down the cliff. Brown smashed the spine of one of them as he gathered himself for his last leap, but the other two reached the water's edge—and safety—unhurt save for gashes and scratches. Three men now crouched in the steam pinnace; they were the only unwounded survivors of a landing party of twenty-one.

But to the puzzled, fuming officers on *Ziethen*, their appearance by the pinnace meant relief from the worry of guessing what had happened to the landing party. The bridge semaphore began sending question after question to the dazed, conscience-stricken trio crouching in the lee of the rock edge. Sitting (for if they stood their signalling hands came into Brown's view and within reach of his bullets) they produced a couple of handkerchiefs and signalled back.

"Where is the rest of the party?"

"Dead."

"Where is Lieutenant Sturmer?"

"Dead."

"How many men opposed you?"

"One."

One question, however, the gesticulating semaphore demanded again and again. "Where is the escaped prisoner?" And the wretched men in the pinnace struggled vainly to satisfy their persistent captain.

"Up the cliff", they signalled, and "Hidden", and "We do not know", and "In the same place as he was this morning", and similar answers which drove Captain von Lutz into a state of blind fury, which was not alleviated by the knowledge that part of the crew was reading off the answers and that the whole would know of them within the hour.

Exasperated officers raked the face of the cliff with powerful glasses, but there was no possible chance of their finding Brown in that way. The crew were furious at the killing of their friends. They were annoyed with their officers, and they thirsted for the blood of the man who had put this shame upon their ship. Von Lutz knew this insolent runaway had undone all the good effected by the victory over *Charybdis*, and only his death would restore good feeling. Von Lutz appreciated the need of good feeling in a crew about to set out on a voyage of half-senseless destruction with certain defeat sooner or later. Therefore he had every possible motive when he issued orders to prepare for a landing at once of the largest party *Ziethen* could put on shore without entirely crippling herself—two hundred men. The news ran round the lower deck to the accompaniment of a buzz of joy.

Meanwhile the work of repair must go on. Some sort of screen for the workers must be arranged, so that they could be hidden from the view of the rifleman on the cliff. A working party hurriedly fell upon the task of preparing booms and awnings—further delay for *Ziethen*.

Brown in his eyrie on the cliff might have found time heavy on his hands were he not so wholly absorbed in the possibility of the need for immediate action. The sun was slowly roasting him alive. More than once he was forced to have recourse to one of his two water-bottles, and it was a worse torture to tear his lips away after a couple of grudging mouthfuls than it was to bear the thirst which preceded and followed them. Already one bottle was half empty, however, and Brown refused to allow himself anything approaching indulgence in the warm, metal-flavoured fluid. He sternly thrust back the cork and buckled the bottles to his belt. He set his teeth while the sweat ran down his face and caked the streaked lava dust which grimed it, his rifle ever to his hand, enduring without regret or hesitation.

He took advantage of the lull to run the pull-through down his rifle barrel again. He looked with attention to the breech mechanism, for the lava dust was a serious clog to its smooth working. He counted his cartridges and settled them more handily in his pouches. He thought about having a meal, but put the idea aside; he was not at all hungry, and the excitement and the sun pouring down onto his back were not likely to allow him to be hungry for some time.

Still time dragged on.

Meanwhile, bent over the meagre charts of Resolution, Captain von Lutz and his officers were planning the new attack upon Brown. This time nothing was to be left to chance. There was to be no repetition of the blunder of the morning, when too few men were flung idly upon an impossible climb in the face of a weapon of precision.

The campaign was mapped out with real German thoroughness. All men were to carry food and water. Each landing party was allotted a different section of the island to beat through. As the small-arm supplies were limited, each party was carefully arranged in sections of beaters and riflemen. Brown was to be forced upon the move first before he was directly attacked. The riflemen in *Ziethen* were to continue their watch for him—a bullet could travel from there to the island as easily as from the island to *Ziethen*. The hunt was to be continued all night if necessary. All possible arrangements seemed to have been made; the only flaw was that the men who made the plans still did not understand the difficulty of movement upon the island.

Brown became aware of great activity on board *Ziethen*. The semaphore messages in German had of course been unreadable to him, and they had occurred two hours ago. Now men began to show themselves here and there on the upper decks. They exposed themselves no more than they could help, and Brown, firing rapidly when opportunity occurred, kept them harried. He hit at least four men and his shots were answered from the ship by hidden riflemen—who, all the same, had no knowledge of his exact position, and whose efforts in consequence caused him little trouble. A boom suddenly was run out on the starboard side abaft the bridge (Brown got two shots into the little group he could see) and from it dropped a long strip of awning which screened the damaged area from his present position.

At the same time another canvas screen was run up across the upper deck at the stern, and he could not quite see over it. He sent three bullets through it before he realized that this was a waste of ammunition. The bridge semaphore wagged again, and the result of its message was seen shortly, when the three wretched men in the steam pinnace left their shelter under the rock and made a wild dash back to the ship. The pinnace steered an erratic enough course, for the helmsman was lying flat on his back under the gunwale in his desperate anxiety to avoid fire, although Brown could do her no harm, and she soon shot round *Ziethen's* stern into safety. The sound of activity came across the lagoon to Brown's ears, but the screens hid everything from view save the ship's stern, upper works, and starboard side as far as the outboard screen, and he could not form any accurate idea of what was going on. He soon knew, however.

Out from *Ziethen*'s port bow shot four boats. The steam pinnace led, towing the other three, and they were all crammed with men. Rifle fire rose from *Ziethen* at the same time and now a new menace was added—machine-guns. Two of these raved at him from

Ziethen's fore-top, traversing slowly backward and forward across the suspected area, at each new traverse taking a line lower down the cliff. Bullets were sending the dust and cactus flying everywhere. Under that leaden hail Brown forced himself to think clearly. He could do little to stop those boats and to fire he must expose himself a little in that deadly horizontal rain. It was not worth the risk. Brown crouched down into his hollow behind the twin lava blocks which had served their turn so well. The sharp rap of a bullet upon one of them and the sound of others close above him made the propriety of the movement apparent immediately after. Then the hail passed on.

Brown peered between the blocks, could see nothing, and squirmed round to where he could see farther. The string of boats, instead of making straight for him, had dashed out through the opening of the lagoon, and even as he caught sight of them, had swung round to port, to his part of the island but on the outside sea face. His position was to be taken in reverse. It was then that Brown looked anxiously at the sun; there were still three hours more of daylight—only three hours, thank God.

The persistent beating of the machine-gun bullets started a little avalanche of rock thirty yards away on the right, and this disturbance attracted the attention of all the marksmen on the ship; bullets rained upon the spot until a wide dust cloud arose from it, drifting away on the hardly perceptible wind. Then the firing stopped; even small-arms ammunition must not be allowed to run short on a raiding cruiser. From the ship came a rattle and buzz of machinery and the creaking of tackle as repairs progressed. Brown knew it would be hard for him to interfere. While his face of the cliff was being raked by a dozen glasses, and while a score of marksmen, finger on trigger, were waiting anxiously for any sign of movement, he dared not make an open attempt to shift his position so as to be able to fire round the screen. Behind him, too, he knew that men were being landed, soon they would be climbing up the outer face of the island. Then they would reach the crest. His saddle of rock was dominated from one or two points on the crest. If the enemy reached one of those points in daylight he was certain of death. If he moved from where he was by daylight he was certain of death. His life depended upon the coming of night. All he prayed for was the opportunity to continue to delay *Ziethen* at Resolution. He lay upon his ledge of rock waiting for night—or for the firing from the crest which would presage his death. There is a sublime, hard satisfaction in awaiting death when one has done all that can be done to avert it.

Chapter Thirteen

The steam pinnace, towing empty boats this time, suddenly shot into view through the break in the cliffs and dashed up to *Ziethen*; in a quarter of an hour she shot out again with the boats full of men once more. Machine-guns and rifles opened again from the ship upon the cliffs to prevent Brown from firing, but, as before, he had no intention of doing so. He saw the boats turn to port as they had done the first time before the cliffs cut them from his view. That meant that the sweep across the island by a line of men would only take place across a limited length; if Brown could only move along the island sufficiently far he would evade the sweep. Two hundred men, which was Brown's accurate estimate of their number, at ten-yard intervals cover two thousand yards and the outside edge of Resolution is about four thousand yards in circumference. Brown realized that he must transfer himself to a point rather more than halfway round the island if he were to have any chance of escape.

Yet he could not move at all till nightfall. He waited on with patience, not knowing from one minute's end to another when fire would be opened upon him from the crest of the island. He cast anxious glances upward at the sun as it sank steadily in his face.

The seaward face of Resolution is very like the inner face, save that the angle of ascent is much less steep, as it is the hardened remains of the lava flow rather than the wall of the throat of a crater. But on the outer face the blocks of lava resulting from sudden cooling are just as razor-edged and the cactus is just as impenetrable. The landing party proceeded with German thoroughness. The first half was lined out along the seashore at accurate intervals, and was kept waiting until the second half was brought from the ship and lined out in continuation of it. Every man knew his job, which was to push straight up the face of the island keeping correct alignment and spacing, scanning every bush and cranny for the fugitive. The lieutenant in command raced from one end of the line to the other in the steam pinnace, saw that everything was in order, and took up his position in the centre of the line. He gave the word and the line began its ascent.

Alas for the accurate alignment! The weary climb up the seaward face was of necessity reduced in pace to that of the slowest. Not until it was attempted could anyone guess the fiendish difficulty involved in moving about on Resolution. The frightful heat radiated from the rocks—which were nearly too hot for the naked hand—was the least of the difficulties. Cactus and lava combined to lacerate feet and hands. Two ankles were sprained in the first half-hour. Thirst descended upon the sweating, swearing sailors. The fuming officers did their best to keep the men on the move, but cramped living in a cruiser in the tropics is not the best preparation for difficult mountaineering. Here and there parts of the island were unscaleable, and men were compelled to move to one side to climb at all; but as soon as the difficulty was evaded the petty officers with the pedantic adherence to orders resulting from an over-strict discipline, held up their section of the line until the intervals were corrected. Bound by its rigid orders, the line crawled up the face of the island at a pace much slower than even the slowest among them could have proceeded alone.

An hour before nightfall (at least an hour, that is to say, later than he had expected to reach the crest) the exasperated lieutenant sent word along the line for each man to push on as best he could. But it takes time to pass orders from mouth to mouth along an extended line, and only one-third of the distance had been covered when they were issued. The sun sank gaudily into the purple sea and night fell with dramatic rapidity to find Brown still unfired at, and two hundred German sailors spread out and tangled in the darkness over a mile of leg-breaking rock.

Brown waited for complete darkness. Throughout the afternoon he had been mapping out in his mind a path down the cliff—a handhold here, a foothold there, a slide lower down. When night came he was ready; his hands were bound about with strips torn from his jumper, his equipment fastened about him, his mind as resolute as ever. He climbed off the shelf which had been his fortress for twelve hours. The lava hacked at him as he slid and tumbled down the cliff. The razor edges tore through his shoes and cut into his feet. The cactus spines scratched into his body, making lines like the marks of a tiger's claws. He wrenched ankle and knee so that they pained him excruciatingly. Yet he kept in his mind the various points to be aimed at, and it was not long before he had covered the three hundred feet of descent.

The first, ill-fated German landing party had reached the island a hundred yards away to his right, and it was there that the bodies of its dead lay along with the dozen wounded whose pitiful cries had climbed the rock to Brown's ears all the afternoon. Gladly would Brown have gone to them, have tried to tend their hurts and given them the water for which they had moaned unceasingly, were it not that to do so would have imperilled the execution of his duty. As it was, he shut his ears to the pitiful sounds and proceeded with his task. Nothing could weigh in the scale at all against his conception of what he had to do.

His two lifebelts still lay in their cactus clump, and he picked them out and buckled them round himself and his rifle as on the preceding night. Then he lowered himself into the water and set out across the lagoon. The sea-water added intensely to the pain.

Brown paddled steadily round the lagoon fifty yards from shore, keeping away from the ship. Far behind him, on the unseen face of the island, the wretched German sailors were toiling over the lava. The island was alive with the clash and clatter of dropped rifles and stumbling feet. No one knows who fired the first shot. Most probably it was an accident, the result of a stumble by some fool who had slipped a cartridge into his rifle. The noise of the shot echoed through the darkness. Brown, paddling across the lagoon, heard it and wondered. The example was infectious. Iguanas, nocturnal creatures, scurrying over rocks and round bushes, gave frights to various people, and there was quite a respectable bubble of musketry round the island before the shouted orders of the officers brought about a cessation of fire. On board *Ziethen* the sound was accepted as a welcome proof that the murderous fugitive had met his fate, the while Brown steadily made his way round the lagoon to a point on the shore broad on *Ziethen*'s starboard beam. Here, with some difficulty, he found a place where he could land, and once more he let drop his lifebelts into a cluster of cactus. Then he set his teeth and began to climb the steep cliff.

But his cuts and bruises and stiffness and the awful rawness of his feet reduced his activity to a pitiful minimum. Climb he must if he were to be able for another day to beat off attacks from the shore and to dominate *Ziethen*'s deck. Also he must be close in to the foot of an overhanging bit of cliff if he was to have any security against fire from above, and it would be as well if he had cover to his left and right in addition. What he needed was something like a cave halfway up the cliff, and for this, in the light of the late-rising moon, he peered about anxiously between his convulsive efforts to scale the cliff.

His rifle and ammunition, too, were serious hindrances to his progress, and his face was distorted with strain at each heart-breaking struggle. Both his feet and his hands left bloody imprints upon the rock where they touched it. Yet he struggled on to where in the faint light he thought he could make out a shallow vertical cleft in the cliff face which might be suitable for his purpose. It was long past midnight before he reached it, passed judgement upon it, and roused himself to climb yet a little higher to a better place still. There he fell half-fainting upon the harsh lava.

Even then, after half an hour's rest, he fought his way back to consciousness again and raised his head and eyed *Ziethen*, whose malignant bulk, black in the faint light, swam on the magical water of the lagoon.

On her starboard side, square to his front, hung a faint patch of light, and the noise of riveters came to his ears over the water. The hole in the ship's side, screened forward and aft, and partly screened in front, had been lit by electric lights dangled over the side. Through the gaps in the outer screen Brown could just see human figures moving back and forth. He slid his rifle forward. But he checked himself even as his finger reached the trigger. He was too shaky after his exertions to be sure of hitting hard and often.

Besides, a rifleman, however invisible by daylight, shows up all too plainly by night by reason of the flash of his weapon. He laid his rifle down, and then, before even he could settle himself comfortably, he collapsed onto the rifle butt. Meanwhile the two hundred men of the landing party stumbled and swore as they endeavoured to sweep across the island, and still fired a stray shot or two when the strain became too much for their nerves.

Chapter Fourteen

Brown woke, or regained consciousness, just as dawn was climbing brilliantly up the sky. His first action was to drink temperately from the dwindling supply in his second water-bottle. Then, doggedly, he began to make sure of his position and situation. Looking out of his notch in the cliff face, hoisting himself cautiously on his knees to do so, he saw a dozen white figures creeping slowly on the very crest of the island a quarter of a mile from him. On the inner face of the island, round about his previous position, he saw a dozen others perched precariously here and there, still endeavouring to carry out their orders to sweep the island from one sea to another.

Of the rest of the landing party Brown could see nothing, but he could guess shrewdly enough. They were scattered hither and thither over the outer face of Resolution, perhaps still struggling on, perhaps nursing cut feet or broken ankles, perhaps sleeping or dodging duty in the way unsupervised men will. Brown shrank down into his notch again, he was safe enough from observation, and out of sight, indeed, of nearly every point of the island.

In front, however, *Ziethen* was in full view. The screens hung out over the damaged part were like a box applied to the ship's side—a box defective down one edge, however. Through the gap Brown could see occasionally a white figure appear and disappear, although for the moment the noise of the hammers had ceased. The operation now in progress was the lowering down of the new plates to be riveted into position. It was in consequence of the demands of the tackle for this business that the booms of the screen had been shifted to leave the small gap Brown noted; and as Brown had not fired at the ship for fifteen hours a certain carelessness had been engendered, to say nothing of the fact that *Ziethen* believed that the landing party had killed Brown hours ago.

Brown pulled the oily rag through his rifle barrel; he oiled the breech, which was beginning to stick badly, and then he sighted carefully for the gap in the screen. He awaited the most favourable moment and then fired twice, quickly, and he killed the two men he could see. Then, to make the most of his surprise, he fired again and again through the screen scattering his shots here and there across it. He hit one or two men, and scared into jumpiness the men he did not hit. The moment when a ten-ton steel plate is swinging in tackles is a bad moment to be shot at.

The killings and the wounds and the interruption roused *Ziethen* to a pitch of fury previously unreached. Those on board were maddened by the deaths and furiously angry with the landing party. Captain von Lutz set the bridge semaphore into staccato action, and the wretched lieutenant in command on shore, staggering along the crest after a sleepless night of fevered action, read the messages with a sick feeling at his heart. The vivid sentences poured out by Captain von Lutz, vehemently demanding what on earth the lieutenant and landing party were about, stung the wretched officer to the quick. A Japanese lieutenant would have committed suicide; a German merely called out his last reserves of energy and gathered a body of the less faint-hearted to push on round the island to where Brown lay hidden.

On board *Ziethen* work was suspended temporarily—another triumph to Brown's credit. Too many skilled ratings had been lost already for the captain to order his remaining ones to chance the bullets which Brown was sending at intervals through the screen. Instead he decided to turn *Ziethen* away from the point of attack. To turn an unwieldy armoured cruiser, with her five hundred feet of length, and listing badly at that, in a lagoon wherein the tide was swirling in a whirlpool, was an operation calling for care and consuming much time. The two anchors had to be raised, the propellers set in motion, and *Ziethen* gently nursed into position, one anchor dropped, the set of the current combatted, and then the other anchor dropped—and good holding ground was scarce. Altogether it was an hour before the mooring was completed and the delicate operation of lowering the new plates into position was resumed. Brown heard at length the clatter of the riveting, and he knew that the delays he had imposed upon *Ziethen* were ending at last.

But the labours of the landing party were still in full blast. The lieutenant's two hundred men were scattered over a mile of almost impossible country, and the problem of supplies now added another burden to the lieutenant's overloaded shoulders. Every man had landed with a day's water; they had been violently exerting themselves for nearly twenty-four hours, and nine men out of ten had consumed the last drop of their water several hours back. The unhappy lieutenant signalled to his captain that he could not hope to move without water. Captain von Lutz signalled back in blistering fashion, but the lieutenant held to his contention. The captain, raging, sent off water to him round the island and his commander as well to take over control, under strict orders not to return without bringing back Brown, dead or alive.

For the morale situation was serious. No captain could dream of setting out on a long and arduous cruise with a crew in such a temper as *Ziethen*'s was. Thirty-four men killed and wounded and two ignominious reverses had upset discipline. If *Ziethen* were to sail away without taking vengeance on Brown the crew would lose all respect for their officers. Captain von Lutz decided that Brown must die, even though killing him meant postponing their ravening onslaught upon British shipping.

So the water was sent, and the commander took over. He did not find it an easy task. To distribute water among his scattered, weary command consumed hours of time and much of the strength of the twenty men he brought as reinforcements. It was afternoon before he was ready to make his first move, and by that time the riveting on *Ziethen* was completed and she was ready to steam away. Brown could now credit himself with further delays to her—all the length of time, in fact, which he occupied in dying.

The commander acted with energy. He sent his casualties down the cliff to where the first landing had been made. There the men

Brown had wounded the day before at last received attention and water: the dead and wounded were sent back to the ship for care or burial. Having purged his force of its weaker elements, the commander proceeded to make his way along the crest of the island, while a boat with full crew lay ready to dash to any point to which it might be signalled, and another one landed more men across the opening of the lagoon to cut off any attempt Brown might make to evade attack again.

The commander did not care how much time the business consumed as long as it was done thoroughly. From *Ziethen*'s bridge he had watched the failure of the first frontal assault, and he was not going to throw away another dozen lives in that fashion. These long, weary flanking movements were the alternative, and he accepted it stoically. All the same, most of the heart had been taken out of his men, and, as before, they made woefully slow progress. Night found them still tangled utterly in the crevasses of Resolution. It found Brown, too, lodged in his cleft in the cliff, tormented with thirst, running a dry tongue round his cracked lips, agonized by the pain in his hands and feet, bitten in every part of his body by vicious flies, but all the same without a thought of surrender. That simply did not occur to him. It was not consonant with his heredity nor with his childhood training.

Chapter Fifteen

Albert Brown spent a weary night. Before morning he had used the last of his water and his thirst occupied nearly all his thoughts. Hunger led him to eat some of his tinned provisions, and that, of course, increased his thirst. From the cessation of the noise of the riveting on board *Ziethen* he deduced that repairs were completed, but as long as a landing party was on shore it was his duty to keep it occupied, and so detain *Ziethen* longer still. He fought down his thirst, and he fell now and again into a troubled sleep, from which he awoke each time with a start, hearing the clamorous noises made by the landing party.

When morning came and found Brown still alive and untaken

(he informed every one of the fact by sending a couple of bullets along *Ziethen*'s bridge, narrowly missing the officer of the watch), pleasant expectation on board changed to furious consternation. Captain von Lutz abruptly sent the last fifty men who could be spared in a dash for the inner shore in an assault upon the place where he judged Brown to be. He was only one hundred yards out in his estimate; that was good judgement considering that he had only the noise of rifle shots echoing from a cliff to guide him, and that *Ziethen*, which had turned away, was now nearly half a mile from Brown.

Brown saw the boats coming and turned his rifle upon them, but now, with his teeth chattering with fever and his hands trembling, he could not aim even moderately well. He looked along the rifle barrel and saw the foresight dancing like a live thing in the U of the backsight, and shot after shot went wide. The boats rushed in to the foot of the cliff and the boats' crews bundled out, scattering a little swarm of marine iguanas who had been comfortably feeding on seaweed at the water's edge regardless of the din of battle echoing round the island.

Even at a hundred yards Brown dropped two men only in five shots. Then, reaching into his pouches to refill his magazine, he realized that he had only twenty rounds left. With such a small reserve he knew that he could hardly stop this close attack—and the one which must develop soon out on his left would be able to push forward unopposed. It was the last, desperate death grapple. He marshalled his failing strength for one more effort, and tried to shoot the attackers down deliberately, one by one.

More than one of the struggling attacking party dropped, but far more by reason of the difficulties of the ascent than in consequence of the casualties the forward impetus died away. Just as before the climbers crouched down in hollows; from the sound of Brown's firing they had formed some idea of his position, and they began to fire back at him. Once more Brown heard the sharp noise of bullets passing close beside him, and once more little puffs of lava dust arose here and there where the bullets struck. But on this occasion the attack had begun farther off to one side and Brown was not perched quite so high up, so that his position was not nearly so dominating, and he could not overlook the lumps of rock behind which lay his enemies. He caused another two casualties, but these did not deter the forty men who were firing at him, and when he had filled his magazine with his last cartridges he had to keep these in reserve to use against the last rush. He lay as close to the lava as he could, waiting in uncomplaining patience for the end to come, while the bullets cracked and sang all round about him.

Soon his quiescence was noted by those below; the bolder and the stronger among them heaved themselves up and made little advances up the face of the cliff out of one crevice into the next. Before long most of the line was bellying forward, up the cliff, and working along it. Peering with one eye over the edge, Brown could see two or three men only fifty yards away. Soon one of them would get a clear sight of him, and that would be the end. He felt no resentment; he had done all he could.

At that very moment the battle was interrupted. A tremendous braying from *Ziethen*'s siren clamorously called everyone's attention to the signal which was being wigwagged repeatedly from her bridge semaphore. It was the general recall.

For some minutes the attackers hesitated. It was hard to go back when success was so close at hand. But the siren brayed again, and no one could act in independence of orders so definite. Reluctantly the officer commanding the landing party blew his whistle and the attackers slowly turned back down the cliff, crawling back perilously, and dropping down little precipices.

Brown saw them go, and as a last effort he raised himself and sent a bullet through the shoulder of the officer in command—which had the desirable effect of delaying the retreat while the landing party turned and wasted ammunition upon him until further trumpetings of *Ziethen*'s siren recalled them to duty. They dropped down to the boats, lifted in their wounded and dead, and pulled back to the cruiser.

It was not the evacuation of the island by the landing party which took up so much time; the real delay was caused by the huge straggling mob on the outer face. After the commander in charge had read the signals from his vantage point on the crest, he had still to pass the word for retreat throughout the length and breadth of his command, and having done so he still had to get his men down to the beaches. Most of them had been straying loose over Resolution for nearly forty-eight hours; they were dispirited, lame, fatigued, and woefully undisciplined. The commander and the lieutenant raved and swore as much as their dry throats permitted, while the sweat drenched their soiled ducks; the petty officers struggled to keep the men within earshot of them on the move; but it was a painful, hopeless task. A man a hundred yards away might as well be ten miles away for all the use it was giving orders to him—there was no going back to him without wasting another hour.

To the wretched commander on the crest the hours after noon seemed to race by; the sun seemed to sink towards the horizon at three times its usual speed, while the messages spilled out by the semaphore became more and more caustic. He watched the incredibly slow descent of his men to the boats with fever consuming his soul.

Seaman Muller, the ship's bad character, came struggling along the top of the crest past the commander. His feet were very sore and his clothes were in tatters. With his rifle hitched over his shoulder he was picking his way along the more easy stretch of small lava at the top of the island. He came within fifty yards of the blaspheming commander, who shouted to him to get away diagonally down the slope to the boats, but Seaman Muller made an inaudible reply. He would keep along the crest until he was above the boats, and then he would, perhaps, graciously go down the steep slope. He was certainly not going to plunge down into that awful inferno of rocks and cactus until he had to.

A hundred yards past the commander he stopped to rest. He sat down where a lava block now cast a fair amount of shade, thanks to the setting of the sun. He mopped his streaming face, and his eyes roamed about carelessly over the tangle of cliff across the arc of the lagoon. A quarter of a mile away, one-third the way up the cliff, he seemed to see a speck of something which was neither cliff nor cactus. It might be the head and shoulder of a man. Seaman Muller unslung his rifle and threw himself upon his face. He slipped a cartridge into the breech.

The red splendour of the setting sun illuminated the speck of target presented to him. Muller was neither a good shot nor a musketry enthusiast. He took aim and fired just as he would have thrown a stone at a stray cat or bird. He did not even see whether he hit what he aimed at, for at the sound of the shot the empurpled face of a petty officer shot up from a hollow close beside him and an order bellowed into his ear roused even the undisciplined Muller to his feet to continue his slouching march back to the boats. For firing the shot against orders he was very properly run into the punishment cells as soon as he and the commander had reached *Ziethen* again.

But that last shot had reached its billet. It hit Brown high up on the right shoulder; it smashed a rib and a shoulder-blade on its way through, and flung him back into his crevice. At first he was merely numb. He put his hands to his wound and was surprised to find them red with blood. It was some time after sunset before the pain came.

Chapter Sixteen

It was as the direct result of the arrival of certain coded wireless messages that Captain von Lutz had ordered the immediate recall of the landing party. The messages came from the German agent in Panama—a Herr Schmidt—who had received information that the battle cruiser *Leopard* and her attendant light cruiser *Penzance* were even now making the passage of the Canal from the West Indies, the first British warships to make use of the waterway—one month open, only. *Leopard*'s twenty-four knots and her 12-inch guns meant death to any German ship in the Pacific; small wonder then that Captain von Lutz, with certain disaster cruising after him in this fashion, had decided to stay no longer within sight of land, and had issued such urgent orders for the landing party's recall.

Those orders nevertheless were more easily issued than obeyed. It was past three o'clock by the time the inner landing party had reached the ship with a fresh load of wounded and dead, and by the time night fell on Resolution only the smallest driblets of the other force had trickled down to the boats; there were still many men hopelessly entangled on the slope. And with the coming of darkness the task of getting the weary men to continue the descent became hopeless.

Messages flashed to *Ziethen* did nothing to allay the impatience of Captain von Lutz as he strode about fuming. With very little additional motive he would have taken the ship out and abandoned what was left of the landing party, but it was really too much to risk. When he had them all back, *Ziethen* would still be short-handed, and the loss of another fifty men would be extremely serious. Captain von Lutz had to bear in mind the prospect of strenuous coaling at sea and of sending away prize crews, to say nothing of having to fight further battles. He could only fret and fume and send orders to get the men into the boats as soon as possible while he calculated the chances of the British battle cruiser setting a course for the Galapagos and the time it would take her to get there.

THE BROAD LIGHT of day was pouring upon the tortured rocks before the last worn straggler came stumbling into the boats; it was almost high noon before *Ziethen* had her anchors up and was heading out of that accursed lagoon to the open sea with a depressed, weary crew and exasperated officers. For once the magnificent German efficiency had come to grief; the stern German discipline had failed. Much may be made of the rocks and thorns of Resolution, but most of the credit for the achievement undoubtedly belonged with Leading Seaman Brown, who had voluntarily opposed himself to the might of an armoured cruiser, and had foreseen that the enterprise would cost him his life.

For Brown was dying surely enough. A night of torture had followed his wounding. The pain came steadily, growing stronger and stronger as the numbness following the initial shock had died away. He was in a high fever, and the pain made him toss in pitiful efforts to get away from what was tormenting him. He had been thirsty enough before, but that thirst was nothing compared to the suffering he now experienced. Several times that night he had struggled back to consciousness, obsessed by the thought that he might have a little water left. Each time he had writhed himself about until he could grasp the water-bottles and draw the corks and raise each in turn to his cracked and swollen lips. Once only had this agonizing effort encountered success; three or four drops of fluid, cool and delightful, trickled out of the bottle into his furred mouth, but that was all. There was never anything in either of the bottles afterwards, but Brown always hoped there was.

As Brown held his left hand to his riven shoulder a troubled memory drifted into his mind of the German boy he had shot the day before yesterday. Brown recalled just how that boy had rolled out from behind his cover, trying to hold his shoulder just as Brown was doing now. He remembered the pain upon the boy's pleasant face, and he remembered how all day he had lain in the torturing sun with the flies thick upon him, calling feebly for water. The heartbroken cries of the German boy echoed persistently in Brown's ears; he felt he must rouse himself to satisfy them.

The effort was easy enough: there had descended upon him a God-given ability to float quietly through the air. He floated down to the German boy, lying with the sun on his pale hair; he took his hand, and the boy opened his eyes and smiled with blue, child-like eyes. Brown lifted him easily by his hand, and together they drifted away from the ugly rocks into a pleasant shady place. They went on to where tall trees reared themselves over a meadow of green grass, and there, beside the trees, there was a little, deep river of clear water. They drank, and it was perfectly cool and wonderful. They drank and laughed with their happiness, and then they lowered themselves into the clear stream and drifted, lapped about with water. Everything was friendly and blissfully perfect.

Then Brown turned and smiled at the boy again, but he did not smile back. Instead his face was contorted with pain and he glared at Brown with wild eyes, and Brown found that the cool water had fallen away, leaving him on the rocky bottom. And it was hot again, and the rocks beneath him were sharp—oh, and his shoulder hurt him so! With a start and a groan Brown came back to consciousness and thirst, thirst, thirst.

The good things of this world had passed him by. He had never had an eye for the wonder of a woodland triumphant with primroses or mysterious with bluebells. He had never known woman's love, and he had never known the love of a child. Good food and good wine and the glory of Rembrandt had alike passed him by. Never even had he known liberty; he had been all his life the slave either of a mother's ambition or of a Navy which demanded her servitors' all. His happiness, his talents, his life itself, had been swept away in the Age of the Twelve-Inch Gun. The achievements of Brown at twenty embraced nothing older than death and destruction.

He never knew the satisfaction of success; he never knew what stupendous results would eventually crown his efforts. Later on that last day he came back to consciousness; he swept the flies from his face and, under the impulse of his one consuming motive, he edged himself to the brink of the rock and peered out over the lagoon. The blue water luxuriated in the drenching sunshine; the grim cliffs danced and wavered in the shimmering heat before his reeling eyes. At the water's edge the marine iguanas browsed upon the seaweed as their Stone Age ancestors had done. Far out at sea the gulls wheeled and sank over the grey line that marked the ocean currents' edge. But of *Ziethen* Brown could see nothing; the jagged cliffs cut off from his view the smudge of smoke which marked where she was heading out for the horizon. She had gone; she had got clear, and all his efforts to detain her had only ended in a trivial forty-eight hours' delay, of no importance at all in a six months' cruise. Brown fell forward onto the rock again with a groan of broken-hearted despair; thirst and pain wrapped him about once more. They killed him between them, did pain and thirst, before the end of that day. He had been a long time dying, but he was dead at last.

Chapter Seventeen

Captain Richard E. S. Saville-Samarez, C.B., M.V.O., sat alone in his cabin at his desk pondering the problems set before him by the terse Admiralty instructions received by wireless and cable, by the small Pacific chart before him bearing the estimated positions of von Spee and his squadron, and by the various possibilities which had gradually accumulated in his not highly imaginative brain. His passage of the Panama Canal in H.M.S. *Leopard* with *Penzance* in company had caused very considerable stir. Already *Leopard*'s presence would be notified to Berlin, and the German Admiralty would note the information and weigh anxiously the effect of this slight dispersion upon the crushing superiority of the Grand Fleet at Scapa, where thirty Dreadnoughts awaited the emerging of the High Sea Fleet from its minefields and protected harbours.

Captain Saville-Samarez was not very different in appearance from what he had been twenty years before; he was not of the type that alters greatly with age. Responsibility and authority sat lightly on his shoulders; he was never a man for deep thought, and the steadiness of his nerve had brought him out of whatever difficulties he had found himself. Little jobs like picking up moorings in a twenty-thousand-ton battleship in a crowded harbour with a full gale blowing he had simply accepted and carried through with automatically acquired skill and without any frightening picture of what might happen if he made a mistake.

But just at present he was thinking deeply and trying his utmost to use all the imagination he possessed. He realized how fortunate he had been; the command of a battle cruiser was perhaps the biggest plum in the service open to one of his rank. Moreover, he held an independent command at present, and *Penzance* was under his command as well.

His instructions gave him a free enough hand; what he had to do was to hunt down von Spee and his squadron. The only tie upon him was the emphasis laid in his orders upon the necessity to keep *Leopard* from damage, no destruction of armoured cruisers being worth the loss of a battle cruiser. If he allowed either *Leopard* or *Penzance* to be seriously damaged, the rage of the authorities and of the British public would be unbounded.

So that a battle, were one to take place, would demand caution—but this need for caution was only one of the factors worrying the captain. Von Spee had last been heard of three thousand miles away, and to find a squadron hidden in three thousand miles of water was not an easy matter. Von Spee might even turn northward again and slip past *Leopard* and gain the Panama Canal—and that would mean Captain Saville-Samarez's professional ruin. The captain realized that he needed all his wits to be sure of encountering the enemy.

And he needed to encounter them. With the age limit steadily pursuing him up the captains' list, he could see plainly enough that unless he did something to distinguish himself he would end his life as rear-admiral on the retired list like fifty others he could name. He needed to do something to make his name remembered, and the surest way would be to sink a German ship or two. Then the public would know him as "Saville-Samarez, you know, 'im 'oo sank the *Scharnhorst*"; and the captain knew how valuable such a label tied on to him would be. With the reward of success so rich, and the penalty of failure so severe, it behoved him to devote all possible energy to the solution of the problem.

Characteristically, he was making his final decision by himself. He had run through the meagre data with the captain of *Penzance*, and heard his opinion, but he had left the final making up of his mind until he was alone.

He looked at the map, whereon von Spee was noted as last heard of at Valparaiso. The wireless room of *Leopard* was continuously reporting powerful messages in an unknown code, and it seemed extremely likely that they were warnings of his approach sent out to the German squadron. That made it possible that the German agents on the mainland thought it conceivable that German ships were near.

Now von Spee had fought at Coronel and had entered Valparaiso with only two armoured cruisers, *Scharnhorst* and *Gneisenau*. That was certain. Therefore his smallest armoured cruiser, *Ziethen*, had been detached before Coronel. Whither would von Spee be likely to send her? Northward? Not likely, with the whole Japanese navy on the lookout for her, and not much plunder to be obtained in the Northern Pacific. Westward, to the Indian Ocean? That was the richest field of all; but *Charybdis* lay on that route and had made no report of meeting German ships. South-westward, to New Zealand and Australian waters? Quite likely. But in that case Captain Saville-Samarez had no business with her; his duty was to get into touch with the main body. But supposing *Ziethen* had not been sent anywhere like this? Suppose she was still near the South American coast? She might have been in collision or had engine-room trouble. Certainly it was odd that she had neither fought at Coronel nor been reported elsewhere. Now supposing she had been damaged, where would she try to effect repairs? Captain Saville-Samarez looked at the map just as Captain von Lutz had done a week before, and came to exactly the same conclusion. The Galapagos Archipelago presented the most opportunities to a ship in need of repair.

Captain Saville-Samarez went on to consider ways and means. The Archipelago lay a little out of his direct course south from Panama. But *Penzance*'s most economical cruising speed was far in excess of *Leopard*'s. The ships would overlook far more water separated than in company. And *Penzance*'s speed was far larger than that of any one of von Spee's squadron. She could look after herself and keep out of danger unless she experienced the very worst of luck. Captain Saville-Samarez reached his final decision with promptitude and did not think about it again. His signal flew for the *Penzance*'s captain to come on board *Leopard*, and a few quite brief sentences explained to that officer what Captain Saville-Samarez wanted done.

So, when the captain of *Penzance* reached his own ship again he set a fresh course which gradually took his ship westward away from *Leopard*. Leading Seaman Albert Brown at this moment was only thirsty; Muller's bullet did not hit him until sunset that day, when *Penzance* and *Leopard* had diverged until they were quite out of sight of each other.

Chapter Eighteen

Nelson once wrote that five minutes make the difference between victory and defeat. It was hardly more than five minutes which made the difference in this case. Had *Ziethen* sailed only half an hour earlier she would have got away undetected. For as *Penzance* came down upon Resolution from the northeast, *Ziethen* was steering northwest away from the island. Just as Resolution came in sight a pair of keen eyes on *Penzance* detected a little trace of smoke far away on the westerly horizon. Smoke in that lost corner of the world was uncommon, and therefore suspicious, and *Penzance* headed after it in all the pride of her twenty-seven knots. In half an hour *Ziethen* was definitely identified, and the air was thrilling with the news as *Penzance* broadcast her information.

Vain it was now for *Ziethen* to try to jam *Penzance*'s messages. *Leopard* was only a hundred miles away; besides, the men who built and equipped *Penzance* had a very clear idea of the duties she was to perform. She was a battleship's eyes, a battleship's message bearer, and her immense speed and her powerful wireless installation were given her solely for these ends. Her news trickled in to *Leopard* hardly mutilated, and that great ship swung her twenty thousand tons round in pursuit.

The captain of *Penzance* knew his duty. Although his ship could match *Ziethen*'s 6-inch guns with 6-inch guns of her own, it was not his business to put her fragile hull within reach when there was a battle cruiser no distance off who would do the business for him without any risk of damage. *Ziethen* carried armour far more effective than *Penzance*'s fragile protective deck. *Penzance* could only possess the speed she boasted by reason of abandoning nearly all other protection; *Ziethen*, built in an age when the naval mind was a little muddled, had tried to combine all factors, speed (twenty knots at the time of her launching was a high speed), hitting power, and armour, with the result that now she was helpless against a specialist.

She challenged action boldly enough; she wheeled, with her guns trained out upon *Penzance* and the range-takers eagerly chanting the ranges; she charged forward, but *Penzance* was not inclined to accept the challenge. Not a man on board would not gladly have fought *Ziethen* to the death, but what was the use of incurring senseless losses when *Leopard* was pounding up behind with her 12-inch guns? *Penzance* kept away. Her seven knots advantage in speed was overwhelming. No possible manoeuvre of *Ziethen*'s could inveigle her into range. It was not very long before *Ziethen* sullenly abandoned her attempt to make a fight of it and turned southward at full speed in the hope of shaking off pursuit or of closing in to a fight when darkness came. And in reply to *Penzance*'s reports *Leopard* turned away to a converging course, working up to her full twenty-four knots, edging rapidly up to the two ships which were cleaving their way through the blue Pacific.

It was then, perhaps, during that long pursuit, that Captain von Lutz tasted defeat and failure and self-contempt at their bitterest. One single man had caused this disaster; one man armed with a rifle had brought about the destruction of *Ziethen*. Captain von Lutz looked back over those three days at Resolution. A single one of them would have sufficed to repair *Ziethen* and set her off again upon her career of destruction. Now, because one wretched English sailor had held her up at Resolution for forty-eight hours longer than was necessary, *Ziethen*'s career was being ended. Captain von Lutz had no illusions about that. He knew that a battle cruiser and a light cruiser had passed the Canal; the light cruiser had arrived and was keeping him under observation, so the battle cruiser could not be far away. And a battle cruiser would have no difficulty at all in finishing the work which Albert Brown had begun. The tea ships and meat ships and sugar ships, the ships carrying troops and the ships carrying bullion, would pass to and fro across the southern waters without *Ziethen* to sink and burn them.

Yet although Captain von Lutz was so convinced of the approaching destruction of his ship, he had no thought of giving up without at least a final struggle. Vigorous messages passed to the engine-room, and soon *Ziethen*'s boilers were filled up with every ounce of steam they could bear. Night was not far off, and if thick weather came with it *Ziethen* had a chance of escape, or might have a chance of closing with her adversaries and doing as much damage as she herself received.

The pursuit must be prolonged until dark, and it was with an anxious eye that Captain von Lutz scanned the horizon as he paced about the bridge, while officers and men laboured furiously making every preparation for a fight for life, stripping the ship of every conceivable combustible material, handling ammunition, and testing range-finders and gunnery controls. Such is the queer nature of mankind that the imminent prospect of a fight in which every one of them might lose his life cheered the ship's men immensely, and the depression and indiscipline which had settled upon

Ziethen after the ineffective attempts upon Resolution vanished like mist.

Night came while *Leopard* was still out of sight, and *Ziethen* began her attempts either to throw off *Penzance*'s pursuit or else to close with her. But the night was clear and moonlit and it was an easy enough matter for the lookouts on *Penzance* to pick up the loom of the big cruiser in the darkness. Before midnight *Leopard* came with her 12-inch guns and twenty-four knots. Then the two English ships were able to take up positions comfortably on *Ziethen*'s port and starboard quarters so that the wretched cruiser's chances of escape became negligible.

All through the night the three ships drove on southward through the Pacific. The Germans had no friends at sea within two thousand miles, and they were acutely conscious of the menacing, silent presence of the British ships. Twice already that night, in the hope that the shadowy cruiser which had hovered after them was within range, had they switched on searchlights and blasted the night with a salvo, but each time they had gained no profit from the performance.

With the first faint beginnings of daylight Captain Saville-Samarez gave orders to reduce speed below the nineteen knots at which *Leopard* had been ploughing through the sea. He was going to take no chances, and daylight was not going to find him anywhere nearly in range of *Ziethen*'s 6-inch guns. Even he, phlegmatic and confident though he was, had found the tension and excitement too great for sleep. He had been pacing about all night, while the crackling wireless was sending through the relay ships to the Admiralty in Whitehall the glad news that one at least of the German Pacific Squadron was within the grip of the British Navy. Before dawn a reply had reached him, and he knew that the K.C.B. he desired would be his by the end of the year—if only he did what was expected of him.

And when daylight was almost come Captain von Lutz on *Ziethen*'s bridge knew that his last hope was gone. Far away on the horizon, almost dead astern, his powerful glasses could make out the unmistakable tripod mast of a Dreadnought battle cruiser. There was death in that insignificant little speck.

Still there was some chance of doing damage. *Penzance* lay closer in, on the starboard quarter. *Ziethen* wheeled, with her guns reaching up to extreme elevation. As the sun's disc cleared the sea a crashing salvo broke forth from her side, but the range was too great. The columns of water where the shells fell rose from the surface of the sea nearly half a mile short of target. Five seconds later *Penzance*, in obedience to an irritated signal from *Leopard*, had turned away and was racing out of danger at her full twenty-seven knots, clearing the range for *Leopard*'s 12-inch guns.

On *Leopard*'s bridge stood Captain Saville-Samarez. The whole business would be as dangerous as shooting a sitting rabbit. Now he saw *Ziethen* swing eastward racing towards the level sun in one last hope of distracting the aim of the English gunners. But *Leopard* turned eastward too, steering a parallel course with the sun dead ahead and her guns training out to port. Eight 12-inch guns composed *Leopard*'s main armament; and the 12-inch gun had twice the range of the 6-inch gun and fired a shell eight times as heavy, with a shattering effect twenty times as great.

Leopard turned two points to port to get *Ziethen* comfortably within range, resumed her original course, and battle began. One gun from each turret volleyed forth in its deafening, appalling thunder, and four 12-inch shells went soaring forth on their ten-mile flight towards *Ziethen*. Each shell weighed half a ton, and between them contained enough explosive to lay all the City of London in ruins.

"Short," said the gunnery commander up in the gunnery control tower, watching with detached professional interest the shooting of his beloved guns. "Up two hundred."

The other four guns bellowed in their turn, and the half-ton shells shrieked out on their flight—ten miles in half a minute, reaching two miles up in the air as they went.

"Short," said the gunnery commander again. The four immense columns of water were well this side of the racing armoured cruiser. "Up two hundred. This blasted climate's played Old Harry with the cordite!"

At twenty-five-second intervals the salvoes blared forth from the fifty-foot-long turret guns.

"Over," said the gunnery commander. "Short. Hit. Hit. Hit. Over."

Three times in a minute and a half *Ziethen* was struck by a ton of steel containing a ton of high explosive. The wretched ship's upper works were shattered and flung about, the steel plates were twisted and torn as though they were sheets of paper in a giant's hands. One shell burst fair and true on the breech of a starboard side 6-inch gun, wiped out the gun's crew and pitched the gun overside. But there was still life in the ship; the black cross still streamed out on its white ground from the tottering mast. Round she came, trying feebly to close with the enemy—just as, five days before, *Charybdis* had tried to do. But *Leopard* did as *Ziethen* had done then; she turned away at full speed, keeping her distance while the target moved slowly back abaft the beam. It was a hopeless effort to seek to close even to 6-inch gun range; there was no chance at all of being able to use torpedoes with effect.

"Hit," said the gunnery commander. "Over. Hit. Hit. My God!"

The 12-inch shells had blasted great holes in the unarmoured upper works; one had blown a gap in the horizontal protective deck. The gunnery commander saw her lurching through the waves, smoke pouring from every crevice; but she was still a ship; she still moved, she still floated; she might still fire her guns. But two shells from the last salvo crashed through the protective deck and burst amid her very vitals. Boilers and magazines alike exploded in one huge detonation. The rending flash was visible in the strong tropical sunshine for a tiny instant as the ship blew apart before black smoke bellied out and hid everything from view. Then, as this cleared before the fresh breeze, there was nothing to be seen, nothing. *Ziethen* had gone the way of *Good Hope* and *Monmouth*, the way *Scharnhorst* was to go, and *Defence* and *Black Prince*, armoured cruisers all, sunk with all hands by gunfire. Twelve salvoes had done it—hardly more than five minutes' firing. Every man on board had perished, including two Englishmen, the leading signalman and Ginger Harris whom Brown had tended; but of course the English ships did not know of their existence on board—and never would.

The black smoke eddied away, and *Leopard* and *Penzance* raced for the spot where *Ziethen* had bcen. They found little enough: a dead man, a few floating bits of wreckage, and nothing else. *Leopard*'s wireless proclaimed the news—a welcome little victory, just in time to counter the depression resulting from the defeat of Coronel. It was England's proclamation of the mastery of the seas, to be confirmed within a week by *Sydney*'s fortunate encounter with *Emden*, and within a month by Sturdee's annihilation of von Spee, where once again 12-inch guns blew armoured cruisers to destruction.

Then Captain Saville-Samarez was free to turn his ship back to England. He was to take *Leopard* into the clamorous, bloody confusion of Jutland and he was to stand watch and ward with the others amid the tempestuous Shetlands, but that was his great day. As he had foreseen, he became known as "the man who sank the *Ziethen*". But nobody was to know to whom the destruction of that ship was really due.

C.S. Forester

Cecil Scott Forester was born in Cairo in 1899, but moved to London with his family when he was only a few years old. He went to school at Dulwich College and then studied medicine at Guy's Hospital (but failed to qualify as he could not recognize a single bone in his anatomy examination!).

His first successful novel, a murder story called *Payment Deferred,* was written at the early age of twenty-four, and, with Charles Laughton in the lead, was put on stage in 1931 and later filmed. *Brown on Resolution,* published in 1929, was filmed in the '30s and made the name of a young actor called John Mills.

By 1932 Forester was spending thirteen weeks a year in Hollywood on a script-writing contract, and was also a foreign correspondent for *The Times.* On the outbreak of World War II he entered the Ministry of Information, later sailing with the Royal Navy to collect material for *The Ship* (Condensed Books 1964). He then made a voyage to the Bering Sea to gather material for a similar book on the U.S. Navy, and it was during this trip that he was stricken with arteriosclerosis, a disease which left him crippled and in constant pain.

Though C.S. Forester wrote many varied and excellent books, both fact and fiction, his name will always be linked with the unforgettable Horatio Hornblower. In 1927, Forester, a hard-up, landlubber novelist, found in a second-hand bookshop a bundle of old naval magazines which supplied the exact, practical documentation of sailing in a British ship of the line in Nelson's age. As a result of this chance discovery, Forester, over a period of twenty-five years, wrote a series of novels about Hornblower, and felt sometimes the same kind of exasperation with his hero as Conan Doyle felt with Sherlock Holmes. Forester died in California in 1966, and it is perhaps fitting that he left, locked in a London vault, a short story telling of Hornblower's last days, with instructions that it was not to be published until after his own death. He could not let Hornblower die before himself.

WHERE ARE THE CHILDREN?

A CONDENSATION OF THE BOOK BY

Mary Higgins Clark

ILLUSTRATED BY NANCY OHANIAN

Published by Talmy Franklin, London

In the little Cape Cod town to which she had fled, Nancy told her terrible secret to one person and one only: Ray Eldredge, the young estate agent who helped her to buy her new home, who fell in love with her, who married her. The past, the dark shadow of suspicion that still lay over her, was safe enough with him. Ray loved her, and believed her innocent.

Slowly, over seven safe, happy years, her tragic memories faded. She and Ray had children of their own. The past was left behind, the future was golden.

Then suddenly, one wintry morning, Nancy found herself trapped once again in the horror of a waking nightmare. Once again the police were asking, "Where are the children?" And once again, afraid for her little family, afraid for her own sanity, Nancy couldn't answer, didn't know.

PROLOGUE

HE COULD feel the chill coming in through the cracks around the windowpanes. Clumsily he got up and lumbered over to the window. Reaching for one of the thick towels he kept handy, he stuffed it around the rotting frame.

The incoming draft made a soft, hissing sound in the towel, a sound that vaguely pleased him. He looked out at the mist-filled sky and studied the whitecaps churning in the water. From this side of the house it was often possible to see Provincetown, on the opposite shore of Cape Cod Bay.

He hated the Cape. He hated the bleakness of it on a November day like this. He had hated it the one summer he'd spent here—waves of tourists sprawling on the beaches; climbing up the steep embankment to this house; gawking in the downstairs windows.

He hated the large FOR SALE signs that Ray Eldredge had posted in the front and back, and the fact that now Ray and that woman who worked for him had begun bringing people in to see the house. Last month it had been only a matter of luck that he'd come along as they'd started through, that he'd gotten to the top floor ahead of them to put away the telescope.

Time was running out. Somebody would buy this house and he wouldn't be able to rent it again. That was why he'd sent the article to the paper. He wanted to be here to see her exposed for what she was . . . now, when she must have started to feel safe.

There was something else that he had to do, but she kept such a close watch on the children. Tomorrow . . .

He moved restlessly around the room. The bedroom of the top-floor apartment was large. The whole house was large. It was a bastardized evolution of an old captain's house, begun in the seventeenth century on a rocky crest that commanded a view of the whole bay.

For six years now he'd rented this apartment in the late summer and fall. It had been ideal for his purpose—until this year, when Ray Eldredge had told him they were actively trying to sell the place for a restaurant and it could be rented only with the understanding it could be shown at any time.

Raynor Eldredge. The thought of the man brought a smile. Had Nancy ever told Ray who she was? Maybe not. Women could be sly. If Ray didn't know, it would be even better. How wonderful it would be to actually see Ray's expression when he opened the paper tomorrow!

Impatiently he turned from the window. His thick, trunklike legs were tight in shiny black trousers. He'd be glad to lose some weight, though it would mean that awful business of starving himself again. And he'd be glad when he could let his hair grow back naturally. The sides had been thick and would probably be mostly gray now.

He paced restlessly around the apartment, finally stopping at the telescope in the living room. The telescope was especially powerful—the kind of equipment that wasn't available for general sale. He bent over and peered into it.

Because of the darkness of the day, Nancy's kitchen light was on, so it was easy to see her clearly, in front of the window over the sink. Maybe she was about to get dinner. She was standing quietly, looking in the direction of the water. What was she thinking of? The children—Peter . . . Lisa . . . ? He'd like to know.

His mouth felt dry. He licked his lips nervously. She looked very young today, with her hair pulled back from her face. She kept it dark brown. Someone would surely have recognized her if she'd left it the natural red-gold shade. Tomorrow she'd be thirty-two. But she didn't look her age.

He swallowed, gulped, then swallowed again. The sound evolved into a chuckle that shook his body, jarring the telescope. Nancy's image blurred, but he wasn't interested in watching her anymore.

Tomorrow! He could just see her expression at this time tomorrow. Exposed to the world for what she was; numbed with fear; trying to answer the question—the same question the police had thrown at her over and over seven years ago.

"Come on, Nancy," the police would be saying again. "Tell the truth. Tell us, Nancy—where are the children?"

CHAPTER ONE

RAY came down the stairs pulling the knot closed on his tie. Nancy was sitting at the table with Missy on her lap. Michael was eating his breakfast in his poised, reflective way.

Ray tousled Mike's head and leaned over to kiss Missy. Nancy smiled up at him. She was so darn pretty. There were fine lines around those blue eyes, but you'd never take her for thirty-two. He noticed the traces of red at the roots of her dark hair. A dozen times in the last year he'd wanted to ask her to let it grow out.

"Happy birthday, honey," he said quietly.

He watched as the color drained from her face.

Michael looked surprised. "Is it Mommy's birthday? You didn't tell me that."

Missy sat upright. "Mommy's birthday?" She sounded pleased.

"Yes," Ray told them. "And tonight I'm going to bring home a big birthday cake and a present, and we'll have Aunt Dorothy come to dinner. Right, Mommy?"

"Ray . . . no." Nancy's voice was low and pleading.

"Yes. Remember, last year you promised that this year we'd . . ."

Celebrate was the wrong word. He couldn't say it. But for a long time he'd known that they would someday have to change the pattern of this anniversary. At first she'd withdrawn completely from him and walked the beach like a silent ghost in a world of her own.

But last year she'd finally begun to talk about the two other children. She'd said, "They'd be so big now . . . ten and eleven. I try to imagine how they would look, but I can't. Everything about that time is so blurred. Like a nightmare that I only dreamed."

"Put it all behind you, honey," Ray had told her. "Don't even wonder what happened anymore."

The memory strengthened his decision. As he bent over and patted Nancy's hair gently, the appeal on her face changed to uncertainty. "I don't think—"

Michael interrupted her. "How old are you, Mommy?"

Nancy smiled. "None of your business," she told him.

Ray took a quick gulp of her coffee. "Good girl," he said. "Tell you what, Mike. I'll pick you up after school and we'll go get a present for Mommy. Now I'd better get out of here. Some guy is coming up to see the Hunt place. I want to get the file together."

"Isn't it rented?" Nancy asked.

"Yes. That Parrish fellow has it again, but we have the right to show it anytime. It'll make a nice commission if I sell it."

Nancy put Missy down and walked with him to the door. He kissed her lightly, got into his car and drove onto the narrow dirt lane that wound through an acre of woods until it terminated on the road to Adams Port and his office.

Ray was right, Nancy thought as she walked back to the table. There was a time to stop remembering and look only to the future, but a part of her was still frozen. It was as though the entire time with Carl were a blur. It was hard to remember the faculty house on the campus. Peter and Lisa. What had they looked like? Dark hair, both of them, like Carl's, and too subdued, affected by her uncertainty; and then lost—both of them.

"Mommy, why do you look so sad?" Michael gazed at her with Ray's candid expression, spoke with Ray's directness.

She glanced around the cheerful kitchen with the old brick fireplace and the red curtains, then looked at Michael and Missy. "I'm not sad, darling," she said. "I'm really not."

She scooped Missy up in her arms, feeling the warmth and sweet stickiness of her. "I've been thinking about your present," Missy said. Her strawberry-blonde hair curled around her ears and forehead. People asked where she got that beautiful hair—who had been the redhead in the family?

"Great," Nancy said. "But think about it outside. You'd better get some fresh air. It's supposed to rain later."

After the children were dressed, she helped them on with their windbreakers. "Now, Mike, I'm going to straighten up," she said. "You be sure to stay with Missy."

"Okay," Michael said cheerfully. "Come on, Missy. I'll push you on the swing first." Ray had put up a swing for the children in a massive oak tree at the edge of the woods.

Nancy pulled Missy's mittens over her hands. They were bright red; fuzzy angora stitching formed a smile face on their backs. "Leave these on," she told her. "It's really getting raw. I'm not even sure you should go out at all."

"Oh, please!" Missy's lips began to quiver.

"All right, all right, don't go into the act," Nancy said hastily. "But not more than half an hour."

She opened the door and let them out, then shivered in the chilling breeze. She closed the door quickly and started toward the staircase. The house was an authentic old Cape, and the stairway was almost vertical. But Nancy loved everything about this place.

She could still remember the feeling of peace it had given her when she'd first seen it, over six years ago. She'd come to the Cape after the conviction had been set aside. The district attorney hadn't pressed for a new trial because Rob Legler, the vital prosecution witness, had disappeared.

She'd fled here, across the continent—as far away from California as she could get, far away from the college and the whole academic community—the friends who had turned out to be hostile strangers who spoke of "poor Carl" and blamed his suicide on her too.

She'd come to Cape Cod because she'd always heard that New Englanders were reserved and wanted nothing to do with strangers, and that was good. She'd cut her hair and dyed it sable brown, to make her look completely different from the pictures that had front-paged newspapers all over the country during the trial.

She guessed that fate must have prompted her to select Ray's real estate office when she looked for a house. "I have a rental on an authentic Cape in excellent condition," Ray had told her. "It's fully furnished, and can be bought eventually. How much room do you need, Miss . . . Mrs. . . . ?"

"Miss Kiernan. Nancy Kiernan." Instinctively she used her maiden name. "Not much, really. I won't be having visitors."

She liked the fact that he didn't pry. "The Cape is a good place to come when you want to be by yourself," he said.

Then Ray had brought her up here, and immediately she knew that she would stay. She loved the large combination family and dining room with the table in front of the window that looked down over the harbor. She was able to move in right away, and that night, for the first time in months, she slept deeply—a peaceful sleep in which she didn't hear Peter and Lisa calling her.

That first morning here, she'd made coffee and sat by the window. It had been a clear, brilliant day—the sky purple blue; the only movement on the bay the arc of sea gulls hovering near the fishing boats. The tranquillity of the scene enhanced the calming sense that the long, dreamless sleep had begun. Peace. Give me peace. That had been her prayer during the trial; in prison. Let me learn to accept. Seven years ago . . .

Nancy realized that she was still standing by the staircase. It was so easy to get lost in remembering. Slowly she began to go upstairs. How could there ever be peace for her, knowing that if Rob Legler showed up they'd try her again for murder; take her away from Ray and Missy and Michael? "Don't think about it," she told herself. "It's no use."

At the top of the stairs she shook her head determinedly, walked quickly into the master bedroom and threw open the windows. Clouds were starting to form, and the temperature was dropping rapidly. Nancy was enough of a Cape person now to know that a cold wind like this usually blew in a storm.

Was it still clear enough to leave the children out? She liked them to have as much fresh air as possible in the morning. After lunch Missy napped and Michael went to kindergarten.

Nancy deliberated an instant, then started to pull the sheets back and off the big double bed. This frantic anxiety that was her constant albatross had to be conquered. Besides, it would take only ten or fifteen minutes to change the beds and turn on a wash. Nancy quieted the feeling that nagged her to go to the children *now*.

JONATHAN Knowles walked to the drugstore to pick up his morning paper. His outing always took him past the old Nickerson house, the one Ray Eldredge had bought when he married the pretty girl who was renting it. In nice weather Nancy Eldredge was out early in her garden, and she always had a pleasant greeting.

Jonathan sighed. He was a big man, with thick white hair and a broad face that was beginning to fold into jowls. A retired lawyer, he'd found inactivity depressing. The Cape had lakes and ponds and the bay and the ocean. But you couldn't do much fishing in the winter. And poking around antique stores wasn't the fun it had been with Emily. They had always spent vacations here at the Cape and looked forward to the day when they could stay the year around. But for Emily it wasn't to be.

In this second year of his permanent residency at the Cape, Jonathan was writing a book. It was a case study of famous murder trials, begun as a hobby. But a publisher friend had read a few chapters and promptly sent him a contract. Now Jonathan worked on the book five hours every day, seven days a week.

The wind bit against him. He pulled out his muffler, grateful for the watery sunshine he felt on his face, and glanced toward the bay. With the shrubbery stripped, you could see clear to the water. Only the old Hunt house on its high bluff interrupted the view—the house they called The Lookout.

Jonathan squinted as he turned his head. That fellow who rented the house must have something metallic in the window. It was a nuisance. He felt like asking Ray to mention it to him, then ruefully thought that the tenant might just suggest that Jonathan look at the bay somewhere else along the way.

He was directly in front of the Eldredge house, and Nancy was sitting at the breakfast table by the window talking to the little boy. Jonathan glanced away, feeling like an intruder. Oh, well, he'd pick up the paper and get to his desk. Today he'd begin working on the Harmon murder case—the one that he suspected would make the most interesting chapter of all.

RAY pushed open the door to the real estate office, unable to shake a nagging sensation of worry. It was more than making Nancy acknowledge her birthday and risking the memories it aroused. It was something else—a feeling of foreboding.

"Oh, no! What does that mean?" Dorothy Prentiss looked up from one of the desks in the outer office. Her hair, more gray than brown, casually framed her long, pleasant face. Her sensible sweater and tweed skirt had an almost studied casualness.

Dorothy had been with Ray ever since he had opened this office. "You do realize that you're shaking your head and frowning," she told him now.

Ray smiled sheepishly. "Just morning jitters. How are you doing?"

Dorothy immediately became businesslike. "Fine. I have the file all together on The Lookout. What time do you expect that fellow who wants to see it?"

"Around two," Ray said.

"That house would make a marvelous restaurant if anyone wanted to renovate it. You can't beat that waterfront location."

"I gather Mr. Kragopoulos and his wife have built up and sold several restaurants and don't mind spending the dollars to do everything the way it should be done. . . ." He went on into his private office. Thoughtfully, he sat at his desk for a few minutes. Then he dialed Dorothy's extension. "If the coffee's made," he said, "would you mind bringing yours in here and a cup for me?"

"All right."

Ray opened the door for her when she came in with the steaming cups, closed it and gestured to the leather chair by his desk. "How would you like to come to our house for dinner tonight?" he asked. "We're celebrating Nancy's birthday."

He heard her sharp intake of breath. Dorothy was the only friend on the Cape who knew about Nancy. Nancy herself had told her and asked her advice before she had agreed to marry Ray.

Dorothy's voice was speculative. "What's the thinking behind a celebration?"

"The thinking is that you can't pretend that Nancy doesn't have birthdays! Nancy has got to break with the past, to stop hiding."

"*Can* she break with the past? *Can* she stop hiding with the prospect of another murder trial hanging over her?"

"But that's just it. The *prospect*. Dorothy, do you realize that that fellow who testified against her hasn't been heard of for over six years? For all we know he may be just as anxious as Nancy not to start the whole business up. Don't forget, he's a deserter from the army. There's a pretty stiff penalty waiting for him."

"That's true," Dorothy agreed.

"Take it one step further. Level with me now. What do people in this town think of Nancy?"

Dorothy hesitated. "They think she's very attractive, and always pleasant . . . and keeps to herself pretty much."

"That's a nice way of putting it. I've heard cracks about my wife thinking she's too good for the folks around here. Last month I finally got her to go to the realtors' dinner, and when they took the group picture, she was in the ladies' room."

"She's afraid of being recognized."

"I understand that. But if there is another trial, I want the people here to feel that Nancy is one them and that they're rooting for her. Because after she's acquitted she'll have to come here and take up life here again. We all will."

"And if there's a trial and she *isn't* acquitted?"

"I simply won't consider that possibility," Ray said flatly. "How about it? Have we got a date tonight?"

"I'd like very much to come," Dorothy said. "And I agree with most of what you've said. But I think you've got to ask yourself how much of this sudden desire for a more normal life is for Nancy and how much is because of other motives."

"Meaning what?"

"Ray, I was here when the secretary of state of Massachusetts urged you to go into politics because the Cape needs young men of your caliber to represent it. I heard him say that he'd give you any help possible. It's pretty hard not to take him up on that. But as things stand now, you know you can't."

Dorothy left the room without giving him a chance to answer. Ray sat at his desk feeling depressed and ashamed of himself.

He thought of the times in the last few months when he'd blown up unreasonably at Nancy. Like the day she had shown him the watercolor she'd done of the house. She should study art. Even now she was good enough to exhibit locally, but she was afraid to call that much attention to herself.

"It's very good," he'd said. "Now which closet are you going to hide it in?"

Nancy had looked so stricken he'd wanted to bite his tongue off. He'd said, "Honey, I'm sorry. It's just that I'm so proud of you. I want you to show it off."

How many of these flare-ups were caused by his weariness of the constant constriction of their activities? He sighed and started going through his mail.

At quarter past ten Dorothy threw open his door. Her usually healthy complexion was a sickly gray. He jumped up to go to her. But shaking her head, she pushed the door closed and held out the paper she'd been hiding under her arm.

It was the weekly Cape Cod *Community News*, opened to the second section, the one that always featured a human-interest story. She dropped it on his desk.

Together they stared down at the large picture that was unmistakably Nancy. It was one he'd never seen before, in a tweed suit, with her hair already darkened. The caption under it read, "Can this be a happy birthday for Nancy Harmon?" Another picture showed Nancy leaving the courtroom during her trial. A third was a snapshot of Nancy with her arms around two young children.

The story began: "Somewhere today Nancy Harmon is celebrating her thirty-second birthday and the seventh anniversary of the death of the children she was found guilty of murdering."

IT WAS TIMING. The whole universe existed because of split-second timing. Now his timing would be perfect. He backed the station wagon out of the garage. It was such a cloudy day it had been hard to see much through the telescope, but he could tell she'd been putting the children's jackets on.

He felt in his pocket and the needles were there—filled, ready to use, to produce instant unconsciousness.

He glanced over his shoulder. The canvas raincoat was the kind many Cape men kept in their cars around fishing season; so were the rods that showed against the back window. But that coat was big enough to cover two small children. He giggled excitedly and swung the car toward Route 6A.

Wiggins' Market was on the corner of this road and Route 6A. Whenever he was at the Cape, he shopped there. Of course, he brought most of the staples he needed with him. It was too risky to go out much. There was always the chance he'd run into Nancy and she'd recognize him even with his changed appearance. It had almost happened four years ago, in a supermarket in Hyannis Port. He was reaching for a jar of coffee, and her hand went right up next to his as she took a jar from the same shelf. She was saying, "Wait a minute, Mike. I want to get something here," and while he froze she brushed against him and murmured, "Oh, I'm sorry."

He didn't dare to answer—just stood there—and she moved on. After that he had never risked a meeting. It was necessary, though, for him to establish a casual routine in Adams Port, because someday it might be important for people to dismiss his comings and goings as routine. That was why he bought milk and bread and meat at Wiggins' Market always about ten in the morning. Nancy never left the house before eleven. And the Wigginses had begun to greet him as a customer of long standing. Well, he'd be there in a few minutes, right on schedule.

He was almost to Route 6A, and slowed to a full stop. The incredible luck. There wasn't a car in either direction. Quickly he accelerated, and the station wagon shot across the highway onto the road that ran back of the Eldredge house.

Nine minutes to ten. He turned into the dirt road on their property.

The paper would be delivered in a few minutes, with that article exposing Nancy. Motivation for her to explode into violence . . . everybody in town talking in shocked tones. . . .

He stopped the car halfway into the woods, got out quickly and hurried to the children's play area. Most of the trees were bare, but there were enough evergreens to shield him.

He heard the children at the swing before he saw them. The girl was calling, "Higher, Mike—push me higher."

He stole up behind the boy. In that last second he had an impression of startled blue eyes and a mouth rounded in terror before he covered both with one hand and with the other plunged a needle through the woolen mitten. The boy tried to pull away, then crumpled to the ground.

The swing was coming back—the girl laughing. "Push, Mike—don't stop pushing." He caught the swing by the chain and encircled the small, uncomprehending wiggly body. Carefully stifling the soft cry, he plunged the other needle through the red mitten. An instant later the girl slumped against him.

He didn't notice that one mitten was caught on the swing as he lifted both children in his arms and ran to the car.

At five minutes to ten they were hidden under the canvas raincoat on the back deck. He backed out to the paved road, then cursed as he saw a small red Dodge sedan coming toward him. It slowed up slightly to let him pull into the right lane, and he turned his head away.

Damn the luck. As he passed the other car, he got a fleeting, familiar impression of a sharp nose and thin chin silhouetted under a shapeless hat. He watched through the rearview mirror until the Dodge rounded a curve and disappeared. With a grunt of satisfaction he adjusted the mirror so that it reflected the canvas raincoat, apparently tossed casually over fishing gear. Satisfied, he flipped the mirror into place without looking into it again. If he had he would have seen that the car he had just been watching was coming back.

At four minutes past ten he walked into Wiggins' Market and grunted a greeting as he reached for a quart of milk.

CHAPTER TWO

NANCY came down the staircase precariously balancing an armful of towels and sheets and underwear. On impulse she'd decided to do a wash that could be hung outdoors to dry. She loved the fresh smell of sheets dried outside; the way they captured the faint scent of cranberry bogs and the salty smell of the sea.

In the laundry room off the kitchen, she tossed the sheets and towels into the machine, added detergent and pushed the button to start the cycle.

Now surely it was time to call the children. But at the front door she detoured. The weekly Cape Cod *Community News* had just arrived. She picked it up, shivering against the wind, and hurried into the kitchen. She turned the burner jet under the still-warm coffeepot. Then she tumbled quickly to the second section of the paper. With the season over, there might be some good antiques available and not at tourist prices.

Her eyes focused on the blaring headline, the pictures: of her and Carl and Rob Legler, the one of her with Peter and Lisa. Through a roaring in her ears she remembered vividly the time they'd posed for that one. Carl had taken it.

"Don't pay attention to me," he'd said. "Pretend I'm not here." But they'd known he was there and had shrunk against her as he snapped the picture.

"No . . . no . . . !" She reached out her hand, and it hit the coffeepot, knocking it over. She drew it back, only dimly feeling the searing liquid on her fingers.

She had to burn the paper. Michael and Missy mustn't see it. She ran to the fireplace in the dining room and reached unsteadily for the matches on the mantel. A flame and a wisp of smoke—then the paper began to burn as she stuffed it between the logs.

Everyone on the Cape was reading that paper. One picture they'd surely recognize. She didn't remember that anyone had seen her after she'd cut her hair and dyed it. Tomorrow in Michael's class the children would be whispering, pointing their fingers.

The children. She must save the children. No, *get* the children. They'd catch cold. She stumbled to the back door and pulled it open. "Michael. Missy. Come here. Come in now!" Her wail heightened to a shriek. Where were they?

The empty swing was still moving in the wind. A mitten—Missy's mitten—was caught in the metal chain.

Then she thought of the lake. They weren't supposed to go there, but maybe they had. They'd be found. Like the others. In the water. Their faces wet and swollen and still.

She grabbed Missy's mitten and pushed her way through the woods back of the house onto the sandy beach.

In the lake, a little way out, something was glistening below the surface. Was it something red . . . another mitten . . . Missy's hand? She plunged into the icy water as far as her shoulders and reached down. But there was nothing—only the numbing cold.

She staggered back and fell onto the ice-crusted sand. Through the mist that rose in front of her eyes, she looked into the woods and saw his face—*whose* face? Then the mist closed in.

Ray and Dorothy found her lying on the sand, clothes plastered to body, eyes blank, clutching a small red mitten to her cheek.

WHEN Jonathan Knowles had gotten the idea for his book, he had asked Kevin Parks, a free-lance researcher and old friend, up for a weekend. Jonathan had selected ten controversial criminal trials, and he'd proposed that Kev put together a file of court transcripts, newspaper accounts—anything he could find. Jonathan planned to study each file thoroughly and then write the chapter—either agreeing with the verdict or rejecting it.

He'd already finished two chapters. The first was "The Sam Sheppard Trial." His opinion: not guilty. Too many loopholes. The second chapter was "The Edgar Smith Trial." Jonathan's view was that Edgar Smith was guilty but deserved his freedom after fourteen years of rehabilitation on death row.

Now he sat down at his massive desk and reached for the thick cardboard folders labeled THE HARMON TRIAL.

A note from Kevin was stapled to the first one:

Jon, I have a hunch you'll enjoy getting your teeth into this. The defendant was a sitting duck for the prosecutor; even her husband broke down on the stand and practically accused her. If they ever locate the missing prosecution witness and try her again, she'd better have a stronger story than last time.

Jonathan remembered that just reading the testimony at the time of this trial six or seven years ago had left many questions in his mind, questions he wanted to concentrate on now.

He began to lay out the meticulously labeled items on the desk. There were pictures of Nancy Harmon taken during her trial. According to the papers she was twenty-five at the time of the murders, but she seemed scarcely older than a teenager. Her dresses were almost childish. Probably her attorney had suggested that.

Funny, ever since he started planning this book, he'd felt that he'd seen that girl somewhere. Of course. She looked like a younger version of Ray Eldridge's wife! Wouldn't it be a small world if there was some family relationship?

His eye fell on the typewritten page which gave a rundown on Nancy Harmon. Born in California, raised in Ohio . . . that probably let out any relationship. Nancy Eldredge's family had been neighbors of Dorothy Prentiss, in Virginia.

Dorothy Prentiss. He felt a dart of pleasure at the thought of the handsome woman who worked with Ray. Jonathan often stopped by their office when he picked up his evening paper. Ray had suggested some sound land investments to him, and also interested Jonathan in town activities. They had become good friends.

Still, Jonathan realized that he went into Ray's office more often than necessary. Dorothy had a penetrating humor that he enjoyed. After her husband died she'd come up to the Cape to open an interior-decorating shop, then had started working with Ray.

Jonathan had often thought of suggesting that Dorothy join him for dinner. Yet all those years of living with Emily's total femininity had not prepared him to react on a personal level to a terribly independent woman. What was the matter? He was so easily diverted this morning. Resolutely he picked up the Harmon file.

An hour and fifteen minutes passed. The silence was unbroken except for the ticking of the clock and Jonathan's occasional snort of disbelief. Finally he went to the kitchen to heat up some coffee. Something smelled about this trial,. some undercurrent that made it impossible for the facts to hang together in any cohesive way.

While he waited for the coffee, he walked to the front door and picked up the Cape Cod *Community News*. Back in the kitchen, he poured the coffee and began to sip as he turned the pages of the paper. When he got to the second section, his gaze froze on the picture of Ray Eldredge's wife.

Jonathan sadly accepted two facts: Dorothy had lied to him about having known Nancy as a child in Virginia; and retired or not, he should have been enough of a lawyer to trust his own instincts. Subconsciously he had always suspected that Nancy Harmon and Nancy Eldredge were the same person.

IT WAS so cold. There was a gritty taste in her mouth. Sand. She could feel Ray cradling her against him . . . "Nancy, what's the matter? Where are the children?"

She tried to raise her hand, then felt it fall by her side. She tried to speak, but no words formed on her lips.

She heard Dorothy say, "Pick her up, Ray. Take her to the house. We have to get help looking for the children."

The children. They must find them. Nancy tried to tell Ray, but the words wouldn't come. She heard him say, "What's happened, Dorothy? What's the matter with her?"

"Ray, we've got to call the police."

"The police!" Nancy heard the resistance in his voice.

"Of course. Ray, hurry! Every moment is precious. Don't you see—you can't protect Nancy now. Everyone will know her from that picture."

The picture. Nancy felt herself being carried. Remotely she knew she was shivering. But that wasn't what she had to think about. It was the picture of her in the tweed suit she'd bought after the conviction was overturned. The state hadn't tried her again. Carl was dead, and the student who'd testified against her had disappeared, and so she'd been released. But the prosecuting attorney had said, "Don't think this is over. If I spend the rest of my life, I'll find a way to get a conviction that sticks."

Afterward, and when she'd received permission to leave the state, she'd had her hair cut and dyed and gone shopping. She had always hated the kind of clothes Carl liked her to wear and had bought that suit. Then she had left on the last evening bus for Boston. The picture . . . it had been taken in the bus terminal.

She hadn't known that anyone was taking a picture of her. She'd really thought that she could just slip away and try to begin again. I want to die, she thought. I want to die.

Ray was walking swiftly, trying to shield her with his jacket. The wind was biting through the wet clothes. He couldn't shield her; not even he could shield her. It was too late. Maybe it had always been too late. It was like last time, and they'd find Michael and Missy the way they'd found Peter and Lisa—with the wet seaweed and the plastic bags over their faces and their bodies swollen.

They must be at the house. Dorothy was opening the door and saying, "I'll call the police, Ray."

Nancy felt herself sliding back and away. No . . . no. . . .

OH, THE activity. They were all scurrying around like ants—milling around her house and yard. He licked his lips anxiously. They were so dry when all the rest of him was wet. Perspiration was streaming down his neck and back.

He'd brought the children right up to the room with the telescope. He could keep an eye on them here until they woke up.

Maybe he'd give the little girl a bath and rub baby powder on her and kiss her. He had all day to spend with the children. The tide wouldn't be high until seven tonight. By then it would be dark, and no one would see or hear. It would be days before they'd be washed in. It would be like last time.

He watched more police cars swarm up the dirt road into Nancy's backyard, and felt wonderfully gratified. He wondered if she was crying. She had never cried once at her trial until the very end—after the judge sentenced her to the gas chamber. The court attendants had snapped handcuffs on her, and her long hair had spilled forward, covering the tear-stained face.

He remembered the first time he's seen her walking across the campus. He'd been immediately attracted to her—the way the wind blew her strawberry-gold hair around her shoulders, the enchanting blue eyes that looked out from sooty lashes.

He heard a sob. Nancy? But of course not. It was coming from the girl. Nancy's child. He turned from the telescope. She looked a lot like Nancy. Well, it was about time for the drug to wear off; they'd been unconscious nearly an hour. Regretfully he left the telescope and laid the children on opposite ends of the musty-smelling velour couch. The little girl was crying in earnest now. He sat her up and unzipped her jacket. She shrank away from him. "There, there," he said soothingly. "It's all right."

Now the boy stirred and sat up slowly. "Who are you?" he demanded. He rubbed his eyes. "Where are we?"

An articulate child—well spoken. That was good. Well-trained children were easier to handle. Didn't make a fuss. Like the others. They had knelt in the trunk of the car so unquestioningly when he had said they were going to play a game on Mommy.

Now he told this little boy, "It's a game. I'm an old friend of your mommy's and she wants to play a birthday game. Did you know it was her birthday today?"

The boy—Michael—said, "I don't like this game." Unsteadily he got to his feet and reached for Missy. She clung to him. "We're going home now."

"Let go of your sister," he ordered the little boy. He yanked her away, then pulled Michael over to the window. "Do you know what a telescope is?"

"Yes. Like the glasses my daddy has. It makes things bigger."

"That's right. You're very smart. Now look in here." The boy put his eye to the viewer. "Tell me what you see."

"It's looking at my house."

"What do you see there?"

"There are lots of cars, police cars. What's the matter?"

He looked down happily at the worried face. A faint pinging

sound came from the window. It was starting to sleet. "Do you know what it's like to be dead?" he asked.

"It means to go to God," Michael answered.

"That's right. And this morning your mother went to God. That's why the police cars are there. Your daddy asked me to mind you for a while and said for you to help take care of your sister."

Michael's lip quivered. "If my mommy went to God, I want to go too."

Running his fingers through Michael's hair, he rocked the still-wailing Missy. "You will," he told him. "Tonight."

THE first reports went over the wire-service tickers at noon. Newscasters seized upon the story and had researchers scurrying to the files for records of the Nancy Harmon murder trial. Publishers chartered planes to send their top crime reporters to Cape Cod.

In Boston a prominent psychiatrist, Dr. Lendon Miles, was enjoying the beginning of his lunch break. Mrs. Markley had just left. After a year of intense therapy, she was finally achieving some insight. She'd even made a joking remark about herself.

Pleased, Lendon switched on the radio next to his desk to catch the news. He was just in time to hear the bulletin.

A shadow of an old pain crossed his face. Nancy Harmon, Priscilla's daughter. After fourteen years he could still see Priscilla Kiernan so clearly: the slender body, the smile like quicksilver.

She had started working for him a year after her husband's death. She'd been thirty-eight then, two years his junior. Almost immediately he began taking her out to dinner when they worked late, and soon he realized that for the first time in his life the idea of marriage seemed logical and even essential.

Gradually she'd told him about herself. Married after her first year in college to an airline pilot, she had one child, a daughter. The marriage had obviously been a happy one. Then on a flight to India her husband had come down with viral pneumonia and had died within a few days.

Lendon never met Priscilla's daughter. She had left for college in San Francisco soon after Priscilla came to work for him.

In November, Priscilla had taken a couple of days off to visit Nancy, and Lendon had driven her to the airport. "You know I'll miss you terribly," he said as they stood waiting for her flight.

"I hope so," she answered, and her eyes were clouded. "I'm worried. Nancy's letters are so down lately."

"Maybe I should be going with you."

"Oh, no. It's probably me being a mother hen." Somehow their fingers had become entwined.

"Don't worry. Kids straighten out, and if there are any real problems, I'll fly out over the weekend if you want me."

"I shouldn't bother you. . . ."

A voice came over the loudspeaker: "Flight five six nine now boarding for San Francisco."

"Priscilla . . . don't you realize that I love you?"

"I'm glad. I think . . . I know . . . I love you too."

Their last moment together. A beginning—a promise of love.

She had telephoned the next night to say she had to talk to him. She was at dinner in a restaurant with Nancy, but would call again as soon as she got back to her hotel. Would he be home?

He waited all night, but the call never came. The next day he learned about the accident. The steering apparatus of the car she'd rented had failed. The car had careened off the road into a ditch.

He probably should have gone to Nancy. But when he finally got through to where she was staying, he spoke to Carl Harmon, the professor who said he and Nancy were planning to marry. He sounded perfectly competent and very much in charge. They had told her mother of their plans at dinner. Mrs. Kiernan had been concerned about Nancy's youth, but that was natural. She would be buried out there, where her husband was interred; their families had, after all, been residents of California for generations. Nancy was bearing up well. He thought they should have a quiet wedding immediately. She must not be alone now.

There had been nothing for Lendon to do. This Professor Harmon sounded fine, and undoubtedly Priscilla had simply been worried about Nancy's taking such a decisive step as marriage at barely eighteen. But surely he, Lendon, could do nothing about that.

He had then accepted an offer to teach at the University of London, and had been out of the country for several years. That was why he'd never learned of the Harmon trial until it was over.

At the University of London he had met Allison, who was also on the faculty, and the sense of sharing that Priscilla had begun to show him had made it impossible to go back to his solitary life. From time to time he had wondered about Nancy Harmon's disappearance. He'd been in the Boston area for the past two years, and here she was only an hour and a half away.

His intercom buzzed. He picked up the receiver. "Mrs. Miles is on the phone, Doctor," his secretary said.

Allison's voice was filled with concern. "Darling, did you by chance hear the news about the Harmon girl?"

"Yes, I did." He had told Allison about Priscilla.

"What are you going to do?"

Her question crystallized the decision he had already made subconsciously. "What I should have done years ago—try to help that girl. I'll call you as soon as I can."

"God bless, darling."

Lendon pressed the intercom button and spoke to his secretary. "Ask Dr. Marcus to take over my afternoon appointments, please. Tell him it's an emergency. I'm driving to Cape Cod immediately."

CHAPTER THREE

"WE'RE dragging the lake, Ray. We've got bulletins going out on radio and television, and we're getting manpower from all over to help in the search." Chief Jed Coffin of the Adams Port police tried to adopt the hearty tone he would normally use if two children were missing.

But it was difficult to sound reassuring and solicitous. Ray had decieved him—introduced him to his wife, talked about her coming from Virginia. He'd filled him with talk and never once told the truth. And the chief hadn't guessed—or even suspected.

To Chief Coffin, what had happened was clear. That woman had seen the newspaper article, realized that everyone would know who she was and had gone berserk. Did to these kids the same thing she'd done to her others. Studying Ray shrewdly, he guessed that Ray was thinking pretty much the same thing.

"Doc Smathers still upstairs with her?"

"Yes. . . . Oh, God!" Ray sat down at the dining-room table and buried his face in his hands. Had he triggered something in Nancy by demanding she celebrate her birthday? And then that article. Had . . . ? "No!" He looked up, turning his head away from the sight of the policeman standing by the back door.

"What is it?" Chief Coffin asked.

"Nancy is incapable of harming the children. Whatever happened, it wasn't that."

"Your wife when she's herself wouldn't harm them, but I've seen women go off the deep end, and there is the history . . ."

Ray stood up. His glance went past the chief, dismissing him. "I need help," he said. "Real help."

The room was in chaos. The police had made a quick search of the house, and a police photographer was taking pictures in the kitchen, where the coffeepot had fallen, spewing streams of coffee on the floor. The telephone rang incessantly.

The policeman answering the calls came over to the table. "The wire services have the story. We'll be mobbed in an hour."

The wire services. Ray remembered the haunted look that had only gradually left Nancy's face. He thought of the picture in this morning's paper, with her hand up as though trying to fend off blows. He pushed past Chief Coffin and hurried upstairs to the master bedroom.

The doctor was sitting next to Nancy, holding her hands. Her eyes were closed. Dorothy had helped Ray strip off the wet clothing and put a fluffy yellow robe on her, but she seemed curiously small and inert inside it.

Ray bent over her. "Honey, please, you've got to help the children. We've got to find them. Try, Nancy—please."

"Ray, I wouldn't." Dr. Smathers' sensitive face was deeply lined. "She's had a terrible shock. Her mind is fighting against confronting it. I've given her a shot to relieve her anxiety."

"But we've got to know what it was," Ray said intently. "Maybe she even saw someone take the children. Nancy, I'm going to help you sit up, honey. You can. Now, come on."

She felt so heavy and vague. This was the way she'd felt for such a long time—from the night Mother died . . . or maybe even before that. She could remember the many nights her eyelids would be glued together—so weary. Carl had been so patient with her.

But she didn't want to think about that now—not about Carl; not about Rob Legler, the handsome student who'd seemed to like her. The children had been so gay when he was there, so happy. She had thought he was a real friend.

Ray was lifting her. "That's it. That's right, Nancy. Doctor, do you think a cup of coffee . . . ?"

The doctor nodded. "I'll ask Dorothy to make it."

Coffee. She'd been making coffee when she saw that picture in the paper. Nancy opened her eyes. "Ray," she whispered, "they'll know. Everyone will know." But there was something else. "The children." She clutched his arm. "Ray, find them."

"Steady, honey. That's where we need you, to tell us. Every single thing. Just get your bearings for a few minutes."

Dorothy came in with a cup of steaming coffee. "I made the instant. How is she?"

"She's coming round."

"Chief Coffin is anxious to begin questioning her."

"Ray!" Panic made Nancy clutch Ray's arm.

"Darling, we have to find the children. It's all right."

She gulped the coffee. If she could just think . . . just lose this terrible sleepiness. Her lips felt rubbery, but she had to talk. She wanted to go downstairs, make them find the children.

She stood up unsteadily. With a supreme effort she groped toward the door. Ray's arm around her waist steadied her. She couldn't feel her feet. They started down the stairs.

Chief Coffin was in the dining room. She could feel his hostility. It was like last time.

"Mrs. Eldredge, how do you feel?"

A perfunctory question, noncaring. "I'm all right."

"We're searching for the children. I have every confidence that we'll find them quickly. But you must help us. When did you last see the children?"

"A few minutes before ten. I put them outside to play and went upstairs to make the beds."

"How long were you upstairs?"

"Ten minutes—not more than fifteen."

"Then what did you do?"

"I came downstairs and turned on a wash. Then I saw the boy deliver the paper and I went to get it."

"And you saw the article about yourself."

Nancy stared straight ahead and nodded.

"How did you react to seeing that article?"

"I think I started to scream. . . . I don't know."

"What happened to the coffeepot?"

"I knocked it over. I didn't mean to. It was just that I was going to burst. I knew that everyone would say I killed the children. And Michael mustn't ever hear that. I pushed the paper into the fireplace. It started to burn. Then I ran to get Michael and Missy."

"Did you see the children?"

"No. I started calling. I ran to the lake."

"Mrs. Eldredge, this is very important: Why did you go to the lake? Your husband tells me the children have never once been disobedient about going there. Why didn't you look on the road for them, or in the woods? Why the lake?"

"Because Peter and Lisa were drowned. Because I had to find Michael and Missy. Missy's mitten was caught on the swing. She's always losing a mitten. I ran to the lake. I had to get the children. It's going to be just like last time. . . ." Her voice trailed off.

Chief Coffin straightened up. His tone became formal. "Mrs. Eldredge," he said, "it is my duty to inform you that you have a right to legal advice before you answer any further questions and that anything you say can be used against you."

Without waiting for her response, he got up and stalked out the back door. Thin pellets of sleet stung his face as he got into a police car and growled to the driver, "The lake."

Maushop was among the biggest lakes on the Cape, and one of the deepest. The lakeside was crowded with bystanders, silently watching the roped-off area where divers and their apparatus were flanked by police. Chief Coffin went directly to Pete Regan, the lieutenant who was supervising the operation. Pete's eloquent shrug answered his unasked question.

Hunching his shoulders inside his coat, the chief stamped his feet as the sleet melted into his shoes. Men were risking their lives because of Nancy Eldredge. God only knew when those poor little kids would be found. Shows what happens. A technicality . . . a convicted murderess gets off because a smart lawyer gets a couple of bleeding-heart judges to declare a mistrial.

"Pete—how long are those guys planning to keep diving?"

"They've been down twice. They'll try once more, then take a break." He pointed to the television equipment. "Looks like we'll make the headlines tonight. You'd better have a statement ready."

With numbed fingers the chief dug into his coat pocket. "I've scribbled one down." He read it quickly. "We are conducting a massive effort to find the Eldredge children. Volunteers are making a block-by-block search of the vicinity as well as the neighboring wooded areas. Helicopters are conducting an air reconnaissance. The search of Maushop Lake, because of its proximity to the Eldredge home, must be considered a normal extension of the investigation."

A few minutes later, when he delivered that statement to the growing assemblage of reporters, one of them asked, "Is it true that Nancy Eldredge was found hysterical and drenched in the area of Maushop Lake after her children disappeared?"

"That is true."

Then the questions came thick and fast. "Was Mrs. Eldredge aware of the article about her in the *Community News* today?"

"I believe she was."

"What was her reaction to that article?"

"I can't say."

"Were you aware of her identity before today?"

"No. I was not." The chief spoke through clenched teeth. "No more questions."

Before he could get away, a reporter from the Boston *Herald* blocked his path and loudly asked, "Sir, in the past six years haven't there been several unsolved deaths of young children both on the Cape and on the nearby mainland?"

"That is true."

"Chief Coffin, how long has Nancy Harmon Eldredge been living on the Cape?"

"Six years, I believe."

"Thank you, Chief."

AFTER the shock of realizing that Ray Eldredge's wife was the notorious Nancy Harmon, Jonathan Knowles had settled down at his desk and begun to study the Harmon case just as he'd planned.

He started with the article in the Cape paper. With grim detail it reviewed Nancy Harmon's background as the young wife of a college professor . . . two children . . . a home on the campus. An ideal situation until the day Professor Harmon sent a good-looking student to his house to repair the oil burner.

The article contained excerpts from the trial testimony. The student, Rob Legler, explained how he had met Nancy. "When Professor Harmon got that call from his wife about the oil burner, I was in his office. There's just nothing mechanical I can't fix, so I volunteered to go over. He didn't want me to, but he couldn't get the regular maintenance service."

"Did he give you any specific instructions concerning his family?" the district attorney asked.

"Yes. He said that his wife wasn't well and I shouldn't bother her; if I needed anything, I should call him."

"Did you follow Professor Harmon's instructions?"

"I would have, sir, but I couldn't help the fact that his wife followed me around like a little dog."

"Objection!" But the defense attorney was too late. The point had been made. Then the student was asked if he had had any physical contact with Mrs. Harmon.

His answer was direct. "Yes, sir."

"How did it happen?"

"Well, a few days later I went back with a new part. And when I was showing her the emergency switch on the oil burner—"

"Didn't Professor Harmon tell you not to bother Mrs. Harmon?"

"She insisted on knowing about it. Said she had to learn how to manage things in her house. She was leaning over me to try the switch, and I figured, why not? So I made a pass."

"What did Mrs. Harmon do?"

"She liked it. I could tell."

"Will you please explain exactly what happened?"

"I sort of spun her around and kissed her—and after a minute she pulled away, but she didn't want to. I said something about that being pretty good."

"What did Mrs. Harmon say?"

"She just looked at me and said—almost like she wasn't talking to me—she said, 'I've got to get away.'"

"I figured I didn't want to get in any trouble. I mean, I didn't want to do anything to get kicked out of school and end up being drafted. So I said, 'Look, Nancy, we can work something out so we can get together without anyone ever guessing. You can't leave here—you've got the kids.'"

"How did Mrs. Harmon respond to that statement?"

"Well, it's funny. Just then the boy, Peter, came down the stairs. He was a real quiet kid—didn't say boo. She looked mad and said, 'But the children are going to be smothered.'"

"Mr. Legler, this is crucial. Are you sure you are repeating Mrs. Harmon's exact phrase?"

"Yes, sir, I am. But of course you don't believe anyone means it when they say something like that."

"On what date did Nancy Harmon make that statement?"

"It was on November thirteenth. I know because when I went back to school, Professor Harmon insisted on giving me a check for fixing the burner."

"November thirteenth . . . and four days later the Harmon children disappeared from their mother's automobile and eventually were washed in on the shores of San Francisco Bay with plastic bags over their heads—in effect, smothered."

The defense attorney had tried to reduce the impact of the story. "Did you continue to embrace Mrs. Harmon?"

"No. She went upstairs with the kids."

"Then we have only your statement that she enjoyed the kiss you forced on her."

"Believe me, I can tell when a babe is receptive."

Then Jonathan read Nancy's testimony. "Yes, he did kiss me. Yes, I believe that I knew he was going to and I let him."

"Do you also remember making the statement that your children were going to be smothered?"

"Yes, I do."

"What did you mean by that statement?"

According to the article, Nancy looked past her attorney and stared unseeingly over the faces in the courtroom and said in a dreamy voice, "I don't know."

Jonathan shook his head. That girl should never have been permitted to take the witness stand. She did nothing except damage her own case. What had been the matter with her? he wondered. It was almost as though she didn't want to get off.

After he'd finished the article, Jonathan turned his attention to the voluminous file Kevin had sent him. He read rapidly, assorting and assimilating information, lightly underlining cogent facts he wanted to refer to later.

The doorbell rang. Jonathan got up from his chair, surprised at how stiff he'd become from sitting.

To his amazement, his visitor was a policeman. The young officer accepted his invitation to step inside, then said, "Sir, I'm sorry to bother you, but we're investigating the disappearance of the Eldredge children."

Then, while Jonathan stared at him, he pulled out a notebook. His eyes darting around the orderly house, he began his questions. "You live alone here, sir, do you not?"

Without answering, Jonathan reached past him and opened the massive front door. At last he became aware of the unfamiliar cars driving down the road and the grim-faced men in heavy rain gear swarming through the neighborhood.

"JUST SIP THIS, Nancy. It will help you. You need your strength." Dorothy's voice was cajoling. Nancy shook her head. Dorothy set the cup on the table, hoping the aroma of fresh vegetables, bubbling in the spicy soup, might tempt her.

"I made that yesterday," Nancy said tonelessly, "for the children's lunch. The children must be hungry."

Ray was sitting next to her, his arm slung protectively across the back of her chair. "Don't torture yourself, dear," he said quietly.

After giving his statement to the news media, Chief Coffin had returned to the Eldredge house, coming in just in time to hear Nancy's words. His practiced glance took in the staring quality of her eyes, the ominous stillness of her hands and body. They'd be lucky if she was able to answer to her own name before long.

"Ray, can I see you privately?" Coffin asked brusquely.

For an instant Ray laid his cheek on Nancy's. "Just sit tight, honey. I'll be right back."

Jed Coffin felt an unwilling admiration for the tall young man who followed him into the living room. There was something so gut-level self-possessed about Ray even in these circumstances.

Stalling to regain his sense of authority, Jed looked slowly around the room. The wide oak floorboards shone softly under hooked rugs. The walls were covered with paintings of familiar scenes. The large one over the fireplace was Nancy Eldredge's rock garden. A painting near the couch had caught the homecoming flavor of Sesuit Harbor at sundown with the boats sailing in. The watercolor of the cranberry bog had the old Hunt house—The Lookout—in the background. Jed had occasionally noticed Nancy Eldredge sketching around town, but never dreamed that she was any good.

"What do you want, Chief?" Ray's voice was cold.

"Who is your wife's lawyer, Ray?" Jed asked curtly.

A flicker of uncertainty betrayed the answer. Just as Jed figured, Ray was still trying to pretend his wife was the average distraught mother of missing children.

"We haven't contacted a lawyer," he said, his tone more subdued. "I hoped that maybe, with everyone searching . . ."

"Most of that search is going to be suspended soon," Jed said flatly. "With this weather, no one is able to see anything. But I've got to take your wife down to the station for questioning. And if you haven't arranged for a lawyer yet, I'll have the court appoint one."

"You can't do that!" Ray snapped, then made an obvious effort to control himself. "What I mean is it would destroy Nancy. For years she had nightmares: she was in a police station being questioned and then she was taken to the mortuary and made to identify her children. My God, man, she's in shock right now. Are you trying to make sure that she won't be able to tell us anything?"

"Ray, my job is to get your children back."

"Yes, but you see what just reading that cursed article has done to her. And what about that article? Anyone vile enough to bring up that story might be capable of taking the children."

"We're working on that. That feature is always signed with a fictitious staff name, but the articles are actually free-lance submissions that if accepted involve a twenty-five-dollar payment."

"Well, who is the writer, then?"

"That is what we tried to find out," Jed replied angrily. "The covering letter instructed that the story was offered only on condition that if accepted, it would not be changed at all, and that it would be published on November seventeenth—today. The editor told me that he agreed to the conditions and had sent a letter of acceptance and a check for twenty-five dollars on October twenty-eighth to a J. R. Penrose, care of General Delivery, Hyannis Port. Two days later it was picked up."

"Man or woman?" Ray asked quickly.

"We don't know. No clerk seems to remember the letter, and so far the check hasn't been cashed."

Ray stared at the fireplace. His eye fell on the cameos on the mantelpiece that Nancy had painted of Michael and Missy when they were babies. A stinging lump closed his throat.

"Ray," Jed said quietly. "Nancy has to get dressed and come with us to the station house."

"No . . . no . . . please. . . ."

The chief and Ray whirled to face Nancy, who was at the

entrance to the room, one hand against the carved oak archway for support. Her eyes had an almost detached expression.

Dorothy was behind her. "She wanted to come in."

Ray pulled Nancy against him. "It's all right, Dorothy," he said briefly. His voice became tender. "Honey, just relax. Nobody's going to hurt you."

Dorothy sensed the dismissal in his tone. She felt useless here. "Ray," she said stiffly. "It's ridiculous to bother you about this, but the office just phoned to remind me that Mr. Kragopoulos wants to see the Hunt property at two o'clock. Shall I get someone else to take him up there?"

"I don't give a damn," Ray snapped. Then quickly he said, "I'm sorry, Dorothy. I would appreciate it if you showed the place; you know The Lookout and can sell it if there's real interest."

"I haven't told Mr. Parrish that we might be bringing people in today."

"His lease clearly states that we can show the house at any time. Give him a call and tell him you're coming."

Reluctantly she turned to go. She wanted to stay and share their anxiety. Ever since that first day when she'd walked into Ray's office, he'd been a lifeline for her. After twenty-five years of planning her every activity with Kenneth or around Kenneth's schedule, she'd been so rootless and frightened. But working with Ray, helping him build the business, had filled so much of the void. She couldn't have thought more of him if he'd been her own son. And when Nancy had come, she'd been so proud that Nancy trusted her. But now she felt like an unnecessary bystander. Wordlessly she got her coat and scarf and went out the back door.

As she hurried toward her car, she saw the swing at the edge of the property. How many times had she pushed the children on that swing? Just yesterday she had offered to mind Missy and pick up Michael at kindergarten while Nancy looked at drapery material. "I have to go to the courthouse for some title-search papers anyway," she'd said, "and on the way back we'll get some ice cream." Only twenty-four hours ago. She stared at the swing, unmindful of the wet sleet stinging her face. . . .

"Dorothy."

Startled, she looked up. Jonathan must have cut through the woods from his house. "I just heard about the children," he said. "I've got to talk to Ray. Possibly I can help."

"That's nice of you," Dorothy said unsteadily. The concern in his voice was oddly comforting. "They're inside."

"I saw the article in the paper."

Belatedly, Dorothy recognized there was a coolness in Jonathan's tone that reminded her she had lied to him about having known Nancy in Virginia. Wearily she got in her car. "I have an appointment," she said. Without giving him time to answer, she started up the engine. It was only when her vision blurred that she realized there were tears in her eyes.

CHAPTER FOUR

THE clatter of the helicopters was pleasing. It reminded him of the last time, when everyone for miles around the college had fanned out looking for the children. He stared out the front window overlooking the bay. The gray water was caked with ice near the jetty. Earlier the radio had spoken of gale warnings and sleet. For once the weatherman had been right. He watched a flock of gulls trying futilely to make headway against the wind. The helicopters wouldn't be up much longer in this.

High tide was seven o'clock tonight. He'd take the children up through the attic then, to the widow's walk. The water at high tide covered the beach below, broke furiously against the retaining wall and was sucked back to sea by the violent undertow. That would be the time to drop the children . . . over . . . down.

In the meantime he had five hours: five long hours to be with them. Even the boy, come to think of it, was a beautiful child.

But it was the little girl. She looked so much like Nancy. He turned from the window abruptly. The children were lying together on the couch. The sedative he'd put in the milk had both of them sleeping. The boy's arm was protectively over his sister. But the boy didn't even stir when he picked up the little girl.

Carefully he carried her into the bedroom and laid her down. He went to the bathroom and turned on the faucets in the tub. When it had filled he tested the water with his elbow. A little hot, but it would cool in a few minutes.

He sucked in his breath. He was wasting time. Swiftly he opened the medicine cabinet and pulled out the can of baby powder he'd slipped into his coat pocket at Wiggins' Market this morning. As he was about to close the door, he noticed the little worn rubber duck behind the shaving cream. . . . Why it had been used the last time. Laughing softly, he tossed the duck into the tub.

Grabbing the can of powder, he hurried back to the bedroom. Easily he slipped the turtleneck shirt over Missy's head, bringing her undershirt with it. Three years old. Just a beautiful age. He picked her up, hugging the limp body to him.

The phone rang.

Angrily he tightened his grip on the child. He'd let it ring. He never, never got calls. Why now? His eyes narrowed. Suppose it was someone asking him to volunteer in the search? It might be suspicious not to answer. He tossed Missy back onto the bed and closed the bedroom door before he picked up the phone in the sitting room.

"Mr. Parrish? This is Dorothy Prentiss of Eldredge Realty. I'm sorry to give you such short notice, but I'll be bringing over a prospective buyer for the house in twenty minutes. Will you be there or shall I use my passkey to show your apartment?"

ALL the way down from Boston, Lendon Miles had kept his radio at a news station, and most of the news was about the missing Eldredge children. When at last he turned into Paddock Path, he had no trouble finding the Eldredge home. Halfway up the road, a television van and several press cars were parked across the street from a house that had two police cars stationed in front of it. The entrance to the semicircular driveway was blocked by one of the police cars. Lendon stopped and a policeman came over. His tone was brusque. "State your business, please."

Lendon had anticipated the question. He handed out his card

with a note scrawled on it. "Please take this to Mrs. Eldredge."

"If you'll wait here, Doctor . . ." The policeman returned promptly. "I'll move the squad car out of the way. Park in the driveway and go into the house, sir."

Lendon shoved his way through a group of reporters and into the house. Nancy Eldredge was standing at the living-room fireplace with a tall young man, undoubtedly her husband. Lendon would have known her anywhere: the finely chiseled nose, the profile so like Priscilla's. Ignoring the hostile look of a police officer and the scrutiny of the craggy-faced man at the window, he went directly to her. "I should have come before," he said.

The girl's eyes had a staring quality. "I thought you would come last time," she told him, "when Mother died. I was so sure you would come. And you didn't."

Expertly, Lendon measured the symptoms of shock: the enlarged pupils, the monotone quality of her voice. "I thought you might resent me," he said. "I should have tried to help you."

"Help me now!"

He took her cold hands in his. "I'll try, Nancy, I promise." She sagged, and her husband eased her down onto the sofa. Lendon watched as a shiver made her entire body tremble.

Ray tucked a coverlet around Nancy. "You're so cold, darling," he said. For an instant he held her face between his hands. Tears trickled from under her closed eyelids.

The craggy-faced man spoke to Ray Eldredge. "Have I your permission to represent Nancy as her legal counsel? I assure you I am qualified," he said dryly.

"Legal counsel," Nancy whispered. She could still see the face of the lawyer last time. He'd kept saying to her, "You must tell me the truth. You must trust me." Even he hadn't believed her. But Jonathan Knowles was different. She liked his bigness and the courtly way he always spoke to her. "Please," she said to Ray.

Ray nodded. "We'd be very grateful, Jonathan."

Jonathan turned to Lendon. "Doctor, may I have your medical opinion as to the advisability of allowing Mrs. Eldredge to be taken to the police station for questioning?"

"Highly inadvisable," Lendon said promptly. "I would urge that any questioning be done here."

"But I can't remember anything," Nancy said wearily. She looked up at Lendon. "Can you help me to remember? Is there any way?"

"What do you mean?" Lendon asked.

"I mean isn't there something you can give me so that if I know, or saw . . . Even if there is some awful part of me that could hurt my children . . . we have to know that too."

"Nancy, I won't let—" But Ray stopped when he saw the anguish in her face.

"Is it possible to help Nancy to remember what happened this morning, Doctor?" Jonathan asked.

"Perhaps. She is probably suffering from a hysterical amnesia as a result of what to her was a catastrophic experience. Under an injection of Sodium Amytal, she would be relaxed and probably able to tell us the truth as she knows it."

"Answers given under sedation would not be admissible in court," Jed snapped. "I can't have you questioning Mrs. Eldredge like that."

The telephone rang and had the effect of a pistol exploding. They all waited silently until the policeman on duty at the phone came into the room. He said, "Long distance for you, Chief."

"This is the call I've been trying to place," Jed told them. "Mr. Knowles, I'd appreciate it if you'd come with me. You too, Ray."

Lendon Miles watched as relief drained from Nancy's expression. "Every time it rings, I think somebody has found the children."

"Steady," Lendon said. "Nancy, tell me when you started having trouble remembering."

"When Peter and Lisa died—maybe even before that. It's hard to remember the years I was married to Carl."

"That could be because you associate those years with the children and it's too painful to remember them."

"But during that time I was so tired. Everything was such an effort. And after the children disappeared, I couldn't remember . . . like now." Her voice had begun to rise.

Ray came back into the room. His voice was strained. "Doctor, could you speak with Jonathan for a minute?"

"Certainly." Lendon hurried into the dining room.

Chief Coffin was still on the phone, barking orders to a lieutenant at the station, "Get down to that post office and round up every clerk who was on duty October thirtieth and don't stop questioning them until somebody remembers who picked up that letter from the *Community News* addressed to J. R. Penrose. I need a full description, and I need it now." He slammed down the receiver.

There was new tension in Jonathan too. "Doctor," he said, "we can't lose any time in trying to break through Nancy's amnesia. To fill you in, I have a very complete file on the Harmon case because of a book I'm writing. I've spent the last three hours studying that file and reading the article that appeared in today's paper. Something struck me, and I asked Chief Coffin to phone the district attorney in San Francisco and check my theory. His assistant has just returned the call."

Jonathan reached into his pocket for his pipe, and clamped his teeth on it. "Doctor, as you may know, in criminal cases the police often withhold a piece of information so that they have some help in sifting through the meaningless clues they receive. I noticed that all the newspaper accounts seven years ago described the children as wearing red sweaters with a white pattern when they disappeared. Nowhere in the newspapers is there an exact description of that pattern. I surmised—correctly—that the motif of the pattern had been deliberately withheld."

Jonathan looked directly at Lendon, wanting him to understand immediately the importance of what he was about to tell him. "The article which appeared in the Cape Cod *Community News* clearly states that when the Harmon children disappeared they were wearing red sweaters with an unusual white sailboat design. Now, Nancy, of course, was aware of that sailboat design. But only one other person outside of the top people on the San Francisco investigative staff knew about it." Jonathan's voice rose in pitch. "If we assume Nancy's innocence, that person was the one who kidnapped the Harmon children seven years ago—and who wrote the story that appeared in today's paper!"

"Then you mean—" Lendon began.

"Doctor, I mean that if you can break through Nancy's amnesia, do it—quickly! I have persuaded Ray to waive any immunity. The overriding necessity is to find out what Nancy may know before it is too late to help her children."

"Can I telephone a drugstore and get something delivered?"

"You can, Doctor," Jed said. "I'll send a squad car over to pick up whatever you need. Here—I'll dial the drugstore."

Quietly, Lendon phoned his instructions. When he finished, Chief Coffin was saying, "Remember, Jonathan, I'm going to have a tape recorder on in that room when that girl is questioned. If she confesses to anything under sedation, we may not be able to use it directly, but I'll know what to ask her later."

"She's not going to confess anything," Jonathan said impatiently. He lit his pipe and puffed at it vigorously before going on. "But I do believe Nancy knew more than she told about the disappearance of her children seven years ago."

Lendon raised an eyebrow, and Jed frowned deeply.

Jonathan slapped his hand on the table. "I'm not saying that the girl is guilty. I am saying that she knew more than she told; probably knew more than she was aware of knowing. Look at the picture of her during the trial. Her face is an absolute blank."

Jed was clearly out of patience. "In one breath you tell me Nancy Eldredge's too sick to be questioned and in the next one that she knows more than she ever let on. Look, Jonathan, writing a book about questionable verdicts is a hobby with you. But those children's lives aren't hobbies with me."

"Hold on." Lendon put a restraining hand on the chief's arm. "Mr. Knowles—Jonathan—you believe that whatever knowledge Nancy has of the death of her first family may help us find the Eldredge children?"

"Exactly. Dr. Miles, is it possible you might be able to have Nancy reveal not only what she knows of this morning's events—which I suspect will be nothing—but also information about the past that she doesn't even know she has herself?"

"It's possible."

"Then I beg you to try."

WHEN DOROTHY WAS readmitted to the house an hour later, the dining room was deserted except for Bernie Mills, the policeman charged with answering the phones. "They're in there," he said jerking his head toward the living room.

Dorothy hurried down the hall, and took in the scene before her. Nancy was lying on the couch, her eyes closed. A stranger was sitting beside her, speaking softly. An anguished-looking Ray and grim-faced Jonathan were side by side on the love seat. Jed Coffin was sitting at a table behind the couch, holding a microphone pointed toward Nancy.

As Dorothy realized what was happening, she sank into a chair. Numbly she slipped her chilled fingers into the deep side pockets of her coat, unconsciously gripping the scrap of damp, fuzzy wool in the right-hand pocket.

"How do you feel, Nancy? Are you comfortable?" Lendon's voice was tranquil.

"I'm afraid. . . ."

"Why?"

"The children . . . the children."

"Nancy. Let's talk about this morning. Did you sleep well last night? When you woke up did you feel rested?"

Nancy's voice was reflective. "I dreamed. . . ."

"What did you dream about?"

"Peter and Lisa. They'd be so grown up." She began to sob. Then, as Jonathan's iron grip held Ray back, she cried, "How could I have killed them? They were my children!"

CHAPTER FIVE

NORMALLY, Dorothy took prospective clients on a brief tour of the neighborhood before showing a property. But today, with the sleet beating a sharp tattoo on the car roof, she had headed directly for The Lookout.

As she drove along the treacherously slick road, she stole an occasional glance at the swarthy-complexioned man beside her. John Kragopoulos was somewhere in his mid-forties, and there was an innate courtliness in his bearing that complemented his slightly accented manner of speaking. He told Dorothy that he and his wife were anxious to settle in an area where well-to-do retired people could be found for winter business as well as the summer resort trade.

Mentally reviewing these points, Dorothy said, "The Lookout has unlimited possibilities as a restaurant and inn. During the 1930's it was renovated extensively and turned into a country club. People didn't have money to join expensive country clubs at that time, and so it never caught on. Eventually, Mr. Hunt bought the house and grounds—nine acres in all, including one thousand feet of waterfront property and one of the finest views on the Cape."

"The Lookout was originally a captain's house, was it not?"

"Yes," Dorothy said. "It was built by a whaling captain in the 1690's for his bride. It still has the original widow's walk near the chimney, and an exquisite fanlight over the front door."

"Is there a dock with the property?" her passenger asked. "If I relocate up here, I plan to buy a boat."

"A very good one," Dorothy assured him. "Oh, dear!" The car skidded dangerously on the narrow, winding road that led up to The Lookout. She managed to straighten the wheels, and glanced anxiously at John Kragopoulos. But he only remarked that she was a brave lady to drive on such icy roads.

"I don't mind driving," she said thickly. "I'm just sorry Mr. Eldredge isn't with us. But I'm sure you understand."

"I understand very well," John Kragopoulos said, "What an agonizing experience for the parents to have young children missing! I am only sorry to take your time today. As a friend and co-worker, you must be concerned."

Determinedly, Dorothy did not let herself respond to the sympathy in the man's voice. "Here we are," she said instead.

They rounded a curve, and The Lookout was in full view, looming above the shrouded embankment, its weather-beaten shingles, peeling shutters and sagging steps mercilessly revealed.

She was surprised that Mr. Parrish had left the doors of the big garage open, but it was a break for them. She'd drive right in and park her car beside his old station wagon. "I've got a key to the back door," she told John Kragopoulos as they got out of the car. "Let's make a dash for it."

To her annoyance, Dorothy found that the door was double-locked. She rummaged through her bag for the second key and gave a quick yank at the bell to let him know they had arrived.

Her prospective buyer seemed unperturbed as he brushed sleet from his coat. She had to will herself not to sound nervous or overly talkative. Every fiber of her being made her want to rush this man through the house. See this . . . and this. Now let me go back to Ray and Nancy.

Deliberately she reached for her handkerchief to dab at her face, aware suddenly of her new gray suede coat. She'd decided to wear it because of this appointment. She knew that it complemented her pepper-and-salt-colored hair. And something else—she had wondered if Jonathan Knowles would stop in the office. Maybe this would be the day when he'd suggest they have dinner together. She had daydreamed like that only hours ago. . . .

"Mrs. Prentiss?"

"Yes. I'm sorry. I guess I'm a bit distracted." To her ears she sounded falsely cheery. "This kitchen does need modernizing, but it is very well laid out and roomy."

The wind was howling mournfully around the house. From somewhere upstairs she heard, just for a second, a wailing sound—this place upset her today. Quickly she led the way to the front rooms, to give Mr. Kragopoulos an impression of the water view.

The savagery of the day only enhanced the breathtaking panorama from the windows. Angry whitecaps churned, crashed on the rocks below, pulled back. "At high tide these rocks are completely covered," Dorothy said. "And just down to the left, past the jetty, is a beautiful sandy beach that is part of the property."

She took him from room to room, pointing out the magnificent floors, the massive fireplaces. On the second floor he examined the large rooms that could be rented to overnight guests. He was interested. She could tell by the way he opened closet doors and turned on water taps.

"The third floor just has more bedrooms, and Mr. Parrish's apartment is on the fourth floor," she said.

He was pacing off a room and did not answer. Dorothy walked to a window. Hurry, hurry, she thought. The need to be back with Ray and Nancy was overwhelming. Suppose the children were out somewhere, exposed to this weather?

When Nancy had left Missy at the office yesterday, she'd said, "Please make her keep her mittens on when you go out. Her hands get so cold." Nancy had laughed as she handed Dorothy the mittens, saying, "As you can see, they don't match—this kid is always losing mittens." She'd given her one red mitten with a smile face and a blue-and-green checked one.

Dorothy remembered the cheerful smile with which Missy had held up her hands for the mittens when they'd gone for their drive. Later on, when they'd picked up Mike and stopped for ice cream, she'd asked, "Is it all right if I take my mittens off when I eat my cone?" Blessed little baby.

She turned to John Kragopoulos, who had finished making some notes. "Let's go up to the apartment," she said abruptly. "I think you'll like the view from there." She led the way to the front staircase, and they walked up the two flights quickly.

"Here we are—just down the hall." Dorothy knocked at the door of the apartment. There was no answer. "That's strange. I can't imagine where he'd go without his car. But I've got the key."

The door was opened abruptly from the inside, and she looked into the perspiring face of the tenant, Courtney Parrish.

"What a dreadful day for you to have to come." Parrish's tone was courteous. He held the door back to let them pass.

His eyes darted from one to the other. Had they heard the little girl—that one cry? He was such a fool, getting too eager. After the phone call he'd had to hurry so much—picking up the children's clothing. Then the can of baby powder had spilled. He'd had to wipe that up.

He'd given the children some more milk containing sedative, then tied their hands and feet and taped their mouths, and hidden them in one of the deep closets in the bedroom. He had put a new lock on that closet, and this fool of a real estate woman couldn't possibly have a duplicate key.

They'd dallied downstairs long enough for him to make one last inspection of the apartment; he hadn't missed anything, he was sure. The tub was still full, but he'd decided to leave it. Let Dorothy think he'd been just about to bathe. . . .

"John Kragopoulos."

Clumsily he tried to dry his perspiring palm on his trouser leg before grasping the outstretched hand that he could not ignore. "Courtney Parrish," he said sullenly.

Seeing the fleeting expression of distaste come over the other man's face when their hands touched, he became more courteous. "I am pleased to meet you, Mr. Kragopoulos, and rue the weather in which you first observe this wonderful house."

The tension in the small foyer relaxed tangibly. He realized that most of it was emanating from Dorothy. Why not? He'd seen her countless times these past years, in and out of the Eldredge house: one of those dreary middle-aged widows trying to be important; a parasite. Husband dead. No children. A miracle she didn't have a sick old mother. Most of them did. That helped them to be martyrs. And if they had children, they concentrated on them. The way Nancy's mother had.

"As you can see," Dorothy was saying to John Kragopoulos, "this is a charming apartment, quite suitable for two people."

"You are an astronomer, perhaps?" John Kragopoulos spoke to Courtney Parrish.

Belatedly, Parrish realized that the telescope was facing the Eldredge house. Seeing that the visitor was about to look through it he gave it a push so that it tilted upward. "I enjoy studying the stars," he volunteered hastily.

John Kragopoulos squinted as he looked through the lens. "Magnificent equipment," he said. Carefully he manipulated the telescope to its earlier position. Then he straightened up and began to study the room. "This is a well laid out apartment," he commented.

"I have been most comfortable here," Parrish volunteered. Inwardly he was fuming. Once more he had suspiciously overreacted.

Dorothy said, "I'd like to show the bedroom and bath."

"Of course." He'd straightened the coverlet on the bed and shoved the can of baby powder into the night-table drawer.

"The bathroom is as large as most of today's second bedrooms," Dorothy was saying. Then, as she stared down at the filled tub, "Oh, I'm so sorry. We did catch you at an inconvenient time."

"I have no rigid schedule." Despite the words, he left the impression that she had indeed inconvenienced him.

John Kragopoulos stepped back into the bedroom hastily. That duck floating in the tub. A child's toy. He winced, disgusted. His hand touched the satiny wood of the closet door. Really, this house was beautifully constructed. They wanted three hundred and fifty thousand for it. He'd offer two ninety-five and come up to three twenty. He was sure he could get it for that.

The decision finalized in his mind, he began to take a proprietary interest in the apartment. "May I open this closet?" he asked, turning the handle.

"I'm sorry. I changed that lock and can't seem to find the key. If you'll look in this other closet . . . they're practically identical." Parrish had to clamp his lips together to keep from ordering this nosy man out. The children were just on the other side of the door. Had he tightened their gags enough? Would they recognize that woman's voice and try to make some sound? He had to get rid of these people.

But Dorothy wanted to go too. She was aware of an indefinable fragrance—one that made her acutely aware of Missy. She turned to John Kragopoulos, who was peering into the other closet. "Perhaps we should start, if you're ready."

He nodded, "Quite ready, thank you." They started to leave, Mr. Kragopoulos this time obviously avoiding shaking hands.

In the garage, Dorothy walked between the station wagon and her car and opened the door on the driver's side. As she began to slide into her car, a bright red scrap of material on the garage floor caught her eye. She picked it up, then slumped into the car seat, holding the object against her cheek. John Kragopoulos, sounding alarmed, asked, "My dear Mrs. Prentiss, what is wrong?"

"It's Missy's mitten!" Dorothy cried. "She must have left it in the car yesterday. I guess I kicked it out when we drove in here. She was always losing her mittens. And this morning they found the mate of this one on the swing." She began to sob.

John Kragopoulos spoke quietly. "There is little that I can say except to remind you that a merciful God is aware of your pain. He will not fail your need. Somehow I am confident of that. Now, wouldn't you like me to drive?"

"Please," Dorothy said. She pushed the mitten deep into her pocket as she slid over. She wouldn't want Nancy or Ray to see it; it would be too heartbreaking. Oh, Missy! She'd taken it off when she started to eat the cone yesterday. She could see her dropping it on the seat. The poor little kids.

Upstairs, Parrish watched from the window until the car had disappeared. Then, with trembling fingers, he unlocked the closet door and reached past the boy for the little girl. He lifted out her limp body and laid her on the bed—then shrieked in outrage as he saw her closed eyes and pinched blue face.

CHAPTER SIX

NANCY'S hands were clenching and unclenching, pulling at the coverlet. Gently, Lendon covered her fingers with his own.

"Nancy, don't worry," he said. "Everyone here knows that you couldn't hurt your children. That's what you meant, isn't it?"

"Yes. How could I kill them? They are me. I died with them."

"We all die a little death when we lose the people we love, Nancy. Think back with me before all the trouble started. Tell me what it was like when you were growing up in Ohio."

"Growing up?" The rigidity in Nancy's body began to relax.

"Yes, tell me about your father. I never knew him."

Jed Coffin moved restlessly. Lendon shot him a warning glance. "I have reason for this," he said. "Please bear with me."

"Daddy?" A lilt came into Nancy's voice. "He was fun. Mother and I used to drive to the airport to meet his flights. He never came back from a trip without something for Mother and me."

Ray could not take his eyes off Nancy. He had never heard her speak in that tone of voice—animated, amused, a ripple of laughter running through her words.

Jonathan Knowles listened intently, approving of the technique Lendon Miles was using to gain Nancy's confidence before asking about the day the Harmon children had vanished. It was agonizing to hear the soft ticking of the grandfather clock, a reminder that time was passing. He was finding it impossible not to look at Dorothy, huddled in her chair. He knew he had been harsh to her, and now he felt that he owed her an apology.

The lights in the room flickered, then went off. Jed said, "That figures," and Ray lighted the antique lamps on either side of the mantel. They bathed the couch where Nancy was lying in a warm glow and threw deep shadows on the corners of the room. This is unreal, Ray thought, impossible. The children missing. Nancy sedated. What was she saying?

Her voice still had that eager lilt. "Daddy used to call Mother and me his girls. . . ." Her voice faltered.

"What is it, Nancy?" Dr. Miles asked. "Your father called you his little girl? Did that upset you?"

"No . . . no. . . . He called us his girls. It was different . . . it was different." Her voice rose sharply in protest.

Lendon's voice was soothing. "All right, Nancy. Don't worry about that. Let's talk about college. Did you have many friends?"

"At first. I liked the girls, and I dated a lot."

"How about your studying? Did you like your subjects?"

"Oh, yes. They all came pretty easily . . . except bio." Her tone changed. "I never liked science, but it was required."

"And you met Carl Harmon."

"Yes. He . . . helped me with bio. He said I must stop dating so much or I'd be sick. He was so concerned, he even gave me vitamins. He must have been right; I was so tired . . . and started to feel depressed. . . . I missed Mother."

"But you knew you would be home over Christmas."

"Yes. . . . But all of a sudden it got so bad . . . I didn't write about it, but I think she knew. She came for a weekend because she was worried about me. . . . And then she was killed . . . because she came out to see me. It was my fault . . . my fault—" Her voice broke into a sob.

Dorothy turned her head, trying to bite back tears. Why was she here? She'd be more useful if she went out and made coffee. She started to her feet.

"Carl helped you when your mother died?" Lendon Miles asked.

Nancy's answer was quiet. "Oh, yes. He was so good."

"And you married him."

"Yes. He said he'd take care of me. And I was so tired."

"Nancy, you mustn't blame yourself for your mother's accident."

"Accident?" Nancy's voice was speculative. "Accident? But it wasn't an accident. It wasn't an accident."

"Of course it was." Lendon's voice stayed calm, but he could feel the tightness of his throat.

"I don't know. . . . I don't know."

"Tell us about Carl."

"He was good to me."

"You keep saying that, Nancy. What did he do for you?"

"I don't want to talk about that."

"Why, Nancy?"

"I don't. I don't."

"All right. Tell us about the children. Peter and Lisa."

"They were so good . . . too good."

"Nancy, you keep saying 'good.' Carl was so good to you. And the children were good. You must have been very happy."

"Happy? I was so tired."

"Why were you so tired?"

"I was sick. Carl wanted me to get better. He said I had to be a good little girl. He helped me."

"Helped you how?"

"I don't want to talk about that."

"But you must, Nancy. What did Carl do?"

"I'm tired. I'm tired now."

"All right. Rest for a minute, then we'll talk some more."

Lendon got up. Chief Coffin jerked his head toward the door, and when they were in the dining room he spoke abruptly. "This isn't leading us anywhere and it could take hours. If you think you can find out anything about the Harmon murders, get to it. Or else I question her at headquarters."

"You can't force. . . . She's starting to talk. There's a great deal that even her subconscious can't face."

The chief snapped, "And I can't face myself if those kids are still alive and I've wasted precious time here."

"All right. I'll question her about this morning. But first let me ask her about the day the Harmon children disappeared. If there is any link between the two, she may reveal it."

Chief Coffin looked at his watch. "It's almost four. Whatever visibility there was will be gone in half an hour. Where is a radio? I want to hear the newscast."

"There's a transistor in the kitchen, Chief." Patrolman Bernie Mills walked into the kitchen, where Dorothy was making coffee. He turned on the radio, and instantly the voice of Dan Phillips, the newscaster for WCOD in Hyannis, filled the room.

"The case of the missing Eldredge children has just taken a new twist." Phillips' voice pulsed with unprofessional excitement. "A mechanic, Otto Linden, from the Gulf station on Route Twenty-eight in Hyannis, has just phoned us to state positively that at nine a.m. he filled the gas tank of Rob Legler, the missing witness in the Harmon murder case of seven years ago. Mr. Linden said Legler appeared nervous and volunteered the information that he was on his way to Adams Port to visit someone who probably wouldn't be glad to see him. He was driving a late-model red Dodge Dart."

Jed Coffin swore. "And I'm wasting time here listening to this claptrap." He picked up the phone just as it rang. "Yes, I heard it," he said to the caller. "I want a roadblock on the bridges to the mainland. And put out a bulletin on the red Dodge." He slammed the receiver down and turned to Lendon. "Now I've got a question for you to ask Mrs. Eldredge. It's whether or not Rob Legler got here this morning, and what he said to her."

Lendon stared. "What are you getting at?"

"I mean that Rob Legler is the person who could dump Nancy

Eldredge back into the middle of a murder trial. Suppose he's been hiding out in Canada with the other army deserters. Suppose he somehow finds out where Nancy is. He's sick of Canada, wants to come back here and needs a stake. How about going to Nancy Eldredge and promising to change his testimony if there's a new trial? That's the same as making her give him a blank check for the rest of her life. He sees her. She doesn't go for the deal—or he changes his mind. And she cracks."

"And murders her Eldredge children?" Lendon's voice was scornful. "Have you thought about the fact that this student who nearly put Nancy in the gas chamber was in the vicinity when both sets of children disappeared? Give me one more chance," he pleaded. "Just let me ask her about the day the Harmon children disappeared."

"You have thirty minutes—no more."

Quickly, Dorothy began pouring coffee into cups on a tray. She carried it into the living room. Ray was sitting next to the couch, holding Nancy's hands. Jonathan was standing by the mantel, staring into the fire.

Dorothy set the tray on the round pine table by the fireplace. "Will you have some coffee?" she asked Jonathan.

He looked at her thoughtfully. "Please."

She knew he took cream and one sugar. Without asking, she prepared the coffee that way and handed it to him. "Shouldn't you take your coat off?" he asked her.

"In a little while. I'm still so chilled."

Dr. Miles and Chief Coffin had followed her in. Dorothy carried a cup of coffee to the couch. "Ray, please have some."

He looked up. "Thank you." As he reached for it, he murmured to Nancy, "Everything will be all right, little girl."

Nancy shuddered violently. Her eyes flew open and she cried out in the desperate tone of a trapped animal, "I am not your little girl! Don't call me your little girl!"

COURTNEY Parrish turned from the small, unmoving figure on the bed, sighing heavily. He'd taken the adhesive from Missy's mouth and the cords from her wrists and ankles. Her fine, silky hair was matted now. He'd been planning to brush it when he bathed her, but now there was no point. He needed her response.

The little boy, Michael, was still on the floor of the closet. Courtney picked him up and laid him on the bed. He undid the bindings on his ankles and wrists and with a quick pull yanked the adhesive off his mouth. The boy cried out in pain, then bit his lip. "What did you do to my sister?" The belligerent tone made Courtney realize that the boy hadn't drunk all his milk.

"She's asleep."

"Let us go home. We want to go home. I don't like you. And Aunt Dorothy was here and you hid us."

Courtney lifted his hand and slapped Michael across the cheek. Michael rolled away from the man's grasp. Swiftly he ran toward the door, opened it and raced through the sitting room.

Courtney lunged after him. Michael threw open the apartment door, which Courtney hadn't locked, and darted down the stairs into the protecting gloom. Courtney, rushing frantically after him, lost his balance and hurtled down six steps before he managed to grasp the banister. Shaking his head, he picked himself up.

The boy was probably hiding in one of the third-floor bedrooms, but first he had to make sure the kitchen door was locked. The second lock on the front door was too high for the child, anyway. "I'll be right back, Michael," he called. "I'll find you. You're a very bad boy. You must be punished. Do you hear me, Michael?"

He lumbered down the two remaining flights of stairs and raced into the kitchen. This door had not only a double lock but a high bolt. With trembling fingers he shoved the bolt into place. The boy wouldn't be able to move that. There was no other way out.

Courtney switched on the overhead light, but an instant later it flickered and went off. He realized that the storm had probably pulled down some wires. It would make it harder to find the boy.

He bit his lip in fury as he struck a match and lighted the kerosene lamp on the table. The chimney was red, and the light cast an eerie glow against the thick-beamed ceiling. "Michael," he called, "it's all right. I'm not angry anymore. Come out, Michael. I'll take you home to your mother."

THE CHANCE TO blackmail Nancy Harmon was the break Rob Legler had been needing from the day he'd gotten on a plane to Canada after carefully shredding his embarkation orders for Vietnam. For six years he'd worked as a farmhand near Halifax—the only job he'd been able to get—and he loathed it.

He needed to cut out for someplace like Argentina. He wasn't an ordinary deserter who might slip back into the States with faked identification. Thanks to that blasted Harmon case, he was a hunted man.

Rob couldn't let that scene happen again. Last time the DA had told the jury that there was probably more to the killing than Nancy Harmon wanting to get out of a home situation. "She was probably in love," he said. "We have here a very attractive young woman who since the age of eighteen has been married to an older man. Her life with this devoted man might well be the envy of many a woman. But is Nancy Harmon satisfied? No. When a student-repairman comes in, sent by her husband so that she will not have to endure even a few hours' discomfort, what does she do? She follows him around, responds passionately to his overtures, says she has to get away . . . and then when he tells her that raising kids isn't his bag, she calmly promises him that her children are going to be smothered.

"Now, ladies and gentlemen of the jury, I don't for a minute believe that Rob Legler's unholy passion for this woman ended with a few kisses. But I do believe him when he quotes the damning phrases that fell from Nancy Harmon's lips."

Rob felt sick fear in the pit of his stomach whenever he remembered that speech. The DA would have given anything to make him an accessory to murder. All because he'd been in old Harmon's office the day his wife phoned about the furnace. Rob wasn't usually given to volunteering his services, but he'd heard some guys talk about what a doll that old creep's wife was.

So Rob had gone over. It was true: Nancy Harmon was a real looker. He'd gotten there about noon. She was feeding the two little kids and didn't pay much attention to him.

He realized that the only way to get to her was through the

kids, so Rob turned on the charm and in a couple of minutes he'd had them all laughing. There wasn't much wrong with the furnace—just a clogged filter. He got it working, but he said it needed a part and he'd be back and do the job right.

He got out fast the first day. No point in getting old Harmon upset. Went back to his office and told him, "I'll be glad to pick up the part you need, sir. It's one of those little things that if you call in a regular service, they'll make a big production over."

Harmon fell for it, of course. And Rob went back the next day and the next day. He got Nancy talking, and she told him that she'd had a nervous breakdown after her mother died. "But I'm sure I'm getting better," she said. "I've even stopped taking most of my medicine. My husband doesn't realize that. He'd probably be annoyed. But I feel better without it."

Rob had told her how pretty she was, kind of feeling his way. It was obvious she was bored with old Harmon and getting restless. He said maybe she should get out more. She'd said, "My husband feels that at the end of the day he doesn't need to see any more people—not after all the students he has to contend with." That was when he'd known he'd make a pass at her.

Rob had an airtight alibi for the morning the Harmon kids had disappeared. He'd been in a class of only six students. But the DA had told him that if he could find one shred of evidence, he'd hang an accessory charge on Rob. Plenty scared, Rob had hired a lawyer. The lawyer had told him that his posture had to be that he was the respectful student of a distinguished professor; had tried to stay away from the wife, but she had kept following him around. That he never took it seriously when she talked about the children being smothered. Actually, he'd thought she was just nervous and sick, the way the professor had warned him.

After Nancy Harmon was sentenced to die in the gas chamber, Professor Harmon had committed suicide. He abandoned his car on the same beach where one of the kids had been found, and left a note inside saying that it was all his fault. "I loved my wife so dearly," he wrote, "that I thought I could cure her. But I was wrong; I meddled beyond my depth. Forgive me, Nancy."

Then a mistrial was declared, because two women jurors had been heard discussing the case in a bar midway through the trial and saying she was guilty as sin. However, by the time a new trial was ordered Rob had graduated, been drafted, given Vietnam orders and bolted.

But there was something that bothered Rob. He didn't buy Nancy Harmon as a murderess. She'd been like a clay pigeon in court, and Harmon certainly hadn't helped her, breaking down on the stand when he was saying what a great mother she was.

In Canada, Rob was something of a celebrity among the draft evaders he hung out with. He'd told them what a dish Nancy was and showed them the press clippings and her pictures. He said she had some dough—it came out at the trial that her folks left her over a hundred and fifty grand; that if he could find her, he'd put the arm on her for some money to split to Argentina.

Then he got his break. One of his buddies, Jim Ellis, slipped home to visit his mother. The mother lived in Boston, but because the FBI was watching the house, she met Jim in Cape Cod in a cottage she had rented on Maushop Lake. When Jim got back to Canada, he was bursting with news. He asked Rob what it would be worth to him to know where he could find Nancy Harmon.

Rob was skeptical until he saw the picture Jim had managed to snap of Nancy on the beach. There was no mistaking her. Jim had done some digging too. The background checked.

They worked out a deal. Rob would see Nancy. Tell her that if she'd stake him to fifty thousand bucks, she'd never have to worry about him testifying about her. Jim wanted twenty percent for his share. While Rob was seeing Nancy, Jim would arrange for phony Canadian passports and reservations to Argentina.

Rob shaved his beard and cut his hair for the trip. Jim warned him that the minute you looked like a hippie, every cop in New England was ready to clock you with radar. Then Jim had made a map of Nancy's street, including that driveway through the woods where Rob could hide the car.

When he hit the Cape, he stopped at Hyannis to refuel. The attendant at the gas station checked everything, cleaned the windows.

When he was settling the bill, the attendant asked if he was down for some fishing. Rob babbled that he was going to Adams Port to see an old girl friend who might not be glad to see him. Then he settled his bill and drove off.

He reached Adams Port at quarter to ten. Even with Jim's map he almost missed the dirt road leading to the woods behind her property. He realized that after he'd met an old Ford wagon that was pulling out from it. So he had turned into the dirt road, parked the car and started walking toward the house, when Nancy came running out like a madwoman. He followed her to the lake and was about to go in after her when she dragged herself out and fell on the beach. He knew she looked in his direction, but he didn't know what was happening, and didn't want to get involved.

Back in the car, he'd cooled off and decided to check into a motel and try to see her the next day.

In the motel, Rob promptly went to bed and fell asleep. He awakened late in the afternoon and switched on the television set to catch the news. The screen focused in time for him to see a picture of himself. A voice was describing him as the missing witness in the Harmon murder case, reportedly seen on the Cape that morning. Numbly, Rob listened as the announcer recapped the disappearance of the Eldredge children. For the first time in his life he felt trapped. Now that he'd shaved off his beard and shortened his hair, he looked exactly the way he had in the picture.

If Nancy Eldredge had actually killed her new family, who would believe that he hadn't had something to do with it? It must have happened just before he got there. Rob thought of the old Ford wagon that had backed out from the dirt road just before he turned in. Heavyset guy behind the wheel.

Rob Legler's instinct for self-preservation told him to get off Cape Cod, and not in a bright red Dodge that every cop was looking for. He packed his bag and slipped out of the motel. A Volks Beetle was parked next to the Dodge. Rob opened the engine lid of the Volks, connected a few wires and drove away.

Six minutes later he ran a stoplight. Thirty seconds after that he saw a flashing red light reflected in his rearview mirror. He was being chased by a police car. For an instant he considered surrendering; then the overwhelming need to bolt from trouble overcame him. As he rounded a corner, Rob slipped open the door, wedged the accelerator down with his suitcase and jumped out. He was disappearing into a wooded area when the police car, its siren screaming, chased the careening Volkswagen down the road.

CHAPTER SEVEN

MICHAEL knew that if he wanted to get away, he mustn't make any noise. He remembered the time Mommy had had the carpet on the stairs at home taken off. "Now, until the new treads go down, you kids have to play a new game," she'd said. "It's called civilized walking." Michael and Missy had made a game of walking down the stairs on tiptoe. They got so good at it they used to sneak down and scare each other. Now, walking that same way, Michael slipped noiselessly down to the first floor. He had to get out of this house and bring Daddy back here for Missy.

At the bottom of the stairs Michael looked around, confused, then darted toward the kitchen. The outside door was over there. He rushed to it and was just about to turn the lock when he heard footsteps approaching. His knees trembled. If the door stuck, the man would grab him. Quickly, Michael raced out of the kitchen and into a little back parlor. The light in the kitchen was snapped on and Michael shrank behind a sofa. Dust tickled his nose. He wanted to sneeze. The light in the kitchen went out suddenly, and the house was black dark.

A moment later there was a reddish glow in the kitchen, and the man called, "Michael, it's all right. I'm not angry anymore. Come out, Michael. I'll take you home to your mother."

JOHN Kragopoulos had intended to drive directly to New York after leaving Dorothy, but a vague sense of depression coupled with a headache made the five-hour trip seem suddenly insurmountable. It was the weather, of course, and the intense distress Dorothy was suffering couldn't help transmitting itself. She had shown him the picture she carried in her wallet, and the thought of those beautiful children having met with foul play left a sickening feeling in the pit of his stomach.

He was driving down Route 6A toward the mainland. Ahead on the right an attractive restaurant was set back from the road. Impulsively, John swung into the parking lot. It was common sense to have a decent meal before starting home. And it was good business sense to try to strike up a conversation with the personnel of a restaurant in a vicinity he was considering.

He went directly to the bar. There were no customers yet. He ordered a Chivas Regal on the rocks; then, when the bartender brought it, he asked if it was possible to get something to eat.

"No problem." John liked both the bartender's obliging answer and the way he kept the bar immaculately neat. A menu was produced. "Technically, the kitchen is closed between two thirty and five, but if you don't mind eating right here . . ."

"Sounds perfect." Quickly, John ordered steak and a green salad. The Chivas warmed his body, and his depression began to lift. "You make a good drink," he said.

The bartender smiled. "It takes real talent to put together a Scotch on the rocks."

"I'm in the business. You know what I mean." John decided to be candid. "I'm thinking of buying the place they call The Lookout for a restaurant. What's your top-of-the-head opinion?"

"Could work. Good atmosphere, good booze, a good menu. . . . You could charge top dollar and keep it packed."

"That's my feeling."

"Of course, I'd get rid of that creep on the top floor."

"I was wondering about him. He seems somewhat odd."

"Well, he's supposed to be up here every year for the fishing. I know because Ray Eldredge happened to mention it. Nice guy, Ray Eldredge. He's the one whose kids are missing."

"I heard about that."

"Damn shame. Nice little kids. But like I was saying, one day, a few weeks ago, this guy—the tenant at The Lookout—comes in and orders a drink. I know him, I see him around. Well, just to make conversation, I ask him if he was here in September when the blues were running. You know what that stupe said?"

John waited.

"Nothing. He didn't have a clue. Do you believe anyone can come fishing to the Cape every year and not know what I meant?"

The steak arrived. As the taste of the prime meat combined with the warm glow of the drink, John relaxed and began to think about The Lookout. He had enjoyed going through the house. The sense of uneasiness had begun only in Mr. Parrish's apartment.

John finished the steak and paid his bill. Turning up his collar, he went to his car. Now he should head right toward the mainland. But he felt a crazy impulse to return to The Lookout. Courtney Parrish had been nervous—desperately anxious for them to leave. And that telescope. Parrish had changed the direction it was pointing in, but when John put it back in place, he's seen the police cars around what must have been the Eldredge home. What an incredibly powerful telescope for a Peeping Tom.

Could Courtney Parrish have been watching through the telescope when the children disappeared? Had he seen something? But if so, of course he would have called the police.

John reached for a cigar and lighted it with the small gold lighter. He was a suspicious fool. What did one do? Phone the police that a man seemed nervous and they should look into it? And if they did, Courtney Parrish would probably say, "I was about to take my bath and disliked being disturbed." Perfectly reasonable. People who lived alone tended to become precise in their habits.

Alone. That was the word. That was what was nagging John. Something had made him sure Courtney Parrish was not alone. It was the child's toy in the tub. That incredible rubber duck. And the cloying scent of baby powder. . . .

He knew what he had to do. He took his lighter from his pocket and hid it in the glove compartment. He would drive back to The Lookout unannounced and ask permission to look for his lighter, which he must have dropped somewhere. That would give him a chance to look around and either allay a ridiculous suspicion or have something more than suspicion to discuss with the police.

SHE DIDN'T WANT to remember . . . there was only pain in going back. But the questions, persistent, asking about Carl . . . about Mother. She had to answer, if only to stop the questions.

She heard her voice, far away. It was like watching a play. Mother in the restaurant . . . the last time she saw her. Mother's face troubled, looking at her, at Carl. "Where did you get that dress, Nancy?" She could tell Mother didn't like it.

The white wool. "Carl picked it out. Do you like it?"

"Isn't it a bit . . . young?"

Mother left to make a call. Was it to Dr. Miles? Nancy hoped so. She wanted Mother to be happy. . . . Maybe she should go home with Mother. . . . Maybe she would stop feeling so tired. Did she say that to Carl?

Carl leaving . . . "Excuse me, dear." Mother back before him.

"Nancy, you and I must talk tomorrow . . . when we're alone. I'll pick you up for breakfast."

Mother getting in the rented car, driving down the road.

Then the call. "There's been an accident. . . . Steering mechanism."

Carl . . . "I'll take care of you, my little girl."

The funeral . . . then the wedding. She'd wear the white wool dress. It would do for just going to the mayor's office.

But there was a grease stain at the shoulder. "Carl, where could I have gotten grease on this dress? I only wore it to have dinner with Mother."

"I'll have it cleaned for you." His hand, familiar, patting her shoulder.

"No . . . no."

The voice. "What do you mean, Nancy?"

"I don't know. . . . I'm not sure. . . . I'm afraid."

"Afraid of Carl?"

"No . . . he is good. Drink your medicine. . . . The children . . . all right for a while. . . . Carl was good."

"Was Carl good to the children?"

"He made them obey. He made Peter afraid . . . and Lisa. . . . 'So my little girl has a little girl'."

"Is that what Carl said?"

"Yes. There's something wrong. I mustn't have medicine after dinner. . . . I get too tired. . . . I must get away."

"From Carl?"

"I'm not sick. . . . Carl is sick."

"How is he sick, Nancy?"

"I don't know."

"Nancy, tell us about the day Lisa and Peter disappeared."

"Carl is angry."

"Why is he angry?"

"The medicine . . . he saw me pour it out . . . made me drink more. So sleepy. . . . Lisa is crying. . . . Carl . . . with her. I must get up. Crying so hard. . . . Carl spanked her . . . said she wet the bed. . . . I have to take her away . . . in the morning. . . . My birthday."

"Didn't you love Carl, Nancy?"

"I should. But Lisa so quiet. I promised we'd make a birthday cake for me. . . . She and Peter and I. . . . We'd go out and get candles. It's starting to rain. . . . Lisa may be getting sick."

"Did Carl go to classes that day?"

"Yes. He phoned. I said we were going to shopping center . . . then after that I was going to stop at the doctor's to let him see Lisa. I was worried. I said I'd go to the Mart at eleven . . . after the children's television program."

"What did Carl say when you told him you were worried about Lisa?"

"He said it was a bad day . . . didn't want Lisa out. I said I'd leave them in the car while I shopped. . . . They wanted to help with the cake. . . . They never had fun. . . . I shouldn't have let Carl be so strict . . . my fault. Rob made children laugh."

"Were you in love with Rob, Nancy?"

"No. I was in cage . . . wanted to talk to someone. Then Rob said what I said to him. Wasn't like that . . . wasn't like that."

Her voice began to rise.

Lendon's voice became soothing. "Then you took the children to the store at eleven."

"Yes. I told them to stay in car. . . They said they would. . . . Such good children. . . . Never saw them again . . . never."

"Nancy, how long were you in the store?"

"Not long . . . ten minutes. . . . Hurry back to car. . . . The children gone." Her voice was incredulous.

"What did you do, Nancy?"

"Don't know what to do. . . . Maybe they went to buy present for me. . . . Peter has money. . . . Look in candy store . . . hardware store . . . look for children."

"Did you ask anyone if they'd been seen?"

"*No.* Mustn't let Carl know. He'll be angry. . . . Don't want him to punish children . . . and Lisa didn't wet the bed."

"What do you mean?"

"Bed dry. . . . Why did Carl hurt her? Doesn't matter. . . . Children gone. . . . Michael . . . Missy gone too. . . . Look for them."

"Tell us about looking for Michael and Missy this morning."

"I must look at the lake. . . . Hurry, hurry. . . . Something is in the lake. . . . Something is underwater."

"What was under the water, Nancy?"

"Something red. . . . Maybe Missy's mitten. I must get it. . . . Water is so cold . . . can't reach it . . . not a mitten."

"What did you do?"

"Get out . . . get out of water. . . . I fell on the beach. . . . He was there . . . in the woods . . . watching me."

Jed Coffin stood up. Lendon held up a warning hand. "Who was there, Nancy?" he asked. "Tell us who was there."

"A man . . . I know him. . . . Rob Legler . . . looking at me." Her eyelids fluttered. Ray turned white. Dorothy inhaled sharply.

Lendon stood up. "The Amytal's about worn off."

"Doctor, may I speak with you and Jonathan outside?" Jed's voice was noncommittal.

"Stay with her, Ray," Lendon cautioned. "She may wake up."

In the dining room, Jed faced Lendon and Jonathan. "Doctor, how long is this to go on?" Jed's face was impenetrable.

"I don't think we should question Nancy any further."

"What have we gotten from all this other than the fact that she was afraid of her first husband, and that Rob Legler may have been at the lake this morning?"

Lendon stared. "Good God, didn't you hear what that girl was saying? Don't you know what you were listening to?"

"I only know that I haven't heard one thing that will help me find the Eldredge children. I heard Nancy Eldredge blaming herself for her mother's death, which is natural under the circumstances. Her reactions to her first husband sound pretty hysterical."

"Chief, do you know what pedophilia is?" Lendon asked quietly.

Jonathan nodded. "That's what I've been thinking."

Lendon didn't give Jed time to answer. "In layman's terms, it's a deviation involving sexual activity with a child."

"How does that fit in here?"

"It doesn't . . . not completely. Nancy was eighteen when she married. But she could have looked quite childish. Chief, is there any way you can run a check on Carl Harmon's background?"

Jed Coffin looked incredulous. He pointed to the sleet that was beating a steady staccato against the window. "Doctor," he said, "somewhere out there two kids are either wandering around freezing or they're in the hands of God knows what kind of kook and maybe they're dead. But it's my job to find them. And you want me to waste my time running a check on a dead man?"

The telephone rang. Bernie Mills, who'd been standing unobtrusively in the room, hurried to answer it. It was Sergeant Poler at the station. "Put the chief on."

Lendon and Jonathan looked at each other while Chief Coffin listened, then asked quickly, "How long ago? Where?"

Lendon realized he was praying—an inarticulate, fervent prayer that the message was not bad news about the children.

Jed slapped the receiver back into the cradle and turned to them. "Rob Legler checked into the Adams Port Motel around ten thirty this morning. A car we believe he stole has just been smashed up on Route Six A, but he got away. There's an all-out search and I'm going over to direct it. I'll leave Officer Mills here."

After the door had closed behind the chief, Lendon stood for a long minute trying to sort out what Nancy had said. I am too close to this, he thought. I see Priscilla at that phone . . . calling me. Carl Harmon left the table after her. Where did he go? Did he overhear what Priscilla said to me? Nancy said her dress was smeared with grease. Hadn't she been saying in effect that she believed Carl's hand must have been smeared, and when he put his hand on her shoulder her dress got dirty? Had Carl Harmon done something to Priscilla's car? But what purpose would such knowledge serve with Carl Harmon in his grave?

THE five-o'clock television newscast that night was largely devoted to the disappearance of the Eldredge children and old film clips from the Harmon murder case. Special attention was focused on a picture of Rob Legler leaving the San Francisco courthouse with Professor Carl Harmon after Nancy Harmon's conviction for the murder of her children, and the commentator's voice became urgent.

"Rob Legler has been positively identified as being in the vicinity of the Eldredge home this morning. If you believe you have seen this man, or if you have any information which may lead to the person or persons responsible for the disappearance of the Eldredge children, we urge you to call this number: KL 5-3800. Let me repeat: KL 5-3800."

The Wigginses had closed their store when the power failed and were home in time to catch the broadcast on their battery-operated television set. "That fellow seems kind of familiar," Mrs. Wiggins said. "Certainly is nothing to look at."

Jack Wiggins stared at his wife. "I was just thinking he's the type that might turn a young girl's head."

"Him? Oh, you mean the young one. I'm talking about the other fellow—the professor."

Jack spoke condescendingly. "Nobody's talking about Harmon. He committed suicide. They're talking about the Legler fellow."

Mrs. Wiggins bit her lip. "I see. It's just—oh, well . . ."

Her husband got up heavily. "When'll dinner be ready?"

"Oh, not long. But it's hard to worry about food when you think about those children, God knows where. It makes our little annoyances so unimportant, you know."

"What little annoyances?" His tone was sharply suspicious.

"Well . . ." Mrs. Wiggins hesitated. They'd had so much trouble with shoplifters this past summer. Jack got upset even discussing it. That was why, all day, it just hadn't seemed worthwhile to tell him that she was absolutely certain that Mr. Parrish had stolen a can of baby powder from the shelf this morning.

The five-o'clock news was also on in a modest home in Hyannis Port, which had not been affected by the blackout. The family of Patrick Keeney was about to start dinner when the picture of Michael and Missy Eldredge filled the screen. Involuntarily, Ellen Keeney glanced at her own children—Neil and Jimmy, Deirdre and Kit. When she took them to the beach, she never stopped counting heads. God, don't let anything happen to them, ever, please.

"He got awful fat," Neil said.

Ellen stared at her oldest child. "Who got fat, dear?"

"That man, the one in front. He's the one who gave me the dollar to ask for his mail at the post office last month. Remember, I showed you the note he wrote when you wouldn't believe me."

They were looking at the picture of Rob Legler following Professor Carl Harmon out of the courthouse. "Neil, you're mistaken," Ellen said. "That man has been dead for a long time."

Neil looked aggrieved. "See. You never believe me. He's a lot fatter and his hair's all gone, but he had his head kind of pulled down on his neck like that man."

The commentator was saying, "Any piece of information, no matter how irrelevant you may consider it . . ."

"Turn off the television, Neil," Pat ordered his son. "It's time to say grace."

Through the prayer that followed, Ellen's mind was far away. They had pleaded for any information, no matter how irrelevant it seemed. When the prayer was over, she asked, "Neil, do you still have the note the man gave you? Didn't I see you put it in your bank with the dollar?"

"Yes, I saved it."

"Will you get it? I want to see the name on it."

Pat was studying her. When Neil left he spoke over the heads of the other children. "Don't tell me you put any stock . . ."

She suddenly felt ridiculous. "I guess I just have a case of nerves."

CHAPTER EIGHT

IT WAS all going so badly. That foolish woman coming here and then the little girl; having to wait till she woke up, if she woke up. Then the boy—squirming away from him, hiding.

Courtney's sense of pleasure and expectation had changed to resentment. The boy was a threat. If he escaped, it would be the end. Better to finish with them both right away.

The sense of danger always heightened his perception. Like last time. He hadn't really known what he would do when he had slipped across the campus to the shopping center. He'd only known that he couldn't let Nancy take Lisa to the doctor. He'd parked on that little supply road between the shopping center and the campus. He'd seen her drive in, go into the store. Not a soul around. In a moment he'd known what to do.

The children had been so obedient. They'd looked startled when he opened the car door, but when he said, "Now, quickly—we're going to play a game on Mommy for her birthday," they'd gotten into the trunk and in an instant it was over. The plastic bags slipped over their heads, his hands holding them till they stopped squirming; the trunk shut and he back in school. The students intent on their lab experiments—no one had missed him. A roomful of witnesses to testify to his presence if need be. That night he'd driven to the beach and dumped the bodies into the ocean. Opportunity seized, danger averted. And now danger to be averted again.

Afterward he'd be here safe with nothing to threaten him; here to enjoy Nancy's torment. And tomorrow night, around dusk, he'd drive to the mainland. And probably some little girl would be walking alone and he'd tell her he was the new teacher. It always worked.

He was still in the kitchen. Holding up the lamp, he called again, "Michael, don't you want to go home to your mother? She didn't go to God—she's all better."

He started into the hall, then thought of the back parlor.

He walked into the room, holding the kerosene lamp high above his head, his eyes picking objects out of the gloom. As he turned around he swung the lamp. Then he let out a high-pitched whinny.

The shadow of a small figure huddled behind the sofa was silhouetted like a giant rabbit across the faded floor. "I found you, Michael," he cried, giggling, "and this time you won't get away."

AS JOHN Kragopoulos left Route 6A on the hilly ascent that led to The Lookout, visibility was very poor. He drove carefully, feeling the tendency of the car to skid on the slick road.

A few minutes later he turned into the driveway back of The Lookout. As he stopped the car, he was struck by the forebidding blackness of the big house. Even the top floor was completely dark. There must have been a power blackout, but surely the man had lamps. Power failures in bad storms couldn't be unusual on the Cape. Suppose Parrish had fallen asleep and didn't realize the electricity had failed? Suppose—just suppose—there'd been a woman visiting him who had not wanted to be seen? It was the first time the possibility had occurred to John.

Why hadn't he thought that Parrish might have a visitor who would be embarrassed at being seen? Suddenly feeling foolish, John decided he'd get out of here before he made a further nuisance of himself.

He was about to drive away when he saw a glimmer of light from the far-left kitchen window. It moved swiftly, and a few seconds later it seemed to go into the hall. Someone was walking around the house with a lamp.

John took a flashlight from the car and, opening the door softly, edged across the driveway.

Mentally he reviewed the layout of the house. The back staircase was reached through that hall, and so was the small parlor on the other side. Sheltering against the weathered shingles, he moved quickly along the back of the house, to the window that should be that of the parlor. He shrank back as the lamp became visible. He could see Parrish now. The man was calling to someone. John strained to hear. "Michael," Parrish was calling. "Michael!"

Chilling fear raced along John's spine. Those children *were* in the house. The lamp was arching in circles now, illuminating Parrish's bulk. John was aware that he was no physical match for this man.

Should he go for help? But if Parrish found Michael, even a few minutes might make a difference.

Then, before his horrified eyes, John saw Parrish reach behind the sofa to pull out a small figure who tried desperately to escape. Parrish put down the lamp and, as John watched, closed both hands around the child's throat.

Acting as instinctively as he had when he'd been on combat duty in the Korean War, John pulled his arm back and smashed the window with his flashlight. As Parrish spun around, John reached his hand in and forced the lock open. With superhuman strength he pushed the window up and vaulted into the room. He dropped the flashlight as his feet hit the floor. Parrish grabbed for it and raised it over his head like a weapon.

"Run away, Michael. Call help," John managed to shout, an instant before the flashlight crashed down on his skull.

NANCY sat upright on the couch, staring straight ahead. Ray had lighted the fire, and the flames were beginning to lick at the thick twigs and branches. Yesterday. It was just yesterday, wasn't it? She and Michael had been raking the lawn and he'd picked up the broken brush. "This is good for fires," he commented.

He was so good, so like Ray. Nancy realized that in some incredible way there was comfort in knowing that Mike was with Missy. If there was any way to do it, he'd take care of her.

"Oh, God."

She didn't know she'd spoken aloud until Ray looked up startled. He was sitting in his big chair. His face showed the strain. He seemed to know that she didn't want him to touch her now—that she needed to think. She must not believe that the children were dead. They could not be dead. Why was she feeling some tiny lick of hope?

"Rob Legler," she said. "I told you I saw him this morning."

"Yes," Ray said.

"Is it possible I was dreaming? Does the doctor believe me?"

"The doctor feels you gave an exact account of what happened," Ray said. "And Nancy, you should know, Rob Legler has definitely been seen near here. He left a stolen car two miles down on Six A. But don't worry, he won't get far on foot in this weather."

"Rob would not hurt the children," Nancy said flatly.

Lendon came into the room, Jonathan close behind him. "How do you feel, Nancy?" Lendon studied her closely. She was more composed than he'd expected.

"I'm all right. I talked a lot about Carl, didn't I?"

"Yes."

"There was something I was trying to remember; something important I wanted to tell you."

"Do you know what it is now?" Lendon asked.

"No." Nancy got up and walked restlessly to the window. She wanted to clear her head. She looked down, realizing for the first time that she was wearing the fluffy yellow robe. "I'm going to change," she said.

Upstairs in the bedroom, she felt light-headed and leaned her forehead against the coolness of the wall. The door opened, and she heard Ray cry, "Nancy!" He hurried over and turned her to him.

"I'm all right," she said. "Really."

He tilted her head up. His mouth closed over hers, and she arched her body against his.

It had always been like this. She'd wanted him so much, right from the beginning. Not like Carl. Poor Carl, she'd only tolerated him. After Lisa was born he had never again . . . not like a husband. Had he sensed her revulsion? She'd always felt guilty.

"I love you." She didn't know she'd said it—words said so often, words she murmured to Ray even in her sleep.

"I love you too. Oh, Nancy. It must have been so bad for you. I thought I understood, but I didn't."

"Ray, will we get the children back?" Her voice shook.

His arms tightened. "I don't know, darling. But whatever happens, we have each other. Nothing can change that. . . . Nancy, they found Rob Legler, in the woods near the bay. Dr. Miles went over to the station house, and Jonathan and I are going too."

"I want to go. Maybe he'll tell me—"

"No. Jonathan has an idea, and I think it could work. But if Rob sees you, he might refuse to say anything."

"Ray . . ." Nancy heard the despair in her voice.

"Darling, hang on. Just a little while longer. Dorothy will stay with you. I'll be back as soon as I can." For an instant he buried his lips in her hair; then he was gone.

Mechanically, Nancy walked into the bathroom and turned on the water in the shower stall. She took off her bathrobe and, twisting her hair into a knot, stepped inside. The needle spray made a steady assault against the rigid tension of her muscles. Gratefully she lifted her face to the warm water. A shower felt so clean.

She never, never took a tub bath anymore—not since the years with Carl. A vivid recollection came as the water splashed against her face. The tub . . . Carl's insistence on bathing her. Once when she'd tried to push him away, he'd slipped and his face had gone under the water. He'd been so startled that for a moment he couldn't pull up. When he did he'd begun spluttering and trembling. He'd been so angry, but mostly frightened. It had terrified him to have his face covered by water.

That was it. That was what she had tried to remember: that secret fear of water. Oh, God. Nancy stumbled out of the shower and began retching uncontrollably.

THE desk sergeant at the station looked up as Ray and Jonathan entered. "Didn't expect to see you here tonight. I'm sure sorry about the kids, Mr. Eldredge."

Ray nodded. "Where are they questioning Rob Legler?"

The sergeant looked alarmed. "You can't have anything to do with that, Mr. Eldredge."

Ray said evenly, "Tell the chief that I have to see him now."

The sergeant's protest died on his lips. He turned to a policeman who was coming down the corridor. "Tell the chief Ray Eldredge wants to see him," he snapped.

Ray glanced across the room at two people sitting on a bench. They were about as old as he and Nancy—a nice-looking couple. He wondered what they were doing here. The guy looked embarrassed, the woman determined. Was it possible they had had a fight and she was pressing charges?

Chief Coffin rushed into the room. "What is it, Ray?"

Jonathan answered. "You have Rob Legler here?"

"Yes. Dr. Miles is with me. Legler's asking for a lawyer. Won't answer any questions."

"I thought as much. That's why we're here." In a low voice Jonathan outlined his plan.

The chief shook his head. "Won't work. This guy's a cool one."

"Let us try. Can't you see how important time is? If he had an accomplice who has the children now, that person may panic."

"Well . . . talk to him. But don't count on anything." As Ray and Jonathan started to follow the chief down the corridor, the woman got up from the bench.

"Chief Coffin." Her voice was hesitant. "Could I speak to you for just a minute?"

The chief looked at her appraisingly. "Is it important?"

"Well, probably not. It's just something my little boy . . ."

"Sit down please, ma'am. I'll be with you as soon as I can."

Ellen Keeney sank down on the bench as she watched the three men leave. The sergeant at the desk sensed her disappointment. "Maybe I can help you, ma'am."

But Ellen didn't trust the sergeant. When she and Pat had first come in, they had tried to tell him that they thought their little boy might know something about the Eldredge case. The sergeant had looked pained. "Do you know how many calls we've had? You just take a seat. The chief'll talk to you when he can."

Now Ellen shook her head. But she was determined to sit here until she got a chance to tell her story.

The station-house door opened and another couple came in.

"Hi, Mr. Wiggins. Miz Wiggins," the sergeant said.

"You won't believe it," Wiggins snapped. "On a night like this my wife wants to report that somebody pilfered a can of baby powder from the store this morning."

Mrs. Wiggins looked upset. "I don't care how stupid it sounds. I want to see Chief Coffin."

"He'll be coming out soon. Just sit down, won't you?" He pointed to the bench where the Keeneys were waiting.

As they sat down Mr. Wiggins muttered angrily, "I still don't know why we're here."

Ellen Keeney's ready sympathy made her turn to them. "We don't really know why we're here either," she said. "But isn't it an awful thing about those missing children?"

In the office down the corridor, Rob Legler stared through hostile eyes at Jonathan Knowles. Fear knotted Rob's stomach. The Eldredge kids hadn't been found. If anything happened to them, they might try to pin something on him. But nobody had seen him near the Eldredge house. Nobody except that fat slob in the station wagon.

"You are in a very serious situation," Jonathan was saying. "You are a deserter who has been taken into custody. No matter how guilty or innocent you are in the disappearance of the Eldredge children, you stand right now to spend years in prison."

"We'll see about that." But Rob knew Jonathan could be right.

Ray stood up and leaned across the table until his eyes were on a level with Rob's. "Now listen, bum, and listen hard. My wife saw you at our house this morning. So that means you've got to know something about what went on. If you level with us now, and we get our kids back, we won't prosecute a kidnapping charge. And Mr. Knowles, who happens to be one of the top lawyers in the country, will get you off with as light a sentence as possible on the desertion charges. Now how about it? Do you take the deal?" Ray moved forward until his eyes were inches from Rob's. "Because if you don't—and if I find out that you could have helped us get our kids back and didn't—I don't care what jail they throw you in, I'll get to you and I'll kill you."

"Ray." Jonathan pulled him back forcibly.

Rob knew when he had no cards left to play. He shrugged and looked at Jonathan. "You'll defend me?"

"Yes."

Rob leaned back. He avoided looking at Ray. "Okay," he said. "This is how it started. My buddy up in Canada . . ."

They listened intently as he talked. Rob chose his words carefully when he said he was coming to ask Nancy for money. "See, I never believed she touched a hair on the heads of those Harmon kids. She wasn't the type. But I got the word that they were trying to pin the rap on me out there and I'd better just answer questions and keep my opinions out of it."

"Get to this morning," Chief Coffin ordered. "When did you arrive at the Eldredge home?"

"It was like a couple of minutes before ten," Rob said. "I had been driving real slow, looking for that dirt road my friend drew a picture of, and I had to slow down for this other car. Then I realized that the other car had come off that road, so I turned around and went back."

"The other car?" Ray repeated. "*What* other car?"

The door of the room burst open. The sergeant hurried in. "Chief, I think it's real important you talk to the Wigginses and that other couple. I think they have something to tell you."

FINALLY, Nancy was able to get up, wash her face and rinse her mouth. . . . The children. Not again, not like that; please.

With lightning speed she dressed, stuffed her feet into sneakers and hurried downstairs. Dorothy was waiting in the dining room with sandwiches and a pot of tea.

"Nancy, sit down. Just try to have something—"

Nancy cut her off. "I have to see Chief Coffin. There's something I have to tell him." She clenched her teeth together, having heard the hysteria rising in her voice. She turned to Bernie Mills, who was standing in the doorway of the kitchen.

"Please call the station," she begged him. "No, I will." She ran to the phone and was just reaching for it when it rang. Bernie Mills hurried to take it, but Nancy picked it up.

"Hello?" Her voice was quick and impatient.

Then she heard. So low she had to strain to make out his words. "Mommy. Mommy, please come and get us. Missy is sick."

"Michael!" she screamed. "Michael, where are you?"

"We're at . . ." His voice faded and the line went dead.

She jiggled the phone. "Operator," she shrieked, "don't break the connection! Operator . . ." But it was too late. The dial tone buzzed in her ear.

"Nancy, what is it?" Dorothy was at her side.

"It was Michael. He said Missy is sick." Nancy could see doubt on Dorothy's face. "Don't you understand? That was Michael!"

Frantically she dialed the operator. "Can you tell me about the call that just came here? Where was it from?"

"I'm sorry, ma'am. We have no way of knowing that. In fact, we're having a lot of trouble because of the storm."

"I've got to know where that call came from."

"There is no way we can trace the call once the connection is broken, ma'am."

Numbly, Nancy put down the receiver. "Somebody may have broken that connection," she said. "Whoever has the children."

"Mrs. Eldredge, are you sure it was your son? You're kind of upset." Bernie Mills tried to make his voice soothing.

Nancy grasped the edge of the table to steady herself. She said quietly, "You may think I'm hysterical, but that was my son's voice. What is the number of the police station?"

"Call KL 5-3800," Bernie said reluctantly. The chief would have his head for not having gotten to the phone.

The number rang once. A crisp voice said, "Adams Port Police Headquarters. Sergeant—"

Nancy started to say "Chief Coffin" and realized that she was speaking into nothingness. "The phone is dead," she said.

Bernie Mills took it from her. "It's dead, all right."

"Take me to the police station. No, you go. If the phone comes back on and Michael can call again . . . Please go to the police station. We'll stay here. Tell them Michael phoned."

"I can't leave you."

"Officer. Please. How far is the station in your car? Five minutes. You'll be gone ten minutes in all. Please."

Bernie Mills thought carefully. The chief had told him to stay here. But if that was the kid on the phone and he didn't report it . . . He considered asking Dorothy to drive to the station, but the roads were too icy and she looked so upset.

"I'll go," he said. "Stay right here." He didn't take time to look for his coat, but ran out the back door to the patrol car.

Nancy said, "Dorothy, Michael knew where he was. He said, 'We're at.' What does that mean to you? If you're on a street a road, you say, 'We're *on* Route Six A,' or 'We're *on* the beach.' But if you're inside, you say, 'We're *at* Dorothy's house,' or 'We're *at* Daddy's office.' Do you see what I mean? Oh, Dorothy, there must be some way to know. There must be something. . . .

"And he said that Missy is sick. I almost didn't let her go out this morning. But I thought just half an hour. And I got her red mittens, the ones with the smile faces, and told her to be sure to keep them on because it was so cold. I remember thinking that for a change she had a matching pair. But she did lose one by the swing. Oh, Dorothy, if only I hadn't let them out!"

Dorothy's face was working convulsively. "What did you say? I thought Missy only had one mitten with a smile face on it."

"She did. But I found the mate last night."

With a sob, Dorothy covered her face. "I know where they are. Oh, God, I was so stupid." She reached into her pocket and pulled out the mitten. "It was there, this afternoon, on the floor of the garage. I thought I'd kicked it out of my car. And that awful man—"

Nancy grabbed the mitten. "Dorothy, where did you find it?"

Dorothy sagged limply. "At The Lookout, when I was showing it today."

"The Lookout . . . where that Mr. Parrish lives. I've never seen him except from a distance. Oh, no!" In an instant of total clarity Nancy saw truth and realized it might be too late. "Dorothy, I'm going to The Lookout. *Now.* Maybe I'll be in time. You go for Ray and the police. Tell them to come. Can I get into the house?"

Dorothy's voice became calm. Later she could indulge in self-recrimination. "The kitchen door has a bolt. If he put it on, you can't get in. But the front door—I never gave him a key. She dug into her pocket and came out with a set. "This one will open both locks." Together the women ran out the back door.

It was almost impossible to see. Squinting against the pelting sleet, Nancy raced her car down the road, across Route 6A to the cutoff for The Lookout. As she entered up the winding incline, the car began to slip on the ice. A tree loomed ahead. She managed to yank the wheel in a half circle. The front end of the car pulled to the right and with a grinding crash hit the tree. Nancy pushed open the door and started up the precarious hill.

At the approach to the driveway she slipped and fell. Ignoring the sharp pain in her knee, she got to the house and ran around it toward the front entrance. Her numbed fingers fumbled with the key. Let it turn; please, let it turn. She felt resistance as first one, then the other rusty lock finally turned. Nancy pushed open the door.

The house was dark—and terribly quiet. She resisted the impulse to shriek Michael's name.

Dorothy had said something about two staircases in the hall past the big front room. Uncertainly, Nancy started forward, her hands in front of her in the pitch-darkness.

The stairs . . . three flights. She yanked off her sneakers. They were so wet they'd make a squishing noise.

At the foot of the top staircase, Nancy stopped to control her harsh breathing. The door at the head of the stairs was open. Then she heard a voice—Michael's voice. "Don't do that!"

She ran up the stairs silently, furiously. Michael! Missy! At the top of the stairs she hesitated. A flicker of light was coming from down the hall. Still silent, she hurried through the shadowy living room toward the candlelight in the bedroom, toward the gross figure with his back to her who was holding a small, struggling figure on the bed with one hand, as with the other he pulled a shiny plastic bag over a blond head.

Nancy had an impression of Michael's startled blue eyes, of plastic clinging to his eyelids and nostrils as she cried, "Let go of him, Carl!" She didn't know she'd said "Carl" until she heard the name come from her lips.

The man spun around. Missy's tousled figure was lying on the bed, her windbreaker a bright red heap beside her.

She saw the look of stupefaction on the man's face replaced by cunning. "You." He started toward her menacingly.

She felt his thick grasp on her wrist, pulled away and threw herself onto the bed, her fingernails tearing at the tight plastic sheet that was making Michael's cheeks become blue. She heard his gasping breath as she twisted around to meet Carl's attack. His arms crushed her tight against him. She felt the sick warmth of his body.

As she tried to pull away, she could feel Missy's foot under her. It was moving. Missy was alive.

She began to scream—a steady, demanding call for help; and then Carl's hand covered her mouth and nostrils, choking out air and causing great black curtains to close in front of her eyes.

Abruptly the hands loosened. She choked—great gurgling sounds. From somewhere, someone was shouting her name. Ray! It was Ray! She tried to call out, but no sound came.

"Mommy, Mommy, he's taking Missy!" Michael's voice was urgent, his hand shaking her. She managed to sit up as Carl swooped past her with the small figure that had begun to squirm and cry.

"Put her down, Carl. Don't touch her." But he looked at her wildly and, holding Missy against him, ran into the dark of the next room. She staggered after him, trying to shake the dizziness. There were footsteps racing up the stairs now. Desperately she searched for Carl, saw his dark shadow silhouetted against the window. He was climbing the stairs to the attic.

"Up here, Ray. Up here!" At last she made her voice carry. She stumbled blindly up the attic stairs after Carl. But now he was climbing the thin, rickety ladder that led from the attic to the widow's walk. She thought of the narrow, perilous balcony that circled the chimney between the turrets of the house.

"Carl, don't go up there. It's too dangerous. Come back!"

But he was at the top of the ladder, pushing up the door that led to the roof. Missy was crying now—a loud, frightened wail—"Mommmmmmmy!"

Carl thrust his body onto the balcony. Frantically, Nancy scrambled after him, trying to pull him back from the low railing. If he fell or dropped Missy—"Carl, stop. Stop!"

Sleet beat against him. He turned and tried to kick her, but stumbled backward, grasping Missy tightly. He lurched against the railing and regained his balance. She could hear his harsh breathing, the high-pitched sound that was between sob and giggle.

He was holding Missy on the railing. "Don't come any nearer," he said to Nancy. "I'll drop her if you do. Tell them they must let me go away. Tell them they must not touch me."

"Carl, I'll help you. Give her to me," she pleaded. "I'll tell them you're sick."

"You won't help. You'll want them to hurt me." He swung one foot over the rail.

"Carl. No. Don't do it. Carl, you hate water. You don't want water to cover your face. When your body wasn't recovered, I should have known you didn't commit suicide. You couldn't drown yourself."

Then she heard the cracking sound. The railing was breaking! Carl's head went backward; he swung his arms forward.

As he released his hold on Missy, Nancy darted forward. Her hands caught in Missy's long hair—caught and twisted and held. She was teetering on the edge of the walk; the rail was crumbling. She felt Carl grab her leg as he fell, screaming.

Then firm arms came around her from behind. A strong hand pulled Missy's head against her neck, pulled them both back, and she collapsed against Ray even as, with a last despairing scream, Carl slid off the balcony, across the icy, sloping roof and down to the angry surf below.

CHAPTER NINE

THE fire licked hungrily at the thick logs. The warm hearth smell and the scent of freshly made coffee permeated the room. The Wigginses had opened the store and brought up cold cuts for sandwiches, and they and Dorothy had prepared a spread while Nancy and Ray were at the hospital with the children.

When they got home the television crews had taken films of Nancy and Ray carrying their children in from the car, and had been promised an interview the next day. "In the meantime," Ray said into the microphones, "we want to thank everyone whose prayers through this day kept our children from harm."

Now Nancy sat on the couch, tightly holding Missy, who was sleeping peacefully, the ragged blanket she called her bee clutched to her as she nestled against her mother.

Michael, in Ray's arms, was talking to Lendon—telling all about it. His voice was a little boastful, "And I didn't want to go away from that house without Missy when the nice man started fighting with the other man and yelled at me to get help. So I ran back up to Missy and called Mommy on the phone. But the phone stopped working. Then the bad man came. . . ."

"Good boy. You're quite a guy, Mike." Ray couldn't keep his eyes off Nancy and Missy. Nancy's face was so serenely beautiful that he had trouble swallowing over the lump in his throat.

Chief Coffin put down his coffee cup and reviewed the statement that he would make to the press: "Professor Carl Harmon, alias Courtney Parrish, was pulled out of the water still alive. Before he died he made a statement confessing his sole guilt in the murder of his children, Lisa and Peter, seven years ago. He also admitted that he was responsible for the death of Nancy Eldredge's mother. Realizing that she would have prevented his marriage to Nancy, he jammed the steering mechanism of her car while she was in the restaurant with Nancy. Mr. John Kragopoulos, whom Professor Harmon assaulted today, is in Cape Cod Hospital with a concussion, but is expected to recover. The Eldredge children have been examined and were not sexually molested, although the boy, Michael, suffered a bruise on the face from a violent slap."

The chief felt fatigue settling into the very marrow of his bones. Tomorrow, he reflected, he would have to judge his own culpability. He had prejudged Nancy because of pique that he hadn't recognized her. By prejudging her, he had closed his mind to what Jonathan and Ray and the doctor and Nancy herself were telling him.

"Coffee?" Jonathan repeated Dorothy's question. "Yes, thank you. I don't usually have any this late, but I don't think I'll have trouble sleeping tonight." He studied Dorothy closely. "How about you? You must be pretty tired."

He watched as an indefinable sadness crept over her face, and understood the reason for it. "I think I must tell you," he said firmly, "that any self-recrimination you have is unwarranted. We all ignored the facts today. This very morning I considered asking Ray to speak to the tenant at The Lookout about whatever he had glinting in his window. An investigation would have led us to The Lookout very quickly.

"And one irrevocable fact is that if you had not elected to keep that appointment and bring Mr. Kragopoulos to that house, Carl Harmon would not have been deterred from his evil intent."

Dorothy listened, considered, and a weight of guilt dissolved. "Thank you, Jonathan," she said. "I did need to hear that."

Unconsciously she clasped his arm. He covered her hand with his own. "The roads are still treacherous," he said. "When you're ready to go home, I'd feel better if I drove you."

It is over, Nancy thought. It is over. Her arms tightened around the sleeping Missy as she looked at Michael, leaning back against Ray. From the wellspring of her being, prayer permeated her mind and heart: Thank You, thank You, thank You. You have delivered us from evil.

"Mommy," Michael said, and now his voice was sleepy. "I didn't get your birthday present."

"Don't worry, Mike," Ray said. "We'll celebrate Mommy's birthday tomorrow, and I know just the presents to get for her." Miraculously the strain left his expression, and Nancy saw a twinkle begin in his eye. He looked directly at her. "I'll even tell you what they are," he volunteered. "Art lessons from a really good teacher from the kids and a color job at the beauty parlor from me. I have a hunch you make quite a redhead, honey."

Mary Higgins Clark

Mary Higgins Clark herself has five children, so she understands very well the agony of her heroine in this book. Indeed, it was the strength of her feeling for her family that gave her the original idea for *Where are the Children?* "Every mother worries about her children getting lost," she says. "Then, one day I thought, suppose a woman not only lost her children but also was accused of killing them. . . ."

As well as outstanding talent, Mrs. Clark possesses rare courage and determination. Widowed in 1964, when her youngest child, Patty, was scarcely a year old, she has cheerfully shouldered the combined responsibilities of mother and breadwinner ever since.

Brought up in New York, Mrs. Clark worked as an air hostess —on the Europe-Asia-Africa route—until her marriage, when she and her husband moved to New Jersey. It was then that she began to develop the writing abilities that were going to be of such crucial importance in the future, attending writers' workshops and evening university courses, and eventually publishing several successful short stories. Her marriage lasted fifteen years, and was wonderfully happy. "I was very lucky," she says.

With the death of her husband, however, she was obliged to turn her satisfying hobby into a serious profession—as much full-time as the demands of her young family would allow. She wrote mainly for radio, but found time to research a very well-received children's biography of George Washington. She also became a partner in a New York radio-script agency.

Where are the Children? is her first novel, written over a period of three years, mostly between five and six thirty in the morning, before getting her children off to school and herself off to her job in New York. As a way of working this must suit her, for she is already well into her next book, another mystery thriller. And—now that her children are growing up and she mightn't have quite enough to do—she's planning to write a play as well. And after that? "That's the big book," she says. "The one I'm working up to." And that's *all* she'll say about it.

AMONG THE ELEPHANTS

A condensation of the book by

IAIN and ORIA DOUGLAS-HAMILTON

Published by Collins & Harvill Press, London

"A huge, bow-tusked female came headlong around the foliage. Without uttering a sound or pausing in her stride, she plunged her tusks up to the gums into the body of the Land-Rover. . . ."

For five years Iain Douglas-Hamilton lived among the four hundred and fifty elephants of Tanzania's Lake Mangara National Park. What started off as a purely scientific study, soon turned into a series of extraordinary African adventures. He camped in woodlands among tree-climbing lions, was trampled by a rhino, tracked the elephants by radio, on foot and in the air. He watched mothers bring up their babies, and tuskers rush to the help of the stricken and dying. He came to know (and respect) elephants such as the great matriarch Boadicea, the four terrifying Torone sisters and the gentle Virgo. He also came to know (and love) the beautiful girl with "long dark hair and slanting almost Oriental eyes," who gave up the comforts of civilization to help him in his work.

The book that they wrote together has won universal acclaim.

"The Douglas-Hamiltons have written in popular style a major work of zoological research, and the close-up pictures of wild elephants are unequalled." —Peter Grosvenor, *The Daily Express*.

"It reads more like an adventure story than a text book."—James Fox, *The Sunday Times*.

"A book of great humour, empathy and delight." —Christopher Wordsworth, *The Observer*.

PART I: Iain Douglas-Hamilton

CHAPTER ONE

It all started in early 1965 when I went to see John Owen, the director of the five great national parks in newly independent Tanzania. He was on a brief leave in England, and I had badgered him into granting me an interview. I was then a zoology student at Oxford.

I met him in his small well-kept Sussex garden. A powerfully built man with grey hair and steely blue eyes, he was vigorously stoking a bonfire with garden junk. Turning a little reluctantly from his labours, he offered me a seat and called to his wife, Patricia, to make us some tea. Then, his large frame crammed into a small chair, he puffed at his pipe and listened patiently while I put to him my research programme.

The summer before, I had worked for Owen on a research project in the Serengeti National Park. My experiences there had captured my imagination, and with graduation coming I could think of no career other than rejoining this élite band of scientists. Since nobody had yet made a field study of the behaviour and ecology of lions, this seemed an obvious choice.

But now Owen said, "No, Iain, I'm sorry. We have the American zoologist, George Schaller, coming to study lions."

"Well surely there must be something I can do?"

"We don't need anyone in the Serengeti right now." He paused, then, almost as an afterthought, added, "But we *do* need some research done in Lake Manyara National Park, on elephants."

He went on to describe Lake Manyara, and that thin strip of land along the northwest shore which was the national park. Although among the smallest parks in Tanzania, its density of animals made it one of the most popular in East Africa. The main tourist attraction was the tree-climbing lions, and what concerned John Owen was that recently elephants had started to strip bark off the acacia trees which the lions used as resting places. Nobody knew why, or what would happen if they continued this destruction, though it had recently been suggested that the elephants were overcrowded and might have to be regulated by shooting.

Elephant ecology was something entirely new to me, and between sips of tea I listened with growing interest. John Owen told me that it was not known exactly how many elephants there were, but he'd heard that during the dry season, from June to September, most of them disappeared into a huge cloud forest, the Marang, on the top of the Great Rift Valley escarpment just outside the park boundary. He wanted to know if this migration really did occur and what its significance was.

"You will have to finance yourself, Iain," he said. "But we can give you an old Land-Rover and you can set up your camp anywhere in the park, provided the tourists can't see you."

To live in a national park and to follow the elephants on their migration routes sounded like a great proposition to me. I accepted gratefully.

Returning to Oxford, I set about getting my degree, and also finding some money for the project. On a bulletin board in the zoology department was a list of opportunities for postgraduates, among them a Royal Society Leverhulme Scholarship which would pay for travel and a certain amount of equipment, in addition to £500 for living expenses. I drafted a research outline and submitted it to the Royal Society. I left my proposed study methods vague, for much would depend on how close I could get to the elephants.

In a few weeks I was summoned to London and ushered into

a dark panelled room where six distinguished-looking men faced me across a polished table. One wanted to know if it was dangerous to approach elephants on foot. This I couldn't answer, never having tried it. Another asked, "What, in your opinion, is the use of studying elephants?" I replied that all over Africa elephants had been declining in number and range for the last two thousand years, and that even now, within the sanctuaries, they were possibly threatened with extinction from overcrowding. Only research could show a way for their proper management.

I was very grateful when in November I learned that I had been awarded the scholarship for a year. By this time I was already in East Africa, where I was learning to fly. On receiving the letter, I hitched a lift in a tourist's car to Manyara.

As we crested the northern end of the escarpment above Lake Manyara, I looked out over miles of forest stretching towards the south, broken only by glades of short grass, and rivers which carved their way to the lake. At that distance herds of elephants looked like parties of termites. The bush was so thick that I wondered how I was ever going to keep track of their movements. Two miles on we reached the village of Mto-wa-Mbu, which was as far as I was to go by car.

As I was buying some bananas, a dilapidated Land-Rover drew up. The driver was a sturdily built man in a green bush jacket and large brown jackboots. Dark glasses concealed his eyes, giving his lined face and grey hair a mask of stern authority. On his chest he wore the leaping impala badge of the Tanzania National Parks. This was Desmond Foster Vesey-Fitzgerald, known to his colleagues as "Vesey", and to the Africans as "Bwana Mungosi" (Mr. Skins) which referred to the boots in which he was always seen. I introduced myself and discovered that he was staying at the rest house at park headquarters, where I was to be based until I had built my own camp.

Over a refreshing cup of tea we talked. Without his dark glasses Vesey didn't look stern any more. He was cheerful, friendly, and humorous. Only when we discussed the current theory that Manyara's elephants were overpopulated did he become aggressive. All these years the national parks had been trying to protect the animals, he said, and now at last when the numbers had built up to a nice density the cry of overpopulation was raised.

When I asked him about the damage to the lions' acacia trees, he snorted, "Good God, man, that's not damage, that's habitat modification." The elephants, he said, were an essential part of nature's scheme. By opening up thick bush, they also opened a way for other animals and for more palatable plants which could not otherwise penetrate these areas. The best way to manage the park was to interfere with nature as little as possible.

The two schools of thought were directly contradictory. On the one hand, the proponents of shooting could not prove that there were too many elephants simply because their density was higher than elsewhere in Africa. On the other, Vesey had no figures to show that the elephants were not in the process of wiping out the acacia trees.

After a supper lit by hissing gas lamps, I collapsed onto my bed and did not wake until the sun shone the next morning. We then made an early start so that Vesey could show me the entire park in one day.

THE DUSTY ROAD from the rest house wound down to the main road. A little farther on, at the entry gate, a clerk sat in a small booth selling tickets to the tourists. Behind the gate an area called the groundwater forest began, and at once we entered the cool shade of tall canopies of trees. Rivulets coruscated between black volcanic boulders to flow into ice-clear pools, where water-cress floated; the pools were fringed by elegant fronds of papyrus that nodded like slaves wafting a pharaoh's fan. Little blue crabs with orange legs eyed us from the rocks, and yellow-barked fig trees deepened the shade.

At first, as we bumbled along in Vesey's faded grey Land-Rover, the ebullient forest looked in no way fragile, nor as if it were crumbling under pressure from legions of voracious elephants. But a few miles south the scenery changed; the springs diminished and the forest gave way to more arid *Acacia tortilis* woodland. These beautiful flat-topped thorn trees where the lions rest epitomize Africa to me. Usually they are found in groves or spaced out with savannah grass which gives a parklike appearance. Now the first portents of elephant destruction were to be seen. Ghostly white trunks stripped of their rough bark offered a glaring contrast to the greenery.

The road meandered on, at times coming close to the foot of the rift wall, at others running along the lake shore. Close up, the lake waters were dark brown and muddy. Halfway down the park, just past a broad sandy river, the Ndala, the escarpment reached almost to the lake edge. Then came another river, the Bagayo, after which the space between lake and cliff widened into a grassy plain devoid of game. This we crossed and entered thick, sweet-smelling bush. On our right the escarpment once more loomed near, and a huge waterfall cascaded down its side: the Endabash River, which supplied the whole of the southern end of the park with water. We forded it at a place where a concrete causeway had been built.

The track ended nineteen miles, as the pelican flies, south of the main gate, at some hot springs which oozed out of the ground. Here the escarpment reared straight up from the lake for a full three thousand feet. It was capped with a tangled mass of dark green trees which marked the edge of the Marang Forest Reserve, an area of eighty-two square miles. The steep slope of the escarpment was covered with dense vegetation and broken by slabs of rock and huge boulders. It formed an apparently insuperable barrier to any movement of elephants up to the forest.

A mile farther on at the southern boundary of the park, was a fence made of three strands of steel hawsers. It had been erected in an attempt to contain the elephants within the park, and to prevent their visiting parts of their former range which had been given over to farmers. But from the numerous tracks and the way the fence was twisted out of shape, it was obvious that elephants had no difficulty in passing through.

On our way back, as the slanting evening light began to turn the bushes into pure gold, a group of elephants crossed the road in front of us. The long-awaited moment took me by surprise.

An orderly column of some ten cows, towering above young of all sizes, filed thirty yards in front of the car, their flanks blue-

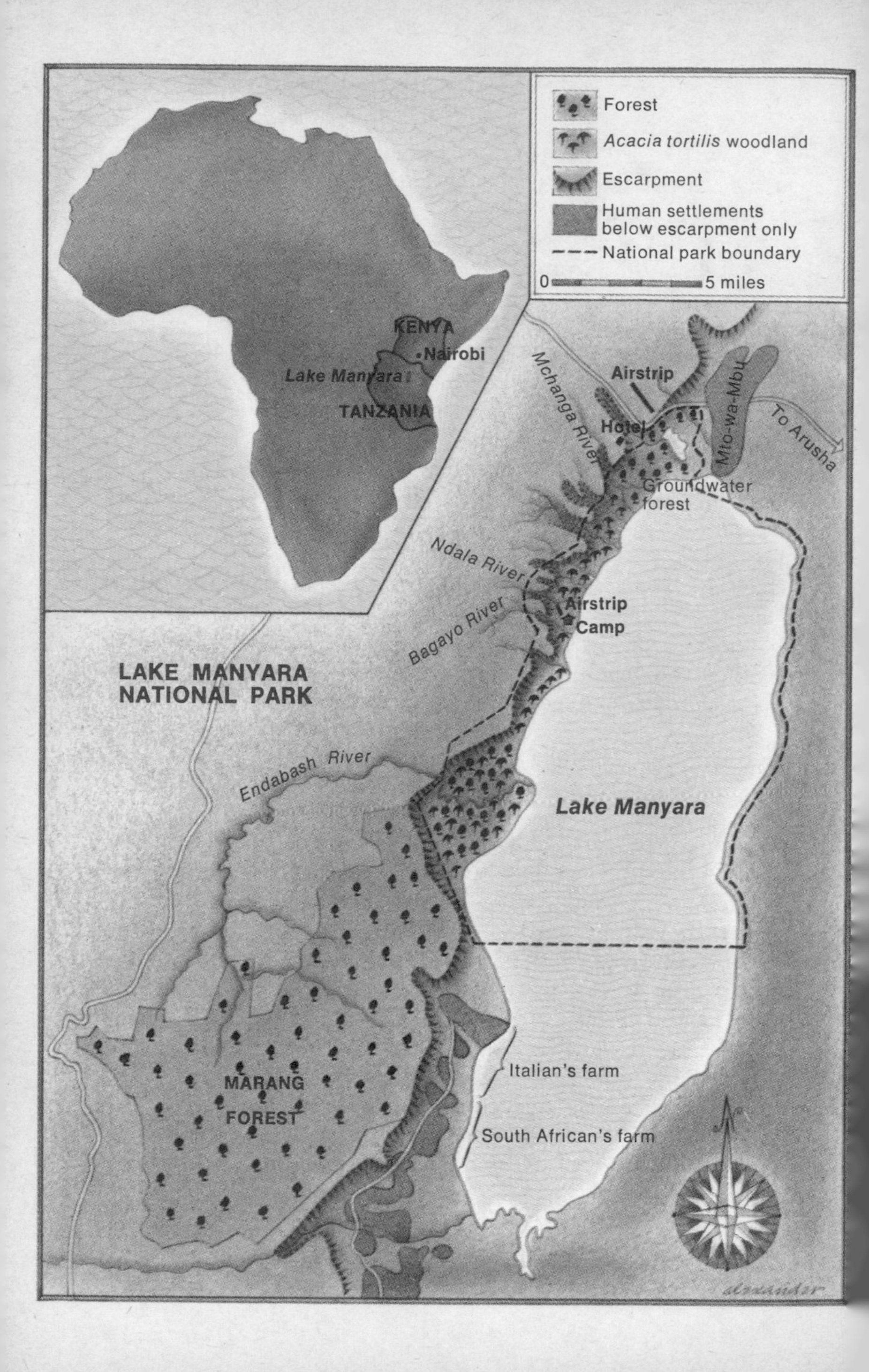

Forest
Acacia tortilis woodland
Escarpment
Human settlements below escarpment only
National park boundary
0
5 miles
KENYA
Nairobi
Lake Manyara
TANZANIA
Airstrip
Mchanga River
Hotel
Mto-wa-Mbu
To Arusha
Groundwater forest
Ndala River
Bagayo River
Airstrip
Camp
LAKE MANYARA NATIONAL PARK
Endabash River
Lake Manyara
MARANG FOREST
Italian's farm
South African's farm

grey in the shadow. Then some younger females scurried over, turning to look at us with heads high and backs arched. As soon as they were all safely across, they wheeled in unison as if at an order. A gust of wind had wafted our scent in their direction. Ears flared and a row of trunks performed a snake dance, waving sinuously above the line of their massive heads, sampling our smell, and afterwards expelling their breath with a *whoosh*. I could no longer see the youngsters except for glimpses between the legs of large cows, who formed a solid wall facing us. We were obviously worrying them. But after a while they became less disturbed, the young ones peeped out, and I was able to examine the whole herd through my binoculars.

THAT EVENING, as we drank coffee after dinner, with the moths dancing around the pressure lamp, my ideas began to fall into place. The controversy between those who wanted to regulate the elephants and those who wanted to let everything alone had suddenly made my research seem vitally urgent. Hundreds of elephants' lives, or the fate of whole woodlands, were at stake.

First, I would have to count the number of trees injured and destroyed. But the long-term effect of the elephants on their environment would depend on *their* numbers, on their birth and death rates, and their movements in and out of the park, especially into the Marang forest. There was only one way in which I could measure these factors. I would have to be able to recognize large numbers of individual elephants with no more difficulty than I could recognize men.

This, I realized, would be my first priority, and the method upon which all my research was to be based. The plan was exciting for it was something that no one had yet attempted.

AFTER CHRISTMAS I started going out on my own in the battered old Land-Rover which John Owen had lent me. I wanted to photograph the elephants so that I could learn to recognize them. But the Manyara elephants were elusive; they spent much of their day in a dark cloak of vegetation, in which only a few backs were visible, or a piece of an ear, or the gleam of a tusk.

The first I saw was a bull quietly feeding by the road. He was slightly obscured by some low-lying bush but if I could approach him on foot, I would get a clear view. I crept silently out of the car, closing the door gently behind me. The wind was perfect, blowing steadily from the elephant to me. I tiptoed towards an anthill halfway between us.

As I rounded the anthill, with the elephant momentarily hidden, a terrifying deep growl reverberated in my ears. Convinced that he was after my blood, I fled helter-skelter back to the car. But when I looked round, the elephant was peacefully munching a palm frond, unaware of my existence. I felt like an idiot. It was the first time I had heard an elephant rumble. Later I learned that this was simply a contact call by which they keep in touch while feeding.

Earlier I had noticed two dugout canoes cast up on the beach, and I decided to try elephant-viewing from the lake. The mud looked so hard that I drove out confidently. Within ten yards of the nearer canoe the car suddenly broke through the surface and all four wheels settled into thick treacly mud. Any attempt to drive forward or backward only dug the wheels in deeper.

Broiled by the relentless sun, I wandered along the beach in search of some debris to put under the wheels. Finally I found a heap of bleached buffalo bones left behind by lions and hyenas, which reminded me that this was no spot to spend a night out. Seizing a couple of well-chewed scapulae and a massive tibia, I trudged back to the car, and inserted them under the tyres. To make doubly sure that it would not bog down again, I laid a carpet of thickly matted acacia branches beyond the bones. The car popped out of the mud, over the branches, and back onto hard ground. I heaved a sigh of relief, wiped the sweat off my face—and then heard a hissing noise. The thorns of the acacia branches had punctured a tyre.

Luckily I had a spare. After jacking up the car I replaced the tyre and drove back to the rest house, arriving exhausted and frustrated. For all its small size Manyara was not so tame as I had thought. I would welcome assistance from someone who knew the area.

Next morning at park headquarters I spoke to Jonathan Muhanga, the African park warden. He suggested that I take out one of his rangers every day until I had set up my camp, at which time one of them would be permanently stationed with me. This arrangement proved a great success.

ONE DAY A sharp-eyed young ranger called Mhoja Burengo came with me. I asked him if we could go close to the elephants on foot.

He spoke only a little English, but answered, "We can try."

The elephants spent much time in the groundwater forest, and at Mhoja's suggestion we went there. Coolness bathed us as we entered the forest. We stopped and listened. Elephants are never silent. A rumble from a member who is separated from the herd, a squealed protest from a calf: such sounds betray their location.

Moving slowly towards a sound of breaking branches, we caught sight of some massive ears flapping behind a screen of palm fronds. We climbed a tree and were rewarded with a clear view of a group of bulls only ten yards away. Delighted, I took many pictures, after which we both retreated.

Mhoja pointed out how white the bulls were. He said that the colour of elephants was a sign of where they had been for the past twenty-four hours. White meant a wallow in the forest beside the tall termite mounds that stick up like rude fingers amid the soft greenery. Burnt ochre signified a mud pool in the acacia woodlands, while a dirty grey characterized the mud of the Endabash River.

At four in the afternoon Mhoja suggested that we move to the short grass area at the mouth of the Ndala River; many elephants would be there at this hour. Sure enough, there were several small groups of cows, with their calves, and some bulls. We were able to approach into the steady breeze that blew across the lake, and sat on the grass with nothing between us and the herd.

Towering over the others was a bull with a shattered right tusk; three feet of the nerve cavity were exposed. This must be painful and likely to make him savage. He also had a large rent in his left ear. His appearance was so distinctive that I took eleven pictures of him, though I should hardly need them to identify him again. I named him Cyclops.

EVERY DAY I accumulated more pictures. I had brought developing equipment from England, and I rigged up a darkroom in my bedroom at the rest house. As the prints came to life in the developing dish, I scanned them eagerly.

The first batch was not very good. Too often the elephants' ears were spattered with mud, so that they merged into the background of leaves and bushes. However, the photographs did show one thing—the degree to which elephants varied in appearance.

The outlines of some elephants' ears resembled Norwegian fiords. Other ears would be almost smooth, with only one or two small nicks, but the shape of a nick provided useful material. There were also large rents caused, I learned, when the animal was young by the sharp tusks of some intolerant old cow. With time, I found, the details changed. Over a long period an elephant might obtain sufficient new cuts on his ears and chips off his tusks to become unrecognizable.

An elephant's tusks continue to grow all its life. It has been calculated that during a sixty-year life span they would reach a length of sixteen feet in the female and twenty feet in the bull, providing they did not break. One is generally used as a master tusk and is worn down faster than the other. Often it acquires a groove near the tip where the elephant habitually pulls grass over the same place.

One evening on the beach I met a large concourse of forty elephants in the open. Here was a chance to get some close-ups outlined against the sky. They were all standing, some eating the short spiky grass, others drinking from small holes which they had scooped out. Among them were two beautiful cows with long curving tusks that swept together in great gleaming bows. One cocked her head and looked at me intently.

I was about two hundred yards away and clearly the car was worrying her. She began to pace back and forth. Then she stopped and shook her head rapidly, so that her ears flapped like dusty blankets. Gradually she worked herself up, weaving to and fro, edging her way in my direction. A few of the other cows followed, spreading their ears and twirling their trunks. They reminded me of some massive Biblical phalanx with a champion standing out in front of the army. The ground was flat, so knowing that I could leave my escape to the last minute, I decided to test their intentions.

When the great cow came to within forty paces, she drew herself up to her full height. I switched on the engine. She broke into a lumbering charge, her trunk rolled up beneath her tusks like a coiled spring. I let her come to within ten yards to see if she would stop, but she kept on towards me at full speed so I let out the clutch and raced away. There seemed little doubt that she was in deadly earnest. After some fifty yards she stopped, stood tall again, and emitted a resounding trumpet.

Her posture was perfect for an identification picture, and, shaking slightly, I took it. She looked such a fine warrior queen that I named her Boadicea, after the ancient British chieftainess who, "earnest, rugged and terrible" had defied the oppression of the Romans.

HALFWAY through dinner that night, Vesey mentioned that an abandoned elephant calf had wandered into the camp of some VIP guests of the parks.

I nearly shot out of my chair. "What! If only I'd known, I would have brought it in." I had been hoping that I might have an opportunity to raise a young abandoned elephant, for there is no better way of getting to know any animal.

The VIP guests were Charles Lindbergh, the first man to fly the Atlantic alone, and his family. They had supported John Owen's campaign in America for the preservation of African wildlife, and in return Owen had invited them to visit the national parks. I had kept away from Lindbergh's camp imagining that he would want to enjoy the park undisturbed, so I had missed the sight of a diminutive elephant calf wandering in while they were putting up their tents. Bewildered, lonely, and too young to have learned to fear man, it had attached itself to Lindbergh's

daughter. But John Owen, concerned that she might be trampled by an anxious elephant mother, had ordered some rangers to drive the calf away. Vesey told me it had last been seen in some bushes not far from the camp.

At first light I drove to the camp and found the Lindberghs heating up their morning coffee. They could not tell me where the little elephant was. I explained that its chances of survival were zero unless it could find its mother, assuming that she was still alive. Lindbergh at once offered to help me look for it and we set off in his car. We found no trace of the calf, but some rangers said they had heard sounds of squealing in the night, mixed with deep growling. I asked them to show me where, but they were afraid to go into the thick bush. So I walked in the direction they indicated, with Lindbergh close behind me.

I rounded a bush and suddenly came face to face with a large black-maned lion sitting on the remains of the elephant calf. He crouched down, and glared at us over the top of his prey. His muscles twitched, and then with a bound and a deep-throated *whoof* he catapulted sideways and vanished from view.

We beat a discreet retreat, before the lion came back. He was known as Dume Kubwa (big male) and was the larger of two grown lions that roamed the northern end of the park. Usually he could be found up a tree, lolling on a branch with his full stomach bulging out on either side.

The death of the baby elephant was most depressing. However, I did not remain downcast for long as I was now absorbed in a search for a camp site. I hoped to find a remote place with fresh drinking water, a river for swimming, a good view, plenty of animals nearby, shade for the hot season and a low density of biting insects. So far none fulfilled all these conditions.

One day I went back to the mouth of the Ndala River. I arrived in the midday heat, too early for the elephants to come out on the beach, so I decided to explore the white sands of the dry river by following it as far as the escarpment. Rounding a bend, I heard a musical sound and, looking towards the escarpment,

Left: The great matriarch Boadicea charges the camera.

saw a silver thread of water cascading down a sheer rocky gorge. A little farther on water plants were growing at a place where the river sank beneath the sand. A wide game trail led on between tumbled boulders to a great pool at the foot of the waterfall. On one bank, to my delight, were some flat-topped acacia trees casting shadows on a level spot ideal for a camp.

A collection of labourers, masons, and carpenters went to work, and I moved out of the rest house and lived at the site in a large tent, so that I could supervise construction. The design of the house was simple: two large rondavels linked by a thatched veranda. One rondavel I would make into a laboratory and the other into an office, with living space on the veranda in between.

The Ndala riverbed was an ideal place to watch elephants. The camp was near a narrow waist between the lake and the escarpment, which had the effect of channelling all elephants moving north or south towards the most convenient watering spot, right below my camp.

CHAPTER TWO

One problem was how to estimate the elephants' ages. Unless I could tell how old they were, I could not get an idea of the rate of their breeding. Hunters passing through the park told me that elephants lived to a hundred years or more. You only had to look at their wrinkles, they said, to appreciate their age. Beyond this sort of belief, little information existed on how to judge the age of an elephant.

Fortunately, a well-known scientist, Dr. Richard Laws, had recently switched his attention to the African elephant. His main study area was in Uganda, at the Murchison Falls National Park (now renamed Kabalega). He was already developing a reliable index for measuring elephants' ages.

I obtained John Owen's permission to take my Land-Rover to Uganda. After a day-and-a-half's drive I arrived in Kampala, and was lucky enough to intercept Laws who had come there to lecture. Despite a tight schedule he gave me an hour of his time.

The key to an elephant's age, he said, is in its peculiar tooth structure. Each elephant has six teeth in each side of its upper and lower jaws, making twenty-four in all, but no more than two of the six are in use simultaneously. As the earlier teeth wear down, they are superseded by others growing forward from the back of the jaw. The first tooth, nearly twice as big as a human wisdom tooth, is replaced before the end of the first year. The second molar then comes into use and lasts until the calf reaches the age of four, when it is replaced by molar number three. At the other end of the life span, which appears to be sixty to seventy years, molar six can be easily recognized because no more teeth erupt behind it.

Laws's next step was to relate age, as determined by the teeth, to body growth. He constructed a growth curve which showed what the average shoulder height would be at different ages, up to the age of fifteen years. He even made me a sketch of the heights of young elephants ranged alongside a fully grown adult female whose average height would be eight feet five inches.

Laws and his associate, Ian Parker, had killed many elephants to obtain this material, but the facts could be determined in no other way. I was delighted with this information and eager to drive up to the Murchison Falls National Park to see the elephants and their habitat at first hand.

Half a day's drive northward brought me to the park. Entering it, I crossed wide grasslands where once woodlands had grown. They appeared to offer rich bounty to the clusters of elephants flung across the landscape, yet compared with Manyara there seemed to be very few calves. I thought of what Laws had told me about the elephants' shrinking environment in Uganda and their extraordinary response to it. By examining the females he shot, and learning whether or not they were pregnant, he had concluded that the breeding rate was depressed. Was this due to the fact that there were no more trees to eat, or to the social effect of overcrowding? Laws himself was undecided, but if it could be shown that elephants had the capacity to regulate their own numbers, then it might be possible to avoid cropping.

I drove on to Ian Parker's camp. Here I realized for the first time what cropping elephants—whether for research or for ecological reasons—really meant.

PARKER, with typical East African hospitality, offered me supper and a bed for the night. Over hippo steaks he explained his rationale for game preservation. He not only accepted the need for cropping, but also recognized that although it was dirty, repugnant work, it was not to be shirked by those who professed to be committed to the preservation of elephants.

He had once been employed by the game department in Kenya to run an elephant cropping scheme, but had decided that private enterprise would be more effective. He had resigned from the game department and started his own company, Wild Life Services. The concession to crop elephants in the overpopulated Murchison Falls National Park had been his first big contract, and under Laws's scientific guidance he secured material for research, while at the same time conducting an efficient and profitable business.

Parker's method of killing came of long experience with elephant reactions to gunfire. Cautiously approaching a group, he and his hunters would deliberately cough or break twigs. Hearing this, the elephants would move into a defensive circle with the mothers facing outward and the young ones stowed safely behind. The hunters would then close in and open fire with semiautomatic rifles of the type used by NATO. A group of ten animals usually took no more than thirty seconds to kill. No survivors were ever left and consequently the bad news never spread from one group to the next. Altogether more than two thousand elephants were to be killed in this way.

The carcasses were utilized with the utmost efficiency. Laws and Parker performed speedy postmortems, extracting any parts needed for scientific examination. The meat was sold for local consumption around the park; the feet were made into umbrella stands; and the entire skin and ears were tanned to make an unusually hard-wearing leather. The ivory was the most valuable commodity of all, and found a ready market.

Ian Parker believed that emotion should be ruled out when dealing with large populations of animals. Game, in his view, should be regarded purely as a resource, to be used in the most economical way, through tourism, research, or hunting. In areas where the increasing human population made the presence of any game undesirable, he advocated eradication programmes based on sound utilization practices.

When I left his camp the next day for the long journey back to Manyara, I had much to think about. I profoundly disagreed with his view that sentiment can have no place in the policy of national parks, since the very reason for their existence is the result of sentiment, whether of an aesthetic nature or plain affection for animals. I realized, however, that this visit had given me an important key to my study. The crowded elephants of Murchison had slowed down their birth rate, which in time would reduce their total numbers. Would the Manyara elephants do the same? They appeared to live at an even higher density, but there was as yet no shortage of food, water, or shade. Only time would provide the answer.

WHEN I RETURNED to Manyara, the rains had begun in earnest. Slate-grey clouds lowered, and the Ndala River ran red and angry. As soon as the roofs of my houses were up I moved in, glad to evacuate my dripping tent. The walls were painted white, and geckos soon made their homes in the eaves. A desk, a table, some chairs, and a bed were sufficient furniture.

I organized my patrols to take me to every part of the park, and day after day increased my score of known elephants. One of my first questions was: What constitutes a stable group? Once I knew this, I would be able to see how these basic building blocks of elephant society interacted under the crowded conditions. The smallest groups I encountered consisted of several cows with their young. The largest contained eighty to a hundred elephants, with bulls on the outskirts and cows and young calves in the centre. But these herds never stayed together for more than a few hours, before breaking up into smaller groups.

About a month after I had first seen her on the beach, I found Boadicea again, this time in the woodlands. From the uppermost branches of a tree I was able to watch her enjoying a midmorning siesta. On her right stood another large cow, with fat convergent tips to her tusks, and two calves at heel. The largest cow in the group also had convergent tusks but these were thin and sharply pointed. Another, whom I named Right Hook, had a tusk that curved sharply inward, and there was a small one-tusker female, Virgo. All had been on the beach together, and now I quietly took their pictures for a second time. I could only see twenty-two elephants. On the beach there had been forty. A hundred yards away was another fine matriarch with long white tusks very similar to Boadicea's. Her ears had relatively smooth edges, but her temples were sunken. She was the most beautiful elephant I had seen, and I named her Leonora. I remembered that she, too, had been on the beach. There was now a distinct unit of eight around her. I compared them mentally with the pictures I had taken before. Sure enough, next to her was a cow whom I had named Slender Tusks.

Under a tree two hundred yards from Boadicea I discovered a third distinct unit that had also been on the beach, led by a large one-tusker I named Jezebel. I counted up this group with growing excitement. The numbers came out right; there were exactly nine. This made forty elephants altogether. The only difference was that now they were arranged in three groups. My puzzle was beginning to work out. The groups were stable.

During the next few months of 1966 I established that a similar family-unit organization applied to all the other cow-calf groups in the park, of which there were at least forty-eight. The average size of the units was ten, and most of these belonged as well to larger kinship groups. Family units might split off from their kinship group for a few days, but they would always rejoin later.

This discovery came as a great surprise to me, because up to this time it had never been suggested that larger herds were anything but random aggregations. My observations provided the first proof of unit stability and showed that family ties were far wider and more lasting than had been thought.

The largest kinship group was Boadicea's, which I observed on three hundred and fourteen separate days in the years 1966 to 1970—and which numbered nearly fifty before I left. For the group to reach this size the kinship ties had probably lasted over a hundred years and possibly for much longer.

I had no means of estimating Boadicea's age exactly, for elephants, by the age of thirty, are within ten centimetres of the height they would reach if they lived to be sixty. Also some are tall for their age, others short. Boadicea's tusks were as large as any other female's in the park and I thought she was probably between forty-five and fifty years old. She was still actively reproductive and had a small calf at heel.

The individual elephants varied greatly in character. Although Boadicea was the matriarch with the fiercest threat displays, within the same family unit was the tamest, gentlest, and most curious elephant in the park. This was the small one-tusker, Virgo. She gave the impression of being intensely curious about me and on one occasion advanced to within two elephant paces of the Land-Rover. I was entranced. Never before had I been able to see the hairiness around the jaw, nor smell the warm scent of elephant which now wafted over me in concentrated waves. I wondered if, after all the centuries of men killing elephants, she would ever accept my presence on foot. To be able to move around the elephants unrestricted by the car was an intriguing hope, but I certainly did not expect it would be possible.

In my first year of study there were six breeding cows in Boadicea's family unit, and fourteen immature animals. The younger calves were tightly glued to their mothers' sides and could walk clean under their bellies. Larger calves with toothpick tusks also seemed tightly attached to their mothers, but once they were half as high as an adult it was often difficult to see to which female they belonged.

Before I could use Laws's method of estimating a calf's age by comparing its height to its mother's shoulder height, I had to find an accurate system of measurement. On a visit to Dar es Salaam, Tanzania's capital, I met a forestry officer who was a specialist in photogrammetry, the science of measuring objects by photography. Foresters have long used overlapping pictures of trees taken from aeroplanes, which when laid side by side and viewed through a stereoscope stand out in three dimensional relief. I suddenly realized that by adapting stereophotography to ground conditions I would be able to measure the heights of elephants. I found that I could get good stereoprints by manipulating two mirrors and a prism in front of the camera. I constructed an apparatus with two long arms with a mirror on each and a prism halfway between, which reflected light into the camera. Through the lens I could now get a double image. The calculation relied on two simple measurements on the photograph —the height and separation of the twin elephant images.

One useful property of my measuring apparatus was its defensive potential. I discovered this when stalking a bull who caught sight of a glint of silver, tucked up his trunk, and charged. At the last minute I tilted the mirror so that white-hot sunlight flashed in his eyes. Quite unable to see what he was doing, he ground to a halt and swung his head to try one eye after the other, only to be dazzled in both. Finally, rather bemused, he strode away.

Early on I learned that threat charges were usually not as much in earnest as they looked. Boadicea had easily the most impressive display, but after some four months in Manyara I decided one day to call her bluff, and remained rooted to the spot when she charged. I was delighted to see her skid to a halt just ten paces from the Land-Rover. Since she was so much more aggressive than the others, I made the mistake of thinking that any elephant with a lesser display must be less dangerous.

By mid-1966 I had met almost all the elephants who frequented the northern section of the park. Consequently, one morning when I caught sight of a new group standing placidly in some long grass, I was anxious to record them. A strong wind drowned the sound of my engine and I approached near to them before they knew I was there. I had switched off the engine and sited myself on the roof when all of a sudden the four cows swung their heads around, with ears like hostile radar scanners. Then with no trumpeting or threat gestures of any kind they charged.

I sat happily on the roof and waited for them to stop. They didn't. When the first elephant was less than ten yards from the car and still going at full speed, I dropped through the roof hatch like a meteorite, and pressed myself flat against the far side of the car. At the last possible instant they stopped. One smashed a dead branch to smithereens with her tusks and, towering above me, let out a strangely savage and piercing trumpet.

These elephants were certainly quite different from any others I had met. They were totally hostile to man. Why they stopped I do not know. I have seen them many times again and I have never known them to stop in a charge since that first occasion. I named them the Torone sisters after a shrill queen of Greek mythology.

WHEN THE DRY SEASON came at the beginning of June, the river turned clear again. Down the waterfall came snails like little flat spirals. I bathed in the pools every day, diving in from the pink gneissic rocks. The pools were a snails' paradise. The water ran gently and waterweed provided them with sustenance.

One day I felt itchy after a bathe. The itchiness persisted for most of the day and the following night, wearing off near dawn. Too late I realized that the pools were infected with bilharzia, a parasite carried by snails.

The pools had been surveyed earlier and pronounced clear of infection, but after July everyone who bathed was infected. Over the following months fifteen people, including John Owen and his daughters, began to suffer from coughs, fevers, general debilitation, and lethargy. All had bathed in my pool in the Ndala River. Some of the children nearly died. In the investigation that followed it was shown that the snails had themselves been infected by the park's baboons, who suffered from chronic bilharzia and had defecated into the water.

Having bathed almost every day for months, I was severely infected, and suffered from headaches and vomiting. Work became impossible. I decided that I would have to return to England to try to get cured at the Hospital of Tropical Medicine in London.

Just before I left for England a storm broke and a flash flood thundered down the waterfall, scouring the lower reaches of the riverbed and sweeping away all the snails and the weed they relied on. The pools were once more free of bilharzia.

After a year of work I realized that I had only begun to scratch the surface of the elephants' social life and their ecological problems. I therefore wrote a report to the professor of animal behaviour at Oxford, Niko Tinbergen, with a copy to John Owen, asking if I could continue my study after my treatment for bilharzia.

CHAPTER THREE

The red-brick Hospital of Tropical Medicine at St. Pancras, blackened with London's grime, seemed another world from the woodlands of Manyara. The only link between the two places was the parasites they had in common, conveyed by sallow, emaciated patients suffering from all manner of infestations. Dr. Walters, who looked after me, conducted seminars at the foot of my bed on bilharzia transmission via baboons. My case was one of the few known to medical science.

One day a letter arrived from John Owen with the good news that he had been to America and had interested the New York Zoological Society in my research; I was to be funded by them for the rest of my project. Moreover I shortly heard from Niko Tinbergen, until now a fascinating but distant figure in my life, that he was willing to take me on as a student for my doctorate. Better still, he was coming to East Africa, and he asked if he could stay at Manyara. As co-founder of the science of ethology (the scientific study of animal behaviour), he later shared a Nobel Prize with Konrad Lorenz and Carl von Frisch.

Ten days after my return to Manyara, Tinbergen came to stay with me and became totally absorbed with elephants. Some of their behaviour demonstrated principles he had discovered through observing very different animals in Europe. For instance, there was redirected aggression: two gulls facing each other in a territorial dispute would direct vicious pecks at the ground, and savagely pull grass stalks as if they were feathers from the rival's head. When Boadicea launched one of her threat charges against us, we found she did the same thing. When we remained stationary in the Land-Rover, she swept close past us and discharged her aggression on an innocent gardenia bush with such fury that a shower of leaves fluttered to the ground.

Niko told me that redirected aggression was usually elicited by an object that evoked fear. This seemed to be true of Boadicea who for all her threat never dared to press her charges home. In fact, it was only because of the usually redirected nature of elephant aggression that I was able to study them as I did and survive. I wondered what terrible experience Boadicea had suffered at the hands of man for her to hate and fear us so much.

Another visitor who was deeply interested in animals, though with a different emphasis, was the naturalist and animal collector David Attenborough. He came with a BBC television unit to film the work of scientists at the newly formed Serengeti Research Institute, of which I was by now an outlying member. As we drove south to Endabash, looking for a tolerant family unit for us to stalk, I told him how elephants greatly outnumbered the thirty or so rhinos and sixty giraffes that shared the same habitat.

It was interesting to speculate on why the rhinos only occurred at low densities. Like elephants they chewed twigs, but they restricted themselves almost entirely to woody vegetation, while the elephants sampled the majority of the six hundred and thirty plant species of Manyara. The rhino social groupings were also much smaller, consisting of parties of two and three.

Before long we came across a family group of elephants led by a matriarch whom I named Queen Victoria, and she allowed us to film her. Returning to camp in the twilight, we trundled very close to a large rhino which huffed and puffed on the side of the road. David missed seeing it and since I wanted to show him something special, I stopped the car and reversed.

The rhino was much angrier than I expected. It trotted through the bush towards us, snorting dreadfully, and thrust its horn into my right rear tyre. Then, like a mad hydraulic jack, it tipped the whole car until it teetered on the point of balance before crashing back to the ground. After this it left us.

David had thought it was a deliberate attempt to introduce some local colour, until he noticed how white my knuckles were, gripping the steering wheel. It was the first time that I had ever seen a rhino's aggressive threat behaviour actually carried into physical contact, and it should have been a warning.

ALTHOUGH a wide variety of animals lived at Manyara, none appeared to benefit more from the different habitats than the elephants. They could choose between forest and swamp, nutritious pastures, palm trees in the glades, and a whole fresh range of delicacies on the slopes of the escarpment. Succulent wild sisal and fibrous baobab were found in great abundance. Along the shore grew brilliant green sedge. At the northern end dense reed mace floated out on its matted roots for several miles. If the elephants were not satisfied with all this bounty, there was a whole other forest, the Marang, suspended above their heads, more than twice the area of the park and replete with a new selection of species, provided they could get to it across the farmland.

I came more and more to realize the importance of the trees to the environment and the animals. Yet changes were taking place and nowhere faster than in the *Acacia tortilis* woodlands. In my first year I had numbered, with little metal tags, a sample of three hundred trees, running in straight lines through these woodlands. These lines were my transections. By visiting them periodically, I intended to measure the precise rate at which elephants damaged and killed trees by bark stripping.

The acacia trees were not only important to the elephants, but

Acacia trees, stripped bare by the elephants, stand like skeletons in the living woodland.

also to the diets of rhinos, giraffes, and impalas. But they were perhaps most firmly associated in the tourists' minds with lions, whose bodies sprawled in languid postures along the branches. Like all lions, the Manyara tree-climbing lions looked peaceful and sleepy most of the time, but I always kept a good lookout when walking near them. They had very little fear of human beings, and although at that time man-eating had not yet started, they had been known to chase villagers on bicycles. One lion had actually swiped a man on the backside as he pedalled frantically for his life. He escaped with a few scratches and a story to tell. Later others were less lucky.

I developed a healthy respect for these tough specialized killers. Twice I came face-to-face with their blazing eyes three paces away. Neither time, fortunately, had I crossed the critical distance, within which an animal fights for its life,* and the lions bounded away uttering deep *whoofs*. But the third time, the lion had second thoughts and crouched behind a boulder, with muscles twitching and tail flicking. I stood still and put out my arms to make myself look bigger as he growled, then I slowly backed away.

IF I EVER needed advice in my work, I could now have stimulating discussions with my official supervisor, Hugh Lamprey, and with the other scientists who lived at Seronera, one hundred and thirty miles away by road. Hugh, a pioneer in the study of big game ecology, was director of the Serengeti Research Institute.

In February 1967 Hugh asked me to give a talk to the scientists. As the only full-time elephant biologist in Tanzania, I was to tell them what I had been able to discover in one year, and this would lead to a discussion of the problems posed by elephants in the Serengeti, which were suddenly causing alarm.

I explained the Manyara problem of elephants and trees. So far, I told them, I knew one hundred and thirty elephants by sight. During the year only six calves had been born to the ninety-eight cows entered in my family-unit notebook. This, if

*Lion tamers know this distance and come close enough to elicit ferocious snarls, but they always take care not to cross the threshold where defence switches in a flash to outright attack.

representative, was equivalent to each cow producing a calf every sixteen years: an average which looked like the beginning of a population decline. Was the density affecting the elephants' breeding rate? One year's data by itself meant little.

Then I told of how many *Acacia tortilis* had been knocked down or stripped of their bark. The damage was serious. In the worst-hit areas thirty-five per cent of the trees were dead and more than half of these had obviously been killed by elephants. There were few young trees to replace the casualties; I found that seedlings could not germinate under an adult tree.

The discussion progressed to the Serengeti. Records seemed to show that elephants had not lived in the area until very recently, but over the previous decade their numbers had increased dramatically until aerial counts revealed about twenty-two hundred. It was believed that they had come from the Maswa and Mara areas of Kenya, driven south into Tanzania by the rigorous elephant control practised by the Kenya Game Department.

This invasion of elephants might have been welcomed, both for the enjoyment of visitors and for scientists to study. But groups of bulls had moved along the Seronera River and pushed over numerous fever trees. Seronera's unique attraction was the ease with which tourists could see leopards in their natural state. Now the elephants were knocking down the very trees in which the leopards spent their days reclining. Hugh Lamprey estimated that if the destruction rate were applied to the rest of the park, there would be no trees left in eight years. He went on to say that the situation might now be so serious that there might not even be time to wait for a research project to run its course, before acting to control the situation.

John Owen countered his view. He thought that there should be a minimum of human interference, particularly at this early stage. Perhaps the presence of elephants in the Serengeti might be part of a long-term cycle in which the numbers of animals and plants oscillated. However, as the rate at which young fever trees were replacing those destroyed was obviously a key factor, it was decided to recruit a forester to the staff as soon as possible.

Next day, I took a walk with Vesey through one of the

Serengeti woodlands. He had stated at the meeting that if there were imbalances between woodlands and elephants, they were caused by man and his injudicious use of fire, and not by elephants. As we walked we could see small fever trees sprouting everywhere. We dug up one. The root was well-developed, but the stem looked as if it had been burned back to the roots by the grass fires which scorched the whole of the Serengeti every year. So the regeneration potential was massive after all. Poachers and honey hunters would always light fires, but if the effects could be reduced, these young trees would perhaps in time replace those destroyed by the elephants.

BACK AT MANYARA I turned once again to the question of the elephants' movements and their access to the Marang Forest Reserve. To the south of the park, below the Marang forest, were the fenced-off farms that were formerly part of the elephants' range. It was possible that the elephants that broke through the fence might still find easy slopes to the forest. So I made a safari to this area.

On one farm a South African lived, curiously unbothered by the arrival of Tanzanian independence and a black government. He carried on planting his crops and left a corridor for the passage of elephants. But north of him was an Italian, who was at war with the elephants. His fields stretched unbroken from the escarpment to the lake. No corridor was left, so the elephants had no way of avoiding his crops. He bemoaned the fact that he lost nearly fifty per cent of his maize. He told me that he had shot fifty elephants the previous year. "But still they come."

One elephant who probably ended her life in his crops was a sabre-tusked matriarch named Inkosikaas. She was a great wanderer and one day I found her at the southern end of the park. The next day she vanished and I never saw her again. She was probably shot in the maize, standing out while her family made its escape.

It was obvious to me that, however slowly and painfully for him, the Italian was getting the better of the elephants. In time it seemed inevitable that he or his successor would drive them for ever from their former range. Already the other farmers between them had shot some three hundred to five hundred elephants, and most of the rest were assumed to have fled to the park or up into the Marang forest.

Since the Italian's land presented an almost impassable barrier, I wondered how else elephants could travel between the park and the Marang forest. There was one other possible route. It was at the northern point of the park-forest boundary, near the Endabash waterfall. I had seen trails winding up the hill from below, but had never been there on foot to see where they went.

My mother was staying with me at the time and since she was a keen bird watcher and a strong hill walker, I planned a day's excursion to this area. My ranger, Mhoja, was away on leave, so we took another called Kiprono, who carried a .470 Rigby rifle. We parked the car in a grassy glade below the waterfall and waded across the shallow waters. The path entered thickets of a scrubby plant that closed above our heads so that we had to stoop. Looking ahead, we could see for perhaps five yards. Some fresh rhino droppings reminded us that we were not alone. It was a relief, four hundred yards farther on, to reach the safety of the escarpment. At least here, on the steep slopes, we would be able to run faster up or down than any of the park's larger animals.

We climbed up interlocking elephant trails until the hill rounded out in a meadow of brilliant flowers. Looking back, Kiprono spotted a couple of rhinos browsing near our path. We were fortunate to have missed them, but so far most of the rhinos I had met on foot had been very willing to run away.

The elephant trails faded out in the grass, all except one, which we followed. Over another rise I found the answer to my day's work. The elephant path zigzagged on up the hill almost to the summit, then disappeared into the Marang forest. But less than twenty yards from it was the framework of a new African house. The expanding agriculturalists had already arrived just where the path passed outside the protection of the park. Obviously the elephants' route was destined to be cut.

We trudged on up to the point where the path entered the forest, and sat on a boulder to eat our sandwiches. The damp forest with lichen-draped trees was on the one side and a view over the upper Endabash valley, on the other, all territory outside the park.

Wherever the slope was gentle enough for agriculture, new huts were springing up. Trees had been cut down, and goats and cattle scoured the grass. Without trees to break the force of the tropical downpours, soil was flayed off the surface of the earth and washed away in streams. The erosion was already so bad that the rivers in the park were filling up with silt from these settlements above the scarp.

Starting back, we looked down from the lip of the escarpment upon the thick undergrowth we would have to cross. Just in case the two rhinos might still be lurking, we shouted and whooped as we entered the thickets. Normally, big dangerous animals will make way for noisy human beings. Halfway across the danger area we stopped shouting, lulled into a sense of security by the absence of any response.

Suddenly, almost below my feet, a rhino snorted and burst into my field of vision at full gallop.

"Rhino! Run for it," I shouted and darted around its head.

Out of the corner of my eye I saw it turn after me, and I ran for my life. Twisting and dodging around the bushes, I could not shake it off. Every time I looked behind me it was within a few feet and closing in. I must have covered fifty yards when a strap snapped on my sandal and I pitched headlong on my face. As I fell, I saw a huge dark shape with its long sharp horn bearing down over me. The thought flashed through my mind that in the next instant I would be killed or spared.

A split second of blackness, a shattering blow, the flash of a second rhino streaking past me, and I was lying there agonizingly winded, but deliriously happy to be alive. Luckily, I had been tossed, or kicked, to one side avoiding a second trampling. I knew that the rhinos had merely been seeing me off and there was no chance that they would return to finish the job. The first rhino must have been a female, mother to the second.

I rolled onto my stomach. Pushing my hands on the ground, I raised my body on all fours, but the pain was intense. It was impossible to stand up; my back muscles would not respond. I subsided again and shouted for help.

A minute later my mother and Kiprono materialized, hot and dishevelled. They had run back along the path, and Kiprono had shot his gun in the air in the hope of scaring away the rhinos.

After wiggling my toes to test that my spinal cord was still functioning, I asked my mother and Kiprono to help me walk. Although I could move my legs, I found it impossible to support myself. Several times I tried to walk but I could only stand the pain for a minute at a time. Eventually I asked them to put me under a tree, and to try to bring the Land-Rover, even though it was difficult country to cross and my mother had never driven a Land-Rover before.

As the flies buzzed around my sweaty face, I heard the engine start up in the distance. It changed tone, and I imagined they must be fording the river. I fervently hoped that my mother had remembered to put the car into four-wheel drive. It changed pitch again and I knew they were across and climbing the steep bank. Then came a bad noise: the high-pitched whine that meant one or more of the wheels was in the air. I shouted at the top of my lungs.

They heard me, abandoned the car, and came back. Once more they put their arms under my shoulders and we struggled by stages to the car. My mother had done very well to get so far up the elephant tracks, but the car was now mounted on a small hummock with all four wheels suspended in the air. I lay by its side and told Kiprono how to set the jack to unstick it.

Eventually we got the car going again. I lay across the seat, and we jolted agonizingly back to camp. There, I rolled into a camp bed and consumed a third of a bottle of whisky. A fine Scotch glow seeped through my limbs and I felt a bit better.

The district nurse was called from Mto-wa-Mbu, a pleasant man who assured me that nothing was very wrong. A doctor was located in a tourist party, but he was enjoying his holiday and refused to render first aid. Jonathan Muhanga, the park warden, arrived and offered to drive us to the hospital in Arusha, eighty miles away. We gratefully accepted.

Night had fallen by the time we started. Halfway to Arusha one of the front wheels fell off. The car listed to one side and we gazed up at the incredibly beautiful sky and sang songs to pass the time. The pain had been completely muted by the whisky.

By chance, John Owen had received news that I had been degutted by a rhino, and had immediately driven from his home in Arusha to Mto-wa-Mbu. We must have passed him in the night. When he reached the village they told him we had already gone to Arusha. Some said that the rhino's horn had gone in one inch, some said nearly a foot, and some said it had gone right through. When he caught up with us, he was relieved to find that I had merely been trampled.

We transferred to his Land-Rover and thanked Muhanga, leaving him disconsolately trying to put back his wheel. Thirteen hours after the accident we rolled into the Mount Meru Hospital, Arusha, and that night I slept well under morphine.

CHAPTER FOUR

After I left the hospital I spent some weeks lying flat on my back on the floor of John Owen's Arusha house. It was an opportunity to improve my Swahili and I put my hands on a phrase book written for pioneers in the 1920s. Soon I had no trouble in reproducing such phrases as "Split the skull and give the brains to the cook," and "Make way for the master," but I found little in it that could be of use.

A bone specialist flew down from Nairobi to inspect me and immediately released me from the plaster in which the Arusha doctors had encased me from chest to rump. He told me that the walk back to the Land-Rover, by exercising the damaged tissues at once, had probably taken weeks off my convalescence. As soon as I was fit, I returned to Manyara.

Immediately I checked up on all the family units to see which cows had given birth and which animals had disappeared. After the rhino incident, I was more wary of the south of the park and temporarily shelved my study of elephant movements there. Luckily, Mhoja returned to stay permanently at Ndala. He was as alert as anyone I ever met in the bush and always forewarned me of rhinos.

He became my instructor for the next three years, and a very great friend. He had a good knowledge of the tribal names of the plants and learned English and Latin names with equal facility. He was able to imitate the calls of the birds and was a superb mimic of human beings, too. Once a visiting Russian agriculturist came to my camp and we had to talk through an interpreter. Within minutes Mhoja was able to give a creditable imitation of Russian-sounding expostulations. Without him life would have been more difficult, dangerous, and lonely, and far less amusing.

So far I had recorded few births and therefore I wondered if overcrowding had slowed down the birth rate. Then in 1968 the dearth of baby elephants in the first two years was followed by an avalanche. Practically every cow that could gave birth, and everywhere family units were seen with their half-shut-eyed newborn calves. At the same time the rains fell in a continual downpour that broke all records and carried right on through the dry season.

Elephant births in the wild have seldom been observed. I never saw one, though I was lucky enough to witness the act of coitus. I found that courtship was virtually absent, and that the bull elephant was not the greatest lover in the animal kingdom, despite the fact that he has the largest penis of all terrestrial mammals, weighing about sixty pounds with its skin. Intromission was brief and accompanied by deep groans from the bull, while the cow remained silent and passive.

The gestation period is twenty-two months, but a pregnant cow elephant shows almost no visible swelling. In Asia the birth of a calf to a domestic elephant may surprise even the Indian *mahout* or Burmese *oozie* who lives with her.

My opportunity to study the development of a wild calf from birth occurred in the Boadicea kinship group. One morning I found Leonora's family going down to the river to drink. As usual Slender Tusks was with the old matriarch. Her looks and behaviour were normal and I went on my way.

That evening I saw Leonora's family again. To my great delight Slender Tusks had with her a tiny blue-brown male calf, covered with red wavy hair. He peered out at the unknown world from under his mother's belly. His head had the squashed look of newborn elephants, with a short trunk, and ears resembling maps of Africa. His toenails looked as if they had just been scrubbed. He was two feet nine inches tall and weighed about two hundred and sixty pounds.

The calf still appeared very unsteady. His legs were weak and he placed the round soft pads gingerly as if they hurt when he walked. With eyes half shut, he moved his trunk up and down exploring for a place to suck. Eventually he found a teat beneath his mother's forelegs, but every so often the effort to suck was too much and he fell down. Each time Slender Tusks nudged him gently upright with her forefoot and trunk. She appeared unaffected by our presence in the Land-Rover, but when a giraffe passed by, Slender Tusks shook her head, warning it to keep away from her baby.

After two days he had found his legs and kept up with the family in their continuous amble in search of food. This took them into swamps, forests, and up the steep-sided escarpment along hazardous paths. His mother and the others took great care not to tread on him, and whenever the going became rough, Slender Tusks would reach down with her trunk and push or pull him over the obstacles. By the end of three months he had visited almost every corner of his kinship group's range.

Like all newborn calves he sucked little but often, probably consuming two-and-a-half gallons of milk a day. When sucking, his pink mouth with its triangular hairy lower lip was firmly fastened on the teat, and his trunk lay limply to one side or was held back in an S-bend above his head. At other times his trunk hung down straight, or was brandished like an uncoordinated, whippy rubber hosepipe. Sometimes he just sat down and put the tip in his mouth like a child sucking its thumb.

Weaning was gradual. Already by the end of the first month he was biting at grass, not yet knowing how to use his trunk. But although some of the material may have been swallowed, the activity seemed to be essentially exploratory. Calves continue to suck for as long as they are allowed and long after they have switched to a predominantly vegetarian diet. One of the female calves, Leonora's eldest immature daughter, named Two Holes, was still sucking at the age of nine.

I named the calf N'Dume (male, in Swahili), because he was a real little male. He was very playful, often aggressively attacking his elder brothers and sisters, ramming them with the front of his mouth where the tusks would appear later. They put up with him in a good-natured way and he enjoyed a blissful period of being allowed to do whatever he wished with no discipline.

One evening he was tearing around on the river shore when suddenly the thin crust of mud gave way under him and he sank into thick glutinous mire. His terrified squeal immediately brought Slender Tusks and Leonora, rumbling with concern. Slender Tusks gingerly waded out, her feet ploughing black treacly furrows. Fortunately she found firm ground under the surface layer. First she tried pulling him out with her trunk. When this failed, she placed her tusks under his belly and shoved. He gradually floundered back to firm ground covered from head to tail with a sticky black coating.

By six months he had lost his baby looks. His body grew fatter. The red hair fell out and was replaced by stiff black bristles. And as he continued to grow his relationship with his mother changed. He began to wander, and she became less protective.

One hot afternoon when the family were drowsing through their siesta, he lay down at the foot of an acacia tree and was soon fast asleep. Leonora for some reason was restless, and ambled off with Slender Tusks by her side. The other youngsters scrambled to their feet, but N'Dume slumbered on, all alone except for Leonora's daughter Two Holes. She tickled his tummy with her

Iain observed the progress of calves like N'Dume (above left), who had "ears resembling maps of Africa" and a trunk "like a whippy rubber hose." A calf is nurtured by the affection of its family (above right) until at least the age of ten. N'Dume peers from under his mother's belly (below).

A mother with her first calf. The authors found new mothers very solicitous of their young; they seemed fascinated with the experience of maternity.

forefoot and trunk and he leaped to his feet, realizing that his mother had gone. But for Two Holes he would have been left behind.

Then there was the time he fell sick. I found him walking around and moaning as if in great pain, while the rest of the family stuffed grass into their mouths. Only Two Holes seemed concerned, and would place a reassuring trunk on his forehead. During about a week N'Dume grew quite thin. Eventually he got well, and I never found out what had been wrong with him.

Slender Tusks's apparent indifference did not mean that she would not have helped him had he been in serious trouble. She merely seemed to know that so long as he was somewhere in the confines of the family unit, he was safe.

All the time N'Dume was growing he was learning. His movements were experimental and often comic. His trunk caused him great problems. During the first year he knelt at the river's edge, holding it out of the water and drinking with his mouth. But gradually, by trial and error, he learned how to suck up water, hold it in his trunk as he raised it, and then pour it down his throat.

An elephant's trunk is a most versatile instrument. A combination of upper lip and nose, it possesses thousands of muscles, each of which needs the appropriate orders from the central nervous system to function. No wonder it took N'Dume a long time to master its possibilities. At its tip were tiny hairs for feeling the shape, texture, and temperature of things. He could use it as a scoop when digging for water, or he could use it to hold grass in place while his toes cut through the stems. His trunk also anointed his back with mud and dusted it with sand. Occasionally he put it up into his mother's mouth and sampled what she was eating, pulling some of it out and chewing it. This same action develops into a greeting gesture which elephants use when approaching a superior.

N'Dume also learned fear. When he was very young, he once rushed right up to my Land-Rover and threatened it with his little ears wide apart, head raised, and piggy eyes squinting aggressively. He was not in the least afraid until he noticed he was alone. Then suddenly he lost heart and rushed back to his mother's side, squealing. He never again approached.

At two years the pearly tips of his milk tusks appeared, then dropped out to reveal the permanent tusks behind them. Naturally, like all young things, he was eager to try out a new-found capacity and joined in—rather ineffectively—the next time the family stripped an acacia tree. He also butted his elder brothers, sisters, and cousins.

As the months passed, N'Dume came to know his little world and all the elephants who lived in it. When the matriarchs Boadicea, Leonora, and Jezebel brought their broods together at the river or on the beach in the evenings, there was great excitement for the calves. They would race around in rough-and-tumble play like puppies and take on all sorts of elaborate three-, four-, or five-cornered combinations. If the level of aggression ever threatened to get out of hand, a nearby mother or adolescent female would sidle effortlessly into their midst.

The blissful period of tolerance passed and N'Dume began to encounter occasional hostility from Slender Tusks herself. In the dry season when the Ndala River percolated beneath the sand, the elephants could only obtain water from holes which they scooped out with their trunks. N'Dume seemed unable to accept the idea that Slender Tusks was not digging the water holes exclusively for his use. He would insist on pushing in on her, and in his clumsiness he would crumble the edge of the sandy hole, so that Slender Tusks had to dig it again. She was very skilful at keeping him out, and once shoved him away with her trunk eighteen times in five minutes. She also used her feet to thwart N'Dume. He would try to get around the foot, and when that failed, just collapse in a heap with his trunk still creeping like a hopeful caterpillar towards water.

For at least the first ten years of their lives elephants continue to be nurtured by the love and protection of their family. The calves continue to play and fight. This playfighting probably teaches an animal its exact strength relative to others in the same area. In this way a hierarchy originates in which each individual knows his place. In later life when competitive situations occur over water or food, the dispute is usually settled by a mere threat display. Serious fighting is extremely rare.

As adolescence approaches, at about eleven to thirteen years, bull calves indulge in bouts of mounting each other and the female calves. This is the last burst of activity before they become totally independent and leave the family units for ever. Their story I discovered when I started radio-tracking.

CHAPTER FIVE

From 1967 to 1968 thirty-four calves were born to my special sample of ninety-eight cows. Only eight had been born the year before, so it was apparent that the birth rate fluctuated wildly. Eventually, I came to the same conclusion that Richard Laws reached in Uganda, that the better the rains the more cows would conceive. Meanwhile, I also wanted to know how movements affected elephant density. For this I needed some method of following elephants in the thick and dangerous Endabash thickets. After my encounter with the rhino, I had avoided foot patrols in Endabash, with the result that while I now knew a great deal about the elephants in the north, I couldn't even identify all the fierce man-shy southern elephants.

When I confessed this to Hugh Lamprey, he replied, "Well, Iain, you had better get to know them. You have chosen your method and you had better make it work." After that, however much I disliked the idea, there was no alternative to meeting the Endabash elephants on their own ground.

Down some of the trails Mhoja and I were able to force a passage with the Land-Rover, until we came to the river. Here we would wait for thirsty elephants to come, and here one day I encountered Queen Victoria and her family. Evidently they had been attracted to this area by the desert dates which were then in full fruit. They were following a bull elephant who was going from tree to tree shaking the dates down with his trunk.

I had a friend, Katie Newlin, who belonged to the American Peace Corps, staying for the weekend. She was delighted to see elephants at such close quarters. Mhoja, who was standing in the back of my stripped-down Land-Rover, with a labourer named Simeon, spotted another group of elephants through the foliage. I drove towards them, crushing branches in the way. A young female with a small calf ran off in alarm behind a gardenia bush. Seconds later a huge, bow-tusked female came headlong around the foliage. Without uttering a sound or pausing in her stride, she plunged her tusks up to the gums into the body of the Land-Rover. Mhoja and Simeon saw the tusks appear beneath their feet. With the huge shape looming over them, they jumped out of the car and vanished into the bush.

The first shock threw the car half around. The elephant pulled her tusks out and thrust them in again.

"Don't get out of the car," I shouted to Katie. She lay down on the floor.

Now more elephants burst out of the bush on the right and joined in the attack. Tusks were thrust in and withdrawn with great vigour. Trumpeting rent the air, together with the sound of tearing metal. However, I was not thinking just then of what John Owen would say about my park Land-Rover, because an enormous brown eye embedded in gnarled skin appeared on the see-through roof. A cow was using the weight of her head to force down the roof of the cab. I was relieved when the eye disappeared; its owner could have picked off our heads like bananas off a bunch.

A huge latecomer with as much zeal as the rest put together now came into contact with the front of the car. One fender folded up like paper and a tusk went through the radiator. She wrenched her embedded tusks upward like a demented forklift. Then, digging her tusks in again, she charged, and the Land-Rover was carried backward at high speed for thirty-five yards until it squashed up against an anthill.

They left us adorning the anthill, and after a few excited trumpets and growls dissolved into the bush with streaks of green paint on their tusks.

My Peace Corps friend picked herself up and dusted her blouse with sangfroid. She was a little shaken, but unharmed. My first awful thought was, What had happened to Mhoja? The car looked a write-off, but I pressed the starter and to my amazement it worked. We limped off on a flat tyre to begin our search.

At the point of the first impact we stopped and shouted. A faint mocking echo came back from the woodlands, or was it a shout? I drove on deeper into the bush and tried again. This time there was a definite answer. Eventually, after about a mile, Mhoja's green uniform materialized out of the twilight.

We were all relieved, and in the relaxation of tension doubled up with laughter. Mhoja described how he had dodged between the legs of the oncoming elephants, and run after Simeon, trying to stop him. Simeon's one thought was to get out of this horrible place and it took Mhoja a mile to catch him.

"Who were they?" Mhoja asked.

In the excitement I had not even looked at their features, but I could make a pretty good guess. Only once before had I seen four equally large cows start an attack with no threat display, in total silence. They must have been the Torone sisters.

We escaped lightly that time. After some panel beating, the patching of a number of round holes, and the installation of a new radiator, the car was almost as good as new.

SOON AFTER this rather alarming experience my chance came to follow the elephant movements in what I hoped would be a safer way. Over in the Serengeti the American zoologist George Schaller was in contact with an American electronics expert called Howard Baldwin, whom he had engaged to make radio transmitters suitable for tracking lions and hyenas. When I heard one day that Baldwin had arrived in the Serengeti, I went straight over to meet him, and asked him if he could spare one of his radios for an elephant.

Howard Baldwin is a man fired by wild enthusiasm to do

unusual things. He was sure he could adapt the lion equipment to withstand the rigours of elephant life, so long as we could first catch our elephant. Fortunately, there was a vet in East Africa named Toni Harthoorn who had spent ten years perfecting methods of immobilizing elephants. He was already associated with Schaller's lion project, advising on the dosage rates of tranquillizing drugs. He, too, immediately consented to come.

Toni arrived early one morning with his attractive, dark-haired wife, Sue. I took them on an introductory tour to meet Boadicea, always an acid test for my visitors. After the initial shock of one of her threat charges, the Harthoorns settled down to enjoy the interactions of mothers and infants. Howard, who had arrived with his wife the night before, remained in camp all day tuning the elephant radios and receivers.

We had three guns suitable for projecting the syringe which would automatically inject its contents on impact with an elephant. Toni had brought a powder-charged gun that could be fired from a distance, and a gas-powered pistol for extremely short ranges. A Capchur gun, operated by compressed carbon dioxide, would take care of the intermediate ranges.

Next day it was agreed that I would do the driving, Toni the shooting, and Howard, his wife, and Sue, would stay in a second Land-Rover, ready to be called up on the walkie-talkie as soon as the elephant was down. It was not until afternoon that we sighted some bulls and cow-calf family units near the Ndala River mouth.

I selected a peaceable bull named Chisel Tusks as our target. He was mature and independent, and I thought it unlikely that any other elephant would come to his aid.

Thirty yards distant, Toni fired at Chisel Tusks through the window. The dart embedded itself in the bull's rump, clearly visible there as a sliver of silver with a red tuft at the end. Chisel Tusks rushed into some bushes and disappeared. There was no hope of following by car so we went on foot. Many elephants were around and we moved cautiously between them.

Soon our quarry slowed to a gentle amble and then stopped under a tree. We waited for the drug to take effect. Twenty-seven minutes after darting, Chisel Tusks's eyes closed. He hung his head and his hindquarters started to droop. Then he awoke with a jerk and started to walk once more. After one and a half hours he seemed fully recovered and we gave up.

That evening we discussed increasing the dose. Toni was against it. The margin between an ineffective dose and a lethal one might be narrow, even though the drug we were using, M.99, had recently been employed in the South African national parks to immobilize thirty-one elephants, with only one fatality.

There followed six days of frustration. The trees and bush at Manyara were so thick that elephants usually only became visible at ranges so short that the gun might drive the dart right into the body. The only time we tried a long-distance shot, the report was so loud that all the elephants stampeded. Our selected bull started forward, crashed into a tree, then picked himself up and limped away. Luckily the damage was not serious, but I loathed the unnecessary disturbance and wondered if I was not getting a bad reputation with the elephants. Once the dart bounced off after a perfect shot. Another time the needle snapped on contact. In yet another case the elephant rubbed the dart off on a tree, and when we picked it up we found that the detonator, which was supposed to fire on impact and drive the drug solution into the animal, had not gone off.

When it appeared that Manyara's elephants were more resistant to the drug M.99 than any elephants he had previously encountered, Toni increased the dose. Immediate success was needed, for the Harthoorns had already postponed their departure twice, and now Howard was due to leave.

On the last possible day we located several family units and some independent bulls just north of the Ndala River. We drove up to a lone bull known as M4/3 (I had never properly named him), and put a dart well into his flank.

Presently he began to lag. A young cow seemed to sense there was something wrong. She felt his face and ears with her trunk, then, resting her tusks on his forehead, pushed him gently backward. It looked like a gesture of reassurance to a sick animal. Her two calves also touched him with their trunks. But eventually she and all the other elephants moved on. The young bull now swayed from side to side, picking up grass and throwing it away. His hind legs began to buckle. As it seemed to be taking too long, Toni shot another dart at him. At last he subsided but still remained conscious, his trunk twirling defensively in our direction as we closed in with collar and instruments.

I immediately doused him with water on the back of his ears and along his flanks. Temperature regulation is the major function of the African elephant's ears. With their huge bulk they have solved the problem of heat dissipation by spraying water behind their enormous ears and flapping them in the still air.

Howard had already clambered on his neck to insert a temperature probe under the skin; this had its own transmitter in a pad that had to be sewn to the elephant's head. Sue handed instruments to Howard while Toni took blood samples. Meanwhile, Mhoja attached the collar, which had the major transmitter attached to it, around the elephant's neck.

The elephant's eyes slowly closed and his breathing grew stertorous. He was lying on his belly, which was dangerous. He looked pretty bad now, his breathing only just observable.

"Quick, get the rope," yelled Toni. "Put it round his tusk and tie it to the Land-Rover, then pull him on his side."

I hooked him up as quickly as possible and by rocking the Land-Rover back and forth we heaved his ponderous bulk over. Immediately he gave a deep sigh and a few rapid breaths, after which his breathing steadied.

With the collar and pad both firmly attached, there was just time to take a few body measurements. His shoulder height corresponded to an age of twenty to twenty-five years according to Laws's growth curve.

Sue now handed Toni a syringe containing the antidote to M.99. Toni gave an intravenous injection behind one of the bull's ears, and we all returned to the car. Within a few minutes his ears started to flap, and with a jerk of his head he stood up. His overall temperature must have been very high, for he now did something which I had heard of but never seen before. He put his trunk deep inside his throat and sucked out some water which he then splashed on the back of his ears and shoulders.

Finally M4/3 fingered his collar, but made no attempt to get rid of it. As the twilight faded, the massed families who had been with him in the morning reappeared and surrounded him. Many elephants reached up to touch the collar and temperature pad, curious to investigate the objects that smelled of man. But none of them tried to pull anything off.

At camp we had a celebration and farewell party. The Harthoorns left the next day.

HOWARD AND HIS WIFE stayed one more night, during which we followed M4/3 without cease. It was dark and rainy, and hippos came out at dusk near our elephant on the shore. He kept company with three others of varying sizes. Most of the night the best we could record were the occasional sounds of the elephants breaking branches, and later in the small hours we heard distinct snores.

The *chink chink chink* of the elephant transmitter became engraved in our brains; the only noise that went on nonstop. It had an unearthly quality, pure and electronic. As we sat in the Land-Rover cab lighting our notes with a torch masked with a red filter, which we hoped would be invisible to elephants, we could have been tracking spaceships through a galaxy.

When the long night ended in a drizzly cold dawn, M4/3 was busy pulling a tender green *Salvadora persica* bush to pieces. We returned to camp, where Howard made some last-minute adjustments to the receivers, now fitted to my Land-Rover. After breakfast he and his wife left for the Serengeti.

I now had seventeen wonderful days and nights tailing the young bull as he wandered up the hills and into forests, along the densely wooded gorges that sliced into the escarpment, and down again to the lake front. While plotting his movements on the map, I recorded what he ate and drank, and above all with whom he associated, for bull social organization was still a mystery to me and I was curious to see if he had any special friendships.

The second night out alone in the Land-Rover, after listening

Iain runs to pull out a tranquillizing dart before the elephant lies on it. The drug was M.99, a morphine derivative.

to the monotonous *chink chink* for two hours, I involuntarily fell asleep. I awoke with a start at midnight with the feeling I was not alone.

Moonlight was pouring down on my face and there was a noise like the repeated hitting of a cricket ball with a bat. Silhouetted against half of the stars in heaven were M4/3 and another enormous bull, their trunks entwined. They pushed and prodded, parrying each other's thrusts with their tusks. Each time the ivories hit, they made the sound which had awakened me. They gleamed and flashed in the moonlight while the two giants struggled in mock fury.

M4/3 kept new company every day. Altogether he met twelve bulls, and associated temporarily with four different family units. The longest he stayed with another bull was five days, but at other times he was alone. In other words, he enjoyed a loose shifting association with whomsoever he met or pleased to join for an hour or more.

As the days and nights passed, the transmitter gradually weakened, until finally I had to be within three hundred yards before picking up the signal. When it finally expired, I located M4/3 visually for two more days, which gave a record of twenty-two days of continuous movement.

All in all it was a successful experiment. But I realized that the important questions of population movements could only be solved by radio-tracking cow-calf groups. The difficulty was to circumvent the matriarchal defensive circle, which would inevitably form every time a family member became stricken with the drug.

There was also a possibility of radio-tracking from the air which would allow me to keep a regular check on the number of elephants in the park over every month of the year.

I knew that John Owen could not afford to provide me with a plane. However, I had been left some shares by my father, who died in 1944. With the stock market booming in 1968, I sold them and raised enough money to finish my pilot's training and to buy a cheap plane.

In January 1969 I found the ideal machine at Wilson; the airfield for small planes near Nairobi. It was an eighteen-year-old Piper Pacer, with a 150 h.p. engine. Once the windows were modified so that I could remove them at will, the visibility for elephant counting was excellent. When I was ready I flew down to Manyara solo. The strip there is poised on top of the escarpment cliff near the hotel.

Over the days and weeks that followed, flying gave me a heady sense of freedom. I came to know every square yard of the park from the air. Hanging in space on an upcurrent, diving in a roar close above the waters of the lake, or cruising in the still air above the clouds were equally delightful.

Although he had given me permission to fly, John Owen became anxious for my safety. My reputation at its mildest was that I was "an accident-prone young man", and at its worst "a goddam reckless fool". My mother came out to stay a second time, and while shopping in Arusha one day she met John Owen, who fixed her with a steely glare.

"It's very dangerous for Iain to have a plane, you know," he warned. "We only let our pilots fly in game counts after they have two hundred hours of experience, and at Manyara there's an added hazard from vultures."

But chance plays strange tricks. Two weeks later it was John Owen who struck a stork while flying. Luckily he retained control of the plane. He never mentioned vultures again.

Manyara was not ideal country for counting elephants. In places the forest canopy was continuous, and on hot days more elephants moved under the trees for shade. However, my eye became attuned to the slightest hint of an elephant's shape and my scores increased. And when leaves withered and fell in the dry season, more areas became countable.

The original supposition that Manyara had the densest elephant population of any park in Africa was confirmed. Nearly forty-nine per cent of the large mammals were elephants. Buffalo made up another forty-two per cent while the remaining nine per cent consisted of hippos, zebras, giraffes, rhinoceroses, all the antelope, baboons, and the predators.

Unfortunately, the Marang forest presented mile after mile of closed canopy, broken in places by swampy glades. I once saw a herd of a hundred elephants in such a glade, but could find no way of estimating the total population. I suspected that the Marang forest and the southern farms had both been an integral part of the elephants' range, but I could not tell how important they still were to the elephants until Howard Baldwin returned with some more radio collars.

IN MARCH my plane was due for a fifty-hour check. I flew it up to Nairobi, and that evening I went to a party. City people were packed in a smoky room, chatting over cocktails.

In this throng was a girl with long dark hair, and slanting, almost Oriental eyes that flickered wickedly from one person to another. Wearing an African robe which clung to her lithe figure, she danced with demonic energy, radiating an entirely un-Anglo-Saxon warmth and gaiety.

Before the evening was out I worked my way through her many

admirers and beguiled her with tales of noble elephants, lions in trees, hairbreadth escapes, all set on the shores of a far-off enchanted lake called Manyara. Impulsively she agreed that she would love to see Manyara, and we made an indefinite plan for the future.

Oria Rocco came from an Italian-French family who lived on the shores of Kenya's Lake Naivasha. Country born and bred, she belonged to that city scene no more than I did. Up in the air next day, on my way back to the elephants, my memory was imprinted with those restless, incendiary brown eyes.

Not long after my return, Howard arrived with several new improved elephant collars. They had been tested in Arizona and gave a range of thirty miles. The batteries should be serviceable for six months.

I now had to decide which elephant to select for radio-tracking. My choice lay between the tame groups that lived mainly in the north, and the wild southern groups that wandered I knew not where. It was a difficult decision, but I had two good reasons for choosing a northern group. Behaviour in the darting operation would be more predictable. And, well though I knew them, they, too, disappeared from time to time, and I was curious to see if they wandered out of the park.

Since Boadicea's was the best known group, it was the one I decided to follow. The key to tracking a cow-calf group, I realized, was to select a member who was held in low esteem by the others, and whom they might not defend at the crucial moment. Boadicea's family unit had just such an elephant, a young bull called Robert. I had named him after the young assistant who had just been assigned to me.

At nineteen, the elephant Robert was unusually old still to be attached to a family unit. I was interested to see what would happen to him when he took the fateful step to full independence. Then, after some months, I would take the collar off him and put it finally on one of the truly wild Endabash baddies.

I had decided to try to persuade Oria to come to Manyara and take part in this operation. So I took off for her home on the shores of Lake Naivasha.

PART II: Oria Douglas-Hamilton

CHAPTER SIX

Against a small green hill overlooking Lake Naivasha in Kenya stands my family home, a strange sort of castle painted dark pink with wooden roofs bleached pale by the sun. It is on a three-thousand-acre farm, most of its hills covered with rocks and grey-yellow scrub. We grow vegetables and cattle food on a strip along the water's edge.

Early in 1969 I took a couple of weeks off from the farm to organize a safari for an advertising company, and find locations where they could film commercials. We moved all over Kenya. At a farewell party for them in Nairobi, a stranger suddenly entered the room. Obviously he did not belong in this advertising milieu. Dressed in an ill-fitting tweed jacket and grey trousers, he seemed rather shy. I went up to him and asked what he did. "I do elephants," he said. He told me all about them and added, "I can fly you to Manyara if you want to see them." It sounded exciting but I had to get back to the farm. It was our exporting season, one of the busiest times of the year.

Sunday morning at the farm was always special. Silence surrounded our house, which stood between tall yellow fever trees where black and white eagle vultures called forlornly to each other. Inside, the servants moved like barefoot ghosts. On the veranda overlooking the lawn, the long table was laid with an old blue and white Florentine tablecloth, wine-red glasses, and gay ceramic plates. We had invited some friends for lunch and Moses, our cook, had decided on a cold buffet. At about midday our guests arrived. As lunch began, the house echoed with talk in Italian, French, and English.

All of a sudden a tremendous roar swept over the house. We

rushed onto the lawn, and watched a small red and white plane silhouetted against huge rain clouds. It had turned and was heading back towards us, flying fast and low. Oh, God, I thought, this must be Iain and he is going to hit something! The plane shot over, making some of the guests duck, then circled our cattle *bomas* trying to land.

I jumped onto my motorbike and raced along the road waving an arm to tell Iain not to land. But he swooped down, hopped over the telephone wires, and dropped into a *boma*. Knowing the place was full of holes, I was transfixed with fear as I sat on my bike. The plane came running down the field and stopped in front of me on the other side of the fence. Out jumped Iain, a big grin on his face as he told me how pale I was.

"I told you this plane can land anywhere," he said, "and don't you tell me you didn't enjoy that arrival."

"It was fantastic." I jumped off my bike and threw my arms around him.

"We are going to dart elephants," he said, "and I would like you to take some pictures for me. Can you be ready to leave in a few hours?"

I was still shaking, and had no idea how this could be arranged. We got on my bike and sped home.

I introduced Iain to my parents and to the others. His arrival was an unforgettable event at Naivasha. "Tell me, young man, do you always fly like that," asked an elderly gentleman who had just arrived from Europe.

"Only sometimes," Iain answered. "I just wanted to see what I was going to have for lunch before landing."

Over lunch he told my father about his work with elephants. "Can you spare me Oria for a few days?" he asked.

"Well, you had better make some kind of a strip in the cow *boma* first or you won't be able to take off," my father replied. "I don't want to have any accidents here."

My parents, Mario and Giselle Rocco, had come out to Africa in 1928 to hunt elephants. Due to the imminent arrival of my brother, Dorian, their journey ended in Kenya. Soon after, they bought the farm where my sister, Mirella, and I were born.

For a while they mined gold not far from Naivasha. Then my mother spent her days sculpting, and my father bred and raced Irish horses. I was put in the saddle at the age of four, and taught to ride like a cavalry officer. Our knowledge of elephants came from exciting tales of hunting, or through reading our favourite books, by our cousin Jean de Brunhoff, who created the king of elephants, Babar.

In 1940 Mussolini declared war. The police arrived and took my Italian father away, as an enemy alien. But my mother was an ally, being French, and she was allowed to stay. The gold mine was confiscated, the horses were sold, and pigs took their place as we struggled to remain self-reliant. We three children were sent away from school as we were half enemy alien, so we stayed at home and ran wild. My mother soon found it impossible to control us and asked a young Masai warrior to look after us. He taught us all he knew about the bush.

Eventually we were sent to an American missionary school, the only one that would have us. Then the war ended and my father returned, white-haired, temporarily shattered after four years in a South African prison camp. I was sent to another school from which I was expelled for leading a revolt for better food and living conditions. After that, my mother thought I needed to be civilized, and sent me to finishing schools in Paris and Rome. I was dreadfully bored and longed to return to Kenya.

All my life I have been driven by a burning restlessness to search for new experiences. I travelled, and learned to speak five languages. Inspired by Africa's colours and its people, I designed fashionable textiles and clothes, then turned to photography to try to catch the beauty I loved so much.

No one was working on the Sunday that Iain arrived, so all the people on the farm came to look at the plane. She was marked 5Y-KIX. Volunteers picked up stones and filled in holes in the *boma*. By evening we had a good strip. Iain stayed the night and early next morning we filled Kix with fruit, vegetables, cream, butter, meat, and wine. As the sun rose, the heavily laden aircraft took off, and we headed south across the lake.

It was a beautiful clear day, and we could see the whole Rift

Valley cutting down through Kenya. We dropped to a couple of hundred feet above the plains. Long lines of cattle and sheep were going out to graze, trailing dust behind them. Here and there was a Masai village. Otherwise this vast area was uninhabited. The rainy season was about to break. Massive clouds drifted above us, their shadows moving over the landscape. I gazed spellbound at the beauty of Africa.

Then, through the haze we saw the flat sheet of water that was Lake Manyara. Below were patchy acacia woodlands. Elephants were everywhere. Suddenly I saw the little house pinned against the escarpment. A man was waving at us. We flew on over the park and saw a car already on its way to the strip, so we touched down. I was very grateful to be standing on the ground.

As we were unloading, a Land-Rover pulled up and out jumped Iain's good-looking assistant, Robert. He was about nineteen. Dressed only in shorts, with a knife hanging from his belt, no shoes, and a mass of long black hair, he looked like a jungle boy. He told me he had been an assistant at the Serengeti Research Institute, but had been sent to Manyara because his hair was too long.

As we drove down the escarpment, we could see that many of the elephants we had spotted from the air were still in the same places. Entering the park, Iain selected one group and drove straight up to it. The elephants hardly moved. Then suddenly one great beast emerged, her head held high and her ears stretched out like wings. Her tusks pointing at us, she advanced four terrifying steps, and let out a shrill trumpet. I nearly died of fright. Then she turned and ambled off in a baggy-pants trot.

I asked Iain as coolly as I could, "Isn't that dangerous?"

"Don't worry about Boadicea," he whispered. "She's only bluffing. I wanted you to meet her because she is the most important lady in this park."

At the camp I met Howard Baldwin, Mhoja, and Iain's cook, Mshaka. The house was perched on an embankment under two umbrella trees. Going up towards the waterfall, following a squiggly path through the dense vegetation, we came to a solitary stone rondavel with a thatched pointed roof and a wild gardenia tree beside it. This was my room. Still farther up, next to the waterfall, was the last house. This one had the most beautiful view of all. The water was rushing down into a large pool and the wind blew spray over us. I sat down on a rock where blue lizards kept popping up and looking at me. There was no need to say "how beautiful". Why say something so obvious?

When we returned to the main house, I was introduced to the two mongooses, Pilipili (pepper) and Ndogo (small). They kept biting my toes, and scuttled around underneath the table while Mshaka brought us lunch. It was a typical bachelor meal: canned meat, boiled potatoes, and canned vegetables, but with a big bowl of fresh fruit salad and cream from our farm.

Iain fed scraps to his chickens, which came running when called. These African chickens had a hard life avoiding hawks, genets and other small fierce predators.

Later, while Iain, Howard, and the other men made final preparations for darting the young bull called Robert on the following day, I looked around. I loved this camp. It had a certain toughness about it. Bare rooms, no decorative things except the lamp stand and some knives on the walls, no curtains. Yet there were good books to read, interesting things to look at, and one's clothes were washed every day. It represented the minimum, and maybe maximum, comfort needed for a young man to live in the bush.

As the sun was setting, Iain and I had a swim under the waterfall and then dressed and drove back through the park to the hotel, where he had to entertain some friends. By the time we left the hotel, it must have been past ten. We were about four miles inside the park when suddenly the Land-Rover slumped on one side and came to a jerky halt. There were elephants eating on the slope of the hill about fifteen yards away.

"I'm afraid we've got a puncture," said Iain.

"And what about the elephants?" I asked anxiously.

"They're all right. Rhinos and buffalo are far worse. Come on, let's try to get this tyre off."

We looked everywhere for the jack but couldn't find it. Finally I was offered the choice of spending the night in the car being devoured by mosquitoes, or walking back to park headquarters where there was a rest house. I chose the walk, but I wasn't dressed for walking. Wearing a flimsy *khanga* (a colourful African dress), a belt of red stones with little gold bells around my waist and my loose sandals, I jingled and jangled down the road like a circus monkey.

Our torch barely lit up a small round spot in the middle of the road. Branches crackled, and we heard snorts and barks and the trumpetings of distant elephants. Twice we came across buffalo and had to hide behind a tree and throw stones at them and yell, until they galloped away.

"The best thing to do is to talk all the time or sing, and your bells will help to make a noise," Iain said. He began singing bloodthirsty Scottish war songs about English horses bathing their hoofs in Highland blood.

I realized how utterly vulnerable a man without a gun is in the face of his predators. All we had to rely on were our senses and our intelligence. I imagined the yellow eyes of a hungry hunter gazing at my body, the smell of my skin blowing into his nostrils. We were now very small and very weak in that immense dark wilderness.

But we reached the rest house unharmed. Next morning we were awakened by the voice of Howard, who had come to look for us. As we were driving back through the forest, Iain said, "I didn't want to tell you last night, but there is a man-eating lion near here and a villager was recently eaten on the main road."

When we reached the abandoned car, Robert and Mhoja had already fixed the puncture. We drove back to camp for breakfast.

We got ready to immobilize Iain's fine young bull. Already excitement tingled through my body. Carefully I loaded all my cameras, and had a lens in every pocket of my jacket. Mhoja, Iain, and I set off in one direction, Howard and Robert in another. We kept in close communication with our walkie-talkies.

It didn't take us long to find Boadicea and her huge family. They were in the acacia woods, swishing cool dust over themselves as if it were talcum powder. Boa, ever watchful, stood out and waited to see what we were going to do. Iain pointed out the other prominent females, Leonora, Slender Tusks, Right Hook, and a lovely old cow whom we named Giselle after my mother. About three hundred yards away were three young bulls. The tallest, with the longest trunk, was Robert.

When the dart hit him, the bull staggered around, throwing an odd trunkful of sand over himself. Then he tottered on until he was within fifty paces of Boadicea. Suddenly the whole family surged forward, the matriarch in front, trumpeting and growling. Boa thrust her tusks against the bull, throwing him onto his knees. A couple of other females also attacked him as he tried to get to his feet. But Giselle pushed her way through, and putting her trunk to his mouth, tried to help him up. He raised himself with Giselle by his side, while the other elephants circled them furiously. Iain had never expected such a demonstration. From Giselle's behaviour he guessed that she was his mother.

By now the bull had collapsed. At this point the trumpeting and movement redoubled. Some of the females charged the car. Sitting on its roof, cameras hanging round my neck, my hands trembling with excitement, I clicked away.

In time Boa led her family to a tree about thirty yards distant. The moment she moved away, Iain and Howard worked fast and professionally. Meanwhile, Robert and Mhoja took samples and measurements. As soon as the radio collar was securely fixed, Iain injected the antidote, and we moved off.

We renamed the young bull Radio Robert.

That evening I decided that the men deserved a good meal. In the tiny kitchen Mshaka and I worked for a couple of hours, while flames and smoke puffed out of the wood stove, making me cry, and I tried to stop a million insects from falling into the food. In spite of all this, we produced a cheese soufflé, roast chicken with peppered potatoes and onions, a ratatouille, and, of course, a fruit salad with a bowl of whipped cream from Naivasha.

My first visit to Manyara was a revelation, but I could not stay on. I was needed in Naivasha. Iain offered to fly me to Arusha on the way home, to buy me a pair of safari boots. He said that since I was going to have to do a lot of walking in the bush, it was no use tripping around in sandals. On our way we spotted Radio Robert and marked the second cross on the map on which Iain was to follow his journeyings for months to come.

I was back in Naivasha by Wednesday. The excitement of swooping down in a little cloth-covered plane, stopping practically at my doorstep, was a piece of life no man had offered me before.

FOR THE NEXT COUPLE of months I spent half the week packing green peppers to go off to Britain by air, selling cattle, and supervising the ploughing and planting of maize. The rest of the week I spent at Manyara.

I had to adjust to Iain's way of living. He had a well-established routine: we got up with the sun and stopped working when it set. Breakfast was always served at seven, when a radio was switched on for the BBC news. Only the British could live like this. Iain was a perfect example: eating eggs and bacon with a mongoose on his lap, elephants drinking in the river below his house, and listening to the stock exchange report.

After the news the radio was switched off and we went to work. Iain wanted to show me as much of the park as he could, so that I could get to know it really well and recognize some of the elephants. He had told me about Endabash and the fierce elephants who lived there, especially the dreaded Torone sisters, and one day we drove along the lake to their home.

When we arrived at the river, we found it in flood, the bridge half washed away, so Iain suggested we walk along the bank following a game trail. I told myself that perhaps his stories were no more than masculine showing-off. How could he be so relaxed if this place was really full of baddies? So I gaily walked along the path.

At the mouth of the river a flock of pelicans were swimming and fishing as rhythmically as a trained team. I stood up to my knees in the lake watching. Suddenly I heard the noise of water splashing behind me. I turned and saw—elephants!

I was trapped like an idiot and would never be able to get out of their way in time. All I could think of was to vanish, and vanish I did. I slipped under the water and swam as far as I possibly could. When I finally lifted my head, I turned around to see what was happening.

There was Iain, sitting on a log a few yards away from the elephants, laughing at me. The elephants were lifting their trunks to catch my scent—but not a charge, not a murmur. And here I was in this water full of bird droppings and stinking of fish. I burst out laughing, too.

Iain explained that I had been right to be frightened, but this family was a harmless one down from the north. I couldn't imagine how I would ever acquire his self-assurance.

In the evenings I had to cope with hardly any utensils and a smoking stove which was burning hot. Mshaka was most apologetic about the state of his kitchen, explaining that he had often asked Iain to get him an egg flipper or a roasting pan, but that they never arrived. On one occasion I was looking everywhere for a knife and found a snake curled up in a box. I didn't know what kind it was, but quickly let it slide out into the bush.

Since Iain and Robert always expected one good meal a day when I was there, and on time, too, the only thing to do was improve the kitchen. When I told Mshaka that we were going to make lists of all the things missing, he let out a long "eeeeeeeeeh" and told me, "You are doing much good." I promised that next time I flew back from Kenya I would bring him the lot.

Food was a constant problem, especially fresh meat. The genets that lived nearby fed off our chickens at night. Since it was inconceivable that a piece of good meat should be thrown away, even if half had been chewed off by a predator, the rest of the chicken would appear on the table in a curry or a soup. We discovered a brilliant green garden of cress in the Mchanga River and it was made into salads and soups. In the market of Mto-wa-Mbu I could always find pawpaws, bananas, and avocados for only a few shillings a pile. Gradually our camp began to get the reputation for *la bonne cuisine de brousse* (good bush cooking).

I loved the atmosphere in Mto-wa-Mbu. Iain and I were known there as "Duglass" and "Mama Duglass". Late one evening we stopped at the hotel for a meal. The people in the restaurant were truck drivers, Mbulu herders, Masai elders, and some prostitutes. At a table next to us sat an old Masai. He held his spear in his left hand and ate with his right hand. We had only enough money to buy a plate of soup and a *chapati* (dough cake) between us and when Iain asked for a drink of milk, which he promised to pay for the following day, it was refused. A man at the other end of the room called the waiter, flicked him a shilling, and said, "Give Duglass milk." He waved off our thanks and continued eating. His name was Ali and he had helped build Iain's camp.

The queen of Mto-wa-Mbu was Mama Rosa, who owned the most popular and profitable beer houses in town. She was about five feet seven, must have weighed around fourteen stone, and had a half-moon smile that cut her face in two when she laughed. Many times when there were too many people in our camp, Mama Rosa would lend me her clay cooking pots and give food to help me out.

EACH TIME I arrived at Ndala camp, our life overflowed with activity. Iain was flying every day, following Radio Robert, who in turn was following Boadicea. For the first time it was possible to follow a family unit week after week, and I tried to cover it photographically. Most of the elephants soon paid little heed to this noisy bird buzzing overhead, unless they were in open country where they seemed to feel less secure.

Iain soon realized that he was spending more time driving up and down to the hotel runway than in the air. He now wanted an airstrip near the camp. We found an open area covered with bush, big anthills and some trees. It looked inconceivable as an airstrip but Iain said it would be all right.

Shortly after this, when he was touching down on the hotel strip one afternoon, his left wheel had a puncture. Kix swung off into the long grass, hitting big stones and holes, bending the prop and the undercarriage, and damaging the other wheel. That was the end of Kix for several months—engineers took pieces of the plane to Nairobi for repairs. It was a terrible blow, even though Iain rented a plane whenever possible to continue his tracking and to pick me up from Naivasha.

Flying was becoming so much part of our life that he suggested I should have a plane of my own. He found a little Piper Cruiser tucked away in a hangar in Arusha. It was going cheap, and Iain convinced my brother, Dorian, and me that we should buy it. When it arrived, I thought it was the most beautiful plane I had ever seen: nearly thirty years old, with huge white wings, few instruments, and only a stick between the pilot's knees to fly with. The plane could carry two passengers on the back seat, and had a maximum speed of one hundred miles an hour. We now had more freedom than ever before: if one plane was out of order there was another to jump into.

The next time we flew in from Naivasha to buzz the camp, I saw below me a straight, smoothly graded track, cleared of bush and anthills. Iain had got together a team of workers to prepare the strip. We touched down and taxied to a stop.

Mhoja had made a small enclosure of thorn branches into which we pushed the planes at night. This kept buffalo and elephants from rubbing against their delicate canvas coverings, and the lions from chewing their tyres.

Iain now taught me to fly. At first it was really frightening, having to sit up there in the cockpit all alone, with Iain shouting instructions from the rear seat as I tried to take off. But once we were airborne I was so overcome by the beauty and the feeling of flying on my own in space, that I forgot about my fears.

Ndala was becoming my second home. Having made Mshaka happy with kitchen utensils, I decided to add some furniture to the rest of the camp. A couple of American limnologists (lake experts) studying Manyara had left Iain all their packing cases of American pine, and the park carpenter helped us to make cupboards, benches, a kitchen table, and shelves. Since we lived in round houses, most of the furniture had to be semicircular to fit neatly against the walls. Out of the remaining packing cases, some old inner tubes, and a mattress, we made a comfortable bush sofa which we covered in dark purple cotton.

Partly to show off our improvements, we invited my sister, Mirella, and my brother, Dorian, with their daughters, for the weekend. The planeload of four children was flown in by Iain.

Mirella brought a carful of fresh meat and bacon, vegetables and fruit. Unfortunately, the meat had gone bad, so we threw it to the hyenas.

As dawn broke we drove out into the park to watch life awaken. Hundreds of buffalo spread across the lakeshore, their horns and ears glittering in the sun. Spoon-billed storks and herons strode through the shallow water, looking for food. Giraffes galloped in slow motion along the beach, their legs seeming never to touch the ground. We found Boadicea and her family making their way down a hill. As Boa stood watching us menacingly, Virgo walked up to the car waving her trunk as if trying to make conversation, and the children talked to her.

We drove back to camp for breakfast, and then it was time for our guests to climb up to the waterfall and swim in the pool. Iain complained of cramps in his stomach and asked Mhoja to accompany them. We would join them later. At about midday Mshaka came to tell me that Iain was very sick. I found him sprawled on the floor writhing in pain, vomiting and moaning. I thought he must have food poisoning but we all had had the same meals. Then I remembered that he was the only one who had eaten bacon, which had also come from Naivasha. When he started to spit blood, I realized that I must act swiftly.

The spasms occurred every thirty minutes. If I could get him to the plane in time, he could help me to take off and to land at Arusha between one spasm and the next. I left a note for my sister, then hurriedly drove him to the plane. As soon as he had finished a spasm of vomiting, Iain fell into the pilot's seat and together we took the plane up. Then I was on my own.

When we reached Arusha, Iain managed to help me touch down, after which he collapsed. I found a car and at last we got to a small clinic. "He's all right, he's only been poisoned," the doctor told me.

It was twenty-four hours before Iain was well enough to fly to Naivasha for a few days' convalescence. Then we returned to Manyara.

We arrived in the camp to find that Mshaka, the cook, had disappeared; he had gone to Mto-wa-Mbu and had never come back. A rumour spread that he had been seen walking across the Serengeti because he had been cursed. I knew that living in the bush sometimes has strange effects on people, but it was also possible that Mshaka didn't want to go on working. Iain replaced him with Suleiman, who had been his cook three years previously and was now working as a labourer on the park's roads.

Our spell of ill luck persisted. Mhoja was clearing out the main room, so that we could paint it. As he leaned down to pick up some junk in a corner, a cobra suddenly popped up and spat straight into his eyes. He felt a flash of pain and immediately became completely blind. Crawling along the floor, he yelled, "*Nyoka, nyoka*"—"Snake, snake." Everyone rushed in with sticks and *pangas*, and killed the cobra. Iain broke open a bottle of serum and washed out Mhoja's eyes, then rushed him to Arusha. Mhoja was in hospital in less than an hour. The serum worked and after four days he could see perfectly.

CHAPTER SEVEN

In the last months of 1969 my life was pounded around like a boxing ball. We were expecting a baby, but I nearly lost it in a plane accident. Afterwards I was very demoralized; but at the beginning of 1970 my life took a turn in a new direction. I moved into Manyara for good.

I slipped into the camp as if I had never been away. Even my bush clothes were there waiting for me, neatly folded on a shelf. The smiling faces of Suleiman, Mhoja, and Ali, who had come to work at the camp again, greeted me.

A breeze rippled through the two big acacias and they threw a silent shower of golden flowers over me. As I ran to the top of the hill, timid eyes watched through the tall feathery grass. From up there I could see the little stream sparkling in the sun.

When the wind blew up from the river, I heard the noise of flapping ears and snorting trunks as the elephants shuffled along with their babies to the ochre-coloured pool below my bedroom.

I wanted to build up a photographic story of individual elephants' lives. But first I, too, would have to get to know them really well. Iain gave me his family-unit photo files, and Mhoja built me a hide on the edge of the river. In front of the hide the river ran over a flat and sandy area where the elephants would often stop to drink.

To get good photographs I had to figure out what the elephants were going to do seconds before it happened. But for every good action picture, or for the expression I wanted, hundreds of rejects piled up. In the end, I learned to sit for hours with my camera at the ready, never getting bored, observing, waiting.

I had plenty of time to look at the other animals. I learned many things, such as that only when the baboons came to the river was it safe for the shy bushbuck to come out of hiding and drink. They knew then that there were no dangerous predators around. Impalas also arrived with the baboons, walking up in big golden herds, with their ears twitching ceaselessly. Some days even the two rhinos who lived in the Ndala valley would come out, or a giraffe might slowly drift along in the haze of the sand heat.

The first time I saw Boadicea at Ndala, not a single elephant had been there that day and I had gone back to camp for a drink. Then suddenly the whole riverbed was covered with snorting, rumbling elephants. None of us had heard them come. There must have been about one hundred, including Boadicea's kinship group. Instantly I picked out Leonora, Slender Tusks with her son N'Dume at her heels, and Jezebel with her family closely grouped around her. Overcome with excitement, I picked up my cameras and rushed down to my hide, bending as I ran to keep myself concealed.

I found myself in the middle of an elephant world, many of whose personalities I now knew. I could see how each family was organized within the hierarchy that Iain had told me about. Not only was there competition between a mother and her offspring, but also between families. Boadicea's family, having already drunk at the top pool, walked down to where Jezebel's family were drinking from holes they'd dug in the sand. With hardly a movement of her head, Boadicea took over from Jezebel and so did her family. Jezebel's family just moved farther up the river without a sign of annoyance. Boa was a queen whom all respected.

Elephants walking up and down occasionally stopped to greet each other with their trunk-to-mouth gesture, while young babies walked up to a big bull and one by one greeted him. In return the bull put his trunk to each little mouth, or touched the babies on their heads rather as Masai elders greet their children. An elephant's trunk can be as gentle and as loving as the most tender arms. It can greet and tickle, smell and caress. It can also change into an efficient weapon to kill. When it smells man, it rears back above the head like a serpent preparing to strike.

I was relieved that Boa was not near my hide as I was sure she would have smelled me, chased me away, and emptied the whole riverbed of elephants at one signal. But when Right Hook and Virgo walked past me, I wanted to go "psst" to attract Virgo's attention. We were daily becoming more friendly with her, and I felt that soon we would be able to walk alongside her.

To be able to sit quite confidently a few feet from the elephants and not feel afraid was one of the most exciting things about the whole study and our work.

EARLY ONE MORNING Mhoja called through the window that he had something to show me. There, curled up in his ranger's cap at the bottom of a cardboard box, was a fluffy little female mongoose. Her red eyes peered up at me with a look half of fear, half of pleading, because she was so lonely. Even a wild mongoose, separated from its mother, needs love from someone. We stroked and scratched her back every half hour. I was happy to have another mongoose, for Pilipili and Ndogo had disappeared some time ago and since then the house felt only half lived in.

Some rain had brought thousands of grasshoppers, which provided one of the mongoose's favourite meals. We all went out into the bushes, returning with a vast provision for Widgey, as we named her. I don't think she ever ate as many grasshoppers in her life as in those first two days. Her little tummy filled out like a balloon.

After a week she seemed completely happy with her new family. Already she was eating bits of egg, drinking her milk out of our cups, chirruping, purring, and nosing all around the rooms. When she was not in Iain's pocket, she was in my shirt.

The first Thursday of the month was market day in Mto-wa-Mbu. Tribesmen brought their fattest cows, their sheep, and goats to sell. Masai women draped in long plum-red pieces of cloth and wearing bright beaded jewellry, sat under trees selling milk which they had carried for many miles in their calabashes. I nearly always went with Mhoja to buy a few chickens and eggs. One day a tall young Masai, standing on one foot and leaning on his spear, called to me, "*Soba*, Mama Duglass"—"Hello, Mama Duglass." He dragged from behind him a small shiny brown goat. "Take this to Duglass," he said.

I was thrilled with the present. "*Ashe oling. . . . Sidai oling*"—"Thank you very much. . . . it's lovely"—I said.

We named her Biba. To keep her safe from predators, Mhoja built a strong house in which she was shut up at night. Soon she became one of the funniest and fattest pets I ever had. She devoured Iain's notes at such speed that it was practically impossible to save them. Bananas were her favourite fruit and she learned every trick to get at the bunches that hung from a beam in our sitting room, climbing onto chairs, cupboards, and window ledges. After a few weeks Biba paired up with Widgey, and together they came with us on long evening walks.

FROM THE WINDOW of my little hut I could see that everything was yellow straw and sand dust. Down the grey rocks above us, a line of black water sparkled and fell into the shallow pool, from which a trickle made its way along a sandy bed and stopped abruptly. This was the dry season. The wind smelled of dust, the earth's crust cracked. The two acacia trees stood like huge burned umbrellas on either side of our house.

One day in October the tops of the acacia trees were covered in little green leaves—the first sign that the rains would soon be here. The animals drifted from one patch of shade to another, waiting for the cool hours to go out in search of food. Then suddenly great flat clouds filled the sky, rolling, tumbling, and flying past, changing colour and form where the sunshine fell. The wind from the lake met the wind from the hills. All the trees started to bend as the wind rushed and whirled around madly. Elephants trumpeted and shrieked, monkeys screamed, bushes bent, branches broke, animals scattered.

This was the wind of rain. The air thickened, the sky darkened, thunder and lightning crashed around us. In camp, doors and windows were banging, dark figures were running to tie things down, chickens were scattering for shelter. The wind dropped and the hot damp silence waited. I felt as if heaven lay close to the earth and I between them.

Slanting streaks of grey swept up the valley with a rushing sound of rain. Above my head the dried thatch rustled as the first drops fell. This was the marvellous sound we had been waiting for. The air grew cooler and the smell of moist earth filled my nostrils. I could almost feel the beginning of life growing from the earth, and I wanted to sing and dance and make love.

The rain came down and pounded the earth. We listened to the drumming on the roof. Sheets of water swept past and sprayed through the mosquito netting of the paneless windows, forming puddles on the floor. After an hour the rain passed over to the hills. In the stillness, drops from the soaking trees fell with loud splatters on the ground. Patches of blue appeared in the sky, sunlight sparkled on the dripping bushes. The quenched earth sucked in the water and steam rose up from its latent heat.

Far away over the escarpment I heard a rumble that grew louder and louder. Then the side of the mountain erupted, and a thunderous gush of dark brown water leaped over the edge, carrying trees and stones as it rushed down into the pool, pushing itself between the rocks and onto the white sands of the dry riverbed.

After darkness fell, distant thunder shook the world, and

lightning cut across the horizon, revealing the line of dark blue mountains beyond the lake. The rainy season had begun.

With the rains pouring down I decided to build verandas in front of the houses, to give us more space and cover. The park warden gave us permission to cut poles from a tree called *mbaru ya faru* (rhino's ribs) which was the best for the purpose. While Ali and a friend of his got to work on the branches with their *pangas*, I walked away from the car to pick some wild flowers. Suddenly, Ali's friend started shouting, "*Chui, chui*"—"Leopard, leopard." "Bring the gun quickly!"

I leaped to the car and grabbed the gun. I could see Ali and his friend in the tree, but no leopard. "Where is it?" I shouted.

"Right here." Ali's friend pointed to his feet.

I crept up to the tree, my finger on the trigger. In a fork I saw a little nest of leaves, and in it, wet and cold and crawling blindly, two tiny spotted genets no bigger than my fist. So far as I could tell they had been abandoned.

Back in camp we fed them warm diluted milk and glucose. Obviously famished, they sucked hard at the eye dropper, and I knew they would live. I wrapped them in an old jersey and held them close to the warmth of my body. With these young animals we were going to get all the experience we needed to bring up a human baby in the bush, for the mongoose and the genets would also have to be watched day and night, and taken with us wherever we went.

One day Mhoja and Suleiman, looking very serious, came to tell me they had decided I needed a woman in the camp to help me. Moreover the girl would arrive next morning with John, one of the park truck drivers. She was his daughter, and a good girl. Touched by their concern, I thanked them.

The girl was called Amina. She was very pretty and lively, dressed in a tight cotton shift which clung to her round, hard bottom. She knew nothing about housework and I didn't know how to teach her, so Mhoja and Suleiman took over. Whenever I told her to do something, Amina giggled and ran back to the kitchen in a sort of wriggle-trip manner, while with her hand over her mouth, she yelped eehs and aays.

After two weeks Amina had learned how to make beds, sweep floors, wash the dishes, and set the table. It was about this time that I went to Mto-wa-Mbu and learned that she was one of the bar girls from Mama Rosa's establishment. She was certainly not the daughter of John, the driver. In fact Mhoja and Suleiman had cleverly manoeuvred things so that she could keep them company at night. I realized that she would soon get bored. Sadly, after a month she asked for her pay and left.

Ali told me he knew lots of very good women, and could easily get a replacement. So pretty Amina was replaced by fat Amina, supposedly a daughter of one of the park rangers. Fat Amina went through the same routine of learning the camp drill, but she was neither as attractive nor as giggly as pretty Amina. Nevertheless, she stayed with us a bit longer. She loved the animals, and always had one of the cats nestled between her huge bosoms. But the day came when fat Amina complained of nausea and giddiness: she was pregnant, and she left soon afterwards.

MORE THAN A YEAR had passed and much had changed since my early trips to Manyara. The elephants were so much part of my life now I hardly bothered to turn around when I heard their angry trumpeting. Living among animals, one becomes more like them. Our senses became so alert that we could smell and track elephants long before we saw or heard them.

In the forest there were always unexpected meetings. One day we came upon Right Hook, Virgo, and their calves. It was the first time we had encountered Virgo on foot. We slipped from one tree trunk to the other, moving up to her. As soon as she saw us, she stopped eating, perked up her ears, and waited. Iain was a couple of yards away, facing her, and held out his hand. It was a moment of great tension. Virgo let out a loud snort, shook her head, clapped her ears in a cloud of dust, and twiddled her trunk in knots, in much the same way as I wring my hands when I am nervous. Iain stood his ground and Virgo, seeing that her threats had no effect on him, began a little dance with her trunk curling near his hand like a snake. Then, when Iain took a step forward calling her name, Virgo retreated. She pulled grass, rubbed her eye with her trunk, used it to dig in her ear, sniffed the air, and kicked up dust, but she never tried to hit him. It looked as if she were playing for time, unable to make up her mind what to do.

They stood watching each other for a long, exciting moment. Then Virgo walked straight up to us, put out her trunk, and moved it around in front of our faces. I heard a long flowing sound, like wind blowing through a tunnel. Finally, as if she had nothing more to investigate, she walked away, ripping off leaves to eat as she went; the others followed close behind her.

"I knew Virgo would not try to hurt us," Iain said. "She's a fantastic elephant. I'm sure if we ever had enough time we would be able to tame her completely and even play with her baby."

CHAPTER EIGHT

Harvey Croze, the elephant man of the Serengeti, had invited Iain to participate in the big yearly elephant-and-buffalo count which took place at the end of May, during the migration. We decided to go early and spend a couple of weeks in the Serengeti so that Iain could prepare a seminar on Manyara which he planned to give soon after we got back.

We packed up all our books, papers, maps, clothing, and bedding, and stuffed them into the Kix. It was a heavy, valuable load. On my lap was Widgey, and the genets, whom we had named Alicat and Amino, were curled up like furry sausages and pushed into the knotted sleeves of my jersey, so they couldn't bite me on takeoff. Kix sped into the wind and rose like a bird.

The Serengeti Research Institute is a cluster of modern stone buildings surrounded by five thousand square miles of plains and nearly two million head of game. Here, animals, vegetation, climate, neighbouring tribes, and tourists are in the process of being analysed so that a plan can be made for them to live in balance with their environment. At the SRI there are electricity, running water, specialized equipment, and mapmakers, foresters, biologists, ecologists, ethnologists, and all the other -ologists that make a scientific centre efficient.

With the elephant-buffalo count about to begin, the SRI was humming with anticipation as planes flew in from other parks. Harvey Croze held a meeting to brief all pilots, navigators, and counters about the elephants and buffalo, and to give them their cameras and maps of the areas they were going to cover. There were six planes and about ten pilots, who flew in four-hour shifts. Planes could land and fuel on isolated bush strips.

The count took two exhausting days. When it was over, about two thousand elephants and fifty thousand buffalo had been spotted from the air.

On the last evening a big celebration was held. Under a huge faded tent, paper flowers and silver tinsel wrapped around the poles flickered in the light of gas lamps. Large terracotta pots of boiling spicy food and bowls of scented wild flowers decorated the tables. Outside, the meat sizzled on a bed of red coals. Laughing faces were tiger-striped with lights that flashed through the canvas opening. Music blared. People danced barefoot on the lawns, where later that night prowling lions, hyenas, and jackals would lick up the remnants of our feast. Parties like this were rare occasions, so we dressed up in all our finery. Iain discarded his bush-green uniform and wore a long yellow robe with his blond hair flowing. "You remind me more and more of Jesus Christ each time I see you," John Owen told him.

All that night outside my window lions were calling and the galloping hoofs of the migrating wildebeests went by without stopping. Two hundred thousand calves had been born this year. During the peak fortnight of the calving season ten thousand mothers gave birth each day.

My most vivid recollection of the calving will always be that of an earlier visit to the Serengeti. I wanted to see and feel this

massive sight of birth, so I slipped out of the house one morning before dawn and drove onto the plains. It was a vision of the world's creation. Everywhere I looked, long wobbly legs, still steaming from the mother's womb, stood up shakily to learn how to run. There was no time for them to wait.

From the moment of birth the babies were in danger, easy kills for a tender meal. Among the births lay the remnants of death: bones left for the sun to dry. From high in the sky vultures dropped like parachutes, and wherever they dropped there was something to eat. The lions' bellies touched the ground, so that they could hardly walk.

I watched a mother wildebeest lie down; it took between five and ten minutes for the baby to be born. As soon as it was,

Elephants get along with most other animals. Left: Impalas remain unperturbed as two bulls fence playfully. But a tiny blacksmith plover (above) can drive off a bull which invades the bird's territory.

she stood up, made low cooing noises, turned around and began to lick it. I could see the calf's nostrils flare as it breathed in deeply and blinked its wet sticky eyes. It seemed to know that it must get up as quickly as possible and start running. From the baby's birth until it was galloping away at its mother's side, took no more than fifteen minutes.

Driving slowly back through the swarm of wildebeests, I saw three hyenas walking. At first I didn't pay much attention; they looked quite fat and had surely had their fill. Then I saw a female wildebeest lying down, pushing and heaving as her calf came. I said to myself, "This one is not going to make it."

The hyenas closed in. The mother lifted her head, saw them, jumped up, and began to run. But the hyenas leaped for the baby and pulled it out. I saw it kick before they tore it to pieces. I stopped and cried and covered my face with my hands. Then I drove on thinking how awful a mother's life can be.

AFTER THE SRI meeting we flew back to Manyara. On the path from the airstrip we met Kiprono who had been looking after our camp while Mhoja was on leave. He had kept the grass well cut, looked after the houses, and not let the elephants eat the thatch. I was very pleased, for I wanted everything to be clean and ready for our next commitment, a great elephant meeting, when so many scientists were coming to hear Iain.

We spent the following days unpacking, ordering food, and finishing the arrangements for the seminar. I had asked John Owen if the guests could stay in the hotel and park houses. But the answer was no. Everyone would far rather camp at Ndala. We were, however, to be provided with as much help as possible, and we would have a lot of co-operation from our park warden, David Stevens Babu, who had succeeded Jonathan Muhanga.

By June 5 all was ready. That night we swam in the pool, the stars bright, the crickets and frogs singing all around us. Afterwards we walked down the river, drying ourselves in the last of the warm air and listening to the night noises. It was the last walk of this part of our life, one I will never forget. A few days later everything was to change.

As usual I woke at dawn. In the basket behind my head Widgey, Alicat and Amina were chirruping and scratching, waiting to crawl out onto our bed. Iain flew off to a farm across the lake to collect a sheep which had been prepared for our barbecue. Having only a very small refrigerator, I had to get all the meat and food ready beforehand, so that it should not go bad. It was quite a problem to lodge and feed sixteen extra people.

Some of the scientists arrived early; they were given a drink or a cup of coffee, and then put to work. John Owen flew in, and since he was at the top of the hierarchy he was given the top rondavel with the best view. Vesey arrived by Land-Rover from Arusha, completely self-sufficient down to his tin bowl and mug.

Harvey Croze came with his wife, Nani, in a mini bus packed full of kids, pets, tents, and bedding. We settled them in a campsite along the river. Hugh Lamprey, director of the SRI, flew his glider from the Serengeti, twisting and turning with pelicans and vultures on the upcurrents. With tents going up all over the place, Ndala looked like a pioneers' settlement.

That night we roasted the sheep, which had been marinated in oil and herbs. Mama Rosa had lent me large clay pots in which to cook beans with chillies, curried rice, and ratatouille. The feast went on till about midnight, after which there were still a few more beds to be made up. At about one o'clock we finally fell onto our mattresses.

Mhoja woke me with tea; it was a cold day, dark and drizzling. There were only two more things for me to do; get breakfast, and then see that everyone was seated by eight thirty so that the seminar could begin. I stood in the kitchen frying bacon and dozens of sausages, and scrambling about thirty eggs.

When everyone was settled, I went to have a bath, glad that I could now relax. I was on my way back to my little house when all of a sudden warm water came pouring out of me.

I called Mhoja and asked him to fetch Mama Croze immediately. He ran to her tent calling, "Quickly. Mama Duglass is sick."

"You're beginning your baby," Nani said when she came. (I thought, This is impossible.) "I'm going to break up the meeting, and you're going to hospital right away. Babies don't wait."

I begged her not to. We had worked for two months to prepare this meeting; we could not break it up now just because I was having a child. "Please," I said, "wait till the coffee break. Then casually drop a word in Iain's ear."

I lay down on the floor of my hut and waited. At the coffee break Iain came in and offered to take me straight to Nairobi. I knew that owing to some complications I would have to have a caesarean, but I was sure it could wait until the meeting was over. I told Iain I was all right. "O.K., *casa roho*"—"O.K., tighten your heart"—he answered. Then he hurried back to the meeting.

At last the meeting ended. Bottles were opened. Nani was

getting lunch onto the tables. Everyone congratulated Iain on his excellent seminar and the imminent arrival of his baby.

I dressed and walked down to the car. My heart was pounding with anxiety. Whether or not I got inside a clean hospital room for this baby to be born was now a question of chance.

Iain and I drove to the strip. Everyone came to wish us farewell, car following car, filled with bush people, children, and animals. When we got into the plane, each in turn came to kiss me goodbye—all the people, the genets, and the mongoose. We raced down the narrow runway and up over the Great Rift wall.

As the plane dropped and heaved in the empty sky, a great wave of pain started pushing through my body and then disappeared, only to start again five minutes later. Nairobi was still very far away. This, I thought, is where I need that British cool, to pretend that nothing unusual is happening.

Suddenly I heard voices crackle above my head. "This is East Air Centre. Your doctor cannot be found. It is Sunday and he is away for the day. We will try to get you an ambulance."

We arrived at Nairobi at two thirty. As we had flown from Tanzania into Kenya, we had to go through immigration. Then we had to find a taxi, for there was no ambulance to meet us. I felt my heart flicker with waves of panic. It'll be all my fault if anything goes wrong, I thought, because of the way I've been living, never giving a damn about the thing that mattered most—our child.

An hour later I was in a hospital bed, and Iain was calling everyone we knew in Nairobi, telling them to look for our doctor. At six thirty he arrived—Adriano Landra, my friend, a tough, confident, and capable surgeon, with a smiling round face. I knew then I was going to make it.

"Come on, roll her out to the theatre," he said. Needles were stuck into me from all sides. I stared up at the huge white lamp above me. All around me I could see masked faces with white caps looking down at me. I recognized Iain by his black-rimmed glasses. We looked at each other for a long moment. I heard the doctor say, "O.K., you can put her out." And to me, "Now count up to ten slowly." I counted till a whirlwind shook my brain.

Slowly I woke. The room was full of flowers. I could not move for pain. Iain was there, his hair still tousled and covered with dust and sweat from the day before. All my family was there, too.

"You've got a daughter. She's fine. She's in the premature unit. She weighs five pounds three ounces."

The news was sent to my home and the Africans there named the baby Saba (seven, in Swahili), because she was born at the seventh hour, on the seventh day of the week, on the seventh day of the month, and she was the seventh grandchild.

WHEN SABA was three weeks old and weighed nearly six pounds, she and I were allowed to leave Nairobi and go to my parents' farm. There we spent another two weeks building up our strength before returning to Manyara.

Back at Ndala camp, wild flowers filled the rooms and the floor was sprinkled with petals picked from the park. Everything was clean and polished, food was cooking, and all the animals were there for me to hug. Mhoja took Saba from my arms, laughing and welcoming her to the bush. A baby was as important as the elephants. She was given her first bush bath propped up in a yellow basin, half filled with warm brown river water.

Widgey, Alicat and Amina had grown into beautiful strong animals. The genets were jumping from shoulder to shoulder, sniffing Saba from time to time. Only Widgey was unsociable: she would never look at us after we had been away. Nothing else seemed to have changed in Manyara. Iain let the corks go with a loud bang and champagne flowed in the glasses. We drank and laughed, hugged and kissed each other, caught for a moment in a net of happiness by the subtle fingers of life.

Before this, I could never believe Iain when, as a zoologist, he tried to convince me that to have a baby was the most natural biological function in a woman's life. I was sure that it was going to be terribly complicated and that my whole way of life was going to be shattered. But now, like most other mothers, all I felt was a very strong protective instinct.

I had never been interested in child rearing, but instead of buying Dr. Spock's book, I was tutored by Iain on the importance of the mother-child bond, as shown in a recent study of the rhesus monkey. Tactile contact with the mother was essential, or the rhesus baby would grow up into a maladjusted animal, unable to form mature adult relationships. Iain insisted that this must not happen to our child.

Since I did not have a furry body for my baby to cling to, it was up to me to do the hanging on. The best method I could think of was that used by the African women, who carry their children strapped against their bodies with *khangas*. This assures safety from animals and gives the baby as much body warmth and contact as it can get. Had I been living in a city, these ideas would probably never have entered my head, and I am sure that my baby would have been wrapped up in beautiful clothes and put to sleep in a frilly white cot. I wanted to bring her up in a more natural way than our society has taught us.

I had decided to make a film about elephant behaviour and desperately needed some help with Saba during the weeks that we would be shooting. Luckily my sister, Mirella, found me the perfect person, and we flew to Naivasha to pick her up. She was a Seychelloise, Madame Violette Thesée, middle-aged, with decades of experience looking after babies. When she heard that she was going to have to get into a tiny plane, fly out into the bush, and live in the midst of elephants, she bravely settled into the back seat, clutched her rosary, closed her eyes, and prayed.

Violette's arrival was greeted with tremendous enthusiasm by everyone in camp. She did not mind how much work she had to do, provided she was paid the right amount of respect and had a proper escort, for she was convinced that every lion, leopard, buffalo, elephant, and rhino in the park had a personal desire to end her life. In the evening when Violette went to bed, a great ceremony always took place. Mhoja went first with his gun, followed by Violette; then came Ali, with a torch, and Suleiman in the rear, armed with a *panga*. Accompanied by lots of talking and shrieks of laughter, they all made their way to the top house.

In the afternoon Violette did her ironing under the gardenia tree, and held court. She had a powerful character with a tremendous sense of humour. Word soon got around, so that truck drivers and rangers returning to park headquarters would stop by for a cup of tea and listen to Violette's stories.

I now had to learn all over again that few things were ever safe outside. Babies of any kind, pets, chickens, even food, needed to be guarded. Snakes, scorpions, tsetse flies, mosquitoes, eagles, mature genets, leopards, lions, buffalo, all visited our camp by day or night. Only the elephants were no trouble.

Shortly after my return to camp I was dozing in the sun and felt a twitch of fear running up my spine. Something was stirring in the bush. To my horror I saw the flat head of a yellow and grey cobra rising up like a periscope from the grass behind me. My sense of being a protective mother went completely astray. I shot out of my chair leaving my baby asleep in her cot and rushed for Mhoja. He came armed with sticks and *pangas*.

"Don't ever leave your baby like that," he scolded me. "Don't you know snakes like milk and are attracted to small babies by the smell?"

I was very ashamed of myself. I was not going to let this happen twice, so I asked him to burn the bush immediately around the camp area straight away. This flushed out two puff adders, and with the bush and grass kept short enough for Widgey to explore everywhere, we never had snakes in the camp again.

Widgey's little red eyes were vigilant, and she could defend herself against almost anything. If she thought something was dangerous, she'd stand on her hind legs, fur ruffled, ears twitching, and give her war cry, a sort of treble growl. Many a time we were able to save a chicken from the claws of an eagle because of it. Once we even chased away a buffalo.

It was only when we began to make our film that our problems started pouring in. Our isolated life was suddenly invaded, and we were menaced by our own species. Perhaps because we had been living among other species for so long, we were not properly tuned-in to people and our life deteriorated.

The first unhappy incident was the disappearance of Amina, the genet. One evening while playing hide-and-seek with Alicat and Widgey, she dislodged a window pane and fell outside. I called and put out food, but nothing would make her come back. Alicat and Widgey then became very close companions, grooming each other, sleeping, eating, and playing together.

One still night we awoke to hear Mhoja yelling, "*Ali na kufa*" —"Ali is dead." I hurried down the path, following the dim light of Iain's torch. Alicat had got out of the kitchen. Blood was on the ground and on the branches of a bush, and I found Widgey. I picked her up, but we searched in vain for Alicat.

Four days later, as we were having coffee after dinner, a very thin, smelly Alicat limped in. His whole lower jaw was broken, and the bones were sticking out, covered with pus. One of his legs was badly hurt and he had sores on his body. He went straight to Widgey for comfort, but she turned her head and walked away.

We rushed Alicat to Sue and Toni Harthoorn. They were the best vets we knew in East Africa. They amputated the broken tip of Alicat's lower jaw and set the back tooth, vital for his survival later. The operation was a complete success. They taught him to eat with half a lower jaw, and how to catch butterflies and other food. Alicat made a new home with Sue and Toni.

Soon afterwards we had a similar experience with Widgey. One of the film sequences was to take place in Marsabit, in the north, where we were to film a famous elephant named Ahmed, who had the longest tusks known. The film unit departed in their car, and we packed our tiny plane, Iain and I in front, with the baby on my lap, and Violette, the cameras, and our luggage in the back. When it came to Widgey and her little round basket, there was simply no more room. Widgey knew we were leaving without her. As soon as the engine started, she screamed and struggled, biting Mhoja's hand and jumping out of the car. She ran to my side of the plane, jumped onto the wheel, and waited for me to open the door. The wind from the propeller blew her off, but I could still hear her pleas.

By the time we returned to Manyara our morale was low, for we had had great difficulties with the film crew. But in camp things were far worse. We found Widgey demoralized with a skin disease, and covered with ticks. Each time I tried to pick her up, she turned her head away or bit me, as if she had been betrayed. Each day her health deteriorated until finally there was only one thing left to do: take her to the Harthoorns. They found that she had mange, tick fever, and possibly also rabies. This was very serious. Everyone in camp, except Saba, had been bitten by Widgey, and I had visions of all of us going mad and foaming at the mouth.

We waited for three anxious days. At last a radio message came to tell us that Widgey was better and that the rabies tests were negative. But it would be a long time before she was completely recovered.

Only Saba seemed happy and well. She was getting fatter and stronger every day, smiling and reminding us of the important things in life, many of which we were forgetting.

ONE DAY IAIN said to me, "You won't believe it, but the Torone sisters are here."

I had been waiting to meet these baddies about whom Iain had told me so much. Each time they visited the park they caused havoc. I could imagine them charging up the river and attacking the camp like great tanks.

The first warning of trouble came one evening as we were driving through the groundwater forest. A loud shrill trumpet sounded, followed by a swish of bent bushes, then silence. There, a few yards away behind a tree, stood a big Torone female. Iain and I looked at her fascinated. Her eyes burned with hatred as she watched us.

Then she charged at full speed. Deliberately we drove only a few feet in front of her. She must have run for at least two hundred yards, trunk turned under, eyes fixed on us. It was a terrifying sight, and I realized how easily this gigantic animal could squash us into pulp should the car stall. She was so determined to get us that she ran straight over a bridge without noticing it, something Iain had never seen an elephant do before. As we came out of the forest, she swerved off the road, trumpeting and thrashing the bush as if demonstrating what she intended to do to us.

It was very frightening. Now there would be no more walks along the river or roads without a gun. Any time, anywhere, one or more of the Torones might be after us in a flash. They must have been shot at a great many times for the smell of a human being or the sound of the car to arouse their immediate hostility.

Next morning Iain wanted to make some observations on the elephants' eating habits, so he asked Mhoja to accompany him with the gun. I stayed in camp. Suddenly I heard a shot, followed by another, and then those terrible sounds of frightened elephants and of branches and trees breaking under their weight. It seemed to be happening not far from the house. I rushed down the drive, but couldn't see anything. Something awful must have happened because Iain would never shoot an elephant, unless he himself was nearly dead.

After ten minutes the car returned. With tears in his eyes Iain said, "We've shot one of the Torones!"

Iain had been taken by surprise. He had been looking through his binoculars, making notes on what Jezebel's family were eating, when Torone sister number four burst out from the bush and rammed her tusk into the car. Iain reversed away but couldn't do it fast enough. She came in for another bash, and as she was picking up the Land-Rover, Mhoja shot her right through the head. She collapsed practically on top of the car. Then he shot once more—the *coup de grâce*. It was probably inevitable that she would be shot sooner or later; everyone was in danger when the Torones were in the park.

We went immediately to the scene of death. A pool of blood was forming under the head of the dead elephant, pouring out of the holes made by the bullets of the .470. Her tusks were marked with green paint from the Land-Rover. Her breasts were full and she must have been suckling a calf. We wondered if it might come back to her; we waited. There were elephants all around but nothing happened.

After several hours we decided to do a postmortem to try to find out if there was any specific reason for her aggressiveness, like disease or old bullet wounds. Soon we had heart, lungs, and assorted organs laid out in neat piles. But there was nothing to explain the matriarch's crustiness.

We wanted to know if she were pregnant. We carefully slit

Iain gazes at the Torone sister shot by Mhoja after attacking the Land-Rover.

open the ovaries, and were rewarded with the discovery of a little elephant no bigger than my little fingernail. It was still in the fish stage of development with gill pouches, but had four perfect elephant feet, and a tiny pointed nose which could have been the trunk. We put it in a bottle of alcohol and kept it.

Every day I went back to the scene to watch the slow disintegration of this huge elephant corpse, black with flies and crawling with worms. The stench was appalling. Iain wanted to see how quickly all the salts and minerals would return to the soil. I watched the first vultures arrive, looking like old men in winter coats sitting on benches at a murder case. Then the tall pink-necked marabou flew in and gathered on the corpse, walking up and down in slow motion with their wings tucked behind their backs, as if pausing before giving their verdict. More and more vultures arrived and glided onto the corpse. They became so gorged that it was all they could do to flap up into the nearest tree.

As the days passed, the body began to shrink. Lions chewed through the skin to get at the intestines and stomach. The tusks fell out of their sockets. Soon there was only the dried-up skin draped over the bones. It was indeed a sad sight to see the brave, fierce and shrill queen shrivelled into a rotting heap.

The death of the Torone sister made me realize once again how fragile is our existence. The smallest event can change its whole course. The signals for fight or flight flashed in the shrill queen's brain, she made the wrong decision, and charged. If life is so finely divided from death by the uncontrollable workings of chance, then at least we should live life to the full.

Being such a restless creature, I have never been able to accept the stability of a well-planned existence. I hate to stay in one place, feeling the years sliding away towards old age—wasted. As a child I had always longed for a miracle to change me into a Masai. When I grew older, I travelled in search of life. Yet each time I went somewhere, there was a call beckoning me back to Africa.

To have found a life among the elephants meant that my search was at an end. I now had a companion with whom I could share this life, and the urge to wander was constantly fulfilled by the work and the way we lived. Everything was alive and real. And with the birth of Saba inevitably the bonds between Iain and myself were strengthened.

I loved the isolation of Ndala. We lived in a small clan, only six members of our own species among five hundred elephants—a whole society for us to investigate. Was it their size, their power, or their gentleness that drew me to them? I could not tell. I just knew that being surrounded by elephants brought me great joy. I discovered that they showed many of the old-fashioned virtues; loyalty, family unity and affection. I was deeply moved by the constant care that they showed each other: mothers, daughters, sisters, babies, all touching and communicating in a very loving way. As we became so deeply involved with them, we both consciously and unconsciously drew parallels between their society and ours. The bond with my child, the tactile care of each other, the trust in leadership, the group defence if one of us were in trouble, all these increased. I now felt a great deal more civilized.

But even after almost five years of living with human beings nearby, only Virgo actually came into friendly bodily contact with us. The others always stood a few feet away. When Saba was three months old, we met Virgo and her closest relatives one evening. I walked up to her and gave her a gardenia fruit in a gesture of greeting. She took the fruit and put it in her mouth, then moved the tip of her trunk over Saba in a figure of eight, smelling her. I wondered if she knew that Saba was my child. We both stood still for a long while, facing each other with our babies by our sides. It was a very touching moment. I feel sure that Virgo will remain a lifelong friend of ours, even if we do not see each other for years.

Our time at Manyara was running out. I was deeply aware of each day as it went by. The sun faded behind the hill and long shadows lay in belts across the valley. In front of me was the river I had looked on a thousand times. No one was around, no one was walking on the sand. I knew that everything I loved most was here, silently saying goodbye. Life moved on and took us with it like a speck of dust blowing in the wind.

PART III: Iain Douglas-Hamilton

CHAPTER NINE

To me the death of an elephant is one of the saddest sights in the world. The day I met Torone sister number four unexpectedly in the Ndala woods she was a powerful strident member of her species. Next second, separated only by a pinpoint in time, she was a colossal lifeless wreck.

For elephants, as for human beings, death remains significant in the behaviour of the survivors. Many great naturalists including Charles Darwin have thought that animals possess strong emotions, and I have little doubt that when one of their number dies, elephants have a feeling similar to the one we call grief.

Attempts to assist a dying elephant may continue long after it is dead. Mhoja and I, searching one day for more elephant paths up to the Marang forest, heard the loud bawling of a calf in distress about a hundred feet up the Endabash escarpment. We cautiously worked our way nearer and saw a scene of great natural drama. A cow was lying on her side down the slope. Her head was bent backward at a peculiar angle and she was stone dead. Next to her stood three calves. The eldest was bawling passionately. The second just stood dumb, its head resting against its mother's body. The smallest calf made forlorn attempts to suck from her breasts. Then the eldest knelt down and pushed its head and small tusks against the corpse, in a hopeless attempt to move it. I backtracked her path up the slope. It appeared that the cow had stepped into a hole covered in vegetation, lost her balance, and rolled out of control down the slope.

Shortly after this incident Harvey Croze and a photographer

friend of his witnessed the death of an old cow in the Serengeti. Harvey first noticed her lagging behind the family unit. When she fell her family all clustered around her, putting their trunks in her mouth, trying to raise her. The most prominent was an independent bull who happened to be with the cows and calves, and at times he attempted alone to aid her. She died there among her family, and they stayed with her for several hours longer.

A zoologist must always try to explain such apparently altruistic behaviour in terms of the helper's own advantage. Even harder to explain in such terms is the extraordinary interest which elephants sometimes show in corpses even when they are decomposed.

After ten days Torone sister number four was reduced to a foul black cavity enclosed by a bag of skin with bones sticking out. One morning a large number of elephants came up from the south. Curious to see what they would do, I parked the Land-Rover just behind the carcass. After a while a large matriarch named Clytemnestra appeared with her family unit. She was an inhabitant of the south, and she must have known Torone four. All of a sudden she caught a whiff of the corpse and spun around. Her trunk held out like a spear, her ears like two great shields, she strode purposefully towards the scent. Three other large cows came right behind her and they all closed around the corpse. Their trunks played up and down the shrunken body, touching each bared fragment of bone. The tusks excited special interest. Pieces of bone were picked up, twiddled, and tossed aside. All the while they were aware of my presence ten paces away. Never had they come so close to me before.

Long before this incident, I had heard of the elephants' graveyard, the place where they are supposed to go to die. This myth I knew to be untrue after discovering elephant corpses scattered all over the park. I had, of course, also heard that elephants took a special interest in the corpses of their own kind. It had sounded like a fairy tale, but now, after seeing it with my own eyes, I decided to test it further.

I found a carcass and set out the bones on one of the most commonly used trails. After about twenty minutes Boadicea appeared with her kinship group. When a breath of wind carried the smell to them, they wheeled *en masse*, cautiously closed in on the skeleton, and began a detailed examination. The tusks aroused immediate interest; they were picked up, mouthed, and passed from elephant to elephant. One immature male lifted the heavy pelvis in his trunk and carried it for fifty yards before dropping it. The skull was rolled over by one elephant after another. Finally, Boadicea picked up one of the tusks and carried it away in her mouth. The rest of the group followed, many of them carrying pieces of the skeleton, which were all dropped within about a hundred yards. Virgo was the last to leave; she came close by me with a rib in her mouth, and waved her trunk at me as she passed. It was an uncanny sight to see those elephants carrying bones away as if in some necromantic rite.

I have no idea why elephants carry bones. It is possible that the exploration provides information about how the animal died, which could be of survival value, but at present this must remain a conjecture. One of the elephants' most valuable survival techniques is the ability to pass on their experience to succeeding generations. The Torone matriarchs, who had probably been persecuted in the elephant massacres of the mid-1950s, showed their offspring how to react violently to human beings.

Another example of "traditional" learning comes from the Addo National Park of South Africa. Here, in 1919, at the request of neighbouring citrus farmers, an attempt was made to annihilate a small population of about one hundred and forty elephants. A well-known hunter named Jan Pretorius was given the job. Unlike Ian Parker's teams, Pretorius killed elephants one by one. Each time, survivors remained who had witnessed a member of their family in its death agonies. Within a year there were no more than thirty animals left alive. It seemed that one final push would rid the farmers of their enemies. But the remaining elephants had become extremely wary and never came out of the thickest bush until after dark. On several occasions when Pretorius pursued them, he in turn was hunted through the dense thickets and had to flee for his life. He eventually admitted himself beaten and in 1930 the Addo elephants were granted a sanctuary of some eight thousand acres of scrubby hillside.

Few if any of those shot at in 1919 can still be alive, yet even today the elephants remain mainly nocturnal and are reputed to be among the most dangerous in Africa. So it seems that this defensive behaviour has been transmitted to calves of the third and fourth generations, not one of whom has suffered a personal attack from man.

At Manyara, toleration of human beings was most strongly developed in Virgo. For a while we fed her with the fruits of various plants, testing which she preferred. But I discontinued this at John Owen's insistence; he felt that feeding her might attract her to cars, and that if she were refused food she could become aggressive. Although I knew that Virgo was harmless, it was the principle of not feeding wild animals that mattered. My behaviour, though safe enough for me, might have tempted others to think they could do the same with another elephant, and this could have been very dangerous. For this reason I must emphatically warn any visitors to Africa not to walk up to wild elephants on foot. I do not want any fatal accidents to occur because an elephant reacts in an understandably hostile way to its age-old enemy.

AFTER ORIA joined me at Manyara and during the tracking of Radio Robert, I was still pondering on what would happen to our overcrowded elephants. If I could show that they were capable of controlling their numbers below the point where they irreversibly damaged the habitat, then it might not be necessary to shoot them in order to save the trees.

Such control worked with other species of mammals. In a classic laboratory study it had been shown that the antisocial behaviour of mice increased with density. The mice neglected their young, failed to court and mate properly, even resorted to cannibalism. Their experimental community dwindled. It was a far cry from mice to elephants, but if antisocial behaviour among elephants were related to density, it would appear in its most extreme forms here at Manyara. I began to study social problems within the family units and bull groups.

The cows in Boadicea's kinship group seemed to hold each

The Douglas-Hamilton's camp (right) on the Ndala River. The stream there was clear, and supplied fresh drinking water; there were shade trees and few insects. Best of all, there were plenty of elephants nearby (below), and Oria (left) found herself in the middle of an elephant world. Shortly after Saba was born, Oria introduced the baby to the friendly Virgo and Virgo's calf (opposite, below).

other in varying degrees of affection. Boadicea associated with Giselle more than with anyone else. Virgo and Right Hook also went together. The most independent was a young cow named Isabelle who often wandered apart with her three calves. Her eldest calf, a teenage daughter, was growing up fast and shortly became pregnant. As the dry season wore on that year, and food and water became scarcer, cracks and stresses appeared within the family unit. Isabelle got into trouble with the big cows. I saw her receive a sharp jab from Giselle, a shove in the ribs from Right Hook, and a head swing from Boadicea that made her drop a branch; it was promptly eaten by the aggressor. At the water holes she and her three calves tended to stand apart. In effect they had formed a sub-unit within Boadicea's family.

One evening Isabelle's calf produced her baby. We named him Bottlebrush because of his fine bushy tail, and his teenage mother we called Laila. Both Laila and the youthful grandmother, Isabelle, were transported with maternal feelings for this calf, but his arrival seemed to accelerate their drift away from the other elephants.

The day came when Boadicea led one of her forced marches down to the Endabash River. Isabelle and her unit remained behind, quietly browsing and drinking, with no competition from elderly cows. This event was just as exciting as originally finding that the family units were stable. I now knew that stability was not absolute, and that large family units might split.

When Boadicea, Leonora, and Jezebel returned with their families a few days later, Isabelle associated with them just as before. But from then on, whenever the mood took her, she would move off as an independent unit, just as Leonora and Jezebel did.

However, there was nothing to suggest that the splits caused a higher mortality. Rather they illustrated a delicate balance of advantage. A young cow, in choosing a larger distance from the intolerant matriarchs, got the benefits of independence—water and food without competition—without forfeiting the protection of the kinship group should she or her offspring run into trouble.

Whatever occasional bullying the young cows received, it was nothing compared to the treatment meted out to Radio Robert. He only had to come within forty yards of some irate cow for her to shake her head at him. If in the course of feeding a cow came quietly up behind him, he was liable to be startled by a jab delivered out of the blue. He had reached the traumatic stage where a young bull is forcibly rejected by the adults of the family. Eventually, the same would happen to N'Dume—the little bull would become more obstreperous and sexy until the cows turned against him. A series of attacks would gradually drive him away.

The final break between Radio Robert and his family came almost imperceptibly. The family had gone to the thickets along the Endabash River, and one day when Boadicea turned north the young bull turned south. He went straight on until he reached the Marang forest escarpment. I was waiting with great excitement to see if he would climb up when suddenly the transmitter packed up for good. I did not see him again for several months, by which time he had managed to get rid of the expensive collar.

He was now occupied in settling his position in the loose hierarchy of bulls. His relationship with the adults was friendly, but there was no question of challenging them over the ownership of a succulent branch. It was only with those of his own size that he had furious fights.

Adult bulls appeared to have an understood hierarchy based on size, so that mild threat gestures were usually enough to resolve any conflict. And while a bull in danger was expected to look after himself, others would sometimes help him if he were wounded, just as cows helped a member of the family unit.

From all this it seemed to me that, despite their destiny, the elephants got along fine with each other. Far from regulating their population, they were even expanding it slightly with a healthy proportion of young animals. I now turned from their social to their territorial behaviour.

AFTER FAILING to recover the collar from Radio Robert, I begged Harvey Croze to let me have one which Howard Baldwin had sent him, since I had little time before I must leave Manyara.

He kindly agreed, and with it we finally succeeded in radio-tracking one of the fierce Endabash family units.

Oria and I, with Mhoja and Suleiman, managed to immobilize a young Endabash cow belonging to the family of a matriarch named Jane Eyre. She was the first cow I ever tried to immobilize, and I only did so because she lagged behind her unit and presented an ideal opportunity. In fact, as we were sitting working on top of her, to our horror Jane Eyre quietly returned and towered over us. I jumped up, spread my arms, and shouted. Fortunately, she retreated before my demonstration, leaving the prone body of the young cow to our mercy. We named her Radio Evelyn, after a friend of mine whom she had charged.

Most of their days the Jane Eyre family skulked in the Endabash thickets, moving half a mile or so during the day. At night, however, they came alive. It was a curious reversal of the usual elephant cycle, and was probably caused by their fear of man.

Jane Eyre and Radio Evelyn never crossed the park boundary during this time, but they brought me into contact with many elephants I had never seen before. On one morning flight I spotted a huge female tusker on the shoulder of the Marang forest escarpment high above the park. Below, the slope ended in a sheer cliff, at the foot of which Radio Evelyn and Jane Eyre paced back and forth. I never expected to see that strange cow again, but that very same evening I saw her on the shores of the Endabash. She was in a herd of a hundred elephants and all of them were strangers.

That settled my doubts. There must be a very considerable track for so many elephants to move in and out of the park, for I did not think they had passed along the path I had discovered with my mother or even through the Italian's farm in the time available. Next morning I went with Mhoja to the escarpment. Above us the Marang forest was wrapped in cloud and mist, and unrelenting rain trickled down our backs. Eventually we found an elephant path that wound higher and higher between giant boulders and precipices. The air grew cooler and the rain stopped. Trees on either side were festooned with thick hanging lichens. We reached the level of the mists and then to our delight we entered the dark green labyrinth of the forest. There, totally concealed from aerial view, was the largest elephant trail I have ever seen. It was smoothly beaten down and must have been at least twelve feet wide.

I went back to this path many times, and found there was a continual flow of elephants across this crucial boundary. John Owen's original question to me, five years ago in the garden in Sussex, had finally been answered. The elephants migrated in quantity between the park and the Marang forest. The forest was, in fact, a safety valve for the overcrowded Manyara park.

IN JUNE 1970, three months before our final departure, I held the seminar at Ndala that Oria has described.

The primary topic that day was space. Owing to the human population explosion, the parks and game reserves have become the elephants' only refuge. Not only are they prevented from wandering, but their numbers have been swelled by countless refugees fleeing from human persecution. This causes wholesale woodland destruction as typified by the ill-fated acacias of Manyara. What should the national parks do about it?

There were, and still are, the two schools of thought that I encountered when I first arrived at Manyara. The first holds that since man created the problem, he should solve it. The elephants should be reduced by culling until a balance is restored between them and their habitat. Those who hold these views insist that, although shooting elephants is repugnant, it is preferable to thousands dying lingering deaths from starvation.

Those of the second school assert that whenever man intervenes he upsets the balance of nature even further. They argue that the decline of the woodlands is not irreversible, but is part of a long-term natural cycle: elephants knock down trees, establishing grasslands in their place, but then their numbers decline or they move away. The grasslands now burn every year, preventing the regeneration of young trees, and establishing themselves even more permanently. This provides ideal conditions for grazing animals to increase, and they may breed to such an extent that the grass becomes threadbare. Patches of soil appear, where the fire can no longer reach and where bushes and trees can sprout. With no elephants to suppress them, the young woodlands proliferate until, perhaps a hundred years after it began, the cycle is complete.

Those who believe in non-interference must ask themselves this question: Can the cycles continue to work in the confined areas of the present national parks, or will they break down under the strain?

I have come to the belief there is no simple answer to the management of elephants in Africa. Each park should be judged on its own merits according to its size, climate, and the fluctuation of plant and animal numbers. Carefully controlled culling should be tried in some parks and complete non-interference in others. In time, when all the pieces of the jigsaw puzzle have been studied, we may be able to be more precise.

Luckily I was able to suggest a unique solution to the Manyara problem, which was to reverse the usually irreversible—to give the elephants more space. In 1955 elephants living along the southwest shore of the lake had been ousted from their habitual range when it was made over to the farmers. By the time of the seminar many of these farmers were about to leave the country. I therefore proposed that the land be returned to the elephants. This would open up another corridor into the Marang Forest Reserve, which should itself be designated as a refuge for the elephants. I believed that when the elephants spread out and ranged through all three areas, there would be an overall balance.

There remained the problem of the lions and their special trees. Lions are conservative in their habits, and eighty per cent of their tree climbing was confined to a mere seventeen favourite trees. I recommended that these trees be protected individually, wrapped in wire, or surrounded by sharp stones which elephants dislike walking over.

These proposals were adopted as objectives of top priority by the national parks.

OUR LAST MORNING at Manyara came all too soon. The day before, we had officially handed the camp over to the national parks. Vesey was there to receive everything in good order. I was happy to know that this camp was going to be used by scientists, park people, and visitors, some of whom might give back something to the elephants: knowledge, love, or money.

Just before we got in the car to drive to the airstrip, I walked all around the camp, seeing, touching, and smelling the place one more time. Biba, the goat, followed me or ran ahead. She was to find a happy home with the driver of the Land-Rover. It seemed to me a very long time since I had first walked up to the waterfall, my thoughts full of tangled impressions of wonder and beauty, and decided to set up camp there. I had changed a lot in that time. I had arrived alone and as a scientist. But after Oria joined me, I saw things increasingly through eyes opened to the importance of individual and family relationships.

The plane sped down the runway, engine roaring. Oria's arm tightened around Saba, and then Kix lifted off the ground, up and over the trees. I banked around the camp. Mhoja's green uniform and waving hand receded in the distance.

As the Great Rift Valley unrolled below us, my thoughts turned back to the elephants and their future. Perhaps the most important key to their survival is to gain the sympathy of the African people and the politicians who represent them.

But behind all the practical questions there lies a much more fundamental one. Why is the survival of the African elephant, the wildlife, and the wilderness a matter of great importance?

The elephants have shared the land with man since the dawn of history and are an integral part of mythology and folklore; their disappearance would diminish the cultural environment of the African people. Elephants are intelligent animals who resemble us in some of their behaviour. As such they deserve our respect. This is why shooting elephants, to quote Richard Laws, "poses moral and ethical problems and cannot be undertaken lightly." Also, the elephants and their wilderness are very beautiful; it is vandalism to annihilate anything of beauty and unpardonable to deprive others of it. I believe, too, that elephants and other wild animals fulfil part of man's deep need for the refreshment of his spirit—a need felt particularly by those who live in highly industrialized surroundings. Elephants are symbols of freedom.

Postscript

For two years we lived in Oxford, a city of stone whose spires pierced the morning mist. During this time I was working on my thesis, analysing our observations, and writing about elephants instead of living with them. Huddled around electric fires, pale-faced and wrapped in woollen clothes, we grappled with the computers until evening came, the bells chimed, and it was time to go home. Our tight-muscled bellies and strong limbs turned soft as we buttered hot crumpets for tea and ate scones with cream and strawberry jam. Our second daughter, Mara, was born.

Then, at last, in 1972 my thesis was completed, accepted, and deposited in Oxford's Bodleian Library.

Within a few weeks we were back in Africa and the day came when we drove in convoy with the children towards Manyara. The new director of national parks, Derek Bryceson, had given us permission to complete the film we had started in 1970 and Anglia Television had provided us with an experienced cameraman, Dieter Plage. It was our hope that through the film we would be able to publicize the urgent need for an extension to the park.

We arrived at Ndala late at night and saw Mhoja standing in the beam of the headlights. Next day we woke to the sound of water running over the rocks, birds calling, and the noise of branches breaking as some elephants ate behind the house.

The camp looked much as it had when we had left. I walked along the scarred woodlands and found that only forty per cent of my marked trees were still alive; it was the proportion I had predicted. At this rate, by 1980 at the latest, there would be none left. I examined the seventeen trees favoured by the lions. They had been protected by fine chicken wire tightly wrapped around their trunks; the wire was surprisingly inconspicuous and for some mysterious reason the elephants had left it alone, although they could easily have ripped it to shreds with a few gentle pokes of their tusks.

The elephants looked in good condition and I had no difficulty in recognizing any of them. Out filming one day I saw a familiar head and ear outline that made my pulse race; Torone sister number three had come on one of her occasional forays to the northern end of the park. "Watch this one, Dieter," I told the cameraman, "and you may get a good charge."

The ground was flat so I turned the Land-Rover in front of her and waited. She gave one outraged trumpet and then came at us in a relentless charge. Dieter was well prepared; he sat right at the back of the car, holding his camera at hip level with its wide-angle lens pointing backward. The elephant followed us for exactly three minutes, long enough for the film to run its full course, before she broke off exhausted.

In contrast, the other elephants seemed completely oblivious to cars and tamer than ever. We found Radio Robert ambling along the foreshore with M4/3, the first elephant we had radio-tracked. They passed within a few feet of us, and I was happy to see that both were plump and well rounded.

I was especially curious to see whether Virgo would remember us. When I found her, I got out and called to her. She stopped and turned towards me, then slowly she came forward, extending her trunk to touch my hand and letting out her breath in a long *whoosh*. It was impossible not to be moved by her trust after our two-year absence. Both children were brought up to her to be introduced and sniffed at.

To solve Manyara's space problem, it would be necessary to buy the farmland that formed the elephant corridor up to the Marang forest, in particular the farm owned by the Italian. While we were filming, we were visited by Professor Bernhard Grzimek, director of the Frankfurt zoo, and a pioneer researcher in the Serengeti. When I explained the situation to him, he immediately offered, on behalf of the Frankfurt Zoological Society, to raise money to buy the farmland.

With this encouragement, Oria and I set off to visit the Italian. In spite of the divergence in our aims, we found him a sympathetic character. The defence of his maize had resulted in the death of some four hundred elephants. But now he was growing old and he was tired of shooting them.

"It was their land before I came and I cannot keep them away," he told us. "I would be pleased if I could be paid a fair price by the national parks. Then I would go back to Italia."

We conveyed the good news to Derek Bryceson that the Italian was willing to sell his land, that Professor Grzimek had offered to raise part of the sum required to buy him and the others out, and that Anglia Television, too, was prepared to make a substantial contribution to its cost.

It therefore looks as though the crisis at Manyara may be solved in the very near future. Already the Marang forest has been promised to the park, and if the regional authorities agree to the conversion of the corridor of farmland to wildlife conservation, the elephants will be able to return to many of the ranges that they enjoyed a hundred years ago.

Iain and Oria Douglas-Hamilton

It is May 1975. "Duglass" and "Mama Duglass" are in the middle of a two-week trip to England during which they are being "lionized"—or should the word now be "elephantized"? —by literary London, and by herds of journalists and TV commentators. In a few days' time, they leave for a similar schedule in America. Even the Douglas-Hamiltons are beginning to feel exhausted.

Iain, it must be said, no longer looks mildly like Jesus Christ: the beard is gone and, for our lunch, he wears an immaculate blazer and grey flannels (befitting the grandson of a Scottish duke) and heavy, dark-rimmed spectacles (befitting a doctor of zoology). Oria wears a long dress and an exclusive-looking leather waistcoat decorated with many many-coloured beads. (She later explains that it is indeed exclusive—made to her own design in her very own factory).

Apart from giving them a hectic month in civilization and the means to buy a new aeroplane (a £6,000 Cessna 185), the success of their first book and TV film is apparently not going to alter their life-style one jot. They made up their minds long ago that they were not going to let other people run their lives and, as soon as politely possible, they will be back in Africa. They now have a house on her parents' farm at Lake Naivasha, which serves as a base for their projects and expeditions.

Iain next plans to study elephant populations throughout the continent. That done, he favours looking up the great pandas in China. By which time, miniature submarines will probably be perfected and he will be able to get down—quite literally—to the business of studying whales.

Oria intends to accompany Iain as much and as far as possible (taking the children with her) but always bearing in mind her own career as a photographer, author, and, of course, director of the waistcoat-making factory. In fact this enterprise, which employs a work force of Masai tribeswomen, produces a whole variety of garments and ornaments, designed by Oria to be sold in New York boutiques. The prices are high but Oria points out that there are not only wages to be paid and the raw materials to be bought, but also a whole community to be run for the hitherto totally nomadic tribeswomen.

At this rate of activity and creativity, it looks as if the legend of "Duglass" and "Mama Duglass" has scarcely yet begun.

THE GREAT TRAIN ROBBERY: Photographs on pages 8 and 9 by Mike Wells.

The biographical note on page 146 by courtesy of *Book of the Month Club News*, July 1975 (U.S.A.).

BLIND LOVE: Chapter decorations by Fritz Wegner.

AMONG THE ELEPHANTS: The photographs in this book, including those by Lee Lyon on pages 422, 501 (bottom) and 510, are used by kind permission of the authors and William Collins Sons & Co. Ltd.

BB 85